A CHAPTER IN
THE TALE OF SECOND EARTH

* * *

THE WAR FOR THE NORTH

✳ ✳ ✳

WHISPERS OF WAR

✳ ✳ ✳

The War for the North: Book One

SEAN RODDEN

ISBN: 1495492958
ISBN 13: 9781495492952
Library of Congress Control Number: 2014903470
CreateSpace Independent Publishing Platform
North Charleston, South Carolina

For my mother,
who believed.

In Gratitude:

Thanks to my Shorty,

my love and my life,

for the love given

even when none is deserved.

ACKNOWLEDGEMENTS

There are so many people who encouraged, supported and inspired me in the development of this work, from concept to completion, that I cannot hope to give them proper recognition in the small space I have here...but my heart is a much larger place, and know that you are wrapped within an embrace of gratitude there! To my wife Sandra and my children Chelsey, Chantal and Chad, oceans of love and thankfulness...no worries, they're all good swimmers! To my sister Rena and her family, much appreciation for your encouragement and ceaseless scorching sarcasm! To Marc Whitaker of MTWdesign, many thanks for kicking a dying dream alive and for creating the most awesomest of awesome covers ever! All the wonderful folks at CreateSpace for their kindness, help and guidance. And to Herman, Mark, Peter, Stefan and Wolf (and Frank!) of the mighty ACCEPT for the inspiration and fire that will forever burn in this rebel heart!

*Special thanks to **Alex Zekovich,***

my brother in spirit,

without whose vision

my own would be sadly less vivid.

THE WAR FOR THE NORTH

BOOK ONE:
WHISPERS OF WAR

CONTENTS

So it begins...

FOREWORD

*A*ll is changed now. All is altered and has become strange. All things save one.

The World is unfamiliar to me. Beneath my feet, the ground is still and cold and lifeless. Maiden Earth sleeps, her power withdrawn, the land and waters long abandoned to the whims of Nature and the ravages of Man. From among the Wardens of the World, the three Guardian Peoples, I alone remain. The Athair have returned to the Light. The Daradur delve in darkness. And the Fiannar are no more.

I alone might recite the histories of the First World. I alone remember the struggles of the Second. And I alone linger still, gazing out upon this last world, this Third Earth, wondering at whiles whether all that has gone before has been for naught and in vain. The Other, the Ancient Enemy against whom we vied so valiantly, survives and thrives upon the Third Earth. The Shadow might have taken another hue, the serpent may slide in another skin, but its power is no less potent, no less deadly, and I am neither beguiled nor fooled...

Unluvin lives.

Unluvin. The Other. Banished from the Light, then thrust from the First Earth before the glory and the valour of the Athair and the Folk of Defurien, then defied and defeated by the Guardian Peoples of the Second Earth, only to arise and reign over the Third.

Unluvin. The Other. The Ancient Enemy. The Lord of the Third Earth.

Though I may wonder at whiles, I truly believe that the wars against Unluvin were not in vain, for from those unceasing struggles and of their countless battles were preserved the gift of Choice and the luxury of Free Will. And if Man, yet in his spiritual infancy, is so very easily swayed by the lures of Unluvin, then the fault is Man's and Man's alone. For upon the Third Earth, the evil of the Other is permitted to exist solely in the heart of Man, and then only when invited, nurtured by need and greed, and made strong by sin. But the choice is Man's...

The faith and the fury of the Guardian Peoples have made it so.

Man need no longer fear being crushed under the gathered fist of Unluvin's vast armies. Man need neither stand stupefied nor slip swooning before Unluvin's soul-stealing sorcery. Man need only stifle that small seductive voice, heed it not, and hush the alluring whispers that beckon him to his doom.

The blood and the blades of the Guardian Peoples have deemed it thus.

May Man prove worthy of our sacrifice.

a map of the west of **Second Earth**

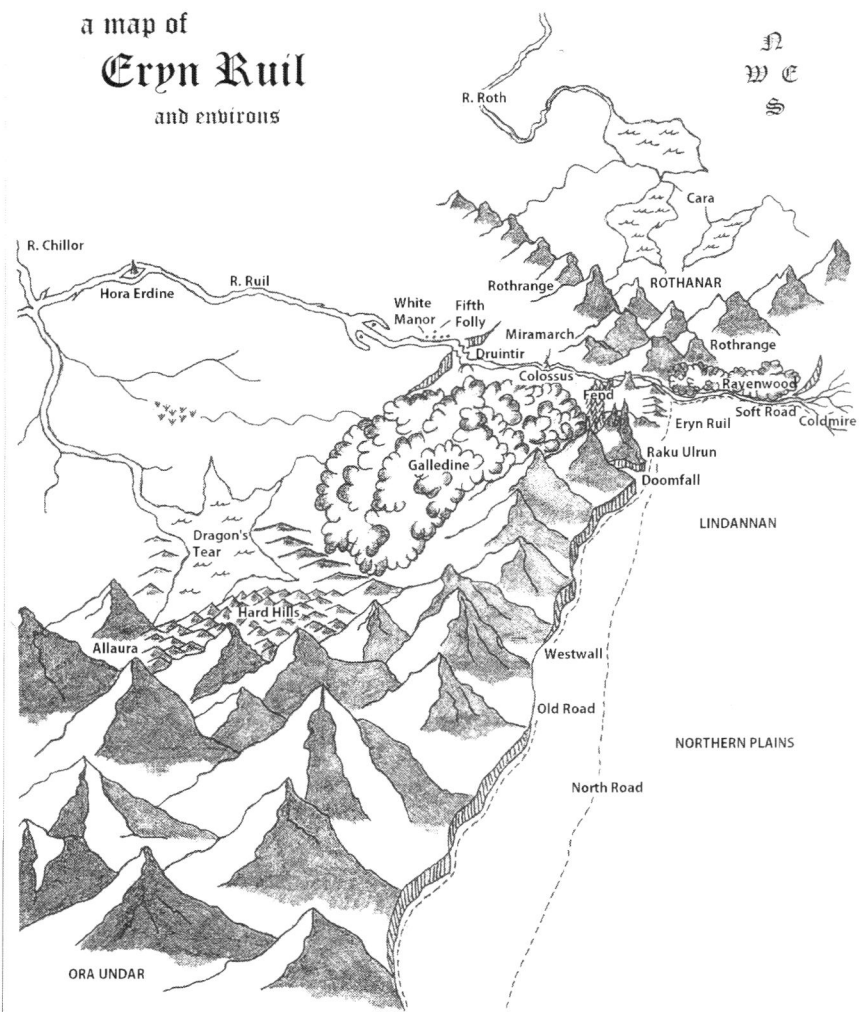

a map of
Eryn Ruil
and environs

DRAMATIS PERSONAE

The Erelians

Axennus Teagh: Ambassador of the Erelian Republic to Lindannan
Bronnus Teagh: Captain of the Erelian Ambassadorial Guard
Runningwolf/Abbawontandontas: Left Tenant of the Ambassadorial Guard, originally from Rheln
Hastiliarius: Right Tenant of the Ambassadorial Guard
Draconarius: an Ambassadorial Guardsman, standard-bearer of the Ambassadorial Guard
Teji Nashi: an Ambassadorial Guardsman, a healer
Regorius: a Decan or sergeant in the Ambassadorial Guard; Whitey
Maddus: an Ambassadorial Guardsman; Maddy
Riffalo: an Ambassadorial Guardsman; Riff
Rooboong: an Ambassadorial Guardsman; Ruby
Lionnus: an Ambassadorial Guardsman; Lio
Anconas: an Undercaptain of the North March Mounted Reserve
Lacius: a Left Tenant in the North March Mounted Reserve

The Fiannar

Alvarion II: Twelfth Lord of the Fiannar, Master of the House of Defurien

Cerriste: Lady of the Fiannar, Mistress of the House of Defurien, wife of Alvarion II

Caelle: Shield Maiden to Lady Cerriste

Sarrane: Seer to Alvarion II, Mistress of the House of Eccuron, wife of Tulnarron

Eldurion: Marshal of the Grey Watch, Eldest of the Fiannar, father of Caelle, uncle of Alvarion II

Taresse: mother of Caelle, wife of Eldurion, governess to Aranion

Tulnarron: Master of the House of Eccuron, Warden of the East

Aranion: son of Alvarion II and Cerriste, heir to the Lordship of the Fiannar

Arumarron: son of Tulnarron and Sarrane, heir to the Mastery of the House of Eccuron

Castadon: a Fian of the House of Eccuron, a forerider in the Host of Arrenhoth

Gornannon: a Fian of the House of Eccuron

Gostullian: a Fian, a scout of the Grey Watch; 'Ghost'

Haldarian: a Fian of the House of Eccuron

Harlastian: a warder of the Grey Watch

Lorradien: a Fian of the House of Eccuron

Milutin: a standard bearer of the Fiannar

Radannan: a standard bearer of the Fiannar

Sandarre: a Fiann of the House of Eccuron**,** cousin to Tulnarron

Silmarien: a warder of the Grey Watch

Spedamon: a warder of the Grey Watch; 'Speedy'

Varonin: a warder of the Grey Watch

The Daradur

Rundul: a Warder of the Wandering Guard
Brulwar: Earthmaster to the Wandering Guard, First Made of the Firstmade
Drogul: Chieftain of the Wandering Guard, Lord of Doomfall; the Mighty One
Dulgar: a Captain of the Wandering Guard; the Wild One
Mundar: a Warder of the Wandering Guard

The Athair

Gavrayel: King of the Athair of the West of First Earth; King of the Athair of Second Earth
Aeline: Queen of the Folk of Gavrayel
Evangael: a Prince of the folk of Gavrayel; a Sun Lord
Thrannien: a Prince of the folk of Gavrayel; a Sun Lord
Yllufarr: a Prince of the folk of Gavrayel; a Sun Lord
Ingallin: Prime Consul to Gavrayel; Chancellor of Gith Glennin
Lalindel: First Knight of the Sun Knights of Evangael

The Bloodspawn

Kor ben Dor: the Halflord, leader of the Bloodspawn, a general in the Blood King's army
Ev lin Dar: a Black Shield of the Bloodspawn
Gren del Mor: a Black Shield of the Bloodspawn

The Rothmen

Ri Niall (of the Thousand Battles): the High King of Rothanar
Connar: a Rothman, Warthane of the *caelroth*
Ciaran: King of the Rothic province of Uladh
Dowdall: Rothic ambassador to Lindannan

The Nothirings

Ingvar Dragonsbane: a prince of Nothira, Earl of Invarnoth, son of Eleric Bloodhand; the Mad Earl
Eleric Bloodhand: King of Nothira
Sunderstrum: the Nothiric Ambassador to Lindannan

The Wraithren

Suru-luk: Blood King of the Wraithren
Kal-suruk: Skull King of the Wraithren
Umun-dron: Demon King of the Wraithren
Zan-zurak: the Death King, most powerful of the Wraithren

Others

Waif: a Leech-possessed child
Urchin: a Leech-possessed child
Arbamas: Prince and ruler of Ithramis
Arn'badt: leader of the Graniants under Earthfall; King of the Giants
Arrowwing: an *elliam*, steed of Thrannien
Drake of Dagoth: greatest surviving dragon of Second Earth
Eveningwind: an *elliam*, steed of Yllufarr
Featherfoot: Runningwolf's Rhelnian stallion
Ongulthuk: an Unman, King of the Unmen from Waldard

Sten Hjerte: a prince of Var

Teraras: the Lord of the *warokka*

Teller of the Tale: the Creator of the universe; Iu

Thunderlight: an *elliam*, steed of Evangael

Thyr: Wulfic / Nothiric god of thunder and war

Umbar'hal: the witchdoctor of the Graniants, shaman of shamans

From Antiquity

Alvarion I: Tenth Lord of the Fiannar, ruled during the battle of Mekkoleth on Sark-u-surum

Amarien: Eleventh Lord of the Fiannar, son of Alvarion I, father of Alvarion II

Andalorian: Fifth Lord of the Fiannar

Andriel: a Sun Knight of the Athair, slain at Mekkoleth on Sark-u-surum

Asrayal: King of the Athair of the South of First Earth

Attametton: the first dragon

Beast of Bazaal: a powerful demon of First Earth

Branne: a Lady of the Fiannar, wife of Vallian, daughter cf Eccuron and Yasminne

Carrinthien: son of Hiridion, took a wife of the race of Man, declared himself King of Erellan

Carrinthien II: founder of the Erelian Republic

Cothra: the Hiath of War

Defurien: First Lord of the Fiannar

Eccuron: one of the Fiannar, dear friend to Defurien

Ferraron: a Fian of the House of Eccuron, slain at Mekkoleth on Sark-u-surum

Fircuine: wife of Defurien

Hiridion: a Fian, founder of Erellan, the South Kingdom of the Fiannar of Second Earth

Idallion: Third Lord of the Fiannar, son of Vallian

Ilurin / Unluvin: brightest and most beautiful of the Hiathir, fallen Hiath of great power, brought war upon the Athair of First Earth

Iu: Athain name for the Teller of the Tale

Majan al Khan: White Mage to the last Turian Emperor

Micyll: King of the Athair of the North of First Earth

Muldarron: a Fian of the House of Eccuron, son of Ferraron; fought at Mekkoleth on Sark-u-surum; renowned for his skill in sculpting

Noth the Red: eldest bastard son of the last Kyetnik king of Var; first King of Nothira

Palladian: firstborn son of Defurien, twin of Vallian

Rafayel: a captain of the Athair of the North of First Earth

Ri Collunn: High King of Rothanar during the Roth-Unman war

Ri Connar: High King of Rothanar during the Fiannar's second war with the Wraithren

Ri Donnal: High King of Rothanar at the time of Noth the Red's landing

Rokkundar: a Darad, slain at Mekkoleth on Sark-u-surum

Sammayal: a follower of Asrayal in the wars for First Earth; Lord of the Shaddathair, First of the Unforgiven

Sithra: a mighty demon in the service of Unluvin

Te'arron: the last King of Erellan

Ulviathon: a fallen Hiath, a demon of First Earth

Unluvin: fallen Hiath of great power, brought war upon the Athair of First Earth

Vallian: secondborn son of Defurien; twin of Palladian; Second Lord of the Fiannar

Yasminne: wife of Eccuron

Yriel: King of the Athair of the East of First Earth

PROLOGUE

"This world is too fragile
to be entrusted to the dubious care of Man.
Thus, even as we diminish,
we must unite in Guardianship of this Earth."

Aeline, Queen of the Folk of Gavrayel, Year of the Strype 1540

F our centuries had passed and another had grown old since the Fiannar had marched upon the great gates of Mekkoleth, the black iron fortress sprawled atop the summit of Sark-u-surum like some great dark dragon perched at the peak of Time. There that dour and dire Deathward folk had brought battle and war back to Mekkoleth on Sark-u-surum, back to its maleficent master. And there, supported on their southern flank by the heavy hammers and angry axes of the mighty Daradur, and from the north by the long bows and longer spears of the high and noble Athair, those fierce Fiannar had faced and fought Suru-luk, Blood King of the Wraithren, and his swarming servants of Shadow.

The battle surged and raged through a day of grey and a night of rain, then a day of mist and a night of wind, tides of constant combat

1

rolling and rushing beneath both sun and moon. War bellowed with a thousand voices: Thunder and wildfire and metal on metal; the ravening roar of blood-raw throats; the siren song of arrows in flight; the calamitous crash of arms; the whispered hiss of death everpresent. The din gathered and grew until there was no sound in the world but the fury of war.

And then the third dawn of battle broke – as did the ranks of the Blood King's hellish host. The subsequent slaughter beneath the morning sun and mustered might of the three Guardian Peoples was appalling, apocalyptic, yet pure in purpose and principle.

Within its crimson cloak, Suru-luk's soulless spirit shuddered.

Then, in desperation, the Blood King sent forth his dragons, the war-worms of Gehennoth, brood of the Drake of Dagoth. But the worms were wingless and far too young to brave the broad blades of Daradun war-axes. The Daradur hacked them to pieces with masterful ease.

Despairing, Suru-luk then summoned a *kuarok*, a monstrous spirit of fire and shadow, the most feared and fearsome of fiends from the First World, only to see it driven into darkness before the white light of the Athain Sun Knights.

And then, at the last, on the blood-slicked precipice of utter defeat, the Blood King of the Wraithren cast wide the gates of Mekkoleth and issued forth himself, a huge incarnadine shadow, to meet the challenge of the Fiannar and their valourous allies. But Suru-luk feared the light shining in the eyes of Alvarion, Tenth Lord of the Fiannar and bearer of the Blade of Defurien. And so the Blood King fled, east and south, swifter than the wind of a summer storm, and the earth quaked in his wake.

Then all fell calm and strangely still as the warriors of the Guardian Peoples marveled in reverent silence at their victory. And slowly, gradually, an oddly harmonious medley of Fiannian horns and Daradun drums rose into the dawn, soaring with the sun, and fair Athain voices lifted in a summer serenade, singing the Shadow away.

In shining triumph and glory, the banners of their proud Houses flying high, the Fiannar returned to their carven city of Druintir at the pass of Eryn Ruil.

The Athair rode north to golden Gith Glennin, the hidden realm of the Neverborn nestled behind the forbidding barrier of the Vallagard Mountains.

Only the Daradur remained at Mekkoleth on Sark-u-surum.

So terrible was the wrath of the Stone Lords that they left not a rock of Mekkoleth's walls and towers and foundations unbroken, not a single stone unshattered, and the dark fortress of defeated Suruluk passed from the world forever. Yet unappeased, the Daradur then turned their formidable fury upon Sark-u-surum itself, and with fist and hammer and through their command of the eldritch energies of Maiden Earth, they brought the very mountain down. Only when mountain and fortress were reduced to ruins of sundered stone and twisted iron did the Daradur turn back to their halls deep in impregnable Ora Undar.

From that time forth, the rubbles of Mekkoleth and Sark-u-surum, like unnumbered fragments of stained glass glinting black and red under sun and star, had been known in the Westspeech of Mankind as the Bloodshards.

And Mankind, for whom in part the Guardian Peoples had gone to war, soon forgot, if indeed they had ever known, what had been done there. Among the Guardian Peoples themselves, few of those who had fought at Mekkoleth on Sark-u-surum ever came there again. For many, the place was too distant and the memory too near. Most had no need, no compulsion, no purpose to draw them back.

Most.

But not all...

1

FLIGHT FROM THE BLOODSHARDS

O cold northern sun and star
Bright eyes of the Fiannar
Hail! Fenders of Light and land
Flash! Brave Blade of Defurien!

Alas! Word of woe and war
Wings of darkness westward bore
Arise! Northmen strong and free
Stand! Faith and fealty!

Hark! The tolling bells of doom
Peal o'er Alvarion's Tomb
Ware! Warders bold and true
Death and ruin beckon you...

Lament for the Fiannar

Late Summer
Year of the Strype 2025

*R**un!*
The thought burned in his mind like a wild white fire fuelled by urgency and fanned by peril. The thought was unsought, unwanted – reviled even. And despite its insistence, its imperativeness, he forced the idea back and down. He could not do otherwise. He was a Darad. The Daradur did not run.

Run!

The concept was alien to him, anathema. He was Rundul of Axar, a Warder of the *mara Waratur*, the watchful Wandering Guard of the warlike Daradur. Squat and bearded, broad and steely muscled, hewn of the metal-veined rock of legends, the Daradur held that even the slightest wound on the back was an indignity surpassing shame. Never in the six hundred years since his Making had Rundul considered running from battle.

He was a Darad. The Daradur did not run.

But none other among that warrior race had ever seen that which Rundul saw in the deep places of the earth that day.

Miles beneath the broken stone of the Bloodshards, Rundul stood cloaked in the shadows of a high stone ledge, staring out and down upon a great cavern steeped in crimson darkness. That which he saw there in that huge hollow of the netherearth moved him – as much as an iron-hearted Darad might be moved by such things. In the flame-reddened unlight, his black eyes flared and flickered.

Urth ru Glir, Rundul swore silently, inwardly. *Earth the Mother*.

Fires burned both without and within. Within him burned alarm, controlled rage and seething hatred, the three coalescing into a single flame of defiant determination – a solitary blaze burning boldly before a dark subterranean wind. Without, red and rotten, vile and so very wrong, burned the foul fire of abomination. Abomination and outrage.

And then, from somewhere at the insidious core of that abomination, a heinous shriek burst from a spectral breast, ripping the air in execration –

"*Daaaaaaaaaaaaarrrrrrrrrrrrrrrraaaaaaaaaaaaaad!!!*"

Rundul's presence was become known.

The Darad remained motionless for a moment, unmoved and unmoving, a boulder of the earth from which he had been Made. He then reached slowly, deliberately, for the great war-axe strapped to his broad back. He held the haft in a fist of iron. And with an inward shrug of his warrior spirit, he stepped forth from the shadows to the lip of the ledge, into the guttering glow of incarnadine gloom.

Thus revealed, Rundul hefted his war-axe with one powerful arm, raising the weapon above his head, bloodlight glittering on its broad blades. Whether the gesture was made in mock salutation or in brazen challenge, its effect was both predictable and immediate.

Unnumbered throats blistered in a single roar of mindless rage. Unnumbered hands reached for unnumbered weapons.

And the thought-voice whipped Rundul's mind:

Run!

Rundul lowered his axe. He blinked languidly, once, twice. Then, with an expression of disdain, he put his back to the cavern and to the horrors it held. One stride took him back into the shadows, into darkness. Another three brought him to the tunnel that had led him to the cavern. He turned into this passage, wrapped himself in the cape of its blackness, and walked back along the way that he had come.

Run!!

The thought directly contradicted, diametrically opposed Rundul's desire, his instinct, his very *need* to stand and fight. Turning from battle, even from one in which he would certainly be slain, came neither easily nor naturally to Rundul. However, that which he had seen was a thing that required telling, that *demanded* telling. Specifically, such ill tidings needed to be delivered to the *kumman ur Korr*, the Daradun Council of Captains at Raku Ulrun.

Had Maiden Earth been present and active in the dark places beneath the Bloodshards, the matter would have been simple enough. Rundul would have extended his awareness through the Maiden's veins of power, through stone and soil, to the great halls at the twin peaks of Raku Ulrun. There his account would have been received by the *uldwar*, the ancient ones of the Firstmade. The Daradur would have been warned. His duty done, Rundul could have remained to do battle, to fight, to strike a blow against the ancient foe. He would have been killed, surely. But he would have died well.

However, Maiden Earth had long abandoned the Bloodshards, and in her absence Rundul knew he could not *send* the message. The message must therefore be *brought*. The enemy would seek to deter him, strive to deny him, that they might shield their sinister secret. Speed was needed. Rundul was swift. But some among the enemy were swifter. A few, perhaps, were stronger. Most were below and behind him. But miles of tunneled stone lay between the Darad and the surface –

Run!!!

The roar of thousands shook the stone, rippling the rock in tremors of rage. The thudding of booted feet on the run, the skittering of sharp claws over stone, the hoarse barking of commands – all flayed the black air in the wake of Rundul's passing, lashing his back with a single desperate decree:

Run!!!

Rundul's stride lengthened, his pace quickened. His black eyes glinted beneath fiercely furrowed brows. There was an intense indignity in such flight, a marked disgrace masked by need, camouflaged by the urgency of the message. Was he not fleeing the foe? The enemy had sensed him, had seen him, and now would seek his death. And he had his back to them.

Ah, the shame! But regardless of the dishonour he would certainly suffer, the *uldwar* at Raku Ulrun *must* be warned.

Run!!!

Must be warned.

Run!!!

Battle and death and grave tidings to be borne.

RUN!!!!!

And so Rundul ran.

Muscled arms pumping, thick legs thumping, the mighty Darad raced up the tunnel into utter blackness. The cries of his pursuers screeched at his back. The howls of the hunters drew steadily nearer.

And he had many long miles to go.

Then the tunnel branched into two greater passages: One led east, back the way Rundul had descended, the way he had come and with which he was familiar; the other led west, in the general direction of Raku Ulrun, but was strange and unknown to him. The Darad gave the matter no thought. The tidings were urgent. And he was a *mara Warator* of the Daradur, a warrior among warriors. He held no fear for that which he did not know.

Rundul went west.

The passage was wide and appeared well and recently traveled. The stench of the enemy was heavy in the thick air. Torches burned intermittently from iron sconces in the stone. Other tunnels led to and from the passage at irregular intervals, intertwining with it until it and they became indistinguishable from one another. But Rundul did not hesitate. He was a Darad, and even in the absence of the Maiden he was one with the rock of the earth.

Upward and westward he ran, his strong legs churning like powerful pistons. Behind him, the screeches of his pursuers clawed at the torch-born halflight, reaching for him with invisible talons and unseen blades. The fleeter among them were drawing nearer. Rundul sensed movement in the maze, shadows in the black, hideous things hunting him in the darkness. He felt them moving in parallel passages, matching his pace, hungering for his life, thirsting for his death.

Rundul knew his hunters were herding him, biding their time, gathering their strength. They waited only for the numbers they felt were necessary for a successful assault upon the solitary Stone Lord. Rundul sensed hundreds on either side of him, and thousands behind. The attack would come soon.

Very soon.

The attack came.

A flash of movement to his left, and an Unman darted out of the shadows, crude weapon raised, the creature's malformed features twisted further with hate and fear. Without slowing, Rundul swung his heavy axe to his left, one great blade splintering the iron of the Unman's helm and splitting its skull in two.

Rundul ran.

Three more Unmen appeared from tunnels before him, grouped themselves together and attacked Rundul as one. A single great sweep of Rundul's axe, and all three Unmen fell disemboweled upon the stone.

And Rundul ran.

Then a dozen of the man-things burst from the catacombs, assaulting Rundul from all sides. Rundul leapt from his feet, turning full-circle in the half-lit air, his war-axe whirling about him like a living thing. Two Unmen fell headless before Rundul's feet touched the ground again, four reeled away ripped and razed, and six ran screaming into the shadows.

And Rundul ran on.

The enemy feared him now. Their quarry was no common Daradun warrior – which would have been unnerving enough – but a Warder of the Wandering Guard. Loathed and feared, dreaded and despised, the warriors of the Wandering Guard made such frightful foes that, ordinarily, the thralls of the Blood King would have let a solitary Warder pass unhindered. But their numbers had swelled their courage, had soothed their natural trepidations. And they were driven by a will greater than their own, compelled by fear far surpassing that which they felt for a lone Warder of the Wandering Guard.

And so they pursued.

Rundul streaked over the rock of the passage floor, a shadowed blur in the half-dark, a strident thunder on the stone. The enemy came upon him in haphazard waves, often more by chance than by choice. The Darad's historied war-axe glowed red with blood and torchlight, and the legend of Rundul of Axar grew wilder with every slice of its great blades. Unmen threw themselves at him in desperate efforts to bodily bear him down. But the great Stone Lord shrugged them from him like water shaken from a wet hound. He was a Darad with a duty, as determined as rock. He refused to be denied.

Rundul ran on.

And then, from both sides and from behind, a choral howl of gleeful hope rent the air of the passage. Something huge and dark moved though the labyrinth of tunnels to Rundul's right, and though it was both lumbering and large, it was far swifter afoot than its quarry. At a twisting bend in the passage, a great black mass burst from the shadows before the racing Rundul.

An Urkrok.

The rock ogre's muscled immensity almost surpassed comprehension. Wielding a great club spiked with shards of iron, it came upon Rundul with the force and fury of an entire tribe of Unmen. Rundul did not break stride. Club met axe with a crash of rage, wrath on wrath, but one weapon's fury was the fiercer. Daradun steel shattered the wood and iron of the Urkrok's club, cutting through and past it with irresistible power, biting into the flesh and bone behind with teeth both terrible and true. The rock ogre roared with rage and pain, one massive fist coming down on Rundul's shoulder, bearing the Darad to his knees. Rundul gritted his teeth as he registered damage to his shoulder and deftly passed his axe to his good hand. Flashing like fire, the weapon's blades ripped into the legs of the Urkrok, severing both at the knees in a single stroke. The Urkrok tumbled like a felled tree.

Rundul ran on.

But the Urkrok had slowed him, and those behind him had narrowed the distance. Arrows screeched in the passage like whistled songs of doom, some finding Rundul's back, only to be denied by the hard *inrinil* mail that all Warders wore beneath their beaten leather. Howls, shrieks, screams of hunger and hatred surrounded him. Ill things moved in the tunnels about him, wretched creatures slunk in the shadows, sightless serpents slithered on the stone. The whole of the netherearth beneath the Bloodshards was alive with things on the hunt. Numberless voices in the stony deeps screamed for Daradun blood.

Rundul thundered on, his powerful legs propelled by purpose and passion, his wake strewn with a slew of blood and broken bodies.

But his ruined shoulder slowed him. Not for pain – for the Daradur knew no pain – but for the detrimental effect the injury had on his balance. So Rundul reached for the power of Maiden Earth inherent within himself, calling it to life – an inner light, an inner flame – and sent its healing fire to his wounded shoulder. Swift and soon a welcome warmth wrapped itself about the wound, mending muscle and binding bone.

His shoulder repaired, the damage undone, Rundul ran on.

The passage sloped upward at a greater angle, its grade becoming increasingly steep with each stride. The air thinned and cooled. Intuitively, Rundul knew the surface to be near. His black eyes blazed. Within him, something grinned triumphantly.

And then he sensed something in the cold stone that chilled his heated heart.

As he slashed his way through a cluster of screeching Unmen, Rundul perceived something darker and more deadly than either Unmen or Urkroks awaiting him in the near distance. But it was no creature, however foul of form, which so effectively cooled Rundul's inner fires. His innate Daradun stone-sense had belatedly warned him of the folly of his flight's path. He had sensed too late where, and to what, the passage he had chosen was leading.

But there could be no turning back. He had come much, much too far.

Rundul ran on.

The passage gradually leveled. Fewer and fewer torches lit the way. Soon there were none. All light faded, fell. But Daradun sight did not depend entirely upon light, and the deep darkness that filled the tunnel neither halted nor hindered Rundul's flight. Indeed, even in the black of the passage, he marked a change in the stone.

The tunnel there had been hewn by hand rather than formed by the natural convulsions and displacement of the earth's crust or by the power of primordial rivers that had run through the rock when the world was young. Rundul discerned that the passage had only recently been riven of the red rock beneath the Bloodshards. And, he intuited, the work had been left uncompleted.

And then the tunnel abruptly terminated before an impassable wall of tumbled and crumbled rock.

Snarling a curse, Rundul slowed, stopped.

He had run many long hard miles. He had slain dozens, scores of the enemy. But regardless of his valour, despite his skill, he had been herded like a beast, hounded, driven to a dead end of collapsed stone that forbade all further flight.

His brows knotted. He eyed the rough and rugged surface of the stone about him. His mind raced, measuring, calculating, devising. An impenetrable barrier before him. The solid stone of endless earth beneath him. Perhaps thirty feet of rigid rock above him. And an entire army of the enemy behind him.

And they were coming.

The corridor's unsullied dark reflected in Rundul's eyes, black on black. A few steps away from the blockade, he turned, braced his stout legs far apart. He took his axe into his left hand, extended that arm, and tapped the spiked head of the weapon against the rock wall. He then moved the axe to his right hand and rapped the other wall. He spat on the stone at his feet. A bestial growl rumbled in his breast. Eyes ablaze with black fire, his axe gripped in both mighty fists, Rundul awaited the enemy.

Let them come.

And so they came.

There are deeds done under sun, moon, star and stone for which the doer is best remembered, that define his existence more profoundly than all else. Such a deed was the battle Rundul of the Wandering Guard fought in the earth at the falling of that day. Long after his passing from the world, the name and deeds of Rundul of Axar would be honoured in sonorous song in the deep halls of the Daradur – but of all his many heroics, Rundul's solitary stand in the deep darkness beneath the Bloodshards would ever be the most renowned and recalled.

They came upon him in one endless wave, driven by rage and madness, forced forward by the crush of the throng behind them. They whelmed against the dancing defense of Rundul's axe with the weight of thousands. Dark forms leapt down the throat of the tunnel, Unman upon Unman, black manes flying, crude iron blades whirling. The very stone shook with the ferocity of their assault.

They were met with metal thew and living steel. The bitter blades of Rundul's axe dealt death masterfully. The darkness of the corridor seemed to retreat from the energy of his exertion, the battle illuminated by blade-shine and blood-sheen. Bodies and parts of bodies heaped at Rundul's feet, and brackish Unmannish blood made a mire of the stone. Dozens upon dozens died at the hand and steel of the great Daradun warrior.

Still they came.

Unmen poured the length of the passage in a flood of flesh and iron. Black blood flew from Rundul's blades like subterranean rain. But Rundul was slowly forced back by the sheer weight of their numbers and by their efforts to flank and surround him. Blows rained down upon him like insistent fists knocking on the doors of his death. A few evaded his defenses, blade and bolt landing with force upon him, only to be turned aside by the hardness of his *inrinil*. But the frequency of the blows was increasing, and the price of survival threatened to become beyond Rundul's power to purchase.

And still they came.

Rundul fought on. His axe sopped with slaughter. His face and beard were begrimed with blood that was not his own. His eyes were wild black lights of desperate defiance. His throat blistered with roared challenges, exertions and exultations. He only vaguely registered the entry of two enormous Urkroks into the seething sphere of battle. He tore at them with crazed rage, ripping through them with an axe-wrath he had not known since the bloodied fields before Mekkoleth on Sark-u-surum.

And his foes became afraid. They retreated. Scattered.

He was Rundul of Axar, Warder of the Wandering Guard, mighty warrior of the Daradur. Unmen and Urkroks would never defeat him alone.

They were not alone.

Strange ominous sounds scored the tunnel – scraping, clawing, dragging sounds, as though something overly large was striving to negotiate too small a passage. The earth quivered. Dust and debris fell from the coarsely carved ceiling of the corridor. A hot acrid smoke snaked the length of the tunnel, burning the air, singeing the stone.

And there followed the caustic crimson glow of infernal flame, and the black of the passage parted before it. Scarlet shadows stained the stone. Great whips of acidic wind lashed along the tunnel, scorching and sulphuric, like baneful breath from the black maw of a monstrous beast. And then came a terrible titanic roar, a peal of abominable power – the thunder of irrefutable doom and the breaking of the world.

And in the wake of that horrible harbinger came the beast.

Rundul stood alone amidst a chaos of blood and bodies and discarded weapons. His back to the wall of crumbled rock, he leaned heavily on the haft of his axe. His dark hair and beard dripped with blended bloods, one of which was his own now – a deep gash had been opened above his right eye, the skin torn and folded down to reveal the pink-white gleam of bone beneath. He stared down the corridor, his eyes as black as doom and as bleak as despair. There had once been defiance in those eyes. Now there was only death.

For against this thing he knew he could not stand.

Forth came the beast, a terrible thing of darkness and of fire and of impossible power. But all Rundul could see of the fiend were two great crimson eyes, massive fissures of malevolent flame suspended in smoke and shadow. The Darad's heart thudded with such force that his breast ached – for such a thing might move even the boldest of warrior hearts.

And Rundul's warrior heart was indeed moved. But not by fear. Neither by despair nor by doom. And the death in his eyes was not his own.

Rundul met the beast's fiery gaze with eyes of cold black ice. Something of a smile tugged at the corners of the Darad's bewhiskered mouth. And for a moment, a wind of doubt wavered the flames of the fiend's eye-fire.

Must be warned.

Then, with a speed and agility that belied his bulky build, Rundul spun about, putting his back to the beast, and swung his war-axe against the barricade of broken stone to the fullest extreme of his exceptional strength. Steel met stone with the ringing chime of doom, showering sparks like shards of loosed lightning. The rock was firm and sure. But Daradun steel was unlike any other – as hard as the hands of the people that forged it. And it did not give to granite.

The rock of the netherearth shuddered with the memory of impact, the after-tremors of steel on stone causing dark faults in the walls and the ceiling, creeping covenants of destruction.

The beast surged forward in a fury of flame and darkness.

His weapon wedged deeply and firmly in the rock, Rundul flexed his muscles about his frame like metal lattices and summoned from deep within him the quiescent power of Maiden Earth. From the very core of his soul she rose, true, pure, strong. Instantaneously, Rundul's flesh became as stone and his bones were as steel. His being was as hard and as perfect as diamond.

Impervious.

The beast charged.

Maiden Earth arisen within him, Rundul sent her forth from himself, through his arm and hand, through the living steel of his war-axe and into the dead stone. The Maiden's ancient puissance poured from him, flooding the red rock with pure, unsullied power.

Power.

Life.

The essence of Maiden Earth was life, and she was the fundamental foundation of each Darad's being, of each Darad's existence. It was this elemental quintessence that Rundul sent into the stone, altruistically expending his inner force, his spirit, his very life. Rundul's soul beseeched the stone – stone long accursed, long spoiled, long dead – to remember Maiden Earth, to remember her, remember her.

Remember.

The stone remembered. Remembered. And revered.

Alive once more, the rock rose to respond to the call of Maiden Earth and to the selfless sacrifice of the Darad that served her. As Rundul willed forth more and more of his inner being, of his own self, the rock rumbled with a righteous rage too long pent, too long fettered. Alive, awake, and angry. The rock of the vaguely vaulted ceiling pulsed once, twice, like the pounding of a great concave heart. The stone beat with energy, with force, with life.

With Rundul's life.

Thmm-thmmp.

At every beat of the stone heart, the cracks in the rock multiplied, widened, spread, deepened.

Thmm-thmmp.

Great chunks of granite fell to the floor. In the distance, Unmen shrieked with sudden terror. The corridor quaked.

Thmm-thmmp.

The darkness hove. Rock rained from above. The beast aborted its charge, its blazing gaze cast upward. The flaming eyes swelled in sudden comprehension. A roar of rage burst from the behemoth's breast, and in fury and frustration it hurled a massive iron mace at the Darad's exposed back.

Thmm-thump.

And as Rundul's Maiden-armoured back absorbed the impact of Hell-wrought iron, his own roar thundered from his throat, rose into the rippling rock, beseeching the Maiden bestow upon him one final boon.

Thmm.

Silence.

Stillness.

An instant in time and space of precise and precious peace.

And then the earth exploded.

RUN!!!

Rundul was on the marge of unconsciousness when the word ripped into his mind as would a gleaming dagger down black canvas. The darkness in him parted, peeled away. Acuity, lucidity instantly returned.

He registered and recognized grave injuries to his form other than that which marred his brow. Something had torn in the flesh of his left thigh. His right arm was limp and lifeless. And most grievous of all was the wound on his back where the fiend's monstrous mace had ruptured leather and *inrinil* to smite his Maiden-hardened body beneath and brand him with a great blue-black mark of shame. Rundul could feel the bruise spreading as swiftly and as surely as must word of his disgrace.

Fatigue battered at Rundul's will with fists of doubt. He had exhausted the entirety of the essence of Maiden Earth that had been in him, all that had been his to call forth and command. He had spent all but the infinitesimal spark that defined life and defied death. That light he had not doused. And though Maiden Earth had shielded him, and in answer to his plea had raised him up through the rubble of blasted stone, her power was finite, and she had faltered and failed fully five feet below the earth's surface.

There Rundul remained, his prostrate form encased in a sarcophagus of shattered stone.

Rundul had realized the risk, had considered the consequences. He had accepted them. And now the weight of those consequences lay in the form of tons of collapsed rock and earth slowly settling upon him, driving his breastbone in upon itself with each laboured breath, with each passing second.

The spark within him flickered dubiously.

But Rundul's heart yet beat and his fires yet burned. His left hand yet gripped his war-axe. And he yet had terrible tidings to bear.

Must.

Be.

Warned.

Somewhere at the western edge of the Bloodshards, freshly shattered stone stirred. Something struggled for the surface with extravagant strengths of purpose and sinew, and neither could be stayed.

As the ebon of deepening night shadowed the land, a great war-axe was fisted through sundered stone into the cool sweetness of open air. The mingled light of moon and star danced on steel. And then, bit by bit, with an expenditure of energy that would fracture a more fragile heart, a dust-drenched Darad emerged from the earth.

Rising slowly to his feet upon the newly broken stone, leaning wearily upon his axe, Rundul of Axar surveyed his position, considered his condition. He found himself in the middle of a broad concavity of rock and rubble. Blood flowed freely from his forehead. His right arm hung from his shoulder like a dead thing. His left leg protested the weight he compelled it to bear, but held, though moving promised to be slow.

His back burned.

Muttering curses to himself, Rundul climbed to the western rim of the bowl and gazed out upon the night.

Westward the moon was falling, spilling soft white light upon windswept rolling hills. To the south, the terrain flattened to a plain of grass sparkling gently with moonlight on dew. North lay the tundral marshes of Coldmire, drear and dark in descended night. And at his bruised back were the broken ruins of the Bloodshards, desolate and desecrate, a morbid monument to the devastation of war.

Then, amidst that night-mantled maze of shattered stone, a shrill cry of discovery rose into the darkness.

Gazing back into the Bloodshards, Rundul caught flits of shadow, dark flutters of movement in the distance. Myriad voices of malice and malevolence barked in answer to the initial cry, a hungry chorus of hunters in their hundreds.

Rundul groaned aloud.

The chase was not done.

RUN!!!

Spitting a curse punctuated by bloody sputum, Rundul lumbered as swiftly as his injured leg allowed. Westward. Into the hills. The terrain altered immediately, as broken stone gave way to razor grass and bramble. Despite the presence of vegetation, the eldritch essence of the earth had fled that place. The Maiden had long abandoned the Bloodshards and immediate environs. Rundul's boots beat a carcass overgrown with gorse and grave grass. Abandoned without, expended within. The Warder knew he could neither call upon Maiden Earth to heal his hurts nor bear his message to the *uldwar* at Raku Ulrun.

He knew he was alone.

Alone, but for his hunters.

And with every laborious stride that Rundul took, the sounds of their pursuit shrieked nearer at his back. His right arm flapped at his side, limp and useless. Blood leaked into his eyes, into his bristling beard. The wound on his back swelled and small scarlet droplets oozed through his blackened skin. His exhaustion was like that of a pit dog forced to fight far past the limits of its stamina. The night seemed to have the physicality of oil, black and thick and viscous. Darkness weighed upon his shoulders and pressed against his progress. As he struggled down the sixth hill, his left leg faltered and he fell, his muscled mass rolling the remaining length of the grade like a bounding boulder.

Rundul regained his feet slowly. His fatigue was become prohibitive and final. He had drained the well of Maiden Earth within him. He had spent his physical strength in bursting free of the red rubble that was to have been his untimely tomb. And he had lost much blood. So much blood.

He was failing.

Rundul hunched heavily on the haft of his axe and gazed through his own blood at the rise of the next hill before him. The hill was higher than the others, and its benighted crown was marked with the blacker shadows of a scattering of immense boulders and great flat shards of stone. There was an import of design in the placement of those stones, a significance Rundul recognized and recalled.

He had been there half a millennium before, had been there when the warding stones were erected by the Daradur after the fall of Mekkoleth on Sark-u-surum. He had been among those who had gathered the corpses of their slain foes upon a broad flat expanse of the plain, layer upon layer of flesh and leather and iron. In little time the mound of the dead had risen higher than those of soil and stone around it, a small mountain of festering, wasted mortality. Innumerous enemy dead – Unmen and Urkroks, gargantuan Graniants, dragons and demons – were deposited there, doused with oil, and burned. The fires of that polluted pyre blazed for seven days and seven nights, the coals and embers smouldering for a dozen more. And when cinder was reduced to ash, and dust returned to dust, the healing had begun.

Green grass had sprouted forth from the black soil, abundant flowers unfolded and bloomed, and life arose where death had been. And then upon the mound's crown the Daradur erected great grey stones as monuments of remembrance or markers of warning – that neither friend nor foe forget what had been done there, that evil would never prevail over the union of the Guardian Peoples, that the pureness of the Earth was sacrosanct.

And nearly five hundred years thence, the stones still stood.

Fongar ur Piruth. The Teeth of Truth.

Rundul moved toward these grey markers with the shambling gait of the walking dead. Wounded, exhausted, failing, he ascended the hill in slow silence, his blood slicking the grass behind him. He was keenly aware of the swift deterioration of his condition. But his only concern was for the delivery of the message.

Must be warned.

And so he struggled on. On and up.

The gently graded hill was as a sharply raised mountain to the weakening Darad. The howls of his pursuers hammered the hills at his back. In torturous time, he reached the summit and shuffled among the grey teeth of *Fongar ur Piruth*, seeking sanctuary among those stones of death and defiance.

Sanctuary – or a place to stand.

Rundul knew his condition forbade further flight. He could not continue. He felt a hollow humming through his boots – the earth there was not dead, but dormant, slumbering, a comely maid adrift in the blissful oblivion of deep sleep. Rundul stamped haplessly, but he could not waken her; the power within him to do so was exhausted, spent. His only recourse was to stand and fight and hope for aid. His axe might purchase him a little time. The hill gave him the high ground, the stones some semblance of defense. And if luck and chance and providence would have it, the nightwind might bear the din of battle to friendly ears.

Luck and chance and providence.

Nonsense.

Rundul turned to face the east, his blood-soaked beard become stiff in the turgid chill. The howling of his hunters drew nearer. Rundul gripped his axe as tightly as his waning strength allowed. *Fongar ur Piruth* was good ground. Despite his exhaustion, he might send a few of his pursuers to share the fate of their ancient forebears before he died.

Let...them...come.

Rundul did not see the hulking shadow detach itself from the stone to his left. He sensed movement in the air too late to avoid the blow of the mighty fist that took him fully in the face. The force and the fury behind that fist sent Rundul sprawling to the ground, his axe flying from his grasp. His nose split open, spewing fresh and precious blood. His head swam in a turbulent blackwater of shadow and darkness. The backs of his eyelids were bedecked with twinkling lights, and in his ears roared rivers of rushing blood.

The assailant knotted a fist in Rundul's torn tunic, hauling the massive Darad to his feet with extraordinary strength and ease. The night whirled. Rundul felt hot angry breath on his face. He opened his eyes, striving to still the swirl of darkness in his mind. He willed his eyes to focus. But all he saw was blood and shadow.

"Why do you run?"

The voice was harsh, guttural, thick with vehemence and accusation, laced with danger and fire. Spittle spattered Rundul's eyes. He was entirely at the dubious mercy of his attacker. But flares of familiarity spurred Rundul from his swoon, pulled him back from the brink of insensibility. The ruthless roughness of the voice, the power in the fist at his breast, the irresistible sense of peril and rage that emanated like flame from the presence of his assailant – all were known to Rundul. Known and loved.

Dulgar.

Dulgar. *Garun-tar*. The Wild One.

A Captain of the Wandering Guard, an ancient one of the Firstmade, Dulgar was wrath incarnate, rage and might conjoined and personified in the form of an indomitable Daradun warrior.

Dulgar! Chance, luck and providence! I beseech you, forgive this fool his doubt!

Rundul's sight swam into focus. And he immediately wished it had not. The face of his Captain was racked with rage, contorted with contempt. In the midst of a flaming red mane of hair and beard, Dulgar's lone eye burned with a mad black fire.

"You *run!*" accused the Wild One, spitting the word with spite and venom. He spun Rundul about. "You fuckin' *run!* And your back is marked. *Marked!* You *flee* enemy blades. Speak! Explain this shame! Or I'll kill you right where you fuckin' stand and regret only that I once considered you a brother."

Rundul gritted his blood-smeared teeth against the accusation. But Dulgar could not be blamed for his vehemence. The charge was neither false nor unfounded. Rundul *had* run. His back bore the brand of his disgrace, but the wound to his proud heart ran deeper. Yet it had been pride that had borne Rundul so far from the abomination beneath the Bloodshards. That pride had served him well, and would not fail him now.

"I have seen things," Rundul hissed into the knotted face of his Captain. "But" – a wave of dizziness took him – "I don't...don't have the strength." He gasped for air. "I need...need you to see. Dulgar. *Garun-tar*. Can you *see*?"

Something in Dulgar's hard face softened. "Fuck you, Rundy."

"I'll take that as a 'yes'," sighed Rundul. "Look. See inside, brother. See what I have seen."

Dulgar's red brows twisted downward. "I don't fuckin' like..."

"*Look!*"

Dulgar looked. Looked upon the memory-tale reflected in the black mirror of Rundul's eyes. Looked and saw. Saw all that Rundul had seen in the deep places of the earth. Saw all that he had done. Dulgar saw all.

And understood.

"Ah," grunted the Wild One. Feral light flared in his solitary eye. "Fuck."

Rundul waited.

"A fuckin' army, is it?" The Wild One's lone eye narrowed. "No fuckin' *dwar-Durka*?"

Rundul shook his head.

Dulgar glowered. "Fuck. I feel the desperate need to kill some of those ugly fuckin' bald fuckers."

Rundul waited once more.

Momentarily, "So you aren't a total fuckbeard, Rundy," the red-maned Captain growled gruffly. "I'll send word to Raku Ulrun."

Rundul nodded. He expected no apology, and received none.

Dulgar stooped to ground, placing the flat of his hand against the hard dormant earth. He remained there momentarily, motionless – but power pulsed from him into the stone and soil, waking the earth, then streaking westward. When he straightened once more, Dulgar held Rundul's axe in one hand.

"Done," the Wild One said lowly. "Drogul's fucked off up north, but Brully's been warned."

Rundul almost smiled. Relief assuaged his heart and soul. His flight had not been futile, had not been in vain. The scars of his back might be less sorely worn. Knowing that he had not failed in his purpose, Rundul might eventually learn to endure his shame.

But Dulgar was not done.

"You're not off the anvil yet, mudfucker." The Wild One's tone was flat, bereft of inflection.

Rundul said nothing, only lowered his head.

Then he felt his Captain's hand grasp the forepart of his wounded, useless arm. A surge of heat coursed from Dulgar's strong grasp into the immobile flesh of Rundul's limb. Almost immediately, health and power returned to Rundul's arm, and his own hand answered the Wild One's vigourous clasp. Invisible tongues of healing flame licked Rundul's assortment of wounds. The gash in his forehead closed, the strength of his leg was restored. And the burning of his back cooled.

From somewhere at the edge of the euphoric glee he felt at his healing, Rundul heard Dulgar deadpan, "Like I said...fuck you, Rundy."

Rundul's eyes were at once blacker than the night and brighter than any star when he raised them to his Captain's fierce face.

Grinning wildly, madly, Dulgar held forth Rundul's axe.

"Time to get off the fuckin' anvil." A twisted grimace that served as a smile. "Brother."

A cold wind battered at the stones of *Fongar ur Piruth* as Rundul reclaimed his weapon. The night shrieked with rage as his pursuers flooded over the sixth hill. Rank upon roiling rank of Unmen, a phalanx of enormous Urkroks, Graniants as tall as oaks. They poured down the last slope like a black sea of savagery and slaughter.

Within him, Rundul's warrior heart pounded in anticipation. His eyes and axe-blades shone in the night.

There would be no more running.

Let the come, Rundul insisted one last time.

Dulgar released his own axe from its bindings at his back. The weapon's steel was as red as the Captain's wild mane of hair, as crimson as freshly spilled blood. A sound like laughter rumbled in the back of the ferocious Darad's throat. The laval fire of madness burned in his solitary eye. As the thralls of Shadow swarmed up the grassy shoulders of *Fongar ur Piruth*, blood seeped from beneath the cracked iron of his eyepatch like a tear-stream of joy.

Together, shoulder to shoulder and axe to axe, the two Stone Lords faced the rising tides of night, onslaught and death.

Chuckled the Wild One, "Stupid fuckers."

And so.

2

THE ERELIAN AMBASSADOR

"Honour the nation that has heroes
And pity the hero who has no nation."

Valerian, first King of New Erellan

Cold and hard and sheer was the rock face of the great Westwall. One and a half thousand feet high and as many miles long, an ancient product of the earth's deep and dangerous volatility, the colossal cliff cut in a roughly northeastern arc from the Erelian capital of Hiridith in the south to the abrupt break at Doomfall in the north. Behind and above the Westwall, near its precipitous rim, rose the gargantuan stone masses of the Haunted Mountains – a vast and towering range wreathed in the mists of time and the myths of men, casting the final three hundred leagues of the Westwall's northern run in evergloom and deepest silence.

But nigh unto dark Doomfall that silence was to be ignominiously broken.

The grey mizzle that had dogged the mounted company of Erelian guardsmen since their departure from Hiridith had done nothing to douse the flames of their captain's ire, an ire the revered veteran of both Trade Wars had endeavored mightily to contain. But forty long grey days and thirty-nine cold damp nights on the rough trail beneath the Westwall had effectively eroded the fetters of Captain Bronnus Teagh's self-imposed silence. Five hundred leagues of wet difficult riding through endless scree of fallen stone had corroded his iron determination to leave the matter alone. Only his martial discipline, hardened by years of warfare, honed keen by bitter lessons learned on distant battlefields, had enabled him to stay his tongue and say nothing.

But no longer.

"The Senator's daughter!"

The baritone bellow echoed off the stony face of the Westwall like a series of thunderclaps.

Startled, the guardsmen on the path before Bronnus swung their mounts to face their seething captain. Those behind him immediately reined in their steeds. There ensued a hushed and nervous stillness broken only by the wet breaths of horse and wind. But Captain Bronnus Teagh's outburst had not been entirely unexpected. The guardsmen braced themselves, a collective tautness gripping their throats. One hundred seasoned soldiers felt their hearts pound just a little faster.

And then the heavy, anxious air was pierced by the most incongruous hoot of unmitigated glee.

Grinning like a fool, resplendent in cerulean cloak and silver chain of office, a young man of evident distinction nudged his lean grey mare forward to touch noses with Bronnus' powerful roan stallion.

"Teller of the Tale!" exclaimed Ambassador Axennus Teagh, chuckling. "The giant of my brother's wrath at long last wakes from its overlong slumber!"

The Captain glowered in the drizzle.

The Ambassador's handsome, expressive face then sank swiftly to a mask of exaggerated dejection.

"But alas, dear brother, you have lightened my purse considerably – and fattened that of good Decan Regorius – for in lasting ignorance of my own sibling's nature, I had wagered you would suffer through no fewer than forty-*one* days of silence on the subject." Axennus smiled, a smile both beautiful and infuriating, then glanced at the dreary skies. "Alas, I had not foreseen this weather…"

Some among the guardsmen lowered their eyes, stifling the laughter reflexively swelling in their bosoms. Not least among them was Regorius, a stocky, muscular albino with a penchant for gambling, whose horse now hoofed at the ground as though she were an equine extension of her master's own apprehension.

Another guardsman leaned across the neck of his mount and muttered, "Cap's gonna remember that, Whitey."

Stark white eyebrows knotted above piercing pink eyes. "So what, Maddy? I bet *on* him, not against him."

Maddus leaned back and grinned. "Goin' a little pale there, mate."

Regorius growled something obscene.

But the entirety of the Captain's attention, the whole of his anger, was focused solely on Axennus, his proverbially precocious younger brother.

Axennus sat astride his mare, grinning.

A flush took Bronnus' broad stubbled features, his teeth grinding in his jaws. He held the reins of his steed in white-knuckled fists. Disregarding his brother's characteristic mirth, Bronnus slowly, emphatically repeated his concern:

"*The Senator's daughter.*"

Newly appointed Ambassador of the Erelian Republic to the Fiannian land of Lindannan – the first to ever hold that lofty title – Axennus Teagh was an exquisitely handsome man who seemed years younger than the thirty-five summers he had seen. Tall and lean, he wore his fine dark hair long and loose, and his keen hazel eyes sparkled with fiendish intellect. The perennially whiskerless face was agile and emotive, and its perfect smile ranged easily from the beatific to the cold and deadly. His presence exuded both a limitless energy and an almost boyish hunger for adventure.

It was no great wonder that such a man of passion, action and irresistible diablerie would find himself embroiled in more than a proprietary allotment of controversy.

Thus the Senator's daughter.

Axennus slumped slightly in his saddle, long fingers folding casually about the polished horn. His features reassumed the look of disappointed hurt.

"My dear brother, it would appear that you believe me to be the cause of some...discomfiture."

Bronnus snarled silently, but refused to leap to the bait.

The Ambassador's flexible features swiftly transformed his face into that of a grinning imp. The laughing light of his eyes was so very bright in contrast to the damp misty gloom of the boulder-strewn trail. Neither the imposing Westwall nor the corporeal darkness of the Haunted Mountains could cast a shadow on Axennus' indomitable spirit.

"However, as is your wont," continued the Ambassador, "you have founded your conclusion upon haste and half-knowledge."

"My conclusion?" Bronnus frowned his confusion. "Half-knowledge?"

"Half-knowledge," affirmed the Ambassador, eyes flashing gleefully.

"Nonsense!" Bronnus waved his hand dismissively. "I have half-knowledge of nothing!"

The Ambassador actually giggled.

Strange strangled sounds escaped the throats of several guardsmen as they struggled to fight their laughter back and down. Regorius coughed. Maddus sputtered into his gauntlet. Others turned away, torn between love for the Ambassador and respect for their captain.

Realizing belatedly that he had, despite his greatest efforts, swallowed his brother's bait and resembled a hooked trout flopping helplessly on a rocky shore, Bronnus inhaled deeply, effectively burying the colourful barrage of profanity that threatened to explode from him. He crossed his thickly muscled arms about his chest and glared at his tormentor.

"Consider yourself fortunate, little brother," rumbled the Captain, "that I, in my folly, swore an oath to our passing father that I would never cause you actual physical injury."

"A good and wise man was Jophus Teagh," nodded Axennus, smiling in warm reflection. An eyebrow then rose roguishly. "And also a man of some intellect who would not have missed my meaning."

Bronnus' frown deepened, darkened. "Missed your meaning? Of what, exactly?"

"Half-knowledge," replied Axennus promptly.

Bronnus cast a beseeching gaze to the grey indifference of the gloomy skies. He sighed. "Half-knowledge again."

The Ambassador nodded, feigning impatience.

"Yes, Bron, half-knowledge."

Bronnus glowered. He knew instinctively, and from more than a little experience, that his brother was manipulating the conversation in a particular but as yet unrevealed direction. And just as instinctively, and from equal experience, Bronnus rued treading that path. Nevertheless, in the company of the inimitable Axennus, such journeys were often brutally necessary.

"To what half-knowledge, specifically, do you refer, Axo?"

The laughing light sparkled playfully in the young Ambassador's hazel eyes.

"Why, to that concerning the question of the Senator's daughter, of course."

Bronnus closed his eyes. The discussion had come full circle, and along the arc the flames of the Captain's original anger had been doused, leaving only the embers of everpresent aggravation. And from that char and ash was sprouting the seed of understanding.

"I see," grumbled Bronnus. "You are saying that I know only half of the story."

The Ambassador clapped his hands together in delight.

"Precisely!"

The Captain pondered in momentary silence, the wet wind cooling the ruddy heat in his face. *Half of the story.* And then, suddenly,

Bronnus' dark eyes widened in something akin to horror – for what had been but a seed had flowered and bloomed. And with that understanding came shock and disbelief, twin leeches sucking the blood from Bronnus' countenance, leaving him uncharacteristically pale and waxen.

"Teller of the Tale," he whispered, more prayer than curse, "you did *not!*"

Axennus assumed a posture of disinterest, apparently distracted by an imperfection in an otherwise flawlessly manicured fingernail. Then his eyes flicked back to his brother, two little lights dancing with glee.

"Oh, but I did," he said softly.

Bronnus' mouth fell open, his jaw flapping like the wing of a wounded bird.

"The Lady Prescia *and* the Lady Cartia? *Both?*"

"The very two."

Axennus winked in wickedness at Regorius who was veritably choking on the laughter suppressed in his bosom. Several other guardsmen were likewise afflicted.

The Captain's mouth clapped shut.

The Ambassador absently stroked the mane of his steed. The grey nickered, as though she shared her rider's amusement.

"The two lovely daughters of the esteemed Senator Fallus," Axennus confirmed in a tone of fond reminiscence. "Musically gifted, as you may have heard. Voices like a cool rain on desert sands. Exquisite! Their tongues work together in such beautiful harmony –"

"*Enough!*"

Flames of ire flushed Bronnus' mien with heat once more. The sheen of thin rain steamed from his cheeks. His dark eyes flashed in the quarterlight of swiftly falling dusk.

"Your banter, little brother, beguiles and befuddles but signifies nothing. Ever have you tried my patience and the goodness of my nature. Though our features betray our shared blood, you have aged me before my time – so much so that I appear more the father than the brother. But you *are* my brother and I am honour-bound to love you."

Axennus pursed his lips. "How very generous of you...brother."

Bronnus was undeterred.

"Nevertheless, I am not so compelled to *like* you. Neither you nor what you do. Fraternal love need not render eternal tolerance. And I will tolerate your antics no longer." He leaned closer to his younger sibling. "You must *learn*, Axennus, that people – my own lost cause notwithstanding – are not your playthings. Nor are women your toys, objects of pleasure and pretty little keepsakes to be petted and then tossed aside when your whims alter. No action is without consequence, dear brother, and your own has earned us disgrace and exile!"

"Disgrace and exile," echoed Axennus, raising a hand to his mouth. "Dear me, I *am* a menace! I should be locked in an oversmall cage and poked with pointy little sticks!"

Bronnus glared.

Axennus smiled.

Bronnus blinked. His broad shoulders sagged. His chest heaved a heavy sough as his anger passed from him once more. All semblance of intelligent discourse with his irrepressible sibling had been ever futile. This particular discussion had, in a matter of minutes, rendered Bronnus emotionally spent. Silently, he cursed the misty drizzle and wished he had said nothing.

In a tone of fatigued surrender, Bronnus said, "Would the one daughter have not sufficed?"

The Ambassador cocked his head to one side. Mercifully, he did not gloat upon his victory. His smile remained, but was soft and silent.

The Captain waited, straight and square in his saddle, his oilskin cloak drip, drip, dripping.

At some small length, the young Ambassador chuckled softly. "The question, dear brother, was one not of sufficiency but of opportunity."

Bronnus shook his head and grimaced.

"Are your nocturnal needs so insatiable, Axo? Indeed, I am somewhat surprised that no invitation was extended to the mother!"

Axennus arched an eyebrow.

"Oh, you did *not!*" exclaimed Bronnus.

The Ambassador laughed, and glibly waved a hand.

"Unfortunately, the Senator's lovely wife was otherwise occupied with a pressing concern in the sleeping chamber of a nobleman other than he to whom she is lawfully wed."

"I see."

"But do not find fault with the Lady Evia's indiscretions. Her esteemed husband, the principled Senator Fallus – an unfortunate name, that, yet somehow exceedingly appropriate – reserves his affections exclusively for athletic young men, thereby relieving the lady of any real blame in the matter. Indeed, the paternity of the daughters Prescia and Cartia should be the subject of some intriguing debate, think you not?"

"I do not trouble myself with the private lives of politicians and their spouses."

"No?"

The Captain of the Ambassadorial Guard chortled in spite of himself. "*You*, dear brother, are no politician."

"None at all, nor do I desire to become such a creature," agreed the Ambassador. "I am, however, the Erelian Republic's chosen representative to the Fiannar at Druintir in Lindannan, this world's most noble and storied people and land, and the founders – should you believe the histories – of our own great and wondrous nation."

Bronnus grunted. "You speak of your appointment as though it were reward and approbation rather than penance and banishment."

"I speak of it as I see it."

"Nevertheless, your bedding and deflowering of the ladies Prescia and Cartia –"

"Bedding and deflowering?" interrupted Axennus, straightening, seemingly truly taken aback. "To the former I readily admit, but in regard to the latter I must protest my innocence! Your knowledge of women in general, and of the ladies Prescia and Cartia in particular, is scant and found wanting. Believe me, dear brother, there were no flowers of which to speak."

"*Nevertheless*," persisted Bronnus, frowning, "had it not been for your lecherous interlude with the Senator's daughter –"

Axennus grinned

"– *daughters*," growled Bronnus, glowering, "the glorious North March Mounted Reserve would not have been disbanded, you would not have been exiled as delegate to a land of faded legends and little else, and – most significantly – I and these good men would not be nearly fifteen hundred miles from home, cold, damp and miserable, and with no foreseeable prospect of return." He leaned forward. "Forgive me, please, should I appear underjoyed and a little lacking in gratitude."

Axennus Teagh's grin faded, fell. He studied his brother with slightly narrowed eyes, the cunning light that swam in those grey-green pools flickering sharply. Then he turned his gaze away.

The dusk had thickened the gloom beneath the Westwall. High above the towering cliff's precipitous lip, the violet vanguard of night merged with the huge shadow of the mist-crowned Haunted Mountains, a mating of eternal powers, a primordial bond bearing all into inevitable blackness.

Axennus Teagh, Ambassador of the Erelian Republic to ancient Lindannan, watched the deepening darkness in sobre, almost medita-tive silence. The wind rose and tousled his long hair. When, in time, he returned his hazel gaze to his brother's rough visage, Axennus was no longer the young rogue prone to impish trickery and verbal play. Rather, he had once again become the intelligent, precise man who had brilliantly commanded a force of twenty-two hundred men in the recent Second Trade War against the invading hordes of the Southfleetian Empire. His face was rigid, stony, and his eyes were deep with knowledge.

Then, his voice sifting like an invisible sea upon the bemurked sands of twilight, the Ambassador said softly, "I was unaware that wisdom and reason abandon you so readily, dear brother." His tone was utterly bereft of banter, yet free of condescension.

Sensing the end to mirth, all impulse for laughter departed the men of the Ambassadorial Guard, and they sat mounted in quiet, def-erential stillness.

Bronnus seethed did not speak.

"Be you truly of the opinion that our fortune, past or present, is dictated by the vivacity of my loins, then your ignorance is severe indeed and should not be so flagrantly and willfully flaunted."

Bronnus said nothing.

The Ambassador's voice, though he did not raise it, carried clear and strong so that all would hear and know:

"The glorious North March Mounted Reserve was *not* disbanded for the reason proffered here. Our term of service ended when the war ended. We were neither a professional nor a voluntary force, but rather one conscripted of the idle, the unruly, the criminal and the simply odd. We were assembled solely to relieve the garrisons in the north, enabling the regular Legion forces stationed there to engage the Southfleetians at the front. Little more was expected of us than the policing of the provinces, and none would have even predicted that we would see battle.

"I would like to believe I was awarded my original commission as a tenant in the North March Mounted Reserve by Legion Command because they wanted a young officer of some intelligence to whom this motley assemblage of misfits could relate. The truth of the matter is likely something else entirely, and is neither here nor there nor anywhere. But imagine my surprise when I learned the legendary hero of the Four Forts had *also* been assigned to the Reserve. I am still unraveling how my overly protective elder brother managed that, but it likely has something to do with debt owed our father's estate by certain men of influence within Legion Command. That would explain the 'how'...the 'why' remains a mystery to this very day. Whatever the reason, old Commander Cassus was ecstatic to have a true hero and proven warrior in the person of Bronnus Teagh as his second in command – so came the Iron Captain to the North March Mounted Reserve.

"But when the old man came to the end of his tale, and no replacement was forthcoming from Legion Command, Captain Bronnus Teagh, in wisdom or in folly, declined command in favour of *me*, a junior officer with little practical battle experience, but whom the Captain considered a decent strategist and tactician. Again, it is unknown – to me – how a mere tenant came to be promoted to Commander, but diligent forensic accountings of the Teagh family fortune and Legion Command's war chest would probably shine some light on this dubious mystery.

"Yet what need had a policing force in the provinces for an able battle-planner? None. But Captain Teagh well knew I could not sit idle in the wilderness when the enemy was breaching Erelian defenses to the east and threatening the lands all along the River March. Thus it must have come as no surprise to him that my first decision as Commander was to muster the entire Reserve and ride east to the succour of beleaguered Northkeep."

Night was falling fast. The eastwind carried a dark chill. But neither dark nor cold caused the shivers that took each and every soldier of the Ambassadorial Guard.

"The North March Mounted Reserve broke the siege of Northkeep. The Mounted Reserve made possible and performed the Miracle at Anthum. The Reserve came timely and unlooked-for to the Battle of Silver Bridge, wresting Republican victory from the black grasp of defeat and destruction. And the Reserve, war-weary, sleep-deprived, famished and exhausted, held the centre of the line in the final, decisive battle at Rhille-haven in the Delta.

"Thus a legend was born."

The Men of the Ambassadorial Guard listened fixedly, absorbed, their attention rapt; the memories too near in time and dear in heart to have faded.

Mists of the falling night, or of another origin altogether, dampened Captain Bronnus Teagh's eyes.

As one entranced by his own voice, the Ambassador to Lindannan continued.

"The Reserve fought thirteen major engagements of the war, Erelian victories all, and we were ever foremost into the fray. Early on, we had simply, somewhat dismissively and often inimically, been called 'Bronny's Bastards' by those few in Legion Command who acknowledged our existence. But soon, when referring to the Reserve, both friend and foe were to hiss the epithet 'Ghost Brigade', the former in prayer and hope, the latter in horror and despair. Forsooth, the very rumour of our proximity to the field came to cast the Southfleetians in fear and doubt, and soon their velvet-hatted masters put prices of ten thousand gold rods upon my head and another ten upon that of the invincible Iron Captain." He glanced at his brother, and Bronnus lowered his eyes briefly. "A further ten thousand would have been awarded to the Southfleetian who might wrest our standard from us, so feared and notorious was the Blue Banner. But the Teller was to tell a different tale, and all these prizes would go unclaimed.

"Remarkably, of the twenty-two hundred men that first rode to the relief of Northkeep and two years of war, *twenty-one hundred and sixteen* returned whole and hale to their grateful capital of Hiridith. And when the Republican Legions paraded in triumph and splendour through the streets of the Silver City, the people's loudest, most raucous cheers were saved for the men of the North March Mounted Reserve – the grand and glorious Ghost Brigade.

"Indeed, we had become more than a collection of unlikely heroes. We had become icons – men of steel, polished in legend and mythos. Men revered us, children adored us, women desired us. Balladeers, bards and poets immortalized us. Our coin was of little or no worth in the taverns, inns and brothels of the Republic – our acclaim was our currency. And the passage of time did not diminish our standing – to the contrary, our renown grew with each tale of our deeds retold.

"But even in Hiridith – nay, *especially* in Hiridith – not all ears that heard these tales were particularly friendly."

The darkness deepened, seeming to slide from the starless firmament as though down a slope greased with midnight. The wet wind whistled eerily against the blackened face of the Westwall. The chill intensified to a more bitter cold. The horses nickered and snorted. But the Erelian soldiers said nothing. Only the white mists they exhaled betrayed they breathed at all.

"Men of small minds in high places, namely the Senate, Legion Command, and – Teller forfend – the Temple of the Tome, grew wary of our popularity, and eventually came to fear the fervour of our fame. However foundless this fear may have been, for none among us possessed any political aspirations or want for power, our leaders deemed it wise to release us from service. The war won, the day of the North March Mounted Reserve, however bright it may have been, was done.

"But what to do with the more than one-hundred-score veterans of the Reserve in their midst at Hiridith? Our presence in the Silver City made the men in power increasingly nervous, as they well knew their own popularity had waned, that the people had grown weary of the leadership's self-serving ambitions.

"Indeed, prior to the war, the Senate had so neglected the military that the Southfleetians, the wounds to their pride yet sore from their inglorious defeat in the First Trade War, had been understandably emboldened. Legion Command was rife with fools and imbeciles, puppets of the Senate whose only claim to command was fostered in so-called noble blood and nepotism. So when the Southfleetians struck, not only was the military ill-prepared and under-equipped, but incompetently led. The valour of the Legion soldiery and the Reserve notwithstanding, but for the intervention of the Nothirings at sea and the ride of the Rhelmen to our aid at Rhille-haven, the Republic would most certainly have been lost.

"And the people of the Republic *knew* this to be so. They shouted down the legitimacy of the establishment. Dissentient voices called for change. And they cried my name in the hope that I might enact such change. And the Blue Banner became a symbol for that change. It is no great wonder that the small-minded men believed we were preparing an insurrection, conspiring to replace the incumbent powers with a military dictatorship – for that is what *they themselves* would have done.

"My father, in conveying to his sons the virtue of honesty, once said, 'The true punishment for the dishonest man is not that he is not trusted, but that he can trust no one else'. Would that Jophus Teagh had saved some wisdom for the fools in power before he came to the end of his tale. Not that they would have listened.

"Those same fools and small-minded men sought to end the peril we supposedly posed to their power. But they could neither execute nor banish us without dangerously inflaming the populace. They could not discredit us publicly, as our conduct while in uniform and in active service was exemplary. Admittedly, some of our activities since our discharge from service have been colourful, but no more so than those of any other group of Legion veterans. The powers were at a loss for a way to deal with us – and then, as is often her wont, Fate intervened on behalf of all.

"One day in mid-summer, an emissary from the Fiannar in Lindannan arrived in Hiridith and approached the Senate with a proposal. The Lord of the Fiannar had invited all the Free Nations of the world to establish embassies in Druintir, grand city of the Fiannar at the Pass of Eryn Ruil. Nothira, Ithramis and Rothanar had already accepted the invitation – would the Erelian Republic care to be represented at Druintir by a delegation of her own?

"Those that lack vision due to the smallness of their minds do not necessarily also lack cleverness and agility of thought. Indeed, I am told that Senator Fallus was extraordinarily swift to suggest that I be selected to lead the Republican delegation in the new Erelian Embassy at Druintir. His motion was quickly seconded, and in a matter of moments, the decision was unanimous – confirming my father's oft-offered notion that fools seldom differ.

"And so the dilemma presented by the Reserve was solved – behead the beast and the body will die. I was to be appointed Ambassador of the Erelian Republic to the ancient Fiannian land of Lindannan ostensibly as a reward for my service to the Republic during the war. I accepted the honour graciously – for an honour it truly is, however maliciously intended. Lindannan! Druintir! The Fiannar! Strangely enough – and it hurts me sorely to admit this – my desire and that of the Senate were and remain one and the same.

"With me to Druintir would go five-score men of my choosing as an elite Ambassadorial Guard, the only stipulation being that said hundred were to be drawn of the veterans of the North March Mounted Reserve. I requested volunteers. To a man, the other twenty-one hundred and fifteen veterans of the Ghost Brigade – *including* the Iron Captain – offered me their services. I was permitted only one hundred. I chose only those men who had neither wife nor offspring, nor binding ties to the Republic of any kind, and whose only great romance was with life itself.

"And so, amidst great fanfare and aplomb, we rode forth from the Silver City. Rather than follow the well-traveled North Road with its taverns and brothels and sordid way stations, I chose the Old Road under the Westwall for its beauty, its quietude, its remoteness. None protested. Along this ancient way of our forefathers, there is wonder even in the rain, and magic in the mist.

"I am contented – even should there be some among us who are not."

The falling darkness, though tangible, was not yet complete, and through its ermine folds Bronnus saw the shadowed mask of his brother's face. Whether a result of Axennus' monologue or a trick of the night, the young Ambassador appeared older in some way. There was a certain depth, a wisdom that comes seldom to the young, underlying that youthful, malleable countenance. Bronnus saw something of their beloved father in his brother's night-dimmed visage.

"Well told, little brother," he said sincerely, the stillness of the gathered guardsmen silently echoing the sentiment. "Perhaps I have been overswift in finding fault with you. Should all be indeed as you say, then I would withdraw my harsh words, naming them false and unfounded."

"But you are not entirely convinced."

"No," replied Bronnus. "I am not. There remains the matter of the Senator's daughter...ahh...daughters."

The Ambassador gazed at his brother, his eyes glinting in the night.

"Ah, dear brother, the skull truly does thicken with age, does it not? Admittedly, I am not without my human failings, foremost among them my predilection for beautiful women, and second most, my inability to forgive a maliciously intended wrong done me. When Senator Fallus named me Ambassador, in effect exiling me from the nation I love – however pleasant that exile might prove – he sparked in me the fires of my two greatest flaws. Thus, in the matter of the

Senator's daughters, I look to the old adage of felling two game fowl with but one arrow."

Bronnus' brows furrowed as comprehension once again eluded him.

"You see, good Captain Bronnus," the Ambassador explained blandly, though laughter pranced joyously in his eyes, "we were not ushered from our country because I bedded the Senator's daughters – rather, I bedded the Senator's daughters because we were ushered from our country!"

Amidst the uproarious laughter of one hundred guardsmen, the Ambassador flashed his perfect smile and, in a dark swirl of cloak and hair, swung his mount away from his gape-mouthed brother.

And in that moment the persistent miseries of the mizzle and the Captain's ire both sighed themselves away.

"The Captain was not amused."

"No surprise there, Whitey," shrugged Maddus. He shook the little leather pouch filled with pebbles and finger bones. "He's called the Iron Captain, and iron's got no bloody sense of humour. It's not like he's called the *Happy* Captain."

The night was old and cold and bitterly damp, and a hoary chill gnawed both flesh and bone. While most members of the Ambassadorial Guard not posted as pickets or paddock wards had long retired to the comparative comfort of their bedrolls, a small group of determined diehards remained huddled on their haunches around the low orange glow of the last surviving campfire. All about them, from within weather-stained tents, rumbled the snores of their comrades, some deep and droning, others wet and wheezing.

Maddus spat against the resulting sonorous buzz in his brain.

"I dunno, Maddy," replied a long gangly youth, his whiskerless cheeks ruddy from the chill. "Maybe he just hides it well. I like to give Cap a little more credit."

Maddus snorted and shook the small bag more vigorously.

"Always lookin' on the bright side, aren't ya, Riff? Gets bloody annoying after a while. Look, the man was in a huff for *forty days*, mate.

He isn't gonna get over it anytime soon. And by the Teller's tongue, *we'll* be the ones paying the price, *that* I promise you. Probably catch the rearguard gig tomorrow."

"Just toss down already, Maddy," grumbled Regorius impatiently. "Shake that thing any more and it's gonna burst in your hand."

"Bet he's used to that, Dec," commented the huge black-skinned man beside him.

The albino Decan chuckled softly. "Even I wouldn't take that bet, Ruby."

"Rooboong."

"What?"

The big man frowned. "My name is Rooboong."

"So?"

"So call me Rooboong."

"Why? We've been calling you Ruby for, what, almost four years now..."

"I'm black. A ruby is red. Maddy might get confused. He's only just wrapped his head around calling you 'Whitey', after all."

Regorius and Riffalo shared a snicker.

Maddus scowled, the lines upon his brow seeming like actual cracks in his weatherworn skin.

"Sometimes I'm sorry the Legion broke your buggered black ass free of those 'Fleetian fetters, Ruby. Other times it just pisses me right off."

"Maybe you should toss down before Ruby decides to step on you, Maddy," suggested Riffalo banally. "My annoying optimism notwithstanding, I doubt you'd survive the experience."

Maddus made a face, gave the bag a final furious shake, then spilled its contents on a clear patch of ground by the fire.

The four guardsmen stared in startled silence.

Thirteen stones, each flat and round and carved with a number on one side, had landed bare face up in a perfect circle. Within that circle, a dozen intricately etched finger bones had come to rest in the distinct formation of a cross, three to an arm, with the fourteenth and largest stone at the origin, its numbered face down like all the others.

Two further phalanges, the smallest ones, had fallen some distance outside the circle, one resting against the other.

The four guardsmen rose as one, each backing away a step, then two, exchanging quick anxious glances.

The game they had been playing was called 'Stones and Bones', a confoundingly complex pastime popular among the more cerebrally gifted members of Legion soldiery, its rules differing slightly with each platoon, with each squad, often in the decided favour of the resident 'bagmaster'. As a game, beyond the very real possibility of making paupers of reckless players – and for those who tossed down under the sharp eye and very malleable rules of a certain albino bagmaster that possibility leaned quite heavily toward probability – Stones and Bones was usually relatively harmless.

But Stones and Bones had not always been just a game, and losing a month's pay was not the cause of the deep discomfort the four veterans gathered about the guttering campfire now experienced. Each man was aware that the game had derived from an ancient method of divination, a method still employed by some seers and soothsayers in Hiridith's seedier sections. None of the guardsmen knew the specific relevance of the circle-and-cross portent that had so peremptorily presented itself. Nevertheless, all felt a chill colder than the dark damp night sliding like black ice over their souls.

Eventually, Maddus cleared his throat. "That's...ahh...odd."

"Very," affirmed Riffalo, nervously brushing a wayward shock of wheaten hair from his eyes.

"Know what it means?"

"It means Whitey don't win for once, Maddy," Rooboong offered jauntily, but his smile was awkward and crooked.

Decan Regorius gazed at the strange configuration, pink eyes narrowed and uncharacteristically nervous, then stepped forward and swept the formation apart with the instep of one weatherworn boot.

"Bag 'em up, boys. No one wins tonight."

When the foursome had finally settled for the few remaining hours of night, a solitary shape issued from the deep shadows between two tents, knelt, placed a palm on the earth beside the ebbing embers of the fire. A hiss escaped clenched teeth, the hand snapped back, flashed an emphatic sign of warding, and the figure hurriedly rose and strode into the cold, cold darkness.

No one wins tonight.

The sun emerged from the eastern horizon, red and radiant, slowly soaring into a cool clear sky, a sky free of cloud for the first time since the Erelian company had departed the grand city of Hiridith. Axennus Teagh had risen before the sun to bear reverent witness to the first glimmerings of the nascent day. He stood at the eastern edge of camp, cerulean cloak wrapped close against the morning chill, grey-green eyes fixed dawnward. At his side was an officer of the Ambassadorial Guard, also gazing into the growing erubescent glow of the new morning sun.

"A red dawn," murmured the officer stoically.

He was significantly shorter than the Ambassador, of dun complexion, his countenance flat and round, his long black hair pulled straight back and tied with a leather thong. The brown of his large, round eyes was deep and dark, earthen, the rich hue of damp loam.

Axennus nodded. "Indeed."

"Such a sunrise bodes danger to the traveler."

The officer's voice was low, somewhat alien in inflection, his words slow and deliberate as of one unaccustomed to the Westspeech.

"That warning pertains to the sea, Left Tenant," replied Axennus. "Mariners only should beware a red morn."

The smaller man did not immediately respond, apparently giving thought to the Ambassador's contention – a courtesy only, in keeping with the ancient customs of the officer's people.

Then, "I know little of the sea, Master Teagh," said he, undeterred, "but in the lore of my people, the sun that rises over the wide waters also rises over the land."

The Left Tenant was a Rhelman, a native of the broad green fields of Rheln, time-honored homeland to the tribal Horse Masters of the West. The Rhelnian civilization predated the Erelian by more than two thousand years, and was steeped in olden tradition, knowledge and wisdom. The Rhelmen were a proud and noble people, highly attuned to the complexities and simplicities of nature – lovers of peace, though fierce and fearless when pressed into battle. And their native tenacity was a thing of legend.

Axennus smiled. "So it does, Left Tenant," he acquiesced softly.

The Rhelman had come to the North March Mounted Reserve in much the same manner, though differing in detail, as most members of that fabled company. Banished from his tribe and ostracized by his people for a transgression in his youth, he had endured years of solitary survival in the wilderness before chance and happenstance brought him to Hiridith, the sparkling Silver City of the Erelian Republic. And there he had been rejected and outcast by Erelian society for his strangeness and his inability – or unwillingness – to conform. For the Rhelman, ostracism was certainly not an unfamiliar thing.

"I would be wary this day, Master Teagh."

Characteristically undaunted by the sheer enormity of the great walled metropolis, the Rhelman had nevertheless been unaccustomed to the closeness of urban society, an existence so distantly removed from the nomadic life of his youth and his subsequent exile in the wilderness. Discovering that Erelians found his Rhelnian name difficult, if not impossible, to pronounce, he had reluctantly adopted its Westspeech translation – a thing that further removed him from those about him.

"Wary or weary, Left Tenant Runningwolf?" Axennus reprimanded lightheartedly. "I do not doubt you slept little or not at all. I suspect you kept a vigil upon this little party of ours once again. Discover anything of interest?"

"I saw some of the men playing with themselves in the night," Runningwolf reported laconically.

The Ambassador actually bit his tongue before risking a reply. "*Amongst* themselves, surely, Left Tenant."

"I discern no difference, Master Teagh."

Axennus simply smiled and decided the semantics of the matter did not elicit immediate explanation.

"Decan Regorius and some of his squad were playing the game they call Stones and Bones, Master Teagh. The one named Maddus threw a circle of thirteen stones, within which was a crux of a dozen bones with the sun stone at its heart. Two little bones landed outside the circle."

The Ambassador stiffened, brows knotting slightly. "Odd."

"So said the one named Maddus." Then, "You are aware that the pieces used in this game called Stones and Bones are the same that were used in antiquity in divining the Fist of Fate?"

"I am, Left Tenant," said quietly, his bright hazel eyes narrowed against the crimson glare of the rising sun. "Fourteen finger bones to a fist, thirteen moons and one sun to a year."

Runningwolf nodded almost imperceptibly. "Master Teagh, the formation I described –"

"The 'Crucible'."

"Yes."

Something in the solitary word prompted the Ambassador to deduce, "There is more."

"The stones settled with their numbered faces down. All of them."

The Crucible of the Dying Man. Followed by a red dawn. Not good.

"That is all, Left Tenant?"

"The ground was cold to the touch. Very cold. It should not have been so cold there by the fire."

The Ambassador nodded, waited. *No, not good. Not good at all.*

"That is all, Master Teagh."

Axennus nodded. He gazed into the crimson light, his face reflecting the red of the rising sun. He pursed his lips pensively.

"We are to be tested, Left Tenant. Severely so. And soon."

"This is possible, Master Teagh."

"Or perhaps Guardsman Maddus only."

"Also possible. However the red sun shines on us all."

"Or it could all mean nothing."

The Rhelman did not reply.

The two stood in silence together, watching the sun slowly stain the sky with skeins the pale pink of thinned blood. Beneath his breastbone, Axennus felt a rime rise over his thudding heart. He stifled an involuntary shudder, then looked to Runningwolf with a conciliatory smile.

"At least the rain has departed us and the wind has died, Left Tenant."

"The wind sleeps," retorted the Rhelman, "but does not die."

The Ambassador's smile slid from his face.

In Hiridith, Runningwolf had briefly found gainful employment in the stables of a kind and wealthy merchant, but his benefactor soon passed to the Great Spirit, and shortly thereafter, fickle fortune had failed the Rhelman again. Extremely adept with his fists and feet, the Rhelman, in defending his deceased employer's honour and good name, had beaten a visiting Genduri trader to the brink of death. Runningwolf was arrested, hastily tried and convicted, and thrown into the dank dungeons beneath the White Tower, where he languished in chains for many long months.

When war came from the South, the Rhelman was unceremoniously escorted from his cell, hurriedly granted conditional Erelian citizenship, then conscripted into the Legion Reserve. Military service to the Republic would, at war's end, earn him a pardon and his freedom. He and the mounted policing body to which he had been assigned were then deployed to the remote North March – the obvious irony of drafting felons and convicts into law enforcement largely lost upon the men in power who made such decisions.

"We must beware the wind's return."

To this, Axennus Teagh simply sighed softly.

But some small good fortune had, at last, come to Runningwolf, for the sons of his former employer, the late Jophus Teagh, were officers of high rank in the North March Mounted Reserve. Axennus and Bronnus Teagh were known to the Rhelman, known and dear. Both had ever been kind to Runningwolf, and immediately upon the Rhelman's assignment to the North March, the industrious Axennus had remarkably arranged for him to be presented with a true Rhelnian stallion, an extreme rarity beyond the borders of green-grassed Rheln.

In turn, Runningwolf had made a gift of his loyalty, given first to the sons of Jophus Teagh, then to the men of the North March Mounted Reserve, but never in sooth to the Erelian Republic. Such fierce and faithful fealty might only be earned.

"Peril awaits us, Master Teagh," affirmed Runningwolf, the sun reflecting red upon the loamy brown circles of his eyes.

"Perhaps," conceded the Ambassador, "but life would be decidedly uninteresting in its absence."

Runningwolf turned his gaze from the sunrise to the Ambassador. The Rhelman's flat face was characteristically devoid of emotion, the bare canvas of a masterpiece gone unpainted. He blinked languidly.

"I must go, Master Teagh," he intoned in his slow, alien voice. "The Captain will want me to ride ahead."

The Ambassador nodded.

"Before I ride, I will instruct the men that they must cease playing with themselves at night."

Axennus bit his lip. Hard.

"Umm...unnecessary...Left Tenant."

"As you will, Master Teagh."

Raising to his forehead the leather totem-pouch that hung about his neck, Runningwolf saluted the Ambassador in Rhelnian fashion, a concession both Teagh brothers not only tolerated, but encouraged, in respect for the ancient customs of the noble People of the Plains.

"Reserve your salute for the Captain," Axennus said gently. "I am become little more than a glorified civil servant, and neither require nor desire such military formality."

Runningwolf said nothing, but only blinked slowly once more, hand and totem yet at his temple, waiting with the imperturbable patience of his people.

The Ambassador smiled, then submitted, twice tapping his breast with a closed fist in the Erelian fashion.

"Each to our tasks, then," spoke Axennus lightly, the smile on his lips reaching his eyes. "Abide the Captain's wishes, as all here must – my own self being the sole and significantly gratifying exception."

Runningwolf lowered his hand, his totem settling back to its place near his heart. He did not otherwise react, but a subtle shift in his stony visage gave Axennus the impression that the Rhelman was momentarily pondering the Teagh brothers' strange relationship. Then, perhaps attributing the brothers' unending verbal contest to simple sibling rivalry, or – considerably more likely – concluding the odd relationship was not worth pondering, the Rhelman turned upon his heel and swiftly moved away.

The Ambassador smiled at the smaller man's back, for Runningwolf was a treasure in the trove of Axennus' heart, a true and loyal friend, a rugged rock in a world of shifting sands.

Clad in the traditional deerhide leggings and footwrappings of the Rhelmen, and cloaked and shirted in Erelian blue, Runningwolf appeared as one existing in both the old world and the new, yet belonging to neither. His double-curved Rhelnian bow and leather quiver at his back, small iron hand-axe and bone-hafted knife at his waist, Runningwolf bore no other weaponry, and he eschewed armour altogether. The Rhelman relied solely upon his reflexes, both in defense and attack, and by those reflexes he was ably served. Axennus had never seen a man so quick, so easy in motion, so very swift of hand and foot, so dexterously deadly in battle. The Ambassador found it unsettling that a man whose people were devoted to peace and freedom should find his only sense of worth in war and service.

Axennus' smile faded as he watched Runningwolf leap agilely astride the bare back of his amber Rhelnian stallion and, with another mounted guardsman at his side, ride northward into the morn.

"One day you will find cause for joy again, my friend," Axennus whispered in the Rhelman's wake. "One day."

The soaring sun was high and white in the northern noon sky, long having shed the foreboding red of its rising. The ambassadorial company followed the rough Old Road northward along the rocky foot of the Westwall, the dual-headed White Eagle of the Republic stretching its stiff wings in the bright blue heavens of the standard-bearer's banner. But for in battle, Erelian law, both civil and military, decreed the colours of the Republic be unfurled only in weather free of falling rain, sleet or snow. Thus, this was the first day in more than forty that the White Eagle had flown.

Another banner, the double-blue of the North March Mounted Reserve, the same standard-bearer had lovingly folded and secreted close to his breast, in the forlorn hope that it might one day fly again.

"We approach Doomfall, Draconarius," advised the Ambassador, eyes agleam with enthusiasm. "History is made this day. The White Eagle has seldom soared so far to the north."

"And proudly she flies, Commander," responded the black-locked, prominently-nosed standard-bearer.

"No longer a commander, Draconarius. You must find another title for me. 'Ambassador', perhaps. 'Master Teagh' seems to work. Or, should you prefer, something of your own design."

The standard-bearer sniffed. "As you say, Commander."

"In your own time, of course." Axennus grinned, absently running a hand through his mare's long grey mane. His eyes gleamed. "When the morrow's sun is down, we will be in Druintir."

"A journey's longest hours are its last, Commander. Ambassador. Sir."

"Verily, Draconarius, verily." Axennus laughed brightly. "But before we achieve Doomfall, let alone Druintir, there is a thing I must do."

The Ambassador fell back among the mounted company, his mare slowing her gait until she came to the flank of the dour Captain's destrier.

Atop the roan's broad back, Bronnus Teagh did not so much as glance at Axennus. The younger Teagh endured his brother's scorn with quiet dignity, the corners of his mouth twitching with repressed humour. The brothers Teagh rode side by side in shared silence for a time, their comrades casting quick looks their way. Some of these looks were curious, some wary, a few clouded with concern. The brothers had not spoken to one another since Axennus' monologue of the previous evening, a speech that had inspired ninety-nine men and had humbled one. None could foresee the Iron Captain's delayed and nervously anticipated response, but the thunder of his silence was ominous.

After some time, Axennus sent his brother a sidelong look.

Bronnus stared straight ahead.

Moments passed, then the Ambassador glanced again.

Looked away.

Glanced once more.

Looked away.

Glanced –

"*Whaaattt???*"

Axennus brought his palm to his chest and made a 'Who, me?' face. "I didn't say anything."

The Captain grimaced. "First time for everything."

"You wound me."

"You could have told me, little brother."

"You're confusing me, Bron," frowned the Ambassador. "First you tell me I talk too much, then you insist I don't say enough."

The Iron Captain made a rumbling sound reminiscent of summer thunder. Glowering, he grinded his teeth, continued staring straight ahead, a storm rolling in his dangerous dark eyes.

Axennus was far from unnerved.

"Nevertheless, I will bite. Reluctantly. What, exactly could I have told you, dear Bronnus?"

From between tightly gritted teeth, "Which came first, our deportation or the Senator's daughter."

"*Daughters*, dear brother." The Ambassador's smile was entirely bereft of even an inkling of ruth. "It really does take you a while, doesn't it?"

"Careful, Axo."

The younger man heaved a weary sigh.

"Do you truly believe that, given the opportunity, I would deny myself a moon and more of a mute Bronnus Teagh? Teller, still Thy tongue! The trek to Druintir is sufficiently long and difficult without the added hindrance of requisite fraternal verbosity."

At last – and grinning broadly – Bronnus reached over, one large hand coming down heavily to grasp his younger sibling's shoulder.

"Little brother, you will never quite fathom the extent to which I agree with that last assertion."

And together, they laughed.

Relief swept through the ranks of guardsmen like a cool soothing wind, and soon the greater number of them were laughing as well. And, as was its wont among most veterans of the inimitable Ghost Brigade, laughter soon gave way to song. Nearly one hundred voices possessing disparate degrees of ability sprang from gladdened breasts, praising in turn the glories of the Republic,

> *"O Hiridith! O Hiridith!*
> *Thou Silver Lady fair!*
> *May thy marble wings cover me!*
> *O Hiridith, sweet Hiridith!*
> *Lay with me if you dare,*
> *And cast wide thy gates in love for me!"*

the triumphant might and valour of the North March Mounted Reserve,

> *"To Northkeep! To Anthum!*
> *To Silver Bridge we ride!*
> *For freedom! For honour!*
> *For glory and pride!*
> *Blaze fire! Flash iron!*
> *To Rhille-haven we ride!*
> *The Blue Banner above us*
> *And Death by our side!"*

and their great fondness for the brothers Teagh,

> *"For the valiant Iron Captain*
> *We would forfeit our very lives,*
> *And for the wily March Fox*
> *From Death we would surely rise!"*

Axennus leaned conspiratorially toward his brother.

"I think they like us."

Bronnus made a gruff dismissive sound.

"You are the one they love, Axennus. I demand and claim only their respect."

"I did not know the two were necessarily mutually exclusive."

"And *I* did not know they call you the March Fox."

"Hah! Likely, that. The wax in your ears has always been rather thick. No need for envy, though. A simple result of the poet's imaginative license, I'm sure. He must have been in need of a clever name for me."

"He should have sought my counsel, then," grated the Iron Captain. "I have amassed a wealth of clever names for you."

Axennus grinned boyishly, and though many razor retorts leapt instantly to the tip of his tongue, he resisted the reflexive instinct to respond. The day was bright and clear, the White Eagle was awing, the Iron Captain's temper had been temporarily tempered – the Ambassador could afford his brother the laurel of the last word. And so with the most serene of smiles on his lips and in his eyes, Axennus Teagh rode at his brother's side in quiet contentment.

The scenery was magnificent. Axennus' gaze happily absorbed the beauty and splendour that the surroundings yielded to his eyes: To the left towered the sheer rock of the Westwall, and beyond it the ominous orogeny of the Haunted Mountains, slate-grey stone and night-black shadows soaring skyward like a gathering of gigantic hands knotted into massive, gnarled, white-knuckled fists; eastward rolled the broad expanse of the sun-gilded Northern Plains, intermittently punctuated by green stands of oak and maple and birch; north twisted the stone-littered trail of the Old Road, hewn of the very rock many centuries before by hands of those long lost to most men's minds in the murk of myth and legend. But as a student of history, Axennus Teagh knew that the ancient Fiannar had carved that road, a lengthy link in excess of five hundred leagues between that noble people's southern and northern dominions of antiquity.

And southward Axennus did not look, for he knew whence he had come, and was not ungladdened that Hiridith was distant in days and miles.

"Master Teagh! Captain!" called Draconarius from atop a rocky rise before them, an undercurrent of awe accenting the excitement of his tone. "Behold!"

As the Teagh brothers mounted the hummock, their steeds coming to rest beneath the unfolded wings of the White Eagle, the standard-bearer's outstretched arm hastened their attention northward.

There, some miles distant yet, lay the abrupt terminus of the Westwall's northerly march, the great cliff turning sharply to the west, and swiftly melding into the hulking masses of the Haunted Mountains until the two were indistinguishable. Though not discernable from his present perspective, Axennus knew the angular conjuncture of the Westwall's northern and western runs formed a sharp corner that was precipitous and precise, both faces cloven smooth and sheer as though by Cothra's own blade. Vaguely visible in the distance, to the north of the Westwall's sudden end, a great grey twin-peaked mountain rose like a monstrous horned skull hewn of stone, its cracked crown wreathed in cloud, its granite bones pocked by the elements and worn by time. Between the Westwall's cessation and the broken feet of the great horned mountain was a breadth of mist and shadow, a dark divide smothered in a seething haze of rolling black and grey. At that distance, the break appeared to be a great dark hole in the earth, a place of nothingness and nihility, the end of the world and the portal to oblivion.

"Doomfall," breathed the Ambassador in quiet satisfaction, his eyes gleaming keenly. The reality of the place surpassed even his own imaginative expectations.

Bronnus' countenance was grave and graven.

"What manner of place is this Doomfall, Axennus?" the Iron Captain queried lowly, warily.

"I know little of Doomfall, but I will relate what I may. The Fiannar name it Eryn Drun, which I believe translates from the Old Tongue to 'Pass of the Guard'. Doomfall is the smaller and more southerly of the two passes leading upward and westward into the higher lands behind the mountains. Behind that haze is a defile, a cleft in the stone which divides the Haunted Mountains from the Dragon's Head, that visually disturbing mountain to the north. Few have ever attempted Doomfall, but it has been reported that the defile narrows as it ascends until it is but the width of a single horse-breadth when it achieves the High Land."

Bronnus grunted. "What is that fog?"

Shielding his eyes from the sun with the flat of one hand, the Ambassador gazed northward for a moment, squinted in silent study, then nodded to himself.

"The dark fog you see is actually ash, smoke and steam forced upward by thermal pressures from deep beneath the earth's surface and emitted through fissures in the stone. The release of these is discontinuous and periodic, and not all need be released together, the shade of the haze varying with the mixture."

"You are well-read, brother."

"The result of an active and enquiring mind."

The Iron Captain peered northward, his frown as dark as Doomfall's fogs.

"I mislike the look of this Pass of the Guard. I have one hundred men and an official Republican delegate in my charge. Their safety in this strange and foreign land lies with me." His sharp eyes swept over to his brother. "What dangers await us, little brother?"

Above the brothers, the White Eagle ensign dangled limply in the sun-warmed air.

The Ambassador stroked the mane of his mount.

"I know of no specific dangers, Bronnus – only that Doomfall is shunned, and its way has been untried and untrod for generations. All who seek passage to the High Land do so either by sea or by way of Druintir at the pass of Eryn Ruil."

Bronnus' frown blackened. "Why is Doomfall shunned?"

Axennus shrugged. "Man is a naturally superstitious creature, possessed of the primal fears of the dark and of the unknown – and Doomfall is both dark and unknown."

"There is wisdom in caution, little brother," the Captain commented softly. "Is the land before us peopled?"

"It is rumoured that the same spirits that ward the Haunted Mountains also infest the Dragon's Head and lurk in the mists at Doomfall."

"The Daradur."

Axennus raised an eyebrow. "Do you believe the old tales, Bron?"

"My beliefs are irrelevant," growled the Iron Captain. "Suffice to say we have long ridden beneath the shadow of the Haunted Mountains, said to be the domain of the Daradur, and we have had no sign of them." Bronnus returned his gaze to the shifting shadows of Doomfall. "And I see no sign of them now." He paused in thought before continuing. "Nevertheless, I cannot shirk a foresense of peril that has hounded me since waking this morning."

"You are not alone in this foreboding," said Axennus, the grey-green of his eyes taking a contemplative light. "Left Tenant Runningwolf also spoke to me this past dawn of impending danger."

"Indeed? The Rhelman knows his omens. It is settled, then. We must heed the warnings in our hearts." The Iron Captain straightened in his saddle, his shoulders square, his head high. "Come! We will give this Pass of the Guard a wide berth."

Axennus seized his brother's reins before he could move away.

"Rider!" he exclaimed, one long finger pointing.

In the distance, riding hard southward, galloped a guardsman. Bent low over the steed's neck, his cloak of pale Erelian blue flying behind him, the rider raced toward the company on the hummock with all the speed his mount could muster.

"He is Lionnus," stated Bronnus flatly. "An outrider. He rode ahead in reconnaissance with Left Tenant Runningwolf."

"He returns alone."

"That in itself is of little concern," responded Bronnus. "Runningwolf is more than capable." His dark eyes narrowed and the set of his mouth was grim. "It is the fervour of the outrider's return that alarms me."

Axennus nodded and released the reins of his brother's horse.

"Then let us ride to him."

With no further words exchanged and no formal command given, the company surged forward and down, descending the rocky hill at speed. Swiftly, and with both precision and economy of motion, the Ambassadorial Guard assumed one of many oft-practiced formations – a score of riders swept forward, a dozen more thundering on either side of the Teaghs, another group closing ranks behind them, the remaining riders falling back in reserve. Considering the disrepair and poor condition of the Old Road, and the roughness of land flanking it, the speed of the company may have been reckless – but all were master horsemen, and well knew the abilities and limitations of their mounts. Their swiftness posed them little hazard.

As they approached the onrushing outrider, Bronnus raised his fist, and the hoofed thunder of the ride quieted to a soft rumble. The forward score of riders parted smoothly along its centre, and the Captain rode this corridor to the fore, the Ambassador ambling at his side.

"Hail, Lionnus!" called Bronnus, his voice as sharp and hard as an iron blade. He reined his great roan to a halt. "What urgent word warrants such haste?"

Reined to a sharp and sudden stop, the guardsman's horse skittered on the stone surface of the Old Road. The tall young rider swiftly swept off his bronzed steel helm, his long blond locks falling free, and brought one fist to his breastplate. Sky-blue eyes flicked from Bronnus to Axennus and back again, as though Lionnus was unsure to whom he should disclose his tidings.

"Be easy, good Lionnus – the Captain is the commanding officer here," Axennus answered the unspoken question. "Mine will be the authority in the embassy at Druintir. Here I am but your ward and your charge."

Bronnus fisted his breast once, something of impatience in the gesture.

"Captain, I bring word to you on the orders of Left Tenant Runningwolf," spoke the outrider, his tone tight with forced calm, his youthful face flushed with excitement and the exertion of his ride.

The Iron Captain nodded. "What word, guardsman?" His voice was denuded of emotion, but his withered patience was manifest upon his mien.

"They are come, sir!" was Lionnus' immediate and impassioned reply, his careful control cracking. The outrider's eyes were bright with enthusiasm and wonder. Bronnus' features clouded darkly.

"*Who* are come, Lionnus?"

At the Captain's side, Axennus Teagh's handsome face was alight with anticipation, excitation.

"The Fiannar, sir!" announced Lionnus exultantly, his voice breaking at last with unfettered fervency.

And again, almost shouting:

"*The Fiannar are come!*"

3

THE FIANNAR

"We are a warrior people, and we will make war
in this Second World even as we did in the First.
For in any world besieged by Evil, by Darkness,
it is only through the sheer strength of our arms
that the Shadow might be lifted from us forever."

Vallian, Second Lord of the Fiannar

"The Fiannar are come."

Rundul's voice was low and laborious, thickened with fatigue. The Darad leaned wearily against a blood-spattered standing stone of *Fongar ur Piruth*, his bearded face begrimed with the filth of battle. His back burned. He was bruised and bloodied, his *inrinil* rent and torn, but the black fire of his eyes blazed brightly still, and his strength of sinew was yet unspent. In one balled fist, his great war-axe dripped with death.

Dulgar grunted in response. Standing upon the slick slaughter-ground of the Teeth of Truth amidst unnumbered enemy dead, the one-eyed Wild One appeared as a war-god come to Earth. His massively muscled chest and arms were bared and sopped in blood, some of it his own, most not, and his hair and beard were pasted wetly to his skin. Chunks of raw flesh yet clung to the crimson blades of his killing axe.

About them, here and there, warriors of the Daradur stood among their butchered foes, bloodied axes and hammers at the ready, steel death in iron hands. They were *mara Waratur*, Wandering Guard of the Daradur, and they had come singly and in pairs to the aid of their embattled brethren throughout the previous night, dawn and morn. Together, the Daradur, sixteen all told, had engaged hundreds of the enemy in a ferocious battle for the high ground of *Fongar ur Piruth*.

Come noon and the zenith of the sun's sailing, the enemy had withdrawn and the Daradur had emerged bloodily triumphant.

Kicking the hewn body of a dead Urkrok aside, Dulgar's savage solitary eye followed the direction of Rundul's gaze.

Cresting a hill to the northwest, below the southern marges of desolate Coldmire, a band of riders appeared. Some sixty strong, they were as grey and as silent as smoke, more mist than mounted men. The silver-maned steeds they rode were as fluid as cool waters, sleek magnificence defining strength and grace. Blades and spearheads glinted, gleamed, and above the party the golden-striped standard of the Fiannar rippled in the sunlight.

Rundul pushed himself away from the rock and moved to stand at Dulgar's shoulder. Together, in silence, they awaited the riders from the north.

At length, Dulgar nodded, more to himself than to Rundul, as though confirming an unspoken supposition. For a second standard had become visible close upon the Golden Strype – the Crimson Fist of the House of Eccuron.

"Tulnarron," rumbled the Wild One. "He's always the first to act. While others debate and delay, he rides to war with fuckin' admirable abandon."

"Tulnarron is young yet," Rundul grunted, wiping blood from his eyes. "He'll learn."

The band of Fiannar halted near to the foot of *Fongar ur Piruth*. The foremost among them whispered his steed forward. The rider was black of hair and broad of shoulder, his eyes as grey and hard and flat as stone. His countenance was square and stern, yet noble, and the thrust of his jaw was given to a haughty pride approaching arrogance.

A Darad's Fian if ever there was one.

The rider surveyed the slaughter atop and about the mound of the Teeth of Truth. Something of a smile touched his eyes.

"We are late in coming, I see," said he, his voice deep, mellifluous. "I am ill-pleased that Fiannian steel must remain unstained by enemy blood this day."

"Late or timely," growled Dulgar, stepping forward, "your presence is always fuckin' welcome, Tulnarron of the Fiannar, Master of the House of Eccuron."

"And the day is only half-old," added Rundul with a grumble. "Your steel may yet taste blood before night falls on this place."

Tulnarron dismounted in a single smooth fluid motion, the billowing of his grey woolen cloak revealing a flash of light beneath – the shine of his *rillagh*, the finely knitted sash of purest gold that all Fiannar wore in symbolic remembrance and reverence. Across his back was strapped a great sword with blade both wide and long – indeed, the weapon was nearly as long as Tulnarron was tall, and he was counted as tall even among his own people.

Behind him, rows of Fiannian spears bristled bright and terrible.

Stepping over the gargantuan carcass of a felled Graniant, Tulnarron took the hill with long, sure strides. He came to stand before the Captain of the Wandering Guard and the Warder at his side, looming above them well more than a foot, nearly two. But that which the Daradur lacked in height, they compensated with breadth, width and muscular mass. Despite Tulnarron's powerful build, Rundul and Dulgar each easily outweighed the tall Fian.

But all had hearts of like size, all burned with the same fire.

They clasped forearms in fealty and fidelity.

"This place has the smell and feel of an abattoir," observed Tulnarron. "A battle of these proportions demands its stipend of blood. Have you any casualties, friends?"

Dulgar spat pinkish sputum.

"A few of us fucked up, let the mudfuckers get a few shots in. Fuck."

The bruise upon Rundul's back pulsed with a sensation as close to pain as a Darad could experience. His companions had seen the rent leather and battered *inrinil*, but had said nothing. Shame is a poison most potent when its fangs sink in silence.

I can't blame them. I wouldn't speak to me either.

"Some are more damaged than others." Rundul's teeth were clenched. "None are wounded so gravely that they might soon return to the embrace of Earth the Mother."

Dulgar made a rumbling, guttural sound. "Give it fuckin' time."

"So there are more of the enemy, then?" Tulnarron's words were more statement than question. "I see only the dead." A sparkling darkness swam beneath the grey storm-seas of his eyes.

"There are more of the enemy yet living than there are dead," confirmed Rundul. "They huddle even now in the shadows of the Bloodshards. One thousand, at the least."

The tall Fian whistled lowly, placed his hands on his hips, and gazed eastward to the red ruins of Mekkoleth and Sark-u-surum. Nothing moved in that dead land – nevertheless, the Master of the House of Eccuron sensed, felt, knew the enemy to be there, watching, waiting.

"Why do they tarry so? What call do they await?"

Rundul grinded his teeth, but made no reply, only gripped his axe more tightly.

The Wild One's red brows knotted. "What've you been told, Fian?"

"Only that there was battle west of the Bloodshards," replied Tulnarron tersely. "I was at Arrenhoth when the messenger came, and there I did not linger. I would be ill-contented to learn through thrice-relayed messages that which I might see with my own eyes.

I gathered the nearest folk of my household and forth we rode as swiftly as the *mirarra* would bear us."

Began Rundul, "Had you waited a little longer –"

But Dulgar interrupted gruffly, "Don't be such a fuckbeard, Rundy. The Daradur aren't the people to preach the fuckin' prudence of patience. Fuck."

Some of the nearest Daradur chuckled roughly.

Laughter, at least. Better than silence.

Rundul's beard parted in a grim, blood-grimed smile. "Nevertheless, Tulnarron, you might have saved yourself the bother."

"Riding to war is never a bother, Stone Lord," stated Tulnarron flatly. "I would learn what you have to tell."

Rundul and Dulgar exchanged a glance, and something passed between them as waters flow through fissures in stone. Then the Wild One nodded.

Rundul faced the Fian, and said simply, "The Blood King is returned."

The Master of the House of Eccuron showed no outward reaction other than the slight dilation of his pupils.

"I see," said he, softly, dispassionately.

Behind Tulnarron, the ranks of *mirarra*-mounted Fiannar were statuesque in their stillness, in their silence.

Rundul continued, "Suru-luk has amassed an army in the hollows of the earth beneath the Bloodshards."

Again, without inflection –

"I see."

"The Blood King readies for war."

The sun was high, the skies were clear, the wind was quieted and resting – a day of late summer that but for the blight of death about *Fongar ur Piruth* would have been halcyon, serene, without stain.

"So war comes, then," spoke Tulnarron. His voice was as ice, smooth and cool. Crystals of cold light twinkled in his eyes. "The House of Eccuron will welcome the thralls of the Blood King with the kiss of northern steel."

Rundul's night-black eyes narrowed.

"They are forty thousands and more." A brief but poignant pause. "And among them is a *kuarok*."

Tulnarron stared at the Daradun Warder for a moment, meeting his eyes levelly, grey on black, ice on obsidian.

"Even so."

And then the earth screamed.

The Iron Captain held up one hand, and the ambassadorial company halted at the foot of a gently sloping hill.

"Over this rise, Lionnus?"

The young guardsman nodded his head enthusiastically. "Yes, Captain."

"Very well, then."

The stony façade of Bronnus Teagh's face masked the scowl that lay beneath. He did not share the outrider's eagerness. The Fiannar were an unknown entity to the Erelian captain, and the unknown was untested, and the untested untrusted.

"Draconarius, Lionnus, you are with me," Bronnus commanded. "Hastiliarius, Regorius, remain here and ward the Ambassador."

"Oh, *that* will happen," smiled Axennus Teagh, his voice veritably dripping with sarcasm. His lively hazel eyes sparkled sardonically. "The Right Tenant and the Decan, for all their exceptional ability, may find my warding rather difficult *here*, when I am with you *there*."

His nod indicated the rise before them.

The Iron Captain glared at his younger sibling.

"Brother, you are the Ambassador, and your safety –"

"– is assured at your side," interjected Axennus, casually, craftily, "more so than otherwhere."

Bronnus glowered.

Axennus grinned.

And in the Teagh brothers' unending war of wills, Bronnus may have been iron, but Axennus was steel.

"Hastiliarius!"

"Yes, Captain."

"Remain here. Command is yours should something ill befall me."

"Yes, Captain."

"Regorius!"

"Aye, Cap. Ahh...yes, Captain."

"The Ambassador will be coming with us," growled Bronnus. "Ward him well."

"Yes, Captain."

"Really, my dear brother," Axennus sighed with exaggerated disdain, leaning forward, arms crossed upon the neck of his grey, "I assure you, the Fiannar will raise no hand against me."

"Perhaps," responded Bronnus, unsmiling. "But *I* might."

The Ambassador laughed.

"Draconarius!" barked the Iron Captain.

The banner-bearer nudged his mount forward.

"Ready the flag!" ordered Bronnus.

The White Eagle rippled in reply.

And so, five abreast – the Ambassador middlemost, the Captain at his right shoulder, the White Eagle above his left, and Lionnus and Regorius on the flanks – the company ascended the grade in the Old Road.

Axennus' heart pounded in anticipation. Long had he dreamed of the Fiannar, that warrior race of myth and song from whom in part the Erelian people were believed to have descended. His face glowed with childlike wonder, his eyes shone in delight. And as they attained the hill's crown, Axennus' spirit soared.

Directly to the north, upon the rounded crest of the next rise, backdropped by the dark mists of Doomfall, two grey riders sat astride magnificent mounts beneath the lordly banners of their people. Upon the left fluttered the noble standard of the Fiannar, a deep green field bisected by a diagonal stripe of brightest gold. And to the right flew the ensign of the ruling House of Defurien, a flaming sword, blade downward upon a field of steely grey, like a crux of fire in a storm-gripped northern sky.

And in the valley between the two hills, the figure of Runningwolf knelt upon the stone road, his chin to his breast, his totem at his temple. At the Left Tenant's side, his proud Rhelnian stallion had likewise lowered his head as though in reverential deference.

For there, before man and horse, were two further grey-cloaked Fiannar upon splendid silver-maned *mirarra*. One rider was evidently tall, bright of both face and hair, and carried a long-shafted spear. The other was smaller in comparison, dark of lock though fair of complexion, and wore a long sword at the waist and a small oval shield upon one arm. Both were women.

Axennus beamed. He had never seen such grandeur, such grace, in living breathing beings. The Fiannar and the *mirarra* were incarnations of courage and elegance, so very fine of form, one complimenting the other so perfectly, so seamlessly. *Ah, such glory!* The Ambassador had dreamed of this moment, this meeting, since before he could differentiate between the real world of the awakened child and the fantasia of the sleeping one. In some small way, the moment seemed more a memory, a thing of the long past, a reenactment, or a returning.

The Iron Captain was not so moved.

"What manner of beings are these Fiannar that Left Tenant Runningwolf pays them such homage?" Bronnus' visage was as dark as a thundercloud. "Why does he prostate himself so?"

"Prostrate, dear brother. *Prostrate.*"

"If you say so."

Smiling, the Ambassador shook his head. "Whatever regard Runningwolf may hold for the Fiannar, I suspect this display of respect is not for their benefit."

"For whose, then?"

Axennus' eyes sparkled.

"For that of their steeds," he replied softly. "I believe Runningwolf bows before the glory of the *mirarra.*"

"The *mirarra*?" The darkness upon Bronnus' mien deepened. Incredulity knotted his brows. "He bows to the horses?"

"Not horses, dear brother," contended Axennus. "No mere beasts are the *mirarra*. They are to horses as the Fiannar are to Men. Apart and above. The Rhelman, being what he is, sees this." The Ambassador's keen gaze flicked to Runningwolf's Rhelnian stallion, the creature's noble head low upon its powerful chest. "Evidently, Featherfoot sees this also." Axennus glanced to his brother and smiled impishly. "Can it be that a simple beast might understand that which you do not?"

Bronnus growled and his knuckles whitened on the reins.

Decan Regorius shifted uneasily in his saddle.

The Ambassador's grin moved from the Captain down to the valley. Across the short distance, his gaze met eyes as grey as smoke and as bright as nightbound starlight.

The smaller, raven-haired Fiann returned Axennus' smile in a flash of perfect pearl-white teeth. The taller blonde woman sat astride her *mirarran*, still of face and form, the light in her own eyes turned inward as though upon her very soul.

His gaze yet fastened to the faces of the Fiannar, Axennus placed one long hand on the Captain's shoulder.

"Shall we, brother?"

Bronnus nodded curtly.

"As we must." He then reached up to grasp Axennus' wrist in a grip of iron. "You *will* behave," the Iron Captain commanded coldly.

Axennus blinked innocently.

"Oh dear," muttered he, more than a shade of mockery to his tone, "it is as you have said – you *are* more the father than the brother!"

"*Axennus!*"

The Ambassador sighed.

"You need not concern yourself, Bronnus," he assured, his voice impatient, purposefully patronizing. "I am become a diplomat of the Republic. I will be" – he paused briefly, cocking his head to one side – "*diplomatic.*"

The Captain grunted, choosing to respond to the words rather than the tone.

"Very well," said he coarsely, releasing Axennus' wrist. "We will go down to these people, these Fiannar – and their horses."

The five descended the grade at a canter and approached Runningwolf and the two grey figures of the Fiannar.

That which had not been entirely evident from the vantage of the hilltop became plainly and pleasantly obvious when the fore-company drew near to the two female Fiannar. Both women seemed relatively young. And both were beautiful. Exquisitely so. Their drab raiment of grey and forest green did little to mask their feminine forms, the one long and slender, the other small and shapely. The Erelians halted as they came before the women, each man finding that his thoughts had been stilled as though held in awe by objects of transcendent splendour.

The smaller of the two had her raven hair pulled back and away from her soft oval face, the grey of her large eyes specked with sapphire, her pink lips things of which men might only dream. Her greymantled shoulders were slight, but square and proud, possessed of secret strength, and her bosom was high and full. One fine small hand was wrapped about the hilt of her sword in a perfect union of delicacy and danger, and the silver shield upon her arm was light but sure. The gold of her *rillagh* lay across her uncloaked breast like a stroke of sunlight.

The other was tall, her bright golden tresses free and long, her brow high and fair. Her features were more precise than her companion's, but no less fine, no less feminine. She was long of trunk and limb, like a sapling of the forest, as straight and as rigid as the spear she held balanced in the crook of one arm. Her soft white hands were folded before her as one might do in deep thought or prayer. Grey were her eyes, ringed in violet, fathomless pools of faith and fortitude, with an introspective turn that bespoke knowledge and wisdom. The golden gleam of her sash shone past the close wrap of her woolen cloak as though its light, its strength, could not be concealed.

And the eyes of the *mirarra* shimmered silver in the sunshine.

The smaller Fiann's lips curved into a smile, soft and sweet.

"Hail! Men of the South, cousins of the long past!" Her voice was as a song, or as the flow of a mountain spring. "The Fiannar welcome you."

Silence.

The small one turned to her companion.

"It seems that our friends from the South have remembered their blades, but forgotten their tongues."

Her companion responded with but the smallest of smiles.

The speaker turned again to the men.

"Long has been your coming along a road seldom taken by your people."

Axennus Teagh was the first to recover his voice.

"I have oft been accused of taking the road less traveled," said he quietly, as though from a great distance.

The Fian's smile broadened whitely.

"Your reputation precedes you, Ambassador Teagh." Her speckled grey eyes flicked to Bronnus. "As does yours, Captain. The sons of Jophus Teagh are not unknown to the Fiannar."

"Then you have us at a disadvantage, my lady," the Ambassador complained gently.

The speaker returned her gaze to Axennus and laughed lightly.

"My apologies, Master Ambassador," said she cordially. "I am Caelle, Shield Maiden to the Lady Cerriste of the House of Defurien. With me is Sarrane, Mistress of the House of Eccuron and Seer to the Lord Alvarion. In the names of Lord Alvarion and Lady Cerriste, we welcome you to Lindannan, land of the Fiannar."

The Iron Captain regained his voice at last – and immediately wished he had not.

"I did not know, Shield Maiden, that your people claimed ownership of any of the Middle Land under the Westwall."

Caelle peered at Bronnus thoughtfully, though not reprovingly, and there was no malice in her gaze.

"The Fiannar claim ownership over nothing, Captain Teagh," she countered casually, "but all land under our immediate protection and care we call Lindannan. And this –" she spread her arms "– is Lindannan."

"I intended no offense, Shield Maiden," atoned Bronnus.

"And I took none," she replied. "Much of what once was commonly known is now forgotten in the South." Then she smiled widely once more, playfully this time. "There is some irony in that you instructed your brother to 'behave', think you not, Captain?"

Bronnus' eyes widened and his jaw fell slack.

"How did you...?"

Caelle's laugh was akin to a young girl's giggle, and a childlike light danced in her eyes.

"Even at a distance, Captain, the movement of your lips and tongue might be easily read by one capable of doing so."

Reflexively, the Captain's mouth clapped closed, and he said no more.

The Ambassador's grin threatened to split his face in two.

The black-tressed Fiann's attention returned to Axennus.

"Ambassador Teagh, know that the initial intentions of Lord Alvarion and Lady Cerriste were to greet you themselves, as they hold your coming to be a great honour," she stated with irrefutable sincerity. "However, their attentions have been," and for but the briefest of moments the smile departed the Shield Maiden's lips, "deflected by matters unforeseen and of some consequence."

Axennus' malleable mien deftly adopted an expression of appropriate tact.

"Be assured, Shield Maiden," replied the Ambassador with practiced adroitness, "we came bearing no such expectation, therefore we suffer no disappointment."

The Fiann's smile returned, a knowing one. Something akin to mischief coloured the light in her eyes and tugged at the corners of her finely formed mouth.

"I did say that your reputation precedes you, Ambassador."

Axennus made no reply, as he had none. Instead, his eyes dropped to the yet motionless kneeling form of Runningwolf, then returned to Caelle with one brow raised.

"Master Abbawontandontas communes with the *mirarra*," explained the Shield Maiden. "I cannot be certain, but I would guess the Rhelman's totem animal is the *mirarran*."

The Ambassador raised his other brow.

"He named himself to us in the Rhenian fashion," Caelle imparted. "And it is well possible that a *mirarran* came to him during his Rite of Becoming in the wilderness, the Rhelnian ritual of passage from child to man. Understand that the *mirarra* are not wholly unknown upon the fields of the Horse Masters. Indeed, is not the Rhelnian breed of horse descended in part from the noble *mirarra* from Erellan of antiquity?"

Abruptly, wordlessly, Runningwolf rose and fluidly mounted Featherfoot, the stallion then moving to one flank of the Erelian party. The Rhelman's countenance bore a certain excitation beneath its characteristically taciturn exterior, and his loamy eyes gleamed with renewed life and light. Both Caelle and Sarrane nodded to him. And the intelligent argent eyes of the *mirarra* glittered in recognition of what had passed between beast and man.

"You are well, Master Abbawontandontas?" Axennus Teagh grinned.

Regorius, Lionnus and Draconarius, though yet captivated by the majesty of the Fiannar, found themselves able to chuckle.

"I am well," responded Runningwolf, his tone as flat as ever.

In that instant, silent Sarrane's head snapped eastward as though startled by a scream that had passed the ears of the others unheard. Her comely but stern countenance tensed, becoming suddenly severe. The violet that encircled the grey of her eyes blazed like rings of fire. Her hands unfolded only to wrap tightly about the shaft of her spear. She sucked a breath inward with an audible hiss.

The laughter upon the lips of the Erelians died swift deaths. The Iron Captain edged nearer to his brother. Ambassador Teagh instinctively gripped the haft of his sword.

Both *mirarra* turned and took two, three paces eastward.

Caelle looked upon her companion with visible concern.

"What is it, Sarrane?" asked the Shield Maiden gravely. "What do you see?"

The Seer of the Fiannar did not immediately respond, but only peered eastward, her widened eyes straining in their sockets as though shocked by that which only they could see. All gazes followed the Seer's, only to fall upon the sun-gilded grasses of the rolling Northern Plains, a picturesque pasture of peace and tranquility. The summer skies were without cloud, the air warm and carried on a soft breeze. All was still and soundless, so very serene.

Moments passed, and still Sarrane made no reply. Her eyes grew impossibly large, their rings of violet fire swirling violently. Yet she remained as rigid as a rod, as silent as the hush of death.

And then, with a sharp and salient suddenness –

"Ware! Ware!" cried the Seer, her voice fell and terrible. "A red wind comes!"

Ambassador Teagh met Runningwolf's knowing brown gaze.

We must beware the wind's return.

The Rhelman blinked placidly.

Peril awaits us.

"There is sorcery at work," continued Sarrane, her voice fallen to a chill calm. "A red wind is spawned of blood magic and carries terror to the west on crimson wings." And colder, calmer still, "We must resist this thing."

Caelle reacted instantly. She swung her *mirarran* to face Bronnus.

"Captain! Your men are in danger! You must summon them. This valley may provide some shelter."

Bronnus Teagh hesitated, for he neither saw nor sensed any peril. And he had ever given mindsight and sorcery little thought and less credence.

"Captain!"

Whether for the urgency in the Shield Maiden's voice, for the iron of the command it held, or for Axennus' imperative tug on his arm, Bronnus raised a silvered battle horn to his lips and blew. The blast battered the hills like the peal of a southern storm. The rumble of massed hoofbeats was evident before the note's echoes ended. Four-score and fifteen guardsmen crested the hummock, bronze armour aglitter, and galloped down the hill's northern grade in a wave of Erelian blue.

A subtle gesture from Caelle, and the Fiannian standard-bearers descended to the Shield Maiden from atop the northern rise, two tall warriors grey of eye and mantle.

Eastward, yet invisible to all but the long-sighted Fiannar, a crimson blot stained the horizon, like a smear of blood on yellow linen.

"Hear me!" cried Caelle, her voice cold and clarion. "Hear me, Men of the South! I am Caelle of the House of Defurien, Shield Maiden to the Lady Cerriste of the Fiannar! And I bid you harken to my words! Will you listen and abide?"

The exigency of her tone could not be denied, could not be defied.

The Iron Captain answered for all: "We will listen, Shield Maiden."

"And abide?"

"Upon our honour, Shield Maiden."

Caelle of the Fiannar nodded sharply and moved her *mirarran* before the Erelian ranks, the creature's silvery mane rippling like water.

"A foul wind rises and rushes upon us with silent speed! Spawned of soulless sorcery, it breeds terror of such dimension as to slay you where you stand! And those that do not die would wish for death if they could – for their minds will be left utterly broken, bereft of all thought but pain and fear!"

A hushed murmur arose among the guardsmen as they glanced from one to another in shared uncertainty. They then gasped as one, a sibilation of unified unease, as the crimson taint of the eastern horizon became visible to all. Beginning as but a narrow line of darkness where sky kissed land, the stain swelled with frightening swiftness, rising like a red wall from the bowels of the earth, or falling like a storm of blood from wounded heavens. The incarnadine ill hurtled westward across the plains with violent velocity. A burning breeze blew in its vanguard, a foul forebreath of despair.

Caelle's midnight tresses flew about her like raven's wings.

"Fear not, Men of the South!" she cried. "The Fiannar are with you and will not abandon you, whatever evil may befall! The *mirarra* will ward your mounts! Think only of me and nothing else! I will shield you if I am able!"

The red wind rushed toward the valley with impossible speed, accelerating in its course with each passing second, an irresistible juggernaut of crimson terror. The air howled in horror, and a sound akin to thunder shook the earth. Brave hearts trembled in trepidation.

Unsheathing her sword, its steel glinting dimly but defiantly in the failing light, the Shield Maiden of the House of Defurien turned her cold sapphire eyefire to the closing darkness. Her voice carried over her shoulder like the war horn of Cothra.

"Stand, Men of the South! Hold fast to your reins! Close your eyes and minds against this sorcery! Think only of me!"

The entire east was as an ocean of blood; earth and sky aflood with gore and grime. Time fled. The party crouched beneath the bloodstorm as though under the curl of a tidal wave of doom.

"Think only of me!"

And the red darkness fell upon the company as would the very hammer of Hell itself.

The earth hove.

A searing screech shook the hills. The Daradur amidst the Teeth of Truth felt pain and fear underfoot – pain and fear that was not their own, for they knew neither – as the ground quailed and quaked before the coming of something impossibly vast and terrible. Rundul and Dulgar exchanged black glances, and behind them assembled the *mara Waratur* of Raku Ulrun, rock amongst rock. They did not waver.

Leaping astride his *mirarran*, Tulnarron rejoined the men of his House, his grey eyes and the steed's silver ones aflame with white fire. The Fiannar remained in formation beneath their banners, sixty strong and as still as stone. A scorching wind came and whipped at hair and mane. The Golden Strype and the Crimson Fist were buffeted with invisible bats. Tulnarron held up one hand, but made no other motion. The Master and the warriors of the House of Eccuron calmly awaited whatever was to follow in the wake of that withering van.

Their wait was not overlong.

First came the red wind. Ill-born beneath the Bloodshards, and blown from the bellows of abomination, it hastened westward with hurricanic force. Enduring the lashes of the crimson blast, the Fiannar and the *mirarra* sensed the terror that rode the wind's phantasmal pinions, bearing death and madness across the Northern Plains. They barred it from their minds, pushed it away and aside, as each was the master of his own heart, and neither mount nor rider would be swayed.

And the Daradur were as the stones of *Fongar ur Piruth*, standing still and stalwart in the face of the wicked wind, as though they felt nothing but a slight breeze brushing coolly upon their blood-slicked skin.

And then the earth split asunder.

The Bloodshards became a chasm, deep and lightless, a dark throat leading down into the blackest of bowels. In an instant, one thousand thralls of the Blood King were swallowed into subterranean night, their death-howls nullified by the shriek of grinding rock.

Then the earth coughed, a powerful spasm of agony and terror, vomiting forth the plague of its torment. Crimson filth exploded upward, a geyser of gore, part laval lymph, part venom, part poisonous puissance. The rotting red ill roared forth in a fearsome fountain of plasmatic power. High and tall spewed the netherspawned surge, putrid, rancid, the waste of ages. Everfoul abomination burst from the heaving guts of the earth as though the entire world was at its ending.

Up from the earth came iron, came steel. Up came rock and stone. Up came bastion and battlement, breastwork and barbican. Arch upon arch, then arcade upon arcade; corbelled bartizans; crenellated parapets capped with great iron fangs; massive, monstrous machicolations. Walls warding walls, each successively higher, stronger, scaled stone and scappled steel. Titanic towers, drum and turret, like upright fists in the face of freedom.

And amidst it all, centermost within the diabolical enceinte, rose a donjon such as had never before been seen upon the face of Second Earth. Skyward soared the great tower, one hundred feet, a thousand, coal black and caliginous. At its pinnacle, six falcated merlons curled about and above a great stone concavity like gigantic iron claws about a colossal cauldron. And within it, a molten magma of malignance roiled and frothed, its crimson power oozing over the brim and sliding down the sheer face of the donjon like blood on skin.

And then the earth shuddered, settled, and was still.

Seven hills away and west, sixteen Daradur and sixty Fiannar bore dark and silent witness to this bitter undoing of the Guardian Peoples' five-century-old victory at Mekkoleth on Sark-u-surum. Although the sun was high and hot and gave short shade, the behemothic fortress shed blackness like a fetid fog, and cast the landscape in cold, deathly shadow.

Near to Tulnarron's shoulder, one of the Fiannar's lips formed quiet words – "Have you ever...?"

To this, another responded, as though from a dark and dismal distance –

"Never".

Growling, turning his broad back to the black stronghold, Dulgar squatted upon his thick haunches and braced his fingers upon the earth. He remained thus for a moment, as power went forth westward to Raku Ulrun. Droplets of hot blood fell from beneath his eyepatch to the back of his hand. In little time, a similar power returned.

Orders from Raku Ulrun.

Dulgar rose, his one-eyed gaze encompassing all Daradur present. Unspoken words passed between the warriors of the Wandering Guard, a silent sharing, then an understanding, and finally assent.

Without removing his eyes from the vast fastness of stone and steel, Tulnarron of the Fiannar raised his voice above the weakening whips of the red wind.

"The Blood King is indeed returned, and he has brought with him the powers of his past – for what can this structure be save Mekkoleth resurrected?"

But Dulgar of the Daradur dissented.

"Fuck that, Fian," rumbled the Wild One. "This isn't Mekkoleth risen from fuckin' ruin. I waded through a lot of fuckin' blood at Mekkoleth on Sark-u-surum. I was there when we threw down that shit-spattered sand castle. I was fuckin' there. No, Mekkoleth was just a big fortress on a small mountain." He paused, his solitary eye burning blackly. "This...this fuckin' thing is a mountain unto its fuckin' self."

Added Rundul of Axar, "And the power that brought forth this thing isn't sourced in Suru-luk himself, but only wielded by him.

I've seen this power, and name it not, but tell you only that it is a mighty evil."

Tulnarron pondered the words of the two Daradur a while. His eyes never left the monstrosity before him. At the great donjon's pinnacle, the vividly red vitriol boiled and bubbled, seeping over the rim of the chasmic chalice like overpour from an unholy grail. Below the claw-bound crown, Tulnarron sensed movement within the darksome fortress, and he soon saw dark ferine forms appear along allure and battlement, behind lancet and loophole.

"Then we are sorely beset," said the Master at last, the deep music in his voice like a martial march. "I take some solace in that, if this thing was fated to be, I am here to defy it. The Fiannar and the House of Eccuron will not abide its existence."

His grey eyes flashed to Dulgar and Rundul and the wrathful Wandering Guard behind them.

"Will we have the aid of the Stone Lords in this matter?"

Blood oozed from under the Wild One's eyepatch. "No fuckin' doubt."

"As ever," granted Rundul of Axar.

Fourteen other deep guttural voices growled in agreement.

Tulnarron nodded his gratitude.

"I would know if this fortress' defenses are beyond the siegecraft of the Daradur."

Responded Rundul, critically, "This thing was built of arrogance and black art, made to inspire awe and dread, but it's neither geometrically nor structurally sound, for its engineering leaves much wanting. However, its sheer enormity is defense in and of itself, and is beyond the skill of sixteen Daradur to overmaster – but not of six thousand, nor even six hundred."

His eyes yet locked on the terrible thing before him, Tulnarron raised one dark brow.

"Have we six hundred?"

Rundul and Dulgar shared a sour look.

Then Rundul replied heavily, levelly, "We have but sixteen."

Tulnarron absorbed the information with a sigh.

"I believe we must choose better ground, then," mused the Fian, his mouth twisted between grimace and grin. "And that choice will be made by those of higher station than my own."

"Any ground is good ground," muttered the Wild One as though impatient for further spillage of blood. "Fuck."

The line of Tulnarron's lips straightened.

"Even so," said he, finally removing his gaze from the fortress. His eyes were cold with chained rage. "Priority precedes pride. We will bear tidings of this thing to Druintir. Lord Alvarion and Lady Cerriste will want word beyond that which they have certainly already heard."

"A decision both wise and prudent, Master Tulnarron," commented Rundul. "When the hammer of war falls, the anvil will surely be Druintir."

"Precisely," nodded Tulnarron. He looked upon the Wandering Guard and their mighty Captain. "What will the Daradur do?"

"What the Daradur have always fuckin' done," grated the Wild One. "We will watch. We will wait. We'll wage fuckin' war."

Expanded Rundul of Axar, "We will remove to Raku Ulrun. As war comes to Druintir at Eryn Ruil, so too will it come to Doomfall. The southern way mustn't be left undefended."

Tulnarron's handsome countenance shone nobly in spite of the looming shadow.

"The Fiannar are glad for the friendship of the Daradur," said he. "When next we meet, may it be in the midst of battle, rather than its wake."

"I'd have it no other fuckin' way, Fian."

"Nor I, Tulnarron of Arrenhoth."

Tulnarron placed one hand over his heart.

"Fare you well, Stone Lords!"

"Stone and steel!" roared the Wandering Guard in response, raising their axes and hammers in fisted fealty and fraternity.

The Master of the House of Eccuron swung his *mirarran* about, his cloak flying open, the gold of his *rillagh* blazing with the same icy fire that burned in its bearer's proud heart.

As loud and as clear as a blast from a battle horn, Tulnarron's voice rose above wind and pall:

"Fiannari! Anh echi Minar Eccuron! To Druintir! Ride!"

And the *mirarra* surged westward as one, a rush of silvery grey, a northern tide flowing fleet and fierce. Rumour of war rumbled in their passing, yellowed grasses whispered warily of wrath and ruin.

Rumour, war, wrath, ruin.

And then they were gone.

"Think only of me!"

Ambassador Teagh heard the voice as though he was submerged in deep dark water. The Shield Maiden's shouted words were muffled, stifled, only vaguely coherent. Still, he heard. He understood. But he did not care to listen. Terror tore at him with icy talons, ripping his mind, rending his soul. He squeezed his eyes shut so tightly that tears burst from their ducts. Within him, his heart thudded impossibly fast, crashing desperately against his ribs, pounding, pounding, wanting out. He threw his head back in violence and madness, his mouth stretched wide in a shrill but soundless scream. Frantically, feverishly, he wished for his own death.

And then she was there.

Hold! Stand fast! Think only of me!

Caelle! Feeble and from afar came her cry, no longer audible to the ear, but to the mind alone. Miraculously, the Shield Maiden had reached into Axennus' inner being with her own, calling him to her, a shadow of light at the edge of his besieged consciousness. Axennus clung to Caelle's presence like a frightened babe at a mother's breast.

Then the talons of terror altered, changed, became wickedly barbed whips that flayed him furiously, mind and soul. In pain, in abject agony, Axennus struggled to heed the Shield Maiden's call, to hold on to her image. But fear forbade him. Terror and torment stripped him of all that he was, of all that he had been. Mind-breaking fear peeled away his power to resist, soul-crushing horror laid waste his will.

And so he fell away from her, away and down, down into darkness.
Stand! This fear is illusion! Heed it not!

But there were none left to hear her. Axennus. Bronnus. The Rhelman. Young Lionnus. All were lost. They had been too many, and the red wind of terror had been too strong – or mayhap she had been overly weak. In her rashness, in her pride, Caelle had believed that she could shield them all. In the end, she had shielded none. All would be taken now in madness or death. One hundred men. All lost. All gone.

I am here.

Sarrane's soft voice fluttered at the marge of Caelle's awareness like a white bird awing on the gentle current of a summer wind. And then Caelle could see her, a ball of cold sunfire, a final beacon of hope in the mistbound seas of despair.

Hail, sister! Caelle welcomed in reborn cheer, her soul bathed in and buoyed by the sure sanguine light of the Seer. *Your strength is needed.*

I am with you, replied Sarrane calmly. Within Caelle's mind, the Seer's voice was crisp and icily clear. *I have not your strength, and cannot hope to reach them. But I would anchor you. Go now. Go to them, lest they be forever lost.*

And so Caelle went to them, to the Men of the South, into the cruel chaos that had claimed them.

Black things, demonic shadows strove to stay her, phantasmal teeth gnashing, talons rending. She struggled. The shadows swarmed. And they were strong, so very strong. But, unlooked for, beyond the scope of the Shield Maiden's most ascendant hope, a great slash of searing white light scattered her assailants, sent them screeching, scurrying away. She knew not the source. She was too elated to wonder. The way cleared for her, she would not be thwarted, could not be checked in her course. Scarlet shadows shrieked in frustration, hunger, loss. But neither terror-spawned soulshade nor windborn devil would deter her, deny her, defy her.

No longer.

For she was Caelle, Shield Maiden of the Fiannar, and the ancestral blood of the Athair was in her, and that blood was Light.

The first to be reached was Runningwolf. The stoic Rhelman possessed the rigid resilience of his people; of all Men, the Horse Masters were among the closest to the eldritch powers that both warded and afflicted the earth. Caelle brought the Rhelman to her and bound him behind her silver shield.

Next came Axennus, then Bronnus, who even in that hellish place had managed to make his way to his brother's side. Regorius, too, was found nearby. One by one, the unfearing Fiann gathered the Erelians to her. Draconarius, Lionnus, dour Hastiliarius. Maddus, Riffalo, gigantic Rooboong. None were forgotten. None were left behind.

And then it was done.

The darkness fled. The wind died. And the sun, white and warm, shone upon all.

Axennus came back to himself still seated astride his sleek grey. The mare was yet atremble, and her flanks were damp. As with all the Erelian horses, Axennus' mount had bucked before the horror of the red wind, but had not thrown her rider, and had not bolted. The majestic *mirarra* had guarded her well, deflecting the main force of the fearstorm from her as a steel chamfron would turn away a volley of wooden bolts.

The Ambassador released the reins, his hands yet cramped for the violence of their grip on the leather, and gently patted the wet neck of his faithful steed. He felt Bronnus' strong hand upon his shoulder and reached up to clasp it in his own. A sweeping glance assured Axennus of the welfare of his fellows – all were unscathed but for the lingering memory of fear paling their faces and reddening their eyes.

Westward, the last gasps of the crimson blast were breaking against the stone shield of the Westwall, then evapourating harmlessly and passing into entropy.

And high above, the cumuli-crowned darkness of the Haunted Mountains soared in immortal invulnerability.

Then Axennus' eyes fell upon the small form of Caelle.

The Shield Maiden was upright upon her *mirarran*, shoulders square and solid, her comely countenance only slightly flushed by fatigue. Her presence exuded courage like a tangible thing, though her blue-flecked eyes were bright with concern. A brave smile took her lovely lips as she sheathed the steel of her sword.

"You are well, Ambassador Teagh?"

In response, Axennus dismounted and knelt upon the stone of the road, his eyes averted, his chin at his chest. One hundred men did likewise.

And in sincere humility, Axennus said softly, "We are in your debt, Shield Maiden. Ours lives are yours to command."

Silence ensued, broken only by horse-breath and heartbeat.

Then, "Rise, Southmen," spoke Caelle. Her voice was silken, serene. "I am unworthy of this gesture. I was not alone in securing your salvation, and will abide no talk of debt or service. I ask only for your friendship."

"That you most surely have," avowed the Ambassador, face yet fixed to the road, "for as long as we play a part in the Teller's Tale."

"Then rise, Men of the South," the Shield Maiden commanded, "and accept the friendship of the Fiannar in return. Among friends, the well-being of one is sufficient reward to the other. All accounts are balanced."

The Men of the South rose, fists at their breasts.

The Iron Captain stepped forward, his dark eyes flashing.

"Nevertheless, Shield Maiden, you will ever have our swords."

"The day may yet come when they are needed, Captain," Caelle responded cryptically. "But enough of this." She turned to the fair Sarrane sitting silent and sedate atop her steed. "What say you, sister and Seer?"

"The peril is passed," answered Sarrane, her tone cool and somewhat removed. Staring to the east, the violet rings of her eyes spiraled like an eddy about isles of grey. "But another, great and terrible, is risen from ruin and calls for our doom."

"The thing you have foreseen?"

Quietly, and with steely calm: "The very same."

An uncharacteristic frown shaded the beauty of the Shield Maiden's brow as she declared, "These tidings must be borne to Druintir with all speed."

Softly, surprisingly, "My husband bore witness to the coming of this thing," said Sarrane.

Caelle's scowl widened to an expression of shocked solicitude. "Master Tulnarron was there?"

"He was." A small pause, a swirling of violet. "He is unhurt, and hastens westward with riders of our House, but even at a gallop their *mirarra* will not gain Druintir for nigh two days. And I fear he will be...distracted."

Caelle turned to the Fiannian banner-bearers.

"Radannan. Milutin. Bring the Seer to Lord Alvarion and his Lady. Slow for nothing and stop for less. Darkness descends upon us swiftly, and we must ever be swifter."

Grey and dour, the two Fiannar inclined their heads to the Shield Maiden, but spoke naught. Above them, the Golden Strype and the Flaming Sword rippled restlessly.

Said Sarrane: "You will remain with the Southmen?"

"I will, sister. I have said that they will not be abandoned. I will keep them behind my shield wherever they might go, until the danger is too distant to consider."

Sarrane did not gainsay her, but the anxiety of the Seer's severe features was explicit.

"Where will they go?"

Before Caelle could reply, the Ambassador did so for himself and for the company of Southmen.

"We go to Druintir," he said casually, as though the matter had never been in question.

Caelle's raven tresses framed a face fraught with concern.

"Ambassador Teagh, it is my suggestion that you return to Hiridith. Your life and the lives of these men will be imperiled in the north."

"Imperiled?" Axennus rubbed the smoothness of his chin in mock meditation. "Indeed." The light in his hazel eyes danced playfully, as the insufferable imp within him rapidly revived. "Left Tenant Runningwolf!"

The Rhelman moved to Axennus' side. "Master Teagh."

"Would you be so good as to share with the Shield Maiden my thoughts on peril?"

Runningwolf blinked slowly.

Axennus could not have been sure, but he thought he detected rare laughter in the loamy light of the Left Tenant's eyes.

Then, his tone as dispassionate and as ineffusive as ever, the Rhelman explained, "Shield Maiden, the Ambassador believes that in the absence of peril, life would be decidedly...uninteresting."

Caelle looked from Runningwolf to Axennus – who was grinning like an idiot – then to Bronnus. The Iron Captain, his face clouded in irritation or embarrassment or both, only shook his head in helpless resignation.

Then, at small length, Caelle laughed aloud. The sound was like silver rain on summer leaves.

"It is said that only the brave and the foolish might laugh in the face of danger," said she, smiling warmly. "You are no fool, friend Axennus. And you bring hope with you as surely as day follows night. It will pride the Fiannar to receive you and your party at Druintir."

Axennus' flexible face deftly adopted a look of appropriate solemnity.

"The honour will be ours, Shield Maiden."

Caelle turned to Sarrane.

"We have delayed overlong," she said, her tone matching the graveness she saw upon the austere Seer's countenance. Then softly, little more than a whisper, "May the *mirarra* bear you swift and safe, sweet sister."

Sarrane nodded staidly. "And you also."

A look passed between them that spoke of love and of trust and of gratitude, of a sorority of souls, of bonds of friendship that could never be severed, come death, come doom.

Then –

"Ride!" cried the Shield Maiden. *"Ei vech aphan! Druintir atinai! Dhir dri, mirarrai! Dhir!"*

Forth and north leapt three magnificent mounts, embodied strength and grace, flashing past the stretching shadows of Doomfall like argent lightning. Enamoured with their beauty, enchanted by their elegance, the Southmen watched them until they passed beyond scope of both eye and ear. Runningwolfs's earthy eyes twinkled damply.

Then the brothers Teagh, one to either side, came abreast of Caelle, Shield Maiden to the Lady of the House of Defurien. The men of the Ambassadorial Guard assembled behind them, a courageous company of bronze and steel and Erelian blue. The Iron Captain nodded in readiness.

Grinned the Ambassador, "Shall we, Shield Maiden?"

Darkness billowed into the sky, a great black mass rising from the earth, swelling, seething, from which ghastly grey tendrils reached across the blue firmament, writhing wraithlike, aloft and almost alive. Pale ash fluttered down, borne over the land on invisible thermal pinions, gliding groundward with a grace that belied the horror of its origin.

The day was old when Tulnarron crested a soot-crusted knoll and cast his icy gaze westward and down. His countenance was grim, his teeth grinding in his clenched jaw. Beneath him, his great *mirarran* hoofed haughtily, nostrils flared, snorting.

"It is as we feared, Tuln," confirmed a Fiannian spearman at the Master's shoulder as the troop of warriors from the House of Eccuron assembled along the ridge to either side of them. Ash dusted the colours of the Golden Strype and the Crimson Fist. "The hamlet burns."

Tulnarron wrinkled his nose against the acrid reek of smoke. He did not otherwise respond.

Below, a shallow creek meandered lazily along the nadir of a broad valley, a forest of conifers and maple rearing on the northern shore, the remains of a small village riotously afire to the south. Of the two dozen wooden buildings that had comprised the hamlet, several were destroyed utterly and lay in blackened heaps, dense smoke issuing from cracks in the blackened char. Others still burned freely, the blaze hungrily devouring both plank and log, crackling and cackling as it fed its voracious appetite for destruction. Only a few structures had escaped the ravenous flames, standing rigid and scorched, like condemned souls awaiting inescapable damnation. Apart from the leaping flames, swirling smoke and floating ash, nothing moved.

Haphazardly, amidst fire and ruin, small bundles of colour lay motionless in littered lanes and ravaged gardens. Slithering underneath the smell of wood smoke, Tulnarron detected the thin caustic stench of seared flesh.

"Corpses," observed the spearman, chewing on an unlit cheroot.

"I am not blind, Gorn." Tulnarron's mighty fists crunched about his *mirarran*'s reins. "Nor have my olfactory abilities entirely abandoned me."

Gornannon said nothing.

The Fiannar lining the ridge sat astride their *mirarra* in solemn silence.

"This place was called Maple Creek," said Tulnarron, his voice uncharacteristically wistful, distant. "Eleven families. Some seventy souls. Many children."

"The little ones called you 'Sheriff'," recalled another of the Fiannar, a woman, a wetness slicking the surface of her eyes, welling at the corners.

Tulnarron's heart was torn between raging and breaking, the inner conflict outwardly contorting his countenance. His cheeks quivered under the cold ice chips of his eyes.

Teller forfend. The children. Red-headed Ceilagh, strapping young Rion. And the little twins...a boy and a girl, gold of locks and blue-eyed, always so happy, always laughing...what were their names?

"I have been remiss in my shrieval duties, Sandarre. Reprehensibly so."

"You could not have known, cousin," comforted the Fiann, somehow forestalling her voice from faltering. "Even the Mistress of our House did not foresee...this."

Tulnarron's jaws bunched.

I cannot so much as remember their names.

"Even so."

Across the sluggish stream, in the concealing eaves of the forest, half-buried in black soil and discarded fir needles, two sets of wide wild eyes stared out from shadow up at the grim grey warriors lining the distant ridge. A stifled whimper. One small hand reached out to another, tiny fingers entwining, gripping tightly.

Hush.

They will see us, sister.

Nay, brother. They will not.

They are Fiannar. They will know we are here, know we are here.

They are distracted.

What if they find us, sister? They will know us. They will know what we are, what we are. We are yet too weak to fight them. They will hurt us, hurt us.

Their leader is a simple brute. All sword and no substance. He is hurried. We are hidden. We will not be found.

They are descending! They come, sister! They come, come, come!

Silence. Remain still. We will not be discovered. They will be gone soon.

But, sister –

Hush, brother.

In pairs and small groups, dour Deathward warriors of the House of Eccuron guided their mounts guardedly through the wreckage of the hamlet of Maple Creek. Some led *mirarra* by the reins and on foot, others remained astride their steeds. Smoke and dust wafted about them, irritating their eyes, assaulting their nostrils. Heat singed their skin. All was silent but for the low roar of flame, the hiss of boiling sap, the crackle of burning wood.

Tulnarron rode slowly along the main way, cold eyes scouring the ground, the ruins, the smoke-spawned shadows. The body of a man lay twisted in a heap, naked, the eye sockets empty, gaping mouth awash in blood. The corpse had no tongue. Tulnarron suspected it yet grasped its eyes in the bloodied balls of its fists. Upon one side of the lane a large hound, or the remnants of one, was scattered in several red chunks of wet flesh across the ground. The beast had literally been torn to pieces. An old woman's decapitated head watched Tulnarron through dead white eyes from the lip of the community well.

Everywhere, the carcasses of animals, the corpses of men, women, children.

"The red wind did this," accused Gornannon, spitting his cheroot into nearby flames. "These village folk were driven mad by terror. Their minds broke. That which they could not kill, they burned. And then they destroyed themselves."

Sandarre peered down sorrowfully upon the ruin of what had once been a pretty young woman. Before dying, the maiden had torn her hair from her head and clawed her face to shreds. Nevertheless, Sandarre knew her.

"Her name was Morgynne. She had seen but sixteen summers. She was to marry in the spring."

Gornannon simply shook his head.

Tulnarron did not respond. His *mirarran*'s ears had twitched, the magnificent head turning westward, silver eyes focused and fixed on something through the haze of smoke and gliding cinder. The Master's own inner sense had been alerted simultaneously, his own steely gaze riveted now upon the gusting smoke before him. Wordlessly, Sandarre nudged her mount to Tulnarron's left side, Gornannon moving to the right.

And then the smoke parted.

There, on the soot-spoiled path, stood a ghoulish figure. A woman. Of middling age. Her plain face begrimed with blood and filth, her simple shift soiled and in tatters, her swollen breasts hanging in pink ribbons of rent flesh. In one hand she held the haft of a wood-splitting maul, the other gripped the ankle of an infant, its doll-like body mangled almost beyond recognition. A ghastly grin split the matron's face, and she raised the baby's battered form toward the three Fiannar. The little skull had been caved in and was dripping grey gore to the ground before the woman's bare feet. The matron threw back her head and shrieked maddened laughter to the heavens.

The infant's body twitched.

"Show mercy," commanded the Master of the House of Eccuron.

Instantly, Gornannon's spear sailed straight into the madwoman's heart, even as an arrow from Sandarre's bow pierced that of the hapless child. Both dropped dead in the dust.

Tulnarron stared for a moment. He closed his eyes. Lowered his head. Exhaled. Raised his head. Opened his eyes. Then turned away.

"These people were of Rothic blood, were they not, cousin?" the Master asked of Sandarre as Gornannon went to retrieve the thrown spear.

"For the greater part. Some Erelian. Perhaps a drop of Nothiring here and there."

"The Roths and the Erelians burn their dead."

"As do the Nothirings, though they do so at sea."

Tulnarron gazed westward, his heart simultaneously haughty and heavy. His broad, square shoulders sagged slightly. Inexplicably, both the *rillagh* across his breast and the greatsword in its harness at his back seemed to weigh a ton.

"There are many more homesteads and villages between here and Druintir."

"I suspect there will be many more...like this," said Sandarre sadly.

The Master of the House of Eccuron fell silent briefly.

Priority precedes pride. Even so.

Then, "We will ride hard. We will send riders to all our kin. Arrenhoth will answer this. The House of Eccuron will visit every village between here and Druintir. None will be forgotten. None will be forsaken."

Sandarre nodded silently.

Gornannon rejoined them then, his steel spearhead freshly cleaned yet gleaming a gaudy scarlet in the sheen cast by the fires. Some blood, it seemed, can never be washed away.

"We will gather the dead," decreed Tulnarron, his demeanor determined and decidedly martial. "We will pray for the repose of their souls. And then we will burn them all."

"As you command, Master Tulnarron," answered Gornannon and Sandarre in solemn unison.

And then Tulnarron tugged the reins of his mount, once, twice, and urged his majestic *mirarran* away.

He failed to mark that the ears of his silver-eyed steed had for some time been turned in earnest toward the woods across the creek.

The forms of two small children emerged from the eaves of the forest and walked hand-in-hand to the pebbled bank of the brook. Their round cherubic faces were grubby and soiled, their golden curls plastered to their skulls beneath a pitch of peat and pine needles. But for abundant dirt and grime both were naked, their bodies entirely hairless, the young girl's small breasts barely beginning to bud. Matching sets of bright blue eyes peered past masks of muck and mud, gazing westward into the setting sun.

They are gone, brother.

Gone, gone.

We must wait now.

Wait for our master, wait, wait.

Not our master, brother. Our summoner. And he will not come. He cowers in the deeps of the earth. No, he will not come. But his armies will.

I'm hungry, hungry.

Did you not devour the human child's soul?

No, sister. The child escaped me, its soul slipped away, slipped away. But I claim the shell. The shell is mine, mine.

The human girl is gone as well. I know not where. It matters not. The shell will suffice.

I'm hungry, so hungry.

As am I, brother. These shells require sustenance. We must eat.

I feel, sister. I feel, feel, feel.

Yes, these corporeal forms are wonders. All sensation is magnified. So brutally primal. So intense.

Yes, yes, yes, yes.

The little girl's azure gaze swept casually across the creek to the smoking ruins of the village. At its centre, a mound of carcasses burned, the sweet reek of cooking flesh rising to greet the falling night.

Let us feast, brother. And then I would have you make use of me.

Yes, yes, yes, yes.

4

IN THE SHADOW OF DRAGONS

"A man looks upon a Dragon and sees a monster,
a terrible beast, a fearsome fiend of terror and fire.
Tell me, what does the Dragon see?"

Majan al Khan, White Mage to the Turian Emperor

They passed Doomfall in silence.

Dark was the shroud of Eryn Drun, a veil of murkish mists that seethed and swirled like a living thing, baleful and brooding. The company skirted the haze, men and mounts warily scanning the vapours and ash for possible peril. The quietude of the place was persistent, pervasive, broken only by the intermittent hiss of heat released from the netherearth and by the hollow clap of hoof on stone. Nothing moved within the roiling earthborn fog, but many among the company could not shake the tingling sensation that they were not passing Doomfall unseen.

"There are eyes in the mist," stated Runningwolf prosaically, as they moved beyond the grasp of Doomfall's most northerly tendrils. He did not elaborate.

Hearing the Rhelman, the Iron Captain directed an enquiring look to Caelle, but the Shield Maiden only smiled blithely and said nothing.

Marking Caelle's reticence on the matter, Axennus restrained his own innate curiosity, stowing his queries for a later time, and of the fog-fettered Pass of the Guard no more was said.

"Creeps me right freakin' out, mate," complained Maddus in the rear of the rearguard of the party. His atypically anxious gaze was concentrated to the left, unceasingly searching the murk and mist of Eryn Drun.

Conceded Riffalo, "The gates of Hell look less menacing."

"Oh, you've been to Hell, have ya, Riff?"

"Every moment he spends with you, Maddy," responded Rooboong.

"Listen, Ruby, you big black –"

Maddus abruptly bit back his words. At a place where the haze of Doomfall briefly thinned and fell away, the guardsman glimpsed a solitary figure, not tall but inhumanly broad, enormously muscled, unbrokenly black, the haft of a huge hammer resting on one massive shoulder. Widely set eyes shone like shards of polished obsidian. One thick finger rose to lips buried beneath a big black beard, and unnumbered fissures in the stone hissed 'shhhhhhhhh...'

And then the shroud of Doomfall billowed, whirled, swirled, and the fantastic phantasm vanished.

Guardsman Maddus tore his gaze away.

"Care to finish that thought, Maddy?" challenged Rooboong, guiding his mount to the side of the smaller man. "Hmmm? I'm a big black...what, exactly?"

"Not so big, Ruby," Maddus answered enigmatically, staring straight ahead. "Not so black."

Upon the company's left, the sun was swiftly sinking behind the rising rock of the Dragon's Head. Rearing huge and hoary, dark and doomsome, the twin-peaked mountain cast the company in the prevenient shadow of a faux dusk. Clustered cumuli wreathed the horns of the Dragon like half-holy haloes that neither absorbed nor emitted light. A mile below the wind-sharpened summits of Southhorn and Northhorn, and an equal distance above the flats of the Middle Land, a great span of stone stretched between the rocky spires, a colossal causeway formed by the twin forces of time and the elements. Millennia of wind and rain had hollowed two cavernous tunnels midway up and through the stone base of the bridge, and in the fall of the evening sun, the eastern apertures glowed crimson like a pair of great flaming eyes.

"The Dragon watches," commented Runningwolf, characteristically detached, his face a mask of dispassion. "There is anger in her eyes."

"A trick of sun and stone only, Left Tenant," muttered the Iron Captain, dubiously. Whether the skepticism in his voice was for the Rhelman's words or for his own was unclear.

Runningwolf shrugged. "I speak only of what I see."

The Ambassador gazed upon the Dragon's stone face in appreciative wonder.

"Trick or no," said he, his tone airy and his eyes bright with boyish delight, "it is a thing of beauty, however dark and dreadful."

"A rare quality, Master Ambassador," Caelle said softly at Axennus' side. "Few are they that may see beauty in the grotesque." A small smile pulled at the Fiann's lovely lips. "I am well-pleased that you are numbered among us."

The Ambassador grinned.

The Iron Captain groaned.

They camped that night beneath the dark imposing presence of the Dragon's Head, the hollow sockets of the Dragon's eyes black and empty, though not unseeing, not unwatchful. The company ate their meal of salted venison and Rhille cheese in intermittent bouts of communal silence and conversation. Less than a day's ride from Druintir, the euphoria they felt at being so near their destination was dimmed by their memory of the red wind, and darkened further by their proximity to the twin-horned hulk of the Dragon's Head. The unblinking gaze of the mountain cast a pall of gloom over the Erelian camp, and few seemed unaffected.

The Ambassador and the Captain moved among the men, the one bringing a smile, the other strength, differing but not incongruous incarnations of the same courage. In time, the camp took an air more typical of the veterans of the notorious North March Mounted Reserve. Many found succour in shared stories and weak wine. Someone produced a pair of gaming stones, and soon the wagering began in earnest, the pandemonium of the players rising with every toss of the numbered nuggets. Reclined before the healer's tent, young Lionnus found comfort in a small fire and an old tome. Nearby, Draconarius painstakingly mended a pennon. And at the eastern edge of camp, stern Hastiliarius instructed a number of younger guardsmen in the arts of weaponless combat. One by one, and in his own way, each man's tension was eased.

The brothers Teagh were contented.

Axennus and Bronnus came to stand at the western edge of camp, just within the thrown glowings of the fires. The brothers were similar, yet dissimilar, in stance and bearing. The Ambassador was tall and lean; the Captain shorter, broad and thickly muscled. Their facial features betrayed their brotherhood, square and chiseled, cheeks and chin like facets of hewn stone, but where Axennus was smooth and soft, Bronnus was bristling and hard.

"The world changed this day, Axo." The shadowlight of the fires flickered orange and amber on the planes of Bronnus' face. "The ill wind altered all."

"Nay, dear brother, the world did not change – only our perceptions. We have been forced to modify our view of things."

Bronnus was quiet for a moment, pensive, pondering.

Then, "The men seem well enough, despite this day's wizardry."

"The healer is happy with our recovery. He seemed rather dismissive of the blood magic behind the red wind."

"Better that such sorcery remain within the vivid imaginations of the tale-tellers," grumbled the Iron Captain.

Axennus smiled softly.

"Even the most fantastic of tales told has its foundation, however deeply rooted, in truth. It is the responsibility of the listener to seek that truth, and to discern the real from the imagined."

Bronnus gazed, blinked.

Axennus sighed.

"Yes, Bron," he said, forsaking philosophy. "The men have endured well. They are buttressed by your strength."

"And by your own."

"And by the Rhelman's," Axennus furthered, nodding to a knot of shadows some distance west of them, where Runningwolf stood, statue-still, staring at the horned black mass of the Dragon's Head.

In spite of the chill of the northern night, the Rhelman had foregone his tunic of Erelian blue, and was standing with his arms folded about his bare chest, thongs of leather and feather dangling from his well-formed biceps. His deep earthy eyes were focused and fastened upon the towering twin-pinnacled formation of night-blackened stone, as though of all wonders of the world, the Dragon's Head was the most compelling.

Wordlessly, the brothers Teagh moved to the Rhelman's side.

Their presence was acknowledged with a nod. The threesome shared a simple, soothing silence under star and moon, each man intent upon his own thoughts, each finding a certain calm in the moment.

Then Runningwolf spoke.

"There is movement on the mountain."

Bronnus looked at Axennus dubiously, then to Runningwolf.

"You see this despite such distance and darkness, Left Tenant?"

"Not with my eyes, Captain."

Axennus grinned. "You have said you speak only of what you see."

Runningwolf blinked slowly. "A man may possess sight other than that provided by his eyes, Master Teagh."

"So we are learning," muttered the Iron Captain.

Intrigued, Axennus asked, "What do you see, Left Tenant?"

"Spirits," replied the Rhelman. "Spirits of stone and fire."

The Iron Captain frowned his doubt.

The Ambassador smiled and starshine played in his eyes.

"Long have the shamans of my people spoken of such beings," Runningwolf continued in his removed alien tone, "masters of rock and flame that reside in the ancient mountains, waging eternal war against the deep-dwelling demons of darkness that would destroy the beauty of the world. The old teachers tell that but for these *akanga*, these spirits of rock and fire, all light and hope in the world would be lost."

His chiseled chin in his hand, Axennus said, "The most ancient of Erelian histories also speak of these beings, Left Tenant, though they were called Daradur by our forefathers."

The Iron Captain grunted.

"Only this past morning I would have said that one man's history is another man's legend, and legends are but lies graced with time." He paused, then sighed, almost sadly. "But one red wind can alter things."

"An open mind is a wonderful thing, brother," smiled the Ambassador. "Unbelief is most often a misnomer for nescience, even ignorance. A thing not experienced is a thing not understood, and a thing not understood is oft not believed and relegated to the realm of fancy. Is it not wiser to believe in reasonable possibilities? Do not mistake me, I do not mean to encourage blind faith. Hardly that. Faith is but another face of the same folly. Surely, there can be no excuse for any form of willful ignorance."

"Sagely spoken, Master Ambassador," came a fourth voice.

The trio turned to find the Fiann Caelle with them.

Come the setting of camp, the Shield Maiden of the Fiannar had ridden alone into the twilight upon concerns of her own. Having tended to these, she had returned in search of the Teagh brothers, soon spotting them in the company of the Rhelman half a thrown stone beyond the reach of the firelight.

She had approached, listening to their discourse, a wry smile taking her comely mouth – for the Daradur had been the purpose of her venture into the night, as she had sought to garner information and secure safe passage from the mighty Stone Lords.

After some gratuitous grumbling, both had been granted.

She had then, almost in afterthought, questioned the Daradur as to the source of the slashing white light that had secured the Southmen's salvation from the ravages of the red wind.

But the Daradur, in their own irascible way, had only assured her that the credit was not theirs.

Don't go blaming us for that, Fiann.

She almost smiled at the memory.

Caelle of the Fiannar stood before the two Erelians and the Rhelman, and for the first time since their initial meeting she was unhorsed. She came only to Axennus' shoulder, and a little above that of Bronnus, but she was straight of back and high of head, of powerful presence, and her stature seemed to surpass their own. Her physical beauty was exquisite and explicit, the curves of her form silhouetted against the warm radiance of the campfires behind her. One fine hand upon her hip, the other about the haft of her sword, she watched the faces of the men before her with a small smile on her lips and a knowing gleam in her eyes.

"Shield Maiden," the Ambassador said simply.

He and his brother inclined their heads, and Runningwolf raised his totem to his temple. All averted their eyes.

"I expected to find you discussing war and women," Caelle quipped, "rather than musing upon the mysteries of a mountain."

The brothers straightened, relaxed. Axennus Teagh laughed. Even Bronnus risked a smile.

Only the Rhelman remained remote.

"It surprises me as well, Shield Maiden," admitted Axennus.

"My own surprise is the greater, Shield Maiden," gritted the Captain. "I am discovering that the beliefs I carried with me from Hiridith dwindle in their worth with each northward mile."

Caelle smiled beautifully.

"Beliefs unfounded on fact can be cumbersome, Captain," said she airily. "As the Ambassador has said, it is knowledge that truly enlightens."

"Oh, is that what he said?"

Axennus glibly waved one hand. "Your wisdom is wasted on this one, Shield Maiden."

Bronnus growled and glowered. Obscenities burned the tip of his tongue.

"Captain," Runningwolf interjected calmly, "I will take my leave. I must inspect the paddock, tend to the watch."

The Rhelman raised his totem to his temple once more. His jaw clamped tightly, the Iron Captain nodded, fisted his breast. And with no further word the Rhelman turned and blended into the night.

"An interesting man," said Caelle, her eyes following Runningwolf's shade in the darkness. "Quite remarkable, actually. Aside from the Fiannar, few are they that might commune with the *mirarra*."

The Ambassador smiled. "The Left Tenant is a special man."

"Tell me, Ambassador, have you many special men in your party?"

"Shield Maiden?"

"A sorcerer of your own, perhaps? A wizard, a mage? Maybe a dabbler in the arcane arts?"

Bronnus barely checked a guffaw before it escaped.

Axennus was understandably perplexed. And concerned.

"Did the red wind wound you, Shield Maiden? If so, we have a healer. Quite a competent one at that. But we count no sorcerers in our number."

Caelle looked away, concealing the heightened, brightened sheen of interest in her eyes.

"Competent. Yes, he would be. The North March Mounted Reserve, I recall, suffered so very few losses in the recent war."

"You remember rightly, Shield Maiden. None who entered the healing house of Teji Nashi alive left it...otherwise. My brother and myself included. We are fortunate to have him with us."

Caelle looked again upon the Erelian brothers, her smile a bright slash of white in the dark.

"Fortunate indeed, Ambassador."

Axennus gazed upon the Shield Maiden in curious silence.

Unlocking his jaw at last, Bronnus grumbled, "Fortune, both good and ill, has befallen us all this day."

Caelle's smile did not falter. "You have questions, of course."

The Iron Captain said simply, "I do."

The Shield Maiden looked from the Captain to the Ambassador, and there was grace even in that slight movement of her head. She marked the warmth in the younger Erelian's smile and the shine in his eyes, comprehended these things, knew them for what they were and for what they might become. She briefly wondered whether he saw the same upon her own countenance.

But she knew the risen shadows forbade he see these things.

And the risen Shadow forbade she show them.

She looked away.

The brothers followed the Shield Maiden's gaze eastward past the camp and into the night, saw nothing, then looked upon her once more. And it seemed to them that the fair Fiann's visage had darkened. But the mingled silvers of star and moon fell upon her hair with splendour, soft and smooth and shining. And when she returned her gaze to the Teaghs, that same splendour was in her eyes.

"There will be time enough for answers at Druintir." Caelle's voice held an irrefutable tone of finality, irrevocability. "We shall dine there tomorrow, though I fear I will find the place greatly changed. Rest now, for we are to ride early. Be easy in the knowledge that this place is well warded."

And shield on arm and hand on hilt, she strode westward into the night.

When she had gone, Axennus murmured, "The Shield Maiden is troubled."

Bronnus nodded darkly. "Only a matter of some gravity would trouble one such as she." His brows furrowed. "I would know the nature of this peril into which we ride."

Axennus eyes gleamed as they focused on the portion of night's darkness into which the Fiann's form had faded.

"I trust we will know soon enough, dear brother."

Lionnus looked up from the tattered, dog-eared tome in his hands. Years of reading by insufficient firelight had caused fine lines to prematurely web about his eyes, lending the lad a precipitately scholarly look. But the eyes themselves, blue and piercingly bright, remained young. And above those eyes, fair brows now arched.

"Sirs?"

"Lio, is it?" asked Regorius.

"Yes, sir."

The Decan nodded mutely, his hand fidgeting at the few fine white hairs that had managed to sprout from his chin. His pink eyes peered past Lionnus to the sprawling, strangely shaped tent at the young outrider's back. Beside and behind Regorius, three exceedingly disparate guardsmen shuffled uncomfortably in their boots. None of them seemed inclined to speak.

"Is there something you want, sirs?"

Regorius jerked his head toward the tent. "Is he in there?"

Lionnus peered up at the Decan, blinked slowly, then gently closed his book.

"Sir?"

"The little Diceman. The healer. You know, with the slanty eyes."

"Teji Nashi."

"Yes, of course. Teji. Is he in there?"

The young outrider set his tome aside, almost tenderly, then uncrossed his long legs and leisurely rose to his feet. Though slimmer, Lionnus was of a height with Rooboong, standing a head and a half higher than the albino Decan.

"Are you injured, sir?"

"What? Injured? No, no, I'm not injured." The Decan seemed flustered. "I – we – we need to speak with the...we need to talk to Teji."

"But sir, if you aren't hurt –"

"*Is he in there or not, soldier?*" Regorius' pink eyes reddened irritably.

"I'm not actually in the army any more, sir," Lionnus replied placidly, maddeningly.

"Oh bloody hell!" spurted Maddus at the Decan's shoulder. "Ruby, punch the little poof right in the gob!"

But Lionnus inclined his handsome head to one side, as though hearing something the others could not, remained thus momentarily, then smiled wanly, stood to one side of the odd tent's entrance and pulled the flap aside.

"Sirs. The Doctor will see you now."

Grumbling, the four guardsmen filed into the strangely shaped tent, throwing the young outrider murderous looks as they went.

Across the fitfully sputtering fire from Lionnus, Draconarius grinned up from his sewing.

"Lambs to the slaughter, Lio. Lambs to the slaughter."

The interior of the canvas enclosure was quite spacious, twice as long as it was wide, the fore and rear walls rounded, those on the flanks curved and narrowing toward the middle, effectively creating a shape evocative of an hourglass on its side.

The first chamber was unlit, unoccupied and evidently little used. The air was cool and still. To the right was a neatly prepared bed of blankets and furs; upon the left an elaborate armour stand displaying a gilded helm, padded gambeson and bronzed plate, and a more modest rack upon which dried a freshly cleaned cloak and clothing of Erelian blue. A grand, intricately carved wooden chest rested at the foot of the bed. Atop this, within an ornately enameled sheath, lay a *katana*, the proprietary weapon of the warrior class of the distant Dice Islands – a three-foot sword, the single-edged blade slender, curved and razor-sharp, the guard square, the leather-bound grip of sufficient length to accommodate two hands.

Led by a resolute Regorius, the four guardsmen quickly traversed the forechamber, then ducked beneath the low, narrowed midsection of the tent and passed into the space beyond.

This second chamber was of like size and shape to the first, but there all similarity ceased. Soft white light, gentle on the eye, illuminated the space, and the air was warm, humid yet not cloying, much like that about the Gendurii baths in Hiridith. Unfamiliar floral fragrances floated almost visibly, weaving and wafting, tingling, not unpleasantly, in the nostrils of the foursome.

Two long wooden tables dominated the chamber; one close upon the entrance and extending the entire width of the room, effectively prohibiting the guardsmen from proceeding any further; the other was pressed against the rear wall of the tent. The nearer table was heaped with tomes, manuscripts, scrolls, codices and tablets, a tumultuous turmoil of papyrus, parchment, bamboo, hide, vellum, wood, wax, clay and stone. The far table was correspondingly chaotic, the whole of its surface covered by hundreds of containers of myriad shapes and sizes; ampules, bottles, flasks, bowls and basins of glass, fired clay, copper, bronze, silver and even gold, holding fluids and powders of every imaginable colour. From several of these vessels, held aloft in the arms of alien apparatuses, steam and smoke of various shades and densities seethed and slithered toward the ceiling.

Between the two tables, in the centre of the room, beneath a veritable jungle of hanging herbs, weeds and grasses, upon a tall slender stool, sat Teji Nashi.

The Diceman's small frame was hunched over, his back to the quartet. He was clad only in an indigo *yukata*, a shimmering serpentine shape stencil-dyed in a winding pattern upon the delicate Dicese cotton. His clean-shaven head was lowered, apparently intent upon an item on the table before him, or upon something in his hands.

Decan Regorius was reminded of a scholar absorbed in reading.

"It is an illusion of the epicanthal folds, you see," said Teji Nashi, neither straightening nor turning around to face his visitors. His voice was quite soft, low, almost a hum, only slightly inflected with the distinctive accent common among natives of the Dice.

Regorius cast his three companions a confused expression punctuated by two arched stark white brows.

Riffalo simply shrugged.

Rooboong's black eyes nearly disappeared beneath an even blacker frown.

"The epicanthus, you see," explained Teji Nashi, remaining seated, hunched and averted, "is a feature common to us all when we are born, but one which those who are not of Elder Eastern origin will eventually lose. The Elder East was a frigid place, you see, and the epicanthal folds functioned to protect the eyes of my people's ancestors from the extreme cold and the harsh glare of the sun reflecting off overly abundant snow and ice. You might also note a fold of skin of the upper eyelid partially covering the inner corners of the eyes of the coastal Toshi people and many of the tribes of Rheln, yes? All cousins, you see, all kin, however removed and estranged. We have lost much, very much, but we retain the epicanthal folds."

Maddus mutely mouthed, *What the bloody hell?*

"Healer. Teji." Regorius' tongue seemed to have thickened in his mouth. "We don't...we didn't..."

Teji Nashi straightened, stood.

"You didn't come for a lesson, yes? Ah, but every moment is a lesson, you see. Every moment, every breath. And you, my honoured guests, have now learned that the eyes of the Dicese people are not so – how do you say? – *slanty*, after all."

Regorius' pale features went deathly white.

"You...you heard that? From here?"

Teji Nashi turned and smiled.

His face was round, his smile white and without flaw, his thin dark eyes veritably dancing with light. His smooth round skull was shaved to a shine, his skin a glowing burnished shade. He appeared to be of middling age, but he could have been a decade older as easily as a decade younger.

At the waist of his light cotton kimono was tied a *wakizashi*, the companion blade to the *katana*, identical to its mate in all detail save length. The *wakizashi* was the smaller of the pair of swords that comprised the *daishō*, the deadly duo of weapons exclusive to the esteemed warrior class of Dicese nobility.

The serpentine stencil decorating his *yukata* revealed itself to be the image of a great golden dragon entwined about the man's small frame, the beast's head resting comfortably on one shoulder.

"I have been expecting you, friends."

The four guardsmen stared in startled shock at Teji Nashi's hands.

The diminutive Diceman held his arms before him, elbows bent square, hands shoulder-width apart, index fingers pointing inwards toward one another. From the tips of each extended digit, a thread of golden flame arced toward the other, burning softly, casting little light and less shadow.

Teji Nashi then lowered his hands and the string of golden fire was gone.

The foursome remained riveted where they stood, slack-jawed and wide-eyed.

The Diceman smiled sweetly.

"Left Tenant Runningwolf told me you would come, you see. He visited me last night, after your little experience with the Fist of Fate. I sought to ease his concerns, but the Rhelman is a stubborn fellow. Did the Left Tenant speak to you tonight?"

The four guardsmen were able to exchange odd glances.

"Well, yes, healer. Teji. He was very...strange."

"Oh?"

"Yes, Nashi...Teji...healer. He said we should come see you. Then, for some bizarre reason, he insisted that we stop...uhh...pleasuring ourselves."

Teji Nashi's smile was saintly.

"Despite his intellect and estimable efforts in the matter, the Rhelman's developing mastery of the Westspeech has yet to embrace many inherent idiosyncrasies and subtleties of the language. A difficult thing at times, you see."

Regorius frowned. He did not see. He did not understand, not at all.

"I think so, healer...Teji....uhh...what do we call you?"

"Ah, yes, Decan, we have had little opportunity to socialize, you, your friends and I, so it follows that you would not know. Your martial prowess and good fortune are such that you have seldom been in need of a healer. Thus, four years of service in the same company notwithstanding, our paths have crossed but infrequently. Would it surprise you to learn that I was of the rank of undercaptain while in the Reserve? No, no, do not salute, the trappings of military hierarchy neither become nor interest me. Those who have had the misfortune to require my services simply call me 'Doctor', often abbreviated to 'Doc', a moniker of which I have admittedly become rather fond."

The four men lowered the fists they had raised to their hearts and managed dumb nods.

"But come, come, friends. I am remiss. My preoccupations render me rude, you see, and I forget my more hospitable nature."

Teji Nashi gestured to the right with one hand, and the four guardsmen found themselves edging past a gap between the end of the interposing table and the tent wall, a gap that each would have sworn had not been there a moment earlier. When they had come around, there awaited them four stools identical to that upon which the Diceman had been sitting. These, too, each man would have insisted had not been present when they had entered.

"Do sit, friends, and share with me your troubles."

The four companions settled silently upon the stools. All seemed to have wilted somewhat. Withered. Regorius appeared to have gone yet another shade paler. Even Rooboong looked a little less black.

None spoke.

"Forgotten your worries so soon?" said the Diceman, something like delight prancing in his bright brown eyes. "Good, very good. Stress is such an unhealthy burden, you see, and in this case so very unnecessary."

Teji Nashi seated himself once more, his hands folding together into the billowed sleeves of his dragon-emblazoned *yukata*.

"Perception is paramount, yes? Thirteen stones in a circle, another at the centre, a bone cross held within, two more bones without. So many would see this as a disturbing portent, the terrible Crucible of the Dying Man. An understandable interpretation, as the cross is indeed evocative of a crucifix, you see. Understandable, even excusable, but awfully erroneous. The Left Tenant and the Ambassador must be forgiven their conclusions, yes?"

Dumb nods.

"Often, we see that which we wish to see, or that which we fear to see. Our ability to decipher truth objectively is incessantly afflicted with preconceived notions, prejudices, desires, dreads. It is in our nature to follow the easiest path, to leap to the simplest conclusions. The committed investigator must avoid such snares, yes?

"Allow me to demonstrate.

"Three men might perceive a thing in three very different ways, yes? Take this tent, for example. What image might it evoke in their individual minds, minds molded by uniquely personal histories and experiences? The first might see an hourglass knocked over on its side; the next, the figure of the number eight; the last, the mathematical symbol of infinity, eternity. All would be correct in their perceptions. But all err, also. The error is in not what they see, but rather in that which they do not."

Silence.

"Perhaps an example with which you can more easily identify might be more helpful, yes? In the cities of Southfleet, the Decan's albinism would be seen as an imperfection; worse, a curse, a mark of evil. Erelians differ in that they regard albinism to be an oddity, generally, grotesque perhaps, but not an overly foul affliction. I, however, see a man simply stricken with the hereditary inability to produce a particular pigment necessary for the more common peachy-beige colouring of the skin and whatever hue the hair and the eyes might ordinarily take.

"As an aside, Guardsman Rooboong, obviously, does not suffer this same deficit; in fact, he produces the essential pigment in some plentitude, yes?"

Utter silence.

"Do I digress? Please forgive me, honoured guests. I will strive to make myself more easily understood.

"The thirteen stones of the circle represent the moons of the year, the fourteenth being the sun, properly situated at the centre, around which all things are bound and revolve. The bones divide the circle into four equal sections – what else, but the four seasons, yes? There is a craftsman in Toshi who has created a most intricate mechanism, so compellingly similar in appearance to the circle and cross portent in question, a mechanism whose sole function is to measure and trace time. No, you would not know that, but the information is essential if you are to comprehend the true significance and import of the portent.

"It is, in simple sooth, nothing more than a symbol of Time."

The little Diceman grinned.

"Ah, I must infer from your silence that the revelation has captivated you so thoroughly that you now meditate upon its momentousness, yes? Good, good. Ponder the Circle of Time, friends. The curious mind must ever be nurtured.

"But there is more, you see.

"The stones all landed smooth side up, yes? This is significant, as it indicates that the immediate future has yet to be determined, that fate, destiny, predetermination have nothing whatsoever to do with what may occur over the next year. For good or ill, we are our own masters, you see. We will decide what is to come. Given the goodness of our natures and the innocence of our intentions, this can be seen only as a positive thing, yes?

"But there is indeed a darkness to the portent, one which all have overlooked – all, save my own humble self, of course."

The four guardsmen fidgeted quietly upon their stools.

"Consider the two little bones that fell outside the circle. A random roll, perhaps? Unlikely. I can only conclude that a pair of entities, yet to be identified, lying *outside* the Circle of Time, beyond its moderating sphere of influence, are to play an integral part in our futures. Unbound and unknown. Disturbing, yes? Not good, not good.

"But do not trouble yourselves, friends. I will think on this."

The four guardsmen nodded as one.

"Oh, and pay the red wind no mind. Simple blood magic, inexpertly wielded. Nothing to lose sleep over."

A minute gesture.

Regorius and his companions rose.

"Dwell no more on these things. And speak of our little chat to no others, yes? I would not wish to be thought of as anything more than a medic of some modest skill."

They nodded once more.

The Diceman's smile was exquisite.

"Good, very good. I must think now. That is all, friends."

Moments later, as the four guardsmen moved away from the Doctor's tent, in a burst of unpent emotional and physical tension –

"What the bloody hell just happened in there?"

"I have no idea."

"Me neither, Riff. How 'bout you, Ruby?"

"Not a clue, Whitey."

"We barely got a word in!"

"Did we even ask him a question?"

"I think you asked his name or something."

"Where'd the bloody light come from? There were no lanterns!"

"Not even a candle."

"No fire, neither."

"So how was it so bloody warm?"

"No idea."

"Well, there was that string of fire between his hands. I mean, did you *see* that?"

"Freaked me right out!"

"Me, too!"

"Where did the chairs come from?"

"There wasn't even any bleedin' poles holding the bloody tent up!"

"Anyone else see the table shrink?"

"Just where the hell did all that stuff *come* from, anyway? He's only got the one goddamn horse!"

"I swear that bloody dragon on his robe *winked* at me!"

In their wake, as the four befuddled men picked their way through camp back to the comparative haven of their own tents, Lionnus met Draconarius' amused gaze across the guttering flames of the campfire.

Both men smiled.

"*Baaaaa-aaaaa-aaaaa...*"

5

ERYN RUIL

"Behold Colossus:
Carved of intellectual steel and emotional stone,
Hewn of granite sinew and iron bone,
A monument to unyielding will –
'Tis but a strong man standing still."

Rodannus, Poet Primus of Hiridith

The drums came with dawn.

Sourced deep within the Dragon's Head, their low thunder reverberated through earth and stone, a rhythmic rumbling in the rock.

Dun-dun-dun-doom.

There was a primal beauty to the sound, a primitive simplicity akin to flame and flowing blood. And the thrumming of the drums was accompanied by a rolling requiem, vociferous voices in the earth chanting a death dirge in harmony with the heartbeat of the mountain.

Dun-dun-dun-doom.

The Iron Captain threw aside the flaps of his tent, his brow furrowed, his face flushed.

"What devilry is this?"

Axennus appeared at his side. "Hardly devilry, Bron."

"What then?"

The Iron Captain's hand instinctively strayed to the pommel of his sword. His chest swelled.

"Drums, brother," grinned Axennus. His tone was light, free of care.

Dun-dun-dun-doom.

Bronnus' frown darkened. "I know of no drum that can make this sound."

"Really, brother, one should not flaunt one's ignorance so liberally."

The elder Teagh turned upon his brother, his countenance dark with anger.

But he then saw Caelle's curiously unconcerned smile at Axennus' shoulder, and his wrath deserted him, the blood of his ire ebbing from his face.

"You hear the drums of the mighty Daradur, Captain," the Shield Maiden elucidated. The light of the dawn sun played over her like a halo of gold. "Seldom are they heard, and never by mortal man, save only in times when need is most dire."

Dun-dun-dun-doom.

The Iron Captain's frown became a black thing. "These drums are...*in the earth.*"

"The Daradur are of the earth, brother," Axennus explained.

"The Daradur *are* the earth," corrected Caelle.

"Surely that cannot be," Bronnus protested softly, though the thrumming in the ground underfoot was as real as the rock.

Caelle of the Fiannar placed one small hand on Bronnus' arm.

"I do not intend to further diminish the value of your beliefs, Captain."

Bronnus closed his eyes and was briefly silent as he willed himself to absorb and accept the latest alterations to his reality. He was a soldier, and adaptation was survival. And physically, intellectually, spiritually, Bronnus Teagh was a survivor. When he opened his eyes once more, they shone clear and bright, twin orbs of determined defiance glowering at the twin-horned enormity of the Dragon's Head.

"These Daradur must be commended on their courtesy, at the least," Bronnus grumbled reluctantly. "They waited for dawn to commence their drumming. I will give them that."

"Courtesy." Caelle laughed softly, truly amused. She released the Captain's arm. "Not a quality often attributed to the great Stone Lords."

"What purpose do these drums serve?"

"I am uncertain of their purpose, Captain, for even the Fiannar are not privy to the myriad mysteries of the Daradur. But I would suggest this drumming is a calling, a summons of sorts, becking all Daradur abroad to hasten to Raku Ulrun, this mountain that men call the Dragon's Head."

Dun-dun-dun-doom.

"And what dire need now compels them?"

The Shield Maiden smiled, and for the first time her smile seemed forced, even false. And her only reply was, "Time will tell that tale." A small pause, and a blue light swam in the grey pools of her eyes. Then, "Dawn is done. We will depart."

And she strode swiftly away.

Dun...

Alone with his brother, Axennus followed Bronnus' gaze to the mountain, hearing the hollow thunder of the Daradun drums, feeling the earth rock and roll beneath the hard leather heels of his boots.

"The truth of our own ancient histories is oft obscured by time and mistelling," he offered Bronnus in consolation, "but of the Daradur one detail is constant, and that is that they are roused from their stone halls by two things only."

Dun...

The Iron Captain looked upon his brother's intelligent, handsome face. Quietly, "And those two things are...?"

Dun...

A peculiar gleam brightened Axennus' eyes.

"Wrath and war."
Doom.

The drums in the earth were indeed a summoning.

The threnody of netherearthen thunder thrilled through stone and soil to all Wandering Guard that had ventured away, urging them to return to the rearing rock of Raku Ulrun, beckoning them back into the bosom of the Dragon.

Wrath and war.

They had been called. The *mara Waratur* of the Daradur. Mighty of the mighty, guardians among Guardians.

Had been called.

And were coming.

They came from the foot of the hoary Peacekeepers. They came from the blasted wastes of far Horachia. From the murk and dark of Mroch Durva. From the fetid Fen of Zelrecha. From the burning dusts and sands of the Dunelands. From all the wicked and wretched places to which their unceasing war of watchfulness had taken them.

And they came from beneath the blood-drenched standing stones of *Fongar ur Piruth.*

Bearded faces set with grim resolution, eyes bits of heated obsidian, Dulgar and his troop of Wandering Guard had chased the sun across the Plains, had seen it fall, had raced the risen moon in the descended darkness, running on through the night and into the dawn. Their short, stout legs churned like powerful machines beneath the considerable weight of their heavily muscled frames, propelling them tirelessly across the Plains. Their feet hammered the earth, making it a drum of their own, pounding, pounding, heedless of any who might hear them, might see them.

Such was their haste. Such was their need.

Like juggernauts of war, the Wandering Guard raced before the rising sun, mighty revenants riding the spearpoints of dawn. Hours passed. Leagues passed. They did not tire. They did not slow. The sun sailed toward its zenith. And the Daradur rushed onward. Onward and westward.

Harkening to the heart-song of the Dragon.

"You tarry, mudfucker," growled Dulgar as he fell back to Rundul's side at the rear of the race. The crimson-maned Captain's solitary ebon eye seemed to flare in disapproval, in accusation.

From between clenched teeth, Rundul replied, "You don't need to be reminded of my shame. Neither do they. Dishonour and disgrace are things better left unflaunted."

Dulgar snorted, spat.

"Shame is for those *without* fuckin' honour, Rundy." His words were punctuated by the heavy rhythmic thudding of his footfalls. "And I've already told you that what you did was honourable. You fuckin' doubting me, fuckbeard?"

Rundul scowled into the wind, and he asked bitterly, "I wonder, brother, would *you* have run?"

Abruptly, the Wild One laughed, and there was something of madness in the sound.

"You *know* that I wouldn't have fuckin' run, brother," he responded fiercely, his beard and hair flaring wildly about him like fire in a whipping wind. And again, with certainty, "I would *never* fuckin' run."

Rundul said nothing. The pounding of his feet on the turf returned him in mind and time to his furious flight from the Bloodshards, from the abominable secrets within its dark deeps. The shrieks of past pursuers echoed in his ears, careening within his memory, cackling. Each thump of boot on earth seemed to emphasize and reiterate his unworth, as though the very ground shuddered in a shared and sorry shame.

"Yeah, I would've stayed," continued the Wild One. The light in his eye took a maniacal sheen. "I would've fuckin' stayed. I would've feasted on blood and death and the fuckin' slaughter of the foe. I would've hewn a fuckin' holocaust in the hollows of the earth. The catacombs would've become veins gushing with the blood of my fuckin' enemies. I would've stood until I could stand not one fuckin' moment longer. When I could stand no more, I would've fought from my fuckin' knees. And then I would've been killed." A small pause punctuated by the percussion of feet flailing hard earth. "And I would have died with fuckin' *honour!*"

Rundul cringed inwardly. The wound on his back burned. Shame scorched his soul, something other than wind seared his eyes.

He condemns me.

And Dulgar concluded, "And in doing so I would have fuckin' sacrificed us all for the sake of my terrible fucked-up pride."

Rundul glanced sidelong at the fierce and ferocious *kor uri Warator* running at his side. The Wild One's face was hidden within a hurricane of red hair, and nothing but black light and the sharp gleam of lunacy could be seen in his solitary eye. Yet there had been something in his words, in his voice. Something like understanding. Perhaps even forgiveness.

Do you absolve me, brother?

And then, without forewarning, Dulgar declared, "Our *uldwan Dor* has sent word that when the foe descends upon Doomfall, you won't number among those who are to stand against them."

Rundul's heart broke.

His damnation was complete.

Fuck.

Well past middle-morning, when the shadows on the stone were short and shrunken, the drums in the earth fell silent.

An invisible wave of relief rippled through the riders of the ambassadorial company. The air appeared to warm in the ensuing quietude, and the sunlight seemed stronger, brighter.

Caelle rode in solitude and aphony at the head of the column, her raven locks flowing behind her like a cloak of midnight. The Fiann took little notice of the abrupt end to the Daradun drumsong. She had been unusually reticent since the breaking of camp and had insisted upon riding alone at the fore of the company for much of the morning. She had set a quick pace, leading at a trot.

Neither the Ambassador nor the Captain had pressed her for reasons, diffidently falling in a few lengths behind the Shield Maiden's magnificent *mirarran*.

"The lady rides as one pursued by demons," observed Bronnus coolly.

Axennus nodded. "Or as one pursuing them."

Upon the left, the Dragon's Head moved steadily southward, its twin horns honed and horrible, its dark and angry eyes ever watchful. The company drew parallel with Northhorn at midday, where the stone of the road gave way to hard packed earth, and then forked, the one branch continuing north to where the River Ruil rushed fast and frothing, the other breaking eastward toward distant Arrenhoth, seat of the noble House of Eccuron.

But no path led into Eryn Ruil.

The Ambassador, the Captain and the Shield Maiden gathered amidst a cluster of large broken stones some distance from the Road. Caelle sat atop a sizeable boulder, legs crossed beneath her forearms resting easily on her knees. Axennus settled upon a stone, his back against another, booted feet atop a third, sipping from a waterskin. Bronnus remained standing, soldier straight, though he relaxed his martial bearing enough to lean one hand against a rearing rock.

"We have come to the pass called Eryn Ruil," stated Caelle as she accepted Axennus' offered skin with a minute but gracious nod. "The pass is bounded by the Dragon's Head to the south and, to the north, by the River Ruil beneath the knee of Rothrange. The eastern approach to Eryn Ruil is warded by a series of rises called the Seven Hills, by the golden Field of Cedorrin and by the ancient evergreen forest of the Fend." She paused, sipped the water, and smiled. "You need look neither far nor overdeeply to find much beauty here, my friends."

"Truly spoken, Shield Maiden," responded the Ambassador, his eyes absorbing the green of the land about him. "The glories of Eryn Ruil and, indeed, of all Lindannan, are not altogether unknown in the South."

Caelle's smile widened whitely.

"What way to Druintir?" interposed Bronnus gruffly.

Axennus laughed aloud.

"You might forgive my brother's blunt nature, Shield Maiden. Though he holds little appreciation for delicacy, he possesses a certain fondness for directness and clarity."

"Not unseemly qualities in these troubled times," mused Caelle.

And for a moment her mind seemed to wander elsewhere.

Then, "Here the Old Road ends, my friends. We will take the path to the river, skirt the eastern edge of the Hills, then turn west again along the southern bank of the Ruil, behind the Maples, around the Warwatch, across the Field of Cedorrin, up and through the Fend and on to Druintir."

Bronnus frowned. "Sounds very...indirect. Can we not cross the Seven Hills themselves? Surely, the way of the Hills would be the shorter journey in both distance and time."

The Shield Maiden shook her head. "The Hills are forbidden," she averred flatly.

No further explanation was forthcoming.

Momentarily, Axennus pursued a different course of conversation.

"You have said that the Hills are seven, Shield Maiden. This is true also of the Hills of Hiridith, though they have not the greenery of those before us now." He pursed his lips. "Where another might see coincidence, I see pattern."

Caelle smiled demurely, and her manner lightened. She tossed the waterskin back to the Ambassador.

"Your mind is seldom idle, Southman."

"As is his mouth," muttered Bronnus.

Caelle grinned for the brotherly banter.

"The histories of your people and mine are long intertwined, Master Ambassador."

Axennus gazed appreciatively, almost longingly, at the oak-crested escarpment of stone rearing near to the north.

"Painful is it that such beauty be forbidden."

The Shield Maiden only smiled and said, "All will be made clear in time."

The Captain frowned.

"You tantalize us with many promised revelations." He leaned forward ever so slightly. "You demand much blind trust, Shield Maiden."

Caelle cocked her head to the other side, twirling a long lock of ebon hair around one fine finger. The gesture was disarmingly innocent, charmingly adolescent.

"Not blind, Captain," she said softly, "but simply...delayed in seeing. I ask only for patience."

"Passive ignorance, dear brother," grinned Axennus. "Something with which you are not unfamiliar." And then to Caelle, "Again, I ask forgiveness on my brother's behalf, Shield Maiden. He is a suspicious man and abrasive by nature. Perhaps our father spanked him too often."

Bronnus directed a look toward Axennus that would have chilled the blood of any but the bravest of men.

"The Captain's concern is not misfounded, Ambassador," replied the Fiann. "His is the responsibility for many brave good lives, and such a charge frequently inhibits forbearance." Her sapphire-speckled eyes swam over to Bronnus. "His instincts reveal to him that I am troubled, yet he knows not why. I will answer him this. I have sent word to Druintir with Sarrane, but have received none in return. I ride blind – or delayed in seeing – knowing only that a time of grave peril is upon us and that my proper place is at my Lady Cerriste's side."

The Iron Captain said nothing, but his brow smoothened, and he inclined his head slightly toward the Shield Maiden. Bronnus Teagh knew something of the burdens of responsibility, of duty.

Of worry.

The Ambassador, however, seemed distracted as he sipped at his waterskin. His bright hazel eyes appeared to belong to a face other than his own, as though his thoughts were focused not on the present, but on the past, or on the future. He ran a hand through his long dark hair, steadying himself in the aftermoments of a difficult decision made. He then met Caelle's steady inquiring gaze.

"Shield Maiden, it is my belief that we are come to Eryn Ruil in a time of war."

Bronnus Teagh's jaw clenched, shut fast in shock.

The Shield Maiden's smoke-grey eyes peered coolly past her own surprise to the Ambassador. Her smile faded, but did not altogether fall. The hair twirled about her finger sprang free.

"I can neither confirm nor deny that assertion, Master Ambassador," Caelle replied quietly, gently, her voice the sigh of the very wind. She rose gracefully to her feet, dropped lithely from the boulder, her hand falling reflexively to the haft of her weapon. "I know only that *we* are come to Eryn Ruil. However, should war be come also, the enemy will find me at my Lady's shoulder – and will have cause to wish that I was not."

A chill ran the length of each Erelian's spine. The cold in the wake of the Shield Maiden's words would surely have made the empty eternity of the Neverending Ice seem decidedly tropical.

Axennus swallowed. Hard.

War it is, then.

In the rearguard of the company, three of the four friends dutifully inspected their armour, their weapons, their gear, their mounts. Regorius, however, stood with his arms crossed upon his bronzed breastplate, a shock of white hair falling over his severely knotted brow. One foot tapped the earth repeatedly.

"I don't understand," he muttered aloud to himself. "I just don't get it."

Hearing the Decan, Maddus followed his gaze past many milling guardsmen and mounts to where the little Diceman sat placidly astride a small steed, practically a pony, patiently awaiting the imminent call to ride.

"No surprise there, Whitey. You don't understand much."

The Decan did not respond to the joust.

"What doesn't Dec understand, Maddy?" asked Riffalo, mounting his charger in his usual awkward manner.

"Didn't I just say 'everything', you long-shanked shite?"

"Well, no," said Riffalo, grimacing, "not actually."

Regorius shook his head.

"I don't get the Doctor, Riff. Aside from his armour, his swords and his clothing, the only thing that man has with him is the chest that was at the foot of his bed. It's there, strapped behind him. But even that looks smaller than it did."

"Maybe all his stuff is in the chest," shrugged Rooboong.

Maddus laughed aloud.

"Ruby, you're even stupider than you are black, mate."

He didn't even see the huge fist that knocked him silly.

Seeing the most abrasive of his four former visitors go down, Teji Nashi casually turned his back to the rearguard, lest the increasingly curious and vigilant Decan see his smile.

And in doing so found himself face to face with the Shield Maiden of the Fiannar.

The Doctor's smile died.

Oh. Dear me.

Caelle only peered at the Diceman from aback her great grey steed, her marvelous mien a mask of marble, her steely stare like a sharp and shining spear.

Probing, piercing, penetrating.

A moment only. Then those lovely lips curved into a small and knowing smile. And she whispered –

"Thank you."

Then a horn sounded the resumption of the ride, and her magnificent *mirarran* turned and bore the Shield Maiden away.

Teji Nashi sighed softly.

Most welcome.

As they moved east and north, then north and west, upon the outer marches of the Seven Hills, the men of the ambassadorial company shared a collective wonder for the lustrous landscape of Eryn Ruil. The southmost of the seven rises was crowned in oaken splendour, sylvan stands rising heaven-high into the crisp light of the afternoon sun. Then came one, two, three softly rolling hills, each blanketed in whispering waves of green and gold, grassy seas rippling before a gentle wind. Behind these and westward could be seen two formations of stone – the majestic crag of Sentinel Ridge and the imposing weather-hewn rise of the Warwatch. And lastly and northmost came a hill crested with mighty maples of height and girth and strength to rival those of their great oaken cousins to the south.

Shortly before the party reached the Maples, there came a change in the afternoon air, a subtle cooling and a dampening. Soon the breeze brought the sound of wildly rushing waters, of rapids cutting through rock. The roar rose as the men rode northwestward, a cacophony of crash and crush, the shouted surge of the white-crested River Ruil. They came upon the run of the Ruil with risen hearts and brightened eyes, each man an awestruck witness to the river's white-watered rush from the upper land down into the east. Steep upon the Ruil's northern shore, above the swift current's mist and spray, rose the great grey rock of time-weathered Rothrange, the mountainous southern boundary of the highland kingdom of Rothanar.

A subtle gesture from Runningwolf directed the Ambassador's attention skyward. There, level to the soaring summits of Rothrange, the great winged form of a *throkk* floated effortlessly on the high northern breeze.

"Magnificent," marveled Axennus beneath the sailing silhouette of the lordly warbird. Both sunlight and wonderment reflected in the Ambassador's upturned eyes.

"The very wings of the Fiannar!" he called to Bronnus.

But his voice was taken and drowned in the roar of the Ruil, and his brother rode onward at his side, unhearing and oblivious.

The company turned westward along the Ruil's stony southern bank, the lush green of the Maples to their left, the rush of the river and the rising rock of Rothrange upon their right. The ground began to slope noticeably upwards as the Erelian party moved past the treed hill toward the towering flat-topped stone of the Warwatch. Leaving the riverway, the Shield Maiden of the Fiannar led the Southmen about the stony base of the Warwatch, the clamour and crash of the Ruil's white waters receding with each falling hoof.

"Curious," said the Captain as they rounded the Warwatch. "We are so near to the city, yet neither soul nor sign do we see."

"Quite singular," agreed the Ambassador. "One would think the land unpeopled." He raised an eyebrow toward Runningwolf. "What say you, Left Tenant?"

Runningwolf was momentarily silent, his loamy eyes caressing the landscape as would a loving hand.

Then spoke the Rhelman, "Captain. Master Axennus. Are you familiar with the *ketterk*?"

"Of course," replied Axennus. "The large flightless bird of Rheln."

The Rhelman said, "When disturbed, the *ketterk* will often bury his head in loose earth, reasoning perhaps that because he cannot see, so too can he not be seen."

Bronnus sent Axennus a questioning glance.

"You riddle with us, Left Tenant," accused the Ambassador.

Runningwolf blinked slowly.

Then, in his strange alien monotone, "Like the *ketterk*, we are unseeing." A poignant pause. "But we are not unseen."

Behind the western foot of the Warwatch, the company came before a graded glade of grass and flowing flower, green and gold and glorious – the fragrant scents of blade and bloom entwining themselves about one another in an aromatic dance upon the glen. The flowered field rose gently but steadily westward for half a league, coming to an abrupt end in the shadow of a great wall of giant conifers.

"The Field of Cedorrin," stated the Fiann. "And beyond and above Cedorrin," – her slight nod indicated the tall jagged line of pine and fir and northern spruce – "stands the Fend." Her lips formed the semblance of a grim smile. "The final bulwark of Druintir's eastern defenses."

"Doubtless Druintir is walled, Shield Maiden," remarked Bronnus, uncertainly.

"Verily, she is walled, Captain Teagh," replied Caelle, her grey eyes asparkle with a distant blue light, "though fir be her brick, and pine be her stone." Her smile was gentle but grim. "The Fend is the only wall this land has ever known."

The sun was long into its westerly arc when the ambassadorial company approached the dark perimeter of the Fend. The trees rose high and tall, many soaring hundreds of feet skyward, and were set so

closely together that they seemed of one gargantuan nettled growth –
a solid mass of evergreen whose lowest needled branches swept the
earthen floor and whose coarse canopy scraped the sky. And though
the company halted no more than a dozen yards from the Fend's rough
edge, the men could discern no aperture, no pathway into the trees.

"A wall in sooth, Shield Maiden," grumbled Bronnus. "The trees
give way to neither horse nor man."

Heedless, Caelle of the Fiannar threw back her head, her long
dark hair spilling across her shoulders and down her back, and the
gold of her *rillagh* blazed beneath the shadow of the Fend like fire in
night.

"Hear me, ancient Faendomin!"

Her cry was clear and strong, like a hornblast, or a song.

"I am Caelle, Shield Maiden to the Lady Cerriste of the House
of Defurien! With me are friends to Lindannan – the sons of noble
House Teagh, a champion from the plains of Rheln and friend to the
mirarra, and nigh upon five-score of the Fiannar's long-sundered kindred from the land called Erellan in antiquity!

"Noble Faendomin! We beseech you. Grant us passage."

But the Fend remained still of sound and motion, and from the
forest's deep green darkness there came no reply.

Nevertheless, Caelle seemed contented as she visibly relaxed and
threw a quick smile toward Axennus.

"A courtesy only, Ambassador Teagh," said the Shield Maiden.
"The Fend stood here long before the Fiannar came to this land. I
offer the reverence and homage that is due."

"Of course, Shield Maiden," replied Axennus respectfully.

Bronnus endured in dubious silence at his shoulder.

And then, her *mirarran* nosing aside a densely nettled branch,
Caelle led the Southmen into the green darkness of ancient Faendomin.

Ascending steadily, the company filed through the Fend, each
man's mount near upon the next. The way through the forest was
dark and close, more tunnel than path and certainly no road. Barely
wider than the breadth of a horse's breast, the sylvan passage was

walled by tightly woven trunk and limb, like the skin-side of a grotesquely knitted sleeve. In places, the men found it necessary to bend low upon the neck of their mounts in order to avoid snagging helm or hair in the low-hanging overgrowth. Underhoof, the ground was soft and spongy with millennia of fallen nettles and cones, and the only sounds made by the horses were the heavy huffs of their breath. Little light penetrated the Fend's dense cover, the way lit largely by patches of luminescent moss that clung to the barbed bark, casting the tunnel and those traversing it in an eerie emerald half-shadow. The air, though, was clean and cool, sweet with the scents of pine and cedar. And rather than feel claustrophobically enclosed, most men of the company were struck with a sensation of solitude, of serenity, of security.

One, however, was otherwise disposed.

"I feel like a rat in a hole," muttered a scowling Bronnus.

Axennus saw no cause for restraint.

"Really, brother. A gentleman keeps his deviancies to himself."

Behind them, guardsmen shook in a bout of laughter. Their merriment, however, was short-lived – the sharp steel of the Iron Captain's subsequent hindcast glare spoke little of sport.

On the path ahead, Caelle kept her smile to herself.

They had been ascending through the Fend for near upon an hour when they came to the forest's western fringe. As the entrance had been from without, the egress from the shadowbound trees was undetectable from within, the light from the outer world shuttered and sealed away by the thick interwoven growth of fir and pine. But Caelle's *mirarran* pushed aside some spiked sprigs of spruce, and one by one the members of the company emerged from the strange green darklight of the Fend into the warm red glowings of sunfall.

Before them, some miles distant still, the half-ring of a great ridge of grey rock marked the horizon, the final rise to the upland plateaus of the High Land. And cascading from the western lip of the precipice fell the River Ruil, cool crystalline waters plummeting six hundred feet in three distinct stages, then racing in foam and fervour eastward.

The tri-tiered waterfall cast up a vast veil of mist and spray, like the shroud of a faerie fog, across which the monolight of a golden rainbow arced nobly into the evening air. And despite the weight and white of the falling waters, the three-throated shout of the cataract seemed surprisingly soft – a ceaseless silver song, or the sound of serenity.

"Behold!" rang Caelle's clarion cry. "Friends of the Fiannar, I give you *Dhir Ruill en Thir*. Druintir of Lindannan!"

And as though in well-rehearsed reply, the cold northwind rose and bellowed, parting the masking mists, scattering the gold of the spray's spectral sash.

And lo!

Beneath the northern sky, in the red-gold glamour of the sinking sun, the last city of the Fiannar was revealed in all her grace and grandeur.

Grey and ancient she was, hewn of the hard metamorphic stone about the Silver Stair, shimmering dimly in the evening glow like sun-bleached bone. Every curve and corner of the city's chiseled stone spoke of age, as though Druintir was but a brittle relic in the rock, the great fossilized remnants of a behemoth of olde. Yet she spoke also of strength and sufferance, of indomitable endurance, for her pale cold marble had weathered twenty centuries of wind and war.

But it was neither Silver Stair nor carven city that stilled the heart of Axennus Teagh within him, that bated his breath and bereft him of voice. Rather, he was awebound and bewildered by another sight, by another beauty – a beauty that no man might behold and remain unchanged.

So it was that Axennus Teagh of Hiridith, Erelian Ambassador to Lindannan, first gazed upon the Colossus of Defurien.

Nearly two hundred feet soared the stone likeness of the First Lord of the Fiannar from the rushing waters of the River Ruil – one hundred feet from knee to bewinged helm, a further one hundred thence to tip of upraised blade – and the sheer power of its presence was taller still, well beyond measure of Man. Towering in both welcome and warning, the graven monolith reared regally from the foam at the foot of the Silver Stair, long legs entrenched knee-deep in the surge, fair yet fearsome face fastened eastward, sacred sword upthrust in triumph and proud defiance. And, glory upon glory, of purest gleaming gold were Defurien's shining blade and royal *rillagh*, blazing in the dusk over Druintir like bolts of fire in the cold northern sky.

Some time passed before Axennus found his tongue once more. And when he did so, his speech was stilted, stunted, as one intoxicated, or entranced.

"Never in my life –" the Ambassador managed with some effort, and left the remainder of his thought unspoken.

"Nor mine," agreed his brother quietly, simply.

And for a time no more was said.

At length, Caelle of the Fiannar broke the still of shared silence. "There are some wonders for which no words suffice."

She looked upon Axennus of Hiridith and smiled in understanding and fellowship, her eyes reflecting the ruddy light of the sinking sun.

The Ambassador only nodded.

"Come," Caelle said softly. "Let us proceed."

They rode northward, a line of blue and bronze following the dark eaves of the Fend, then turning west along the southern bank of the River Ruil. In their van the White Eagle of the Republic fluttered listlessly as though humbled by the splendour of the land into which it had been so boldly borne.

North of the Ruil, from riverbank to receding Rothrange, a broad expanse of golden grassland danced to the whispered song of the wind.

"The Miramarch," nodded Caelle. "The pastures of the *mirarra*."

And momentarily a riderless rush of the noble silver-maned creatures thundered from the concealing shadows of the mountains, fleet and fierce and ever free.

And south, below the river road, was a vast wilderland of tree and rock and rolling grass, of oak groves and cedar stands and clusters of gleaming marble and limestone, of reed-banked rivulets and spar-kling streams.

"The Gardens of Galledine," said the Shield Maiden.

Though few in number, there could be vaguely discerned in Galledine strange structures of blended arbor and gorse; willow-walled halls with flowered floors; open-sided shelters formed of stone, grand dolmens raised to private purpose; magnificent manors that married living wood and rock so perfectly as to obscure where the one ended and the other began.

"By nature, mine are a people of the wilderness," explained the Fiann. "Few are they that prefer the stone ceilings of Druintir to the leaf-caressed skies over Galledine."

West were the majestic marvels of Druintir and the Silver Stair, the way there paved of finely set slabs of stone that shone as though with a light of their own. The half-circle of sunset crowned the bluff above the city, colouring the cataract, the caps of the Ruil's waters glittering scarlet it their race eastward, save where the long shadow of the Colossus fell dark upon their surface – for soaring above all was silent stone Defurien, vast, vigilant, eternal.

So taken were the Southmen with the manifold wonders of the land, many failed to mark one that most certainly should have been evident.

Should have been, but was not.

"Where are your people, Shield Maiden?" the Iron Captain grated from beneath knotted brows. "I see only horses."

Caelle looked upon Bronnus, her head tilted, her smile small.

"My people are here, and many, Captain. When outlanders approach, the custom of the Fiannar is to remain concealed until the warders of the Grey Watch, guardians of our Lord and city, deter-mine whether they be friend or foe. Trust that you would have been challenged long since had not word been sent with Sarrane of your coming, and had I not been at your fore." Her smile broadened, bright and beautiful. "Patience, Captain. The Grey Watch will make their presence known soon enough."

"Pardon my brother, if you please, Shield Maiden," excused Axennus once again. "I believe he imagines himself to be a *ketterk*, a childhood quirk he has never truly outgrown."

Bronnus bit back a hot retort.

For the quickness of his side-sight, the Ambassador detected the smallest and briefest of lights spark in the loam of Runningwolf's dark eyes.

Not quite a smile. But close enough.

As they drew nearer and night settled upon the earth at last, the titanic statue of Defurien soared higher and higher from the waters of the Ruil, and murmurs of excitement and expostulations of awe ran through the troop of Erelians. Of surpassing beauty was Defurien, though cold were the eyes and grim the mouth, the expression stern and set of purpose. When the company came beneath the glittering gold of the First Lord's risen sword, they halted, their heads cast back on craned necks, theirs eyes straining upward into the blacklight of fallen night. All were silent, all were still, their only sound the muted beating of ascendant hearts, their only movement the slow blinking of wonder-widened eyes.

"He is Defurien," said Caelle softly, her silken voice quiet but clear, "Father and First Lord of the Fiannar."

The Southmen remained silent, staring skyward.

"There is much mystery to the Colossus of Defurien," continued the Shield Maiden. "We know nothing of its making, neither its true composition nor the manner of its crafting, only that it was fashioned by the Daradur and gifted to the Fiannar in recognition of our friendship and fealty. For the Daradur are not a forgetful folk, and ever has there been great love between our two peoples."

She paused, looked upon the Ambassador's upturned face, and something swirled in her eyes.

"But seldom do the Daradur share their secrets. And if the crafting of the Colossus is one, then the subject of the sculpture is the greater. Often has it been said that the resemblance of the Colossus to the Father of the Fiannar is striking, that the Daradun masters superbly captured Lord Defurien, countenance and character. But how can this be so? For though his skill in stonework and metallurgy be unrivaled and unsurpassed, how might even the most gifted of masters reproduce so unerringly something he has neither seen nor heard described? For the Daradur are beings of this Second Earth alone, and to these shores Lord Defurien did not come."

Caelle waited a moment for her words to be absorbed, but expected no reply and received none. Her glittering gaze subtly assessed the Southman at her side.

"A marvel and a mystery, both," she said, ever so softly.

The Shield Maiden then unsheathed and raised her sword to the Colossus.

"*Emni lea, Defyrine!* Your lost sons of the South are returned!"

"And the people of the Father bid them warm welcome," came a voice as hard and as smooth as oiled iron. The tone failed to achieve the kindness of the words.

As one, the men of the ambassadorial party tore their attentions from the countenance of the Colossus to the marble road before them.

There, mounted upon a noble *mirarran*, was a tall strong figure, cloaked and clad in whetstone grey, the blade of a long silvery sword lying naked across his thighs. The grey figure's face was completely concealed within the cowl of a heavy woolen hood, save two points of light where the steely glitter of eyes shone forth.

"You are long in coming, Caelle," spoke the voice of iron, something of displeasure, of disapproval underscoring the statement.

"And you, Marshal Eldurion," retorted the Shield Maiden, sheathing her sword, the sapphire specks of her own eyes flaring brightly, "are short on courtesy."

"Truly spoken, Shield Maiden," growled Bronnus Teagh blackly as he kneed his roan to the Fiann's side. "Word of welcome speaks the Marshal, yet his unsheathed blade gainsays him." The Iron Captain's hand fell to the pommel of his own sword. "But forthmost, he belittles you in arrogance, and chastises you as though you were a child. I am mindful of the hand you had in our so recent salvation, and would not have you so ill-treated."

The grey Marshal neither moved nor spoke, but within the shadows of his cowl twin sparks flashed coldly.

"Hold, Captain Teagh," commanded Caelle calmly, sternly, turning her blue-flecked eyefire upon Bronnus. "You act rashly in the face of custom with which you are unfamiliar. And though I recognize your fair intention, I would tell you that where one lacks familiarity, one might exercise prudence."

The Iron Captain's visage hardened for the gritting of his teeth. But he said no more, and his hand loosened about his sword-haft.

"You will understand, Captain," continued Caelle, her voice softening, "that though it be bare, the Marshal's blade is not unsheathed, for neither sheath nor scabbard has ever touched its steel. Always are the swords of the Grey Watch as naked as they were at their forging, and they are ever in or near to the hands of their wielders. That the weapon of the Marshal of the Grey Watch slumbers in his lap is welcome enough, and few are the strangers that are greeted with such honour."

Bronnus said nothing, his tongue stilled by the bitter taste of swallowed pride. He lowered his eyes. He released the handle of his weapon entirely.

Grey Eldurion remained as still and as silent as stone.

Caelle reached across and placed one hand on the hard muscle of Bronnus' forearm. Her touch was soft but firm. And then she smiled upon him in something akin to sympathy.

"And alone of all men," said she, her voice soothing the Captain's aching dignity as would a heated cloth upon sore sinew, "Eldurion of the Grey Watch might be forgiven his fatherly scolding of me. For you see, Captain" – and a childlike giggle slipped past her smile – "I am his daughter."

Bronnus' jaw fell slack.

And from somewhere behind the Captain's sagging shoulders there issued a single yelp of such perfect glee that many a well-mastered mount started and stamped in surprise.

"At last!" burst Axennus, his eyes shining with hilarity. "Doughty Bronnus Teagh is silenced! My dear Shield Maiden, you have accomplished in little more than a day that for which I have striven these past thirty years! Wonder of wonders! Would that I were a bolder man and beg of the good Marshal your fine hand!"

Caelle's smile instantly vanished. Her eyes widened and whitened. An expression like fear flashed over her face, colouring her countenance. A rustle of uncertainty rippled through the troop of Southmen as all there followed the Shield Maiden's anxious gaze to the tall grey form of her father.

Eldurion did not move.

A quiet ensued, a silence that would have been utter and complete but for the whispers of wind and water.

Then slowly, ever so slowly, the Marshal of the Grey Watch raised his hands and pushed his hood back upon his broad shoulders. Long locks of silvered hair fell free, and a face that once had been fair, but had since been weathered by time and the elements, was revealed. His eyes were glittering chips of ice, his mouth a thin line that suggested little forbearance and less humour. Eldurion slowly lowered his hands to rest upon the flat of his sleeping sword, and his chill gaze fastened Axennus in the frozen grip of tundral winter.

"Fortune well favours you, Ambassador Axennus Teagh," came the smooth hard voice, "if only because you are not a bolder man."

Horrified with himself, the Ambassador dismounted and fell to one knee, his abashment manifest upon his mien.

"My apologies, Marshal Eldurion," Axennus extended sincerely, his eyes lowered to the marble of the road. "I spoke rashly, and with neither thought nor wisdom."

Grave Eldurion peered at the Ambassador. Probing, piercing, penetrating. But his eyes were no longer overly ungentle.

"There is goodness in you, Ambassador Teagh," said he, "but you are yet unskilled in the conventions of the office that has been thrust upon you." A small movement of his thin lips that might have been a smile momentarily softened the Marshal's rough visage. "But if wisdom was gifted to the young, what need would be served by the old?"

Relief like a wave of sun-warmed water washed over the ranks of Erelians and the raven-haired Fiann who had come to be their friend.

"Arise, Axennus Teagh of Hiridith," bade Eldurion, "and think no more on this. The hospitality of the Fiannar awaits you. Will you accept our welcome?"

The Ambassador rose to his feet. "We will."

"Then you shall have it," avowed Eldurion. "Varonin! Harlastian!"

Two tall figures, wrapped in grey and mounted upon *mirarra*, melted silently from the shadows behind the Marshall. Until then, the pair and their steeds had gone unseen and unsensed, had been little more than subtle shadings of night. They bore long gleaming swords in their hard hands, and within the cowls of their cloaks could be seen only darkness.

"Harlastian and Varonin of the Grey Watch will guide you and your party to the halls of your Embassy," stated the Marshal. "There you will find food and drink, bathing basins and beds – all the comforts that might be desired at the end of a long road."

"We are grateful, Marshal Eldurion," said the Ambassador.

"Lord Alvarion and Lady Cerriste send their regrets that they cannot join you this night, nor even on the morrow, but are desirous of an audience with you two days hence."

"We will be...we are honoured," responded Axennus, bringing his fist to his bosom.

The Marshal of the Grey Watch nodded curtly, and to the Erelians he said no more. He instead turned to Caelle, and the tautness of his face loosened with love.

"I am glad for your safety, daughter."

"As I am for your own, father."

"Come, daughter. Our Lord and Lady await in counsel with the Masters and Mistresses of the Houses – all save Tulnarron, who in his usual recklessness and incaution still finds himself abroad. But Sarrane is come, possessing sight and insight little congruent with the irresponsible folly of her husband. Your golden friend, daughter, is the true grace of the House of Eccuron."

Caelle smiled for the word of Sarrane's safe return, though the conveyance of the message had been obscure and indirect. Overt sentiment was not in the grey Marshal's nature.

The Shield Maiden then waited as Axennus remounted his grey mare.

The Ambassador appeared weary, worn perhaps by his ordeal with Eldurion. Many were the young and bold who had been stripped bare before the Marshal's withering glare and lashed by his razor tongue – and oft had a rambunctious young girl named Caelle been counted among them.

And that impetuous young girl was not wholly gone.

"I trust, Ambassador, you found the final leg of your journey to have been not overly...*uninteresting*."

Her smile was a devious slash of white in the night, and there was laughter in the stars that were her eyes.

A flustered look took Axennus' features.

"More than adequate, Shield Maiden."

Caelle laughed, a clear pure sound like the chiming of bells or the singing of a summer stream.

"That is well, friend Axennus." Her face was alight with humour, and the black of her hair glistened in the glow. "I will bid you a good night, then. And you, Captain. You also, Left Tenant."

Bronnus saluted.

The Rhelman touched his totem pouch to his temple.

The Shield Maiden of the Fiannar then raised her hand to the men of the Ambassadorial Guard.

"Southmen!"

And they hailed her in turn, a hundred voices crying as one.

"Shield Maiden!"

Caelle turned then, smiled brightly, nodded to Axennus.

"Until the morrow, Ambassador."

And father and daughter galloped into the silver shadow of the nightbound city.

Beneath the imposing figure of stone Defurien, the brothers Teagh shared a soundless sigh.

"These people are beyond us, little brother," muttered the Iron Captain sullenly.

To which Axennus replied simply, "They are the Fiannar."

Before them, ancient Druintir, last city of the Fiannar, glimmered gently in the light of the woken stars.

Then, "Come," commanded Varonin of the Grey Watch.

And they went.

6

THE ROAD TO FOLLY

"The difference between a fool and his horse
is that the latter shites while it walks
and the former shites when he talks."

Anonymous, Rothic Proverb

Wisps of smoke rose from the wreckage of the hamlet, slithering into the night, sleek and serpentine. Wraiths of the wrongfully ruined. Rising, reaching. Seeking salvation in a star-spangled sky that simply did not care.

The twins stood atop the ridge overlooking the ruin of Maple Creek. They remained naked despite the deepening cold, their freshly scrubbed skin glowing pallidly beneath a waning white moon. Their little bellies were swollen, distended.

The girl cradled a cracked, charred object close to her breast. Something slick and black seeped slowly down her inner thighs.

The boy seemed almost giddy.

Settle, brother.

But sister, I can hear them. The army. They are coming, coming!

Your new senses confuse you. The army does not come. Not yet.

But I hear them, hear them.

A scouting party, only. A small one.

The boy emitted a thin whine.

The girl's eyes were luminous lanterns.

Ah, that is interesting.

What, sister? What, what?

The Halflord leads them. He would see for himself what awaits the army. Do you sense his power, brother?

Yes. Yes, yes. He is magnificent.

Quite. He and his Bloodspawn will decide this war. Of that, I am certain.

Then we cannot lose, sister. We cannot lose, cannot lose.

The girl clung to the burned thing at her breast.

Indeed. Smile now. The Halflord approaches.

The marble road leading to Druintir gleamed with moonlight, silken and silvery, the sound of hooves hitting the stone's smooth surface distinctly muted, somehow softened by the sheen. The Shield Maiden and the Marshal of the Grey Watch rode the road side by side. They shared a protracted silence, calm and comforting, the quietude of two long-sundered souls sufficiently contented by simple reunion, an affable aphony ending only when Caelle reached over to place her hand on Eldurion's. The old Fian's lips twitched toward a smile, then pressed themselves into a thin grim line once more.

"Daughter –"

"I am well, father," she assured softly.

"So you have said, Caelle," returned the voice of oiled iron. "But a father has his fears. There was vast power in the red wind."

"Barring that you and mother are withholding something of import from me, I remain a scion of Defurien. I am able to resist such things."

The Marshal grunted.

"That you were able to resist the red wind does not surprise me. That you were able to shield one hundred men..."

"Impresses you, father?"

Eldurion looked to his only child, his frown concealed in the deep lines of his weathered face.

"Should you have accomplished the feat alone, daughter, I would be duly impressed."

Caelle remained quiet for a moment, remembering a certain slash of white light, shadows flailing, fleeing. She bit her lip reflexively.

"Alas, I did not accomplish the feat alone. Sarrane –"

"Anchored you, only. I have had her report."

The Shield Maiden grimaced inwardly. She did not know why she was so reluctant to reveal the sorcerer amidst the Erelians. Certainly, she was bound to report the man's presence and his power. To her father. To the Lady. To Lord Alvarion himself.

But betraying the little Diceman feels so very much like...well... betrayal.

"There is a sorcerer among the Southmen," she sighed.

Grey Eldurion said nothing for a few lengths, his bright gaze focused on the pale scape of the city.

Then, "The Diceman. Yes."

Caelle looked to her father, surprise reshaping her eyes, her lips.

"You know. Of course. Of course you know."

"I am Marshal of the Grey Watch."

Caelle smiled. "That you are."

"You sensed him, daughter? Should that be so, then you would make a fine Marshal one day."

"No, father. I deduced. And then there is the small matter of his name."

"Oh?"

"He calls himself Teji Nashi."

"Ah. Teji Nashi. *Tejinashi*. The Dicese word for sorcerer. Hiding in plain sight. It has ever been his way."

"You know him, father?"

"We are acquainted."

"Will you inform the Lord and Lady?"

"Assuming they do not already know."

"He wishes that his power remain concealed. I was strangely hesitant to reveal him. I felt compelled to protect his secret."

"Unlike our friends the Daradur, we Fiannar are not insusceptible to sorcery. We are resistant, but not immune. Thus his...suggestion... to remain silent had some effect upon you."

"He suggested nothing of the sort."

"Not to you, daughter. But to someone, assuredly. You would only need to have been in the vicinity."

"He is as powerful as I suspected, then. Strange, then, that the Daradur let him pass Doomfall unhindered."

"For the same reason they did you, daughter. He is a friend."

Caelle peered at the grim grey figure of her father.

"Why is the Diceman here, father?"

"I do not know. The sorcerer has ever kept his own counsel. Long has he been a friend to the Fiannar, but only few among us know of him. The Lord and Lady, certainly, myself, a few others – and now you. We have an understanding. We leave him to his ways, and do not include him in our councils. He likely would not come, even should the invitation be extended. He communicates with us sporadically, usually when something specific is asked of him, but he has not visited Druintir in many years. I can only guess why he has come now. Perhaps he will have some hand in Aranion's education, as he did Alvarion's. And my own."

Caelle's eyes widened.

"Revelations abound, father."

"Your Teji Nashi will reveal himself in due course, daughter. When the time is come."

"From whom does he hide?"

"He hides?"

"In plain sight, apparently."

"Ah. A manner of speech, only, daughter."

"I would remind you that I am Shield Maiden, Marshal Eldurion."

Eldurion grimaced. *Ah, I have taught the girl too well.*

"And I would remind you that I am Marshal of the Grey Watch."

"So you have said. Twice now."

"You are being impertinent, Caelle."

"A matter of perspective."

Eldurion gritted his teeth. *So much like her mother. Teller forfend.*

"There are those who would see the Diceman dead, daughter. He does not share that specific desire. Nor do we."

"Ah. A mystery."

"And I will have it remain so."

"For now, at least."

"Yes. At least."

The Shield Maiden's glanced at the grave warrior at her side, the graver set of the lines of care on his face. Her bright eyes glittered. Despite the dark, she well knew the expression making a stormy mask of the Marshal's weathered mien.

And what it meant.

Coyly, she quipped, "Fear not, dear father. I am as much your daughter as I am mother's."

Dour Eldurion almost succeeded in concealing his smile.

Varonin and Harlastian of the Grey Watch led the ambassadorial company from the Colossus of Defurien toward Druintir. But rather than enter the city, they escorted their charges south along the foot of the great bluff to a narrow cleft that climbed upward through the rock. The company followed their dark and dour guides up along the defile, the slivered moon shimmering down upon them through the slit in the stone. The way was steep and treacherous in places, loose chunks of stone scattered on the path, the pocked floor made slippery by a skin of moss. Frequently, where the way became overly perilous, the Erelians found it necessary to dismount and lead their steeds cautiously by the reins, while above them, the two grey guides astride their surefooted *mirarra* waited with something like but not quite patience.

"They're called horses, not bloody mountain goats," complained Maddus, after skinning the heel of a hand while bracing a fall.

THE WAR FOR THE NORTH

"You're such an unhappy soul," said Rooboong. "Funny how one punch can make two shiners."

Maddus' frown made him look like an angry raccoon.

"You'll get yours, Ruby."

"Whatcha gonna do, Maddy? Climb up a ladder and hit me with those doll-sized fists of yours? Flail away, little man, if it makes you feel any better."

"Enough, idiots," interjected the Decan. "This climb is arduous enough without you little girls bickering like...little girls."

"Oh, I dunno, Dec," mused Riffalo, thoughtfully, "I find their banter rather entertaining."

"Then you're an idiot, too, Riff. Big surprise there."

Guardsman Riffalo frowned, a shock of yellow hair falling over a wounded gaze.

"What's eating you, Dec?"

"Been thinking, is all," glowered Regorius.

"About?"

"The Doctor. He's a sorcerer. And we are ensorcelled."

"I don't feel ensorcelled, mate," argued Maddus.

"Me neither," echoed Rooboong.

The Decan ignored them.

"It all makes sense now. All those battles the Reserve fought, always outnumbered, always appearing where we were least expected, coming out of nowhere like ghosts, surprising the enemy regardless of the lack of any real cover, never losing despite what frequently should have been impossible odds. And our casualties, or lack thereof – thirteen major battles, countless skirmishes, and we lose *fewer than one hundred men*? The March Fox is a genius, given, and the Iron Captain is a crazy good soldier, but what the Ghost Brigade did, what *we* did, was nothing short of *magical*."

The other three guardsmen exchanged glances.

"Well, when you put it like that..." said Rooboong.

"I would've sworn I'd lost my right hand during the fiasco at Ball's Falls," remembered Riffalo, "but when I awoke in the healing tent, there was barely a scar on my forearm."

Nods and murmurs as the others recalled similar situations of their own.

"So the Doctor is a sorcerer. Makes sense, Dec. But what makes you think he's bewitched *us*?"

"Before this ascent, I approached Left Tenant Runningwolf to tell him what we all saw, tell him what happened in that damned tent. Because if anyone would understand, I figured the Rhelman would. He's like that. But I couldn't tell him. No, no, you don't understand – I *could not* tell him. I mean, I was *unable* to. I opened my mouth to speak, and nothing came out. Like a stutterer stuck on a word starting with a vowel. My tongue just wouldn't move. I couldn't get a sound out. I couldn't talk at all."

Maddus snickered. "Bet that looked funny as hell." His countenance then clouded. "What's a 'vowel'?"

Regorius closed his eyes briefly. Breathed.

"Well, the Doctor did suggest we say nothing, Dec," offered Riffalo.

Regorius looked up, pink eyes shining.

"Suggest? No, that was no suggestion. That was a *forbidding*. A verbal ward of forbidding. And a powerful one."

"I've seen the same or something like it in the slave nations of 'Fleetian Empire," nodded Rooboong, his heavy brows dropping in a pensive scowl. "Such magic is not unknown in my homeland of Unga Boon."

"Neither is dancing naked around fires and eating boiled babies," sneered Maddus.

The grinding of teeth in Rooboong's jaw was an audible thing.

Regorius sighed. Closing his eyes and breathing would not likely work again.

"One day Ruby really *is* going to kill you, Maddy. And I will not only permit it, I will *insist* upon it. And I'll pin a medal on his breast when it's done. Happily. Now shut your ugly mouth!"

Maddus' mouth closed with an audible clap.

As though nothing had happened, "Why would the Doctor do it then?" wondered Riffalo.

"Do what, Riff?"

"Why would he reveal himself to us, but forbid us to share the information with anyone else? Why not just wipe the memories from our minds?"

"Only one reason that I can see," said Rooboong. "He wants us to know. And he wants us to know because he has a use for us. A purpose. A need of some kind."

"Very true, Ruby," conceded the Decan. "He must want us to know. He obviously has a plan for us."

The four fell silent then, save grunts and curses, as they scrambled over a particularly treacherous stretch of moss-slicked scree.

All shared the same simple thought.

Shit.

Attaining the High Land, the ambassadorial party once again turned north along the lip of the precipice above the city toward the head of the Silver Stair, then west against the flow of the River Ruil. In some time, the company came to a broad bridge of carved stone spanning the Ruil, and they crossed through mist and moonlight to the northern shore.

There, along the riverbank, were a series of disparate structures, generously distanced from one another, each surrounded by a cluster of outbuildings. Each main structure was distinct from the next in character and architecture, and all were very unlike the Fiannian delvings and design at Druintir. Though neither Harlastian nor Varonin spoke aught of the buildings – they were men not given to unnecessary narration – Axennus readily deduced the nature and purpose of each building.

The Embassies of the Free Nations, structures as diverse and as defined as the cultures they represented.

Eastmost was a greathouse walled of large stones and roofed with thatched sedge. The sound of flute and harp, of laughter and song, rode the glowing wings of lantern-light through glassless openings set into the stone. A group of men and women decked in coloured woolen wraps danced and frolicked upon the dew-silvered grass, pausing in their ribaldry only long enough to watch the Southmen pass, marking every movement of the outlanders with bright suspicious eyes. Above the greathouse, light of moon and star revealed a sunburst against a field of green, the flag of redoubtable Rothanar proudly aflutter in the northern nightwind.

The company then passed a great manor of clay-packed pine-wood, a tall chimney of mortared stone rising at the rear, from which a thick oily cooking smoke slithered snakelike into the night. The heavy odours of pork and port emanated from the main doorway, about which stood a knot of tall, thick-bodied men, long of hair and beard, and clad in fur and leather, one of whom raised a closed fist to the Erelian troop and shouted, "Sea and slaughter!" From a pole of pine undulated a scarlet sea serpent in an ocean of blue, the binding banner of the wild and warlike Nothirings.

Then came a small keep of carven stone, polished and pristine. The design of the structure was simple and sound, the styling sensibly subtle, consisting of a central donjon encircled by low walls that connected a series of crenellated turrets. The wrought iron gate set into the front wall had been thrown wide in trusting welcome, though a pair of helmed, armoured and halberd-bearing sentries were at rapt attention, one to a side. From the spire of the main tower reared a trio of white lions upon a plain of gold, one major rampant flanked on either side by a minor – the brave banner of the neophyte city-state of Ithramis.

And lastly and westmost was a whitestone citadel worthy of the most gifted artisans of Hiridith. Consisting of a single tower of gleaming marble rising betwixt two long wide wings with white-limed outer walls, and fronted by an impressive colonnaded stair, the structure was very much in character with the most modern of Erelian designs. From the spire of the tower rose a tall brass flagstaff, a lustrous arm reaching toward sky and heaven, the lofty but yet unclaimed perch of the noble White Eagle of the Republic.

"The Erelian Embassy, Ambassador," Varonin of the Grey Watch monotoned, the first and only words either Fiannian warder had uttered since departing the Colossus of Defurien.

"Surely, this is the work of Erelian hands," the Iron Captain stated.

To which Harlastian contended, "We may be a people much diminished, Captain, but skill in stone and timber has not wholly forsaken the Fiannar."

And with no further word of either wisdom or welcome, the two Watchers turned and rode back into darkness, grey ghosts of power and peril, extraneous essences of the very night.

The brothers Teagh shared a shrug.

The younger said, "Should they be a diminished people, one can only wonder what they may have been in the days of their glory."

And the elder replied, "A little less lacking in courtesy, perhaps."

"Their invitation was a courtesy in and of itself, dear Bron, and this marble manor with which they have gifted us is a gesture beyond compensation. There can be no doubt that our own Senate had neither word nor hand in the erection of this palace."

"Very true, Axo," Bronnus grudgingly admitted. "Only two nights past, I went to my bedroll with visions of pitched tents upon grasses browned by horse dung."

Axennus laughed. "You are beset by strange demons, Bron."

Fresh feed and clean water awaited the wearied horses, and within the White Manor – for that was the name swiftly bestowed upon the Embassy – an array of sweet fruits and spiced meats and casks of chilled summerwine had been set out in the mess for the men. Beyond the mess, within the eastern wing they found the barracks, four guardsmen to a chamber, and past these were beautiful Gendurii baths. The western wing likewise held the bedchambers, baths and offices of the Ambassador and the men of rank.

And located centrally toward the rear, beneath the belly of the tower, the tiered seating of a grand oval theatre sloped downward to the Council Circle, a large round table of polished stone about which had been placed thirteen tall-backed chairs of knotted ash.

The Circumforum.

"Thirteen," Axennus muttered thoughtfully. "A number of peculiar choosing. I wonder of the significance."

"Perhaps none," Bronnus replied dismissively.

"Perhaps," Axennus conceded, though his tone evidenced some skepticism – for the Fiannar had impressed upon him that they were a people not given to practices without purpose.

Lionnus approached.

"Ambassador. Captain. We have guests, sirs."

Axennus and Bronnus followed the young guardsman to the pillared front hall of the White Manor and found waiting for them there a group of rugged, bonhomously curious Rothmen.

"Welcome, Southfolk," said their apparent leader, his distinctive acrolect particular to the court at Cara. The Rothman's eyes sparkled with innate inquisitive intelligence, their bright green light ever appraising, assessing. "I am Ambassador Dowdall." And he thrust a flagon of ale into Axennus' hand. "Get that down ye, and it will surely do ye good."

Knowing something of Rothic custom, Axennus threw the bitter brew back at a guzzle, wiping the residual froth from his lip with the back of his hand.

"Up the High King!" he praised loudly.

"Up the Republic!" grinned the Rothmen as one.

Axennus smiled in turn.

"That rolled easily off your tongues, my friends."

"Aye, it did," replied the Rothic Ambassador. "Sure, didn't it just sound right? One day, perhaps. Nothing against the present regime, of course."

"I think I would prefer *pocheen* to politics this night, Ambassador Dowdall."

Dowdall's green eyes gleamed.

Bronnus' dark ones rolled in their sockets.

The Rothmen laughed in recognition of Axennus' kindred heart, convened an impromptu conspiratorial collogue, then urged the young Ambassador and his retinue to accompany them to the Fifth Folly, the local common house, where there had gathered "such a rabble of salt-suckers and iron-asses as to make ye wish ye could shite out yer eyes!"

The poetic parlance of the Rothmen was often beyond even their own comprehension.

When the horses had been rubbed down and stabled, and the men fed and quartered, Axennus and Bronnus gave the guardsmen leave from all duties for the night, and all but an abstaining few followed their newfound friends to the promising delights of the Fifth Folly.

Set some distance north of the embassies of the Free Nations, the common house was little more than a ramshackle tavern of weathered pine plank and pillar, loud with shout and song, and warm with the odours of drink and man and Rhelnian tobacco. Nothirings there were in number, tall and broad and raucous; and Rothmen, verbose and volatile; and Ithramen, though few, relatively reserved beside their Nothiric and Rothic counterparts.

Warders of the Grey Watch observed in sepulchral silence from the shadows.

"Preservers of the peace, I presume," said Bronnus as he surrendered his weapons to a watchful warder. The Iron Captain's tempestuous glower had seemingly become a permanent fixture on his face.

"Welcome to the Fifth Folly," beamed Ambassador Dowdall, unstrapping his sword belt. "What the first four may be, sure, I have no idea, but the fifth likely has something to do with what we Roths call the *craythur*."

"The *craythur*?"

"The 'creature', Bron. We call it drink."

"Of course. Silly me."

Axennus clapped a hand on his brother's broad shoulder. "The task set before us is clear, noble Captain."

"It is?"

"Yes."

"What task is that, Axo?"

"Effective compotation and jollification, dear brother. We must bring some southern civility to these northern barbarians," Axennus resolved, ignoring Bronnus' disapproving scowl and accepting from a decidedly delighted Dowdall a proffered jug of unidentified inebriant.

"Let the lesson begin!"

And thenceforth, the events and particulars of Axennus' initial night above Druintir became increasingly resistant to recollection.

Father and daughter had halted beneath the natural glory of the Andalorian Arch, the marble masterpiece marking the entry to the ancient city of Druintir. Carved by neither hand nor iron, but by millennia of wind and the primordial run of the Ruil, a course long since altered, the stone arc soared sixty feet at its highest, six-score across its base, raw, resplendent, regal. The Arch spanned the marble road, softly aglow in pale moonsheen, its thick northern pier rearing from the south shore of the Ruil, plinth and haunch and crown all formed of the same unbroken stretch of bedrock. Named for the Lord of the Fiannar who had wisely forbidden forever any carving or working of the natural rock formation, the Arch remained as it had been long, long, long before any mortal creature applied measurement to Time.

There were no guards, neither inspector nor inquisitor, none to record who came, who went. Any who approached the Andalorian Arch, the gateless gateway to Druintir, would have successfully endured the icy-eyed scrutiny of the Grey Watch – or would have somehow destroyed those several hundred shadowy sentinels utterly.

Caelle glided from the back of her *mirarran*, landing lightly, quickly relieving the shimmering stallion of his trifling tack. She ran one loving hand through the long silvery mane, the silken strands like warm wind sliding between her fingers. The beautiful beast lowered his noble head, touching temples with the Fiann. Caelle patted the sleek grey neck, smiled for the answering nicker, then whispered the animal away to the fair fields of the Miramarch.

The Shield Maiden stood beneath the Arch, her *mirarran*'s tack slung across her slim shoulder, mist from the falls and light from the moon silvering her dark hair. One fine hand curled about the haft of her sword.

Grim Eldurion remained mounted, his bald blade upon his lap.

Caelle gazed up at him, her shining eyes speckled with sapphire starlight.

"You spoke harshly of Tulnarron, father."

153

"I spoke of the Master of the House of Eccuron as I see him. He is rash and impetuous. He acts without thought, is reckless and unheeding of any counsel but his own. He mistakes boldness for bravery. Tulnarron is the Warden of the East. His place is here."

"But father," she smiled impishly, pointing, "east is that way."

Grated grey Eldurion, "Impetuosity, it seems, is not the province of Master Tulnarron alone."

"Tell me, father," mused the Shield Maiden, "how is it that the very qualities you consider reprehensible in Master Tulnarron, you find so endearing in me?"

"Not so endearing, daughter."

But beneath the iron in his voice was a belying softness and warmth.

"I just might tell mother you said that."

High atop the back of his *mirarran*, Eldurion's arctic eyes glittered in the black tundral night of his hood. Caelle *felt* her father smile. There are some things even the deepest shadows cannot conceal.

She pointed once again.

"East."

A tempting lure, but the Marshal did not bite.

"What of the Daradur, daughter?"

"Brulwar will come," she replied, lowering her hand to rest on the grip of her sword once more. "And Mundar. Rundul, also. It was the latter who discovered the abomination beneath the Bloodshards. We agreed it would be wise to have the Wild One remain at Doomfall. Though he does not name them foe, Dulgar harbours no great abiding love for some among the Athair. Assuming the Neverborn answer our call."

"Prudent," nodded the Marshal. Whether the prudence was in the remaining or in the harbouring was unclear. "And Drogul? Will the Lord of Doomfall come?"

Caelle shook her head.

"Drogul was not there. He is somewhere in the Far North. I know neither why nor where, and Brulwar did not seem inclined to share."

Eldurion was silent for a moment. Within the shadows of his hood, the brightness of his eyes seemed to decathect.

"Drogul will be missed. Both at the table and on the field."

"He may yet come, father. He has never failed us before."

"You possess your mother's optimism, daughter."

"Balanced by a fair share of my father's cynicism," she chirped. "Each in moderation, of course."

"Of course. And the Southmen?"

Caelle could not suppress a smile.

"Well, you saw them, father."

"I did."

"And?"

"I seek your opinion, daughter. I am aware of my own."

The Shield Maiden cocked her head to one side.

"They are an interesting pair, father. Nay, intriguing. Ever at odds, yet never so. Always competing, but truly cooperating. Constantly quarrelsome but never quarreling. However unaware of it they may or may not be, their love for one another is abundant and absolute.

"The elder is the simpler of the two, but only for the lack of superfluous complexity of character. He is direct, honest and sincere. Neither his courage nor his care for the men in his command may be questioned. His prowess in battle is the stuff of legends.

"The younger is complex, intelligent, and his seeming immodesty is in truth a douce humility. He surfeits in daring and diablerie, yet he is also a man of reason, of cold calculation, and this balance served him with notorious lethality in the last Trade War. Indeed, he is a man of many humours, each captivating in its own way. He possesses and wields an almost fiendish intellect, yet can at whiles appear absurdly foolish. Forsooth, he is frequently a contradiction unto himself, at once a carefree child and the wisest of elders."

"A young spirit but an old soul."

"Precisely, father."

"The very man Sarrane saw in her vision."

"More." Caelle smiled devilishly. "Not exactly hard on the eyes, either."

The Marshal's mount stamped.

The Shield Maiden cocked her head once more, disarmingly demure, waiting.

The shadows in Eldurion's woolen hood revealed nothing. His breath came as algid steam from the hollows of the cowl. One breath, two breaths, three. Then the Marshal's *mirarran* tossed its regal head and turned.

Rasped grim, grey Eldurion:

"Welcome home, daughter."

And the night took him.

"So what did he say, Dec?"

Regorius looked up from his third jug of Nothiric mead. Or was it his fourth? The pink of his eyes had darkened to a distinct and disconcerting red. The chatter and laughter infusing the boisterous Fifth Folly hummed harshly in his head.

"What did who say to...? What?"

"The Left Tenant. Runningwolf. What did he say when you tried to tell him about the Doctor? He must have thought it very odd, you standing there, mouth open, saying nothing."

"That certainly is bloody odd," muttered Maddus between swigs of undiluted *uisce beatha*. The vacuous aspect of his grizzled face indicated he had no inclination that he had spoken aloud. "Bloody Roths know their spirits, I'll give them that."

Regorius ignored him.

"Yeah, it was the strangest thing, Riff. He just stared at me in the way he does. You know the look, lads. Like he's weighing your very soul – and judging it highly combustible. He just stared and stared. And then...well."

"Well, what?"

"Well, then he just shrugged and ordered me to stop playing with myself."

"Again? What the –"

"Aye, mate. It's like he *knows*," mumbled Maddus into his whiskey.

As though struck, Regorius, Riffalo and Rooboong stared at their companion.

"What?" Maddus looked up, left, right. Blinked. "What'd I say?"

Rooboong turned to Regorius.

"Listen, Whitey, we know you're a Decan and everything, but can Maddy sleep in your tent from –"

"Not a chance."

There had been a burning.

The night reeked of sour smoke and fired flesh. The lingering memory of madness slashed the darkness with phantom blades, silent shrieks of terror tore at the edge of awareness, echoes of horror dragging cracked fingernails down the black slate of night.

Kor ben Dor raised his milky white gaze from the soot-soiled trail he had been following. The spoor was old now, too old to have been of any actual interest, but he had followed it for the last few hours, doggedly even, though he did not know why, nor was he entirely aware he had been doing so. Darkness did not diminish the keenness of his vision, not in any physical sense, but it often drew a portion of him away and apart from himself. When this happened, he would drift in a half-haze, sometimes for hours, principally alert and acute of thought, but also separate, remote, removed. It had been so since his first real memory, a memory of agony, of penetrating pain, early in his twentieth year. A long time ago now. A very long time.

But Kor ben Dor remembered.

The Halflord shrugged a kink from his massive shoulders. His eyes widened, whitened, brightened. Beneath him, the monstrous *mar render* he rode snorted.

The sixty-odd Fiannar that had passed that way were not Kor ben Dor's concern. They were gone. He cared nothing of them, for them.

Not so the two small figures atop the western ridge.

The Halflord's huge hand tautened about the haft of his massive mace.

"Remain."

His voice was unexpectedly smooth and soft, seeming almost alien in one so huge and powerful, yet it wanted for neither severity nor finality. The company of Bloodspawn at his back halted instantly.

Kor ben Dor's immense *mar render* moved forward.

He is beautiful, sister, beautiful, beautiful.

Yes, he is, brother. A true prince. He is...exquisite.

Below the tiny twins, the Halflord approached astride a terrible nightmare steed.

The Prince of the Bloodspawn was gigantic. Had he been standing he would have towered in excess of nine feet, his shoulders square and broad, his arms and thighs thick with muscle. His seeming winged helm was actually his own hair, long tresses artfully wrought to form outspread pinions blacker than the very heart of night. Tattooed talons gripped the brow and temple of a flawless face chiseled into planes and facets, cheeks and chin shaved smooth and shining, as hard and as implacable as diamond. His skin was the colour of damp ash, greying towards black, and his eyes glowed a luminous solid white. He was sheathed in gleaming black steel, save his huge hands and corded thighs and biceps. His cloak was slit into several long broad strips, thrown back now to reveal a pair of opposing sashes upon his breastplate. These bands formed an X, the greening copper arm crossing the heart from lower right to upper left, the blackening silver one atop and opposite. The mace he held was a weapon a god might wield.

The *mar render* the Halflord rode was a creature of corruption. An equine atrocity. The demonic destrier stood nearly thirty hands high, massively muscled, its neck arched, its withers high, the shoulders sloped. The hindquarters were powerful, the back relatively short, the bones iron-strong. Beneath the steel chamfron its face was straight, broad of forehead and wide of muzzle. Its coat was black, roaning in places, its mane and fetlocks a bright blazing red, a red surpassed only by the crimson fire in its widely set eyes. Foamy froth dripped from jaws which were significantly longer than those of any true horse, a crocodilian maw gaping to bare teeth more leonine than equine, long and white and wickedly sharp. Its fore-hooves were not hooves at all, but were hideous clawed hands, though hands that served as hooves when balled into fierce ferric fists.

Rider and mount halted a short distance from the rocky knoll where the children waited.

The Halflord gazed upward, his white eyes aglow like small moons. The render razed the earth between tearing talons; its snort was stridulant, a deep drakish snarl, so very unlike the nicker of a horse. The head of the giant's mace thudded to the ground, stirring gusts of ash and dust from the grass, so many grey ghosts roused from spectral slumber. Still astride his steed, the Prince of the Bloodspawn casually rested a forearm on the upright end of the weapon's extended collapsible shaft, his hand dangling loosely. He regarded the little twins from between talon tattoos, a silent scrutiny, his hard-hewn features revealing nothing.

"Come."

Oh, but he is good, brother. So very good. He sees human children, but knows we are not such. He tells us to descend to him because we have the high ground. He is cautious, yet unafraid. Does he know our power? Or is he simply sure of his own?

Let us go to him, sister. Let us go, go, go.

Do you feel that? That energy in the air? That is the essence of him, so vital, so vibrant, vivacious. Such power, such sweet power.

Yes! Let us go to him. Go, yes, go, yes.

Patience, brother. The mortal can wait. We will make him –

"Come."

The girl clutched the burned thing nearer to her breast. Her cherubic face clouded with indignation.

Impertinent barbarian!

Nevertheless, she took her brother's little hand and together they nimbly descended the rocky rise, stone scraping at the soles of their feet. Reaching the foot the hill, they moved across the grasses toward the Halflord. His white eyes marked their progress, moving from the boy to the girl to the burned thing and back again.

"No nearer."

The children halted. Smiled up beatifically, blue eyes wide and wet. Her pique passed, the girl parted her lips to speak.

But the Halflord preempted her.

"Names."

The girl's mouth remained open, yet she did not speak.

The boy looked at her, his angelic face pleading.

Do you know our names, sister? Do you know, know, know?

I cannot recall, brother. Have we ever had names? I do not remember.

I do not know, sister. What of the human children? Might we take their names as we have taken their bodies? Might we take them, take them, take, take, take?

There are none here to tell us what their names were, brother. And we do not possess their memories.

We do not have names? No names. No, no no, no.

Be silent!

"Names."

The boy whinged. The girl's nails dug into the burned thing at her breast.

"I know what you are." Kor ben Dor's voice was deceptively tender. "And I know what you are not. I will have your names."

The little girl stamped her foot.

"And we would have your army, Halflord."

Kor ben Dor's handsome head tilted slightly. The great raven's wings of his hair seemed to buffet the night.

"The Bloodspawn are mine, *blutsauger,*" he declared softly. "You may claim the remainder. If they will have you."

He calls us Leech, sister. He knows what we are, what we –

Oh, shut up!

As though he had heard them, the Prince of the Bloodspawn smiled.

"I could have you, Halflord," the little girl blurted. "I could *take* you. I could make you –"

"You have no names."

The little boy whimpered. The girl's eyes flashed with mute fury. Her little fingers ripped into the burned thing.

"I will call you Waif." Kor ben Dor jerked his head. "He is Urchin."

I will make you scream!

"You will need clothing."

You will scream, mortal! I will take you, and you will scream!

The Halflord effortlessly hefted his massive mace, reined his monstrous render about, and headed back the way he had come.

"Follow."

Waif screamed.

7

THE SHIELD MAIDEN'S TALE

"Few are the sorrows that surpass
that of a good tale gone untold."

Old Erelian Toast

Axennus Teagh dreamed of drums and thunder. And beat and peal pursued him across the formless darkness of his slumber, through the fog of waking and into the day. And with them came pain.

He woke in acute agony, every joint in his body aching dryly, his pulse pounding in his ears with the gushing thud of blood on bone. The most minute of movements sent his head aswim, every motion made his stomach turn sickeningly in protest. His eyes cracked open, thin slits of resistance against the gaudy light that sliced past the curtains of the chamber. But daylight pierced his pupils as would a lance, then shattered into long narrow shards of sharp steel that embedded themselves in the back of his skull like a rain of bright white arrows.

He threw one arm over his eyes and rolled away from the light, but found no succour in shadow, only a different pain.

And then, amidst the chaos of anguish and affliction roiling behind his tightly clamped eyes, memories of the previous night slowly seeped back to Axennus like lava creeping on the earth.

Let the lesson begin!

Axennus groaned.

"I would tell you that one should not marry the fruitwines of the South with the dark mead of the Nothirings, not to mention the *pocheen* of the doughty Rothmen, but I fear such wisdom will have come to you overlate."

The familiar voice seemed distant, but was not. Nor was the sweet and soothing tone unwelcome, though it came delicately laced with a sarcasm not very much unlike the Erelian's own.

Axennus summoned the strength and the courage to open his eyes once more. The hurt of light returned, but was weakened and had lost its initial violence. His vision was blurred and bleary and seemed limited to black and white and shades of grey. Some moments passed before he could will his sight into focus and once again discern colour, shape, distance.

Then he saw her.

"Caelle."

His voice came thick and pained for his swollen tongue and bile-grimed mouth. His very teeth ached to their roots.

The Fiann smiled.

"The emboldening effect of drink has not been wholly nullified by sleep, I see," said she. "You have never before addressed me with the name my mother bestowed upon me, or I am much mistaken."

Axennus groaned again.

"Nevertheless, young though it may be," continued Caelle casually, her voice the sound of a smile, "I do find our friendship to be sufficiently fast for such familiarity."

Another groan.

Caelle sat upon a finely carved oaken chair by the door, small hands folded demurely upon her lap, her sandaled feet crossed before her. She had foregone the grey of her riding gear in favour of a long gown of cotton, emerald green, an intricate design of white flowers embroidered at the shoulders. Gone also was the broad band of her *rillagh*, though a thin strap of gold gleamed in its place. Her midnight hair was pulled back from her lovely oval face and tied behind her head with a fine string of gold, and a single silvery bloom shone above one ear. She was otherwise unadorned.

"Rise, friend Axennus," commanded the Fiann gently. "I have with me an elixir that may ease your distress."

Axennus pushed himself into a sitting position on the bed of down. Though the linens were soft and silken, they seemed to scrape against his skin, leaving his flesh sore and sensitive.

"Would you also care to remove the pike from my skull?" moaned the afflicted Ambassador.

"Seek pity elsewhere and from others," remonstrated the Shield Maiden.

She stood and took up a plain clay flask from the small table beside the chair, and padded silently to the side of the bed. With her came the scent of sun and summer.

"Drink," she demanded. Her demeanor discouraged discussion.

The flask was warm to the touch and from it arose a fragrance reminiscent of peppermint. Axennus sipped, and instantly his face twisted in repugnance and revulsion.

"Teller of the Tale!" he coughed, sputtering. "Do you mean to poison me?"

"Hardly, Southman," scoffed Caelle, her grey eyes darkening beneath a reproachful frown. "You have proven quite capable of that dubious feat yourself. Rather, it is my own desire to purge you of your poisons."

"A more adiaphorous remedy might purge them sooner, certainly."

But Axennus could already feel the potent properties of the elixir rushing through him, bone and sinew. And as he sipped again at the bitter liquid, his pain was stripped from him like the dried scab from a wound newly healed. A third and longer drink, and he was refreshed, and his mind and sight were clear.

He stared incredulously at the drained clay flask.

"I find myself in your debt once more."

"The root of the *ethacca* plant is a rare but effectual medicine," Caelle answered the unspoken question, "though continued use may prove toxic over time."

"Are you well versed in herb-lore and healing?"

"I am a Shield Maiden of the Fiannar, and the Fiannar are a folk acutely aware of their mortality. Because we are people doomed to die, ever have we sought to prevent and cure those ailments that we can, and to ease those that we cannot."

"A noble quest, Shield Maiden."

"We have returned to formalities, I see," observed Caelle with a wry smile. "Very well, Ambassador. Someone was kind enough to draw you a bath and set out some walking dress for you. I will await you in the courtyard. You will break fast with me in Druintir this day."

Midday's sun was high and the air was crisp and cool when the Ambassador joined Caelle in the courtyard of the White Manor. There they tarried for a time, watching the Iron Captain and the tenants drill the men of the Ambassadorial Guard. Most guardsmen were ashen-faced and red-eyed for the previous night's festivities, but if they sought mercy, there was little to be found in the brusque sharpness of Bronnus' barked commands, and even less in the quiet, exacting manner of the Rhelman.

"There is a price to be paid for pleasure, I see," mused the Shield Maiden.

"So my brother would have them believe," responded Axennus, his eyes twinkling. "He strives to teach them of consequences, of balance – all things in moderation and such nonsense. I would spare all the effort and teach instead the miraculous qualities of the *ethacca* root."

The Fiann frowned, and even in her furrowed brows was there beauty to be found in fair measure.

"You would achieve their deaths far sooner, Ambassador."

"Indeed, Shield Maiden," Axennus conceded, sighing in feigned sadness. "But they would die happy."

Druintir of Lindannan, last city of the Fiannar, was very unlike the urban metropolises of the Free Nations. A single colossal and continuous carving of conjoined caverns and causeways, of myriad manors and mansions, of tunnels and towers, the city had long ago been hewn by hand and heart of the metamorphic stone of the ridge. The marble of which she had been formed was the light grey of a winter dawn, like ice on steel, smooth and gleaming, and throughout her hollowed halls was the cool sweet breath of the stony earth. The tri-tiered waters of the Silver Stair divided the city into north and south, the two portions joined by a series of stone bridges spanning the surface and by a labyrinthine array of tunnels bored through the bedrock. The mist and spray of the Ruil shrouded the city, but did not dampen her, the pristine sheen of the polished stone coming of hand and time rather than the wet of water. And lights of sun and moon and shining star did the doming veil of the Silver Stair admit to the city, though these came softened by their passage through the waterfall's argentine haze.

Within the city, the Fiannar were about in number, tall and proud. Axennus saw many men of that folk, fierce and fair, their faces worn with cold and care. He saw some women, more fair of face and form, but no less hard. And still fewer children did he see, and these had been aged beyond their years by knowledge and northern clime. But all the Fiannar, irrespective of age, sex or standing, were of noble countenance and piercing eye, and decked with golden sash. All were humbly clad in stony grey and forest green. And all were armed in some manner, with even the smallest of children bearing a blade at the hip or bow and quiver at the shoulder.

"You are a people well-readied for war, Shield Maiden," Axennus observed coolly, his discerning eye marking the shadow that darkened the visages of the Fiannar, his ear harkening to the storm of their silence.

"We are a people born of war," replied Caelle flatly. "Where the Fiannar have survived and even flourished, more peaceable and less prepared peoples have been destroyed." She paused. "But do not mistake precaution for predilection, Ambassador."

Sliding shadows signified the ghostly presence of the Grey Watch on the streets of the city, fore and aft and to either side of them. The spectral silence of the grey warders brought an eerie chill to Druintir's stony heart, like a harbinger of winter, or the cold breath of foredoom.

"Be assured, Shield Maiden," Axennus asserted softly, a quirk to his smile, "I mistake little."

The Erelian Ambassador and the Fiannian Shield Maiden shared a light meal of wild berries and goat cheese upon a terrace overlooking the middle tier of the Silver Stair. The muted roar of the waters hummed through the stone, a ceaseless chant invoking the deepest powers of the earth. The sound was calming, comforting, subliminally massaging muscle and mind. The pair spoke little, and little needed to be spoken. They were at peace in one another's company, and found solace in their shared silence, like two old friends who measured their bond in decades rather than in days. But the mood was momentary, as neither protracted peace nor sustained silence were in the Erelian's nature.

"A pleasant place, Shield Maiden," sighed the Ambassador, dipping his fingers in a nearby washing basin. "All the more so for the platter and present company." He glanced up, grinning roguishly. "Both delight the senses."

Caelle cocked her head to one side, her raven tresses shining with the sun's silvered gold, her large round eyes as broad and as bright as the summer skies over Lindannan.

"Either you are a man of remarkable resilience, Master Ambassador," she quipped, "or the *ethacca* root exceeds itself." Her voice was light and playful, her full lips curling at their corners. "Few are they that wholly recover from an encounter with the Marshal Eldurion, and none swiftly. Yet here you are, recklessly playing at courtship once again, though your knees be freshly bruised with yesternight's abashment."

Rather than grimace at the memory, Axennus only shrugged. "I have knelt before both father and daughter, Shield Maiden," he reminded her casually. "Forsooth, what place has pride in the heart that loves?"

Caelle of the Fiannar scowled, but her eyes shone without shadow.

"Speak not of love, Southman," she cautioned quietly. "There are fates worse than Eldurion's wrath for the heart that goes unheard."

Axennus grinned. "You have much to learn of your guest, Shield Maiden. Seldom does the youngest son of Jophus Teagh go unheard."

Caelle laughed. The sound was the light of diamonds, or the spiraling descent of winter snows.

"So the elder one has warned me, Ambassador."

She rose then, flowing to her feet with feline grace, fine and feminine.

"Come, my friend," she beckoned with the wave of one small hand. "I would walk with you in Galledine."

Leaving Druintir by way of the marble road, the Shield Maiden and the Ambassador halted beneath the upraised arm of the Colossus of Defurien. There, following the Fiann's example, Axennus removed his footwear, neatly placing his riding boots beside her sandals at the edge of the river road.

Noticing some discomfiture upon the Ambassador's face, the Shield Maiden smiled reassuringly, saying, "Be easy, friend Axennus. There is no thievery in Lindannan."

"My concern is not for my footwear, Shield Maiden," frowned Axennus, his hazel eyes alight with humour, "but rather for Galledine. The stench of my unshod feet has been known to wilt flowers and wither grass."

Caelle laughed gaily.

"I know of a place where you might wash the offending appendages, Ambassador –"

"And poison waters."

"– and failing that, I have with me a blade in the folds of my gown, should amputation be deemed necessary."

Axennus gulped audibly.

And the Shield Maiden of the Fiannar moved from under the shadow of Defurien and led her guest into the wondrous green wilderland of Galledine.

The Gardens of Galledine were a geological masterpiece, a glacial wake of pitted limestone rising westward in rugged waves of white and grey. Bounded on the north by the Ruil, Galledine rolled southward behind the Dragon's Head, past the crack of Doomfall, to the Hard Hills at the foot of the Haunted Mountains. And westward, the Gardens climbed leagues of escarpment to the pebbled shores of the Teller's Tear, the fathomless lake of glacial meltwaters long misted in myth and mystery.

The sedimentary bedrock had been hewn and fissured by unnumbered millennia of elemental erosion, irresistible forces working the primeval limestone of the land into a petrous eden of crag and talus and rocky rise. But the creviced stone of the Gardens seemed as nutrient as any soil. From the rock rose the green of ancient cedars and noble ironwoods. Stands of supple sugar maple soared skyward, only to sway in the shadow of great groves of hallowed oak. Elm and hickory, there were, and birch and poplar and hoary walnut. The understory was rich with rock sandwort and golden corydalis, and lichen and fern and clinging moss. Where the trees did not hold, hardy grasses flowed over glade and glen, like small seas of gilded green. And everywhere in Galledine did flowers bloom in abundances of kind and colour, nurtured and sustained by songs of spring and stream.

Caelle led the Ambassador along a narrow deer trail that ran alongside the thin silver line of a slow-flowing stream. The ground beneath Axennus' bared feet was surprisingly warm and yielding, more like soft supple carpet than mossy stone and grassed earth. Galledine's vigour and vitality tingled in his soles, his ankles, his calves, swimming his bloodcourse ever upward into his heart; his eyes glittered green in reflection and absorption of the Gardens' enchanting light; his nostrils twitched and thrilled with the myriad fragrances of herb and flower; something like the taste of maple sap teased his tongue, as though the very air were flavoured; and his ears were attuned to the underlying melody of breeze and brook and bird of song.

But for all Galledine's glory and green grandeur, Axennus' senses were more keenly focused upon the small fine form of the Fiann before him.

The daughter of Eldurion seemed to float along the path with an elegant ease of motion, like a leaf on flowing water, fleet and free. And where she walked, there went also the sweet scent of spring, the ethereal essence of femininity. Her small square shoulders and slim muscled arms spoke of a strength that seldom accompanied such singular beauty. The tied tail of her midnight hair fell between the blades of her fair-skinned shoulders like the darkness between stars, and beneath her narrow waist, her hips swayed to and fro as though in tempo with the beat of Axennus' very heart.

Caelle smiled inwardly. She could feel the Southman's eyes upon her as surely as she would the gentle caress of caring hands. But she was neither offended nor affronted by the Ambassador's attention, for her beauty had ever moved the hearts and minds of men, even those of the dourest of Fiannar. Oft was it whispered that the light of the Athair yet shone within her, for hers seemed not a mortal beauty, not one that flowers and fades and fails in the end.

Thus the wonder was small that a man such as Axennus Teagh, a man whose love of the female form approached legendary proportions, might be enamoured of her, might be drawn to her. But he brought with his attentions a sincere respect and unhindered honesty that Caelle found both surprising and refreshing. For all his swagger and showmanship, the young Ambassador was in sooth a man of well-hidden humility, a man in unconscious search for meaning, for enlightenment, for his very self. And apart and aside from these things, Axennus Teagh was not an unseemly model of masculinity, nor was his countenance uncomely. And he was surely a man of intriguing intellect. That he was not of the Fiannar of Lindannan was of little consequence – she knew the truth of his blood. Surely, Caelle of the Fiannar had suffered the unsolicited attentions of admirers less worthy than the Erelian Ambassador.

Caelle's smile fell and a shadow stole across her sight. Such thoughts were for other times.

"I would tell you a tale."

Caelle sat atop an outcropping of rock overhanging a shallow stream. Her arms were braced behind her, her head tilted back upon her fine neck, long hair brushing the surface of the stone. She had hiked her gown over her knees so that she might dangle her legs over the lip of the rock and immerse her small feet in the slow flow of the water. Nearby, a turtle basked lazily on a log, long neck stretched toward the light, small eyes blinking languidly. And closer still, Axennus lay upon the rock, his head pillowed by his hands, his green-glossed eyes peering pensively into Galledine's sun-dappled canopy. He could not recall having known such peace.

"I would be pleased to listen, Shield Maiden." He maneuvered himself into a more attentive sitting position at the Fiann's side.

"Your questions have been many, though not all have been voiced."

"You perceive much, Shield Maiden." Then Axennus, too, dangled his legs over the lip of their stony seat.

Caelle closed her lovely eyes, feeling the cool waters wash between her toes. Something like a sigh slipped past her slightly parted lips.

"I am told you are a man well-learned in history, Ambassador."

"You are misled," denied Axennus, his voice soft and sedate as he tested the chill of the stream with his own tentative toes. "I am no historian, but only a man of some little curiosity, oft intrigued by things found in tomes old and dusty."

"You have some knowledge, then, of the writings of the renowned Erelian philosopher Omereo?"

"A few words only, Shield Maiden," replied Axennus, the little rill licking his toes with light liquid tongues. "From his *Dissertations on Time*: 'The past defines the present, and the present decides the future'. Long has Omereo been revered for stating the obvious."

"Nevertheless, I will tell you now of the past, not as we would have it, but as it truly was – our history unglossed by legend, the truth unsullied by rhetoric religious and political. I will tell you of yesterday, that you might better understand today, that you might approach tomorrow armed with knowledge and armoured with wisdom. I will tell you of Light and of Darkness, of joy and of sorrow, of love and of war. I will tell you as I heard it from my father, who heard it from his own father, who heard it from one whom was there. It is in their words that you will begin to find the answers that you seek, Master Ambassador."

"You honour me, my friend," said Axennus sincerely.

Absently, he slowly submerged both feet into the rippling water. Disturbed by the man's movement, the basking turtle abandoned its perch, hurriedly tumbling into the safety of the stream and swiftly disappearing.

The Fiann opened her eyes, sapphire fire sparking in their fathomless grey depths, like blue stars in a silver sky. And her voice was as the trickling song of green Galledine's very soul.

"Ambassador Axennus Teagh, I would tell you of the making and breaking of worlds."

"Before time, before being, there was The One, whom the Athair name Iu, and whom we call the Teller. The Teller looked about him, and saw no beauty, but only the darkness of the Untold. And in his wisdom he thought to tell a tale, to bring order to chaos, and from darkness Light. And so he began the Tale.

"The Teller first spoke law into the Tale, law to which all the Told must adhere, for without law there can be no order, and without order no beauty. The Untold exploded into light. Time began. The stars, of which our sun is but one of countless billions, shone. And of the dusts of the cosmos worlds were formed, though they were but three, and barren. The First Words spoken, the Teller rested.

"And for a time he was content, but he soon longed for companionship, for he was alone in his creation, and there were none with whom he might share his Tale. So he spoke of spirits, and there came into the Tale beings of such beauty and light as to defy description. The mightiest of these he named the Hiathir, and though they were powerful, they were few. The greater number of the spirits he named the Athair, and they were many. The Hiathir and the Athair gave the Teller companionship and listened to his Tale. And again, for a time, he was content.

"But soon the Teller became restless, for the spirits had no will of their own, but were only extensions of his own thoughts. And so he gifted them with free will, that they might no longer be as slaves, that they be bound to him by love not law, that he might listen to tales other than his own.

"However, of free will came choice, and of choice came rival good and evil. And not all spirits chose to love the Teller, for there were those that were envious of his power, and coveted his throne for their own. Mightiest of these dissenters was Ilurin, brightest and most handsome of the Hiathir. Ilurin whispered against the Teller, naming him undeserving of devotion, speaking the first lies to come into the Tale. And many listened, for Ilurin was beautiful, and his voice persuasive.

"But the Teller was not blind to Ilurin's machinations, and he called the seditious Hiath to him, and chastised him for his pride and envy. Fearful of the Teller's wrath, Ilurin prostrated himself before the throne, begging forgiveness, swearing eternal fealty. But the Teller heard deception in Ilurin's voice, and he cast the wayward Hiath and his followers to the darkness at the Edge of the Untold, there to remain until their repentance became sincere. Peace returned to the Tale, and the Hiathir and the Athair that were loyal to the Teller rejoiced. But Ilurin dwelt in shadow, brooding, nursing his anger, plotting his vengeance.

"There came a time when four who were mighty amongst the Athair approached the Teller, saying that for too long had the Three Worlds been barren, requesting that these places be made beautiful. And the Teller saw the innocence of their desire, the nobility of their intent, and he knew they wished only to beautify the Worlds and not possess them. And so he granted them their request, and thus it was that Life was brought to the Three Worlds.

"And the four Athair gave a name to these Worlds, calling them the Earths: The First Earth was a place of magic and eldritch power;

the Second was a place where magic and nature co-existed; and the Third Earth was a place of nature alone.

"The Athair saw the beauty of the First Earth and came again to the Teller, requesting they be permitted to leave the Light and abide there. And the Teller was pleased with them, and granted their desire, though he decreed that they must take physical form. He warned them that he would not influence the fates of the Three Earths, that the Worlds were beyond the reach of the Hiathir, that the Athair would be alone in guardianship of First Earth. And though they were to remain powerful and immune to Time, they would be susceptible to death by sword or sorrow, lest some among them become as Ilurin, and seek dominion over the Earths.

"To these things the Four Kings agreed, and they came to First Earth with a great host of their followers. Micyll, proud and strong, took residence with his people in the North, a place of mountains and ice. Yriel, lover of living things, made the East his and his people's home, great plains broad and free. Asrayal, dour and deep of thought, brought his people to the South, a land of silver rivers and fertile marshland. And Gavrayel of the Golden Voice went with his folk to the West, where the forests grew tall and mighty.

"The peoples of the Four Realms lived in peace and nurtured the Earth, making that which had been beautiful even more so. And the Teller saw the ways and works of his Children, and he was pleased.

"But Ilurin also saw. Great was his rage and hot his hatred for the Athair of First Earth. However, his hatred of the Teller was the hotter, and with such great numbers of loyal Athair removed from the Light and dwelling upon First Earth, Ilurin deemed his enemy to be weak. So gathering his forces at the Edge of the Untold, Ilurin brought war into the Tale, and moved to usurp the Teller from the throne.

"But Ilurin had misjudged the strength of his enemy, and in a fierce battle the traitorous Hiath's armies were broken, and he was taken by Cothra, who is known now as the Hiath of War, and chained, and brought before the Teller. There Ilurin humbled himself, and he sued for mercy. Cothra spoke against him, as did many Hiathir, and they counseled the Teller to douse the fire of Ilurin's spirit, to remove him from the Tale. But Ilurin shed tears of gold, and the Teller took pity upon him, for Ilurin had once been much favoured, as he was the brightest and most beautiful of all the Teller's Children.

"And so, against Cothra's grave counsel, the Teller forgave Ilurin his evils. But he reaved the rebellious Hiath of his beauty, and dimmed his brightness, and cast him and his minions forever from the Light. These ethereal entities floated across the astral plane, lost and forgotten for centuries, millennia, their rage seething, their hatred growing as they gradually gathered to themselves dusts and detritus of the universe and became corporeal beings, however base and corrupted. And in time, their path intersected that of First Earth, and they showered down upon the dark side of that world, unnumbered fugitive fires falling from the sky.

"So it was that evil first came to the Earths."

The Ambassador smiled.

"An interesting tale, Shield Maiden, but disturbingly like the teachings of the Recitors of the Tome in Hiridith – small-minded men of hypocrisy, immorality and falsehood, bold deceivers who grow fat on the faith of the people."

The Fiann smiled, and touched Axennus' shoulder.

"Though the vulture be winged, Master Ambassador, he is not forever aflight."

Caelle's words played in Axennus' quick agile mind, and in little time his countenance brightened with understanding.

"Ah, I see," he said appreciatively. "Even the most dishonest man is not always lying."

The Fiann nodded, withdrew her hand.

"The Recitors might misemploy the Tome of the Teller for their own selfish purposes, Southman, but such profanation does not make the Tale therein less true."

Axennus stared into the blue-starred grey heavens of Caelle's enchanting eyes.

She smiled sweetly.

He inclined his head.

"Pray continue, Shield Maiden."

"Ilurin came to First Earth and took his abode upon an island in the seas east of the lands of the Athair. There he sat in silent wrath, suckling his hatred, and scheming. The Athair had seen his coming to First Earth, a great blazing star falling from the firmament, a wail of crimson fire in its wake. And the Four Kings took counsel, for they knew of the war in the Light, and they knew of the Teller's decree, and they were worried for their world. And so they sent emissaries to Ilurin, becking his presence, that he be given opportunity to ease their concerns.

"Ilurin smiled unto himself, and he came to the land of the Athair in the guise of a repentant. And though his brightness had been dimmed, his face was yet beautiful and his voice as silk. Weeping, Ilurin bowed before the Four Kings, claiming madness had taken him, but was passed, and he swore oaths of peace and fraternity. And the Four Kings took pity on the Hiath, though some doubted, and they granted Ilurin his island in the sea. And Ilurin smiled, and promised knowledge in return, that together the Athair and he would make First Earth as beautiful as the very Light itself. And smiling like a serpent, he returned to his isle to plan and prepare.

"Of the Four Kings, Micyll was mightiest, and had little cause to fear Ilurin. Gavrayel lived far to the west, and his forests were as a mighty fortress, and he had Seven Princes of great power to ward his land, and felt assured of his security. Asrayal, ever in quest of erudition, had been moved by Ilurin's promise of knowledge, and not intimate with the true nature of evil, he willingly gave Ilurin his trust.

"But Yriel, who dwelt nearest to Ilurin, possessed the instincts of the beasts that he so loved, and he gave little credence to the covenants of the Hiath. Defurien, who was Yriel's confidant and closest friend, warned the King that Ilurin was false, that he was making designs upon First Earth. Trusting in his own wary heart and in the words of his friend – for Defurien was ever an Ath foresighted – Yriel fortified his land, and he raised a great fortress on the cliffs by the sea, and amassed a mighty store of arms and armour. And Defurien, once a student of Cothra, trained the people of Yriel in the arts of war, in sword and shield and shining spear. And the first army of the Athair came into being.

"Ilurin saw the defenses of Yriel, and he laughed, for the seeds of his machinations had taken root. He came to the court of Asrayal, who had befriended him, and he whispered into that dour King's ear words of suspicion and misgiving for Yriel's newfound militancy. For Asrayal had profited much under the tutelage of Ilurin, and had learned to mine and mold the glittering metals and precious stones of the Earth, and his land had become the most wealthy and lovely of all the realms of the Athair. Ilurin warned Asrayal that Yriel had become envious of his wealth, and would have it for himself, by force of arms if not freely given.

"Asrayal looked to the East and saw Yriel's fortifications and armouries in a darker light, for the shadow of Ilurin had fallen across his heart, and he believed others to be covetous of his wealth of shiny things. And so, under the guise of friendship, Asrayal did bid Yriel attend his court, so that he might test the King of the East, and discover for himself the truth of his brother's heart. When Yriel came to the South, Asrayal displayed for him the trove of gold and precious stones he had amassed, and Yriel's eyes widened in wonder and love for the treasure. And though the light in Yriel's gaze was of innocent appreciation for the treasure rather than desire for it, Asrayal saw otherwise, and in a rage he struck down the King of the East and slew him. So came death and murder into the Tale of First Earth.

"Ilurin laughed in blackest joy, and urged Asrayal to make war upon the orphaned land of the East, lest another King rise to power and seek to avenge Yriel's death. So it was that Asrayal marched upon the East with a host of unnumbered thousands. And they were met in battle by Defurien, and the land of the East was made red with blood. And though Defurien fought bravely and well, the enemy were too many, and they had been empowered with rage and hate. Defurien sent emissaries West and North, begging aid, but Gavrayel refused him, saying he would not partake in war, and Micyll debated overlong on the rightness of the issue.

"When Micyll did at last march to Defurien's aid, he came over-late, for the war for the East had long been lost, and Asrayal had taken the fortress of Yriel, and had claimed it for his own. Defurien had only a small scattering of warriors left to him, and with these and the help of beasts of fur and feather, he fought a war of attrition from the wilderness. Upon seeing for himself the devastation of the land of the East, a wasteland of corpses and ruin, Micyll was wroth, and called Defurien to him, and together they besieged Asrayal in his stolen fortress. Of the Athair of First Earth, Micyll was the mightiest, and his host most strong and numerous, and he destroyed the hosts of Asrayal, and broke the walls of his refuge, dragging the usurper from his purloined throne and throwing him upon the blood-grimed ground at his feet.

"There did Micyll hear the truth at the heart of Asrayal's treachery, and knew Ilurin to be the core and cause of it, and he swore to rid the Earth of her enemy or die in the trying. And he forbade the name of Ilurin to ever be spoken again, rather the fallen Hiath would be known as Unluvin the Treacher. But upon Asrayal he took some pity, and left his fate to Defurien, and Defurien declared that Asrayal be banished from the lands of the Athair, that he be as dead in the hearts and minds of all the Earth's Children. And Asrayal laughed, and spat upon Defurien's boots, and fled far into the South and Shadow.

"Unluvin the Treacher saw that the Athair were much weakened, that their eastern and southern kingdoms were virtually destroyed, and that Micyll's entire host was assembled in the East, weary and vulnerable. And so swiftly he attacked – though he dared not sally forth himself, for he feared the great Athain lords – and he unleashed the hordes of demons dark and foul that he had secreted deep in the bowels of the Earth. The valour of the hosts of Micyll and Defurien served them well against all hope, and long they held the field of war against a foe tenfold their numbers. But Asrayal came again from the South with another force, and Micyll and Defurien knew their dooms were nigh.

"But lo! A voice there was awing the western wind, and unlooked for from the forests of the West came the hosts of Gavrayel, the Seven Princes in their van, Sun Lords all, and for each Lord a thousand

Knights. And the Sun Knights of the West fell upon the foul forces of Ilurin and Asrayal like a summer storm. Following a long and costly war, the land was cleansed of evil and Shadow was driven into the sea. Asrayal was taken by Defurien, and in single combat was the traitor slain by that glorious Lord, and in that manner was good Yriel avenged.

"But with his dying words, Asrayal cursed Defurien with the Creeping Doom, a deep and dark magic he had gleaned from Unluvin. And Defurien and his people became afflicted with mortality – death by age and illness, not very unlike the fates of the Men of Second Earth – though Defurien's people remained long-lived and hardy. So it was that the *fiannari*, the Deathward, came into the Tale, and they suffer under the Plague, the Curse of Asrayal, even unto this day."

"I presume, Shield Maiden, the Defurien of which you speak is the same whose likeness stands in stone and gold beneath the Silver Stair – the founder and Father and First Lord of the Fiannar."

"That is so."

Axennus stroked his smooth square chin. Wonder swirled in his hazel eyes.

"Then it is true that the Fiannar are of the Athair, not of Mankind."

Caelle smiled.

"The Fiannar are a people unto themselves, warders of marches and mountains, fenders of forest and fen. We are less than what we once were, but more than what our enemy would have had us become. We are the Fiannar. Neither Ath nor Man, but something there between." She paused, and her smile faded, and something like sorrow stole into her voice. "And we are not long for this world."

"Shield Maiden?"

The Fiann did not immediately respond, but gazed at the Ambassador with deep, damp eyes.

Then, "My tale is not yet done, Ambassador."

Axennus took her small hand in his own.

"You have my ear, Shield Maiden."

"With the Curse of Asrayal came also the blessing of procreation to the Fiannar, for in the law of the Teller, all must be balanced, darkness with light, death with life. Of the love of Defurien for his wife Fircuine came Palladian and Vallian, twin sons, the first of the Born to come into the Tale. Vallian was hale and healthy, but Palladian was a sickly child, and was entrusted to the care of Gavrayel in the West, there to be fostered until such time that he be cured of his ills. Of Vallian much is told, but Palladian's fate remains unknown, and it is thought that he succumbed to his affliction, for his name does not come again into this tale nor any other. And the people of Defurien began to age, and die, but they produced many children, and thereby was the pain of the Plague greatly lessened.

"The Fiannar did not suffer the Curse of Asrayal alone, for the creatures of the Earth that loved and served them also shared in their doom. The ivory coats of their *elliamir* turned grey and their golden manes silvered, and they aged and foaled, and became the *mirarra*; the lupine *tararri*, fierce and loyal, became the savage *warokka*, the great war wolves of the Fiannar; and the *screaethri*, Defurien's wings and eyes, laid their first eggs and became the *throkka* of the skies.

"And in the wake of war, there were those among the surviving people of Asrayal who had not partaken in their King's treachery, or who had done and had since repented, and their fates were debated by Micyll and Gavrayel and Defurien. The Kings and the Lord forgave them the evils of Asrayal, though Micyll and Defurien refused them sanctuary. But Gavrayel was of kinder heart, though four of his Princes and many thousands of his folk had fallen in battle, and he accepted the unhomed as his own, that they not be without kin and King.

"Yet Sammayal, first and fiercest follower of Asrayal, in spite or in shame, refused Gavrayel's forgiveness. And he gathered many of the Folk of Asrayal to him and departed in darkness, never again to be seen upon the First Earth.

"And then the Athair withdrew, Gavrayel going west, and Micyll returning to the North, for they had not the strength to hold the East, nor the heart to remain there amidst the wastes of war.

"Having no land of their own – as the East was destroyed, and the South abandoned for the lingering memory of Asrayal's evil – the Fiannar made their abodes in the farthest eastern marches of the Athain lands West and North, there to remain in wary readiness lest Unluvin return with war. And this line of defense became known as the *Rillaghir Defyrine*, the Pale of Defurien, a golden bulwark against the tide of Unluvin's evil, remembered by the Fiannar to this day in the shining *rillagha* across their hearts.

"Unluvin saw that the lands East and South had been forsaken by the Athair, and he departed his island stronghold, and unchallenged he made his lair in the ruins of murdered Yriel's fortress. And to this he made repair, and a black bastion rose strong and grotesque, and was called Ungloth the Lightless. And darkness came to the East and to the South, the former a desert of Shadow and blasted stone, the latter a poisonous bog of mists and twisted things. And Unluvin gathered his strength, bided his time, eyes ever west and north, with the blackest of hate in his heart.

"And ever did Unluvin test the defenses of those lands, sending innumerable sorties against the Fiannar that held the Pale of Defurien. But the Fiannar were strong and brave, and they had grown in number under the Curse of Asrayal, and the marches of the Athain Lands were become dread places where the minions of Unluvin went to die.

"But the Athair and the Fiannar were wise, and knew that time was no friend to them, for the might of Unluvin was growing. And so they held council about the Stone of Scullain, the Cornerstone of the Earth. Defurien advised open war, but the two remaining Kings of the Athair refused him, as the numbers of their people were finite, for unlike the Fiannar, they bore no offspring, and each life lost to them was a light forever extinguished and removed from the World.

"Micyll recommended the withdrawal of all peoples to his hidden stronghold in the mountains of the North, for he deemed it secret and unconquerable. And Gavrayel advised departure from First Earth, for its beauty was already greatly stained and beyond reclamation, and he deemed its doom certain. And though they each debated long and persuasively, they came to no consensus. So it was that Gavrayel gathered his people and sailed for Second Earth. And Micyll went with his mighty folk deep into the northern mountains.

"But the Fiannar would neither flee nor hide, and they alone remained to hold unto death the Pale of their Lord. A hundred Houses did they have, noble clans proud and true, and of these Defurien's and Eccuron's and Hiridion's were most in might. And the Masters of the Houses of the Fiannar gathered for counsel amongst themselves, for they knew their time was short, that Unluvin would soon come upon them in all his might, and that the Pale could not be long held. And so they mustered the fullness of their force, and in courage or in folly, they marched upon Ungloth, that they might meet the Enemy in a last battle upon the lands that had once been their own, to find there victory – or honour in death and final glory.

"And so war came again to the East. So great was the wrath and courage of the Fiannar that they held the field for forty days and forty nights, and battered the very gates of Ungloth the Lightless. But Unluvin had withheld his most potent weapons, and now he unleashed them upon the Fiannar; great dragons and worms of wing and fire, and the *kuarokur*, most powerful and formidable of all demons. The Fiannar saw the coming of their Tale's End, and they assembled amongst their countless dead in a final stand worthy of great praise and song, though none might remain to remember. And there, beneath a bleeding moon, they awaited their doom.

"But word had come to Micyll in his mountain fastness of the plight of the Fiannar, and so moved was he by their valour that he mustered all his might, and rode to Ungloth in the fullness of his strength. Timely did he come to the aid of Defurien, for few there were remaining of the Fiannar, and these were gathered behind a shield wall atop a hill of death, engulfed in foes one hundred-fold their numbers. But Micyll broke through the hordes of Unluvin, and so came to Defurien's side, and they smiled in love for one another, as brothers in arms do, and together they held back the hosts of Darkness for many sailings of the sun.

"In those days of blood and battle were many great deeds done. Eccuron slew Attametton, the Father of Dragons, with his own hand; Rafayel, Captain of the Folk of Micyll, threw down the Beast of Bazaal, and took its head; bold Hiridion of the Fiannar smote a *kuarok* into a ruin of ash; in mighty contest did Vallian bring Sithra, Lieutenant of Unluvin, to the end of her Tale. And Defurien fought as would Cothra, and none could stay him, and no foe would stand against him.

"But alas, the forces of Unluvin were too many and overly strong. And for all their valour and courage, the Athair of Micyll and the Fiannar of Defurien knew their dooms had been decreed, that their Names were to be removed forever from the Tale. Under banners battered and bloodied, and beneath the battle-call of "*Dooooom!*", they assembled for their own slaughter.

"So it was that the black gates of Ungloth opened, and Unluvin came forth at last to claim his victory, for he felt there was nothing more to fear. In this alone did Unluvin err, for in his pride he deemed himself overmighty, that neither Ath nor Fian could assail him. And he found little cause for thought otherwise when first he strode, a great black shadow of iron and ruin, upon the fields of war.

"The hammer of Unluvin broke the ranks of Athair and Fiannar alike, falling upon them with such force that might sunder the Earth, and none could withstand him, until he came at last to a place where Defurien stood alone. There did the Lord of the Fiannar meet the Lord of Darkness in battle, and long did they fight under moon and sun and star, and Defurien wounded Unluvin with many wounds. But mortal Defurien grew over-weary before a foe that did not tire, and his feet slowed, and Unluvin smote him a great blow that broke him, bone and body.

"But Micyll was of the Athair, and among that shining people he was most mighty, and he knew neither fatigue nor fear. And Micyll fought his way to the side of Defurien, and having splintered his own blade he took up Defurien's sword, and he drew Unluvin away from the smitten Lord of the Fiannar, that young Vallian might tend his father, or hear his last words should Defurien have been beyond recall of healing.

"Athain King and fallen Hiath fought before the walls of Ungloth, and they fought on mountain peak and in ruined vale, in caverns deep and across storming skies, in fire and in sea, on plain and over bog and in forest aflame. Well-matched were Micyll and the Lord of Darkness in might and mettle, for the former was made strong with Light and righteous wrath, and the latter was bloated with hate and rage. But Unluvin had been sorely wounded in his felling of brave Defurien. Dear and costly had been the price paid for his besting of the Lord of the Fiannar, and from Unluvin's many wounds his strength bled as lava from the shattered sides of a mountain. And the Earth quaked with the throes of the combat between Micyll and Unluvin, and split where they passed in mortal contest, until at last Micyll threw his foe into a great crack in the World, and pursued him down into darkness. And at the very heart of the Earth did Micyll at last cast Unluvin down, and stood above his foe in final blazing triumph.

"And Unluvin begged Micyll to spare him, as a mongrel might beg a morsel of its master. But Micyll was mindful of Unluvin's many dishonoured oaths, and was not moved by Unluvin's cries for mercy, and with a mighty stroke of Defurien's sword did he cleave through the ironbound neck of Unluvin, and he threw his foe's severed head and rent body into the fires of the Earth's heart. And the Earth devoured Unluvin, flesh and iron, until all that remained of him was the impotent ash of memory.

"So passed Unluvin the Treacher from the Tale of First Earth. And the slaves of Shadow were bereft of the will that had commanded them, and they looked upon their foes so fell and so fair, and they knew fear, and they fled. The Athair and the Fiannar hunted them, until all that could be found were cleansed from the World, though some it is known escaped into the deepest places where their pursuers did not go.

"Micyll, in triumph and glory, but also in great sorrow, came to the side of dying Defurien, and he kissed the brow of that noble Lord, and returned to him his sword, and wept. But Defurien smiled, as one relieved of a great burden, and with final fleeting breath did he bid farewell his wife and son and friends, and he passed into a sleep from which there would be no waking. So died Defurien, Father and First Lord of the Fiannar, the noblest soul ever to come into the Tale of the Three Earths.

"Few there remained of the Athair, and of these many were gravely wounded, but most would heal with time and care. But the World itself could not be healed, and so there was a hollowness to their victory, and weary with woe and war and the cares of the broken World, the Athair of Micyll made ready to return to the Light whence they had come. For they were a people greatly beloved of the Teller, and he had bidden them return to his side, that they might bask in the Light for all eternity.

"But to the Light the surviving Fiannar could not go, for they yet suffered under the Curse of Asrayal, and will do so until they pass forever from the Three Worlds. And so Vallian, Second Lord of the Fiannar, took leave of Micyll, the Last King of First Earth, and set sail with all that remained to him of his Deathward folk across the mists of time and the seas of space.

"So it was that the Fiannar, the people of Defurien, came to the stony shores of Second Earth."

Axennus looked upon Caelle with the wonder-widened eyes of a child bedazzled. He fought to find his voice, and once found, fought to keep it from shaking with emotion.

"Well-blessed am I, Shield Maiden, to be gifted with a tale of such tragic beauty." He inclined his head reverently. "Once more do I find myself in your debt."

"And I say again, Ambassador Teagh," replied the Fiann, "there are no debts among friends."

Axennus felt something small and soft and warm in the fold of his palm, and was pleasantly surprised to find that he yet held Caelle's hand in his own.

"And we are friends, Shield Maiden. Yes. The dearest of friends."

Caelle smiled beautifully, and gave his hand a gentle squeeze.

"May there come a time that the tale be told of the friendship of Axennus of Hiridith and Caelle of the Fiannar."

"That is a tale I would gladly hear over and again, Shield Maiden."

But then Caelle's smile faded and her eyes clouded, the brightness of their light shadowed in a darkness of doubt, or of foredoom.

"Let us pray, then, that some survive these troubled days to tell it."

And she withdrew her hand.

"Shield Maiden?"

The Fiann sighed, a heavy sound, weary with old sadness.

"When the Fiannar came to the western shores of this world, they soon discovered that evil was not unique to First Earth, that the Second Earth, too, was beset by powers of Darkness and Shadow. And though the Fiannar set themselves against this evil with all their might, they could not vanquish it. Verily, only with aid of allies old and new could they hold the forces of Shadow at bay and keep safe the lands of noble Men, so that these good peoples might grow unhindered into power of their own."

"And what is this evil, Shield Maiden?"

But Caelle shook her head.

"That, Ambassador," she lowered her eyes, "is not my tale to tell. But I will say that for twenty centuries have the Fiannar held vigil over the lands of the Free Nations – for twenty centuries have we held in check the tide of evil that would overwhelm this world. But evil now comes with new strength to find the Fiannar greatly weakened, and their friends far and few."

"Nearer and more than you might think, Shield Maiden."

Caelle raised her eyes to meet Axennus' concerned and empathetic own.

"There are powerful evils at work upon this Second Earth, Ambassador. The red wind that would have taken us below the Westwall was but a taste of these."

"But the ill wind did not have us, Shield Maiden."

Caelle's smile was a cynical one.

"Truly spoken, Ambassador. But, as you have deduced, war follows hard upon the heels of the red wind. And the Fiannar are few and – despite your own fealty – their friends fewer."

"But surely the Fiannar are strong, Shield Maiden," protested Axennus softly. "The blood of the Athair is yet potent in the veins of your people, so much so that some retain powers of mindsight and soulshield. And you yet have the service of the *mirarra* and the *throkka* and, I surmise from the size and depth of tracks I have seen here in Galledine, the *warokka*. And the Daradur, I have learned, are no mere legend. And what of the Athair, Shield Maiden, what of the fair folk of Gavrayel? Did they not come to Second Earth? And forget not the Free Nations of Men that would answer your call for aid."

The Shield Maiden raised an eyebrow.

"Forget?" She then frowned. "Nay, the Fiannar do not *forget*, Master Ambassador." She paused in meaning and something much like melancholy. "But we are *forgotten*."

"Ah, dear sweet Shield Maiden. Fine friend, fair and true. At long last have you spoken false." Axennus took her gently by one wrist, guiding the flat of her palm to come to rest upon his breast. "The realm of possibility does not provide for the forgetting of a people that can produce beauty, grace and strength such as your own."

Caelle's large round eyes dampened, and her full lips curved into the most felicific of smiles, bright and brave and ever so beautiful. The beat of Axennus' heart was warm against her palm.

"Do you know no despair, Southman?"

"Despair, Shield Maiden?" Axennus ran a hand through his long free-flowing hair. His hazel eyes danced with humour, care and kindness. And in their depths kindled the fires of something more. "Despair is the doom of fools."

Caelle looked away.

As is love, my dear friend.

But she left these last words unspoken.

8

THE GUARDIAN PEOPLES

"Alone and apart,
we each represent one of the Four Elements:
The Athair are Air; the Fiannar, Water;
Earth be the Daradur.
But combined and together we are Fire."

Aeline, Queen of the Folk of Gavrayel

T here was a storm in the stone.

The thunderous thrumming in the root-rock of Raku Ulrun was precise, pure, purposeful. The hidden halls of hammer-hewn stone pulsated with power, and an invisible fire burned fierce and insistent in the hot heart of the mountain.

Rundul had been called, had been summoned. He had been beckoned to become one with the earth – flesh and bone and sacred soul. He was to be sent into the strange subterranean sleep of the *urthrust*, the deep dark slumbering of being so like the reunion of soul and stone that was Daradun death. And, because he was a Darad, he could not refuse.

The great war-axe of rugged Rundul of Axar would be sorely missed when war came to Doomfall.

The shadows on the marble of the river road were long and lean as Tulnarron approached Druintir, the grim-faced Master riding tall and terrible at the head of the rumbling Host of his House. His long black hair flew behind him like death pennons in a wild wind, and the cast of his eye was cold and dark. Riding between the rippling furls of the Golden Strype and the House of Eccuron's own Crimson Fist, Tulnarron slowed the gait of his sweat-slicked *mirarran* beneath Defurien's sky-defying Colossus, giving the monument to his people's Father little more than a cursory glance of reflective and reflexive respect.

Defurien's wars were in the past.

Tulnarron's yet awaited him.

A little more than two days had passed since Tulnarron's three-score Fiannar had departed the blood-steeped slopes of *Fongar ur Piruth*, flashing westward across the plains in a blur of grey and silver. And with the passing of every league their numbers had swelled, as warriors of the House of Eccuron answered the calls of horn and heart, racing from north and south and east, under sun and star, to the beck and back of their beloved Master. A day into their wild ride, their ancestral halls at Arrenhoth well behind them, the Host of the House of Eccuron numbered in their hundreds. Another day still, and greater than half a thousand warriors, men and women dark and dour and dangerous, followed the Crimson Fist along the marble road to the carven city of their noble Lord Alvarion.

War was coming to Druintir.

And Tulnarron, Master of the House of Eccuron, was come to war.

"Will you not go to him, mother?"

Violet mists orbited the grey of Sarrane's irises as she watched her husband ride the silvery streets of Druintir amidst welcoming roars and songs of war. The weeks of separation from Tulnarron had been long and many. And oft lonesome. Such was the price of duty, of service.

"Nay, Arumarron," she answered quietly. "The people need him more than do I this day."

Her voice, like her gaze, was misted.

Young Arumarron nodded solemnly.

The Seer peered upwards – for though the mother was tall, the son was taller, and was taller even than the father – into Arumarron's eyes, and saw that he did not, in fact, understand. But she did not expect him to understand. Such insight would come only with age, with wisdom.

Her son's face was so very young. A boy's face, for a boy he truly was. His features were smooth but not soft, a masterpiece of lines and planes and facets, hard and handsome. And although his frame and musculature was that of a very large and powerful man, Arumarron was yet some moons shy of sixteen years. His hair was wild and wavy, somewhere between the midnight black of his father and the morning blonde of his mother, one stray shock partially veiling his youthful visage. And his eyes were a deep dark grey speckled with silver, tempestuous heavens decked with stubbornly sparking stars.

"So Arrenhoth is abandoned, lost, and not a blade to be bloodied in her defence," complained the young heir to the House of Eccuron. His smooth-skinned countenance achieved a scowl. "Is the Rock of Arren not good ground?"

"The Lord and Lady believe the Seven Hills to be better ground," replied Sarrane. "Your father would seem to concur."

Arumarron pondered for a moment beneath a dark and thoughtful frown.

Then, "The enemy can only approach Eryn Ruil from the east," the boy considered, "whereas at Arrenhoth they might surround and besiege us from all sides."

The Seer nodded. The boy's grasp of war lore had ever been impressive.

"And should we have remained at Arrenhoth, a portion of the enemy army could keep us at bay behind the walls," continued

Arumarron, "while the main body marches upon Eryn Ruil, thus removing the House of Eccuron from the defence of the pass. We would become irrelevant...inconsequential."

Sarrane nodded once more. Quite impressive.

And then the lad grimaced as though a thing sour or bitter had offended his palate. "And Eryn Ruil provides us many avenues of retreat, should the need to withdraw from the field arise. Arrenhoth offers only a high walled place where we might make a glorious last stand." He paused, glowered stormily, then added emphatically, "The Daradur would not have abandoned the Rock of Arren. And they would give no thought to routes of retreat."

Sarrane smiled inwardly, though her face remained rigid. She had glimpsed her son's destiny and knew that greatness awaited him, a greatness that would exceed that of his father and rival that of Eccuron himself. She needed no power of precognition to know this – a mother's intuition might often surpass the sight of a Seer. But she knew also the legend of Arumarron of Arrenhoth was yet in the earliest stages of its formation. The telling of her son's tale had only just begun.

"The Daradur do not die in the manner that we die, my son," Sarrane advised quietly, the violet of her eyes aswirl. "We should not aspire to live as they live."

Arumarron absorbed this, comprehended this, but obviously did not entirely agree. He remained silent, however, silvered eyes aglitter as he watched his famed father's proud parade along the streets of the city, cloak and Crimson Fist billowing brusquely behind that mighty warlord, greatsword upthrust and gleaming in the thickening eventide. Arumarron saw a living Colossus, a prince without peer.

"Mother, I intend to fight this coming war."

Violet whirlpools swirled. "We have spoken on this, Arumarron."

"Even so."

Sarrane sighed, a wistful, weary wind. *So much the father's son.*

"Lord Alvarion will forbid you."

"I will petition Father to persuade him. He has the Lord's ear."

Far less than do I, my son.

"Very well, Arumarron. Make your request. And we shall all three of us abide the Lord's word and speak on this no more."

Arumarron smiled. His chest swelled.

"Agreed, mother."

And having caught Tulnarron's bright eye, Arumarron bade farewell his mother and moved to greet his father. And man and child embraced then, *rillagh* to *rillagh* beneath the Crimson Fist, Master and heir, father and son, pride upon pride.

The Host of Arrenhoth roared.

And Sarrane turned silently away.

Rundul was become the Earth, and the Earth Rundul. His flesh was stone, his bones ferric ore, his blood molten magma. He was one with holy Mother Earth, was the fire in her veins, the surge of her heart, hot and wild and full of power. He hurtled northward through ground and granite with mind-crushing velocity, his essence an unbodied rage in the rock, oblivious to and uncaring of all but the compelling call of his summons.

For indeed Rundul had been summoned. And poignantly aware of the need for utmost haste, his caller had reached through stone and space for him, pulling the great Daradun Warder into the earth, then drawing his being northward, body and soul, as water would be drawn from a well.

Such was the caller's command of Maiden Earth.

Such was his power.

They moved across the golden grasses of the Miramarch with the grace of ghosts, elegant and ethereal, like spirits from a realm of wind and whispers. They were tall and fair and of boundless beauty, and light like the starshine of night shone forth from their eyes, for their very souls had been formed of the white words of the Teller. They were borne through the gloaming upon equine creatures from another time, another world, of ivory coat and golden mane, stepping in gallantry, in glory. And about the wondrous party was the music of Light, surreal and soundless, but shaded with a subtle sadness, a melody of melancholic memory arising from the hopelorn harp of dreams.

And though they were but one score and four, power emanated from them like the soft white warmth of a northern summer dawn, a radiance discernable by the soul, if not visible to the eye. The *mirarra* of the Miramarch whinnied in reverent welcome of them, and those blessed among the Fiannar that saw them pass did fall upon bended knee with bowed head and handheld heart, as though before very princes of the Earth.

And princes of the Earth they were, in sooth – for they were nobility of the Neverborn, exalted of the Undying. They were the Light of the World.

So came the Sun Lords of the Athair to Druintir in Lindannan.

Far beneath the nethermost foundations of ancient Druintir, well below the deepest delvings of the Fiannar, a fluid form flowed from the stone, molten and mercurial. Then condensed. Solidified.

Became mighty Rundul of Axar.

Consciousness, awareness swept into the great Daradun warrior, a burning wind, soulfire. His hot heroic heart pounded within him, crashing against his breastbone like a hammer on an anvil. His spirit thrilled and soared. He had endured the peril of the *urthrudd*, a trial long considered the domain of the *uldwar* alone. His massive chest swelled, iron muscles flexing. Mother Earth had found him worthy. Worthy and unwanting.

The shame branded upon his back by the *kuarok*'s massive mace might now be more easily borne.

The first stars of the northern night sparkled softly in their sable sea, their light falling through the spray of the Silver Stair to the pale stone of Druintir, shimmering there like the luminous soul of a dead man about his own moon-bleached bones.

Axennus Teagh, his cerulean cloak wrapped around him against the chill, gazed down upon the marble city from a lofty terrace near its centre. His silver chain of office glittered argent in harmony with the nightlight. Sounds drifted up to him from the stone streets below – the clear, strong voices of the Fiannar, emotive, uplifted, and here and there the music of joyborn laughter. The Ambassador thought it strange for such sounds to have come from a people so dour, so stony of heart. Stranger still beneath the whelming shadow of war.

A subtle fragrance on the wind whispered to him that he was no longer alone, that Caelle had returned to him from an errand to the Lady of the Fiannar. Her scent was near and soft, floating on the night like petals on water. Axennus had neither seen nor heard Caelle return, but even had the night not carried her sweet scent, he would have sensed her there at his shoulder, slightly behind him and to the right. In Galledine he had come to realize that he had become wonderfully attuned to the lovely Shield Maiden of the Fiannar. Attuned and attached. Below Doomfall, she had been in his soul. And in his soul she had remained. He would have known her presence in a faceless crowd of thousands.

"Your people are lighter of heart than they were, Shield Maiden," Axennus observed, not turning, for he wanted the Fiann to know he was aware of her unseen, unheard approach. He could feel her smile.

"They have cause, Master Ambassador," came Caelle's smooth velvet voice at his shoulder. "Tulnarron, husband to Sarrane and Master of the House of Eccuron, is come to Druintir with the greater part of the host of his House beneath his banner. Ancient Arrenhcth, ancestral estate of the line of Eccuron, is emptied. Five hundred swords gleam in Druintir tonight that did not do so this past day. And more will come."

Axennus felt her gaze upon him. He turned then to meet those blue-specked eyes of grey and the face from which they shone. Caelle's appearance had altered, he noticed. The summer gown of the afternoon discarded, the Shield Maiden was clad again in plain green and grey riding garb, and her golden *rillagh* burned across her breast once more. From one hip dangled her long-bladed sword, from the other her small silver shield. But her mouth wore the same blithe smile with which Axennus had become so familiar, and of which he had become more than fond.

"Master Tulnarron was expected, surely." The Ambassador's breath misted slightly in the night. "There is more to your people's risen mood than the return of a wayward son."

"Oh?" Caelle's eyes sparkled. "You are an astute and perceptive man, Ambassador Teagh – that much is certain. For indeed, others have come to us in this dark time, others that were not expected so soon, offering words of wisdom and – it is our hope – swords of valour to aid my people in their plight." She paused, gazing into Axennus' eyes. "You are thinking the glorious Athair, those who were never born and do not die, are in Druintir this night."

"Indeed, Shield Maiden," Axennus replied, smiling wryly, "the reading of words on another's mouth is a thing readily explained, but the reading of another's thoughts is a different thing altogether, a thing of both wonder and witchery."

The Fiann's laughter was light and melodic.

"Little wonder and less witchery, Ambassador, unless the arts of observation and deduction have been branded sorcery in secret, and the secret not shared with me."

Axennus chuckled, folded his arms about his chest, and leaned back against the stone rail of the balcony.

"Or mayhap I am more transparent than I like to believe."

A little laugh. "Mayhap, Southman."

"So the Athair have come, then?"

But before Caelle could give answer, a sharp shout arose from the streets below, a cry of both wonder and welcome, swiftly followed by another, and another, until a hundred voices, a thousand, rose in crescendo into the silvered night.

Axennus Teagh turned and watched an enthusiastic throng of Fiannar move toward the nearby bridge whence the initial call had come. He then cast an enquiring look to the Shield Maiden.

But Caelle simply smiled and shook her head.

"Nay, Southman, this welcome is not for the Athair. The Undying are come already, as you have guessed, and enjoy my Lady's hospitality at this very hour. Moreover, my people's welcome of the fair Athair would be less...exuberant, for the Undying are a folk much reserved."

The roar in the streets below grew to seismic proportions.

"Who, then?" Axennus frowned perplexedly. "What army comes so soon to Lindannan's succour?"

Caelle peered through the argentine gloom to the stone span about which her people were swiftly gathering. She saw a thousand balled fists rise in greeting, in salutation. Her eyes shone brightly, silvery blue, like polished steel.

"No army of warriors marches to the aid of the Fiannar this night, Master Ambassador," she replied quietly. "I can think of one warrior, and one only, who would inspire such a reception. But I was told he is in the North."

Her voice was cool, calm, but evidenced an underlying tone of restrained excitement, and the tautness of her stance suggested a desire in her to join her brethren at the bridge.

And before Axennus could voice his next and most natural question, the crowd of Fiannar at the foot of the bridge roared and parted, moving aside like wind about a megalith, and the starshine of night revealed a fantastic figure in their midst.

Beside the Ambassador, the Shield Maiden inhaled sharply. And Axennus found that his own breath had left him.

For there, approaching along the road below them, came a warrior of incredible might and power. Though he stood no higher than Caelle, the warrior was extremely expansive of chest and shoulder. He appeared to wear no armour, but only a mantle of wolf fur, and tunic and breeches of old leather, though his boots were clad in metal and about his wrists were great bands of black iron. His arms were long and massively muscled, his legs impossibly thick, his hands huge and gnarled. His sun-bronzed skin was as rough and tough as rawhide, and with every unhurried heavy stride, the sinew and thew of his immense frame rippled like living rock. The hair and beard of his broad-browed head were long and wild, a leonine mane falling in unruly tangled waves the hue of red clay. His deeply set eyes were entirely black, pits of burning pitch in a face as hard and as unforgiving as stone. And across his massive back was slung a great war-axe, more than half the height of a man from cutting edge to cutting edge, with shaft and both blades of such a shining black as to have been forged and formed of Death itself.

"Who..." the Ambassador stammered, incredulously, "...*what*...is he?"

The Shield Maiden's breath at his shoulder was quick with excitement.

"Do you not know, Master Ambassador? Can you not surmise?"

His gaze yet glued to the strange and powerful figure below him, Axennus only shook his head in incomprehension.

"The...*strength*...he must possess..."

Caelle's eyes shone.

"Often have you spoken of his people since Sarrane and I did bid you welcome below Doomfall," she revealed, her spirit aroused and eager. "And you woke to the thunder of their drums only two morns past."

Axennus' expressive face both brightened in understanding and slackened in awe.

"*Teller of the Tale*." Wonder was in his whispered words. "*A Darad*."

"Fortune well favours you again this night, Southman," said the Shield Maiden in a tone tense with passion, "for of a mighty race, the one you see before you is deemed most mighty. He is Drogul of Dul-darad, the *kirun-tar*, the Mighty One, Chieftain of the Wandering Guard at Raku Ulrun, and Lord of Doomfall. It is held by those who know such things that no greater warrior ever walked the lands of Second Earth, and that no being born of this world may ever match him in battle."

Axennus could feel his heart race within him.

"Ever have I wanted to believe..." His voice cracked with child-like excitement, and light danced in his eyes. Then, his composure returning, "Erelian mytho-histories describe the Daradur as being either giants or dwarfs. The truth, it would seem, lies somewhere there between."

"The truth always does, Southman."

Drogul of Dul-darad drew nearer to where Caelle and her Erelian companion watched from the terrace above. The great Daradun chieftain strode in resolute silence, and his bearded face was grim and dark. As the Darad approached, Axennus detected a subtle unease in his manner for the fervour of his reception, a certain discomfiture born of a deeply rooted humility, or of a shyness specific to the nature of one accustomed to solitude.

And as he passed below them, the Mighty One glanced up, catching Caelle's eye, and something of a smile moved in the rusty mess of his beard. Then, amidst cheers and shouts and snippets of song, Drogul of Dul-darad moved past and away, deeper into night-domed Druintir, an aura of strength and power lingering in his wake.

"Did I not say, Shield Maiden," spoke the Ambassador after a short shared silence, "that your friends would not abandon you?"

Surprisingly, the Fiann frowned.

"A handful of Athair and a Darad or three will not save the Fiannar, Southman."

But Axennus laughed, ever impish, ever irrepressible.

"Perhaps not, my friend, but a certain charming Southman might."

The outward reflection of Caelle's inner smile took the form of her hand sliding into Axennus' own.

Rundul of the Wandering Guard blinked once, his obsidian orbs focusing and flashing in the dark of the underearth, revealing to him the great black presence of his summoner, powerful, and of another, less so but mighty still – two great shadows in the nethernight, darknesses on the stone. A rumble not unlike the tectonic shifting of the earth's own rocky armour threaded through the gush of blood thudding in Rundul's ears. The low laughter of one of his kind – a rare and welcome sound.

"You have the look and smell of dung, my friend," the amused one chuckled.

A grim smile like a visible grumble parted Rundul's blood-tangled beard.

"I, at least, have cause, Mundy."

Despite his relative youth and comedic nature, Mundar of Dul-darad was a fierce fighter and a fiercer friend, and was mightily beloved of his fellow Wandering Guard. Distinctive among the Daradur for his blond hair and beard, Mundar was also distinguished by un-Daradlike gentleness and kindness, traits not usually overly treasured by that fiery-hearted folk. Still, his sharp tongue could slice apart his friends as swiftly and as skilfully as his axe-blades could cut down his enemies.

But Mundar's reply to his fellow Warder's verbal parry was precluded by a third voice, a voice as hard and as smooth and as sheer as windshorn stone.

The voice of Rundul's summoner.

"I see that you are well, young Rundul," interjected Brulwar of Dangmarth, eldest of the *uldwar*, First Made of the Firstmade, and Earthmaster of the Wandering Guard. "Earth the Mother holds you dear, indeed."

Brulwar stepped forward, his long straight hair and beard as thick and as black as the netherdark, his midnight eyes glinting with an inner shadowlight of their own. Power throbbed from him like invisible fire.

"There are some among the *uldwar* who do not endure the way of the *urthrudd* so easily, even at their most whole and hale, and you are wounded and weary. Maiden Earth is strong in you, Warder Rundul. She has found you worthy."

Rundul inclined his head slightly. *But* you *find me unworthy.*

"You do me great honour, *uldwan Dor*."

Brulwar waved the words aside with one hand and summoned Rundul forward with the other. Rundul felt the Earthmaster's power swell as he approached him. He knew that Brulwar was seeing in the soul behind his eyes that which Dulgar had seen in him on *Fongar ur Piruth*. He knew the Earthmaster saw him run, saw the *kuarok* smite his exposed back. Saw all.

Unworthy.

But Brulwar said only, "You have brought that which I requested, Warder?"

Rundul nodded once, wordlessly raising a large bulky sack in one knotted fist. A sharp stench seeped from the sack, and about its bottom was a dark wet stain. A vile viscous substance oozed from the leather, globs of which intermittently dripped upon the cavern floor in big black spatters.

"Very good," commented Brulwar with satisfaction. "You may leave the bag here, young Rundul. Should my guess not mislead me, its contents will not be needed until the morrow."

Rundul shrugged, then let the sack fall to the stone with a heavy thud.

"Have you your wits with you this night, Warders?"

Rundul and Mundar shared a curious glance.

Then Mundar grinned.

"Our malodorous friend has no wit of which to speak, *uldwan Dor*," he replied. "Luckily, I have wit enough for the both of us."

"Then have wit enough to hold your tongue," muttered Rundul with a growl.

The Earthmaster held up one hand for silence.

"War is upon us, Warders," he announced gravely, "and wisdom rather than witticism is required." Brulwar hefted his great warhammer to his shoulder. "Our Chieftain is returned from the north, and now awaits us in Druintir." He paused. "As do several old friends."

The two Warders of the Wandering Guard exchanged another look.

"Come, young Warders," beckoned the Earthmaster, his heavy black greatcoat billowing slightly as he turned and moved upward into the black of the underearth. "This night you shall sit with the lords of the Guardian Peoples about the Stone of Scullain."

The Stone of Scullain was not of Second Earth.

Formed of white fire at the heart of First Earth long before the coming of the Athair, the Stone was a flawless disc of the most pristine crystal, perfectly circular, some twenty feet in diameter, and waist-high to a man. The Kings of the Athair brought the Stone forth upon their colonization of First Earth, setting it at the mist-crowned summit of majestic Scullain, the tallest of all mountains of that mystical world and the place where the Four Realms of the Athain peoples converged. About it they set thirteen similar smaller stones to serve as seats for the lords of their peoples. There the Athain lords would gather in debate and council in times of both peace and war, and there the fate of the First Earth was oft held in balance.

Vallian, son of Defurien and Second Lord of the Fiannar, brought the shining Stone of Scullain aboard the Fiannian flagship *Dal Starrys* upon his people's departure for Second Earth. Come the founding of the Northern Realm and the sculpting of Druintir from the rock about the Silver Stair, the Stone of Scullain was placed in Hollin Tharric, the great time-carven cavern behind the crashing curtain of the highest of the three tiers of falling waters. And there, as before, the protectors of the Earth met in times dire and dangerous to decide the doom of the world.

Such a time was the night that Rundul of Axar, Warder of the Wandering Guard, came by way of the *urthrudd* to Druintir in Lindannan.

The nocturne sheens of moon and star slid past the cascading veil of the Silver Stair as though through glass, spilling into Hollin Tharric like a tide of argentine twilight. But the pure crystalline lustre of the Stone of Scullain outshone the soft light of night's lofty lanterns, the Stone's inner and innate radiance whitening the walls of the cavern the shade of a cool winter morn.

And it was that very same light that shone in the steely eyes of Alvarion II, Twelfth Lord of the Fiannar, and in the dawn-grey ones of the queenly Lady Cerriste.

"We shall commence with the Gifting of Names," announced Lord Alvarion to the dozen diverse figures seated about the Stone of Scullain.

The Lord of the Deathward spoke the shared Westspeech of the Free Nations, for the Daradur were known to brutally butcher the elegant Old Tongue of the Athair and the Fiannar, and none but the Stone Lords could comprehend their own incomprehensibly guttural language.

Alvarion wore his dark hair long and loose in the old way, tumbling tresses streaked very faintly here and there with the greys of time and care. His long green hunting cloak was thrown back behind his square shoulders, revealing simple scale armour over a padded green gambeson, across which the gold of his chain mesh *rillagh* shimmered in the silverlight. His eyes were shards of steel in his handsomely hewn face, though deeply shadowed by the austerity of the occasion. And beneath that same shadow, below his right eye, the pale hatches of a ragged scar marked yet did not mar the intrinsic beauty of his countenance.

"I am Alvarion, son of Amarien, whose father was also Alvarion, he who fought at Mekkoleth on Sark-u-surum, a Lord of some renown after whom I am so unworthily named."

The Lord's voice, strangely gentle, floated upon the muted roar of the Silver Stair like a longship upon stormy seas. His grey gaze swept over the disparate faces staring back at him from around the Stone. Despite its gentleness, his voice was strong and sure and carried throughout the cavern easily – the voice of one accustomed to authority, to command.

"I am the Lord of the Fiannar, Master of the House of Defurien, and loving husband to the Lady Cerriste."

He paused, ceremoniously drawing his legendary sword from its scabbard, then balancing the wondrous weapon's great golden blade upon the flats of both palms, and laying it reverently upon the surface of the Stone before him. There it burned like fire on ice.

"And I am the bearer of *Grimroth*, the Bane of the Other, the glorious Blade of Defurien."

Lady Cerriste flowed to her feet like the queen of a dream, elegant and elemental. Hers was a classical beauty, fine and feminine, ageless and august – her features angular, her cheekbones high and her eyes large and round, her brow broad and bold. The sun of north-ern summer had gilt her chestnut tresses with gold, and had bronzed her smooth silken skin. She wore a simple gown of supple grey upon which her sash of gold gleamed like a band of sunlight.

"I am Cerriste," said she, her voice soft but strong. There was a depth to her tone that bespoke wisdom, intellect. "I am the Lady of the Fiannar, Mistress of the House of Defurien, loving wife to the Lord Alvarion – and new mother to Aranion, our living pride and future."

She placed a staff of ornately carven whitewood before her upon the sparkling Stone of Scullain.

Tulnarron towered to his feet, holding the haft of his huge grey greatsword in one strong hand. His manner and bearing betrayed no fatigue for his long and wild ride from *Fongar ur Piruth*, though the sheen of his midnight hair was yet dulled with the dust of travel. His eyes glittered with ice and ire.

"I am Tulnarron," he said, his deep mellifluous voice a veritable thunder in the hollow of Hollin Tharric, "Master of the House of Eccuron. Lord of Arrenhoth. Warden of the East."

He lowered his greatsword to rest upon the Stone.

Then stood Sarrane, straight and slim, the strange violet light of her eyes aswirl, her fair hair cast platinum in the silvered light of the cavern.

"I am Sarrane," said she, her tone distant, dreamy, "Mistress of the House of Eccuron, and Seer to the Lord Alvarion."

She set her spear upon the Stone.

And last of the Fiannar to gift his name was Eldurion, as dour and grey as the steel of the longsword in his hand.

"Eldurion," came the voice of greased iron, "of the House of Defurien. Marshal of the Grey Watch." And as though in afterthought, "Eldest of the Fiannar."

He placed his sword upon the Stone of Scullain.

Then, in their turn, one by one, rose the representatives of the mighty Daradur, the stalwart Stone Lords of Second Earth.

"I am Brulwar of Dangmarth," rumbled the midnight-maned Darad, "First Made of the Firstmade. I have held many titles in my time, but am now Earthmaster to the Wandering Guard of Raku Ulrun, for I go where I am needed and I do what must be done."

His black eyes flashed as they briefly met the Lord Alvarion's.

"I bring to the Fiannar and offer to their worthy Lord the ancient hammer *Whulm*." He lowered his enormous weapon to the crystal surface of the Stone. "And the hand and heart and mind that wield it."

Rundul then stood, his great war-axe in hand. Both weapon and wielder were yet bloodied and battered by the battles beneath the Bloodshards and amidst the Teeth of Truth. And the wound upon his back was hot and sore with the memory of his harrowing flight from the Bloodshards. Rundul was certain he could feel a hardness in the eyes of the great ones gathered in Hollin Tharric.

Judgement? Contempt?

"I am Rundul of Axar," he said quietly, "a Warder of the Wandering Guard of Raku Ulrun."

And I am unworthy.

His teeth gritted against his own shame, Rundul placed his steel upon the Stone.

Then Mundar rose, a smaller replica of his fellow Warder's war-axe in each hand. His eyes twinkled with kindled light, and beneath his whiskers his lips curled into a coy, cathectic grin.

"I am Mundar of Dul-darad," said he volubly, "a Warder of the Wandering Guard of Raku Ulrun."

Impulsively, he spun his twin axes in his hands, then crossed them before him on the Stone.

Last of the Daradur to rise was the wilderness-weathered, wolf-mantled Drogul. Drogul the *kirun-tar*. The Mighty One. Chieftain of the Wandering Guard of Raku Ulrun. Lord of Doomfall.

But as the massive and mighty Daradun warrior set his death-black war-axe upon the Stone of Scullain, he said plainly, simply:

"Drogul."

And indeed, no further words were required.

And then the delegates of the high and holy Athair rose to honour those gathered about the Stone of Scullain with a Gifting of Names most ancient and revered. They were a people apart, the Athair, and

Light exulted from them as though their bodies could not contain the brilliance of their souls. And an unheard music, solemn and sidereal, serenaded the Neverborn with the sorrow of a song too sad to sing. And ever about them was the delicate scent of summer rain.

First among the Undying to rise was a warrior.

He was tall and solid of frame, cloaked and mantled in evening blue, his precisely fitted armour formed of an otherworldly white metal that shone hauntingly in the silvered light of Hollin Tharric. His presence was quiet but pervasive, his power primal and pure. And he was beautiful. His shining tresses were long and free, flowing over his strong shoulders like wreaths of golden flame. And his eyes were sunfire in his everfair face.

"I am called Evangael." His voice was ethereal, divine. "I am Prince of the Folk of Gavrayel in Gith Glennin, and a Lord of the Sun Knights of the Athair."

He placed a sword that seemed more sunlight than steel on the cool crystal surface of the Stone.

"I am called Thrannien," spoke the next of the Athair to rise. His voice was dreamy, almost wistful.

Garbed in simple green and brown, he wore neither cloak nor mantle, nor jewel or gem of any kind. He was long and lean, and something in his stance spoke of salient strength and speed. His braided hair was the lustrous hue of polished oak, his features fine and flawless. And his eyes were of gleaming gold, farseeing and forever ashine.

"I am Prince of the Folk of Gavrayel in Gith Glennin, and a Lord of the Sun Knights of the Athair."

He placed a great bow of immaculate ivory upon the Stone of Scullain.

Then rose the third of the Athair to make a Gift of his Name.

He was shorter in stature than the others, but no less possessed of power. He was cloaked and clad entirely in black, yet light still shone from his spirit as the sun shines past the moon of an eclipse. His hair was as shining black as the darkness behind stars, his eyes strangely colourless, his features at once gleaming and gloomy. But there was yet beauty there – beauty, strength and grace.

"I am called Yllufarr." His voice was cold and dark, like the wind of a winter night. "I am Prince of the Folk of Gavrayel in Gith Glennin, and a Lord of the Sun Knights of the Athair," – he withdrew a long silver knife from the shadows of his cloak – "though I have neither sword nor Sun Knights left to me."

He placed the weapon on the Stone with an audible clink.

Tall and regal was the last of the Athair to rise. Though his form was narrow and lean, an ancient puissance pulsed from his presence, a surreal strength slave to neither youth nor sinew. Vestmented in luminescent white, gold upon his brow and woven into his hair, his beauty was beyond both measure and words.

"I am called Ingallin," said he. His voice was the sound of a sigh, a whisper on the wind of time. "I am Prime Consul and Chancellor to Gavrayel who reigns in Gith Glennin." One fine hand moved to brush aside a lock of winter-white hair that had fallen before the shine of his silver eyes. "You may trust that I have the King's ear."

He paused, his argent gaze sweeping the faces of those gathered in Hollin Tharric. And then, and with some ceremony, he set a sceptre carved of perfect diamond upon the Stone of Scullain – the royal wand of the Athain King.

"You might heed my voice as you would Gavrayel's own."

And then there was silence – silence but for the muted roar of the Silver Stair, and for the beating of thirteen mighty hearts. So great a company had not been gathered about the Stone of Scullain since the time of Mekkoleth on Sark-u-surum. The gravity, the significance of that fact was lost on none there. Though one, perhaps, found it to be of less import than did the others.

"Well," muttered Mundar of Dul-darad, casually breaking the soulful silence, "now that we all know one another..."

Rundul found himself in the awkward place between horror and hilarity. Beside him, Brulwar the Earthmaster frowned upon Mundar in the manner that a human father might frown upon a precocious son. Only mighty Drogul allowed himself no reaction to the words of the affable Warder of his Wandering Guard.

And of the Athair, Evangael and Thrannien were smiling thinly; dark Yllufarr's pale eyes shone like a grin; courtly Ingallin glared at Mundar with a coldness approaching contempt.

But Alvarion, Lord of the Fiannar, laughed aloud.

Turning to his wife, "Strange and sturdy is Warder Mundar of Dul-darad, my Lady," he observed, amusement softening the lines of care in his mien. "He bends before neither peril nor practice."

Cerriste's winter-grey eyes twinkled.

"Indeed, husband," she replied, "we are fortunate for his friendship and for his forbearance. A less patient individual might find our age-honoured customs somewhat...tedious."

"Truly fortunate, beloved," said Alvarion, a more staid tone thickening his voice, "as we are for each and every friend of the Fiannar that assembles here in Hollin Tharric in the time of our need."

"Very much so, husband."

The Lord of the Fiannar spread his arms in a gesture of grateful welcome.

"Fellow Fiannar. Mighty Daradur. Noble Athair. Staunch allies tested and true, Lords and Masters all. Please. Be seated."

The Lady inclined her head.

Alvarion's steely eyes took a silvery sheen.

"Let us begin."

9

THE HALFLORD

"The mind is a killing field
Upon which good and evil vie
For the favour of the heart –
And the prize is the soul."

Intimos XIII, Denarro Primus, Tome of the Rock

Dawn seeped in from the east, oozing over the plains like vile violescent sludge, pressing against the risen rock and iron of U'gloch Nur, thrusting its sinister shadow relentlessly westward. All creatures save those which fed on death fled the cold touch of the dawn-spawned darkness. Beneath a crown of standing stones, millions of *bh'ritsi* flies and larvae feasted in the soiled blackness of that shadow, chewing ceaselessly, interminably gnawing, the sound of their mastication a pervasive wet whisper that curdled the blood like rotting red milk.

The troop of Bloodspawn rode into the raw light of the whitening sun. They skirted the black shadow of U'gloch Nur, neither for fear nor loathing, but of necessity, for even among the horrible *mar rendera* there were some that would not abide that sour shade.

The Halflord rode at the head. At his flanks and back were a picked guard of Black Shields, set there not to ward their leader from danger but to prevent his two small charges from approaching and annoying him. Not that the Halflord was easily annoyed. But his preternatural patience was known to have limits that, when surpassed, could result in dismemberment, decapitation and death. And for a reason awaiting explanation, Kor ben Dor did not wish to kill the human children. Yet.

Waif and Urchin rode atop a render in the middle of the company, seated before a watchful and wary 'Spawn warrior. Both children were clad in improvised tunics of sackcloth tied with lengths of rope. The boy sat behind the girl, his little arms clinging about her waist. Waif sat in sulking silence, her angelic face pouty and petulant, her blue eyes intense, angry. She glared away a lone *bh'ritsi* that dared alight upon the precious burned thing at her breast.

Insolent bastard.

Who, me? No, I am not. I'm not, I'm not.

Not you, brother. The Halflord. You're simply irritating.

Oh? I thought he was magnificent...exquisite.

Waif stared straight ahead. She did not miss the lack of superfluous repetition in her brother's words. The little shit was developing a spine.

Be careful of your courage, brother.

I was just saying, just saying, saying.

Of course you were. We approach the camp, brother. It will not do for me to treat with these mortals whilst irritated.

By me? Me, me, me?

Not you, brother. Him. Well, you, too. But you know what I mean. The Halflord has...unbalanced me. I must relax.

Relax, yes. Relax, relax.

Waif guided Urchin's small hands to her thin thighs.

Distract me, brother.

Kor ben Dor did not deign to glance at unholy U'gloch Nur as the party of Bloodspawn passed to the north of the fortress and angled around behind. He knew the castle to be empty. Not devoid of denizens, though indeed most of the Blood King's army were encamped without those black walls now, sufficiently south and east so as to escape the throw of U'gloch Nur's evening shadow. No, not uninhabited, but truly empty. Empty of purpose, empty of meaning. The empty indulgence of an arrogance teetering toward extreme insecurity. Like the pillared mansion of a rich man, a dazzling demesne far surpassing his needs, its functions few and self-serving: To attract attention; to flaunt wealth; to shout his success at the world. Status. Power. Balled fists and a querulous voice crying, *Look at me, look at me, look at me!*

Kor ben Dor did not look.

"This fortress is a monstrosity, Prince Kor," said the Black Shield at his right shoulder. She craned her neck, peering up, up, up into the halflight, seeing the ill incarnadine vitriol froth over the rim of the great foul chalice, seeing it seethe, slither, slowly sliding down the slick black length of the central tower. "Do you think the Blood King realizes what it looks like?"

"No."

"A terrible waste of power, Prince Kor."

"Yes."

"Power that would have been better employed elsewhere and otherwise."

"Yes."

Ev lin Dar smiled at her lord's loquaciousness. Oftentimes, especially at night, Kor ben Dor did not trouble himself to respond at all.

"I believe there is something wrong with those human children, Prince Kor," she said, her pretty brows beginning to knot. "They are... strange."

"Agreed."

Ev lin Dar's ivory eyes regarded the Halflord. "They are not entirely human."

"Wrong."

Neither the deep furrows of her frown nor the tigress tattoo it caused to snarl menacingly detracted from Ev lin Dar's inherent natural beauty.

"How am I wrong, Prince Kor?"

"Backward."

"Backward? I am backward?"

"Your words."

"My...? How so?"

"Not 'not entirely human'. But *entirely not human.*"

Ev lin Dar glanced back, saw the little girl's blue eyes flutter closed, her pouty pink lips part. The Black Shield looked away, the line of her mouth severe and grim.

"Agreed, Prince Kor ben Dor."

The camp sprawled for miles. Camps, rather, as there were at least nine separate and distinct tent towns, divided by a shambolic series of roughly scooped latrine ditches which seemed to emit an anthropogenic haze, a flavescent fog hovering above the blighted plains, offensively odoriferous. The rancid reek of multitudes. Unmen of Waldard, of murky Mroch Durva and the Hebbingore Roots. Urkroks of the Blackbones and harsh Horachia. Gigantic Graniants from the blasted lands beneath Earthfall. Wild Wulfings of icy Var. A spattering of Norian mercenaries. And the Bloodspawn who could claim no country in that world or any other.

"Home," adverted Ev lin Dar sardonically.

The Halflord's render huffed. Kor ben Dor made a similar sound. Ev lin Dar thought to comment on the odd echolalia, but quickly decided against it. Perhaps her Prince favoured her, perhaps he did not; either way, vocally drawing a parallel between the Halflord and his *mar render* was...unwise. Heads had gone missing for less.

"Gren del Mor comes," she said instead, as she caught a knot of Black Shields approaching from the direction of the Bloodspawn encampment. "And he doesn't look overly happy."

"Gren del Mor is never happy, Shield," responded the Halflord. "That 'Spawn makes *me* seem positively giddy."

Ev lin Dar smiled. Her ivory eyes shone. The sound of the Prince's voice was like a bolt of silk fluttering on a warm whisper of wind, as soft as a sigh. There was beauty in him, she knew, a beauty beyond her modest own. A beauty she could not touch.

Gren del Mor and his retinue reined in before the Prince of the Bloodspawn. Above them rippled the Black Jack, the battle banner of the Bloodspawn, a diagonal bar of silver transversing another of copper on a field of deepest obsidian. The background of the ensign, it was rumoured, had been dyed in the blood of the Halflord's victims, blood that had dried coal black, lending the standard a second name – the Killer Krux.

"Report," commanded Kor ben Dor.

Gren del Mor inclined his head. He was gaunt for a Bloodspawn, thin of arm and slender of shoulder, his face long and lacertilian, his black hair fastigiated to a sharp point atop his narrow head. When he raised his white gaze, a look of severe distaste darkened his lizard-tattooed face.

"I have spoken with all the leaders, as you ordered, Prince Kor," the Black Shield grated irritably. "Scum, every last one of them. Worse, stupid scum. Even worse, stupid ugly scum. And still worse –"

"Report."

"The kings and chieftains and generals, if that's what I must call them, assemble in the command tent, as directed. Some really should've bathed first."

"Dissenters?"

"It is an enclosed space, after all."

"Dissenters."

Gren del Mor shrugged.

"The Wulfic pup will not be pleased. The Waldard Unman's loyalty lies not with the Blood King but with the Skull King – he follows none here. And the Graniant – what's his name? Armpit? – will balk, of that I am certain."

The Halflord's *mar render* grunted. As did the Halflord.

Ev lin Dar said nothing.

Kor ben Dor nudged his render forward.

"Follow."

"Scum, I tell you," muttered Gren del Mor as the company rode behind their Prince toward the command tent. "Stupid ugly stinking scum, every last one of them."

Much better, brother.

Urchin slid his fingers from his mouth. Licked his lips. Smiled.

Yes, much better, much, much.

Do you feel, strong, brother?

Yes, sister. I feel strong. Very strong. And hungry, hungry, hungry.

I hunger, also. We will feed soon, I promise.

Feed, feed, feed.

The Halflord remains an issue. He irks me. I cannot tolerate him.

Because he resists you? Or because he dismisses you?

Because he irks me! And I would ware your boldness, brother. Your digits are not as deft as you deem them. My own are the nimbler.

You wound me, sister, you hurt me, hurt me.

Remorse is such a tawdry thing.

You are so hard, so hard, so very hard.

You will recover. As will I. I must ponder this Prince of the Bloodspawn. I did not foresee his recalcitrance.

He gave us the army, sister. Is that not what you wanted, what you wanted?

The army was never his to give. He simply rid himself of a thing he did not wish to have: Command of the Blood King's host.

Command is what we want, what we want.

Yes, but the Blood King's host is a rough lot, brother. And the diamonds in that rough the Halflord kept for himself.

But the army is ours now, sister. Ours, ours.

First we must win these little kings and captains. Win them or ruin them.

Do you think they will bow to us, sister? Will they bend, bend?

That which does not bend, breaks. And you do like to break things, brother, do you not?

I do, yes. I do, I do, I do.

The grey morning yawned over the encampment as the Halflord's party halted outside the command tent. Set at the centre of the comparatively small and orderly Bloodspawn enclave, the enclosure was by far the largest in all the disparate tent towns of the Blood King's host. Dozens of roughly hewn timber poles held aloft a ceiling comprised of hundreds of oiled skins, not all of which appeared to be animal in origin, providing clearance high enough to permit a render and rider to pass unhindered. A crude rail system allowed the canvas sides to be pulled open and closed as weather, warmth and certain olfactory conditions required. That morning, despite Gren del Mor's persistent grumbling, the sides had been slid shut and sealed securely – a room without walls is a room without secrets.

Several Bloodspawn warriors awaited at attention by the entrance to the tent, great grey giants, steadfast and sure.

"All are here, Prince Kor," announced one with a lupine tattoo.

"Perimeter," ordered Kor ben Dor as he dismounted his monstrous *mar render*.

The Bloodspawn near the entry and most from the Prince's company immediately moved to surround and encircle the tent.

The Halflord reached up and folded his hair-wings back on their intricate invisible hinges, so very like a great raven gathering in its glistening black pinions. He briefly brushed brows with his render, patted the behemoth's neck, ushered it away. He then adjusted the massive mace in its harness at his back, loosened the fastenings. Rolled his strong square shoulders. Stamped dust from his boots.

"Bring them."

Ev lin Dar gestured.

The 'Spawn warrior in whose care and under whose watchful eye the children had been placed came forward with his two small charges.

Kor ben Dor regarded the tiny twins, his chiseled features empty of expression, his pearly gaze impassive.

"Down."

The twins glided lithely from the back of the *mar render*, clasped their little hands and glissaded before the Halflord, gazing up with wide blue eyes, smiling. They stood only slightly taller than Kor ben Dor's knees.

He speaks to us as though we are dogs not gods!

Smile, sister. Smile, smile.

The Halflord peered down at them.

"I will speak. You will not."

Waif opened her mouth, but she felt Urchin squeeze her hand, and she clapped her lips closed, clutched the burned thing to her chest. Both children nodded.

"When I am done, you may have your say. Some will not listen. You may find a demonstration of your powers to be necessary. I understand this." The Halflord's eyes narrowed to slits of white fire. "But know this: Any assault upon myself or the Bloodspawn will be met with your swift and certain destruction. Your powers may be vast, but they are yet in their infancy. My own are...not so."

Impertinent half-breed!

"Oh, but we feel strong, Prince of the Bloodspawn," smiled Waif beatifically. Her nails dug into the burned thing. "Yes, indeed, quite strong. Strong enough to inflict a great deal of pain. You do remember pain, do you not?"

Careful, sister. Please, please, please.

Kor ben Dor stared down upon her in silence.

Waif beamed up at him. Her face immaculate, angelic. Bright, shining. Beautiful.

Half-breed shit!

The Halflord only stared.

And then Waif's smile seemed to falter, and lines knotted the pretty brow beneath her gleaming golden curls. Her eyes darkened. She heard Urchin whimper for the tautness of her grip on his hand.

Waif looked away.

From somewhere nearby, Ev lin Dar was certain she heard the Halflord's *mar render* huff. The Black Shield allowed herself a small smile.

216

The Halflord's gaze moved almost leisurely to the command tent's entrance.

"Weapons ready," he instructed. "Ev. Gren. With me. Waif. Urchin. Follow."

The two Black Shields dismounted, tested the draw of their swords in their scabbards, and strode with their Prince toward the tent.

Waif and Urchin lingered, holding hands, one defiant, the other hesitant.

"Come. *Now.*"

Urchin winced at the soul-shredding shrillness of his sister's silent shriek.

Gren del Mor's report had been excruciatingly accurate.

The place reeked. Horribly. Too many unwashed bodies in too small a space with too little in the way of ventilation. Of the several dozen chieftains, captains, petty kings and warlords gathered in the command tent, few had ever seen a bath, let alone taken one. Filth, fetid perspiration, piss. Rotting teeth and rancid breath. Effluvious echoes of vomit and shit.

Ev lin Dar wrinkled her nose and tried in vain to snort the stench from her nostrils. Failing that, she set her soft lips in a firm straight line, inhaled as shallowly and as infrequently as mortally possible, and glowered irritably at the happy place in her mind.

At the Halflord's other shoulder, Gren del Mor was manifestly appalled. His nose was rucked, his mouth twisted, his eyes squinting as though the stink was a visible outrage. His customary dolor darkened to disgust, revulsion, as he surveyed those gathered there with the murderous loathing of one contemplating a massacre.

Of the three Bloodspawn standing just within the entrance, only the Halflord appeared unaffected.

His two tiny wards were entirely at their ease.

The twins stood before Kor ben Dor, little fingers yet entwined, smiling blithely, like two cocksure scallywags, sure of their secrets, with no care in the world. They seemed so small, so insignificant beneath the grey giants of the Bloodspawn, yet their casual smirks and the luminous light in their round blue eyes hinted at something deeper, darker. A thing dripping with dread and cunning. Verily, with no care in the world.

Nor for it.

Before them were assembled the select, the elite, the chosen leaders of Suru-luk's vast army of vengeance and conquest.

A few dozen Unmannish chiefs and elders, even a king or two, squat and dark, low of brow, wrapped in skins and shod in crude iron. The Horachian Urkrok king and his retinue, huge and hulking, constantly grunting like pigs rutting in a sty. His counterpart from the Blackbones, a massively obese bitch, her green-grey tongue repeatedly licking the slime from her pierced nostrils; her fawning entourage. The fur-clad princes and war chiefs of wintry Var, quite tall for humans, broad of shoulder, thick of limb, bloodthirsty of heart and battle-axe. The Norian warlord, small, slim, his skin dark and wizened, his narrow eyes pale slits in a face both shrewd and cruel; his cortege of champing captains.

And the gigantic self-styled King of the Giants, the undisputed ruler of the wastes under Earthfall. Hair the colour and texture of hanging moss, skin the tone and toughness of slate. He and his gathered Graniants dwarfed even the biggest of the Bloodspawn. And he did not look happy.

"Settle," spoke the Prince of the Bloodspawn.

Save the interminable snuffling of the Urkroks, the place fell quiet – though Ev lin Dar was convinced she could *hear* the reek there, an incessant slinking, slithery, slimy sound that seeped through the ears into the soul. And all Gren del Mor heard was the imaginary slippery, slapping sound of his sword slashing, slashing, slashing.

"Good morning, friends," Kor ben Dor said softly.

Both Ev lin Dar and Gren del Mor checked small choking sounds before they escaped their throats.

"I am grateful for your audience."

Kor ben Dor spoke a simple dialect of Eastish, a generic language largely derived from Unmannish which all there would – should, rather – comprehend.

The King of the Giants loomed above him.

"Why are we here, Halflord?" demanded the Graniant, apparently oblivious to the line of drool hanging from his chin. "I am king, and kings do not come when called."

"Yet you are here, Arn'badt," replied Kor ben Dor quietly.

Arn'badt balled his gigantic fists.

An almost imperceptible gesture of the Halflord's hand, and the two Black Shields subtly stepped another stride away from their Prince.

"The only king who rules here," continued the Halflord, unperturbed, "is the one who sits the Blood Throne beneath U'gloch Nur. And I am certain that he does not make a habit of slavering upon himself."

Arn'badt glowered, both in ire and incomprehension, suspicious that he had been insulted – suspicious but unsure.

"I remain a king," the Graniant rumbled, "and you are but half a lord. And half a lord is not a lord at all. I will not follow you."

"You need not do so, Arn'badt. I have neither the intention nor the desire to lead. That is indeed precisely why we are here."

The King of the Giants shook his huge head, sending the string of drool behind him to lash one his lieutenants like a wet white whip.

"Trickery! The Halflord seeks to fool us!"

"The Blood King won't leave his seat, Bloodspawn," interjected Ongulthuk, the Unmannish King of Waldard. "Who will lead us in the field, if you will not?"

Kor ben Dor lowered his gaze meaningfully to the two human children.

Waif and Urchin beamed.

"Babies?" gaped Sten Hjerte, the proud Wulfic prince. "You would have us follow *babies*? This is sheer madness. The girl is obviously simple – simple or touched, and touched hard. Do you not see what she carries? The Wulfings of Var will not follow mad babies. The sum of these children is even less than half a lord!"

Stop giggling, sister. They will see it on your face, on your face, your face.

Oh, but it is funny, brother. So very funny.

Arn'badt laughed. A loud, raucous, ugly sound.

"Do you even know why you are called 'Halflord'? Tell me, if you can, what is this pseudomorphic creature we call 'Bloodspawn'? Do you know what blood flows in your veins? Some good Graniantish blood, that much is clear. But what of the other portion? How was this half-breed bred? Hmmm?"

Ev lin Dar's hand hovered over the haft of her sword. Gren del Mor's gauntleted fist curled about the grip of his weapon.

"I urge you not to lose your head, Graniant," Kor ben Dor said softly.

"*You* do not urge *me*, half-breed. Do you hear me? I am a *king!* You are – what are you, exactly? Hmmm? More a half-bastard than a half-lord, surely. Do you even know who your father is?"

Gren del Mor tensed. Ev lin Dar readied herself.

But Kor ben Dor simply stared.

The Graniant guffawed. "Your pretty white eyes don't impress me, half-bastard."

"There is more than one way to make an impression, King of Giants." Kor ben Dor's voice was soft, gentle, enchantingly tender. "Tell me, if you can, why do they call you 'Arn'badt the Headless'?"

"They don't –"

The Graniant's eyes narrowed, then widened in sudden startled understanding. His hand flashed for the crude flat sword-like weapon at his hip.

And then his head disintegrated.

Blood, skin, hair, teeth, skull shards, grey matter exploded backwards, spattering and splattering over the gathered leaders of the Blood King's army. Shouts and alarmed cries erupted, a cacophony of disgust and revulsion swelling to fear and horror. Arn'badt's decapitated body remained upright for several heartbeats, spouting brownish blood, a grotesque geyser gushing gore, before finally crumpling to the earthen floor.

Gren del Mor made a herculean but futile effort to suppress a grin.

Ev lin Dar grimaced. She looked disdainfully upon the corpse of the King of the Giants. *Half-bastard? Really?* She sighed into the stink.

The Halflord stood, his tattooed face impassive, his massive mace in hand, fragments of flesh and bone pasted to the flanges of its crown. Arn'badt had been the first to reach for a weapon. All there had witnessed that. But none among that mortal company save the Black Shields had seen Kor ben Dor heft his mace from its harness, swing through the space his guards had so casually provided him, and completely obliterate the Graniant's head. The deed had been done with a deftness, force and velocity that untrained eyes simply could not follow.

Did you see that, sister? Did you see, see, see?

Impressive, indeed, brother. Evidently the price for losing one's head around the Halflord is...well...losing one's head. How perfectly appropriate.

Something you should remember, sister.

Oh, shut up.

The Prince of the Bloodspawn lowered the head of his mace to the ground, leaned a thick iron-braced forearm on the butt of the long haft, heavy hand dangling loosely. His pearly white eyes regarded the remaining Graniants calmly. He seemed content to wait upon them, upon their reactions. Upon whatever would come.

Gradually, the roars of revulsion and whines of fear fell away. Even the snuffling of the Urkroks was mercifully muffled.

A stooped giant, longer in years than he was of leg, stepped forward. Bent as he was, the Graniantish elder yet towered over Kor ben Dor, and the muscles of his arms and bowed legs remained corded and tight. Cranial fetishes dangled in his thinning greased green hair, marking him as a shaman of his clan; the withered dragon's heart hanging upon a cord of sinew from his crooked neck named him shaman of shamans. Witchdoctor. Evoker, invoker, provoker of powers primal and eldritch, powers long lost to younger races.

The giant wiped something wet from his cheek. Stared down upon the headless corpse of his dead king. Nudged it tentatively with the toe of one battered boot.

"Seems dead enough."

The gigantic shaman raised his aged eyes. His ivory gaze met Kor ben Dor's own, white on white.

"He was never our king, you know. Not really. No part of any crown ever rested upon his head." The Graniant gestured to the flanged business end of the Halflord's weapon. "It is quite fitting that a crown now wears part of his head."

The Graniants behind the elder laughed, some nervously, some not.

"You have released us, Halflord. You have ended the terror of the tyrant. You will have our allegiance."

But Kor ben Dor shook his head.

"I will not."

The elder giant's milky gaze dipped down to the two human children.

Waif and Urchin grinned up at him.

"Ah. Them."

"Yes."

"This is the Blood King's will?"

"It is."

The Graniant squinted myopically, creamy eyes slitted more for a function of thought than for one of sight.

"They are not what they seem. They are more. And less."

"*Blutsaugers*," said the Halflord in the shaman's tongue.

The shaman shook his head, the skull fetishes rattling hollowly.

"They have been called 'Leech' in many languages by many peoples over many millennia. But they are more *seele-esser* than *blutsauger*. Eaters of the spirit. Devourers of souls." His squint widened slightly, whitely. "Though the souls that once dwelt within these little ones seem to have eluded them."

"Some innocence cannot be taken."

The elder peered at the Prince of the Bloodspawn, his head cocked awkwardly on his twisted neck, oily hair hanging limply, skull fetishes clattering, shriveled drakeheart swinging like a pendulum. Something shrewd shone in his ancient eyes.

"Have they names, Halflord?"

"Waif. And Urchin."

"Ah. Names you gave them. Fitting. And what of the names of the human children before they were…invaded?"

"Unknown."

"Ah. Pity, that. Names have power."

"Yes."

"My name is Umbar'hal."

"I am Kor ben Dor."

There was a sorrow to the shaman's smile.

"I am saddened you will not lead us, Kor ben Dor."

The Halflord lowered his eyes to the headless corpse lying in a lake of dark blood at his feet. The carcass of the King of the Giants had already begun to augment the stench in the tent with its own specific stink.

"You would not want to follow where I must go, Umbar'hal."

The Prince of the Bloodspawn then hefted his gigantic mace and turned away, away from the reek, away from the captains and kings, from Waif and Urchin, away, away, pushed through the tent's hide flaps, out into the gaudy morning beyond. After a dozen strides he stopped, his broad back to the command tent. Ev lin Dar appeared at his right shoulder, Gren del Mor to his left, the former smiling, the latter scowling. The Halflord deftly returned his unwieldy weapon to its harness, unfurled the great black wings nestled in his hair.

"When the Leeches are done, their command over the armies will be absolute," announced Kor ben Dor, his voice become harder and flatter than was usual. "The bodies they have taken require nourishment, so they will pause to feed. But they are impatient creatures, primal in their passions, and other hungers drive them. Ancient hungers gone unassuaged across the ages. They will not wish to linger."

The Black Shields waited. Not long.

"Prepare the 'Spawn. The host will march this day."

Ev lin Dar and Gren del Mor nodded and quickly moved away.

The Halflord turned his tattooed face toward the risen sun, closed his eyes, inhaled deeply.

For a long sweet moment, the world seemed so exquisitely quiet, utterly serene, a place of perfect peace, of true transcendent tranquility.

And then the screaming started.

10

THE STONE OF SCULLAIN

"And at Scullain, the cornerstone of the Earth,
were gathered the Guardians of the Lands,
there to decide the doom of the World."

Rafayel, *Book of Laments*, Chapter VII, Verse 12

"So ends the tale of my gravest trial," concluded Rundul.
A hush hovered about the Stone of Scullain.

The Darad lowered his head.

"I don't have the gift of eloquence, but I've shared with you my knowledge to the best of my ability and recollection. I have left nothing in want of telling."

I have laid bare my shame.

A deep and profound silence.

The Stone of Scullain glimmered like a moon fallen to earth. All eyes – black, silver, gold and grey – were upon Rundul as he lowered himself to his seat. A student of neither Athain nor Fiannian custom, the Darad considered the stern silence of his audience to be censure, condemnation. His back throbbed as though the mark of the beast was a living thing, a salamander writhing in wreaths of fire beneath his skin. Though the Daradur were impervious to physical pain, they felt some agonies more surely and more sorely than did others.

Unworthy.

But Lord Alvarion stood and bowed his head toward Rundul.

The Darad blinked mutely. *Does he mock me?*

Then Alvarion turned to address the gathering. All harkened.

"Hear me, faithful friends and true," declared the Lord of the Fiannar, the ruined cheek tissue beneath his right eye flushing faintly. "We are in the company of one whom history will hold heroic long after the Earth claims our bodies and the Light embraces our souls. Verily, it is only through this Stone Lord's strength and courage that we have had warning of the doom crouching upon our threshold, that we retain any hope of turning that doom aside."

Looking again to Rundul, Alvarion placed a hand over his glittering *rillagh* in acknowledgement, gratitude, salutation.

The Darad only blinked back blankly.

"The Fiannar are forever indebted to you, brave Rundul of Axar, Warder of the Wandering Guard," proclaimed the Lord of the Deathward. "Where there is a Fiannian heart that beats, mind that remembers, or tongue that tells, the Legend of Rundul's Run will endure."

What the...?

And as one, they rose, the great ones of the Fiannar. The Lady Cerriste, the Seer Sarrane, Master Tulnarron and Marshal Eldurion. Hands upon their hearts and love leaping like flames in their shining eyes.

Spoke the Lady Cerriste, "We will always remember, noble Rundul. Truly, we can never forget."

The Darad straightened slightly, found himself nodding.

Beside him, his own brethren said nothing.

Lord Alvarion lowered his hand to his side. The steel of his grey gaze hardened.

"The question remains, however, as to what to do with the warning which Warder Rundul has provided."

All but Alvarion resumed their seats.

As he spoke, the Lord of the Deathward seemed a man made more of metal than of mere flesh:

"The Blood King of the Wraithren has returned. But he has been exposed, and his secret scheme has been revealed. His intent is clear. Long has he desired the destruction of the Deathward and dominion over the lands of Men. He means to bring war to Lindannan, seeking to break the Fiannar and take the Pass of Eryn Ruil. Should my people fail to repel him, and should Druintir fall, the Blood King's conquest of the High Land and the Free Nations of Men can then proceed little hindered.

"But he failed to fathom and factor in to his estimations the valour of our friends – for not only has Rundul of Axar brought us word of the Blood King's clandestine machinations, but the Darad has caused him to act rashly. For whether in despair for his foiled plan or in the arrogance of his nature, he expended vast amounts of power in sending forth his red wind and raising his great black fortress from the bowels of the Bloodshards. He will need to recover.

"And so he waits there now, brooding behind his black gates, unsure of our strength, and gathering his own. Our scouts report that further forces, numbering in the many thousands and fully equipped, march openly now from Mroch Durva, from Waldard and from the Hebbingore, from the harsh countries beneath Earthfall. From the south have come companies of Norian mercenaries, and with them a new threat – Southfleetian munitions. The army of the Blood King grows. As does his confidence." Alvarion's steely eyes glinted darkly. "However long he may need to recover, he will not wait long."

Allowing his words to carry their import, the Lord of the Fiannar stood in silvered silence for a moment, pausing for emphasis, for exigency, before resuming his seat.

Another mute moment passed in the hollowed stone of Hollin Tharric.

Then Chancellor Ingallin, Prime Consul to the Athain King in Gith Glennin, floated to his feet. He sighed imperceptibly, the sound of soft wind on sand.

"Am I to understand, Lord Alvarion," Ingallin inquired, pushing a shock of white hair from his brow with one slim beringed hand, "that this army of the Blood King was assembled with neither sign nor clue beneath the vigilant watch of the Fiannar?"

The Lord of the Fiannar met Ingallin's silver gaze evenly. "That is so, Chancellor." No trace of emotion touched Alvarion's tone.

"How might this oversight, this shortcoming, be explained?"

At Ingallin's side, the Athain Princes Evangael and Thrannien exchanged golden glances, and Yllufarr peered palely at the Prime Consul. But the three Sun Lords of the Neverborn said nothing.

"Readily enough, Chancellor," replied Alvarion calmly. "The minions of the Wraithren came by ways unknown to us, by dark roads far beneath the earth, by paths that our eyes do not see, that Deathward boots do not tread."

"Ah, I see," said Ingallin delicately. "Beneath the earth." He folded his long thin hands together before him. "Thus, were it not for one incompetent Unmannish warlord's decision to lead his troops across the Northern Plains for our heroic Darad to...*chance*...upon their trail and follow them into the underearth, we would have had neither warning of the Blood King's return nor any inkling of his designs for your destruction." Something pulled at one corner of his finely formed mouth. "The fault, then, the blame for this lapse in vigilance lies not with the Fiannar, but with those who watch and ward the dark roads in the earth."

There came an inaudible rumbling from the Daradur gathered about the Stone of Scullain – a rumbling not unlike the unheard, unfelt foreshocks of the earth before it breaks in seismic rage.

"There has been no failure, Chancellor," stated Alvarion quietly but emphatically, one fingertip absently tracing the raised hatches of his scarred cheek. "There can be no blame."

"What, then?" Ingallin's silver eyes flashed strangely. There was a hiss akin to vehemence underlying the velvet of his voice. "Are we to consign our hope to the ineptitude of our foes and to the whims of fickle fortune?"

Thrannien and Evangael traded sidelong looks once more. Yllufarr gazed at Ingallin, and the cast of that Sun Lord's colourless eyes was cold.

But it was the Lady Cerriste of the Fiannar who gave answer.

"Our hope lies in unity, Chancellor," she said, her voice the rush of rain on a torrid summer night, "not in division and derision."

And then Brulwar of Dangmarth, broad and black, lumbered to his feet. The argentine air in Hollin Tharric thickened like cream, and the light of the Stone seemed to dim as though shadowed by the powerful presence of the Daradun Earthmaster.

"The Chancellor's concern is a valid one," came Brulwar's smooth marble voice. His black eyes were as inscrutable as obsidian, as cool as coal in the bosom of the earth.

Ingallin inclined his head, spread his hands.

"I thank you, Earthmaster."

"I might have raised such a concern myself in his place, were I ignorant of the powers arrayed against us." Something moved in Brulwar's black eyes as his gaze fell upon the Athain Chancellor. A flicker, a flash. A reminder to all there that even the coolest of coal might burn. "Fortunately, I cannot boast such ignorance."

A shifting of Ingallin's bone-white brows hinted at consternation, then apprehension. Beside him, the three Athain Princes sat in silence, their faces averted. Slowly, the Chancellor lowered himself to his seat.

"The known ways under the earth are aptly watched and ably warded," affirmed Brulwar. "The minions of the enemy did not come to the Bloodshards by these paths. They came by ways that the Daradur do not know, ways so deep in the earth that no mortal being might safely traverse, for the air there is a poisonous mixture of noxious vapour and toxic gases. These netherearthen paths are below the reach of Maiden Earth's consciousness, beyond her awareness. Thus the army of the Blood King could march in secrecy, well hidden from the wary eyes of the warders of the West."

"But if the air there is poison...?" asked the Lady Cerriste.

"They were protected by a power that until recently was unfamiliar to us," explained the Earthmaster. "Warder Rundul has spoken to you of the earthblight, of the foul force infesting the earth, of the ill incarnadine pool of power in the bowels of the Bloodshards. It was this very power, this *urthvennim*, that permitted and enabled the army of the Blood King to pass unseen and unharmed through the mantle of the earth."

"What is this earthblight?" asked Alvarion gravely. "What is the nature of this...this *urthvennim*?"

"It is the Earth's power and capacity for destruction and devastation," replied Brulwar. "Not evil in and of itself, but tapped and taken by the Blood King, corrupted, twisted, perverted. It is no longer what it once was."

"Do you tell us that Maiden Earth has been corrupted, friend Brulwar?"

"No, Lord Alvarion, not that. Never that. The Maiden is incorruptible. But you might safely suppose her to have a darker, deeper sister with little conscience and a proclivity for destruction."

Cerriste said softly, "In the hands of the Blood King..."

"Precisely."

Alvarion's eyes darkened. "What danger does this power pose us?"

The Earthmaster frowned.

"I do not know how the Blood King intends to wield the *urthvennim*. Thus far he has only used it to make bad air good, and to augment his mastery of blood magic. I cannot be certain, but this enhancement seems to have spawned a hybrid sorcery of blood and fire, red and rotten – an 'Illincarnadine', for want of a better name. It is quite possible that the peril posed by this perverted power, this Illincarnadine, is very great indeed."

Brulwar resumed his seat.

Tulnarron, Master of the House of Eccuron, rose.

"I have seen what this Illincarnadine can do," said the Master from his great height. "The red wind summoned and sent by the Blood King has slain by terror and by madness every man, woman and child of the race of Man between Druintir and the Bloodshards. They died in towns and temples, hamlets and homesteads, on farms and fields, in little lanes and rutted roads, terribly twisted and torn, uncounted corpses, and nary a wound from enemy iron."

Alvarion nodded slowly, solemnly, a movement that seemed to say, *They were under my protection – I have failed them.* His eyes grew colder, harder, and their cast softened only with the caress by Cerriste's hand of his own.

"We will send riders to find each of these unfortunate fallen," Alvarion vowed, "to give them proper service according to their beliefs, that they might find the peace in death that they did not have in dying."

His hand beneath Cerriste's was warm, but the cold did not leave his eyes.

"There is no need, Lord Alvarion," replied Tulnarron. "Arrenhoth has answered these atrocities. Even now, the embers of a hundred pyres crumble to ash on the Plains." A meaningful pause. "Other, more aggressive answers shall follow."

The Lord of the Fiannar nodded in silence.

"I was there," continued Tulnarron, "there upon the hill of the Teeth of Truth, when the Blood King used this Illincarnadine to bring forth his great black bastion from the bowels of the earth. I saw the monstrosity come into being with my very eyes, a thing so vast and foul that I thought I had witnessed the resurrection of unholy Mekkoleth. But Dulgar of the Daradur who was with me, and who had fought at Mekkoleth on Sark-u-surum, assured me otherwise."

Alvarion nodded once more.

"Indeed, Master Tulnarron. Your wife, my Seer, gave us fair warning of this dark and dreadful thing, for of a recent night did its vile immensity haunt her dreams. Only, I failed to heed the boding of her sight, thinking it to be a vision of a time and place past, rather than the shadow of a thing soon to come.

"In this, wise Seer," he inclined his head toward Sarrane, "I erred sadly and sorely."

The violet eddies of the Seer's eyes swirled slowly, silently.

And then rose Evangael, Prince of the Neverborn, bright and beautiful.

"Hold, Lord Alvarion," said the golden Sun Lord of the Athair, raising one hand. "Your natural humility moves you to chasten yourself without cause. You did not err in supposing the object of your Seer's vision to be of the past, for of the past it certainly was, and to the past it surely belongs." His gaze swelled with sunflame. "For it was the shadow of foul Ungloth, ancient lair of Unluvin the Treacher, that tormented your Seer so."

"That cannot be, noble Prince," replied Alvarion, frowning, "for Sarrane saw precisely that which the Blood King has reared from the ruins of the Bloodshards here on this Second Earth. And Ungloth was of the First World."

"Both are true, Lord Alvarion," came Evangael's even response, "for the past and the present need not exclude one another."

"I do not understand, Prince Evangael."

"Neither the Seer Sarrane nor you might be expected to recognize this bastion of the Blood King. And for this you should feel no shame, for blameless are they that know not better. But I beseech you trust in the memory of one who was there when I tell you this black bastion newly raised is the very one in which Unluvin dwelt so long ago and so very far away." Evangael's eyes were like shining suns in the silvered firmament of Hollin Tharric. "It is Ungloth, or it is nothing."

Alvarion looked to the two other Athain Sun Lords and the Prime Consul.

"Do you concur, Princes Thrannien and Yllufarr? Chancellor Ingallin?"

"It is so, Lord Alvarion," answered Thrannien. "As surely as the cruel citadel of the Seer's vision and the bastion of the Blood King are one, so surely are they one also with unholy Ungloth of olde."

Yllufarr nodded his consensus.

Ingallin only brooded behind folded hands.

"How is this possible?" Cerriste quietly asked. "The Wraithren are of this Second Earth, as is this earthbane, this Illincarnadine. Ungloth was of the First, and was rendered in ruin with the fall of its dark master long ages ago."

"I cannot tell you *how* it is so, Lady Cerriste," replied Evangael, lowering himself to his seat. "I can only tell you that it *is* so."

Cerriste looked upon her husband, studied his chiseled countenance, saw his mind move in the depths of his wintry eyes.

"The Athair are of the First Earth, and the Fiannar trace their ancestry there," commented Alvarion, the turn of his tone contemplative, assessing. "The dragons and the *kuarokur* are also refugees from the First Earth, as are the demons against which the Daradur make constant war in the deep places of the earth. There is much memory among these expatriated fiends of First Earth from which the Blood King might have drawn the plan for the rebirth of Ungloth. And the power of the Illincarnadine has enabled him to perform this blackest of resurrections."

Brulwar of Dangmarth shifted in his seat. "A fair supposition, Lord Alvarion."

"The question, friends," grumbled Tulnarron, "is not of whence the Illincarnadine and this New Ungloth came, neither of how nor of why, but of how these things and the Blood King and his army of thousands might be confronted. War is coming, my lords, and the horn calls for swords and slaughter, not for words and wistful thought."

Mundar of Dul-darad chuckled. "You should endeavour to be more direct, Master Tulnarron."

"Needless circumlocution irks me, friend Mundar."

"As haste and rashness do me, young Tulnarron," came Eldurion's iron voice. "One should understand one's enemy as one understands one's self."

"I know my enemy, Marshal Eldurion," retorted Tulnarron. "And I know myself. I only wish to acquaint the twain as speedily as possible."

Lord Alvarion raised a hand.

"In time, Master Tulnarron. In time. But you have ably identified the perils already debated by the Masters of the Houses in your absence yesterday. These perils must now be addressed and answered."

"You have my ear, Lord," acquiesced the Master of the House of Eccuron.

"For the moment, at least, of New Ungloth we can do nothing," Alvarion admitted reluctantly. "We have not the strength – neither to besiege the black fortress of New Ungloth, nor even to meet its dark master's hosts upon the open Plains. We will therefore await the Blood King here, and meet him in battle upon the Seven Hills of Eryn Ruil."

There followed murmurs of agreement from those seated about the Stone of Scullain.

"This is the home and native land of the Fiannar," persisted Alvarion, "our beloved Lindannan, where rock and root are as near and as known to us as our own hearts. Thus the terrain well favours us. The Seven Hills are good ground, my lords, very good ground."

More murmurs of agreement.

"Even so, the centuries have dwindled the Fiannar, and we are only six thousands all told. The army of the Blood King now numbers some sixty thousands, and grows daily. Indeed, our intelligence estimates that an equal number of enemy forces are en route to the encampment behind the Bloodshards." Alvarion paused briefly, his words hanging in the silverlight of Hollin Tharric like the resonant chimesong of doom. "Should the Fiannar stand alone, we have only a fool's hope for victory."

"The Fiannar will not stand alone," vowed Brulwar, *uldwan Dor* of the *mara Waratur*. "Of that, Lord Alvarion, you may be certain."

The Lord of the Fiannar bowed his head to the representatives of the Daradur in acknowledgement and gratitude.

"What aid from the Stone Lords, Earthmaster?"

But Brulwar grimaced.

"Little enough, Lord Alvarion," he grumbled, his smooth marble voice uncharacteristically pocked with rue. "The three Great Cities of the Daradur are sorely besieged from beneath. Umun-dron, Demon King of the Wraithren, assaults Ora Undar with heretofore untold strength. He, like the Blood King, is now empowered by the *urthven-nim*. And he has at his command an army of *dwar-Durka*, warriors of intense and immaculate evil, and possessed of such wrath and might as to rival the Daradur's own."

"Ah, the *dwar-Durka*," intruded regal Ingallin from behind folded hands. "Dwarks. I have had word of these beasts. So very like the Daradur both in name and nature."

An audible growl arose from the Warders of Wandering Guard, but Brulwar quieted his younger kindred with a quick and subtle gesture. The growl fell away into an angry silence. Rundul glowered. Mundar glared. Only the mighty Drogul seemed unconcerned – Ingallin was quite beneath his quiet dignity.

But Brulwar was not so passively disposed.

The Earthmaster peered at the Athain Chancellor, the Darad's night-black eyes and the Ath's silver ones locked in a short and silent struggle for dominance, until Ingallin turned imploringly, almost pleadingly, to the Sun Lords. But not one of the three noble Princes deigned to meet his beseeching gaze.

Turning back to Alvarion, Brulwar continued, "Of the Five Armies of the Daradur, the First and Fourth hold Dul-darad, the Second and Third ward Dangmarth, whilst the Fifth fends Axar. All are powerfully and perilously pressed. None might be spared for the succour of the Fiannar. Indeed, of the forces of the Daradur, only part of that which gathers now at Raku Ulrun may be given in defence of Eryn Ruil."

The argentine air of Hollin Tharric instantly thickened, becoming viscous, oleaginous. The silence that followed Brulwar's revelation was oppressive, ominous, like the soundlessness of stone slowly eroding in a vault of the dead.

Then, quietly, "This bodes ill for us," said the Lady Cerriste. "The Wraithren are not wont to act in such concert. Indeed, they have ever seemed to despise one another as violently and as viciously as they do us. We have lost a goodly advantage should such disharmony among our enemies now be discarded." Cerriste's cool grey gaze met the shimmering silver eyes of Chancellor Ingallin. "Especially should such discord now belong to us."

The Prime Consul's perfect lips curled slightly, but did not part to retort.

Lord Alvarion stared at the sword on the Stone before him. His wife's voice seemed distant, distorted, as he absorbed Brulwar's words. The Lord's strong square shoulders seemed to slump slightly, then straightened as he banished the darknesses of doubt and dejection.

Raising his gaze, Alvarion repeated, "What aid from the Daradur, precisely, Earthmaster?"

The Lord's voice was low and flat, and his eyes had become as frozen pools in whose grey depths dwelt only an unyielding icy resolve.

"You will have my hammer," decreed the Earthmaster of the Daradur, "and the axes and hammers of fifty Wandering Guard. A further one hundred under the command of Drogul the *kirun-tar* will defend Doomfall, for doubtless the Blood King will attempt the southern pass so as to assail the High Land upon two fronts." Brulwar paused, his hand reaching to touch the haft of his hammer. "He will be denied."

"Pah!" exclaimed Ingallin, leaping to his feet. "Fifty? This Darad insults you, Lord Alvarion! Why abide him so? This is *their* world, not ours. Take your people and repair with us to Gith Glennin. Leave this war to the Daradur."

The Sun Lords traded long looks, and there was anger in their eyes.

Alvarion peered at Ingallin coolly.

"That is *not* a consideration, Chancellor."

"What then?" replied Ingallin, his voice nearing shrillness. "Trust in one hundred Wandering Guard to hold Doomfall against unnumbered thousands?" There was something wild in his argent gaze. "Doomfall will be taken, and Eryn Ruil will be assailed from before and behind, both east and west." His voice fell to a serpentine hiss. "Druintir will fall and the Fiannar will be slaughtered."

Alvarion only stared at the Ath in silence.

"It would seem, Lord Alvarion, that you need not look so far as the Blood King to find a foe," interjected Brulwar. His tone was quiet with gathering thunder. "Doomfall will hold."

Ingallin slapped one long hand on the surface of the Stone.

"Folly! You mean to destroy us all!"

Warders Rundul and Mundar growled inwardly, their ire for the Chancellor burning in their hearts and in their eyes, but they were yet bound by their Earthmaster's earlier gesture for silence.

Not so the Mighty One.

Drogul the *kirun-tar*, Chieftain of the Wandering Guard, Lord of Doomfall, rose slowly from his seat. There was neither heat nor cold in the great Chieftain's black eyes, nor pride in his manner, but his presence was commanding, compelling, like the uncompromising ubiquity of a living colossus. All those who had been standing resumed their seats, Ingallin doing so somewhat swiftly.

At his most loquacious, mighty Drogul was curt and taciturn. He spoke seldom and little. But the Mighty One's tongue had been loosened.

Dismissing Ingallin entirely, Drogul turned and addressed Alvarion. The Daradun Chieftain's voice was that of a great boulder rolling in the netherearth, emotionless, petrous, perilous, recking little of life and less of death. He spoke no oath, gave no covenant, swore no promise. He stated only truth, plain and pure.

Quoth the Mighty One:

"Doomfall will hold."

And then he sat down.

The silence that ensued was neither thick nor heavy, but only the stillness of a rumbling rock come to rest.

Lord Alvarion stood once more.

"The security of Eryn Drun was never in doubt, my old friends," he assured the Daradur. "Should the Stone Lords say that Doomfall will hold, then Doomfall will hold. Forsooth, it is not the southern pass that is in question, but the northern one, and it is in my heart that even with the aid of the Earthmaster and half a hundred Wandering Guard Eryn Ruil cannot long be defended."

Alvarion then turned to Ingallin, the Lord's grey gaze holding the Ath's argentine eyes as a steel chalice might hold iced water.

"What aid from the Athair?" queried the Lord of the Fiannar quietly.

Pushing a shock of white hair from his brow, the Athain Chancellor rose once more. He looked about the Stone of Scullain, surveying the faces there, a belated prudence causing him to pause before responding, to choose his words with caution, care, cunning.

"Neither the Princes nor I may speak for our King and Queen," he replied warily, his voice smooth and silken. "We might merely bring word to Their Highnesses of the threat to the Fiannar, and advise them accordingly."

"Did you not say, good Chancellor," interjected Cerriste coyly, "that your voice is as Gavrayel's own?"

Ingallin smiled beautifully.

"In counsel only, dear Lady. Surely you know that none but Their Majesties may commit the Athair to war."

"What counsel, then, Chancellor," asked Alvarion, "will you give to Gavrayel and Queen Aeline?"

Ingallin hesitated.

Then, softly, slyly, "It will be my counsel that the Sun Knights should ride to the aid of the Fiannar with all speed."

The Daradur grumbled as one. Deception was an agent of corruption, and as the Daradur were a people impervious to corruption, they therefore could not be deceived.

But it was the Seer Sarrane who revealed the Athain Chancellor's true intent.

"He speaks falsely, Lord," said she with quiet candour, the violet of her strange eyes swirling slowly. "He means to counsel Gavrayel *against* war, urging caution rather than action."

Ingallin looked at Sarrane surlily. His lips formed a thin, severe line.

Alvarion peered at Gavrayel's Prime Consul silently, searchingly.

Ingallin met his gaze and grimaced.

Then, and at long last –

"He will not be given the opportunity." The Sun Lord Evangael rose from his seat once more, as graceful as a swan, as bright as white fire. "The Chancellor abuses his office. He will no longer speak here, nor in Gith Glennin, on this matter. Indeed, our King will be most aghast and incensed to learn of the words that have been spoken here in his good name."

Ingallin's mouth flapped open in objection. For a moment he remained standing, contesting the Sun Lord's authority in defiant silence. But the strong hand of Prince Thrannien soon compelled him to sit, even as Prince Yllufarr deftly relieved him of the King's scepter.

Sun Lords were not ones to be openly defied.

"The Chancellor has offered nothing here but dissention," Evangael attested apologetically, "and he now compounds this with deception. His scorn for the Daradur is both ill-conceived and ill-concealed. The Chancellor will not be permitted to subvert the will of my folk to his own malicious devices."

Once again, Ingallin opened his mouth to protest, but clapped it closed at a cold colourless glare from Yllufarr.

"I cannot commit the Athair to war, Lord Alvarion," continued Evangael. "That is a decision for Gavrayel and Aeline alone. Though the Athair are an undying folk, we are not immune to sword and sorrow. And we are few. I do not envy my King and Queen their burden in this matter. But I will remind them of the Athair's common blood and cause with the Fiannar. I will advise that the Sun Knights of the Folk of Gavrayel ride in might and speed to Druintir, that they may stand in solidarity with the people of Defurien. Of that counsel you can be certain."

Alvarion nodded grimly. "We are grateful for your friendship, Prince Evangael."

The Sun Lord inclined his head.

"We are also a people for whom time passes differently than it does for mortals. That which might be decided by the Fiannar between the rising and setting of a sun, the Athair might decide in the full cycle of the moon. I can neither foresee nor promise a swift decision on the question of the Sun Knights riding to war. But should we ride, the only thing swifter will be Light itself." He paused, the flame in his eyes burning softly. "I pray only that we do not come overlate."

"As do we all, Prince Evangael." Alvarion's voice, like his eyes, was dark, cold, hard.

"I do have some little aid, however, that I might now offer you, Lord Alvarion." Evangael's words soughed like the soft song of wind on water. "It is my understanding that the children and womenfolk of the Fiannar are not to partake in this war. You mean to ensure that, even should Eryn Ruil be forced and Druintir fall, the Fiannar will not be altogether destroyed. I can help you in this." Alvarion waited silently.

"I offer the women and children of the Fiannar asylum in my sanctuary of Allaura in the Hard Hills at the northern knee of Ora Undar. Should the Lord and Lady of the Fiannar find this to be agreeable, Chancellor Ingallin will repair to Allaura in all haste, as will the score of Sun Knights who accompanied us here, in order to prepare for the arrival and care of my honoured guests."

Ingallin sulked in silence.

"Might Allaura accommodate three thousand women and children?" inquired the Lady of the Fiannar.

"Of course, good Lady," smiled Evangael goldenly. "The need for such shelter for your good folk has not gone unforeseen."

Alvarion and Cerriste glanced at one another, communing as only the most attuned and intimate of couples might do, and something subtle and sublime passed between them. The Lord and the Lady of the Fiannar then rose in unison, hands upon their hearts, heads inclined toward the Athain Prince.

"In the name of the Folk of Defurien, we accept your most gracious and generous offer, friend Evangael," announced Cerriste. "The swords of the Fiannar will be sharper and swifter for the knowledge that the future of their Houses is assured and secure."

White gold was the Sun Lord's smile.

"The Hard Hills are a labyrinthine maze of scarp and talus," commented Brulwar of the Daradur. "Allaura is not easily found, and the way there is fraught with difficulties. Your people will need a guide. I suggest Mundar of Dul-darad serve to escort them."

Mundar frowned but did not protest. The Earthmaster's motive in the matter was clear – the Athain Chancellor was not to be trusted.

Cerriste and Alvarion exchanged a quick glance.

"Agreed, Earthmaster," said the Lord of the Fiannar.

"It is decided, then," said Evangael, his smile like sunshine. "I only wish I could do more, and do so more immediately."

"I can do more," stated the Prince Thrannien, standing with feline fluidity. "The Athair must be active in this war from the advent. The Sun Knights may not ride without Their Majesties' consent. But the Sun *Lords* are not so bound."

Thrannien turned his comely countenance upon the Lord and Lady of the Fiannar.

"I will stand at your side, friends, should you desire it." The Sun Lord's eyes glittered golden. "I humbly offer you my bow."

Another quick glance shared between Lord and Lady.

"We are most greatly honoured, gracious Prince," accepted Alvarion solemnly.

Said Cerriste, "It is told that the bow of Thrannien of the Neverborn was as a thousand swords at Mekkoleth on Sark-u-surum, that the song of its string was that of victory itself. May that same song be heard over the Seven Hills of Eryn Ruil."

Thrannien inclined his head.

"Even so," said Alvarion, "three thousand Fiannar, fifty Wandering Guard and a solitary Sun Lord will not long hold Eryn Ruil against the hordes of the Blood King." He sighed. "We must therefore place our hope in the hands of Men."

"It is fortuitous that Sarrane suggested we invite the Free Nations to establish embassies above Druintir," said Cerriste. "Our relationships with the states of Men have been greatly strengthened thereby."

"I estimate that we will be in need of some seventeen thousand troops, both foot and horse, from the Free Nations," suggested grey Eldurion, "in order for the defence of Eryn Ruil to be successful. Three thousand Fiannar. Seventeen thousand Men. Twenty thousand all told. No fewer."

"We may safely rely upon aid from the Rothmen," stated Tulnarron with confidence. "Though they are isolationist in nature, and participated in neither of the recent Trade Wars, the Rothmen harbour a great love for the Fiannar and an equal hatred for the Unmen. The Roths are fierce and fearless in battle, if wild and unorthodox, and they are ever eager for a good war. Indeed, the Rothic clans fight often amongst themselves, but only for lack of worthy opponents."

"What of the Ithramen?" inquired Alvarion. "Like Rothanar, Ithramis displayed little interest in the wars of the South."

"Prince Arbamas did commit the Ithramian navy to the protection of Nothira's ports," commented Eldurion, "thus permitting the Nothirings to sail to the succour of the Erelians. I doubt he would fail to fathom the peril posed by a war so near his borders."

"Prince Arbamas is bound to us by honour if not by treaty," added Cerriste, "for did we not gift him with our abandoned city of Ithramis? He will not so soon forget our generosity."

"I suggest," said Evangael, "that you might safely depend upon the fealty of Prince Arbamas."

The Lady Cerriste raised an eyebrow.

"Your confidence in Arbamas is quite singular for one so removed from the world of Men, Prince Evangael."

The Sun Lord smiled.

"Prince Arbamas' love for the Fiannar is well known even in far Gith Glennin, my Lady. He will not allow a threat to your people go unchallenged."

"Let us hope that he does not," said Alvarion. "And of Nothira?"

"The Nothirings are a wild and lawless people," replied Eldurion. "They are politically unstable and are only some few generations removed from their years of raiding and pillaging. They have no love for any race or nation other than their own – and even amongst themselves they feud and murder – and indeed their concern in the Second Trade War was purely economic. I do not think we can expect any assistance from the wild Nothirings of the North."

"They are a mercenary folk," said Tulnarron. "Perhaps we might entice their aid with gold."

Alvarion frowned.

"I will not purchase friends for the Fiannar, Master Tulnarron."

Tulnarron shrugged his broad shoulders.

"Then, of the five Free Nations, we depend upon Rothanar and Ithramis alone, for the Erelian Republic and Rheln are too distant to send aid in time, even should they care to do so. We will not have Eldurion's twenty thousands."

"We must trust in our own strength, then, Master Tulnarron," decreed the Lord of the Fiannar, "and in the strength of those who choose to stand with us. And then pray that the Athair come, and come in time."

"There is the matter of the Southfleetian munitions," Eldurion reminded from beneath a grey scowl. "Explosives change the game."

"As does sorcery," added Tulnarron.

"These matters will be addressed," assured Alvarion quietly, his cool eyes flicking from the Marshal to the Master. "Indeed, both are blades that cut two ways, and such things have satisfyingly strange ways of working themselves out."

Eldurion allowed himself a small smile. *Ah. Of course they do.*

Tulnarron cocked his head, pondered, but did not immediately press for clarification.

"And should the Blood King himself come to the field?" asked black Brulwar. "The Daradur are immune, and the Fiannar may resist, but Men are susceptible to his power and cannot suffer it. They will break like autumn leaves in a windstorm."

Alvarion smiled grimly.

"The Blood King is not without fears of his own, Earthmaster. This he did demonstrate at Mekkoleth on Sark-u-surum. He will not go where *Grimroth* burns in the hand of a son of the House of Defurien. He will remain in New Ungloth, and leave the war to his captains and lieutenants."

And then stood Yllufarr, the darkest Prince of the Neverborn. His odd, pale eyes gleamed with a cool light, like moonsheen on still dark waters.

"Then to New Ungloth we must go," the Sun Lord decreed.

All harkened.

"Far too long have the Wraithren bended their will upon this world." Yllufarr's voice was as an astral echo of the endless struggle between powers Light and Dark. "Time and again, the Guardian Peoples have met and defeated their armies, but we have yet to put a permanent end to their evil. I hold that should the beast be beheaded, then the beast will die."

All listened.

"We must therefore bring death and destruction to the Blood King himself, even as he has brought death and destruction to unnumbered others so very much less deserving. To this end we must commit." His eerily hueless eyes flashed. "We must away to New Ungloth and seek out and slay this most foul of lions in the darkness of his own den."

All heard.

A hush fell over Hollin Tharric and the crystalline Stone of Scullain. The still was inner rather than outer – an internal quieting of mind and heart and soul, as each of those gathered about the Stone pondered the possibility of the Blood King's doom.

All understood.

And then the Earthmaster's chesty chuckle slowly slipped into the silence.

"A bold and noble enterprise, good Prince," said Brulwar of Dangmarth, "one to which we might give some little thought."

Yllufarr inclined his head.

"Pretend not that the idea has failed to play in your own mind, Earthmaster," replied the pale-eyed Sun Lord. "Indeed, I would be remiss to presume that you came to this table without the very thought."

"Ah, quite perceptive of you, Prince Yllufarr. And yet there are some who cling to the belief that the Athair will never understand the Daradun heart. But yes, I suggest the Blood King must be slain. And his *urthvennim* neutralized."

"The question, dear friends," said Alvarion, "is how these worthy feats might be accomplished."

"And to this I shall give answer," replied Yllufarr, a dark light dancing in his colourless eyes. "A small company might pass through the moors of Coldmire unseen and undetected by Suru-luk's spies, enabling us to approach New Ungloth in stealth and secrecy. We might then breach the black fortress, find its dark master and bring him to his final ruin. I, at least, will make the effort."

"One does not simply *pass through* Coldmire, Prince Yllufarr," advised Eldurion, "nor does one breach New Ungloth, in stealth or otherwise."

"One has never tried," the Sun Lord retorted.

"Coldmire?" scowled Tulnarron, perplexed. "Surely the Soft Road would be the quicker way."

Yllufarr nodded. "And also the more closely watched."

"The more so the further east you go, especially as you near New Ungloth," agreed Eldurion. "There is no approach that is not well watched and warded."

"That we know of, Marshal Eldurion. But we cannot profess to know everything."

"You will need a guide, good Prince," counselled Brulwar, as though the scheme had been thoroughly considered and decided. "None would be more able than Warder Rundul of Axar, for he has been in the deep dark heart of the Blood King's netherearthen lair. And Maiden Earth is mightily strong in Rundul. With my tutelage I believe he can arrest the power of the *urthvennim* and render it impotent."

Rundul blinked slowly, the sole outward sign of his inner surprise. He looked toward the Earthmaster, but he did not speak the questions in his heart.

"Of course, the negation of the *urthvennim* will not mean the Blood King's doom in and of itself," continued Brulwar, "for the *urthvennim* is not the sole source of his power. But its extirpation from the guts of New Ungloth will surely greatly weaken the Blood King, making his own doom a thing more easily achieved."

Alvarion frowned.

"Is it not true that the Blood King is not a living being, but a dark spirit only, and that he may be slain only with a weapon of mighty power? Such weapons are rare and few. Drogul's axe will be at Doomfall. Evangael's blade goes to Gith Glennin. And Thrannien's bow will be with *Whulm* and *Grimroth* at Eryn Ruil. Unless Rundul's axe or Yllufarr's knives have power of which I am unaware, I know of no weapon upon this Stone that might achieve the Blood King's demise."

Yllufarr's eyes were like white ice.

"Lord Alvarion, the weapon that is to be the bane of the Blood King rests before your very self upon the Stone of Scullain."

The furrows of Alvarion's frown became deeper, darker.

"The Blade of Defurien must remain with me at Eryn Ruil. I cannot go to New Ungloth. I must lead my people in battle with *Grimroth* in hand, lest Suru-luk come forth and wreak riot and ruin among the Men that stand with us."

"It is true that *you* must remain at Eryn Ruil, Lord," reasoned Evangael in his fellow Sun Lord's stead. "Not so the Blade of Defurien. *Grimroth* must go east to New Ungloth, and go in the hand of a son of the House of Defurien."

"*Grimroth* cannot be at Eryn Ruil and New Ungloth, both, Prince Evangael," interceded Tulnarron, his broad brow a veritable thunder-cloud of consternation.

Evangael smiled strangely.

"Perception and reality are not of necessity one and the same, Master Tulnarron," he said, an ageless wisdom awash in his voice like springwater in the heart of a mountain. "Illusion is oft an invaluable instrument of war."

"How might the illusion of *Grimroth* remaining at Eryn Ruil be effected, good Princes?" asked Cerriste. "The Blade of Defurien is a weapon of quite singular qualities, both in beauty and in power."

"*Grimroth*'s power is certainly unique, Lady," replied the Sun Lord Evangael. "Not so its beauty. You might recall that in gratitude for her aid in the penultimate battle of the long war for First Earth, Defurien gifted Aeline with a weapon of like appearance to *Grimroth*, though of lesser power." He paused meaningfully. "The Queen of the Folk of Gavrayel would return this most gracious gift to the people of Defurien, that it be seen ablaze upon the Seven Hills of Eryn Ruil, that it might serve the Lord of the Fiannar in the wars of this Second World even as *Grimroth* served Defurien in those of the First."

And the Sun Lord unsheathed a second sword and placed it on the Stone.

Alvarion stared at the weapon that glistered golden and glorious on the moon-white surface of the Stone of Scullain. The blade was long and broad, of gleaming gold, and light rippled and rolled beneath the plane of its luminous yellow metal like water aswirl, or like twisting tongues of fire. The pommel and quillions were plain, with neither gem nor jewel adorning the entwined red, white and yellow golds that composed the grip of the sword, which was sufficient in size to accommodate two large hands. The brand veritably glowed with beauty and power, eldritch and arcane, and even at a distance Alvarion could feel the familiar and welcome warmth of the weapon on the cool contours of his face.

Grimroth.

The Blade of Defurien.

But not.

The Lord of the Deathward raised his eyes and looked across the Stone into the bright golden gaze of the Sun Lord Evangael. Alvarion silently marked that the Prince's glittering eyes and the gleaming blade on the Stone were of the very same hue and sheen.

"She is called *Findroth* the Gifted, friend Alvarion. A name of twofold meaning. For she is a sword gifted with extraordinary properties and was a gift given by Defurien to Queen Aeline. And now the Gifted is gifted once again."

Alvarion's gaze fell to *Findroth* once more, and a frown furrowed his forehead.

"This is not the Blade of Defurien."

Evangael smiled beautifully.

"Not *the* Blade of Defurien, certainly, but *a* blade of Defurien. More, perhaps, a blade of Defurien than is *Grimroth*, for it was that great Lord's own hands that forged and fashioned *Findroth*, whereas *Grimroth* is the work of mighty Cothra, Hiath of War. Forsooth, it was *Findroth* for which Defurien held the greater love, thus the noble gifting of her unto Queen Aeline was a thing nobler still."

The troughs at Alvarion's temple eased slightly.

"Like in beauty to *Grimroth*, as you have said, good Prince. But you have also said she is lesser in power."

The Sun Lord nodded. The minute movement sent ripples through his hair like undulant sunfire.

"*Findroth* possesses all the powers of *Grimroth*, save two only."

Alvarion waited in silence.

"*Findroth* retains the power to make her bearer immune to most sorcery, but does not reverse and return sorcerous attacks to the sorcerer."

Alvarion nodded.

A small thing only, thought he, *should the Blood King not take the field.*

He waited once more.

"And *Findroth* does not sap the strength of the foe upon each successful strike as would *Grimroth* – nor does she bestow that stolen strength upon its wielder as would *Grimroth*."

The Lord nodded again.

A yet smaller thing – I have ample strength of my own, and need not purloin that of others.

"And *Findroth*'s cutting edges, Prince Evangael?"

The Sun Lord's grin was golden.

"As keen and as sharp as *Grimroth*'s own," replied the Ath assuredly, "and sufficiently sure to cut anything wrought of this Earth, save *inrinil* only." A pause pregnant with purpose. "All else rests in the hands that wield her."

At this, Alvarion smiled grimly. "All else," he echoed.

Evangael cocked a golden brow.

"Is it overmuch, Lord Alvarion?"

The Lord of the Fiannar met the Athain Prince's glittering gaze, and the Fian's grim smile became grimmer still. One callused hand reached toward the fiery *Findroth*, and the sword floated fantastically across the flawless surface of the Stone of Scullain, slowly swinging about, the Lord's fingers finding and wrapping about the golden grip. And he felt *fire*. Fierce, familiar fire.

"It is enough."

"A generous gesture, Prince Evangael," said Cerriste softly.

Lord Alvarion's countenance was as flat as the beautiful blade upon which he gazed, and a swirling golden flame relected in his narrowed eyes.

"I can see both the wisdom and the necessity in this venture to New Ungloth. Slaying Suru-luk will sever his hold over his minions, routing his armies as sword and spear might never do. And though I am loath to part with the sword of my forefathers, I do find that I am compelled to agree to this scheme."

At her husband's side, Cerriste nodded. Her face shone.

"*Grimroth* will go to New Ungloth in the hand of a son of the House of Defurien," resolved the Lord of the Fiannar. He placed the Gifted beside *Grimroth* upon the Stone of Scullain, and indeed there was nothing to visually distinguish one sword from the other. "It only remains that we determine whose will be that hand."

"He will need both strength and wisdom, husband," offered Cerriste, her eyes straying to the long grey figure of Marshal Eldurion. A small smile. "And he will need intimate knowledge of Coldmire."

"My Lady!" exclaimed the aged Eldurion, literally leaping to his feet. "I am Marshal of the Grey Watch of the Fiannar." Pocks and notches marked the greased iron of his voice. "My place and duty are ever by Lord Alvarion's side. My charge is to ward Lord and city. Give the honour of this quest to one younger and abler than myself!"

But Lord Alvarion held up his hand.

"Protest not, Uncle. You are my father's brother, and but for the chance of my birth, the Lordship of the Fiannar would have been your own upon Amarien's death."

"A death that might have been prevented, *had I but been there*."

"We cannot know that, Uncle."

"I will not leave you," grated Eldurion between gritted teeth.

Alvarion then reached for *Grimroth*, taking up the sword that had been his father's, that had been Defurien's, that had smitten Unluvin the Deceiver into ruin. His eyes seemed glazed with golden ice.

"Nothing would more effectively protect my person, my people and my city from doom and disaster than the destruction of the Blood King. And no sword arm within the House of Defurien is more able than your own."

Alvarion extended golden *Grimroth* toward the grey Marshal. Translucent flames licked along the mythic blade and the hand that held it.

"I...cannot."

"Nay, Uncle Eldurion. Yours is a battle-might that belongs to the Fiannar of olde. You will achieve this thing, or no one will."

Eldurion's countenance darkened as a storm gathered behind his iron eyes, his grizzled chin outthrust in defiance. But whether in reverence for his Lord or in reluctant accordance with the rightness of Alvarion's decision, Eldurion did not long dissent.

Slowly, hesitantly, the Marshal reached for the golden haft of *Grimroth*. His gnarled fist curled about the grip beneath Alvarion's hard hand, tentatively at first, gingerly, then tightened as the wild warmth of the metal surged through him. And for a long silent moment they remained thus, both Lord and Marshal sharing the haft of *Grimroth* in a communal grip of determined steel.

Then, in a voice of greased iron that forbade both doubt and disbelief, Eldurion vowed –

"I will do this thing."

And Lord Alvarion released his grasp of *Grimroth*.

At that precise moment, Varonin of the Grey Watch slipped ghostlike into the argentine light of Hollin Tharric. He came before the high ones of the Fiannar and stood at taut attention, martial, unmoving, his sheathless blade in one hand, the other upon the *rillagh* at his breast. All those around the Stone of Scullain rose in anxious and expectant silence. The faces of the Fiannar were grim and grave.

"Marshal Eldurion. Lord Alvarion. Lady Cerriste."

Varonin's voice was perfectly flat, bereft of any inflection, devoid of all emotion.

"Report, Watcher Varonin," Alvarion said quietly.

"Our scouts send word on the wings of the *throkka* that the Blood King begins his march westward. His host now numbers eighty thousands. More will come. Should they proceed unhindered by rain or raid, they will reach Eryn Ruil in twenty days."

Eighty thousands. Twenty days.

The Twelfth Lord of the Folk of Defurien felt blood flee the ragged scar upon his cheek. He drew an even, steady, measured breath. His visage was sere and stark, his mouth set and firm, his eyes as grey and as cold as wintry doom. The eyes of a warrior awaiting battle, expecting death.

Eighty thousands.

Twenty days.

"So begins the tale of my gravest trial."

11

THE HOUSE OF DEFURIEN

"The Fiannar will not flee the Shadow,
nor will we remove to the mountains of the North.
We will remain, and hold the Pale, even should it mean our doom.
But I yet keep faith that the Teller would not abide an evil
that the will of good peoples might not resist."

Defurien, First Lord of the Fiannar

G rand and glorious was the great Hall of the Hallowed. A vast vault hewn of the hard rootrock below and beyond Hollin Tharric, the Hall stretched westward through the metamorphic bedstone beneath the River Ruil, its carven cathedral ceiling soaring to half the height of the Silver Stair, its significant breadth sufficient to accommodate two-score men walking abreast. The palatial Hall was bisected along its length by a colossal colonnade of regularly spaced stone pillars, the marble of these veined and variegated with the most pure of gold. Skilled hands had worked the gold of the columns into a collage of cryptic runes and glyphs, and though the unlearned mind might miss the meaning of these markings, the beauty found in them would surely sear the soul of the beholder forever.

Into the walls between the pillars were hollowed great arched alcoves that housed towering stone statues of the noble Lords and Ladies of the line of Defurien, great golden *rillagha* glittering across their dawn-grey breasts. And all stone within the Hall of the Hallowed shimmered softly, as though with an inborn light of its very own – the cool luminescence of the living earth herself.

"Ah, the splendour," Ambassador Axennus Teagh marveled softly, his eyes ashine with delight and wonder. "The artisans among your people surpass themselves, Shield Maiden. Their skill leaves me bereft of words."

Behind him, the Iron Captain muttered, "Exceptional skill, indeed."

The lovely lips of Caelle of the Fiannar curved into a small smile.

"The Hall of the Hallowed is a sacred place, my friends, hollowed long ago upon decree of Vallian to hold and to honour the lineage of Defurien." Her smile broadened slightly. "A rare exception to the inherent modesty of my people."

"People more prone to pride would not have valid claim to such a shrine, Shield Maiden."

"The Fiannar are not without pride, Master Ambassador," replied Caelle. "Only, we are humbled by the glories of our forebears."

Axennus nodded in understanding, his bright eyes absorbing the transcendent grandeur of the Hall of the Hallowed. The luminous sheen of the stone and the glitter of gold shone upon his face in cool swaths of everlight. He then looked upon Caelle, and in his eyes gleamed an undying light of another source, of another sort.

"A mausoleum, I presume," grumbled Bronnus, "however magnificent. Houses of the dead disturb me."

"Then be not disturbed, Captain," comforted Caelle. "The Hall of the Hallowed is no mausoleum. You will find no crypt here. The Fiannar do not entomb their dead."

Axennus raised an enquiring eyebrow.

"My people do not age in the manner of Men," the Shield Maiden responded to the Ambassador's unspoken question. "We are longer lived, and remain hale and vigorous until our ending days. When one of the Fiannar senses his time is near, he departs of a dark night alone into the Wilderness, there to lie him down into the final sleep, the earth to claim his body, the Light to receive his soul."

"A gentle and noble death, Shield Maiden," mused the Ambassador.

The Iron Captain murmured, "Would that we were all so fortunate."

"But we are not, Captain," said the Shield Maiden. "Not all Fiannar perish in such peace. A disproportionate number of my people meet their deaths in battle. And those that do are immolated in the Pyre, the Fires of the Fallen, and their ashes are cast seaward on the westly wind under the ruby glow of a dusking sun."

"Neither end is in want of grace, of dignity," assured the Ambassador.

Caelle sighed softly.

"One ending or the other awaits my own father in the coming days," said she, a shade of sorrow tinting her tone. "Eldurion is the Eldest of the Fiannar, and has seen nearly three hundred years of this world. Such extreme longevity is rare among my people now. The Wilderness would beckon him should war not be come to the Fiannar. And as a warrior, Eldurion harkens to a horn of another time. Soon he will hear the final note. I have seen it in his eyes."

Axennus bowed his head. "He will be mourned, Shield Maiden."

Bronnus said nothing, but a silent sympathy shadowed his dark eyes.

After a motionless moment, Caelle shrugged. "The Deathward do not mourn, Ambassador Teagh."

Axennus raised his eyes. "Nevertheless."

"Perhaps, Southman." The Shield Maiden shrugged once more. "Nevertheless."

She then touched Axennus' elbow lightly, a brief display of tenderness, of affection, then led the brothers Teagh into the Hall of the Hallowed.

"The worked gold of each central column details the history of the Lord and the Lady whose stone likenesses stand in the alcoves immediately beyond it," explained the Shield Maiden. "Those statues upon the left are of the direct descendents of Lord Defurien, and those upon the right are of their respective spouses. With but one historical exception, the rule of the Fiannar has passed to the firstborn child of the line of Defurien, regardless of gender. But ever and increasingly have more sons been born to the Fiannar than daughters, thus only thrice in our history has the rule of my people passed to a daughter of Defurien's blood."

"Such a discrepancy between numbers of male and female children endangers a people's survival as surely as would war or famine, Shield Maiden," observed Axennus quietly.

"Indeed, Ambassador," replied Caelle. Profound melancholy was manifest upon her mien. "The Fiannar are truly a dwindling people. Few are our women who bear more than one child, and of those born most are male. Thus, in the past, many sons of the Fiannar took brides of the race of Man, as did Carrinthien, son of Hiridion and first declared King of Erellan. In the Men of the South the blood of the Fiannar has thinned over the generations, until it has veritably vanished altogether.

"Here in the Northern Realm, centuries of battle and war have further culled the Fiannar, so that now, of the forty-four thousands that first came to Second Earth, only some six thousand full-blooded descendants, all told, remain. Two generations, perhaps three, and the Fiannar may be no more." She paused, and the sapphire of her grey eyes darkened. "The coming war will only hasten that end."

"We must not consider such things, Shield Maiden," the Ambassador remonstrated, the stoneshine playing damply in his eyes. He then smiled, the odd light of the stone glinting on his perfect teeth. "Are the women of the Fiannar also known to take their spouses from the race of Man?"

Something brightened beneath the sorrow shadowing the Shield Maiden's lovely eyes.

"We must not consider such things, Ambassador."

Axennus grinned.

Bronnus stewed in silence.

Caelle then motioned to the stone semblance of a Fiannian Lord upon the southern wall of the Hall of the Hallowed.

"Foremost upon the left we find Lord Vallian, who missed being the firstborn of all Fiannar by mere moments, that honour going to poor Palladian, Vallian's sickly twin. Vallian fought in the final great battle for First Earth, and was the bringer of the Fiannar to Second Earth."

Axennus Teagh gazed appreciatively upon the regal rendering of Lord Vallian. The chiseled face of the long-dead Lord was fair yet fearsome, the eyes cold, the mouth grim, the expression stern and set of purpose.

"Very much the father's son, Shield Maiden," he remarked, "should this effigy and the Colossus of Defurien be accurate portrayals."

"Aye, he was, Ambassador," assured Caelle, "and, aye, they are." Then, "Across from Vallian is found Branne, his Lady-wife, born of the love of Eccuron for Yasminne. Together Lord Vallian and Lady Branne established Lindannan, the Northern Realm of the Fiannar. Upon their decree was carven the city of *Dhir Ruill en Thir*, 'Where the Ruil Falls', that which we now call Druintir."

Several steps behind Axennus and the raven-tressed Fiann, Captain Bronnus Teagh of the Ambassadorial Guard strode in dour silence, his eyes dark and hard beneath knotted brows. And although he heard the Shield Maiden's ongoing narrative, he was no longer truly listening.

Rather, he had returned in thought to a discourse with his brother at the day's dawning –

"She is beyond you, Axennus," the Iron Captain announced as he entered the Ambassador's chambers.

Axennus glanced up from the task of arranging his cerulean vestment upon his square shoulders.

"And a marvelous morning to you as well, dear brother," grinned the younger Teagh. He picked a fleck of fluff from his sleeve. "Blue certainly compliments me, think you not?"

Bronnus ignored him.

"She is like unto a princess, Axennus. You are but a merchant's son and a soldier. There can be nothing between you."

"Is that so?" Axennus smirked. "Am I permitted no romance?"

"Your great romance is with yourself alone, Axo. Your desire for her will prove but a tangent in the tale of your sundry interludes and sordid adventures."

Axennus placed the silver chain of his office about his neck, taking great care that it rested in perfect symmetry.

"Tell me, Bron, what greater adventure can there be than the epic enterprise of love?"

Love? Bronnus' brows knotted into thunderclouds of consternation.

"I worry for your mind, little brother. Reason oft abandons a man in the presence of beauty such as her own. And should war, as you say, truly be approaching, you will need what little reason you do possess."

Axennus waved one hand dismissively. Laughed.

"Love and war defy reason, both, dear Bronnus. Tell me, what place has reason in a world ruled by primal emotion?"

Bronnus only grumbled something unintelligible in response.

"Ah, Bronnus," Axennus sighed, "your concern is as appreciated as it is unnecessary. You will make some hapless child a fine father one day."

The Iron Captain's countenance contorted into a masque of explicit exasperation.

The sound of approaching footfalls came then, followed by a quick rap and a guardsman's voice announcing the arrival of the Shield Maiden, the brothers' escort to the Hearthhold of Alvarion and Cerriste of the House of Defurien.

"Come, Captain," Axennus said with a sly smile, patting Bronnus on his bristling back and brushing past him in a whirl of Erelian blue. "The Lord and the Lady of the Fiannar await us."

The sight of several grey figures, stone ghosts in the rocklight, recalled the Captain from his reverie. A woman of the Fiannar approached eastward along the Hall of the Hallowed, warded upon each side and fore and aft by a smokelike sentinel of the Grey Watch. And as the Fiannian woman neared them, Bronnus and Axennus marked that she resembled their own escort strikingly, both in beauty and in bearing, though she was taller than Caelle, and lines of silver accented her long dark hair.

The woman cradled a small bundle of soft cloth in her finely toned arms, holding it closely, caringly to her bosom. And as she and her guard came up to them, the brothers noted that within the folds of cloth could be seen a tiny head of full dark curls, and wide eyes of the brightest and most startling grey.

"She is Taresse," the Shield Maiden informed the brothers Teagh, "governess to the infant Aranion, son of Alvarion and Cerriste." Caelle smiled as her gaze fell upon the clear eyes of the little Lordling. "Taresse is also wife to Eldurion, and – of some lesser distinction – mother to my own self."

"Beauty is in the blood," the Ambassador murmured beneath his breath.

"The sun of the morning to you, mother," greeted Caelle cheerily.

"To you also, dearest," replied Taresse. Her voice was like wind on water. "And to our Erelian friends."

The governess did not slow as she passed, and both brothers noticed that the warders of the Grey Watch, long swords naked in their strong hands, eyes coldly alert and aware, had moved minutely, almost imperceptibly nearer to Taresse and her charge. Any threat of harm to the infant Lordling, the Southmen knew, would be met with swift and certain death.

"A handsome child," Axennus said in admiration when Taresse, her charge and their grey guard had passed. "And ably warded, I see."

"Aranion is the future of the Fiannar," Caelle said simply.

The Shield Maiden then proceeded with her narrative of the Hall and of those whose histories it held holy.

"And there we have Lord Amarien, eleventh Lord of the Fiannar, and father to Alvarion the Second who rules now in Druintir. Amarien's time was shorn short by an ill-fated venture excessively south and east into hostile lands. Two hundred Deathward vanished into the arid wastes of the Dunelands, with neither trace nor rumour of their end." The Shield Maiden sighed in sorrow. "The Lost Legion of Amarien. May they forever bask in the Light."

The Ambassador frowned as he gazed upon the stone rendering of Amarien. "With neither word nor trace, how may you be so certain that this Lost Legion is truly fallen?"

Caelle remained silent for a moment, pondering the wisdom of disclosing such information to the Erelian.

Concluding there could be no harm, she responded, "Amarien bore with him into the dusts of the Dunelands the Blade of Defurien. When the bearer of the Blade is slain, and the Blade not taken up by another of the House of Defurien, the gold of the Colossus' sash and sword turns to stone. This the Fiannar did see come to pass one hundred years ago, when Amarien had gone into the East.

"Then, in much haste and with heated heart did Eldurion, my father, ride southeast, and with the aid of Amarien's Seer he discovered *Grimroth*, the Blade of Defurien, buried beneath the shifting sands of the Great Desert. But of the Lord Amarien and his brave company no further sign was ever seen. The sands had taken all."

Axennus stared into the stone eyes of the noble Lord before him. There was a subtle strength there, an elemental endurance – Amarien's majesty immortalized in chiseled rock.

The Shield Maiden sighed once more, her sorrow deepening.

"When Lord Amarien departed on his ill-fated journey, Eldurion remained at Druintir to be with my mother at my birth. To this day, Eldurion feels he failed in his charge as Marshal of the Grey Watch, and he blames Amarien's death on his own absence – a dereliction of duty, of sorts. He has not forgiven himself." A third and saddest sigh. "I fear he may never do so."

Teller of the Tale! Axennus exclaimed inwardly, as the realization struck him: *She is one hundred years old!*

But the Ambassador's agile face suppressed any visible surprise, and his mouth managed, "Eldurion is an honest and honourable man, Shield Maiden. Such a man will oft blame himself more readily than he would others, and where he might find in him forgiveness for another, he might find none for himself."

The Ambassador paused, perceiving the dismay etched upon the Fiann's fine features, a ghostly crepuscule of sorrow in the stoneshine.

He then added, "But the same man will ever have the wisdom to make peace with himself before he comes to the end of his tale. Of that, my dear friend, you may be assured."

Caelle's lips eased into a smile, and light returned to her eyes.

"You are an insufferable optimist, Southman."

"I will give you the 'insufferable' of that statement, Shield Maiden," the Iron Captain grumbled gruffly.

"And I would have you return it to him, Shield Maiden."

The Fiann grimaced. "I could never accept from either of you that which you both obviously find so endearing."

Axennus grinned like an imp.

"I believe we both lost that battle, brother."

"The gold of this last pillar remains ungraven," the Ambassador observed as they came to the end of the Hall of the Hallowed, "and the alcoves stand empty."

Caelle nodded.

"The tale of Alvarion and Cerriste is but partly told. The work of Aranion's own hands will honour them when their tale is ended."

Axennus noted that there remained no allowance of space for a column and statuary to commemorate Aranion's future rule, but of this he said nothing – for an intuitive fear warned him that such an observation might recall Caelle to dismay.

The threesome then came to the Door of Lords, the great arched egress from the Hall of the Hallowed. Upon each side stood what at first glance appeared to be stone statues of warders of the Grey Watch, still and cold and sword in hand – but these were living men, though they were as near to rock as flesh and bone might ever seem.

Axennus leaned toward Caelle.

"Do they blink?"

"Hush, Southman," she reprimanded. "These are men you would not wish to rouse."

Into the shimmering stone of the arch of the Door of Lords had been hewn strange hieroglyphs, to which the Shield Maiden spoke secret words of power in the Old Tongue, then passed beneath, moving between the warders of the Grey Watch unaccosted.

The Erelians followed in silence, twin tingles of trepidation tracing icy trails along their spines. They, too, passed without waylay, but had taken only a few strides down the connecting corridor when they heard the sound of brisk and heavy footfalls approaching them. And following those footfalls was the form of a formidable Fiannian warrior.

The Fian was huge, both tall and broad, his long black hair spilling over his wide square shoulders, and in his hard and grizzled face bright eyes burned with a cold fire. Above one shoulder could be seen the haft of the gigantic greatsword bound across his mighty back, following the diagonal of his *rillagh*, the corresponding sheathless tip of the weapon threatening to score the ground at his booted feet. And about him whirled an air of heated wrath and haughty pride.

"Master Tulnarron," Caelle greeted with a small smile.

But the great Fiannian warrior passed in a storm of silence with no more than a curt and cursory nod.

"The Master of the House of Eccuron is in ill humour this morning," Caelle commented quietly when Tulnarron had gone.

"The power and peril in him," Axennus whispered, "is easily perceived."

"Verily, Southman," replied the Shield Maiden. "Tulnarron is the Fiannar's strongest sword." A small pause, then, "Come, my Erelian friends – the hospitality of the House of Defurien awaits you."

Moments earlier, in the Hearthhold beyond the Door of Lords:

"Nay, Master Tulnarron," the Lord Alvarion said quietly, but emphatically. "That concession I cannot make. My authority on this matter may not be questioned."

The Lady Cerriste, Marshal Eldurion and the Seer Sarrane stood in silence, bearing solemn witness to the struggle of wills between the Masters of the Fiannar's two highest Houses.

Tulnarron glowered, an icy heat flaring in his eyes.

"I question not your authority, Lord Alvarion," he replied, the deep bass of his voice held calm in the rigid grip of respectful self-control, "but rather your wisdom."

"My wisdom, Master Tulnarron?" echoed the Lord of the Fiannar softly. "Please, do elaborate."

Reflexively, Tulnarron drew himself to his full and formidable height.

"You have decreed our women are not to fight at Eryn Ruil, thus denying us twenty hundred able swords. Although I am in disagreement with this decision, I comprehend the reasoning at its core."

Alvarion nodded slowly.

"But denying the Fiannar one of our mightiest blades in this battle at Eryn Ruil defies all reason, all wisdom."

Another slow nod.

"Arumarron's battle-skill may be matched by fewer Fiannar than I have fingers on my hands," persisted the Master of the House of Eccuron, "and you would deny us his sword, and forbid him the fame of his forefathers."

"I forbid Arumarron only the fate that is to find overmany sons of the Fiannar in this fight at Eryn Ruil," responded Lord Alvarion evenly. "Your paternal pride in Arumarron blinds you, Master Tulnarron. Would you see your own and only son slain shy of his sixteenth summer?"

"Arumarron will survive us both, Lord," stated Tulnarron. "Of that you may be certain. Has not Sarrane, your Seer – and my wife and Mistress of my House – seen this?"

Alvarion sighed inwardly.

"She has seen this, Master Tulnarron. But have you not considered that this may be because I hold to our Law that not one of the Fiannar may march to war should he or she have seen fewer than twenty-one summers on this Second Earth? Think you not that my decree *assures*

Arumarron's survival, so that in time he might do proper honour to the name of his father and to his father's House?"

But the Master of the House of Eccuron was unmollified.

"Lord Alvarion, you will have *need* of my son's sword in this coming battle."

Alvarion nodded a third time.

"I will have need of many things when war comes to Eryn Ruil, Tulnarron," he conceded. "But young Arumarron's doom upon my conscience does *not* number among them."

The voice and visage of the Lord of the Fiannar were firm and final.

Tulnarron glared, and in his eyes were fire and ice, both the still and the storm. His heart burned. But the martinet within the Master forbade him any true display of disrespect, any greater degree of dissention. He had pressed Alvarion as tenaciously as the propriety of his position permitted. He had been refused.

Tulnarron lowered his eyes respectfully. Fisting his *rillagh*, he spun on his booted heel, and with no further word the Master of the House of Eccuron departed the Hearthhold of his Lord.

Alvarion turned to the tall bright form his Seer.

Sarrane returned his small smile with a nod.

The Hearthhold was a cavernous chamber wrought of the rock of the earth, its walls arcing majestically to a high and lofty dome. Upon the curvature was carven a forest of stone oaks, branches interweaving overhead like a thousand entwined arms uplifted toward the central circle of a stone sun. The intricately chiseled bark of the trees shimmered softly as though with silvery moss, and amidst the canopy glistened stalactitic mistletoe. Betwixt the mighty trunks of the stone grove were several doors, visible only because they were ajar, indicating a complex of chambers and corridors beyond. At the center of the smoothly polished floor was a great dais of sculpted marble, atop which was raised a cairn of stones. These stones burned with a strangely flameless fire, shedding light and warmth throughout the Hearthhold. And about the dais were several chairs and small tables, suggesting welcome and comfort, despite the unforgiving rock of which these had been formed.

"Lady Cerriste, Lord Alvarion," proclaimed the Shield Maiden Caelle as she entered the Hearthhold of those who ruled in Druintir, "Master Axennus Teagh, Ambassador of the Erelian Republic to Lindannan. And his brother, Captain Bronnus Teagh of the Ambassadorial Guard."

The Lady Cerriste rose from her seat, elegant, splendid, a smile upon her lips and a welcoming light brightening the grey of her eyes.

Lord Alvarion turned from Eldurion and Sarrane with whom he had been speaking. He smiled pleasantly, but the smile seemed not to reach his steely eyes.

Axennus Teagh bowed low before Lord and Lady, the silver chain of his office dangling loosely below his breast, catching and reflecting the ruddy flamelight of the Hearth.

At the Ambassador's side, the Iron Captain lowered himself on bended knee.

"On behalf of the people of the Erelian Republic," said the Ambassador, his eyes upon the floor of polished stone, "I extend to your Lordship and to your Ladyship the most sincere of gratitudes for the invitation to establish a Republican Embassy in glorious Lindannan, for the wonderful hospitality we have received, and for the magnificent White Manor with which you have so generously gifted us. Your kindnesses honour us greatly."

Lord Alvarion waved the words aside.

"Small things all, Ambassador." His voice was cool, infused with a hard softness.

"Be welcome, Masters Axennus and Bronnus Teagh of Hiridith," said Cerriste. Her own voice was gentle and feminine, but was no less possessed of strength, of salience, than was her husband's.

"Rise, friends," commanded Alvarion. "There are no thrones in Druintir."

Axennus straightened. He smiled faintly.

"Nor in Hiridith, Lord Alvarion, not for a long time – though I have oft opined that the Silver City could use one once more."

Bronnus rose, as did the hair at the base of his skull.

A singular gleam crept into the altostrati of Alvarion's eyes.

"Such an opinion is more appropriate than you can possibly know, Axennus Teagh of Hiridith."

Axennus did not comprehend the comment, but he knew hidden import lay in the Fiannian Lord's words. Elucidation, however, did not appear to be immediately forthcoming.

And so, "Not possibly, my Lord," he agreed quietly.

The Erelians gazed upon the two high ones of the Fiannar.

Each was tall and regal, possessed of subtle but sure majesty – austere, commanding, strong. Both were garbed in green and grey. Neither was overly adorned: The Lord with only a single wedding band about one wrist and the *rillagh* of the House of Defurien across his breast; the Lady with these and a simple golden necklace about her throat. Axennus was impressed by their modesty, their simplicity. And oddly, he felt more at ease in their presence than he had upon his awe-marked initial encounter with Caelle and her companions below Doomfall.

"I think, perhaps, we may forego formalities, Ambassador," suggested the Lord of the Fiannar. "You may call me Alvarion."

"And, please," spoke the Lady, smiling pleasantly, "I am Cerriste."

Alvarion gestured toward the Seer and the Marshal.

"You have made acquaintances with both Sarrane and Eldurion, I am told."

The Seer inclined her head toward the Erelians, and grey Eldurion nodded curtly, the light of the Hearth glinting in his eyes like sunlight on steel.

Axennus shivered inwardly as he recalled his recent abashment before the grim Marshal of the Grey Watch.

"I have, indeed. Call me Axennus, if you will."

"Bronnus," said the Iron Captain.

The Lord of the Fiannar nodded, and something of a sigh passed his lips. He seemed a man with many cares, both lesser and greater.

But his eyes were clear and cool, and his demeanor marked by a most steadfast calm. His voice was stolid, steady.

"My cousin tells me you are something of an historian, Axennus."

Cousin?

The Ambassador could feel Caelle's mischievous grin at his back.

Cousin?

Axennus' agile mind processed the information swiftly, efficiently, almost instantly, and then there came laughter to his heart, and light to his eyes.

"Evidently, the Shield Maiden is substantially more liberal in recounting the distinctions of others than she is in relating her own."

The Lady laughed.

"The Fiannar are not a boastful folk, Axennus." She gestured toward the loose ring of empty chairs. "Please, my friends, sit in comfort. Husband, some morningwine, if you would be so kind."

But the Shield Maiden waved Alvarion into his seat.

"Rest yourself, cousin," said she with a smile, and moved toward an aperture between two trunks of sylvan stone.

Lowering himself into a chair, the Ambassador sensed Caelle's presence depart the chamber, like the sough of a softly scented summer wind come and gone.

"A remarkable woman," Alvarion commented quietly, his grey gaze falling upon Axennus like that of a physician seeking a wound. A lone finger tapped the tattered scar tissue decorating one cheek.

The Ambassador lowered his eyes. "That she is," he agreed, his voice little more than a whisper.

Beside him, Axennus sensed Bronnus shift slightly in his chair. But Axennus knew his brother's discomfiture was one of mind rather than of body.

Alvarion's eyes seemed as grey and as distant as a clouded sky.

"There is more of our grandfather in my cousin Caelle than there is in my own self," the Lord mused. "A truth that serves us well in these darkened days. Did you know that the Shield Maiden counts among the Fiannar's strongest swords? Likely not. Remarkable as she is, my cousin remains a modest woman."

"Revelations abound, it seems."

"Indeed, Axennus. Indeed they do."

They sat in silence for an extended moment.

Grim Eldurion remained standing at his Lord's side, his eyes as cold and as gleaming as the bare blade in his belt. Sarrane drifted away, her presence but a brush of silk behind the eyes.

Alvarion peered at the Ambassador from above steepled hands.

Axennus felt as though his very soul was being probed, measured, weighed. He sensed intuitively that there was more to this interview than the cordial reception by one nation's rulers of another's appointed delegate. There was something deeper, and perhaps darker, to his host's intent.

"What know you of the history of our two peoples, Axennus Teagh of Hiridith?" asked the Lord Alvarion.

"Little enough," replied the Ambassador, wondering what possible purport the question might carry. "I know only that which is found in the old tomes, and that which the Shield Maiden has shared with me. Like their years, the memories of Men are far shorter than those of the Fiannar."

Lord Alvarion nodded once, twice – the first in acknowledgement of Axennus' response, the second indicating the dais of sculpted stone.

The dais was old, probably ancient, its intricately chiseled surface a chaotic collage of war, of battle between forms fierce and fair and shapes darksome and demonic, of pain and blood and death, but also of valour and of glory.

"A rendering of the Fiannar's final battle against Unluvin the Deceiver in the long and ruinous war for First Earth," explained Lord Alvarion, "before the coming of brave Vallian to the shores of this world."

"A beautiful piece," complimented Axennus, eyeing the carven rock with appreciation. The invisible fire of the cairnstones reflected upon his pupils, and a question rose in his mind.

"The firestones that burn upon the Hearth," said Alvarion, although the Ambassador had not spoken the question aloud, "like the stoneshine of the Hall of the Hallowed, are a gift from the Daradur. I know not how they burn with benefit of neither fuel nor source – the Stone Lords have an intimacy with the natural powers of the earth to which even the Fiannar are not privy. These firestones were gifted by the Daradur to my grandfather, he whose name I so undeservedly share, following the last great war against the Wraithren." He smiled grimly. "My grandfather was blessed or burdened with a black humour, thus due to its resemblance to the piled stones that oft mark a man's grave, he called this cairn 'Alvarion's Tomb'."

The Ambassador stared in attentive silence, seeking the elusive import of the Lord's words. He had read of the Wraithren, the legendary foe of the Fiannar. He had plunged into the old mythologies as a child, enthusiastic and eager for tales of adventure, giving little consideration to the historical accuracy of those stories of heroes and demons and the great wars of olde. The Wraithren. Were they the enemy that threatened the Fiannar of this day? Had they emerged from the murkish mists of mythos to march upon Druintir, last bastion of the Deathward?

Caelle returned with a flask and goblets.

Axennus accepted the light clear morningwine graciously, sniffing, sipping, then smiling in satisfaction.

"Candiorra White, thirty years old," deduced the Ambassador, "from the vineyards of the western Delta, from my father's own winery, or I am much mistaken."

The Shield Maiden smiled her confirmation, and offered the morningwine to the Lord and the Lady, who accepted, and to the Iron Captain, who did not. She did not extend a goblet to Eldurion, for she knew he would refuse it, nor to Sarrane, who remained aloof.

Caelle then took her place at her Lady's shoulder, standing straight and strong, one fine hand on the hilt of her sword, her fair face become a marmoreal masque of solemnity.

The Lord and the Lady of the Fiannar shared a brief glance that few might mark, a swift look which carried far more in a miniscule moment than words might ever do.

Lady Cerriste smiled approvingly.

Then, and so very slightly, Alvarion nodded.

"*Slan vitha sinn dri clannar.*" The Lord of the Fiannar raised his goblet. "To our two peoples. May we ever be as brothers."

"And sisters," said Cerriste.

"Ever and always," Axennus answered.

They drank.

Something of a shadow swam in the grey seas of Alvarion's eyes.

"My friends," said the Lord quietly, a cool edge to his voice, "we are bound by more than ancestral blood and olden histories. Oft that which seeks to divide only succeeds in uniting, for few are the ties that bind peoples more surely than the threat of a common foe."

"Few in times of peace." Axennus sipped. "None in times of war."

Alvarion fixed his grey gaze upon first one and then the other Teagh.

"Good Men of the South, I would tell you of the Wraithren."

The Ambassador gave Bronnus a quick glance of his own, to which the Iron Captain seemed entirely oblivious.

Ah, the Wraithren. We come to it at last.

And so, in a voice as wistful as a wisp of white winter wind, Alvarion spoke of the Wraithren and of the Fiannar's age-old fight against them, putting into prose the poetry of his father, the *Lay of the Fiannar* that the lost Lord Amarien had penned in his youth.

"Led by Lord Vallian, son of Defurien, the Deathward departed from the war-wrought ruin of First Earth, sailing a thousand tall ships across the seas of time and space, so bringing the few surviving Houses of the Fiannar and forty-four thousand war-weary souls to the shores of the Second World. But Vallian and his folk found only a land besieged and beset by evil not unlike that which had caused the devastation of First Earth, a world thrashed and threshed by the talons of terror and tyranny, where all but a few emerging civilizations of Men had been crushed under the maleficent might that afflicted them. The tribes of ancient Man, yet in their spiritual and intellectual infancy, were scattered and broken, suffering in sorrow beneath the shadow of the Wraithren who held dominion over the world.

"The Wraithren: Kings of War and of Demons and of Blood and of Death, ancient evil entities, sorcerous spirits of unknown origin, each with mastery over formidable and forbidden forces, each with his own massive armies to control and command.

"Kal-suruk, the Skull King, a skeletal shade armoured in steel, feasting on violence and the horror of war, ruled the northeast of Second Earth with an irresistible iron fist. Umun-dron, the Demon King, a baneful and bestial being that had mustered and marshaled demonic refugees of the ruination of First Earth, terrorized the southwest of the Second with fang and claw and wicked wing. Suru-luk, the Blood King, a vile vampiric creature that fed on the bloods of Men and monsters alike, rampantly ravaged the northwest of the world. And Zan-zurak, the Death King of the Wraithren, a phantom that ruled in silence and in shadow in the southeast, a great black wraith of near limitless power, of whom little was guessed and less was known, save only that he was the most formidable of the four.

"The vast armies of the Wraithren raged over range and river, savaging forest and field and fen, making mountain and meadow desolate. They were yet opposed by the defiant valour of the Rhelmen of the South and of the Rothmen of the North, fierce and fearsome folk who would have surely seen their own slaughter before they would have submitted to slavery and shadow.

"And that slaughter, it seemed, was but a matter of time.

"So the Lord Vallian drew forth the flaming brand of *Grimroth*, the Blade of Defurien, and led the Deathward into war once more."

And then Lord Alvarion rested, and the Lady Cerriste took up the tale, her voice like the caress of night, or as the sound of a tear sliding down a cheek.

"The Fiannar joined with the Rhelmen and the Roths and the rallied tribes of Men against the terrible tyranny of the Wraithren, and together they fought a great war for freedom, winning a glorious victory in the vale of Caen-al-Morra. The Wraithren fled into the distant East. A long peace ensued, halcyon days of healing and renewal. Vallian established the realm of Lindannan, where would sit the Lords and Ladies of the Fiannar, and Master Hiridion founded of the realm of Erellan, to be governed by the heirs of his House. Lord Vallian in his wisdom knew the respite would be overshort. The minions of the Wraithren were massing in the East, and the skies over those dark and distant lands was turned black with ash. So Vallian sent his son, Idallion, into the far places of the world in search of the fair folk of Gavrayel and Aeline, seeking the shining spears and singing bows of the Sun Lords and their bright white Knights. And the Deathward and the mustered might of Men marched to war once more, seeking to strike before Shadow became too strong, though Idallion had yet to return and had sent no word.

"So was fought the *Angar ban Maelmorradh*, the apocalyptic Battle of the Barrens, where the Fiannar and their allies suffered disastrous defeat, where fully half the Deathward's Houses were lost, and one hundred thousand bold Men were slain. Idallion and the Sun Lords of the Athair came to Maelmorra overlate, finding only the dead and the despair that watches over them. Turning away with tears in their eyes, they searched for the survivors of that slaughter. Vallian had fought a long retreat to Gan Innivir, the Valley of the Dreams in ancient Eldagreen, where it was decided amongst the Masters of the Deathward and the chieftains and kings of Men that they would fly no more, but would die there in that wondrous place, defiant to the end. The entire valley encircled by the enemy, the doomed allies sung sorrowfully as they summoned the strength for one last stand.

"And then was hope reborn, for Idallion and the Sun Knights of Gavrayel came to Gan Innivir, and a great battle was fought there between Light and Darkness, and Gan Innivir, Valley of Dreams, became Gan Gebbernin, the Valley of the Dead. But the Death King had withheld a great portion of his force until the coming of the Undying to the *Angar ban Gan Gebbernindh*, and he then unleashed all Hell's hordes upon the gathered armies of Light. There Lord Vallian fell, and Master Hiridion, and the Rothic High King Ri Connar was struck down, and the Sun Knights of the Athain Prince Yllufarr were mercilessly massacred.

"And then the very earth broke, and grief-maddened Idallion her-alded the end of all things, declaring the doom of the World, for from the rent earth rose yet another army, one of such might and power that neither Man nor Fian nor Ath might ever resist. This fearsome force fell into the fray like a storm of stone and steel.

"But then a strange and miraculous thing happened, for that army so horrible and hideous to look upon hurtled into the hordes of the Wraithren, hewing and hammering with a fury and ferocity never before seen upon this or any other World."

"So it was," rejoined Lord Alvarion, "that the mighty Daradur first rose from the dark bosom of Mother Earth to defend her from the depredations of those that would destroy her. And neither the Wraithren nor their servants could withstand this new foe, for sorcery could neither slay nor stay the Stone Lords, and to arrow, bolt and dart they seemed impervious. And in close combat the Daradur had – and have – no equal. Even so, the battle at Gan Gebbernin was not soon won, for the very vastness of the Wraithren's armies denied Idallion and his allies a swift victory.

"But in time, and with much sacrifice and slaughter, the Fiannar and their friends prevailed. The Wraithren fled the field, the remnants of their forces scattered, and the *Angar ban Gan Gebbernindh* was at long last won.

"And upon that field in the days that followed was sworn a pact between the Fiannar, the Athair and the Daradur that they would ever stand together in defense of Second Earth, though it would be nearly fifteen hundred years before they would rise again as one to meet the Wraithren in full-scale battle – but Mekkoleth on Sark-u-surum is another tale for another time.

"Fortunately, the Wraithren have long seemed unwilling or unable to act again in such concert as they did at the times of Maelmorra and Gan Gebbernin." Lord Alvarion's eyes shone strangely. "But times change, and things do also."

"In Erellan," Cerriste continued in her husband's stead, "Carrinthien, son of slain Hiridion, declared himself King, and tribal Man flocked to his crown and banner. And the Fiannar of the House of Hiridion took wives of the race of Man, for their own women were few and of close relation. So it was that over the next millennium the blood of the Fiannar in the South became so mingled with Man, that come the death of Te'arron, last King of Erellan, and the establishment of the Republic nearly one thousand years ago, the Erelian Fiannar were no more.

"The Erelian Republic and Mankind flourished while Lindannan faded, though the Fiannar of the North yet held, and still hold, the eastern marches against the Wraithren. Because of the vigilance of the Fiannar, and the indomitability of the Daradur in their eternal war with the demons of the netherearth, the peoples of the race of Man have been permitted to prosper in relative peace, warring mostly amongst themselves and for causes far less noble than the loves of Light and liberty."

Cerriste paused, looking first upon Axennus, then upon Bronnus, then back upon Axennus. Each felt that his worth was being closely considered.

"But it is as my husband has said," she concluded with a sigh. "Times change. Things must change also."

And then the Lady folded her fine hands upon her lap and nodded slightly. Lord Alvarion sipped at his morningwine. The tale was told. And both high ones of the Fiannar watched the Erelians with careful scrutiny, as though awaiting from the Southmen a specific reply, a particular response.

Silence.

Axennus searched for words. Found a feeble few.

"A fine tale, masterfully told. We are grateful."

Alvarion nodded. Cerriste smiled. At their sides, the Marshal and the Shield Maiden stood as still and as silent as the stone oaks etched into the walls. Somewhere on the periphery, the violet-rimmed eddies of Sarrane's eyes swirled soundlessly. The Fiannar waited.

Silence.

Axennus could feel his heart pounding in his breast, like a fist striking against his ribs from within. His mouth and lips were dry. His tongue moved to moisten them.

He sought words once again.

Found a few more. These, not so feeble.

"Lord Alvarion. Lady Cerriste. I suspect that war comes to Lindannan and the Fiannar. And I surmise with some certitude that it is the Wraithren who bring it."

Silence.

But for the gasp that passed the Iron Captain's lips.

The Lord of the Fiannar closed his eyes, then opened them, his gaze straying to the carven dais of the stone Hearth.

"See you there, my Erelian friends, the warrior with the horned helm in mortal contest with the great and horrible demon?"

"I do," replied the Ambassador.

Bronnus nodded but said nothing.

"The warrior is Hiridion. He was mighty among the mighty of the Fiannar of olde, and he slew in single combat one of the *kuarokur*, greatest of all Unluvin's servants of Shadow. As we have said, Hiridion sailed with Vallian, son of Defurien, from the ruin of First Earth and was the founder of Erellan, the ancient Southern Realm of the Fiannar of antiquity upon Second Earth. It is from him that the Silver City of Hiridith draws its name."

"This we know," said the Ambassador.

"The son of Hiridion's grandson's grandson was Te'arron, last King of Erellan before the forming of the Erelian Republic by Carrinthien the Second one thousand years ago."

"This also we know."

The Lord of the Fiannar leaned forward ever so slightly.

"It is from Te'arron, my Erelian friends, that your family inherits its name."

Time slowed.

Axennus' eyes widened. Wonder whitened his visage. Within him, heart and breath were stilled. Words failed him.

And a question glistened in his eyes.

"Yes, Axennus," Cerriste smiled gently in response to the Ambassador's mute query. "Your late father, Jophus Teagh, was the direct linear descendant, from eldest child to eldest child, of Te'arron, last King of Erellan and heir to the House of Hiridion. Were that noble House to yet exist, worthy Bronnus would be its Master."

The Iron Captain blinked dumbly.

The Ambassador's jaw fell slack, then shut tightly. In time, his voice, however strained, returned to him.

"Of this you are certain?"

Both Lord and Lady nodded solemnly.

Axennus' resourceful and resilient mind adeptly adapted itself to the bewildering truth of his heritage. The wonder in him swiftly transformed into pure and profound joy, a joy that soon awakened the intractable imp that had been slumbering peaceably in his soul. The grin that spread across the young Ambassador's face suggested a happiness approaching euphoria.

But there was nothing of gaiety in Alvarion's cold grey gaze.

"Ambassador Teagh."

The Lord's tone was grave, his features graven. The foregoing of formalities seemed itself foregone.

Axennus' glee deserted him instantly.

Beside him, the Iron Captain frowned with a dark foreboding.

The Lord of the Fiannar leaned forward, his shadow falling over the stone frieze of his forebears' war.

"Ever from the time of the South Kingdom's long slow slide into Republicanism and accompanying capitalism, and the thinning of its people's blood by the race of Man, have the Seers of Lindannan decreed that only with the reunion of the sons of the Houses of Defurien, Eccuron and Hiridion might the Shadow be lifted from Second Earth. The Fiannar have therefore taken great interest in the scions of Te'arron, awaiting the time that fate and circumstance might bring the three highest Houses of the Fiannar together once more."

"And months ago," furthered Cerriste, "did Sarrane, who is Seer now, approach us with counsel that the sons of the House of Hiridion would soon be in Druintir." Her eyes glittered. "And so you have come."

Axennus nodded woodenly.

"So we have come."

"And war is come also, Axennus of Hiridith," stated Alvarion flatly, directly. "The Houses of Defurien and Eccuron muster for battle with the Blood King at the Pass of Eryn Ruil." His eyes narrowed into grey slits of dawn at the breaking of night. "We would ask that the sons of the House of Hiridion stand with us upon the Seven Hills."

Silence. Short, succinct, poignant.

Then –

"There is no place, Lord Alvarion of the Fiannar," said the Ambassador with quiet solemnity, "that the sons of the House of Hiridion would rather stand."

But before either of the high ones of the Deathward could respond –

"Hold, brother," interceded the Iron Captain. "Though I do not forget our pledge to the Shield Maiden, I would have you arrest your haste here and not so readily heed these whispers of war. You would commit us to war without the certainty that this Blood King of the Wraithren even exists, or, should he exist, that we need fear him."

Bronnus turned to the Lord and Lady of the Fiannar, and the set of his face was stern.

"I intend no disrespect, but I believe only that which I see with my own eyes, and you tell tales of monsters and of sorcerers, things of legend best served to frighten insolent children at the falling of night."

Alvarion and his Lady wife exchanged a grey and gleaming glance, a question and its answer passing silently between them.

The Lord of the Deathward motioned to grim grey Eldurion.

"Dear Uncle, would you be so kind?"

The Marshal of the Grey Watch reached behind the stone chair of his Lord, and with some small effort he hefted forth the bulky leather bag that contained the thing Alvarion had received from Brulwar, Earthmaster of the Daradur, that it might serve as an instrument of persuasion, a tool to convince the skeptical. The bag's bottom was stained black, its sides stiffened with crusted ooze, and as Eldurion moved it a rancid reek seeped from within, the stench of decay and rotting death. The grim Marshal let the bag fall upon the table with a heavy thud.

"You have said, Captain Teagh," said Alvarion quietly, his eyes agleam with a hard humour, "that you believe only that which you see with your own eyes." He reached forward and knotted one hand in the blackened leather of the bag. "I do not bid you believe, Southman. But I do bid you see. *Behold!*"

And at a powerful jerk of his hand, Lord Alvarion snapped the sack back with such a violence that its content spilled forth – a single dark mass, very large and vaguely round, that wobbled weakly, then came to grotesque and gruesome rest in the center of the stone table.

The huge and hideous severed head of a Graniant stared at Bronnus Teagh with dead white eyes.

The Erelian Captain leapt to his feet, his hard face twisted into a mask of shock and horror, his chair crashing resoundingly to the stone floor behind him. The decapitated head's pale death-glazed gaze seemed to follow the startled Southman, investing him with an acute awareness of pure and pervasive evil. Even in the shriveling rot of death, the Graniant's malignant mien possessed malevolence in magnitude.

Beside the Captain, the Ambassador stared in wonder.

"What –" stammered Bronnus, his face as pallid as the drained flesh of the horrid thing before him, "– what is this...this abomination...this *demon*?"

Alvarion smiled grimly.

"Not a demon, Captain Teagh. But a Graniant. A stone giant from the shattered wastes beneath Earthfall in the eastern reaches of Second Earth. Long ago were they bred by the Wraithren through ill means, selected specifically for their cleverness and cruelty. The tallest of them can stand as high as the combined heights of four men, but most are closer to half that. They are uncompromisingly evil – slaves of Shadow to whom all life but their own means nothing. And many hundreds of them, perhaps thousands, now march upon Eryn Ruil."

The Iron Captain frowned.

"Should we join you, how do you propose we do battle with these giants?"

Alvarion's grey eyes glittered.

"You make every effort to avoid them," he replied. "You leave their dooms to the Deathward and to the Daradur who stand with us. Suffice to say, the Stone Lords are the foe that the Graniants most fear. Indeed, it was a Darad that brought this gruesome trophy from *Fongar ur Piruth* to Druintir, having taken it without expressed consent from the Graniant that was once so dearly attached to it."

There came a wry smile to the lips of the Ambassador.

"I would try my own strength against one of these Graniants."

But Lord Alvarion shook his head.

"To the Free Nations that choose to stand with us will likely fall the burden of holding the hordes of Unmen in check."

The Iron Captain's brows furrowed further.

"And these Unmen of whom you speak, what manner of creature are they?"

"They are the descendants of the Nundulla," replied the Lord of the Fiannar, "a race of hardy manlike beings that evolved alongside Man's own primitive ancestors. The Nundulla were of lesser intelligence than Man, though physically stronger and in some ways more cunning. But they were fewer and less prolific. Following the *Angar ban Maelmorradh*, the Wraithren took the Nundulla, twisted them, warped them, made them into the Unmen. The Unmen remain of inferior intellect, and their cunning has been torn from them and replaced with a mindless cruelty, but they have increased in physical strength, a might made insidious by hate and evil. Thrice in the past two millennia have the Unmen been brought to the verge of extinction – twice in wars with the Guardian Peoples, once in war with the Rothmen – and thrice have they rebounded in population and power. Marshal Eldurion informs me the most recent reports indicate that now ninety thousand Unmen march under the crimson banner of the Blood King upon Eryn Ruil and Eryn Drun."

An inaudible whistle passed Axennus' pursed lips.

Ninety thousand.

The Iron Captain scowled in storm-shackled silence.

Then spoke the Lady of the Fiannar:

"Captain. Ambassador. For two thousand years have the Deathward fought a long and costly war that some might reason is not our war to fight." Her eyes narrowed, gleamed. "The Fiannar fight for *you*. We fight for the Republic, for Nothira, for Rheln and for the High Kingdom, that these sovereign nations might thrive and prosper in peace. We now call upon the Free Nations to begin to assume responsibility for their own defence, to march to Eryn Ruil in force, that they might stand in faithful fraternity with the Fiannar, we whom have ever held the field against the hosts of Darkness in their name. We beseech you –

"Stand with us."

Axennus actually shivered.

Not so Bronnus.

"The Senate would say this war does not concern the Republic," stated the Iron Captain. "They would say that neither Erelian land nor people are at risk. Republican soldiers will not come."

"Republican soldiers are already here, Bron," responded Axennus from behind folded hands. "And as is ever their wont, the Senate would be sorely and severely mistaken. This war *does* concern the Republic. Very much so. You see, the beautiful embassy with which we have been gifted is by default of law Erelian property, and the land upon which it rests is likewise Erelian land, and abiding there are one hundred Erelian citizens. And as a sworn representative of my people, I am honour-bound to stand in their defense, and in defense of their property, let alone for what is indisputably *right*. Would you, a warrior of great strength and courage, counsel that we flee this land in shame and disgrace, and leave the Fiannar to fight for our newfound home? I think not. You would say '*Stand!*' I only say to you now, dear brother, that which you yourself would say to me."

The elder Teagh glowered, grunted, then shrugged, righted his chair and resumed his seat. He crossed his arms upon his chest, and his martial calm returned to him.

The Iron Captain met Alvarion's gaze with cool dispassion.

"I have one hundred warriors in my command. And you say this Blood King's army is ninety thousands."

The Lord of the Deathward nodded stiffly.

"Ninety thousand Unmen. But others march with them. Urkroks, Graniants, Wulfings of Var, Norian cavalry. One hundred and twenty thousand, all told. But the host is ill-marshaled, composed of several camps stretched over a great distance. The nearest sizeable cohesive mass numbers some sixty thousands. But they are early into their march, and we cannot yet be sure which forces will strike Eryn Ruil."

The Iron Captain stared for a moment at the sinister severed head of the Graniant, and for another upon the Hearth's stone relief of Hiridion in contest with the demonic *kuarok*. He then cast a grim glance toward the Shield Maiden, saw the light in her eyes, smiled despite himself.

You will ever have our swords.

"We will approach the men and advise that they stand with you in this thing."

Lord Alvarion nodded gravely.

The Lady Cerriste smiled graciously.

"We will send a rider to Hiridith," said the Ambassador, his innate enthusiasm texturing his tone. "There is little hope of convincing the Senate to march to war, and even less of any assistance from the Legion reaching Eryn Ruil swiftly enough to be of any service, but I will make the effort nevertheless."

But Alvarion shook his head.

"That will not be necessary, Ambassador. We have sent emissaries to each of the five Free Nations."

Axennus smiled strangely, and something sparkled in his eyes.

"Nevertheless."

Alvarion and Cerriste peered at the Ambassador, themselves now seeking secret meaning to the Erelian's words. They found none.

"Nevertheless," echoed Alvarion pensively.

Then the Lord and Lady of the Fiannar stood and put their fists to the *rillagha* at their breasts.

"You do honour to the name Teagh of Hiridith," Alvarion praised, "and to the lost House of Hiridion."

At the Lady's shoulder, the beautiful eyes of the Shield Maiden Caelle met Axennus' own, and hers sparkled with something akin to pride. Her father's eyes glinted at the Lord's side like slits of steel shining in the night. Sarrane floated behind them, the grey of her eyes enswirled by gleaming amaranthine.

The Ambassador smiled, rose, lifted his morningwine in silent salutation.

Bronnus stood as well, soldier-straight, solid, strong.

Then, and with some flourish, Axennus Teagh removed the chain from about his neck, peered at it with curious disdain, and extended it toward the Lord and Lady of the Deathward.

The chain's silver glittered in the strange lustrous light of the Hearthhold.

"Would you be so kind as to hold this in safekeeping for me?"

"Of course," said Cerriste as she accepted the heavy necklace. "But is this not the Erelian ambassadorial chain of office?"

"It is indeed," replied Axennus.

"Then why...?"

Axennus' smile was that of one returning home after too long an absence.

"Because, dear Lady, such a trinket does not flatter the Commander of the North March Mounted Reserve."

12

FAREWELLS AND FORESIGHT

"'Goodbye' is but a contraction of the phrase,
'The God be with you'.
Let it signify nothing else."

Colleareus, Master of Linguistics, School of Languages, Ithramis

T he soft sylvan shadowlight of day in Galledine was like an emerald dusk, deep and green and gentle. The song of bird and the whir of insect lent a lyrical lullaby to the murmuring melody of brook and stream, a soothing serenade summoning weary souls to slumber. To sleep and dream.

The Seer Sarrane slept upon a bed of leaves at the stoop of an ancient oak, her head resting on a root made soft by moss, her arms cradling her spear closely, almost lovingly, to her bosom. The Seer's breathing was slow and steady, and behind their lids her eyes moved restlessly, rapidly, as though she was searching in her slumber, seeking something in her dream.

And she moved there, through the mists of her dreams, very much as one would wade against water. Each step was slow and arduous as she slogged through the fog that fettered her in her sleep. The mists soon swelled and became a black rain, and her feet found themselves mired in muck, in a great dark ooze that strove to suck her down and swallow her.

Then her foot struck something and she stumbled, fell. Brackish mud splattered her hair, her face, her eyes. Her ears rang. A sour stench rose from the slime beneath her. And then she saw the obstacle that had caused her fall – the rotting, maggot-ridden corpse of a Fiannian warrior, his body ripped and ravaged, his *rillagh* rended in shreds. She stood as swiftly as the ooze allowed, retching in revulsion, the ringing in her ears rising to a roar.

And then the rain eased, and she saw the desecration of the Seven Hills, their splendour spoiled, savaged – a slaughterground of the dead and the doomed. The roar in her ears was the distant din of battle, of steel on steel, of men screaming, dying. The Hills and vales were become a mire of mud and blood, a fetid fen brimming with the broken bodies of Fiannar and *mirarra* and Men and horses, their limbs and torsos hacked and hewn, layer upon layer of corpses hammered and trampled into the reeking muck.

Sarrane shuddered, spitting the bitter taste of bile from her mouth. She fixed her gaze toward the war-wracked west, toward Cedorrin, her Seer's eyes straining to see in the murk. But she had been blinded by mud and blood, and all she saw was Shadow.

And then the deep booming roll of a thunderous voice carried clear and cold above the cacophony of war.

"Fly! Fly! Fly to the Fend!"

Tulnarron! gasped Sarrane into the damp dark everdusk. *Husband!*

She could feel herself sinking into the bog of blood at her feet, her body being sucked down, down, down into the rot and decay.

And then another sound came to her, a chaotic chorus of grief and dismay:

"The Fend is burning! Burning! The Fend is burning!"

Down, down, down into despair and ruin.

And then Tulnarron's throat pealed once more, a tempest of pride and power, defiant unto the end of ends.

"Stand! All ye Deathward souls! Good Men of the North! Stand! Stand and die well! And know at your doom that the Teller's Tale does not end here!"

Down, down, down.

Into darkness and death.

Sarrane woke to the wet touches of a cold nose and a warm tongue upon her cheek. Her eyes flicked open, fighting to focus in the foliage-filtered light of Galledine, their violet-ringed grey haunted by both horror and fear. Above her loomed the huge head and feral eyes of a great dark beast, its massive maw agape revealing rows of wicked white fangs. But neither the Seer's horror nor her fear was for the creature before her, but rather for the lingering images of her vision and for the perilous plight of her people.

Sarrane knotted one hand in the tangle of black fur at the beast's neck, and pulled herself to a sitting position.

Ah, Teraras, she sighed in her mind, *my fine and faithful friend. Would that I were not fey, that I was not compelled to see such things.*

Teraras, Alpha of the *warokka*, those ferocious and veracious war-wolves of the Fiannar, sat back on his haunches, cocking his great head to one side, his strangely intelligent eyes reflecting both care and concern. He was enormous, easily the size of a lion, his humped shoulder higher than Sarrane's hip. His pelt was iron-grey but for the great black leonine mane about his neck and throat, and beneath his close coat mighty muscles rippled like floes of stone.

The Seer ran her long fingers along the side of Teraras' large lupine snout. The *warok* growled gently in response. Sarrane's lips formed a small smile, and she stared into the gleaming silver lights of the war-wolf's eyes, past iris and pupil, into his soul.

War is upon us, old friend, she said silently, sadly. *Shadow marches on Eryn Ruil. The Fiannar will need you, will need the courage and strength of your kindred. We will need the* warokka *to fight for us once more*. Her soul sighed, an inner sough of sorrow. *Many, likely most, and perhaps all of you will die. But I would not ask this of you, Lord Teraras, were the need not most dire.*

The great war-wolf cocked his head to the other side, and a more menacing growl rumbled in his throat. A feral fire flamed in his eyes.

Sarrane's smile widened slightly, though her sorrow deepened.

Thank you, old friend, spoke her soul. *The Fiannar are ever grateful for the love and loyalty of the mighty* warokka.

The Seer stood. A single tear sprang from her damp eyes. The *warok* reared on his hind limbs, placing his powerful fore-paws on Sarrane's shoulders, and with a lap of his long pink tongue he licked the salty sorrow from the Fiann's fair face.

The Seer patted the fur of the *warok*'s flank as he fell back again to all fours.

"Go, Teraras, brave Lord of Galledine," she spoke aloud. "Go gather your kind. And should the Teller speak your end so soon into your tale, look for me, and we will meet again in the Light."

And Teraras, Alpha of the *warokka*, wolf-king of Galledine, padded off into the green glory of the Gardens. And as he went, a great howl burst from his bulking breast, echoed instantly in the descending dusk by dozens, scores, hundreds of other *warokkan* throats.

The great maned wolves of the north had been called to war.

Sarrane lingered briefly, listening to the war-song of the *warokka* until it fell again into silence, replaced at little length with the lilting lullaby of bird and buzzing thing.

Then the Seer of the Fiannar took up her spear and moved toward Druintir to bear the bodings of her vision to those who must know.

Alvarion stared out upon the dying day, the pale marble of the last city of the Fiannar shimmering faintly in the falling dusk and rising river-mist. Warriors of the Deathward were about in some number, the metal of their weaponry and the gold of their *rillagha* glinting dimly. And here and there moved the ghosts of the Grey Watch, unsleeping sentries of stealth and steel, shadows warding against Shadow.

Alvarion sighed. The Fiannar were so few – six thousands all told. And they were a dwindling people. Fewer and fewer children were being born, and of those most were male. His own son was four months old, and no Fiann had borne a child since the day of Aranion's birth. The Fiannar were failing – two centuries, perhaps three, and they would be no more. And war promised to quicken that certainty. It seemed to Alvarion that the Deathward were only too aptly named.

A small gurgling sound lured the Lord from his lament. He sensed a presence, no, two presences – one greater, one lesser, both familiar, both beloved – behind him. And then came the sweet velvet voice of she to whom he was forever sworn in body and mind and soul.

"Your son is restless, husband," said Cerriste quietly. "He senses that you are troubled."

Alvarion turned. The hardness of his eyes softened as he gazed upon his wife and child. They were beautiful – she lustrous of lock and long of limb, he a bundle of fair flesh and dark curls. And the grey of their wide round eyes was as polished steel.

The Lord of the Fiannar smiled.

"The days have been long, and the nights longer, my love," he said softly, almost apologetically. "Much has been accomplished. But I am eased in neither mind nor heart." His smile faded, fell. "I fear that I will bear witness to the failing of the Fiannar. Sarrane has seen our doom."

The Lady's brow darkened.

"Sarrane has seen no such thing, husband," she remonstrated. "Her vision was of blood and destruction, as must be all visions of war. A Seer's visions of the future are largely symbolic, metaphorical, and must be carefully interpreted lest we be overcome with unwarranted despair – or, perhaps more dangerously, false hope. That she heard the cry of the Fend aflame certainly cannot mean that Faendomin will burn." She then smiled coyly, saying, "Or is it another thing that bothers you so? Perhaps that Sarrane heard Tulnarron's voice rather than your own rallying the defenders of the Pass...?"

Alvarion grinned grimly.

"That was of some small, almost inconsequential concern to me, yes." His voice held the same dark humour for which his grandfather had been notorious.

Cerriste laughed lightly, waving one hand in dismissal.

"That a woman hears the voice of her husband in her dreams should be of no surprise to you, for to whom is a woman more connected than her spouse and children? That Sarrane did not hear your voice does not foretell your death, good husband. Rather, it speaks well of Sarrane's love for Tulnarron, think you not?"

The light of reluctant concession came to the Lord's eyes.

"Ah, woman," he sighed softly. "You gladden me so. But we dare not disregard the sight of our Seer."

"No, we daren't," agreed Cerriste. "We must understand what she has seen. But mayhap that understanding will only come with time."

"I only hope that such understanding is not overly tardy in its coming."

"Better late than not at all, husband." A strange smile touched her lips. "Much like a certain old friend."

Alvarion regarded his wife momentarily, then nodded.

"Ah. You speak of the Diceman."

"He rides with the Southmen, serving as their healer, and has done since the formation of the North March Mounted Reserve. That he has come here with them at this time of all times is not simple coincidence, husband. There is purpose to everything the Diceman does."

"He has yet to speak to us. We know nothing of his intentions."

"We know he is our friend."

"Yes," mused Alvarion. "That we do. But he has never fought beside us before."

Cerriste's lips twitched. "Not that we know of, husband. But the Diceman's ways have ever been...subtle. And we cannot pretend to know everything."

Alvarion's eyes narrowed. "Speak for yourself, woman."

Cerriste smiled lovingly and extended the infant Lordling toward her husband.

"Your son is become heavy, beloved, and your wife is old and weak and weary."

The babe Aranion made a laughlike sound as Alvarion took him tenderly into his strong arms.

"You neglect to mention that my wife is also haggard and hard on the eyes," chided the Lord.

The Lady laughed brightly. "And depreciating in value with the passage of every day."

Cerriste watched with adoration as Alvarion brushed his lips upon their son's soft brow. She allowed them a moment of perfect peace, the kind that is found in the bond of father and infant.

Then, "Let us go, husband. We will find Taresse, and deliver unto her your precious burden. Then we must attend our duties. Night falls, and many of our guests prepare to depart Druintir. We must bid them farewell."

Lanternlight glossed the stone walls of the Marshal's quarters with fluttering banners of tarnished gold. Despite the warm amber shadows, a chill crisped the sparely furnished chamber, an invisible breathless breeze. The run of the Ruil was a soundless song rumbling in the rock, deep and sonorous, like a threnody arising from terranean throats, a dirge to the departed. To the departing.

"You have decided?"

The timbre of Taresse's voice made the question a statement.

Eldurion nodded, but said nothing. He felt different, older. Other than he had once been. Less than he had once been.

"Varonin will perform the Marshal's duties well," affirmed Taresse. She stepped forward, fastidiously adjusting the clasp of her husband's cloak. "As ever, you have chosen wisely."

Eldurion looked over his wife's shoulder to the nondescript leather bundle on the table, shapeless and impotent, untouched somehow by the golding gloss cast by the lantern beside it.

Grimroth. The Blade of Defurien.

His now. His to wield. But asleep. Idle.

Impotent.

"You will speak with our daughter, husband?" Again, a statement.

And again, a nod.

Taresse placed her hand upon the clasp at Eldurion's breast. She peered upward into her husband's bright but strangely distant eyes. Within her, something shuddered, threatened to break.

"One might say farewell without saying goodbye, Eldie."

At last, the second son of the first Alvarion spoke, but his iron voice was become strangely soft, almost molten.

"Our customs can seem unnecessarily...harsh, at times."

Taresse shrugged. The movement was one of a younger soul, more of the daughter Caelle than of the mother Taresse.

"The life of the Fiannar is harsh," she replied, too casually. Something like mourning underlay her calm. Or perhaps mournfulness was her calm. "Our *world* is harsh." She lowered her hand but not her eyes.

Eldurion met Taresse's gaze, held it – or was held by it, bound by the sapphire sparks that spoke so eloquently, so very profoundly in the silvery silence of her irises.

"She has your eyes," the Eldest of the Fiannar said with a gentleness that none but his wife and daughter had ever heard pass his thin grim lips. He raised his hand as though to touch Taresse's cheek, hesitated, lowered it again. He saw his wife's eyes moisten, glisten. He stepped back, away.

And his wife whispered, "Eldie...beloved..."

But the former Marshal of the Grey Watch turned from her, from the appeal in her voice, in her eyes. He moved to the table, lifted the anomalous grey bundle and bound it to his back. He took his own sword in hand. And the steel hardened within him once more.

"Look to your own death, woman."

Taresse lowered her eyes, stared at her folded hands, saw them tremble. But they soon stilled, settled, and she stifled the plethora of passions assailing her soul.

And she said only: "You must promise me one thing, my husband."

Eldurion waited.

Taresse raised her gaze once more. Strength and defiance were etched upon her comely countenance as surely as runes riven in rock.

"Promise me that you will die well, Eldurion son of Amarien of the House of Defurien."

Eldurion spared himself a small smile, and a light as keen and as clear as madness flickered in his eyes.

"And you also, beloved wife."

Taresse actually laughed. "Of that, you may certain, dear husband."

And then she glanced toward the door.

Eldurion followed her gaze.

"Yes," said he. "They are coming for you, my love." His grey eyes were now impossibly bright, like silver slivers in stone. "They bring the child."

Taresse sighed. "So they are. So they do."

"Ward him well. And our daughter also, while you are able."

"I will."

Eldurion moved back to his wife, embraced her, bent low, brought his lips to her own one last long, lingering, loving time.

"Until the Light, my wife."

"Until the Light, husband," she whispered breathlessly.

And he was gone.

Night had gathered the Gardens of Galledine in a shroud of mist, a fine fog silvered by the mingled lights of starshine and moonsheen. Reared from the rush of the Ruil, the luminous mists seeped southward through the trees, gently swirling and seething about the broad trunks of maple and elm.

Somewhere near to the bank of the river, in a glade ringed by great and ancient oaks, were assembled the bright company of the Undying, those who had come to Druintir in the time of the Fiannar's need. They were fine and fair, the folk of Gavrayel from Gith Glennin – the Sun Lord Evangael, Prince of the Athair; his one-score Knights; and the white-locked Chancellor Ingallin. All were mounted upon glorious golden-maned *elliamir*, elegant equine entities of the First Earth, their star-white coats shimmering in the shadows. The Sun Knights wore the colours of their Prince Evangael, sky blue cloak and mantle over ivory-white armour, their long lustrous hair gleaming in the argentine gloom of night. Their spears were tall and terrible, a grove of shining steel leafed with colourful ribbon. About them was the silent sound of bells, the song of starlight, the whispered sigh of snow dancing in glow of moon. And above them fluttered fine silken pennons, swaying in the nightwind like soft angelic wings.

Before the Athair, astride their regal *mirarra*, were the Lord and the Lady of the Fiannar. Their countenances were clear and calm, carven of a solemnity not far removed from sorrow.

"We are grateful for your kindnesses, good folk of the Neverborn," spoke Alvarion, "though we are, as ever, saddened by your leaving."

"When we are able, and time and circumstance allow," appended Cerriste, "we will return your generosity, if not in kind, then certainly in intent."

"We have done little more than nothing, Lady," replied Prince Evangael, his voice a song, music in the night, "and far less than we are able. Reserve your gratitude for when my one thousand ride to Eryn Ruil, rather than for when my one score ride to Allaura."

Alvarion nodded grimly.

"I do pray the day will come when I may thank you for the ride of your one thousand to Eryn Ruil in my people's hour of need." The Lord's grey eyes gleamed. "*Will* you ride to us, Prince Evangael?"

The Sun Lord said only, "That is my intention and my desire, Lord of the Fiannar."

Alvarion sighed. "I wish for your desire to be fulfilled, good Prince, but doubt gnaws my heart, if only for the vision of my Seer. She saw the battle's ending hour – and the Athair had not come."

Evangael smiled curiously.

"Mindsight is a strange and fickle thing, dear friend," said the Athain Prince, his melodic voice as soothing as salve. "Believe in the rightness of your cause and the strength of your arm, and all will be made clear to you in time."

Alvarion nodded once more, sighed again.

"In time," he echoed softly.

Prince Evangael turned to his twenty Sun Knights, and to the Chancellor Ingallin mounted upon an ostentatiously bejeweled *elliam* off to one side and slightly apart the company.

"In my absence, command of the *Sul Athaifain* falls to First Knight Lalindel, who in turn shall hear the counsel of Prime Consul Ingallin. First Knight, listen carefully to that counsel."

Lalindel met Evangael's golden gaze, bowed his head.

"I will hear him, my Prince."

The other Sun Knights did not stir, and no emotion played upon their fair faces. The bright eyes of the Athain warriors reflected the lights of moon and star as dispassionately as would clear still waters. They said nothing. And there was acceptance, if not approval, in the synchronicity of their silence.

And then the Sun Lord Evangael turned to the Prime Consul Ingallin. The former Ath's mien was stern and stolid, the latter's shrunken and sullen.

"Sulk not, Chancellor," commanded the Prince. "Your duties are to make ready Allaura for our guests and to accommodate them with the hospitality which is due them. Perform these responsibilities with all care. I will advise His Majesty of your new concern, and of the cause of this appointment."

Ingallin pushed a shock of winter-white hair from his brow.

"I cannot promise, my Prince," said he, a soft serpentine hiss to his voice, "that His Majesty will be well-pleased."

Evangael smiled. And his smile was as cold and as bright as a midwinter morn, as passionate as a soul-sworn oath.

"Nor I, Chancellor. But I can promise any displeasure the King may display will not be for *me*."

The implication in Evangael's words was explicit, as was the warrior's ire simmering in his golden eyes. Ingallin's ungraciousness in Hollin Tharric, his deception and dissention at the Stone of Scullain, had not been forgotten – and word of these failings would not pass the King's ear unspoken.

Ingallin lowered his head.

"I will do as you bid, my Prince," said he quietly. A smile, small and bereft of both joy and humour, played upon his pink lips. "The Laws of our folk must be upheld."

The Sun Lord stared at the Chancellor for a moment, seeking hidden meaning to the sallow Ath's words. But Ingallin did not deign to meet his gaze, and Evangael detected untruth in neither the Prime Consul's deference nor his demeanor.

"Very well," spoke Evangael at length. "Ride with speed, Chancellor."

And then to his loyal Sun Knights –

"Ride, *im Sul Athaifain!*" Evangael raised an open hand in farewell. "*Ya'Iu en inte vui! Dhir!*"

And the Lord and the Lady of the Fiannar put their fists to their *rillagha*.

"Fare well! Fare free!" cried Cerriste.

"May your tale not go untold," extoled Alvarion.

And the Sun Knights of Prince Evangael turned like fluid starshine and flowed into the trees of Galledine, a procession of power, the soundless music of Light playing in their passing.

Ingallin lingered for a moment, raised his gaze to Evangael's, and smiled. But his smile was more an underscore of the coldness in his eyes, a curving not far from contempt. And he said only, "My Prince," then turned with a jingle of jewelry and slid into the shadows of the night.

"A strange and disturbed soul, that one," mused Alvarion after the darkness had closed about Ingallin. "All bitterness and venom."

Lady Cerriste was more direct: "The King's Chancellor has been touched by the Shadow."

Prince Evangael of the Athair peered toward the blackness into which Ingallin had gone, and the light of the Sun Lord's golden eyes dimmed.

"Ingallin is of the Forgiven," he explained softly, "those folk of fallen Asrayal, they whom Gavrayel absolved, whose sins were shriven by him, but whose shedding of Athain blood goes not unremembered."

"Ah," understood Alvarion.

But Cerriste's eyes narrowed. "Is he to be trusted, Prince Evangael?"

The Sun Lord remained staring into the darkness of Ingallin's departure.

"He can do no harm in Allaura," Evangael replied at length. "He will receive your people warmly, and will abide by the Laws of Gavrayel, laws which he himself shared in the making. Your sanctuary is assured."

"Yet you seem troubled, my friend," Cerriste observed coolly.

Evangael paused before replying. Then, "Ingallin is an Ath foresighted," he revealed. "I believe he has seen something that he has not chosen to share."

The three sat mounted in a protracted silence.

Then Alvarion shrugged.

"You have said, good Prince, that mindsight is a strange and fickle thing. Should I, as you have advised, not concern myself with the shadows of a yet unfolded future, then nor should you."

The Sun Lord smiled slowly, beautifully.

"Verily, Lord of the Fiannar, verily. You possess the cunning of your grandfather, whom I knew and loved well."

Alvarion sighed. "Would that I possess also his strength and courage."

Cerriste's own sigh was one of impatience.

"Enough self-flagellation, husband." She sniffed the dampening night air. "A storm comes, and we have tarried overlong. Let us remove north of the Ruil to Ravenwood where those who carry our greatest hope await our farewells."

Chastised accordingly, Alvarion sent Evangael a daring wink, and the Ath's answering laugh was the sound of Light itself.

They then turned their splendid steeds about and rode with swiftness northward into Galledine's besilvered night.

The night upon the Field of Cedorrin was at its deepest and most dark, and black rain-bloated cumuli had rolled swiftly in to blot out both moon and star. Far below the heavy storm-swollen skies, essentially invisible in the darkness, two broad and burly figures descended the long flowered slope of Cedorrin. They moved with a surety that belied the absence of light, and about them was the silence that oft accompanies great strength. Then, where Cedorrin met the gap between Warwatch to the north and Sentinel Ridge to the south, the pair halted.

"The storm gathers, brother," grumbled Brulwar, Earthmaster of the Wandering Guard, his black *inrinil* greatcoat billowing in the risen eastwind. He rested his massive forearms upon the equally huge heads of his hammer. "When it falls upon us, we must weather it without breaking."

Drogul the *kirun-tar* nodded silently, and folded his monstrously muscled arms across his chest. His ink-black eyes stared eastward into the wind, peering past the night-shackled Seven Hills into the deep dark distance. He did not speak.

"Doomfall must hold, brother," Brulwar emphasized, eyeing the tempest brewing in the night skies, the smoothness of his voice the still of his own inner storm. "At all costs."

The Mighty One only nodded once more. The wind whipped at his hair and beard, roughly ruffling his mantle of wolf's fur.

"Young Rundul bears a grievous burden," continued the Earthmaster, accustomed as he was to the Chieftain's reticence. "Maiden Earth is strong within him. But the *urthvennim* is a potent and powerful poison. Rundul will need aid." He paused, his deep black eyes scanning the grasses at his feet. "I will arm him in such a manner as to ensure the *urthvennim*'s negation."

There followed a short silence, complete but for the rush of the wind through the grasses of Cedorrin.

Then, "Rundul will succeed," Drogul stated plainly. "Not every Darad is bound to fail in his given quest."

Brulwar frowned blackly.

"Your mission into the polar north was not an utter failure, brother. That the *urthrath* refused you does not speak to any unworthiness in you, but rather to my own deficiencies in both understanding and judgement. A weaker Darad refused by the *urthrath* would have been destroyed, but you have returned with the knowledge of *how* the Fury of the Earth is to be harnessed." The Earthmaster placed a strangely gentle hand upon the Mighty One's broad shoulder. "Come this war's end, another will be sent, brother. One whom I am confident the *urth-rath* will not deny." He followed the Chieftain's gaze eastward. "Then we shall see."

Another nod.

"But now we will tend to the troubles at hand," Brulwar vowed.

Nod.

"Make all haste to Raku Ulrun, brother, where Dulgar marshals the *mara Waratur* in your absence. Send Gulgrum to Druintir with fifty Wandering Guard. Then prepare for war."

One last nod that malleably morphed into a slow shaking of the head.

"Who's the Chieftain here, you or me?" grumbled the Lord of Doomfall.

Brulwar's black beard parted in a white grin. His hand dropped from Drogul's shoulder to grasp the Mighty One's forearm in firm and fond farewell.

"Stone and steel, my Chieftain."

Drogul gripped the Earthmaster's forearm in return.

"Stone and steel, brother."

And then the *kirun-tar* moved toward the break between Warwatch and Sentinel Ridge, slipping his great black war-axe from its strappings as he went. And as he left Cedorrin and entered the Seven Hills, the Mighty One broke into a run, a juggernaut of the night racing to war.

Somewhere above, thunder rolled ominously in the storm-swollen skies.

The ghostly warders of the Grey Watch that saw the great Daradun warrior enter the Seven Hills – lands forbidden to all but the Fiannar – made no move to stay him, but only marked his passing with a degree of dour dismay.

The mightiest warrior of all Second Earth would not be standing with the Deathward at Eryn Ruil.

Brulwar lingered momentarily, listening to the long rumbling peal of the nightbound heavens. He then stooped to retrieve a small stone from the grasses at his feet. Slipping the rock into the folds of his greatcoat, he hefted his huge war-hammer to his shoulder, summoned the power of Maiden Earth within him, and sank swiftly from sight into the fertile soil of Cedorrin.

And then the storm burst.

The rain fell from night's enraged firmament at a hard angle, raking into the squinted eyes of the three riders like little slivers of iron. The trio carefully picked their way along the narrow stone path between the rising rock of Warwatch and the crashing rush of the River Ruil. The stone was slick with rain, and the going was slow and perilous, the shod hooves of the roan stallion and those of the grey mare slipping and sliding intermittently. The heavy oilskin cloaks in which two of the men were closely wrapped shielded them from the greater bite of the driving rain, but their faces, bent low within the refuge of their cowls, were already raw with wet and wind and cold. The third horse, an amber stallion, was surer of hoof, and its rider rode upright and capeless, his muscular chest and arms naked to the rain.

The threesome made their way past the towering rock of the Warwatch to the foot of the forested hill directly eastward, and there they halted beneath the shelter of a mighty stand of maple.

The man on the roan glanced upward dubiously, rivulets of rain running from the rim of his cowl.

"Should we not beware of lightning here?" the Iron Captain asked, an uncharacteristic trace of trepidation to his tone.

"Hardly, brother," replied Axennus as he wiped rain from his eyes. "There are places higher than here that would draw the wrath of the storm. We are more likely to be stricken with exposure than we are with lightning." He looked to the third man. "You will excuse my brother's perturbation, Left Tenant. The Captain yet harbours a neurotic fear of thunderstorms – a trait he shares with the family cat."

Bronnus scowled.

Runningwolf paid the brotherly banter no heed.

"The white fire of the storm will not fall here," he stated with the self-assured stoicism of his people.

An incoherent grumble issued from Bronnus' throat, the sound of a stubborn and lingering doubt, but the Captain trusted the word and wisdom of the Rhelman – if not that of his own brother – and he did not pursue the point.

"It is most unfortunate that you must depart in such foul weather, Left Tenant," Axennus apologized, "but an hour is as a day, and a day is as a year, and word of war must be brought to Hiridith as quickly as possible."

The Rhelman shrugged.

"The rain causes me no concern, Commander," he said flatly, his alien voice seeming even stranger amidst the surrounding sounds of the storm. "I mislike only leaving your side in time of battle."

"You are our swiftest rider, Left Tenant," Axennus stated simply.

"And our most dependable," added the Iron Captain. "Should any man among us be capable of reaching the Silver City and returning in time to engage the enemy at Eryn Ruil, that man is you."

Runningwolf shrugged once more.

"As you wish."

The Commander reached within the folds of his oilskin, and brought forth a small square package, extending it toward the loamy-eyed Rhelman.

"A token from Guardsman Draconarius," he explained. "He wanted you to have it. He said you would understand."

The Rhelman accepted the leather-bound packet wordlessly, slipping it into the roll bound behind him.

"And I give you this, Left Tenant," said the Iron Captain, removing his silver battle horn from his shoulder, "to hold until such time as we meet again." A rare smile softened his hard countenance. "I look forward to the day when next I hear its silver song."

Runningwolf hesitated only a moment before taking the Captain's battle horn and sliding its strap over his bare shoulder. He then bowed his head, and raised his leather totem pouch to his temple.

Axennus and Bronnus put their fists to their hearts.

And with no further word, the Rhelman nudged Featherfoot about, and rode into the wind and the rain and the dark of the cold northern night.

Night was approaching the small black hours before dawn when the worst fury of the storm passed, its electrical rage flashing farther to the west, followed some moments later by the muffled rumble of thunder over the High Land. Beneath the imposing rise of Rothrange, where the Ruil angled south and away from the mountains, sprawled the dark tangled wedge of Ravenwood. The last surviving remnant of Eldagreen, the ancient forest that had once spanned the northern Middle Land from Eryn Ruil to the Peacekeepers, Ravenwood was a place of stillness and shadow, where epigeal mist crept, writhed, swirled through the twisted labyrinth of hoary root and mossy trunk, like the sorrowful soul of devastated Eldagreen seeking her lost and forgotten eminence.

And assembled there, in a small clearing in the befogged eaves of Ravenwood, were gathered the great ones of the Deathward – the noble Lord and Lady of the Fiannar, the taciturn Master and Mistress of the House of Eccuron, the Shield Maiden Caelle and grim Eldurion.

"You may inform Varonin," spoke the latter to the Lord and Lady of his people, "that he is Marshal of the Grey Watch now. He will serve you well."

"It will be done," Alvarion responded quietly.

Eldurion nodded curtly. The Eldest of the Fiannar was very much his father's son, his brother's brother, and his nephew's uncle – tall and strong, determined, though dourer of nature and of a keener pride. He was cloaked and cowled in grey, the gold of his *rillagh* concealed within the dull cladding of his traveler's trappings. He held his long sword in one hand, the cold steel of its naked blade greased black against gleam and glitter. A far greater weapon was wrapped in inconspicuous leather and strapped at his back – *Grimroth*, the Blade of Defurien. He bore no other burden. His was to lead the company through Coldmire and to slay the Blood King. Each was burden enough, and both would demand all the agility his body might command.

Then spoke Tulnarron:

"Beware the Moor Walkers, Eldurion. They have been seen near the southern marges of Coldmire by both your warders and my warriors, but they do not leave the fen. Though they have raised no hand against us, they may be spies of the Wraithren, and possess some considerable skill or sorcery, or they would not have been able to elude us for so long."

Eldurion nodded once more.

"Marshal."

The voice was that of Sarrane, wife to Tulnarron and Seer of the Fiannar.

The Eldest of the Deathward looked upon the Seer, and he saw the strange swirl of her eddied eyes, knew that she had seen something that he had not seen, that he could never possibly see.

"Marshal no longer, good Seer," he corrected, his voice cool and cautious.

Sarrane disregarded the correction completely.

"The road you take is fraught with foes, Marshal," said she. "But even in the most hostile of places, and among the most bitter of enemies, one might find a friend."

Eldurion nodded again, storing the Seer's words for a future time, when their wisdom might become more apparent.

Then spoke the Lady Cerriste, saying only, "My love to you, dear Uncle."

"And mine to you, my Lady," he replied.

Of the gathering of Deathward in the darkness of Ravenwood, only Caelle, daughter of Eldurion, said nothing.

Nearby, at the trunk of a towering redwood were assembled the Athain Princes Evangael, Thrannien and Yllufarr, noble Sun Lords all.

"I remind you to not exceed your duties, my brother," spoke golden Evangael. "The Illincarnadine is the Darad's. The Blood King is Eldurion's. Yours is but to enable our friends to perform these worthy feats, and to keep removed the Blood King's eyes from the North."

"There are those in Coldmire who will not appreciate your presence there," advised Thrannien. "Though you will surely hear them, do not heed the voices in the fen. Leave the winsome ghosts of the Unforgiven to their wanderings."

Yllufarr's oddly achromic eyes swam with pale light.

"The Teller's Tale be told," he replied softly. There was a darkness to his voice deeper than the black of night.

"His Tale be told," echoed Thrannien.

And the three Athain Princes joined hands in a triangle of Light and Love, and ancient eldritch power pulsed through them, puissance that in the World to come would be reserved for angels in Heaven alone.

And some distance away were Brulwar and Mundar and Rundul of the Wandering Guard, mighty of the Daradur.

"There's nothing right in this world," complained Mundar of Duldarad, his black eyes glowering beneath their thick blond brows. He folded his huge arms defiantly across his massive chest. "Not only does this mudfucker rise in rank due to luck and happenstance, and maybe some marginal skill with the axe, but he's then sent upon a mission crucial to the fate of the world, while I'm appointed guide and minder to a flock of whining women and snot-nosed children." He growled something as incoherent as it was foul. "Tell me, *uldwan Dor*, where's the justice?"

"The Daradur create their own justice, young Warder," returned black Brulwar of Dangmarth patiently. He well knew Mundar's gentle love for the Fiannar, specifically of their women and children, a love only made greater for the Daradur's lack of women and children of their own. "Where we will it, we will find it."

Mundar grumbled something that might have been "Captain Rundul, my fuckin' ass..."

Rundul's dark beard parted in a wide white grin. Despite Mundar's bombast and brashness, Rundul knew his voluble friend was immeasurably gladdened for him, and that the Warder's protest was pretended.

"Take care, *Warder* Mundar," chided Rundul, "lest envy stain your beard a permanent green."

"Bah!" dismissed Mundar, struggling against a smile. "I envy you only the obvious but inexplicable favour of our Chieftain."

And Rundul smiled in reverie.

For earlier that day he had been summoned to walk with Drogul in Druintir –

They strode in silence through the marble streets of the sun-washed city, admiring the stonecraft of the Fiannar, their black eyes gleaming in approval for the skillfully chiseled statuary, the finely formed fountains, the single continuous carving that was Druintir of the Deathward.

The men and women of the Fiannar left the pair of Daradur unmolested, the earlier euphoria of the Deathward for the coming of the Mighty One replaced by a more reticent reverence, their grey eyes agleam with a forlorn hope. Some of the smaller Fiannian children had approached, fair faces bright with wonder, and were received with quiet kindness by the legendary Lord of Doomfall. They held his huge hand, touched his great black war-axe, then sped off to boast of the encounter to their families and friends. Such was the extent of their esteem for Drogul the *kirun-tar*.

Rundul's own esteem for his Chieftain was not far removed.

The two Daradur tarried in their tour at the base of Muldarron's Monument, a realistic rendering in rock of the allegiance between the three Guardian Peoples and of their avowal to stand united in defense of life and land and liberty. The skilled hands of Muldarron had deftly depicted an Ath, a Darad and a Fian positioned in a tri-angular formation, back to back to back: The first lowered to one knee, an arrow nocked upon the bent string of his long bow; the next bristling with battle-fury, a war-axe in one hand, a huge hammer in the other; the last wielding a broad-bladed greatsword, a war horn raised to his lips.

"The Ath is the Sun Knight Andriel," the Daradun Chieftain said, his rough voice infused with a quiet respect. "He was slain upon the field before the black gates of Mekkoleth on Sark-u-surum. The Fian is Ferraron of the House of Eccuron, father to Muldarron. Ferraron fell also at Mekkoleth on Sark-u-surum." Drogul turned his dark gaze from the Monument to the Warder beside him. "And the Darad is Rokkundar, whom I knew well, and who returned to Earth the Mother on the final day of battle at Mekkoleth. Rokkundar was a great warrior who never ran from nor turned his back to enemy blades."

Rundul lowered his head to keep secret the shame stinging his eyes. The bruise on his back burned then, searing past flesh and bone into his soul – the eternal brand of his betrayal. Despite the honour that had been paid him by the high ones of the Fiannar, no amount of remorse or regret could ever return to him his dignity. Such disgrace could never be justified, never be forgiven.

"But then," Drogul considered, a white gold glinting where the midday sun met his midnight eyes, "Rokkundar was not in the belly of the Bloodshards four days ago. He did not see what you saw."

For against this thing he knew he could not stand.

Rundul raised his eyes to those of his Chieftain.

"There are many definitions of courage, young Warder," Drogul said. "Is it nobler to die a warrior's death and keep intact one's honour than it is to sacrifice that honour for the survival of unnumbered thousands at the risk of one's own lifelong shame? What would I have done in your stead? I cannot say. But the customs of the Daradur are very clear on this matter, and leave me with little to consider."

Rundul lowered his eyes once more, the shame that seared his soul burning at their corners. Drogul *did* know. Of this, Rundul was certain. The Mighty One would not have turned from the *kuarok*.

"I therefore have no choice, Warder Rundul," the Chieftain continued, his voice completely devoid of emotion, "but to promote you to *kor uri Waratur* – Captain of the Wandering Guard. When next the *kumman ur Korr* sit in council, Captain Rundul of Axar will be welcome to sit with them, the first and only Darad not of the Firstmade to hold such honour."

Rundul stood dumbfounded, his mouth falling agape in astonishment.

The Mighty One's thick moustaches twitched with the suppression of a smile.

"We are a people made of Earth and Fire, Captain, a people gifted with War and Love, and these latter two need not be mutually exclusive. You have proven this. Your deeds in the Bloodshards define selfless love for kith and kin, and for the Earth herself, and can go neither unacknowledged nor unrewarded. Wear the mark upon your back with pride, Captain. It is the brand of a courage unsurpassed by any Darad that has gone before you."

Rundul blinked in disbelief.

"And," Drogul the *kirun-tar* furthered, "a mission such as the one upon which you embark tonight for New Ungloth must be undertaken by a Darad of no lesser rank than Captain." A smile finally broke past the Mighty One's heavy beard. "So you see, Captain, as I have said, I am given no choice in the matter."

Rundul's burning ceased, though his eyes yet stung, but of a cause polarly removed from shame.

Absolution.

Rundul managed a mute nod, the sole expression of his acceptance and gratitude.

The Mighty One grasped Rundul's shoulder strongly, assuringly.

"I will not be with you in Ravenwood this night, Captain," Drogul rumbled lowly. "I must depart for Raku Ulrun where Dulgar awaits me with some impatience. But I will leave you with this, bold Rundul – the *urthvennim* must be neutralized. Brulwar will give you the power to do this, though it may seem inconsequential, even impotent, when he does so. Hear and heed the wisdom in his words, Captain, and when the time comes, the way will be made clear." The sheen of the Mighty One's black eyes seemed shadowed with something akin to sorrow. "The answer lies in your own self only, my brother. *You will not fail.*"

Releasing him, and with no more said, the great Chieftain of the Wandering Guard of the Daradur turned from Rundul and moved away into the sculpted stone of the city.

Staring into the stone eyes of long-dead Rokkundar, Rundul of Axar, Captain of the *mara Waratur*, stayed standing where he was, silent and still, slowly recovering from the stupefying shock of his absolution.

Breath in, breath out. Willing his hammering heart to slow.

I will not fail.

In the blackened murk of Ravenwood, Rundul smiled at the memory. There were no medals, no stripes, no insignia of any sort to mark his rise in rank. The Daradur, regardless of their regiment, wore no uniforms, bore no symbols to signify their individual status or bond of service. Their inherent aura spoke to others of their race of these things for them. Beyond that, no more was necessary.

"Favour, indeed," echoed Rundul. "But fret not, brother Mundar. The day might come that you surpass me. Ungrgoth, demesne of the *dwar-Durka* and the demon hordes, remains hidden. Perhaps it is in your destiny to have a hand in the finding of that abominable place, that the besiegers might themselves become the besieged."

Mundar grinned and an odd light oscillated in his obsidian orbs.

"Ahhh," mused the blond-bearded Warder of the Wandering Guard. "A fine and fitting fortune, that, and one well worthy of me.......
Captain."

Whether Mundar's closing word was in recognition of Rundul's recent rise in rank or for the garrulous Warder's envisioning of his own possible promotion, Rundul did not – and would never – know.

"The time is upon us, my brothers," interjected Brulwar, his voice as smooth as polished obsidian. "You must depart now, Captain. The horrors of New Ungloth await you, and the way there is long and hard. Yours is to guide your companions from Coldmire to the cavern of the Blood King, and to render impotent the *urthvennim*. In the former you must rely upon your own knowledge and experience, but in the latter I give you some little assistance."

The Earthmaster removed from a fold in his greatcoat the small stone he had retrieved from the grasses of Cedorrin. He held it forth upon his open and heavily calloused palm. There it rested, small and grey, no more spectacular than any other little chunk of rock.

Rundul peered closely and curiously at the stone. He then frowned doubtfully, and raised his gaze to the Earthmaster, an unspoken question in his eyes.

"The *urthvennim* may be negated only through the spirit and strength of Maiden Earth, Captain," explained the First Made of the Firstmade. "And Maiden Earth resides in this rock. You need only cast it into the pool of the *urthvennim*, and Maiden Earth will see the evil destroyed."

Rundul blinked slowly. Any misgivings he may have had faded, fell away. The word of the *uldwan Dor* was ever irrefutable, beyond all circumspection.

The Earthmaster took Rundul by one wrist, opened the Captain's hand and placed the stone upon his palm. Rundul closed his thick fingers about it. Brulwar then wrapped his own hard hands about the Captain's fist.

"You will not fail, my brother." The Earthmaster's statement was as the seal of his soul, an oath unbreakable. "The power is within you."

Rundul of Axar, Captain of the Wandering Guard, nodded. He slipped the stone into his *inrinil* tunic, secreting it close to his heart.

You will not fail.

"As you deem it, *uldwan Dor*, so it will be done."

Mundar of Dul-darad veritably beamed with empathetic joy and pride.

The Earthmaster returned the Captain's nod, then turned to where the Fiannar and the Athair had come together and now awaited the Stone Lords.

"We're ready," Brulwar called into the blackness of Ravenwood.

Rundul hefted his ponderous pack, shrugged his massive shoulders into its bindings, took up his great war-axe and, with Mundar at his side, followed Brulwar to the awaiting ennead of Athair and Fiannar.

Lord Alvarion greeted the Daradur with a small nod, weariness evident in the lines about his eyes.

"I am told some congratulations are in order, Captain Rundul," he smiled dimly. "I can think of none more worthy."

Rundul nodded, brought his fist to his chest.

Alvarion's eyes then swept across the gathering of great ones before him. Even he, noble Lord of the Deathward, seemed humbled in that mighty company.

"There is little left to say, my friends. Know only that our gratitude for the friendship of the Stone Lords and for that of the Neverborn knows no bounds. Your aid in this, the great test of my time, will not go unremembered."

"We shall all be tested, old friend," responded Evangael. "None more so than those who now embark upon this unenviable journey to New Ungloth."

"Well said, good Prince," said the Lady Cerriste. "Though they seek the place of gravest peril, they carry with them our greatest hope."

"And this hope is ever fragile," Alvarion added, his fatigued eyes flicking from Rundul to Yllufarr to Eldurion, "and relies upon absolute stealth and secrecy. Suru-luk's spies are about and abroad, but are likely to avoid the bitter bogland of Coldmire. Once within that morass, assuming the Moor Walkers have not allied themselves with the enemy as Master Tulnarron fears, you should be safe from the Blood King's many eyes. The *throkka* will patrol the skies above you, and that you go afoot will allow you to avoid the attention that mounts would surely draw. But you must refrain from all use of magic and Maiden Earth, and especially the Blade of Defurien, lest those powers swing the Blood King's awareness toward you. You must depend upon the mights of mind and muscle alone – and upon one another as surely as those who do not go with you depend on you."

The grim former Marshal of the Grey Watch stepped forward then, his eyes but points of cold light within the blackness of his cowl. He looked first upon Tulnarron and Sarrane, then upon Cerriste and Alvarion, all of whom he acknowledged with the slightest of nods.

Lastly he looked upon Caelle, his lovely and loving daughter – the greatest joy in the three long centuries of his life. He raised one hand to her cheek, then bent to kiss her beautiful brow, strangely gentle gestures for such a decidedly ungentle man. But he spoke no words, and a moment later he turned his back upon his child, his folk and his friends, and slipped away and eastward through blackbound Ravenwood toward the wet and wintry wastes of Coldmire.

The Shield Maiden's round blue-flecked eyes grew large as they followed the form of her father vanishing into the firs of the forest, into the Wilderness. Each of the Fiannar there knew, and Caelle better than any, that whether in success or in failure, Eldurion of the House of Defurien, Eldest of his folk, would not be coming again to Druintir of the Deathward. Caelle felt first Cerriste's then Sarrane's hand slide into her own. She swallowed against the threat of a swelling tear.

The Fiannar do not mourn.

Alvarion looked away from the place of his uncle's departure into the trees. His dry grey eyes fell upon Rundul of the Wandering Guard.

"So, Captain," said he stiffly, "we call upon you to once again save us from certain doom." He shifted his gaze from the Darad's broad bearded face to the enormous pack at his back, and managed a wry smile. "Your burden is a weighty one, I see."

Both Mundar and Brulwar chuckled for the Lord's humour.

"There's no burden I wouldn't willingly bear for a friend, Lord Alvarion," Rundul gruffly replied.

"This we know, Captain." Alvarion brought one fist to his *rillagh*. "Stone and steel, brave Rundul of Axar."

And the Deathward there echoed, "Stone and Steel!"

Rundul turned then to the Sun Lords of the Athair and inclined his head respectfully. The Princes of the Neverborn returned the subtle salutation, accompanied by smiles both bright and beautiful.

Rundul then found himself enveloped in an embrace that would have broken the body of a lesser being.

"Stone and steel, Captain," rumbled Mundar, releasing him. Then, and with definitively un-Daradun delicacy, "My love goes with you into war, brother."

307

"Remind me upon my return," grumbled Rundul, "to *plead* with Earth the Mother that she Make for you a woman."

All there laughed aloud, and Warder Mundar most loudly of all.

Rundul looked to Brulwar then, and the great black-bearded Earthmaster held his eyes as though in a vise of black iron. And somewhere within his soul Rundul heard repeated –

The power is within you.

And then Rundul was freed from the grip of the Earthmaster's gaze, and he turned upon the heavy heels of his iron-shod boots, and walked in Eldurion's wake into the enfolding darkness of Ravenwood.

The remaining Daradur and Deathward turned to the Sun Lords then, the three surviving warrior princes of the Seven once sworn in service to Gavrayel and Aeline who ruled in Gith Glennin. Even in the midnight murk of Ravenwood, the Sun Lords shone with an inner light, though Yllufarr's luminescence was veiled by his black garb, and the cool glow of his pale eyes was the only shining that slid past cloak and cowl. About the noble Neverborn was the song of strings and bells, sweet and soft, laced with a subtle yet profound sorrow. Were tears of both love and loss to come together in a melody, the mystical music that was the Light of the Athair would be the soul within that song.

"Ward them well, brother Yllufarr," said Evangael, his voice like the flowing of mist on a meadow. "They possess the means to fulfill their missions. You must only ensure them the way. And when the Sun Knights ride, they must ride unseen. Therefore the Blood King must be blinded. That which he does not see will not cause him concern, will not move him to alter his plans. That he acts as we have predicted is essential."

Prince Yllufarr nodded, his pale eyes flashing. "So it will be done."

The Sun Lord Thrannien sang a soft sad song of sending, the sound the whisper of a warm summer wind, or the rustling of leaves in the night.

And Prince Yllufarr slid into the benighted forest like one of the black avian creatures after which that ancient wood was named, sailing the darkness on wings of silent speed.

Then, in answer to an unspoken summons, one of the elegant *elliamir* seemed to materialize from nothingness in the darkness of the trees, her golden mane like fire in the night, her coat as bright and white as a winter sun. The Sun Lord Evangael leapt lightly upon the *elliam*'s silk-shirted back, his own mane of flaming gold blazing about him like a flag of fierce and unfailing hope.

"Fare free, my friends," said he, raising one hand to his heart, "and when all farewells are done, remember me as I remember you."

Alvarion stood to one side of the Sun Lord's glorious mount, and raised one hand in farewell.

"Make haste, good Prince."

Evangael reached down and placed one strong hand upon Alvarion's shoulder.

"Faendomin will not burn, my friend," he vowed.

"You will come, then?" The deep melodious voice was Tulnarron's.

The Prince of the Neverborn, mightiest of the warriors of the Athair of Second Earth, moved his golden eyes to the Master of the House of Eccuron. Silence swirled in like fog from the mountains. Then Evangael smiled a most beautiful and beguiling smile.

"Look for me, Master Tulnarron," said he eerily, as though from a great distance, or from the mists of a dream, "when the sun rises in the west."

And then the very trees seemed to part to permit the enchanting *elliam* passage, and the night gathered at the backs of steed and rider, and in an instant both were gone.

Nothing was spoken among those that remained in the eaves of Ravenwood. They had been left to ponder in silence the puzzle of Evangael's parting words.

When the sun rises in the west.

And all there, all but the Sun Lord Thrannien, shared the same dark, dismal, disturbing thought, a thought that brought them to a conclusion near to doubt and not very distant from despair.

The Athair would not come.

Thunderlight, *elliamian* steed of the Sun Lord Evangael, flew through Ravenwood like a white wind, and the tangled twisted trees parted for them as they passed. Within minutes, they came to the River Ruil. And without hesitation, Evangael urged his gallant mount out upon the rushing waters, and Thunderlight rode the Ruil as easily as she would a grassy plain or a flowered meadow. Westward against the current she ran, galloping over wave and whitecrest as though the river were elemental earth, and she recked little or naught of the warders in the night that saw her pass.

But two who saw the white flash of Thunderlight on the water marked her going with quiet careful words.

"What in the Teller's Tale was *that*?" asked the Iron Captain of his brother as they made their way westward through the storm-shivered night to Druintir.

"I know not," came Axennus' reply, following a pensive pause. "But I have a suspicion."

"Never mind, little brother," frowned Bronnus, retracting his question. "I am of the considered opinion that I would rather not know."

Onward, upward, westward raced Thunderlight. And then, beneath the upraised sword of Defurien's Colossus, she turned north upon the golden grasses of the Miramarch. Evangael marked the invisible sentries of the Grey Watch, allowed them to witness Thunderlight's wild run, but when mount and master passed the northern limits of Fiannian vigilance, the Sun Lord turned Thunderlight westward again, whispering –

"Like the wind, *Cel-lumin!* As swift as lightning, as silent as sunrise, as sure as death to the deserving! *Fly!*"

And abandoning the northerly path that would have led to the regal rises of the Vallagard Mountains and mystical Gith Glennin that lay hidden behind them, Thunderlight raced westward, swifter than a windborn storm, but as softly quiet as a mother's lullaby, and no more visible to the eye than the scent of flowers in summer air.

Westward they went, mount and mounted, bearer and borne, steed and Sun Lord. Westward, ever westward. Away from Gith Glennin where ruled good Gavrayel of the Golden Voice and his Queen Aeline, where the shining *Sul Athaifain* awaited command. Westward, where the sun died each day and the wind was scented with salt.

Westward, ever westward.

To the sea.

13

SERENDIPITY

"There is the thing we see,
There is the thing we perceive,
There is the thing we believe –
And then there is the thing that is."

Omereo, *Schematas*

An involution of consciousness.

Ascending into the astral skies, sailing the soul of the universe. A solitary spark among millions of roaring stars, darting through the darknesses between blue giants and white dwarfs, betwixt pulsars and pulsating cepheids. An etheric vessel possessed of deliberate volition, soaring across the cosmos. This subtle body, alert, self-aware, intent, seeking a darkness among shadows.

Swirling down upon the earth like an angel of death. Arcing through the atmosphere, plying the physical plane. Descending upon the gross world to a place where the earth reflects the sky, where thousands of seeming stars shine on yellow seas. Fires. So many fires. So many thousands of fires. This subtle body, alarmed, apprehensive, resolved, sensing a darkness among shadows.

Tents. Thousands upon thousands of tents. One tent greater, so much vaster than all the others. Floating, fluttering down, finding the flaps. Slipping inside. Into the shadows. Into *those* shadows. Blind in the black. Feeling about with phantasmal hands. Feeling and finding – one, two. Touching. This subtle body, revolted, recoiling, fleeing, having discovered such terrible darkness among shadows.

A man called Teji Nashi opened his eyes.

His jaws bunched, biting down upon a most bitter word.

Leeches.

The perfumed air seemed to sour.

"Oh, dear."

Did you feel that, sister? Did you feel it, feel it, feel?

Waif looked up from the massive meaty mess upon which she perched, her small form hunched on her haunches. Rivulets of blood slicked her chin. Her fine fair brows twisted together. She clasped the burned thing tighter to her breast.

I am not sure, brother. I think I felt...something. Something may have touched me. A prodding, perhaps. Or a poke.

Yes! A poke. Poke, poke, poke.

The little girl rose to her feet atop the putrefying carcass. She looked about the interior of the command tent. Cocked her head to one side, listening. She sniffed, then licked the fetid air. She then shrugged, tucked the burned thing beneath one thin arm, crouched once more, and with her bare fingers she tore a strip of raw red flesh from the rotting remains of the King of the Giants. Her teeth ripped into the shred ravenously, maggots falling from her scarlet lips as she chewed.

There is nothing here, brother.

But I felt it, sister. I felt it, felt it.

These bodies are so sensitive, brother. They betray us. Always feeling. Feeling so much. Feeling and needing.

Yes, sister. Feeling and needing, needing and feeling. Feeling so much, so much, much, much.

The little boy moaned.

The little girl glanced up.

Do you ache, brother? We have but little time before the Halflord comes. Tell me, brother, tell me – do you ache?

Urchin's wide blue eyes met Waif's across the dead King's huge hollow chest cavity. Met and held, shining, shining. One small red hand reached for another.

Yes, yes, yes, yes.

And down they sank into the crimson sludge.

Night on the Northern Plains was growing old, growing cold. The camp was unnaturally quiet. Even the snores and occasional night terrors of the slumbering warriors seemed muted, strangely subdued. From the rough rock-rings of unnumbered extinguished campfires, the sibilant sound of embers disintegrating to ashes hissed and slithered into the star-pricked darkness. Vipers dying in the night. There on the Plains, in a world awaiting war, the everpresent eventuality of dissolution was an audible, tangible thing.

"I don't like this."

Mounted upon her monstrous render, Ev lin Dar raised one fine brow toward her habitually dolorous companion.

"You don't like anything, Gren del Mor."

"Untrue. And unfair."

The second brow raised. "Oh?"

"I like raw meat. I like black wine. I even like you, Ev. Sometimes."

"I see that I'm in good company, at least," sniffed Ev lin Dar. "I'm flattered."

"You should be," returned Gren del Mor with no hint of humour.

Ev lin Dar cast her sharp white gaze back toward the closed entrance to the immense command tent. Two enormous half-Urks flanked the fastened flaps, chaotic corruptions of nature, brutal bestial beings spawned of abominable ambition and blood magic. Small yellow eyes set deep in yet yellower faces radiated a wanton lust as their cruel gazes devoured the dark beauty of the female Bloodspawn before them.

Ev lin Dar disregarded them entirely.

"Our malformed friends are enamoured of you," grinned Gren del Mor. "Come, Ev, a small boon, a sweet smile for your admirers."

She ignored that as well.

The half-Urks leered and lapped their bulbous black lips.

"Sorry, fellas,' sighed Gren del Mor with a shrug, "not tonight."

Indecipherable voices, smothered and muffled by heavy skins and canvas, issued from within the command tent.

Between her muscular thighs, Ev lin Dar's *mar render* shifted slightly, terrible talons tearing into the dark earth. When she stroked the creature's neck, she felt a slow silent thunder reverberate in its throat. The beautiful Black Shield's fine brows crumpled into a frown, her tigress tattoo contorting apprehensively.

"The beast is uneasy," observed Gren del Mor, "despite its unequivocally enviable position."

The tigress snarled.

"Your cone is crooked, Gren."

Gren del Mor jolted, his hands jerking upward to hastily yet thoroughly inspect his perfectly tapered hair. Soon satisfied, he lowered his hands.

"That was uncalled for, Ev," he chastised in a hurt tone. "And you have the audacity to call *me* disagreeable."

Despite the night's distinct chill, despite the lascivious leers of ogling ochre ogres, despite the serpents in the dark, both Ev lin Dar and the tigress smiled.

And then she recalled the man facing demons within the hide and canvas structure before her.

All smiles die.

The little girl smiled.

"Are you appalled, Halflord?" she quipped, the pitch of her voice high, the sheen in her eyes bright. "Do you find us...abhorrent? Do we disgust you? Repulse you?"

Kor ben Dor looked up into Waif's grinning eyes, the dead white of his own betraying no emotion, the set of his tattooed countenance as flat and as impassive as painted stone.

Waif giggled, clutching the burned thing closer to her barely budding breasts.

"Dear brother, I do believe we have at long last truly offended the Prince's lofty sensibilities."

Somewhere beneath her, Urchin sniggered.

"Offended him, yes, yes. Oh, what naughty brats we are. Bad, bad, bad."

The Halflord inhaled slowly, deeply. He rolled one immense shoulder, grinding away a bothersome knot in the thickly layered muscles. The motion seemed a careless shrug, but was actually something more, so much more.

Yet he did not otherwise respond.

"The dead are infinitely simpler to inhabit than are the living, Halflord," the little girl imparted almost pleasantly. "Simpler, but much less...satisfying."

The ruined corpse of Arn'badt, King of the Giants, loomed before Kor ben Dor, animated and erect, swathed in strange sorcerous shadowlight. Waif sat perched atop the cadaver's headless shoulders, her spindling legs dangling casually, tiny feet bare but stained dark with what could only have been blood. Well below her, crouched in the hideous hollow of the dead Graniant's disemboweled belly, Urchin rocked rhythmically back and forth, bloodied arms curled about his knobby knees, his cherubic face plastered in a gruesome grin.

"The dead offer no resistance, the souls having fled the shell." Waif smiled beatifically, despite a solitary maggot wriggling awkwardly across her blood-streaked chin. "Though this particular one did not fly far."

"We caught him," giggled Urchin within the corpse's abdominal cavity. "Caught him and ate him. Chewed him, ate him, ate him up."

"His terror was...delicious," Waif beamed. Her slim pink tongue flicked out, snapping up the pale slug. The thing made a sickeningly wet, gushing sound as she crushed it between her teeth. Viscous fluid oozed from one corner of Waif's smile. "My brother and I extend to you our sincere gratitude, Halflord."

Slowly, deliberately, Kor ben Dor cracked a crick from his neck.

And he said softly, "Speak."

Waif blinked, clasping the burned thing closer.

"But we *have* been speaking, Prince of the Bloodspawn," she complained. "Some of us more loquaciously and eloquently than others, of course."

"Speak."

The little girl frowned.

"Your single-mindedness is admirable, Halflord. Admirable but annoying. Do you seek to irritate me?"

A purposeful pause, then –

"Speak."

Waif scarcely suppressed an infuriated scream.

Calm yourself, sister. Calm –

"You impertinent *shit!*" Waif shrieked. "You were summoned *two days ago*, and you only now deign to darken our door with your dour and despicable self! Prince or no, I will have you flayed alive!"

A genuine shrug.

"The messenger indicated that I should come at my own convenience," the Halflord said, his melodious voice as soft and as smooth as silk. "Until now, it was not."

"Not what?" seethed Waif, her eyes burning.

"Convenient."

"Not convenient? Not *convenient?* And should I have the skin peeled from your flesh?" Spittle and grub guts flew as Waif raved. "Would that...*inconvenience* you, Prince of the Bloodspawn?"

"Momentarily, perhaps."

"Momentarily? You think too highly of yourself. You would do well to remember that you are but half a lord."

"Unnecessary." Kor ben Dor made a dismissive gesture. "Others insist upon reminding me."

Waif glowered down upon the Bloodspawn, her large eyes glimmering, deep dark blue lamps, baneful and lurid.

"I shall instruct you in inconvenience, mortal." Her hiss was the sound of a soul slipping from a dying man. "And your very hide will be the instrument of your enlightenment."

The Halflord shrugged once more, seemingly aloof, without care – but at his sides his huge hands stretched deliberately, long strong fingers spreading and flexing.

"You would find me a poor student, *blutsauger* – my skin is thicker than you might suspect." His white gaze wandered impassively over the repugnant ruination of Arn'badt's corrupted carcass. "Thus my lack of outrage."

Waif glared, her jaws chomping, champing.

Easy, sister. Still your anger. He purposefully baits you. You must calm yourself, calm, calm, ca –

Oh, shut up!

Gradually, the set of Waif's features softened, her eyes dimmed to a gentle gleam, and she smiled the smile of angels.

"Tell me, Halflord, do you know why you were created? The purpose to your design? To your...existence?"

The Prince of the Bloodspawn drew a sharp breath. *Answers? Does this contemptible creature offer me answers?* He willed his hands to relax. *Tell me.*

"I do not pretend to know the motivations of the Blood King," he replied quietly.

Waif's laughter was a shrill song of madness.

"The Blood King...oh, that is *good*. You, for all your pretense and posturing, presume the creative genius, the brilliant intellect responsible for your design, belongs to a meagre half-undead mage with an insatiable blood fixation. Such willfully flaunted ignorance – priceless, purely priceless!"

Kor ben Dor said nothing.

Tell me.

"You do know" – the little girl's eyes narrowed to sapphire slits – "that you were *manufactured*, do you not?"

The Halflord only stared, his face fixed and placid. *Go on, demon.*

Waif grinned wildly.

"The Blood King was neither the architect nor the engineer of the Bloodspawn, but only the manufacturer. Suru-luk does not create, he does not...*dream*. He merely constructs. The fool's sole duty is to mindlessly, mechanically follow the plans provided him. And even then he gets it wrong more often than not, a truth to which those horrid little half-Urks out there so capably attest. No, sweet Prince, the Blood King is but the hammer in the hand of another, of one far greater than himself."

Kor ben Dor nodded, silent and speciously serene.

Ah. Another. But not you, *demon. You, like the Blood King, are but a hammer...only bigger, heavier. Yet you fail to see this – and mock my ignorance, when your own is the greater. Who,* blutsauger, *is the true fool?*

"Suru-luk is the hammer, Halflord," sneered Waif, reddened fingers digging into the burned thing at her bosom. "You are the nail – and the Fiannar were to be the skull."

Yes, the Fiannar. But I knew this. Wait – the creature said..."were"?

Prince Kor suppressed the frown threatening the insensate stone of his countenance, verily biting down on his tongue.

"Yes, sweet prince, you and your precious Bloodspawn were meticulously, fastidiously, deliberately designed to destroy the Fiannar. To meet them on their own ground – meet them, engage them, and annihilate them. The sole reason for the existence of your race is the obliteration of another. Such sweet purpose, such glorious cause, a thing so brutally simple, more pure than fate, more profound than any destiny. The extermination of the Fiannar. This magnificent deed you were to achieve, this splendid feat you were to accomplish. But no longer."

Were, but no longer. Something has happened. Something has... changed.

Waif grinned in insidious silence.

Tell me, demon.

Crouched in the hideous hollow of Arn'badt's abdomen, Urchin slid the side of one bloodied finger along the thin line of his twisted lips, his tongue snaking out to slurp blood from the slickened skin.

Tell me.

"You will not bring doom down upon the Fiannar, Halflord." Waif's voice was light and breezy; her sweet, cherubic face veritably glowed. "No, you will not do this good and glorious thing."

Will not? Or would *not? Choice is implicit in her words, though she would mask it in obfuscation. But why? Why would I not choose to destroy the Fiannar? Why would I turn aside from the only purpose I have ever known?*

"The Bloodspawn are strong, *blutsauger.*"

Atop Arn'badt's headless shoulders, Waif cocked her head to one side, beguilingly demure, disarmingly decorous.

"Of course they are, Halflord. But Eryn Ruil? The Fiannar? No, I think not. I cannot risk it."

Risk it? Risk what? What is it that you fear we will do, demon? Why do the Bloodspawn terrify you so?

Kor ben Dor stared at the Leech, his gaze hard and white. Said nothing. Waited.

Waif beamed.

Urchin slurped noisily at a finger.

And then the little girl sighed, a sound as soft and as sinister as a snake sidewinding on sand.

"I believe, Halflord, that you and your dear Bloodspawn would be more effective...elsewhere."

Elsewhere. Not Eryn Ruil. Not the Fiannar. Where then? And against whom?

The Prince of the Bloodspawn rolled one shoulder, then the other. Muscles bowled and rippled. At his side, his huge hands flexed into boulders of stone.

"Tell me."

And she did.

"Sirs?"

The word tapped at the Decan's consciousness. Like a finger on a tabletop. Incessant and irritating. Regorius rolled over in his bunk, tugged the blankets up a touch higher, closed his eyes just a little tighter, stubbornly clinging to the hypnopompic haze of failing sleep.

"Sirs?"

The tapping became a poking now. More invasive, more insistent. A stick in the ribs. Maddus and Riffalo and Rooboong tossed against the prodding, turning away, groaning, moaning, pushing their faces deeper into the plushness of their pillows.

"SIRS!"

Regorius sprang awake, leaping up only to hear the thud of his head hitting the wooden slatted underside of the bunk above him. He slammed back down onto his mattress, eyes bedecked with tiny twinkling lights. Then the pain came.

Rooboong and Riffalo jerked awake, profaning profusely if not profoundly in their native tongues, instinctively reaching to their hips for weapons that were not there.

Maddus actually yelped, rolled, and plummeted from the top bunk to land in a tangled heap of blankets, arms and legs on the floor. There he remained, groaning.

"My apologies, sirs," said the silhouette of a guardsman in the doorway. His voice sounded suspiciously like a smile. "I was instructed to wake you, wait for you to dress, if necessary, and then escort you. Sirs."

Regorius gingerly tested his scalp for blood, felt none, but could distinctly discern the lump already starting to sprout beneath the shocks of stark white hair.

"Instructed? By whom?" Despite the little stars swimming across his sight, the Decan detected no light seeping around the drawn window curtains. "Is it even morning yet?"

"Very nearly, sir."

"Damn, my head hurts."

"The foreseeable consequence of a third consecutive night of festivities at the Fifth Folly, sir."

"No, dumbass!" snapped the Decan. "The foreseeable consequence of banging one's head against an upper bunk! Now who sent you?"

"The Doctor, sir."

Regorius' pink eyes narrowed. He squinted past his private dance of stars to the tall form framed in the open doorway.

"Ah. Lionnus, is it? The Doctor's bodyguard."

The smile slid into the young outrider's voice once more. "I assure you, the Doctor needs no bodyguard, sir."

"Lackey, then."

"No cause for hostilities, sir."

Regorius stood slowly, teetered, used a bedpost to brace himself as the chamber spun kaleidoscopically around him. Perhaps the third night at the Fifth Folly had indeed been a bit...immoderate.

"No cause for...? You wake me up in the middle of the night –"

"Nearly dawn, sir, as I have said."

"– you make me conk my noggin against wood that seems more like stone –"

"You did that yourself, sir."

"– and you have the balls of steel to tell me there is *no cause for hostilities*?"

The silhouette of Lionnus cocked its head to one side.

"Perhaps I could be a little more empathetic, sir. I will work on it. Will you and your men be pausing to dress, sir?"

"Pausing to...? Teller's tongue, no! We aren't getting dressed, and we aren't going anywhere!"

"Very well, sir. Come as you are, then. Please follow me, sirs."

Regorius was too distracted by disequilibrium and a churning stomach to protest any further. He wobbled woozily after the tall outrider, awkwardly maneuvering around Maddus' huddled prostrate form.

Rooboong and Riffalo fell in listlessly behind the Decan.

As Rooboong stepped over him, unfortunate Maddus raised one hand in supplication, groaned, and wheezed the piteous plea –

"*Come...back...for me.*"

"Come."

Ev lin Dar ducked past the hide flap into the Halflord's tent. When she saw her Prince, her fine brows bunched darkly, giving her tigress tattoo an angry aspect. But there was no anger in her. Not, at least, for the Halflord. No, not for him. Never that.

"You summoned me, Prince Kor."

The Halflord sat on the edge of his cot, shoulders hunched, forearms resting upon his thighs. He held the intricate mechanisms of his hair-wings in his large strong hands, absently working the hinges with his fingers. His magnificently muscled body was bare from the waist up, and bore a sheen of sweat. His head was bowed, his hard handsome face hidden behind curtains of black hair.

"Yes."

Ev lin Dar waited, but the Halflord said no more. He did not move, nor did he seem inclined to do so any time soon. The Black Shield's pearly eyes swept the austere interior of the tent. Armour. Weaponry. Some clothing. A platter of untouched food. Little else.

"Do you dream, Shield?"

Ev lin Dar swung her gaze back to Kor ben Dor. Two white eyes peered up at her past strands of the Halflord's hanging hair. There was a shining in the depths of those pale lights that the Black Shield found disconcerting, disturbing.

"Do I...?" she began, then shook her head. "I don't understand, Prince Kor."

The lights behind the draped hair disappeared. The Halflord had closed his eyes.

"We do not sleep, we Bloodspawn, not in the way that others do. But we rest. And when we rest, we dream." The Halflord's voice was disarmingly soft, silken, and seemed somewhat sad. "The mind wanders. Thoughts scatter, images rise, patterns emerge, themes develop, culminating in complex visions over which we have no conscious control. In the dark, it happens. It happens in the dark."

Ev lin Dar blinked slowly, bit her lip.

"Are you unwell, Prince Kor? Shall I summon..."

The two white lights reappeared, brighter than they had been.

"You do not dream, Shield?"

Ev lin Dar shook her head slowly.

"I do not believe so, Prince Kor." She frowned, then added, "Though sometimes my thoughts do drift, and I...remember things."

The white lights narrowed.

"What things do you remember?"

Ev lin Dar's frown darkened. The tigress snarled. She brushed a shock of midnight hair from her beautiful face.

"I remember...I remember being young. At least I think I do. I cannot be sure."

The Halflord stared at her.

"You remember things from the time before the pain."

The Black Shield nodded.

"I was a child. A little girl. There were others. Not like us. Smaller, paler. Stern. But kind. They cared for me. I felt...I...it is very vague, Prince Kor."

"And then the pain came."

Ev lin Dar winced, nodded.

"And then the pain, Prince Kor. That I remember all too well."

"As do we all, Shield."

Kor ben Dor rose slowly, his muscles rippling like rivers of rock beneath his tight skin.

Ev lin Dar felt a warmth take her, realized she was staring, quickly averted her eyes, looked down upon her hands.

"We have lost much, Shield," mused the Halflord as he languidly stretched subtle aches away. "We cannot know the extent of our loss. However, I believe my dreams may be the ambiguous beginnings of memories from the time before the pain."

The Black Shield's gaze remained fixed on her hands. Strong hands. Strong and hard. Not soft like a human woman's. Not hands made for gentle touches and sweet caresses. No, not the hands of a lover.

"Tell me, do you feel close to me, Ev lin Dar?"

Her head snapped up, her mouth dropped open. Beneath her breastplate, Ev lin Dar's heart fluttered fitfully against her ribs.

"Do I...do...Prince Kor?"

The Halflord rolled soreness from his shoulders, eased an ache in his neck.

"Sometimes when I drift, when I dream, I think I see you. Not as you are now, but as you were then. As a child. Smiling, laughing. Happy."

Ev lin Dar blinked, tried to swallow her nervousness.

"Before the pain, Prince Kor."

"Yes. Before the pain."

The Prince of the Bloodspawn shrugged into his thin grey gambeson. Adjusted the straps and fastenings. He sighed. The sound was more like a growl.

Ev lin Dar watched quietly, apprehensively mindful of the warmth in her cheeks.

"Dawn comes, and with it another day's march. Day upon day. Miles on miles. It numbs the mind, Shield. But it does not soothe."

Somewhere outside, a *mar render* huffed.

"Tell me, when you remember the things that you remember, Shield, do you recall anything about me?"

Ev lin Dar's heart stopped. Her sight went dark.

"I...yes. I do, Prince Kor."

She had closed her eyes, squeezed the lids tightly shut, but she could feel the white heat of the Halflord's gaze on her. She could *see* his eyes.

"Speak."

Ev lin Dar swallowed. Hard.

"Before the pain, Prince Kor. Before the...loss. You and I. We were...friends."

Nothing had changed.

The walls were of canvas, rounded, curving towards a low curtained aperture at the back. The dark air was cool and calm. To the left was an ornate armour stand and a clothing rack, both bearing their appropriate burdens. Upon the right was a tidily made bed, at the foot of which a splendidly scabbarded *katana* rested on an elaborately etched wooden chest. There was a stillness to the place, a certain tranquility, the soothing sensation of seamless serenity, or the deceptive allure of a siren's silence before the song.

The three guardsmen stood bunched in the open doorway of the Doctor's bedchamber in the officer's wing of the White Manor, staring, stupefied, bewildered by the fantastic fixity of the space. *Canvas walls? What the hell?* Then something bumped them heavily from behind and they cried out in alarm, falling inward in a tangled tumble of bodies and bedclothes and accompanying curses.

"Glad you could make it, Maddy," Rooboong snarled sarcastically, fighting free of the human heap, the first to regain his feet.

Echoed Riffalo, "How very good of you, Maddy."

"Dumbass," said Regorius, straightening.

Maddus simply groaned.

The Decan unceremoniously dragged the hapless guardsman up.

"Teller's tongue, you look awful, Maddy."

"I feel worse, mate."

Regorius wrinkled his nose, made a choking sound "Gods, you smell even worse!"

"Thanks, Whitey, you don't stink too good yourself."

Reflexively, Regorius sniffed himself, but before he could rifle a retort, a fifth voice joined the scintillatingly witty repartee:

"Ah, my friends," greeted the Doctor, smiling congenially, his thin brown eyes twinkling despite the dark. "Welcome, welcome. I must apologize for the early rousing from your warm beds, but I found it unavoidably necessary. You will forgive me, yes?"

The four guardsmen nodded woodenly.

Teji Nashi grinned, perfect white teeth gleaming. He was barefooted, dressed comfortably in a *yukata* of magenta-coloured cotton, a golden dragon stenciled on the fine fabric, coiling about his small frame, flattened head perched upon one shoulder, watching. The Diceman's hands were folded before him and hidden in the ample sleeves of the garment. As ever, at his waist was strapped his curved *wakizashi*.

"Most gracious of you. Most gracious, indeed. I am sorely pressed, you see. Time is precious. We must prepare. So much to do in such a short time. Very constrained, frightfully so – but manageable, yes? Mayhap time itself can be made malleable. Come, come. We have a little while before the day's drills, and we must utilize every hour left available to us."

The Doctor turned and ducked through the opening to the back chamber. He moved with silent grace, almost gliding, padding like a panther, quick and quiet.

The four who followed him were decidedly...otherwise.

Like the forechamber, the rear room remained unchanged, or little enough altered as to be unremarkable. The light was a warm white, soft and soothing, with no perceivable source. The air held a tepid moistness, a succulence made sweet by floral perfumes. The pair of wooden tables endured, one near the entrance and heaped with all manner of written things, the other at the back and bearing its baffling farrago of vessels and apparatuses. Varicoloured tendrils of smoke and steam swirled slowly toward the herbarium hovering over the middle section of the room. Beneath this hanging jungle stood the Diceman's tall slender stool. Four more stools awaited the guardsmen.

The Doctor lithely perched himself atop his stool, smiling blithely, the smooth burnished skin of his cheeks and pate radiating health and humour.

"Sit, my friends. Make yourselves comfortable. Rest and relax, yes? Good, very good. I must say, your haggardness ill becomes men so young and so hale. I need neither preach nor teach the of benefits of moderation. A nice carafe of Hellevintan hippocras now and perhaps again on occasion, but drunkenness and loutishness accomplish nothing and less. Indeed, habitual indulgence imperils what we intend to do here, you see. Not good, not good at all. There will be no repetition of the past three nights' revelries, yes?"

The four guardsmen nodded as one.

Teji Nashi clasped his hands, then rubbed them together almost gleefully.

"Excellent. Most excellent. Admittedly, our clandestine council should have been better preconcerted, and I better prepared. Here I must solicit your understanding, my friends, for the fault is mine. I have been very active of late, and my attention to much has been necessarily delayed. I will make recompense. Should a thing need doing, and the doing done well, then give it to a busy man to do, yes?"

The guardsmen nodded.

The Diceman smiled. His hands disappeared once more beneath his billowed sleeves.

"Now, where to begin an allocution to such a select and secret consistory? No need to extend this exordium, and less for couthie circumlocution and attending circumambages. None lament the loss of logorrhea, you see. Dispense with peremptory punctilios and press to the point, yes? Good, good. We will start in the middle."

The Doctor's smile slipped away. His slitted eyes glittered, gleamed.

"You see, my friends, war descends upon us, and very soon the Ghost Brigade must rise and ride once again."

The four guardsmen gawked at the little Diceman. Eyes wide, brows raised, mouths agape. Effectively gorgonized.

"Yes, my friends, a vast and terrible army marches upon Lindannan, upon Eryn Ruil and Doomfall, upon the Fiannar and those allies they may gather to them. Upon us all, yes? The Fiannar will stand and fight, as is their wont, and they are a most fearsome foe. But they are so few, you see. And they are sorely outnumbered. Dreadfully so. Forty to one, in fact. Odds most frightful and made worse by the nature of the enemy they will face: Hordes of Unmen, Wulfings of Var, Norian mercenaries, ogres, stone giants, monsters of myth and legend marching beneath the banner of the Blood King returned. Nevertheless, the Fiannar will stand. The Fiannar will fight. And the Fiannar will fall. Unless we help them, yes?"

Giants? Monsters? The Blood King?

Regorius blinked. Found his voice. Cracked and croaking, but he found it.

"Help them? How can we help them? What can *we* do?"

"What can we do, indeed," echoed the Doctor, his white smile returning. "There's the spirit, my good Decan! Of course, there can be little doubt that the March Fox and the Iron Captain will solicit our one hundred and send for the rest, yes? Every sword counts, indeed it does, but swords and spears will not win this war alone. No, indeed. Our friends the Fiannar will be facing ancient sorceries, you see, foul crafts born of blood and decay and corruption. Regrettably, they have sent away their greatest protection against these things. Whether this was done in wisdom or in folly, it matters not; necessity knows and bows to both, yes? Either way, *Grimroth* is gone. Thus is their shield against sorcery much weakened. It cannot long withstand the combined powers of blood magic, the earthblight and the horror of the Leeches."

Stark white eyebrows arched. "Leeches? Like physicians?"

"Oh, terrors, no! I despise the name – leech, that is, not physician. You will recall the two little bones that fell outside the circle cast by Guardsman Maddus, yes? Not a random roll, that. Not at all. I have discovered that the Blood King's army is marshaled and commanded by two terrible entities, baneful beings long called 'Leech' by many peoples in many languages. These Leeches are beyond ancient, for they existed before Time, and as such they are not constrained by its binding influence. Much like gods. Disturbing, yes? Not good, not good. Thus what we must do becomes most obvious, you see."

The four guardsmen shook their heads in slow deliberate unison.

"Ah, well, such ambiguity can present itself when starting at the middle, yes? Clarity will come, my friends. Admittedly, I could be more succinct. I lose myself sometimes, you see. Now where was I?"

"You were about to tell us how we can help the Fiannar, Doc," suggested Regorius. "At least I think you were."

Teji Nashi smiled. The eyes of the dragon on his shoulder glittered.

"Yes, of course. Well, that is simple enough, my friends. We will provide a shield against the blood magic, the earthblight and whatever foul puissance might be wielded by the Leeches. We will be the wall against which all the Blood King's sundry sordid sorceries crash, break and burn away. An easy thing, yes?"

Crash? Break?? Burn???

The foursome's communal gulp was distinctly audible.

"As you have certainly deduced, my friends, I possess a scattering of sorcerous talents. In point of fact, at risk of appearing immodest, I am rather accomplished in the arcane arts. A lifetime of practice, you see. I do believe I possess the skills sufficient to oppose and negate the dark powers arrayed against us. However, for reasons that would surely bore you to the brink of insensibility and beyond, I can neither be seen nor perceived to be doing so. Thus our newfound friendship becomes most fortuitous, yes?"

The four guardsmen exchanged blank, blanched looks.

"I will need conduits, of sorts. Channels through which to exercise the elemental energies essential for the effective defense of Eryn Ruil. There are many modes of magic, some easier to understand and employ than others. I must insist that the elemental arts are far from elementary, especially when utilizing conduits, yes? Each channel must be specific to the power that seeks to negotiate and navigate it. Earth cannot traverse a Water conduit, nor might Air pass through Fire. Such is nature, you see. There are rules, yes?"

"You...you want us to be...conduits?"

"What I want is immaterial, good Decan. You either are a conduit or you are not. One chooses to be a conduit no more than one chooses one's parents. You are born to it, you see. The ability is inherent. But like a man born with a mole on his back, you may be completely oblivious of its existence for the entirety of your own – unless, of course, you are made aware by another. You are familiar with the term 'serendipity', yes?"

Four heads nodded, then shook.

"A fortunate development of events, occurring strictly by chance, yes? Though there are those who believe said chance is itself orchestrated by the Teller or some other illumined ubiquitous but otherwise anonymous omnipotence."

Four heads bobbled.

"Oh."

"Aye."

"Of course."

"I actually knew that."

The Doctor looked from one guardsman to another, and with great effort refrained from sighing and giving his own weary head a shake. He recalled the old Daradun phrase, *If you're looking for a diamond, you gotta dig deep.* The Diceman's smile persisted. Then he remembered that the Daradur were also wont to say, *Whether digging for gold or cleaning up shit, you still use the same shovel.* The Doctor's smile faded somewhat, but did not falter.

Not fully.

"Our meeting, my friends, was the very definition of serendipity. I did not seek to find you, but find you I did – or rather you found me. We found one another, yes? Good, very good. For I perceive in all men certain potentialities, you see. Some great, some not so. And in a few – a very few – I perceive some latent ability, some innate but inactive acumen for arts eldritch and arcane."

Regorius' pink eyes blinked rapidly.

"You see that in *us*, Doc?"

Light seemed to seep from Teji Nashi's slitted eyes.

"I do."

"In *us*? You're serious?"

"I am."

"Are you sure?"

"Quite."

"Oh...shit."

Regorius seemed totally unaware that he had said the last little bit, that which each of the four guardsmen was certainly thinking, aloud.

Nor did the Doctor appear to hear him.

"In you, good Decan, I perceive a channel for the elemental energy of Air. In Guardsman Riffalo, I detect a canal for Water – you will pardon the particularly poor pun, yes? Guardsman Maddus is a conduit for the powers of Earth. And in Rooboong, a path for Fire."

Oh...shit.

Unspoken this time, but almost as audible.

And then there was Maddus –

"Shite! Bloody shite and rubbish!" Somewhere in the haze of alcoholic aftereffects, Maddus had found some courage along with his voice, and both flooded from him in a tumbling torrent. "I'm a bloody carpenter's son from the streets of Scarshire, for shite's sake! I'm an illiterate oaf, dumb as a stump. I drink, I gamble, I fight. I'm a pain in both bollocks. Everyone will tell you that I'm a royal arse. I'm a lot of things, none of them any bloody good. 'Cept maybe on the battlefield, aye, I'll give me that. But I'm certainly no bleedin' conduit for no bloody earth power!"

Silence, but for the soft hissing of steam from an apparatus or two behind Teji Nashi – or was the sound sourced somewhere at his shoulder? The light in the Diceman's eyes took a golden hue, glittering, glowing.

"You sell yourself disconcertingly short, my friend, and in doing so you cheat the world. That you are a conduit for Earth's energies is inarguable, for did the Earthmaster himself not hail you at Doomfall? True, you can never wield the vast powers of Maiden Earth, but the elemental energies of the Mother are yours to channel, and one day command, if you so choose. Why do you not believe? The world is a much larger place than you, and much exists beyond the limits of your narrow experience. That you do not believe says more of you than it does the world, you see. Many truths in this world can seem unreal. Open your mind. Receive the world, yes?"

"Do I have a bloody choice?"

Teji Nashi's smile exhibited an almost impish quality.

"Well, choice is such an ephemeral thing, you see. Always changing with winds and whims. Commitment and obligation are much more dependable devices, yes? You are satisfied, my friend? Good, good."

Maddus frowned but said no more.

"So," said Regorius dubiously, "you're telling us that we're all conduits. Even Maddy. One for each element. Is that it? Seems too convenient."

"Oh, but it is convenient, good Decan, most decidedly so. Serendipity, you see. A cosmic convergence of sorts. A coming together. Everything for a reason, it is said. The Teller's Tale to tell, yes?"

"Yes. I do see. I get it now. You are going to possess us so you can secretly spin your spells through us..."

The Doctor looked stricken, seemed to actually shudder.

"Possess you? Terrors, no! Whatever would make you think such an abominable thing of me? We are friends, yes? Possession is the work of Leeches and the like, and unlike those foul fiends, I neither defile nor corrupt. I simply ask good things of good men, better things of better ones, and more of you. But be assured that you will neither be coerced nor forced – however, I must reassert that you share our little secrets with no one else, yes?"

Slow, synchronized nods.

"Good, good. We are all agreed, then." Teji Nashi's intemerate smile gleamed beneath glistering eyes. "We have a little time left to us this morning, my friends. I suggest you avail yourselves of the excellent *ethacca* elixir to be found in the vials on the table behind you – it will relieve you of all remnants of last night's revelries. Revive and invigorate, yes? Always beneficial to begin these things with a clear mind, you see."

The quartet stared at the Doctor in something that could have been nothing other than sheer terror.

Teji Nashi's eyes flashed. Smoke issued from the stenciled dragon's nostrils. The Diceman removed his small dark hands from the sleeves of his *yukata*, and strings of golden fire danced between his fingers.

Ohhh...

The dragon winked.

...shhhiiit.

The morning wind whipped across the Northern Plains, the chill bitter breath of hoary white winter near waking. The Halflord's ribboned cloak stretched behind him like outspread raven's wings, inimitably black against the rising sun at his back. His monstrous *mar render* coughed clouds of moiling mist from its nostrils as it breasted through a frosted forest of thick-bladed giantgrass as tall as its rider. The rimed sedge snapped and creaked in protracted protest, protest as fervent as it was futile, then seemed to heave a rattling sigh of relief as the great render emerged from the most westerly edge of the field.

Kor ben Dor halted the beast, rolled his shoulders, his white gaze fixed westward across grasses of more common length. To either side of him, hundreds of black-armoured Bloodspawn mounted on *mar rendera* exited the forest of giantgrass, apocalyptic outriders of the Blood King's massive host. All halted, silent and still, their breath blooming and bleaching the cold morning air as they awaited their lord's lead.

The Halflord's handsome head tilted on his thick neck, his gaze rising, ivory eyes peering into the morning skies. High above, invisible to most mortal sight, several infinitesimal specks circled slowly, gracefully.

Kor ben Dor grunted softly. His render huffed.

Ev lin Dar appeared at his right. Looked up.

"What are they, Prince Kor?"

"*Throkka*. The eyes of the Fiannar."

Ev lin Dar sighed. "We are watched."

"Yes."

"I suppose we could not have expected to march across the open prairie unobserved."

"No."

Ev lin Dar glanced sidelong at her Prince. He had returned to his usual reticence after she had revealed that they had been friends in the time before the pain. He had not asked her to elaborate. He had said nothing, actually, had simply and silently dismissed her. She now regretted telling him. She felt foolish, silly.

Hurt.

Ev lin Dar shifted uneasily aback her *mar render*. Cleared her throat.

"The Fiannar will be ready for us, Prince Kor ben Dor."

"Not for us."

Upon the Black Shield's beautiful face, tattooed tigress whiskers arched.

"Prince Kor?"

"We do not go the Seven Hills."

"Then where...?"

But Kor ben Dor did not answer her. Rather, he closed his eyes, spread his arms, his broad black hair-wings buffeting in the cold morning wind.

And he whispered, "Come to me tonight, Shield..."

Ev lin Dar was too slow and too surprised to check the reflexive whistled gasp that escaped her lovely lips.

"...and bring the Graniant shaman, Umbar'hal, with you."

Instantly, Ev lin Dar's throat tightened. She pressed her lips together and looked away.

"Yes, Prince Kor."

"The shaman of shamans might help me recall something of the time before the pain."

Ev lin Dar could tell by the sound and direction of his voice that the Halflord had turned toward her. She kept her own face averted and away, hiding her hurt.

The Halflord's voice was soft, so soft.

"I would know more of the time before...of the time when we were friends."

The Black Shield turned back to her Prince. The grey skin of her comely face flushed, her lustrous white eyes were damp and wide, threatened tears.

"I will bring the shaman, Prince Kor."

The Halflord frowned, and sincere concern curled the talons of his tattoo.

"Does the wind sting your eyes, Shield?"

Despite herself, Ev lin Dar smiled, nearly laughed.

"Something like that, Prince Kor."

Axennus and Bronnus Teagh turned along the officers' wing of the White Manor, their cloaks yet heavy and damp with the night's rain, their strides slowed by sleeplessness, their booted heels falling loud and hollow against the pale veined marble of the floor.

"When do you suggest we tell the men, Axo?"

"In the morning, brother."

"It is morning."

Axennus smiled wearily.

"That it is, Bron. Tomorrow morning, then. It will give us time to think on things, to absorb what we have learned."

"Time for you to nap, you mean."

Axennus' smile broadened to a grin.

"That, too."

As they passed the door to the healer's chambers, a group of bare-footed and barely dressed guardsmen partly poured, partly stumbled from within.

The brothers Teagh turned, exchanged curious glances.

Noticing them, the guardsmen scrambled to fist the breasts of their nightshirts – those, at least, who were wearing nightshirts.

"Good...uh...good morning, Captain. Good morning, Commander. Combassador...uh...Ambassador. Sir."

"Decan Regorius," the Iron Captain said gruffly, his brow darkening. "Guardsmen." His heavy fist thumped his chest.

Axennus smiled amiably, laughter dancing in his hazel eyes.

"Good of you to dress for the occasion, gentlemen. Lose a bet, did you?"

Regorius lowered his fist, managed a crooked smile.

The others seemed inexplicably stricken, troubled, even traumatized.

"Are you injured, Decan?" frowned the Captain.

Regorius' pallid smile was more of a grimace.

"Not injured, Captain, no."

"Unwell? Ill? Is there something wrong with you?"

"Neither unwell nor ill, Captain," replied Regorius, his voice a fatigued rasp. "But I thank you for your kind concern." He brought his fist to his chest once more. "A very good morning to you, sirs."

Despite his unsatisfied curiosity, the Iron Captain found himself fisting his own breast, inadvertently dismissing the guardsmen.

Regorius and his ragged retinue turned and began to walk woodenly down the hall, back towards their own wing.

Bronnus glowered stormily at their backs.

The amusement in Axennus' smile slipped from his eyes.

Then, absurdly, Decan Regorius laughed aloud, a bleak and barren sound closer to a cackle, carrying over his shoulder, ringing with a resignation not far removed from despondence.

"Oh, but there is *definitely* something wrong with us!"

The brothers watched the guardsmen's half-dressed forms diminish down the corridor, the modest torchlight flickering across their shrinking backs like laughter.

Bronnus' scowl was scurrilous thing.

"Do I even want to know, Axo?"

Axennus' smile slid into a pensive pursing of the lips, the light in his eyes turning inward.

"I doubt it."

As the guardsmen disappeared in the distant dark, the Iron Captain nodded curtly to his brother, turned away.

"As I suspected. Have a nice nap."

14

THE RIDE OF THE RHELMAN

"When the Rhelnian Nation
asked the Allfather for Wisdom,
He made sage our minds.
When we asked him for Strength,
He made powerful our limbs.
When we asked him for Courage,
He made bold our hearts.
But when we asked him for Grace,
He made for us the Horse."

Rhelnian Creation Myth

T he night's brief storm had signaled the end of summer's long slow slide into autumn, and the first dawn of the nascent season was clear and crisp and cool. The sun broke round and red over the horizon, its crimson light seeping westward across the Northern Plains on a brisk breeze, casting the rain-rimed grasses in sanguine shadow.

Runningwolf's loamy brown eyes narrowed as he gazed eastward into the ascending sun. *A red dawn.* The set of his face was as inscrutable as stone. *Such a sunrise bodes danger to the traveler.* The Rhelman adjusted the bow and quiver at his back, loosened the strappings of the hand-axe at his waist, nudged Featherfoot to a fleeter pace, and rode on.

South and swiftly they raced, brown Rhelman and amber Rhelnian, pounding the prairie between the Old and the North Roads, where the ground was firm but pliant, and the grasses were long and soft. The huge hard spike of Northhorn gradually passed them on the right, and come the fullness of morning they had drawn parallel to the stone span betwixt the hollow eyes of the Dragon's Head.

Runningwolf slowed Featherfoot to a more leisurely pace, and the Rhelman met the eyes of the Dragon with his own, peering upon the visage of the stony beast with both wonder and wariness. The anger he had sensed there during the journey to Druintir had grown, swelled, become a palpable rage.

And even as he gazed, Runningwolf felt Featherfoot's flanks tremble for a rumbling in the earth, a deep booming roll in the rootrock.

The *akanga* were wrathful and readying for war.

Runningwolf patted the Rhelnian's muscular neck reassuringly.

Be easy, dear one. Within him, the words were soft, soothing – the ancient tongue of his people playing like poetry in his mind. *Though they do not ride, the* akanga *are friend to both my kind and your own. We have nothing to fear from them.*

Featherfoot snorted as though unconvinced.

Very well, dearest, thought the Rhelman. *We will leave this place.*

And he nudged the great amber stallion from a trot to a canter, and from a canter to a gallop, and in moments they were racing southward beneath the unsleeping glare of the Dragon, hurtling past the great dark beast with a speed approaching abandon. Under the soaring sun and abreast the warming wind, man and mount sailed the gold-green seas of the Northern Plains like a ship on a southerly surge. The Rhelman's long black hair flew at his back, a wind-whipped mane of midnight, as Featherfoot hied forth upon hooves both swift and sure.

As the sun approached its zenith, Runningwolf, though blessed with the rugged constitution of his hardy folk, felt the first hints of fatigue. Nevertheless, he was also inwardly exhilarated, spiritually invigorated – for were freedom a fire, then galloping over open ground under skies calm and clear was the fuel that fed those fine and fervid flames.

His visage set with stony determination, his eyes agleam with quiet glee for the thrill of the ride, Runningwolf of Rheln raced on.

The boy has been in the forest for a day and a night and the greater part of another day. He is huddled in a hollow formed by the roots of an ancient redwood. The hollow gives him some shield from the winds of winter that whip amidst the titanic trees. He has curled his arms about his drawn knees beneath a heavy hide of bison fur. He has packed dry straw under his thick leathers to ward him from the bitter cold. He shivers nevertheless. He briefly considers making a fire, but fire – like food, drink and sleep – is forbidden. The Rite is sacrosanct. And he would rather die than desecrate the treasured traditions of his people.

He watches. He waits. He believes his spirit guide and protector will make itself known to him. It may come as a deer. It may come as a raccoon. A panther perhaps. Or as one of the great mountain bears that infrequently defy winter to forage for food in the forest. He must only meet the animal's gaze in a sharing of souls, in spiritual communion, and then he may return to the village – to the relieved sigh of his mother and the proud smile of his father. He believes his spirit guide and protector will come. It must come.

He believes. It must.

The day wanes. Night comes. The cold deepens. The boy has neither slept nor eaten nor taken water for two days and a night. He is cold. He is hungry. And he is alone.

But he is not afraid.

With a resolve well beyond his few years, the boy adjusts his furs, rubs cold-numbed hands into his eyes against the rearing threat of sleep, and maintains his vigil.

Sometime past midday Rhelman and Rhelnian found themselves at the bank of a slender stream, and there they halted their wild run. Wide-winged dragonflies flitted above delicate water lilies; a gaggle of geese dove for silvery flashes of small fish; a red-winged blackbird sang a scratchy *oak-a-lee* amidst wind-rustled reeds. And upon the far shore, a lone female deer blinked at man and horse warily – then, sensing no imminent threat, she stooped to drink.

Featherfoot watered, then ambled away, wandering the grassy shore to graze, enjoying the sweet clusters of clover-like *siamrach* that grew there in abundance.

Runningwolf squatted and drank of the creek's cool clear waters, then wetted his sun-warmed face. Little rivulets of water trickled down his muscled chest, tickling his tight brown skin like the furtive fingers of a lover.

The Rhelman's flat earthen gaze strayed along the shoreline. Where possible, he, like Featherfoot, would forage sustenance from the land, lest his own supplies become less than meagre. Spotting a small cluster of ripe *ruabarri* nearby, the Rhelman uprooted three succulent reddish-purple necks from the giving earth. He removed the broad green leaves from the *ruabarri* with his knife, then returned to his haunches, chewing the sweetly sour stalks in satisfied silence.

Westward, some miles distant, below Southhorn and above the northern terminus of the Westwall, lay dark and dim Doomfall. Concealed behind its cloak of earthborn cloud, the Pass of the Guard was nevertheless imposing, oppressive, almost menacing. A certain ferment emanated from the fog-fettered gash in the earth, a wringing wrath at once hot and cold that assaulted both mind and spirit, lashing the soul as though with a flail forged of fire and ice.

Rage.

Rage was the second of the Sorrows of the Brave, the fourfold griefs that had plagued every warrior among the Rhelmen since that noble people's emergence from the lost and forgotten East.

Peril. Rage. War. Death.

The folklore of the Horse Masters equated these Sorrows with the Four Winds. Peril ever flew upon the North Wind. Rage rode the

West. Always had War whipped in upon the Wind of the East. And Death ever soared on the dark wings of the South.

As the wind weakened to a whisper, then fell away entirely, Runningwolf nibbled distractedly at his *ruabarri*. Three of the four Sorrows were manifest – for in the north were the Fiannar imperiled by war marching upon them from the east; and to the west, at the Dragon's Head and Doomfall, the mighty *akanga* had risen in wrath. The Rhelman's eyes narrowed. What death lay in wait in the south? What unseen doom lurked there with a patience both poignant and perverse?

Runningwolf rose from his haunches. The movement startled the doe and she dashed away, disappearing into the tall grasses of the far shore. The Rhelman peered southward, marking the ominous stillness of the winds, the superficial heat of the noon sun, the very *feel* of the air. Rain in the night, frost in the morning. Autumn, season of wither, had arrived. Shortening days, fading colours, warmth bleeding away. But fall itself would fall swiftly and soon. For winter, in all its white wrath, was to come early – and with its coming, many things would die.

The Rhelman swallowed the last of his *ruabarri*, slid his bone-hafted knife into his belt, and signalled for the rejuvenated Featherfoot. Leaping aback the great amber stallion, he shrugged his indifference.

Runningwolf of Rheln, citizen of the Erelian Republic, Left Tenant of the North March Mounted Reserve, would not number among those things that were to die.

The winter has been particularly severe, almost preternaturally so – as though the season itself is a malignant beast, a thing ruled by rage and ruling with wrath, intent upon destruction, decided on death. Blizzards have blasted from the north, whirling winds have whipped from the west, a deep cruel cold has settled upon the land like a shroud of white doom – and many are the old and the young and the weak among the People that will come to their ends in winter's bitter and baneful grasp.

The cold in the forest deepens with each crawling hour of night. The wilding gods of winter have marshalled the wrath of the west wind, have gathered unto them sundry storms from the distant sea, have combined these rages and herded toward land such a mass of wintry might that Rheln will see no day for six risings of the white and weary sun. Nature has endowed the animals of both field and forest with wit enough to sense the approaching storm and to skitter and scatter, seeking refuge in the pillared galleries of the forest, hiding and huddling there in mute fear of the icy death they instinctively know may be imminent. Even the sleek grey wolves that haunt the paths of the forest abandon their hunt and sequester themselves in secret and secure havens, stealing warmth from one another and resolutely ignoring the hunger that festers in their hollow bellies.

Like the lupine creatures after which he is named, the boy knows a storm is coming. His young bones ache quietly and his lungs detect a subtle edge to the cold of winter. The storm will be brutal, violent, lethal. He knows this. He accepts this.

The winterborn of the Rhelmen are the hardiest of a hardy people – for only the strongest of newly born infants may survive the trials of the year's most devastative season. His paternal grandfather is of the winter-born. His father and uncle also. They each survived the Rite of Becoming under particularly harsh and severe conditions. The boy is resolved that, though it mean his death, he will do no dishonour to that legacy.

He maintains that his spirit guide and protector will come. It must come.

Must.

The night wanes. The dark dawn comes. The cold deepens further. The boy has neither slept nor eaten nor taken water for two days and two nights. He is very cold. He is very hungry. And he is so all alone.

Yet he is unafraid. And he does not abandon his vigil.

As the day waned and dusk darkened the Northern Plains, the seed of a cold foreboding planted itself at the core of Runningwolf's being. And the Rhelman's sense of dread increased, magnified, sharpened with each length southward. Soon the ruby and indigo glowings of twilight chased the sun down behind the Haunted Mountains and a bitter chill infested the gloaming over the grasses. Runningwolf warily drew his steed to a halt. He peered about his environs cautiously. His nostrils twitched, testing the air. Something faintly acrid had accented the sweet scents of the prairie flora – a nearly imperceptible taint, a pale stain on fresh linen, the transparent tear upon a child's cheek.

Featherfoot snorted in displeasure, and hoofed the earth once, twice. Runningwolf rubbed the Rhelnian's neck reassuringly.

Hush, dearest. It is but the scent of death on the prairie. A predator has made a kill.

The Rhelman sniffed once more, and the slightest of frowns marked his brow. He scanned the southern horizon with sharp and searching eyes. But little was to be seen there – only the rapidly falling shades of a night yet too new for either moon or star.

Runningwolf leapt lightly from Featherfoot's back, and rubbed the amber down.

We will take our night's rest here, dear one.

Featherfoot nickered, then trotted into the rising night to water and graze at leisure.

The Rhelman settled to the ground, his legs crossed in the fashion of his folk, and ate sparingly of his rations. And as night claimed the Plains in the fullness of its dark embrace, Runningwolf rested his forearms upon his thighs, sent his cares away into the distant morrow and calmly closed his eyes.

Curiously enough, words of the Shield Maiden flitted like so many little white moths against the drawing curtains of sleep.

I cannot be certain, but I would guess the Rhelman's totem animal is the mirarran, Caelle had surmised upon their first meeting.

Runningwolf's breathing slackened. His heart slowed.

And it is well possible that a mirarran *came to him during his Rite of Becoming in the wilderness, the Rhelnian rite of passage from child to man.*

The last conscious thought to drift upon the rising seas of the Rhelman's slumber was of how very wrong the Shield Maiden had been.

Anent the storm.

The morning skies heave and erupt in masochistic glee. The winter winds lash the land with frigid force and fury, whipping the snow-strangled air into whirling multitudes of white devils. The storm surges with ever-increasing strength, with ever-deepening cold, ever-intensifying power. Living things long accustomed and well-adapted to bitter Rhelnian winters begin to die. The snows swallow the stiffened carcasses in mere moments. All the land of Rheln, field and forest and frozen rill, is buried, interred, entombed in pallid darkness. Nothing moves but winds and snows and the wheeling wights of winter. And ever does the storm grow in its violence, in its maleficence.

In the long-held beliefs of the People, the Ending of the World is to come of a winter such as this.

The boy is past shivering. His face is raw with cold. His fingers and toes tingle painfully. Winter has seeped into him, wringing all warmth from him. His blood flows slowly as though choked with floes of ice. His breath is ragged, raspy, coming in pained wheezes and gasps. He has been in the forest for two entire days, long and cold, and two entire nights, longer and colder. Without food. Without water. And this, the third morning –

And his spirit guide has not come.

The boy no longer moves. He barely blinks. He is aware but he is not alert. He is only partly conscious. His lone thought is the staunch and steadfast resolve to remain awake. To sleep is to die. To die is to bring shame to his family, to his tribe, to the People. Shame. Such a petty human suffering. What shame can there be in a noble failure?

Hours pass. The storm rants and roars with the arctic savagery of a thousand ice dragons. The boy's skin discolours. His flesh and bones are past pain. His heart beats slowly, feebly. His breath is so shallow that it cannot even mist in the frigid air. He struggles to remain wake. He strives. He battles. But he weakens. And even the most resilient and resolute of Rhelmen have their limits. In a moment of stark revelation the boy realizes his folly and abandons his faith. He knows now that his spirit guide will not come.

Will not come.

Alone in the dark and the cold and the suffocating snows of the forest, the boy's chin descends upon his chest. Sleep rises like the ghost the boy is to become. He sighs. The sound is as the chill pale whisper of Death itself.

Will. Not. Come.

Slowly, sorrowfully, the boy closes his bleak unseeing eyes.

The Rhelman rose long before the second sun of autumn. He stretched briefly, flexed, felt the blood in him feed his rested muscles. A wind had risen in the night, sourced in the south, thick and slow, blackened breath crawling over the ground. Runningwolf brought his totem to his temple and spoke a brief and silent prayer. His nostrils twitched, sampling the cool dark air of the small hours. He could smell the frost on the grass, the cool vitality of the black earth, the icy hardness of the underrock that lay still and silent beneath. But above these, around and beyond and throughout them, he detected something profoundly colder – colder, blacker, harder.

Death. Much death. Older than it had been the previous evening. Older and more foul. Rife with rot. Decay. Putrefaction.

A shadow passed over the brown stone of Runningwolf's visage. Something of a grimace tightened in his face. He peered southward into the last deeps of night, but saw only grasses silvered by frost and fading starshine. The Rhelman huffed the viscous oily stench from his nose, dismissing and dispatching it to a dark corner of his cognizance.

Then, at a subtle and silent beckons, Featherfoot emerged from the chill of waning night. The golden bay hoofed the earth in greeting, nickered softly, then snorted his distaste for the repugnant reek. The Rhelman leapt agilely astride the splendid stallion, knotted one fist in the flowing mane, and caressed the noble neck. And he remembered words spoken to him of a winter night long before.

Fear no death. Fear only the dying.

The amber pranced in answer, eager to run.

Fly, now, dearest! commanded Runningwolf. *Fly like an eagle awing the wild wind! Fly, my love!! Fly!!!*

And with a whinny of delight, the great amber leapt forth, virtually transforming into a bolt of yellow fire in the grey gloom of the Plains, striking southward into the risen wind, into the dawn, into the day.

They happened upon the first carcass at middle-day.

The sun shone a cool heat upon the Northern Plains, dry and autumnal, and beneath its white light the long grasses chafed together in a conspiracy of hushed and frightened whispers. A short distance southward from horse and rider, a small dark cloud swirled low over the fields, and a faint but constant hum rode the slow wind. And as man and mount drew nearer the odour of death thickened, became more present, more powerful. And above it all there lingered another foulness – the caustic stench of brimstone, flavouring the air with the acrid fragrance of ash.

Featherfoot slowed at an unworded command from Runningwolf and breasted cautiously through the grasses. Every instinct within the Rhelnian stallion urged him to turn from this place, but the amber's love for and loyalty to the man upon his back were the greater suasions.

Runningwolf eyed the dark cloud hovering and humming over the grasses. His calm countenance twitched imperceptibly.

Bh'ritsi. Scavenger vermin. Thousands upon thousands of the large flesh-eating flies. Feeding. Feasting. Runningwolf knew what he would find beneath the swarm of *bh'ritsi* – the decomposing carcass of a deer, perhaps, or that of one of the great buffalo that migrated across the Northern Plains come new autumn. The sheer number of flies made the latter the more likely of the two.

Runningwolf drew Featherfoot to a halt. Something disturbed the Rhelman, something subtler than massed flies feeding on a dead thing. His gaze moved away from the swarming *bh'ritsi* to the clear autumnal skies. Not a wisp of cloud. Nothing but endless blue, soft and light, with the stark white orb of the sun directly overhead. Perturbed, Runningwolf shaded his eyes with his hand, peering searchingly into the blue, scanning the skies from horizon to horizon to horizon – seeking something that should have been there but was not. Momentarily, he lowered his hand, and then his eyes.

I am troubled, dear one, he confided to his loyal mount.

Featherfoot snorted against the sulphuric stench.

Nay, dearest, it is not the smell of brimstone that worries my thoughts – although that and the cause of my agitation may very well be related in a fashion yet unrevealed to me.

He stroked Featherfoot's mighty neck.

Where are the carrion birds, dear one? Where are the vulture and the buzzard? Why are they not here?

Featherfoot huffed, hoofed the earth.

Sooth, dearest, there is no bird of any feather aflight in this day's sky. What has frightened them so?

The Rhelman's eyes narrowed with dark discerning insight.

Or mayhap some unnamed evil has destroyed them all. And this stench of sulphur is the spoor of these destroyers.

The amber flinched faintly.

Runningwolf leapt gracefully to the ground.

Remain here, dear one.

He paused, producing a pungent yellow root from a pouch at his belt, rubbing the root's oozing oils into the skin at his neck and pits and wrists. Thus warded from the *bh'ritsi*, he then took his bow into hand and nocked an arrow to its string – lest foes larger than flies approach that root-oil might fail to repel. He glanced upwards, only the slightest hint of anxiety clouding his calm countenance.

And beware the sky, dearest. Ware it well.

The Rhelman then moved forward, the deep bronze of his skin melding with the dusty gold of the Plains. He went in silence, in stealth, as though his quarry was alive and alert and not already dead and rotting. Catching the root-reek approaching, the swarm of *bh'ritsi* buzzed and whirled in displeasure, then dispersed. Runningwolf paused, watching the carrion flies scatter, then pushed his way through a tall tangle of brush to the place of the dead.

Immediately, his acute senses were assaulted, and his steadfast heart started, then fell still for a moment.

The stench struck him first – the rancid reek of rot and decay, a palpable thing, pervasive, perverse – like the fetor of an abattoir left too long unclean in a humid heat.

Then were his eyes assailed. The carcass of a plains buffalo lay in a gory heap in its own offal upon grasses bent and broken and browned with dried blood. The noble beast's beauty had been savaged, ravaged. Its vast bulk had been hideously mutilated, its hide partially peeled from putrescent pink flesh, its entrails torn from its rent belly and strewn in scarlet skeins upon the ground like great veins bereft of flesh through which to flow. The creature's lips had been ripped from its skull, its tongue wrenched from between its shattered teeth and protruding grotesquely. One eye had been eaten away, the other gored from its socket and hanging on thin threads of reddened gristle.

And then there was the sound – that *sound* – the slick wet vociferation of teeming thousands of *bh'ritsi* larvae feasting upon befouled and fetid flesh – moiling multitudes of maggots, creeping, crawling, chewing – legions of wiggling white worms devouring body, blood and bone from both within and without.

Runningwolf blinked slowly, purposefully, as though in doing so he might wash the sight of the slaughter from his eyes. He then willed the sound of the voracious vermin from his ears, and the stenches of rot and sulphur from his nostrils. His breathing slowed, silenced, and his heart soon thudded steadily against his ribs once again.

He then moved forward, acutely alert, cautiously circling the carcass, his sharp dark eyes scanning both the ground and the gruesomely gutted beast. Once, twice, thrice he circuited, stopping and stooping now and again to probe either grass or gore with the steel head of his readied arrow. At length he straightened, returned the arrow to its quiver and his bow to his shoulder, and raised his eyes to the vast void of the day's blue skies.

And then Runningwolf walked back toward the place where Featherfoot awaited him, the proud Rhelnian prancing and hoofing the earth at his master's safe return. The Rhelman nimbly mounted, patting the stallion's strong neck reassuringly. Featherfoot stilled and nickered softly at his touch.

Neither wolf nor bear did this thing, dear one, came the Rhelman's silent voice. *Nor panther nor mighty lion – nor even hand of Man.*

The Rhelnian snorted.

But for those of the buffalo, there are no tracks leading to or from this place. The poor animal has been brutally butchered, ripped to shreds – yet nothing has been removed, and nothing has been eaten, save that upon which the flies and the worms have fed.

A slight crease distorted the Rhelman's brown brow.

No, this deed was not done of a natural hunger, dearest, but of evil passions, and for perverse pleasure.

Runningwolf's eyes seemed to darken to a deep black.

And the thing that did this deed was not of the earth, in either sense of the phrase – nay, dear one, the perpetrator of this abomination came from the sky, and is not of this world.

The amber huffed, and Runningwolf steered the steed wide of the slaughter and the rapid return of *bh'ritsi*. The stench of brimstone was yet sharp and hot in the autumn air.

The worms of the bh'ritsi *tell me that the animal met its fate only one day past, dearest,* the Rhelman reasoned. *And the proliferation of the flies speaks less of death and the absence of carrion birds than it does of an evil most foul. This sulphuric stench is the spoor of this evil. And the scent leads south. Into the wind.*

He knotted a fist in Featherfoot's silken mane.

A very mighty evil indeed.

The carcass behind them, the empty sky above them, Runningwolf urged the great amber to a trot, then to a run. Southward they sped.

Southward.

Into the wind.

Death, the boy remembers being told, comes in many forms and along many paths. His own end will come of cold, he knows, of the white pitilessness of winter – and he knows also that it will come soon. He feels nothing – neither pain nor cold. He cannot move. He is only conscious enough to know his heart is failing, his blood but a feeble trickle in his veins. Darkness swells about his spirit, enfolding him in a black unfeeling embrace. One by one, he calmly fares well his mother, his father, his grandfather, his grandmothers, his uncle, his cousins, his many friends. He wonders how they will remember him, what they will say of his life, what will be said of his death.

And then his heart beats one last time and falls still. The blood in him freezes. His spirit detaches from his flesh, hovering above his snow-dusted body, a faint and fragile luminescence, like the fabled coloured lights of distant northern nights. He gazes upon his own corpse, so small, so insubstantial, so very inconsequential. He wonders if he will be remembered at all.

And then he is aware of another thing. A light. Bright and white. Nearing from the north. Bold and so very beautiful. And a voice comes to him like wind in the trees, like a song in the night.

"Abbawontandontas."

The boy feels his spirit smile, and he is at ease – for he to whom no spirit guide came in life would soon have one in death.

As they progressed southward the stench of rancid death grew in its putrescence, its pestilence, and man and mount came upon more and more hideously mutilated remains of hapless buffalo. The brutalized beasts lay upon ruined grasses in heaps of festering flesh, swarming with filthy *bh'ritsi*, the carcasses first appearing singly, then in pairs and threes and fours, then in small clusters, then in larger ones, and lastly upon a slaughterground of hundreds, perhaps thousands – an entire herd utterly destroyed. Similar to the ravaged state of the first carcass, all had been gutted, savaged, ripped apart, left to rot. And though there was no sense to the slaughter, there was yet purpose, and that purpose was pleasure – the twisted pleasure found by things fell and foul in the act of killing, in the maiming of beauty, in the wanton destruction of life.

Runningwolf brought Featherfoot to a slow gait. He viewed the scene through dark heated eyes. The amber huffed and snorted in instinctive repugnance, in revulsion, in wary fear. Runningwolf held him by the mane, steadying him. The stench of sulphur was like fire in the air.

This is where it began, dearest, judged the Rhelman. *The things came from the sky. Likely from the east. And they were many. Very many.*

Featherfoot nickered in quiet trepidation.

Nay, dearest, soothed the Rhelman, scanning the vacant skies in all directions. *They are not here. They have gone. East or south. They did not go north.*

His eyes moved to the distant grey stone of the Westwall and the huge and hoary Haunted Mountains, domain of the mighty *akanga.*

And they will not have gone west.

The stallion stamped one heavy hoof.

Few buffalo escaped the initial assault, Runningwolf continued. *Those that did so fled northward. The first we found was the last to die. The things that perpetrated this abomination suffered none to live.*

He paused, peering into the vast flowing fields south of them. The waystation of Highmarch, the Rhelman knew, lay more than a full day's uninterrupted swift ride down the North Road. Three hundred souls resided there, with little soldiery of which to speak.

Let us hope the things that did this have gone eastward.

The Rhelnian's regal head bowed in agreement.

Come, dearest, nudged Runningwolf, *we will depart this place. We can do nothing here but lament. And we leave lamentation for lesser hearts.*

They rode through the remainder of the day, through the purple-grey glow of evening, into the black heart of night, across the risen glow of dawn, through another long day, and achieved lonely Highmarch as the shades of the following dusk were coming down on the world. Runningwolf halted the fatigued Featherfoot a small distance from the outpost and surveyed the place with weary but wary eyes.

Highmarch – the northmost waystation and trading post between the Erelian Republic and the Free Nations of the North – consisted of a small cluster of buildings closely lining the North Road upon both the eastern and western sides. Each structure was distinct from the next and each was in a differing degree of repair. Faded flags of the Free Nations fluttered at varying heights from poles and porches. Runningwolf noted a traders hall, a pair of inns, a stable, a general store, a smithy, a postal station, lenders offices, a garishly painted brothel – and several other establishments necessary to the continuance of open commerce.

But Highmarch seemed dead, deserted, a town of ghosts and grey wind. Nothing moved within the gloom deepening in and about the town. And despite the hour, Highmarch should have evidenced *some* activity – a vendor bartering with a customer in the makeshift market, a groom rubbing down a weary horse, a drunken merchant shambling down the single dusty lane, a whore peddling her lascivious wares. But all was desolate, disquietingly quiet – nothing moved, save only the slow dark breath of the southwind.

The Rhelman readied his bow and placed it across his thighs, then loosened the hand-axe at his waist. Highmarch had been far enough south to have been spared the sorcery of the red wind of six days past – no, the silence and the stillness of the waystation were sourced in something other than sorcery, a darker thing, a thing far less subtle. And the sour reek of sulphur was its brand burned into the dusk.

Forward, my dear, the Rhelman whispered silently. *But slowly. Ever so slowly. Be watchful of all. Miss nothing.*

They had drawn little nearer when Runningwolf marked the first corpses – all but shadows initially, they swiftly took form in the growing gloaming and became the destroyed and the dead. Three men, one woman, strewn upon the street, each horribly mutilated, torn to pieces, ripped almost beyond recognition. And more beyond. Dozens. Scores. Lying dead in the dust, in the dusk. The ruined remains of lost lives.

Warily, ever watchful of the sky, Rhelman and Rhelnian moved into the town. Beneath the suffusive stink of brimstone, the smell of death was thin yet, more given to the metallic flavour of blood than the rancid reek of rot. No, this slaughter was young, recent, fresh. Even the *bh'ritsi* had yet to come. Some of the butchered bodies still seeped blood. Others remained limp, awaiting the rigidity that comes hard upon the heels of death. All were only an hour, perhaps two, removed from life.

Man and mount moved along the road in hushed horror.

The dead were everywhere, lying in the blood-sullied dirt along the street and between the buildings. Men, women, children. All had been ripped and rended. Dogs, chickens, horses. Everyone. Everything. Destroyed. Massacred.

Runningwolf rode Featherfoot the length of desecrated Highmarch in silence, the soft but heavy thud of the horse's hooves on the road matching the slow pump of the Rhelman' pulse. He then turned the Rhelnian about, and moved into the waystation's dead heart once more. There he halted, his flat earthen eyes absorbing the extent of the atrocity about him, then peering upward into the deepening darkness of the skies, seeing nothing there but grey becoming black.

In some time he dismounted, secreted the amber beneath a blood-spattered awning, and moved afoot about the battered bodies of the slain. Though many evidenced wounds that could only have been caused by long and wicked fangs, none had been eaten, nor even gnawed upon, and no trophies had been taken. All had been slain to satiate an urge other than hunger, other than pride – the sole purpose of the atrocity had been to provide the perpetrators with pure impassioned pleasure.

Evil.

The Rhelman then investigated each structure in turn, thoroughly inspecting all interiors – but he found only more dismembered dead sprawled in swathes of slowly sluicing blood. Stubbornly, he persisted in his search, looking behind every door, in every trunk, beneath every bed, in every closet, in every cellar – all the possible places where one in terror might conceivably flee to hide. But he discovered nothing but further death and the spoors of sulphur and slaughter.

Of three hundred souls and more, none had survived.

Such evil.

Leaving the last building, Runningwolf gathered some feed from the stable-cum-slaughterhouse, returned to Featherfoot, and led the stallion into the dark dingy confines of one of the inns – the only structure where there were none of the slain. The low ceiling there was only barely high enough to accommodate the tall Rhelnian, and Featherfoot nickered against the closeness of the place.

Nay, dearest, we take our rest in the open no longer, explained Runningwolf as he massaged the amber's tired muscles.

The Rhelnian quieted at his master's firm but gentle caress.

And we journey no more by night, nor even beneath skies low with cloud. Should the things that committed these desecrations come for us, it would be well that we have some warning.

Night claimed Highmarch. Featherfoot watered and fed in relative security in the front room of the tavern. Runningwolf stood in the entrance, arms folded across his muscled chest, feathers dangling from the thongs at his hard biceps, weapons loosened and at the ready. His loamy eyes searched the black skies for sign of peril, his ears harkening for the flap of leathery wings. He saw nothing but the white of the moon and the distant shine of a thousand stars. And all he heard was the growing buzz of *bh'ritsi* come to feast.

We will remain here till dawn, my dear, the Rhelman spoke silently over his shoulder. *But for our own selves, there are only the dead in Highmarch now, and the things that killed them have no use for the dead. The things are not likely to return. Indeed, unliving Highmarch is the safest place on the Northern Plains this night.*

Featherfoot snorted skeptically.

Runningwolf then settled to the floor, rested his arms upon his knees, closed his weary eyes, and soon sank into a deep and dreamless sleep.

The boy waits as the light approaches from the north. So white and pure, like living starfire in the night. Beneath his floating spirit, the snow begins to bury his frozen body. He hears an otherworldly music, soft and melodic, the tinkling of tiny bells, the stringing of a harp on a sighing summer wind. The light draws nearer, the song seems closer. The boy's soul warms in the glow, weaves to the melody. But strangely, he is no longer at ease.

I am dead, *he thinks.* But I am not content.

But then a coldness grasps him, bears him down, draws him back into his body. Winter claims him once again, shackling him in ice, wrapping him in polar chains. Pain wracks him. His spirit flails, resists. But the struggles are in vain. He is not dead. But only dying. Slowly. And in agony.

The soundless scream of the boy's floundering spirit shrieks into the frigid heart of the winter storm.

Shrieks, and does not pass all ears unheard.

They departed the horror of Highmarch at dawn. The great amber seemed desperate for the run, relieved to put the devastated outpost behind them, hurling himself heedlessly over the Plains. But Runningwolf was not so enthused to be upon the open grasslands, visible and vulnerable, where shelter was sparse and refuge rare. He continually scanned the southern and the eastern skies; he paid the northern sky less heed, though of its vastness at his back he was ever conscious and aware; and the western heavens he abandoned entirely to the guardianship of the Haunted Mountains and the angry vigilance of the mighty *akanga*.

They ran through the day, into the steady surge of the southwind, galloping over the grasslands with a haste born of urgency, of necessity. Even at a constant gallop – which Featherfoot could not hope to maintain without his heart rupturing within him – the silver city of Hiridith lay many days distant yet, and Runningwolf's duty was to deliver his Commander's dispatch with all speed. He would ware the death that rode the dark wings of the southwind, but he would not fly from it, nor would he turn aside from his Commander's charge.

Despite the swiftness of their run, the day passed slowly for man and mount. The leagues inched past, and the yellowed seas of the Northern Plains differed little from one sun-crested wave of grass to the next. The horizons south and east and north never appeared to alter. And to the right, the Westwall was a single long grey monotonous line, seeming without end; beyond and above, the hulking mass of the Haunted Mountains remained wreathed in the motionless mists of stilled time.

The day was old when Runningwolf marked the minute black blot in the southern sky. Dark and distant. Many long miles away. A small but stark stain upon the deep blue mantle of fading day.

The Rhelman first slowed Featherfoot, then drew the great amber to a halt, staring warily, watchfully, southward into the wind. The horse huffed and snorted. But Runningwolf's own breathing remained measured and even. Hand on axe-head, he sat astride the anxious amber, the pair seeming so very small in the vast and otherwise empty expanse of the Plains. And with the patience and the dispassionate self-possession of his people, Runningwolf of Rheln waited.

And slowly, gradually, the black stain swelled, drawing steadily nearer, like a terrible dark dragon soaring on the southwind. And before it, faint but intensifying with each passing moment, with each furious flap of wings still too distant to discern, came a sinister harbinger in its van – the hot acidic odour of brimstone.

They have come, my dear.

The Rhelman shadowed his loamy oval eyes with the flat of one hand, squinting into the distances both east and south, scrutinizing every vague variation in the grasslands, seeking some semblance of shelter or sanctuary. But all he saw was the endless emptiness of the Northern Plains.

Nor is there haven behind us, dearest.

Runningwolf's gaze flicked back to the sable stain in the sky. It had expanded, enlarged, but had also blurred as the one blot became many, dappling, allowing sullied light to seep between individual forms. Then, as Runningwolf gauged the speed of the things, he detected an infinitesimal but significant alteration in the their course as they neared.

They have seen us, my dear.

Featherfoot neighed nervously as Runningwolf whirled him around to face the faraway heights of the Westwall and the huge and hoary hulk of the Haunted Mountains. The Rhelman's dark eyes flashed in the flat fearlessness of his face.

Westward we shall fly, dear one, for though they are swift, the setting sun may slow them a trifle. And mayhap we shall find some shield in the shadows and the stones beneath the cliffs.

Deftly, reflexively, Runningwolf nocked an arrow to his bow.

But blood, my dear – both theirs and our own – will surely feed the earth this day.

Featherfoot then reared, hoofing the autumn air, and with a whinny born of the rival thrills of exhilaration and trepidation, the great amber of Rheln streaked westward over the grasses, chasing the sun, gold on gold on gold.

Six miles.

Six miles of vacant meadowland lay between the racers from Rheln and the soaring steep of the Westwall. Fleet and furious was their flight – Featherfoot's magnificent muscles rippling and rolling beneath his glistening coat, Runningwolf bent low upon the splendid steed's neck, the golden mane of the former and the midnight hair of the latter flying as one in a wind of the pair's own making.

However, the Rhelman knew only too well that even such utmost speed would not suffice. He needed not look their way, needed not see them adjust their course to know the foul things in the sky were moving, rushing, racing to intercept. He could *sense* them, feel them like the fiery breath of a pursuing dragon on his left shoulder. He could smell their sulphuric spoor. He could taste their evil, their hatred, their very wrongness. He could hear their heinous screeches increase in both frequency and volume as they narrowed the distance between them and their prey. And he knew them for what they were.

They are golgarrai, *dearest,* he revealed in reserved revulsion. *Bewinged demons of the First World, loosed long ago upon this Second Earth. They have not been seen in the skies of this Earth since the battle of Gan Gebbernin twenty centuries ago. Long have we thought them destroyed, extinct, removed from reality to the misted realm of mythos.* His earthy eyes narrowed into slits glossed with hindsight. *Long have we been mistaken.*

Featherfoot ran like wind, like lightning, like no other Rhelnian had run before him. Before them, the Westwall grew steadily taller, certain features and facets of its immense stony face becoming discernible in the shadows as the sun swept over the Haunted Mountains. Runningwolf soon distinguished great rocks heaped at the Westwall's landing, titanic talus creating an abundance of protective crevices and defensible caves.

Refuge was near. So very near.

They were less than half a mile from the Westwall when the *golgarrai* fell upon them from the sky.

"Abbawontandontas."

The voice is ethereal, eurhythmic, surreal. It is not so much heard as it is felt. A soft and gentle caress on the boy's chilled cheek. A summer wind within him. A rich loam upon his soul.

"Awaken, Abbawontandontas."

A revival.

"Awaken, now."

Or a resurrection.

The boy's eyes crack open. He fights to focus. He is aware of a great whiteness – immediate, extreme, excessive. Sunfire. So brilliantly bright. Yet not hurtful. And as the boy's sight adjusts, the light swirls, solidifies, assumes shape and form.

And lo!

There stands before him such a creature as could have only been born of the Light itself. Tall and regal, it is – magnificent, resplendent – an equine entity as far removed from the humble horse as the Sky Spirits are from lowly Man. Its immaculate coat glistens like starshine, whiter than the sun-kissed snow on the mountains, brighter than lightning aflame across the heavens. Its mane and tail and fetlocks are long, lustrous, spun of the finest gold, flowing in wondrous waves and fluttering without avail of wind. And its eyes are as gold-gilt moons, large and round, their innate internal light evidencing intellect, reason, emotion.

And cold and darkness flee the creature in reverence, in terror. The snows and even the trees withdraw from where the equine entity looms

over the prostrate form of the boy. And the boy soon finds himself upon
a green glen in the night, where the grasses are as soft as down, and the
ground is warm and dry. And the boy rises to his knees, his face and eyes
bright with reflected light, and he reflexively extends one small shaking
hand. He well knows what is come for him in the night.

A Spirit Horse.

A thing of legend, of the tales of the elders about the village fires at
night. A Sky Spirit's steed. One has not been seen in Rheln in one hun-
dred generations. But the boy knows that not all things that exist are
seen. His soul soars within him.

But then he becomes aware another thing.

Astride the Spirit Horse's back sits a figure, man-like in shape and
form, and as black as the steed is bright, as baneful as the steed is beau-
tiful. He is tall as well, taller than any Rhelman, and cloaked and clad
in diaphanous midnight. And within the shadowed close of his cowl can
only be seen two cold colourless eyes, flashing like pale pearls in the
depths of a bedless sea.

The boy shudders for a cold beyond any that winter might muster.
His sailing soul falters, falls within him. He knows the Spirit Horse is
not come for him. It is merely the means to an end. And it bears the end
upon its back.

The boy lowers his hand, then his eyes, and submits to the might and
majesty of Death itself.

The *golgarrai* swooped down upon them from the gloaming
firmament, great dark thunderbolts, shattering the air with their
hellish screeches. The grasses withered in the burning wind of
their wings. Runningwolf whirled atop Featherfoot, sensing the
proximity, the immediacy, of the demons. And his bowstring sang
aloud, clear and cold. The Rhelnian bow was small, compact,
recurved, specifically designed for close fighting from horseback,
and none was more its master than was Runningwolf. Swifter than
the eye could follow, one, two, three, a dozen slender Rhelnian
arrows flew into the mass of bewinged beasts that made black and
bleak the broad blue of the evening sky. But the bolts fell harmlessly

away from hard lacertilian hides, dropping haplessly to the earth, broken and unbloodied.

Undeterred, Runningwolf discarded bow and sheaf, leapt from Featherfoot's back, rolled, rising with both axe and knife in hand.

And he gave his loyal steed one final command.

Fly! Fly, my love! came the voice of his soul. *Fly to the Wall! I will distract them if I might, hold them if I may. Fly! And if fate shall have it, we will meet again upon the fair fields of the Otherworld!*

But the great amber slid to a halt on the grasses, turned and reared. Feverish with fear, but ever faithful, Featherfoot would not abandon his master.

And with a searing screech that would shrivel a lesser soul, the first of the foul and fulsome *golgarrai* fell upon the small brown man standing alone in the wing-buffeted grass. The demon was immense, easily thrice the Rhelman's bulk, with wings spanning nearly twenty feet from tip to razor-taloned tip. It was markedly chiropteran in appearance, its vast membranous wings extending from its overlong forelimbs to its short stout hindlimbs. Its head was huge and hideously horned, distorted further by a mangy mane, crimson cancroid eyes and an immense protrusive maw in which long fangs gnashed like rows of great yellow knives. Its mightily muscled body was armoured in ironlike scales, squamous and serpentine, the most dense of these upon its bosom and about its throat, as impervious as any breastplate and gorget forged of steel. And despite its mass and misshapenness, the beast was surprisingly swift, unnaturally agile, and ever about it was the sinus-scorching stench of brimstone.

But Runningwolf was also swift, was also agile, and no reek in the world would ever sway him, could ever stay him.

The Rhelman deftly ducked below the striking jaws of the *golgarra*, slipped inside the deadly arc of a slicing claw, leapt, plunged his long knife hilt-deep into the creature's clavicle, spun, and buried his axe-blade in the side of the beast's skull. The *golgarra* shrieked once and tumbled to the ground, great wings collapsing, the momentum of its fall propelling it to its back. The thing was dead before its brackish blood besmeared the wounded earth. The beast's body slid to a stop, shuddered reflexively, then lay still. Runningwolf, balanced upon its broad breast, tore his steel from the fiend's foul flesh. And then, his visage the portrait of indifference, of insouciance, the Rhelman turned to meet the others.

The *golgarrai* shrieked and screeched at the sight of one of their number slain. They raged in concert, crazed with hate and hunger, frenzied with fury. They plummeted upon the Rhelman, screaming shrilly, buffeting him with their enormous bat-like wings. They reached to rend him with their wickedly curved claws. They strove to shred him in their massive maws. To impale him on their horrible horns.

But their quarry was as a ghost, and the talons and teeth of the *golgarrai* struck only air and earth.

Runningwolf danced among the demons like a wild thing. He was so very fluid, pantherine, ever swift, ever strong. His long black hair flew about him like wings of his own, his body bending, evading, avoiding. His knife and his hand-axe whirled around him, stabbing, slashing, and his legs and feet were as swift as his steel. Runningwolf's battle-style was the definition of grace – artful, effortless, efficient. The *golgarrai* were unprepared for this enemy, one that fought back with such masterful poise and martial proficiency. They screamed as they died. And ever were the dark eyes of the Rhelman aflash with cool fire in his flat unfearing face.

But the *golgarrai* were many. Very many. And they knew little terror but their own, and they were possessed of a cruel cleverness. Though not mortal in and of themselves, they knew the mortal heart, having long fed on the spirits of living things in the darkness of their distant demesne. They knew how to slice and sleave the human soul.

Runningwolf heard Featherfoot's heart-curdling death-cry above the cacophony of combat. *Above.* Ripping his knife from the soft flesh under the jaw of a dying demon, the Rhelman glanced upward into the coming night, saw three *golgarrai* aflight with Featherfoot flailing between them. Saw the bewinged fiends tear the proud Rhelnian to shreds in a crimsoning sky. Felt the stallion's warm blood spatter his skin. Sensed something substantial break within him, felt part of his own self die.

And Runningwolf's stony composure shattered.

Wrath consumed his heart, wildfire exploded within his soul, madness took his mind. The artfulness and grace of the Rhelman's battle-dance gave way to the grotesque, to savagery and butchery. And he thought no more of his own well-being, but only of death – the death and ruin of the vile things that had destroyed his dearest.

Beloved!!!

Blood flew from Runningwolf's steel like acidic rain in a windstorm. He raged through his enemies, his mouth stretched into the horrible battle cry of his forefathers, his war-screams slicing through the screeches of the hellish beasts even as his weapons ripped through their flesh. So swift was he in the slaughter that, despite his disregard for his own person, the *golgarrai* could not touch him. Again and again his keen metal cut past scale into muscle, bone, organ. Again and again the demons shrieked and fell to the blood-blackened grasses. Slow and awkward they then seemed as the grief-crazed Rhelman flashed around them, darted beneath them, leapt above them. And the stipends for their crime and their sluggishness were blood and pain and death.

In the end, Runningwolf's undoing came of not of *golgarraish* might – neither of the demons' strength nor of their skill – but of ill chance.

The Rhelman leapt from the back of a *golgarra*, ripping his knife free of the beast's eye. He rolled away from the stricken thing, momentarily assuming the crouch of a panther about to pounce. He watched the demon as it died, its eye a fountain spewing foul fluids. It writhed upon the ground, retching reflexively, dead but for the last feeble motor responses firing in its broken brain. Runningwolf roared in rage and triumph, and turned away to meet his next foe, his next kill.

But in its spasmodic death throes, the *golgarra*'s black wings splayed widely, flapping violently, and one long steely claw pierced Runningwolf from behind, running him through the middle, impaling him.

The Rhelman gasped, dropped to his knees. His weapons fell from his hands. He looked down at the black barbed thing protruding from his belly, wrapped his hands about it, felt the seep of his own precious lifeblood. Shock was etched upon his flat face, a dark wonder was in his eyes. That he was dying did not surprise him – from the moment he had seen the black blot on the horizon, he had expected to die that day – rather it was the manner of his end that moved him so in those his final moments.

Chance. Happenstance. Fate. The boldest, the strongest, the swiftest, the most skilled of warriors – even these might not choose the particulars of their passing.

The triumphant *golgarrai* circled about and above him, shrieking with glee, closing quickly.

Ah, dearest...I come for you now.

Runningwolf fell to his side on the ground, the thud of his heart overly loud in his ears. He sighed. He felt his heartbeat enter the soil beneath him, felt the earth's own heart pound in answer. Pounding, pounding, pounding. And as his own lifepulse faltered, that of the earth grew louder and stronger, like a thunder in the stone, or like great drums rumbling in the rock.

Dun dun dun doom.

Runningwolf felt the earth quake with rage, heard the demons screech in dismay, anguish, loss – sensed them hurriedly leave him, felt the dark wind of their departing wings fall foul upon his face.

Dun dun dun doom.

Mighty hands pulled him from the claw on which he was impaled, laid him upon the bloodied grass. Guttural voices that he did not comprehend muttered quietly, almost sadly, over his motionless form. And the drums in the earth fell silent.

His cheek upon the grass, his eyes wide and staring, the last thing the Rhelman saw in the growing gloom of dusk was a small speck of white light – so far and so faint, but nearing from the north, impossibly swift, like a fiery comet hurtling through celestial skies.

Then Runningwolf's eyes went blank, empty.

And he died.

"Are you Death?" the boy asks of the figure upon the Spirit Horse.

Something flickers in those cold uncoloured eyes, suggesting a small smile.

"Many would consider me so, child." A short pause. A strange warmth rises in the figure's pale gaze. "You, however, may consider me otherwise."

"But...but you called for me," the boy stammers.

Silence.

Then, *"No, 'twas not I that called your name, child," replies the form in black, "but Eveningwind."*

Eveningwind?

"You are gifted with the talent to commune with all creatures equine," reveals the dark one, "be those creatures horses, mirarra *or* elliamir. *And as I am a Prince of the Athair, so Eveningwind is a prince of the* elliamir.*"*

Prince?

"I am Yllufarr, Sun Lord of the Athair, Prince of the Folk of Gavrayel in Gith Glennin. In the tales of the people of Rheln I am the Sky Spirit called Fyllur Lumin. Eveningwind is my bearer, my intimate and my friend. And he has come here to summon you from Death."

The boy is astonished, struck dumb.

"Thrice in your life will Eveningwind come to you, child. Twice will he claim you from the dark grasp of Death. Once, and for a time, will he bear you."

Claim me?

"Eveningwind has some little power over Death. He is the reason I live, though all my Sun Knights have fallen and are lost to me and to this world. And Eveningwind has taken to you, and will not allow you to die." The smile in Yllufarr's gaze cools, becomes wry. "Your time, he tells me, is not yet come."

The boy blinks in wonder.

"Yours will not be an easy life, child. You will return to your village. You will tell your elders that a Spirit Horse came to you in the wilderness, that the elliam *is your totem creature, your spirit guide and protector. They will not believe you. They will accuse you of sacrilege, of blasphemy. You will be ostracized, banished, sent away. You will cease to exist in the minds of your people, your dearest kith and your own kin. Even in the hearts of your own father and mother, you will become one of the Invisible."*

Tears swell in the boy's eyes.

"But you will survive, child. You will see things that no Rhelman has ever seen. You will go places where no Rhelman has ever gone. You will accomplish fantastic feats, do great deeds. You will become a Rhelman of legend. And in time, when the need is most dire, you will return to your people. And you will return as a hero, a saviour, a messiah – and as a son."

The Spirit Horse nickers. The sound is as a song, soft and sweet. A single gleaming golden strand falls from the elliam's glorious mane, a sliver of the rising sun, and flutters to the ground.

"Rise now, child, and return to your village. Remember what I have told you. Remain strong. Know no despair. Keep faith. Become the man the Teller speaks of in his Tale."

The boy stands, the solitary string of Eveningwind's holy hair clutched tightly in one tiny hand.

"Fear no death." The pale pearly eyes become cold once more. "Fear only the dying."

Eveningwind turns, and Sky Spirit and steed glide into the coming dawn like ghosts. And are gone.

Runningwolf woke to the smell of smoke and burning flesh. His eyes fluttered open, fought to focus. Above him, gliding awkwardly, great dark carrion birds circled slowly in a grey and gloomy sky. Heavily laden clouds had rolled in on the eastwind in the night as the Rhelman slept, undreaming and oblivious, and the dark dawn air was heavy with the promise of rain.

Slept? But surely he had died –

Runningwolf was on his feet in an instant. Memory flooded back to him through the shattered dams of slumber.

Golgarrai. Flight. Battle. Featherfoot. Death.

The Rhelman swiftly surveyed his surroundings. Some distance to the east a great pyre burned upon the plains, the carcasses of the slain *golgarrai* heaped carelessly upon one another and aflame. Burning, burning. The stench of their fired flesh darkened the dawn as effectively as did the hovering cover of cumuli.

Southward a mound had been raised – a burial mound, certainly. And though it was unmarked and anonymous, the Rhelman knew what body lay there in the cool embrace of Mother Earth.

Beloved.

And immediately beside him, neatly arranged on the grasses, was the small assortment of his own trappings. His hand-axe and bone-handled knife, each weapon meticulously cleaned and polished by hands other than his own. His small bow and replenished sheaf of arrows. The silvered horn with which his Captain had entrusted him. The little bundle the Commander had given him. His meagre provisions and scant belongings. All tidily assembled.

But he had surely died...

Runningwolf moved his gaze to his middle, to where the claw of the demon had pierced him. A subtle spark of wonder briefly flared in his deep loamy eyes. The skin of his belly was smooth and flawless, marked by neither wound nor scar. He had healed – or had *been* healed – in the night. Completely so. As though his dying had been but an insubstantial illusion. But he *remembered* – remembered being impaled, remembered grasping the wicked talon, the cold sensation of its hoary hardness in his hands, remembered feeling the fatal flow of his own blood. Reflexively, the Rhelman passed a hand over the place where the claw had run him through. He remembered dying.

And then he remembered another thing.

Drums. *Dun dun dun doom.* Great drums thundering in the earth. *Dun dun dum doom.* The war drums of the mighty *akanga*.

The *akanga* had come to the field of battle and the *golgarrai* had fled before them. The *akanga* had then laid Runningwolf on the earth. They must have also placed his provisions beside him, must have buried faithful Featherfoot's remains, must have gathered and set afire the carcasses of the demons. Had the *akanga*, those great spirits of stone and flame, also revived, resurrected, returned life to the fallen Rhelman?

No – for all their power, for all their might, the *akanga* were destroyers, not healers, of ones other than their own.

Another must have come. Another. One with influence over death. Another...

And then the Rhelman remembered the light that had raced toward him from the north as his life had failed him. A light so white. So bright. So very pure. So very potent and puissant. The light of one whom he had encountered of a winter night so many long years before, of one come again for him upon his falling, come to lift him up, to bear him back.

Abbawontandontas.

A voice in his soul, the very voice Runningwolf had heard in that wintered forest so distant in time and space. Ethereal, eurhythmic, surreal. Playing in his mind like a divine melody once again. Calling to him.

The Rhelman's gaze was drawn westward, to the tumbled talus scattered at the foot of the Westwall, to the great shards of stone standing in the twin shadows of that colossal cliff and of the Haunted Mountains behind. Instantly, beat and breath and blood stilled within him. For there, atop a lofty rise of broken rock, brilliant and beautiful in the gloom of the sunless dawn, was the grand and glorious creature that had come and had called and had claimed Runningwolf from death a second time.

Eveningwind.

And the Rhelman knelt before the power and the glory of that prince of the *elliamir*, raising to his temple the totem pouch that held a single strand of the equine entity's golden mane. And he closed his eyes in reverence of the Spirit Horse's light and loveliness.

Rise, Abbawontandontas.

Runningwolf rose. He lowered his totem pouch to a hammering heart.

Hiridith awaits you, Abbawontandontas. Your errand is yet urgent. Bid farewell to your beloved. But quickly. We must make all haste to Hiridion's Walls. Come rain, come wind, we will achieve the Silver City two days hence. But each hour lost may mean the doom of the Fiannar, and therefore also of this Second Earth.

Runningwolf's eyes opened slowly, but he did not otherwise respond.

Ah, forgive me, Abbawontandontas. Etiquette has eluded me, and I assume overmuch. Wind ruffled the *elliam*'s gleaming mane and tail and fetlocks as he stood tall and terrible atop the great rock. Sunfire burned in his intelligent eyes. *Will you permit me to bear you, Abbawontandontas?*

Eveningwind's unearthly beauty and power swam in the Rhelman's otherwise earthy gaze. Silence. And then another silence accented the first. A second silence so loud that it was deafening. The silence surrounding Runningwolf's unspoken reply.

I will.

Day and night disappeared. The world vanished. Time ended. Runningwolf rode aback Eveningwind through the half-realm of light and shadows. The needs for sustenance, for sleep, even for air abandoned him. He was become at once ethereal and elemental. He was water. He was wind. He was the wilding of the soul. His spirit thrilled to the race.

Once, and for a time, will he bear you.

Runningwolf of Rheln could now go contented and complete when Death came calling a third and final time.

Anconas gazed hazily into his flagon of ale, searching for his reflection there in the amber, seeing none. The tavern was thick with dirty oil-light, with wafting weed-smoke, with indeterminable food odours, some favourable, most not, with the sharp salient scent of spirits, with the bawdy reeks of bad perfume and unclean men. Despite the late hour, the King's Head was busy, though hardly bustling, her Old Quarter patrons the usual assortment of labourers, soldiers, drunkards and whores.

Anconas had been seated there at his regular table in the corner since dusk, having spent the greater part of the day scouring Hiridith in futile search of employment, inevitably drawn to the King's Head in the city's Old Quarter for the odd free flagon that his fame as a former Undercaptain of the North March Mounted Reserve still, though with faltering frequency, afforded him.

The Undercaptain sighed, sipped his ale. Fifty days. Fifty days since the Commander had departed Hiridith under his new mantle of Ambassador to the Fiannar in distant Lindannan. Fifty days only, and how very far the veterans of the Reserve had fallen. Outcasts they had once been – thieves, swindlers, thugs – outcasts and pariahs, until the brothers Teagh had marshaled them, molded them, made them men. But outcasts they had become again. The Senate had no use for them, the Legion did not want them, the people had heard the stories of their valour and had, for the most part, grown weary of the tales of Northkeep and of Silver Bridge and of Anthum.

With no vocations and few marketable skills, the men of the Mounted Reserve drifted as their celebrity waned. Their wives began to leave them. Their children no longer peered up at them with proud bright eyes. Society was in the process of discarding them. Some had disappeared, a few had died. Most, like Undercaptain Anconas, could be found in dimly lit and dingy bars, desperately clinging to a faded fame and a complimentary jar of ale.

A loud bout of mocking laughter drew Anconas' attention to the bar, where Left Tenant Lacius had been attempting to regale the publican with an inebriated rendition of the determining battle for Rhillehaven in the faint hope of another flagon. But the publican, kind as he was, had only shaken his head as a group of unseemly patrons jeered the intoxicated hero of the legendary Ghost Brigade. Anconas watched as an ugly old whore deftly reached into Lacius' pocket to relieve the hapless veteran of what few coins he may have had.

The Undercaptain sighed once more, tilted his head back, throwing the last dregs of his flagon down his throat. He placed the empty jar on the table before him, closed his tired eyes, mentally preparing himself for the compulsory confrontation with the whore and, quite likely, her handler.

But there was to be no confrontation that night. No, not that night. For that night Anconas' life, Lacius' life, and the lives of two thousand veterans of the North March Mounted Reserve were to change irrevocably. Irrevocably and forever.

"Undercaptain."

The voice was flat, quiet, strange. There was an alien inflection to its tone that made it seem at once both distant and near. And though the voice was vaguely familiar to Anconas, he could not place it for the fog of ale. He sighed a third and final time, then opened his drink-blurred eyes.

A man stood before him. Small, dark, muscular. The man's features were as flat as slate, his hair long and black, his eyes the dark of wet earth. He wore a tunic of Republican blue, but his leggings and decorations were distinctly Rhelnian. The man raised a small leather pouch to his temple.

Runningwolf?

"Collect Left Tenant Lacius, Undercaptain," spoke the Rhelman, not bothering to await the customary answering salute. "We must leave this place."

"Runningwolf?"

The Rhelman's patented patience had withered and had worn thin for the trials of his journey. And time was of the essence. He placed an object on the table.

Anconas lowered his eyes and saw before him the silvered battle horn of Bronnus Teagh, the great and glorious Iron Captain. Wonder weaved its way through the Undercaptain's rising awareness. He raised his gaze once more, only to see Runningwolf's back as the Rhelman moved through the dirty smoke and dirtier people, past the King's Head's rickety doors, out into the night.

Anconas remained as he was for a moment, perplexed, pondering the past minute. And then he reached for the Iron Captain's war horn, a slow smile tugging at the corners of his mouth, a new light ashine in clear cold eyes.

"Left Tenant Lacius!"

The Undercaptain's voice was as hard and as clarion with command as the blast of the horn held so tightly in his hand.

Lacius turned, wobbled slightly, raised one brow. He had not heard that tone in the Undercaptain's voice since Rhille-haven in the Delta.

"Come, Lacius. The Commander calls for us."

Lacius willed himself steady, raised his other brow.

"The Commander calls, Left Tenant," repeated Anconas.

The Undercaptain rose to his feet, suddenly solid, sturdy, steadfast once again. His eyes shone.

"And we shall answer."

15

WINDS AND WAYS OF WAR

"And from the East came the wickedest of winds,
unnumbered whispers thundering to a roar,
Hell's herald and harbinger, harsh autumnal
voices promising winter, prophesying war."

Amarien, *Lay of the Fiannar*

The messenger came in the night of autumn's first day.

He came to Ithramis, ancient city on the sea, by ways long secret and hidden, to the palatial Hall of Halmorian, to the chambers of the noble Prince Arbamas who ruled there. He came alone, cloaked and cowled, bearing tidings of looming war and ruin.

The messenger spoke to Arbamas of the return of the Blood King, of a horrible host of teeming thousands, of unholy Ungloth risen anew. He told of the plight of the Fiannar, of the threat posed to Men of the High Land, of the need for the Prince's blade to flash fiercely in the face of Darkness. He revealed that the Prince's long wait was nearly done, that Arbamas must go to Druintir, that he must at long last stand in union with the valiant Fiannar.

That his time was almost come.

Prince Arbamas knelt before the emissary, bowed his head before the bright light of those glittering golden eyes, then rose and embraced him whom he had ever considered a brother.

Arbamas then took up sword and shield and gleaming helm, and strode into the sea-scented night, his countenance set and stern. He rode his great black eastward, across the wondrous Floating Road, over the fertile fields of Sendenna to the fork in the waters where the River Chillor ended and the Rivers Ramis and Ruil began. Having issued specific instructions to his generals, the Prince set sail in the small dark hours before dawn upon the Ithramian flagship *Prodigal*, her great white canvasses harnessing the wind, her smooth prow slicing eastward to the last domain of the Deathward.

Four days and four nights of faring on fast water before a preternaturally generous wind, and come the white-golden zenith of the fifth day's sun, *The Prodigal* eased into port above the roar and fall of the Silver Stair. Escorted by silent sentries of the Grey Watch, the Prince walked to the edge of the precipice overlooking the ancient city of the Fiannar. He gazed there upon the towering Colossus of Defurien, felt a strange stirring in his soul, a certain quickening of his heart. He allowed himself a small smile.

Dhir Ruill en Thir, anen em.

Druintir, I am come.

The fall's first sun soared, sank and set, and in Druintir preparations for war continued in earnest – though in sooth the Fiannar were a folk ever readied for battle. Cold and hard were the eyes of the Deathward as they moved through the stone streets of the city. Swords and spears glinted under sun and star, beneath banners brave, and every heart thudded to the bold beat of war's driving drums. And the very mists of the Silver Stair seemed to swirl with ghosts of the slain, long sundered souls of fallen Fiannar fighting to return to the field of battle one final time.

The small hour before dawn found the Lord Alvarion seated at a table in an antechamber of the Hearthhold, an assortment of maps and charts and scrolls and texts before him. A solitary tallow burned low and yellow at his elbow. The Lord's face seemed haggard in the wavering halflight, drawn, uncharacteristically gaunt and grey. He ground his fists into his eyes and mumbled something incoherent to the swaying shadows of the room.

"You must rest, husband," chastised a concerned Cerriste as she came up behind Alvarion. Both her voice and her step were soft. "Your body must be strong and your mind clear."

The Lord of the Fiannar sighed and leaned back in his chair. The feeble light made a wasteland of his scarred cheek.

"Another council of the Houses convenes come midday, my love," he explained, fatigue thickening his voice as effectively as would drink. "Rest is a thing I can ill afford."

"Hush, husband," admonished Cerriste, standing behind him, her slim yet strong hands gliding over his shoulders, pressing, caressing, massaging away tension and tightness. "You can ill afford *not* to rest. There is nothing that can be said this day that cannot be said come the morrow."

Alvarion sighed once more, though not for fatigue, but for the pleasure of his wife's touch. He sensed her lean in and down. He felt the warmth of her sweet breath upon his ear.

"We have time, husband."

Cerriste reached down, taking her husband's hand in her own, gently compelling him to his feet. The Lady gazed into Alvarion's cool eyes and saw there the anguish, the silent agony of the soul, the struggle between doubt and hope. But resilience was yet there – resilience, refusal and resolve. Pleased with her husband's quiet strength, Cerriste held his gaze, her beautiful eyes capturing and captivating his own, grey on grey, water on ice, silver on steel.

And she then saw in his eyes the flicker of a particular fire that had begun to kindle there.

"Come, husband," Cerriste said softly, almost sultrily, her voice the hushed song of a silken-throated siren. She raised her left hand to his face, her soft cool palm cupping the chiseled, grizzled jaw, the pad of her thumb tenderly tracing the raised ridges of the garish scar. "We have time for many things."

A third sigh passed Alvarion's lips – the sound of anticipation as a certain warmth washed through him. He smiled.

And the Lady of the Fiannar led her Lord and husband away.

The soldiers of the North March Mounted Reserve assembled in the Circumforum of the White Manor at middle-morning. The men of rank assumed their places in the chairs of ash about the Council Circle: Commander Axennus Teagh; the Iron Captain, Bronnus Teagh; Undercaptain Teji Nashi, the healer; Right Tenant Hastiliarius. Conspicuous by his absence was Left Tenant Runningwolf, the laconic Rhelman. And ninety-six men gathered in small groups here and there throughout the tiered seating of the theatre. Although their posture and manner seemed casual, their collective attention was rapt as they gave ear to their Commander's tale of coming war, of monsters and demons and hordes of mythical Unmen.

They listened and spoke no word.

The Commander spoke of the threat to the Free Nations of the North, of the plight of their good friends and hosts, the Fiannar. He spoke of sorcery, of Unmen and ogres and giants, of the strange dark power of the Illincarnadine, of red winds and terrible towers risen anew, of death, of doom, of destruction.

The men listened and spoke no word.

And then he told of the Fiannar themselves, of their coming to Second Earth two millennia before, of their joining with the primitive tribes of Men against the terror and tyranny of the Wraithren, of their grand gifts of knowledge, of wisdom, of civilization. He told of the founding of Lindannan and of Erellan, of the endless struggle by the Fiannar against the forces of Shadow so that Men might live in peace and grow into power of their own. He told of the secret sacrifice of the Deathward, of their fealty, of their faithful fending of the marches of the High Land, and of their selfless defense of the precarious sovereignty of each Free Nation that prospered, blissfully oblivious, behind the invisible wall of Fiannian swords and spears.

The men yet listened and spoke no word.

And lastly he spoke of pride, of gratitude, of debt and service. He spoke of the need for Men to rise with the Fiannar against the approaching Shadow, of the need to unite under common banner in the face of the Blood King's invading army, of the vital *must* that every Erelian there stand in solidarity with the noble Deathward in the desperate struggle for the Pass of Eryn Ruil.

They listened and still they spoke no word.

And the Commander said, "For twenty hundred years have the Fiannar fought a long and costly war that is not, in sooth, their war to fight. They fight for *us*. They fight for the Republic, for Nothira, for Rheln and for the High Kingdom, so that we might thrive and prosper in peace. I now call upon each man here to answer this debt. I call upon you to stand in faithful fraternity with the Fiannar, that fair and fierce folk that have ever held the field against the hosts of Darkness in *our* name. I beseech you, my friends – do not allow them to stand alone."

Silence.

"But no man here is bound to this," stated Commander Axennus Teagh succinctly, his voice ringing out and up from the Council Circle. "Despite your debt to the Shield Maiden, I will commit none of you to this war." His eyes sparkled in the oil-light. "To this war each man here must *himself* commit, and of his own volition offer his sword – and likely his death – or he must decline and leave this place and live, without shame, though he might ever wonder what part he may have played in the greatest battle of our time, had his courage and honour held."

Stone silence.

At the Commander's shoulder, the Iron Captain's hard visage struggled between wry grin and grimace.

"They are soldiers all, brother," Bronnus had told Axennus earlier that morning. "Command them, and they will fight." But the Commander had shaken his head and his white teeth had glinted behind a perfect smile. "Nay, Bron – a warrior unencumbered by the chains and shackles of bounden duty is swifter of sword and lighter afoot than one who fights of obligation alone. They will not perceive this to be their war. They must choose to fight it of their own free will – or at least *believe* that they do so – or of our ninety-eight remaining, none will ever see Hiridion's Walls again." Bronnus had frowned. "Very well, little brother, speak your piece," he had said gruffly, "and then I shall speak mine."

In the Circumforum there was only cold stone silence.

The Iron Captain stood then, his chin outthrust and bristling. His eyes were a deep dark challenge, meeting and holding the gaze of every man there, one by one by one by one. The air of the chamber thickened, became chill.

Then, and with the throated thunder of a battle-cry – which, in sooth, it was – the Iron Captain's bellow burst forth:

"Men of the South, what say you? Aye or nay?"

The stone of the great chamber shook at his shouted plea to the warrior heart.

"What say you?"

And in answer, nearly one hundred throats and hearts erupted as one.

Somewhere in the tiered seating, high up and near the back:

"And there you have it, Dec."

"Yup."

"We're in it now, lads."

"That we are, Maddy."

"Deep."

"Very deep, Ruby."

"Oh, I don't know – maybe not so deep."

"You boys ready?"

"Nope."

"Not at all, Whitey."

"Oh, I don't know – it should be fun."

"I'm looking forward to it, boys."

"Me too."

"Same here."

"And I."

"But now I'm hungry."

"Me too."

"Same here."

"And I."

"We'll go have a bite, then we'll practice some more."

"Sounds good, Dec."

"Agreed."

"Bloody right."

Secreted in the shadows of the upper tiers of the Circumforum, Caelle smiled as the lingering echoes of the deafening and unanimous cry of "*Aye!!*" melted into the marble of the theatre's walls. She waited for the Erelians to disperse, her sapphire-speckled eyes following the long form of Axennus Teagh as the Commander made his departure. She then saw Axennus pause at the great door, turn, and glance upwards toward her place of concealment. The Commander's lips formed a small white grin. He inclined his handsome head in a nearly imperceptible nod, and even at that distance Caelle saw a twinkling in his clear keen eyes. And then he was gone.

Caelle's own smile softened into something else. The Southman had been aware of her presence all along.

Such a remarkable man. Truly remarkable.

The Shield Maiden's visage then darkened, and her smile faded and fell altogether. And a coldness crept into her heart.

One hundred gallant swords, thought she as she rose from her seat, cloaking herself in shadow and silence. *One hundred valiant souls – but despite your fair intention and their own blind courage, friend Axennus, none are they that will survive this thing. None. And no measure of remarkability will spare them.*

And swiftly she went to bring word of one hundred Southern swords to her Lady.

Alvarion woke to the sound of a soft sweet song, a lilting lullaby luring him from the deeps of slumber rather than to them:

> *"Alli, alli, emla mori fithra,*
> *Da'enn mayine mure cullah,*
> *O cullah se mi, den ensyl ain distra*
> *Art sul mayine mori sullagh,*
> *Alli, alli, emla fithra..."*

And the song slipped into silence as Alvarion's eyes slid open.

"You have slept long, husband," came Cerriste's voice, the echoes of song lingering at its edges like the shades of a dream, or a memory. "The day ages."

Alvarion sniffed, smelling the air.

"Verily, the middle of the day is behind us." His brows knotted, though there dwelt no true reproach in the expression. "Woman, you have allowed me to sleep overlong."

Seated before a grand mirror of brightly polished steel, the Lady of the Fiannar ran a comb through her long dark hair, rich waves of ermine ocean parting before the sleek prows of a hundred little ivory ships. Her luminescent locks seemed to gain in gleam and lustre with each supple stroke.

Cerriste's gaze shifted slightly from her own reflection to that of her husband lying upon the furs of their feather bed. The chamber was yet sweet with the scent of their morning love. A smile touched her lips and her eyes.

"Did I not say that we have time, husband?"

Alvarion moved to a sitting position, his tousled hair falling over his taut shoulders, the hard muscles of his chest and arms rippling with every minute motion. He rested his forearms upon his drawn knees. His brow smoothened, and his handsome mouth formed a smile of its own.

"I would do well to heed you sooner and more often, woman."

Cerriste sighed in pretended disdain. The comb slid through her glistening tresses one last time.

"Seventy-nine years of marriage and you are only discovering this now?"

Alvarion chuckled softly.

The Lady put her comb aside, rose from her chair, and turned. Her tall straight form was gowned in grey and shawled in green, and the gold of her *rillagh* glittered gloriously across her bodiced bosom. Her eyes were like silvered steel, her face graven of grace and elegance.

Alvarion's smile faltered before his wife's deep and deadly beauty.

"I convened the council of the Houses in your absence, husband," revealed the Lady of Fiannar. "The Masters surmised that you were in conference with our allies, the Daradur and the Athair." Her grey gaze absorbed the fine form of her husband amidst the rumpled furs, and she fought a smile back and down. "I did not deem it necessary to persuade them otherwise."

Alvarion nodded. "And what has come of this council?"

"Little or nothing," shrugged Cerriste. "Preparations for war proceed, as do those for the departure of the women and children."

Alvarion nodded again, and his brows furrowed slightly.

"Do not mistrust your wisdom in the matter, husband," the Lady commanded quietly, knowing well Alvarion's very thoughts. "The decision has been made. We will away to Allaura. Your logic in the matter is sound."

A small pause, a dismissal of doubt, and Alvarion nodded once more.

"However, following the adjournment of council, two things of some little interest have come to light, husband."

Alvarion raised an eyebrow. "Oh?"

"Firstly – Caelle has brought word that we shall have the Erelian's one hundred."

"Ah," acknowledged Alvarion, "of that determination I was already convinced. The blood of the Fiannar is yet hot and red in the Commander's veins."

"And in the Captain's."

"Verily. And the second thing?"

"Marshal Varonin reports that the High King Ri Niall of Rothanar approaches with haste and several hundred *caelroth* from the north," Cerriste disclosed levelly. "He entered the Miramarch at dawn from the foothills of Rothrange and will achieve Druintir within the hour."

Ri Niall!!!

Alvarion leapt from the rumpled furs of the bed in surprise, bewilderment and kindled hope.

He immediately received a flying towel to the face.

"Wash, husband." Cerriste made a pronounced performance of testing the air, and her fine fair face contorted in a mask of exaggerated disgust. "The bath is readied and waiting, and you are riper than a freshly fertilized field after a warm summer rain."

Alvarion laughed outright, almost gaily.

"You will not attend and aid me in this unseemly endeavour?"

Cerriste's beautiful smile broke past her willful restraint, and her silvery grey eyes sparkled with love and humour – and with faith in him to whom she was eternally bound and devoted.

"Nay, husband," the Lady declined emphatically. "I have experienced your form quite sufficiently for one day, thank you." And she turned, took up her staff. "I will await you in the Hearthhold."

And Alvarion's hearty laughter chased the Lady from the chamber.

The Rothmen sailed the gold-green seas of the Miramarch upon great brown hunters, thick-bodied steeds of shaggy coat and wild mane. They rode one abreast, a long line of worthy warriors, hundreds strong, swords and spears and armour aglitter, hunting cloaks awing in the wind of their passage, their voices uplifted in an ancient song, the melody punctuated by the percussion of their heavy horses' hooves pounding the pliant turf. Amongst them ran huge hoary hounds, dark and dangersome, howling in strange harmony with the battle-hymn of their masters. And above the line flew the proud banner of Rothanar, a golden sunburst upon a field of gleaming green, flanked on one side by the Emerald Trefoil of the High King, and upon the other by the Black Hand of the much-blooded *caelroth*.

Upon the northern shore of the River Ruil, beneath the sun-bright blade of the Colossus and the billowing banners Golden Strype and Flaming Sword, the Lord and the Lady of the Fiannar sat in stillness astride their noble *mirarra*. The Marshal Varonin at the former's shoulder, the Shield Maiden Caelle at the latter's, they watched the approach of Ri Niall of the Thousand Battles and his guard of *caelroth* and great hounds.

"A beautiful thing, is it not, my love?" Alvarion appraised quietly. His eyes glimmered like ice under moonlight.

"It is, husband," Cerriste replied with equal softness.

"Three hundred *caelroth*, at the very least," observed Alvarion.

And Varonin intoned, "Three hundred and thirty-three, my Lord." The Marshal's voice was cool, hard. "And sixty-two Rothic wolf-hounds. The High King himself rides at the centre."

And at that moment the middle figure in the rank of Rothmen, a man broad of back and shoulder, seemed to sight the four Fiannar upon the distant bank of the rushing Ruil, and he raised a clenched fist in salutation.

The Lady Cerriste reached and took Alvarion's hard briefly, tenderly.

"We are not forgotten, husband."

And the song of the *caelroth* flew over the meadows of the Miramarch like the very voice of war.

Upon the Lady's right, in the light of the aging day's sun, the Shield Maiden of the Fiannar smiled.

Do not allow them to stand alone.

Rothanar had come.

The Rothic nation predated the founding of Lindannan by more than a millennium, and had remained essentially unchanged for three thousand years. Comprised of five ancient provinces, each with its own king and united under the supreme rule of a High King, Rothic society had ever been a complex amalgam of mysticism and theology, of militancy and music, of intellectualism and philosophy, of law and chaos. Unlike the primitive southern tribes of the Men, the Rothic people had neither required nor desired the tutelage of the Fiannar upon that lordly folk's coming to Second Earth. The Roths had been sufficiently advanced and structured as a society, and indeed had only looked to Fiannar for trade, some little knowledge of metallurgy, and lasting friendship.

In the ancient wars with the Wraithren, of all the western races of Men, only the Roths had been able to unilaterally resist the forces of Shadow. And a thousand years after the arrival of the Fiannar, an army of Rothmen under the command of the legendary High King Ri Collunn had slaughtered a massive force of invading Unmen in the eastern foothills of the Peacekeepers, essentially eliminating any substantial threat from those thralls of the Wraithren to the High Land for centuries to come.

To many observers and students of human nature, the great Roths of the North were a strange, contradictive, even mad folk who found bliss in battle and sorrow in song. But to others, those more apprised of the true nature of the Rothic heart, the Roths were a noble, cultured, contemplative people, dauntlessly brave, a folk determined to remain forever free, in mind and in body and in spirit, to whom war was but a means of ensuring liberty and perpetuating peace.

As the closing curtain of dusk dimmed the luminous mists of the Silver Stair, Fiannar and Rothmen assembled beneath the great arched and etched dome of the Hearthhold.

Gathered there for the Deathward were the regal Lord and Lady of the Fiannar, and the tall and powerful Tulnarron, Master of the mighty House of Eccuron – for this last had ever held a great fondness for the warlike Roths of the North, and Cerriste had deemed the Master's stoked temper might be cooled by inclusion.

And there for the Rothmen were the High King Ri Niall, small but broad, aged though not bent, of heavy hand and piercing emerald eyes; and Connar, gigantic red-maned Warthane of the *caelroth*, that fierce and fearless warrior sect of Rothic society sworn in service to High King and country.

Having eschewed their light armour and hunting cloaks, each Roth wore the traditional garb of their race – a colourfully checked scarf indicative of clan pinned across one shoulder, a dull woolen wrap about the body that left both legs bare below the knees, a broad leather belt about the waist, and tall boots of sturdy deerhide. They bore thick torques of artfully worked gold around their necks, bands of silver about their wrists and arms, and their long hair was curled, braided and jeweled after the Rothic fashion. Their faces were much scarred by blade and blow, and their weathered skin was marked by many a burned brand and carven tattoo.

And the warm radiance of Alvarion's Tomb reflected in the eyes of all gathered there in the Hearthhold, lending an amber sheen to both green orb and grey.

"Fortune favours us, Niall, old friend," declared the Lord Alvarion, "in that your autumn hunt brought you so far south this year – for the need of the Deathward is dire, and our time short."

"Fortunate, indeed," emphasized the Lady Cerriste.

An odd light played in the emerald eyes of Ri Niall of the Thousand Battles. Then, in the curiously Rothic manner of making statements in the form of questions –

"Sure, are not the giant deer of Rothanar creatures bound fast and forever to the fate of the High Kingdom? And did those same beautiful beasts not draw my hunt to the very borders of the Miramarch, where your emissaries soon found me and informed me of the your wee...predicament?"

"A touch of Rothic luck," mused Lady Cerriste.

The High King grinned strangely – the humour of Rothmen was ever a queer and peculiar thing.

"We Roths are a fatalistic folk, my friends, and we hold that nothing in this world goes unguided by fortune. I was on the borders of the Miramarch this autumn because I was *meant* to be so."

Alvarion's nod was grave.

"I would request aid from you, my old friend," he stated simply.

The heavy golden torque about Ri Niall's throat shock for the High King's chesty chortle.

"And would this request not be overlate in coming? Sure, such an impetration at this late hour would be past redundant and likely avail you nothing."

The Lord and the Lady of the Fiannar shared a swift sharp look.

Ri Niall of the Thousand Battles chuckled again, and furthered, "For have I not already sent in swiftness and urgency word of battle and war to my council at Cara and to the five provincial Kings who rule under me?"

Lord and Lady returned their grey gazes to the battle-scarred and clime-worn countenance of the High King.

The great Roth was grinning widely, almost wildly, and his eyes glittered with something like madness – but not.

And Cerriste surmised, "You would stand with us, friend Niall."

Delight seemed to dance in Ri Niall's every feature.

"Am I not assuring the Lord Alvarion and the Lady Cerriste that the Roths of the North would gladly wade through the hottest of hells to stand at the side of the fair and noble Fiannar? For do I not commit the *caelroth*, who number twenty hundreds, and a further thousand from each of the five provincial armies of Rothanar, to this wee fray at Eryn Ruil? And will the Roths not anticipate this most good and glorious of wars with exultant hearts and voices raised in the merriest of songs?"

Alvarion and Cerriste shared another swift glance.

But it was the Master of the House of Eccuron who gave voice to their thoughts.

"It is a thirty day march from the great hill of Cara, friend Ri Niall," said Tulnarron, "and we have fewer than twenty before war breaks upon us. Indeed, Marshal Varonin estimates seventeen."

"Then we will achieve Druintir in sixteen, Master Tulnarron," shrugged the High King as though the matter was unworthy of discussion.

"Fifteen," came the deep bass voice of Connar, giant Warthane of the *caelroth*. "Fourteen, should the weather hold."

"Aye, good Connar, and have we Roths not accomplished greater deeds in times of lesser need?"

Alvarion, Lord of the Fiannar, inclined his head to the ruler of the Rothic nation. "Your seven thousands will be welcomed with high honour, old friend."

The High King clapped his heavy hands together gleefully, and his lilting laughter soared into the warm light of the Hearthhold like a song.

"Welcome us with whiskey instead, Alfie me lad, and won't we be marching on this fooking New Ungloth itself!"

The blush of the following morning had blossomed into the bleached blue of forenoon over the yellowed fields of the Northern Plains. A cool wind had risen in the east, greasing the grasslands with an invisible chill. Despite the hour, the grey of autumnal frost yet clung to the faded gold of the grasses like leeches sucking on the spent soul of summer.

Commander Axennus Teagh's long dark hair rippled in the wind as he sat astride his grey atop a small rise. He seemed strangely stern and silent as he watched the soldiers of the North March Mounted Reserve drill below him. Upon the Commander's right, the Iron Captain observed the flawless manoeuvres of the men with a masked pleasure and a quiet pride. Upon the left, the sapphire-specked shine of the Shield Maiden's eyes followed the impressive exercises of the Erelians – followed, but did not favour with true intentness, for her concern and her care were elsewhere.

The Commander, Caelle knew, was troubled.

"They are as sharp as a well-whetted blade, Axo," praised the elder Teagh, obviously oblivious to his brother's unvoiced discomfiture. "They have unquestionably mastered the Fox's Feint of Rhille-haven's fame, and seldom have I seen the Scissors and Stones performed so perfectly." The facets of his chiseled face formed a small hard smile. "These one hundred would shred a thousand Southfleetian Light Foot within minutes."

The Commander said nothing, but only stared out and down upon the superbly executed simulations before him.

Marking Axennus' reserve at last, the Iron Captain turned to his brother, the question in Bronnus' dark eyes yet to reach his tongue. He glanced across the neck of the Commander's lean mare, noticed Caelle cock her comely head toward them, saw her pull a wayward tress of midnight hair from her bright and beautiful eyes. He returned his attention to his brother.

The Commander had turned his face away, peering in eerily uncharacteristic aphony, eyes east into the wind. Bronnus' own eyes followed his brother's, but he saw nothing of interest, only an endless expanse of grassland fading into a far and fogged horizon.

Then, and without removing his face from the east, the Commander's voice came as cold and as smooth as oiled steel.

"Shield Maiden."

Caelle started inwardly. *He sounds like father.*

"Commander Teagh."

"Have you a library in Druintir that I might visit?"

Bronnus' jaw flapped open in astonishment, open disbelief.

"Of course, Commander," Caelle replied quietly. "Druintir houses such a place, however modest."

The Iron Captain frowned furiously.

"A library? Teller of the Tale, little brother! War comes soon and swift, and you would trade the blade for *books*?"

Without turning from the east, Axennus nodded slowly, saying simply but emphatically, "Aye, Bronnus, I would."

The Iron Captain glowered in undisguised hauteur.

The Commander felt his brother's fiery glare upon him, but paid that particular and familiar flaming at the hind of his head no heed. He then turned away from the east, looked down once more upon the men of the North March Mounted Reserve drilling on the Plains below him. The skill, grace and horsemanship displayed there excited little confidence within him. Rather, he was moved to dismay.

Bronnus yet broiled beside him, the flushed ire in the Captain's face demanding an answer, an explanation.

Axennus said only, "The foe we are to meet on these fields does not hail from Southfleet."

The Iron Captain burned, and his brow furrowed further in frustration and in his failure to fathom.

At Axennus' shoulder, the Shield Maiden's fine full lips curved into a slow small smile. And her glorious eyes glittered in understanding.

Remarkable. Truly remarkable. A son of the House of Hiridion indeed.

Bronnus grumbled something incoherent but nonetheless obscene.

Axennus reined his mount about, the mare's mane fluttering in the wind. He raised a beckoning brow to the Shield Maiden.

And Caelle laughed aloud.

"The Fiannar's humble Halls of Lore await you, Commander."

The Halls of Lore in Druintir were anything but humble. A vast and intricate continuous carving of gleaming marble, the library of the Deathward was a magnificent monument to that noble people's collective love of wisdom and knowledge. Hewn of the stone of the Silver Stair's higher level, the place comprised a grand central lecture hall and podium and ten surrounding chambers, each of these last a rich reservoir dedicated to one of the denary disciplines of Fiannian lore – Philosophy, Mathematics, Medicine, Physical Science, Astronomy, Languages, Music, History, the Arcane Arts and the Ways of War – the accumulated knowledge of the ages, millennia of inquisitive intellect captured upon scrolls and scripts and held in ornate armaria, each carefully numbered and titled, generations of genius recorded within bound books and orderly sequenced on shelves of graven stone. Each Hall was a place of silence and solitude, where one might seclude oneself and delve without distraction into the combined insight of masterly minds from eras past and present.

And it was in the Hall of the Ways of War that the young Commander of the North March Mounted Reserve had chosen to seclude himself.

"How long has he been so?" whispered the Seer Sarrane, the strange violet eddies of her eyes slowly swirling about seas of grey. A cool concern marked her hushed tone.

Below, amidst a scattered myriad of manuscripts and time-tattered tomes, Axennus Teagh sat cross-legged in the middle of the etched marble floor, his hair hanging long and lank over the yellowed pages of an ancient text. Silently, he leafed through several pages, then stopped, read intently, then leafed once more. Even his muttering made no sound.

The Shield Maiden peered down from the gallery of the Hall of the Ways of War. The care evident in Sarrane's voice was mirrored in the quiet calm of Caelle's comely countenance.

"Two days, two nights – and this morning."

"Has he taken food? Water?"

"Some," replied the Shield Maiden. "Sufficient to sustain him."

The Seer's face was a strange and striking portrait of mystery and lucidity.

"I comprehend his purpose, sister," said she.

Caelle nodded. Something akin to both pleasure and pride danced in her eyes. "The Commander seeks to save the lives of his men."

But Sarrane shook her head slowly, the yellow light of the hall agleam in her golden hair.

"Nay, sister." The Seer's whisper was a wisp of wind. "The Southman seeks to save us all."

The cold eastwind carried night over the Northern Plains. The stink of Shadow was on that wind, the foul forestench of war and ruin. And into the reek of the wind flew the fiery white blur of an *elliam*, a star shooting across the frosted firmament of the nightbound Plains. Arrowwing was his name, and Thrannien, Sun Lord of the Athair, was his master. As white wind into black they sailed, swift and certain, a bolt from the bow, speeding into the night, into the path of peril and pending doom.

To the great rocky rise where reared the forsaken fastness of the mighty House of Eccuron.

Into the emptiness of abandoned Arrenhoth.

"Lord Alvarion. Lady Cerriste. I give you Prince Arbamas of Ithramis."

The Lord and the Lady of the Fiannar rose from their seats before the Hearth and fisted their regal *rillagha*. Their grey eyes gleamed in gracious greeting and welcome. The flameless fire of Alvarion's Tomb flashed, pulsed. The Hearthhold itself seemed to warm inexplicably as the Prince of Ithramis entered the great carven chamber, as though the very rock itself was receiving a long lost friend, or embracing a lover of olde.

"The glory of this day to you, Prince Arbamas," welcomed Cerriste. "It would appear, good friend," observed she, her lips curving coyly, yet elegantly, "that Druintir remembers you."

Prince Arbamas of Ithramis stepped away from the ghostly form of Varonin who had been his escort, and the Marshal of the Grey Watch soon vanished as would mist into fog. Alone before the most high of a majestic and masterly people, the Prince of Ithramis displayed neither discomfort nor discomfiture, but rather the quiet confidence of a man at ease among equals.

"And I Druintir, my Lady," came Arbamas' deep but strangely soft voice – the sound of waves washing over coastal shoals.

Cloaked in the heavy black brush of a great bear, clad and armoured in deepest grey, and about him a hint of darkness and dread, the Prince of Ithramis seemed a son of the very night itself. Ever with him was the scent of sea and salt, as though the essence of the ocean flowed in his veins. He embodied and exuded a great physical strength, being tall and broad, straight of back and narrow of waist, and thick in the chest and arms. His hair and beard were a bright and shining black, worn long and loose, substantially secreting a face that might have been quite handsome. His mouth was grim, his expression stern and set of purpose. And his eyes were as silver stars shining in the darkness of a night that knew no end.

"We welcome you in love and with some little hope, good Arbamas," spoke Alvarion, Lord of the Fiannar. "Your early coming would make it seem fortune yet favours the Fiannar this day."

The dark and dour Prince of Ithramis fisted his chest in the manner of his hosts. His argentine eyes sparkled. Beneath the black of his beard, something that may have been a smile played at the corners of his hard mouth.

Hardly early, my brother, thought Arbamas in silence and shadow. *Rather, I am more than two thousand years late.*

The city-state of Ithramis was the youngest of all the Free Nations, having been founded by Arbamas fewer than thirty years before. An Erelian prospector said to have made a fortune in mining gold and precious stones from deep within the Erels, Arbamas had approached Alvarion and Cerriste with a proposal to purchase from the Fiannar their long-abandoned coastal city of Ithramis, that it might be converted into a place of learning for the people of all the Free Nations. Impressed with the Erelian and intrigued by his idea, the Lord and the Lady of the Fiannar had made a gift of the ancient city.

Arbamas had swiftly set Ithramis in good repair, employed teachers and masters of many and diverse arts and sciences, and soon people from all the nations came as students of lore to the fledgling city in the North. All had been schooled in both their chosen field of learning and in the field of warfare. Their education completed, many had remained at Ithramis, married, raised families, settled land and established commerce, and in short time the city became a nation in its own right.

Arbamas had adopted the honorific of Prince, but only to appease the demand of the people that their leader be held in titular esteem by the Kings and Earls and Senators of the world. The Prince had in his service a sizeable professional army comprised of both men and women, expertly trained and thoroughly disciplined. But the army of Ithramis, however well-drilled, well-armed and well-captained, was yet untried and untested upon the fury-flayed fields of war.

Spoke the noble Prince of Ithramis:

"My Lord. My Lady. I know something of the struggles of the Fiannar. I know of the debt owed them by the Free Nations of Men. Some there may be among the leaders of the Free Nations who would consider the Wraithren and their sorcery and their armies of Unmen to be little more than fancies of legend. But I comprehend the Wraithren to be a real and terrible evil. The Blood King is real, the Illincarnadine is real, the approaching army of Shadow is real. And the peril posed by these compounded darknesses to the Fiannar and to the Free Nations is genuine."

Alvarion and Cerriste listened to the flowing words of the Prince with a wet light in their eyes, and with hope kindling in their hearts.

"But equally real are the gallant spirit and glittering steel of the Ithramen," stated Arbamas in uncontestable certainty. "And they now number fully four thousand foot, bow and heavy horse."

Hope, holy hope.

"My Lord and my Lady of the Fiannar." The Prince's eyes seemed to explode with starfire. "I, Arbamas, Prince of Ithramis, will stand with you."

Hope.

Commander Axennus Teagh clapped the tome entitled *Of the Rise of the Red Wraith and the Battle of Mekkoleth on Sark-u-surum* closed.

He rose, stretched in satisfaction, then moved about the Hall of the Ways of War, carefully returning to its proper place each of the hundreds of items of academia he had perused, studied, absorbed. His face was drawn and lean, haggard, grizzly with three days' growth of beard. But his eyes and the mind behind them were clear and bright, and the set of his countenance calm and cool.

The Commander stepped out into the silvered dusk of Druintir.

And a fair and familiar form materialized at his shoulder.

"You are become my shadow, Shield Maiden," said Axennus, his voice raw and rough, as though his throat was parched and pleading for water.

"There are worse shadows, Southman," returned Caelle. "And darker. Of that you may be certain."

"I am."

Caelle waited briefly, expecting more from the usually loquacious Commander, but the Southman's tongue seemed strangely still.

So, "Though he would never admit it, your brother worries for you, Commander," said Caelle, striding in step at the Erelian's side. "You should go to him."

"And you, Shield Maiden?" retorted Axennus, a slight quirk to his lips. "Do you worry for me as well?"

"I have no cause for concern, Commander," she replied simply, the sound of a shrug to her tone. "I know your purpose."

"Then grant me another audience with your worthy cousin," Axennus responded. "I would have a kindness from Lord Alvarion."

"A kindness, Commander?"

Caelle peered at the Southman at her side. Something had changed in him. Something had altered. She searched the Erelian's face, a face become rugged, become strange and stony with shadow and shades of care. But there were no revelations readily found in the uncharacteristically severe set of Axennus' mouth, neither there nor in the steely line of his jaw. But the light in his eyes remained, though it had been made odd and alien, and was marked by something yet unrevealed.

And the Commander disclosed only, "Shield Maiden, I seek permission to do a thing that has been heretofore forbidden."

Caelle comprehended.

The Southman seeks consent to survey the Seven Hills, that he might know the ground there when war comes.

The Shield Maiden looked away, her own features hardening, steel for steel, stone for stone.

Or that he might know the place of his death.

"Very well, Commander Teagh," she conceded crisply. "Let us hasten to the Hearthhold."

The Commander and the Shield Maiden entered the Hall of the Hallowed as dusk in the last city of the Deathward darkened and deepened into night. The Commander was once again taken by the grandeur of the Hall, struck by its magnificence, and he washed his gaze in the skillfully worked stone of the cavern, bathing his eyes in the silvery shimmer of the wondrously wrought rock. The graven gold of the central colonnade blazed with innate fire, and the royal *rillagha* of the sculptured Lords flamed across stone breasts, bright and brave. And upon Axennus' left, the fair but fearsome features of Vallian glowed as though the soul of that long-dead Lord of the Fiannar burned within the very stone from which his likeness had been rendered.

Very much the father's son, Axennus recalled having said.

"Commander," said Caelle, touching his arm. "Arbamas, Prince of Ithramis, comes."

And there approached a man from the direction of the Door of Lords, a man tall and broad, black of hair and beard and billowing bearskin cloak, a man of masculine grace, of soundness and strength, whose argent eyes shone with intensity and intellect – a man of indisputable power and peril. He passed Caelle and Axennus with a nod and a fist to his breast, but spoke no word, and something in his manner forbade formal greeting and words of welcome.

In silence and stillness Axennus watched Arbamas of Ithramis pass, the Commander's eyes caught and held by the majestic mien of the man – the cold eyes, the grim mouth, the stern and purposeful expression.

And when Arbamas was gone, Axennus muttered, "Ahhh...so there goes the Black Prince."

Caelle tilted a brow.

"You know Arbamas of Ithramis, Commander?"

Axennus smiled curiously.

"Nay, Shield Maiden, I do not know the man."

He looked once more upon to the severe and stony visage of Vallian, son of Defurien, and his smile first broadened, then fell.

And he said softly, "But the face is familiar to me."

The Rock of Arren rose from the flats of the benighted Northern Plains, a bold black fist upthrust in the faces of dark and Darkness. Beneath Arren's invisible shadow, completely encircling the toe of the tor, a great crumbled cromlech grew from frost-greyed grasses, a ruined ring of tumbled dolmens, long-disused dwelling-places of the diaphanous dead. Above this megalithic wall of broken stone, a cladding of conifers clung tenaciously to Arren's steep and stony sides, a suit of sharply spiked armour shielding the Rock from the ravages of wind and winter. And atop the soaring summit rose the walls and towers of ancient Arrenhoth, the magnificent manor of the mighty and militant House of Eccuron.

Abandoned now. Emptied of the sons and daughters of Eccuron.
But not deserted.

Thrannien, Prince of the Undying, stood upon a parapet of Arrenhoth's weatherworn walls, the foul breath of the eastwind flaying his feathered hair. The Sun Lord's golden eyes gleamed eastward into the night, staring into the starless black in silence and solitude until both were shattered by a sound akin to magma moving in the mantle of the earth.

"What do you see, Prince of the Neverborn?" came Brulwar's smooth marble voice as his form flowed from the stone at the Sun Lord's side.

Thrannien displayed no surprise, his golden gaze not moving from the abysmal black of the eastward night.

And he said sorrowfully, "I see the doom of the Deathward, Earthmaster."

Brulwar, *uldwan Dor* of the Daradur, leaned on the huge head of his heavy war-hammer. The only thing blacker than the eastern night was the dark light in the Earthmaster's eyes.

"The enemy are many, Prince Thrannien," he said stonily, "but they are not overmany."

Thrannien's head swayed slowly.

"The army of the Blood King numbers more than one hundred and twenty thousand," revealed the Prince of the Athair. "Graniants, Urkroks, Unmen of Mroch Durva and the Hebbingore, more from Waldard. Ill-bred half-Urks. Norian mercenaries. Wild Wulfings from the icefields of distant Var. And others with which I am unfamiliar, hundreds of great grey giants in black armour riding horrible red-maned beasts. From the breaks in the enemy's formation, I would suggest that at least one hundred thousand will assault the Fiannar at Eryn Ruil, but some twenty thousand more will remove from the main force and strike for the way of Doomfall."

The Earthmaster's massive shoulders shrugged.

"The more that come to Doomfall, the more that Drogul will kill."

"Twenty thousand is an *army*, Earthmaster."

"So is Drogul."

"You have not the farsight of the Athair, Earthmaster," the Sun Lord sighed sadly. "You do not see what I see."

"I do not *see* them, Prince, but I *feel* them. I feel them in the earth, in the rock and stone." The wind fell upon the black of Brulwar's mane, but neither hair nor whisker wavered. "And I feel other things. I feel mud and muck sucking down the blood and bones of one hundred thousand foes at Eryn Ruil. And I feel fire consuming the flesh of twenty thousand more under Raku Ulrun." He nodded knowingly, and his black eyes burned with certitude. "Neither Druintir nor Doomfall will fall to this foe."

They shared a certain silence then, Darad and Ath, Earthmaster and Sun Lord. A silence that forbade further doubt, that abolished dismay, dismissed all despair.

Then –

"And I feel one thing more, Prince of the Neverborn," muttered Brulwar meaningfully. "I feel the foe is lonesome and bewildered in this far and foreign land." The Darad's heavy hand tapped the silver sheaf of arrows at the Sun Lord's shoulder. "Perhaps you should assure him that he is not alone."

And with a dark grin, broad black Brulwar, Earthmaster of the Wandering Guard, slid silently back and down into the stone.

And a smile like sunlight slid across Thrannien's beautiful face.

A single sleek Athain arrow sailed upward and eastward into the unstarred night over the Northern Plains – a solitary missile sailing, sailing, over minutes and miles, singing through the heavens, then plummeting down, down, down into the bloody light of twenty thousand fires.

Thus was Ongulthuk, King of the Unmen of Waldard, welcomed warmly that night – and the warmth of that welcome was the heat of the Unmannish King's own blood as it seeped about the shaft of the gold-feathered arrow that had pierced his heart while he slept.

Verily, winds of war were not the province of Shadow alone.

16

COLDMIRE

"Alas! Eldagreen, fair wood of olde,
Thy glory drowned in waters cold,
Thy grace lost, thy will enslaved –
And grey Coldmire, thy watery grave."

The Song of the Shaddathair

R avenwood, last bastion of ruined Eldagreen, was more than ancient, having stood for untold ages, a remnant of an elder era far
beyond the memory of Man. Legends told that Ravenwood had always existed, aging before Time, growing before Light – great groves
of oak and soaring stands of cedar holding themselves in deathless
darkness, black bark and bough bathing in unending evergloom.

There, and there forever.

The sun never touched there, never marred Ravenwood's perfect
murk, the tightly entwined branches of her canopy forming a solid
shield against the loathed light of the outer world. But Ravenwood

permitted wet and chill to penetrate her – indeed, she welcomed them – and her mossed and matted earth was cold and damp beneath unnumbered millennia of fallen leaves and failed life.

There, and there forever.

And there came into the Ravenwood no whisper of wind, but only a low lethargic mist that crept and crawled about twisted trunk and knotted root – the ghostly gasping breath of a thing near death, or of a thing beyond it. And only the occasional croak of the raven broke the black and baneful silence.

Ravenwood. A place at once both deathless and lifeless, neither dead nor alive, but only *there*. Existing.

There.

And there forever.

The bright and beady eyes of great blackbirds traced the trio's trek through the trees. The avian watchers cawed intermittently in the waning night, restlessly ruffling their inky feathers, alerting one another to the strangers in their midst, to the unwanted outland- ers disturbing the deep dark slumber of ancient cedar, oak and ash. And now and then, they erupted in concerted and raucous protest, a clamourous chorus against the threesome's intrusion into the final fastness of fallen Eldagreen.

Waa-waa-ware!!!

Heedless, the company from Druintir trotted eastward through the trees.

Eldurion of the House of Defurien strode at the fore, pressing ever onward in the misted murk, silent and sure. His thoughts, however, remained at the time and place of his departure, with the lovely oval face of his daughter, with the love and loss shining damply in her wondrous eyes. Caelle was strong, he knew, a true scion of Defurien. Hers was the formidable fortitude and battle-fury of the first Fiannar, of those whose stature was once as gods among men, like rods of steel amidst twigs and sprigs. But hers was also a gentleness and tenderness that belied the bloodied history of her kin and kind – things surely passed to her by her mother rather than by her father. And her heart was like a butterfly fluttering on a sifting summer breeze, bright and beautiful – a heart unfettered, free to be given to whomsoever she chose.

Axennus Teagh.

Eldurion smiled grimly, but there was warmth there, underlying the cool curl of his lips. The Erelian Commander was a good and honest man, a man of courage, skill and intellect. And his love for Caelle was unmistakable. That Axennus was not of the Fiannar mattered nothing – he was of the hallowed line of Hiridion, and the blood of that high House's founding father flowed like fire in his veins. The Erelian was impudent, perhaps, even insolent at whiles. But the coming war would certainly cure him of those things. And the Seer Sarrane had recently confided to Eldurion – with some understandable reluctance – that the Southman would be remembered long after the world had forgotten Eldurion of the House of Defurien.

Caelle had chosen well.

And Eldurion would take that comfort to his death.

For he was aware that his time was near. He well knew that he would not return to Druintir of the Deathward. He would destroy the dark thing lurking under New Ungloth and then he would disappear to die in the Wilderness after the fashion of his folk. Eldurion would never again lie with fair Taresse in the warmth and wonder of love's embrace. And he would never again bask in the loveliness and light that was his daughter, the incomparable Caelle – he would never again see those starry eyes, never hear that angelic voice, feel that slim small hand in his own.

Never.

Never again.

Eldurion's smile faded, fell.

Farewell, my precious Caelle.

The spears of autumn's first dawn assailed Ravenwood's tightly woven canopy, though none passed her leafy armour to strike the narrow animal trail that Eldurion followed toward Coldmire. But the Fian's feet were sure, and the way was familiar to him. And darkness was barrier to neither the Daradun warrior nor the Athain Sun Lord behind him. The Blade of Defurien bundled humbly at his back, his own sword in hand, confidence and determination in his every stride, Eldurion hurried on.

In defiance of dawn and of the impudent invaders who so boldly dared to bring bare steel into that dark domain, the ravens burst into a particularly shrill cacophony of complaint.

WARRRRRRRRRRRE!!!

Hearing and heeding at last, grey Eldurion paused at the fore, and placed a hand upon the *rillagh* across his breast. He then lifted his own voice in answer, singing a light lullaby to the blackbirds in the boughs, his tempered tongue softening into a sweetly sonorous serenade. And in time, the great ravens of the wood were soothed into silence.

Eldurion's lyric lapsed into a warm and wordless hum, and then stilled.

Rundul of the Wandering Guard came close behind the Fian and glowered at the contorted trees. There was an unhappy heat in the fired furnace of the Darad's ebon eyes. He leaned on the haft of his war-axe, his dark whiskers bristling.

"We're not welcome here."

The Eldest of the Fiannar lowered his hand, slipped his naked blade into his belt, then nodded.

"There is both warding and warning in the voice of the forest, Stone Lord."

Rundul glowered blackly. "So I've heard."

Within the hollow of his hood, Eldurion's steely eyes glinted, twin points of silvery light sourced in the sparkings of his soul.

"I have reminded Ravenwood of the glory of Eldagreen, and of those who once defended and died for her. The sacrifice of the Guardian Peoples remains unforgotten. Ravenwood remembers. She will protest our presence no longer."

Rundul grunted dubiously, but spoke no more.

Yllufarr of the Undying was a ghost in the listing mist at their backs, blacker than the birds in the branches, as silent as a shadow. His innate Athain aura was subdued and shrouded within his coal-hued cloak and cowl, but a luminous lustre shimmered on the surface of his eerie eyes. He too had heard the warning in the call of the ravens. And of the three, he alone knew the cause of that cackling caution. But of this dark and distant thing the pale-eyed Prince of the Neverborn said nothing.

They resumed their trek, moving along the path with some semblance of speed, speaking little, sensing rather than seeing the day pass and become night again. They did not rest, but hurried on. Time was precious, vital, of the essence. Each moment lost drew doom near and nigh to Druintir and the Deathward.

Eldurion ate of salted meats and hard cheese from a pocket of his cloak, and drank of the waterskin at his hip, neither slowing nor halting as he appeased his hunger and sated his thirst. He set a swift pace, pressing persistently eastward through the wood, eager and earnest for the fall of the land where forest met fen.

Above deep dark Ravenwood, the second day's sun rose pinkly, whitened into noon, yellowed with the passing day, reddened to dusk, then quickened into the star-specked black of night. But Ravenwood was a place of misted gloom and evergloom, and the cycles of sun and moon signified nothing there.

Eldurion did not slow.

But as the second night aged, the grey warrior of the House of Defurien became fatigued, for though the Fiannar were a rugged and robust folk, they were yet a mortal people and subject to wear and weariness. Eldurion was the Eldest of his race, and his legs had carried him through nearly three centuries of hard living in the wilder regions of Second Earth. Even his iron endurance was not limitless, not without bounds. But the ferriferous Fian had firmly resolved to attain the eastern edge of Ravenwood by the third day's dusk, and this demanded the deferment of both rest and repose.

Eldurion was also propelled by a passionate but purposeless pride that caused him to contend with the constitutions of those that followed him. The Darad would surely need scant sustenance and sleep whilst those heavy ironshod feet trod the living earth – and black

Yllufarr behind was of the immortal Neverborn and would neither tax nor tire ere the world's ending or his own.

Eldurion trudged on.

The third day dawned.

Eldurion's awareness of golden *Grimroth* bound at his back registered as a constant reminder of the oath he had sworn to his nephew, the noble and worthy Lord Alvarion.

I will do this thing.

And though, in the cool confines of his heart, Eldurion believed he had surely failed the father, he would not fail the son. The steely-souled warrior of the Deathward willed weariness from mind and muscle, from body and bone – forsooth, fatigue was a frailty of feebler men.

As middle-morning brightened the world beyond Ravenwood, Rundul of Axar slowed his stride and fell back into the murky mists of the forest. He shifted beneath the great bulk of his pack, more for a certain inner unease than for any true physical discomfort. His heavy brows bunched into a thunderous scowl and he muttered something vaguely profane. His axe-haft was warm in his tightly fisted hand.

And a wraithlike shade appeared at Rundul's side, a thing as ethereal and as formless as the fogs of the forest.

"Calm your thoughts, friend Rundul," whispered Yllufarr of the Folk of Gavrayel, his pale eyes shining with a ghostly light, "lest Ravenwood sense your dislike for her."

"I've got no ill will for this place, good Prince," grumbled the Darad, "though I'll be happy to leave it behind. Sooner better than later. I prefer tunnels fashioned of stone to those formed of timber."

Yllufarr smiled blandly.

"We will agree to differ peaceably on that small detail, good Rundul of the Daradur."

The Darad's grasp on his axe loosened.

"My concern is more for the Fian than for the forest, Prince Yllufarr," Rundul muttered in the mist. "No one appreciates his burden more than I do. I've seen what he must best in battle. I'm just worried that he presses himself beyond the bounds of his body. Oft is hope trod upon by haste and need."

"Ah, but Eldurion's need is great, friend Rundul, and of manifold causes, both obvious and obscure," reasoned the Sun Lord. "And until he engages the Blood King under New Ungloth, haste is the sole weapon that he may wield against the marching might of Shadow." Yllufarr's voice was as a sigh of soft and sorrowful wind. "Haste, good Rundul, *is* his hope."

Rundul grunted.

"The Blood King's army is a behemoth made slow and shambling by its very mass, Prince. We three could march with ease to New Ungloth and back again in time to meet that beast at the battle's beginning. I tell you again, the Fian's haste is unnecessary."

"The Blood King's behemoth does not seek passage through the fens of Coldmire, Stone Lord. I assure you, my friend, you will wish for haste long before the bog is at our backs." Yllufarr paused, his cool colourless eyes peering along the fog-fettered trail before them. "And surely the second son of Amarien knows his limits better than do you or I."

The Darad's massive shoulders shrugged as though the unwieldy weight they bore did not exist. His hand reached within his tunic and curled unconsciously about the small plain stone given him by Brulwar the Earthmaster. He huffed once and abandoned his concern for Eldurion.

The Athain Prince smiled.

"Aye, verily, my friend. We would be well and ably served in looking to our own burdens."

Nearer to his companions than they suspected, Eldurion glowered within the cowl of his cloak, his eyes glittering with a light both cold and hard, like the sheen of star-polished steel. Having paused to relieve himself, he had heard the conversation of his comrades. The Darad's concern for him was genuine and born of love rather than of doubt or of callous criticism. And the Ath's faith in him was clear and unshaking. But that they had even found cause to discuss his evident frailties irked him.

I will do this thing.

His countenance cast of stone, his eyes of iced iron, grey Eldurion slipped into the hovering haze of the path, adjusted the Blade of Defurien at his back, and deliberately lengthened his stride eastward.

I will do this thing.

They emerged from Ravenwood at dusk.

The ancient wood ended abruptly, her eastmost eaves crowning a steep formation of mossy rock that curved northeastward to the snow-maned rises of Rothrange and sloped away southwestward to border the banks of the River Ruil. Oak and ash teetered precariously at the edge of the precipice, leaning perilously into the open gloaming of eventide, dark green giants pondering the pains of life ere leaping in final despair to their doom.

Eldurion stood at the very rim of the ridge, arms crossed over his chest, his hood thrown back, long silvery hair floating on a rising wind. Rundul of Axar rested upon the haft of his war-axe, a living monolith of stone and steel, a mountain of might and muscle. And Yllufarr of the Neverborn was a silent shadow on the wind, a revenant black and baneful, a foreshade of the falling night.

Grey and black and eerily hueless eyes peered eastward, gazing from gloom into gloom. Eastward and away. Away and down.

Down.

Into Coldmire.

Coldmire.

The woeful waste of fallen Eldagreen.

That which had once been the fairest and most formidable forest of the Second World was now but a great grey grave, a monstrous hollow of haze-wreathed heath and fog-fettered fen. The moors were impossibly vast, stretching under the eternal shadow of Rothrange from the ridge at Ravenwood to the broken feet of the Peacekeepers. The fresh flow of the River Ruil that had nourished Eldagreen of olde was become but a confusion of acidic arteries and poisoned veins quickening into quag, seeping into slag.

All was cold there, all was dull and dank, greyed and brittle with everfrost. Low lethargic cloud smothered the moors, a death shroud suffocating all that may once have been beautiful, leaving only those slimy slinking things that might survive in the stillwater of the swamp.

Coldmire was a tomb – and for many long cold centuries the cadaver of once-elegant Eldagreen had lain rotting in the clammy casket of the bogs.

The three stared in silence upon the sunken sweep of Coldmire. Behind them, beyond Ravenwood, the sun slowly slipped under the world. Dusk deepened, dampened, darkened into newborn night. Above the moor the sky tinted to a tattered sheet of sable satin, sadly bereft of moon and star, the lights of night having long abandoned the heavens over that hateful and horrid place.

Something rumbled irascibly in Rundul's bosom.

"Ah, would that you had seen Eldagreen in her glory, my young Daradun friend," spoke Yllufarr of the Undying, a song of mourning to his tone. "This was once a place of grandeur and of unbounded beauty, where the sun swam in the boughs and the stars slumbered peacefully upon the soft forest floor. Often did I tread the wild wonder of Eldagreen, wandering with neither purpose nor destination, content and without care, as though moving through a dream of paradise." The Sun Lord arched one fine eyebrow toward the Captain of the Wandering Guard. "Mayhap, had you walked with me, friend Rundul, you would have forsaken your halls of hewn stone for those grand green galleries of olde."

Rundul peered upon the night-fettered fen below him, a wasteland as wretched and as removed from beauty as a butchered carcass decaying in the damp. Shrugging away the Prince's suggestion, the Darad responded only, "What upon this earth or under might have caused this desecration?"

"War," replied the dark Prince of the Neverborn simply. His pale eyes seemed to glaze and their ghostly gleam retreated as though withdrawing into the mists of memory and melancholy. "For in the heart of Eldagreen, in the golden glen the Athair once called the Valley of Dreams, was the *Angar ban Gan Gebbernindh* fought and sorely won. There broke the greatest of all the battles for this Second Earth. There was slain gallant Lord Vallian, son of Defurien. There your own fierce folk first raised fist and axe and hammer in wrath. And there my Sun Knights fought and fell."

Yllufarr lowered his eyes in remembrance and reverence, and in each pale light there swelled a single silver tear for that which and for those whom would never be forgotten.

"And with them fell the greatness and glory of ancient Eldagreen."

Rundul bowed his head. And when he looked up again the knight-less Sun Lord of the Neverborn was gone. The Darad glanced toward Eldurion.

The aged Fian drew his hood about his head once more.

"We will rest here this night, Stone Lord," came the voice of oiled iron. "Come dawn, we descend into the moors of Coldmire." Eldurion, bare blade at rest upon his shoulder, turned back into the black of Ravenwood. "My pace there will be more to your liking, I assure you."

And then he also was gone.

Alone in the night, Rundul grumbled, spat into the blackness above the bogs and reminded himself of the stealth and heightened senses of the fair and fell folk that were the Fiannar.

Dawn came dull and dismal upon the wastes of Coldmire, the new sun's light veiled and made vague by the ever-hanging haze that haunted the heavens over the grey northern marshes. The escarpment that marked the march of Ravenwood fell away at a hard angle, severe though not sheer, some few hundred feet into the dank and dreary dark of the moors. The descent was treacherous, the rockface of the ridge made slick with moist moss and strange viscous condensation. But each member of the company was footsure and secure for his own inherent ability – the Fian for his intimacy with the wild and for his familiarity with the way; the heavily encumbered Darad for his oneness with rock and stone; the Sun Lord for the astonishing agility innate to all Athair.

The party paused upon a rocky landing at the foot of the fall, tendrils of marshmist twisting and twining about their legs. They gazed in a hush akin to dread across the fogbound flats of the fen. The place was wet and windless, wracked by a tundral cold that seemed a physical being, invisible teeth and talons tearing at the wasted flesh of the earth. The air was at once both thick and thin, and bore the rancid reek of decay, of dead things, of countless corpses rotting in the chill. And ever there arose from Coldmire a wet squishing sound, like that of monstrous thing moving through mud and muck, or of great white carrion worms feasting on the festering carcass of a fallen behemoth.

"Maiden Earth has forsaken this place," muttered Rundul of Axar as he felt the damp creep into his beard. His breath came white into the grey air. "This foul land, this...Coldmire...is not...alive."

"Nor is it dead," appended Yllufarr. His eyes appeared impossibly pale in the grey unlight of the fetid dawn. "But there is death here. Much death."

Eldurion sighed as he slid his sword from his belt.

"All things that come of womb and of egg and of seed die, Prince Yllufarr."

"As do some that do not, Eldurion of the Deathward," responded the Sun Lord quietly, sadly. He peered far into the mists of the mire and of memory to a place and time where many had done that had not. And he repeated, more quietly, more sadly, "As do some that do not."

The stern grey Fian nodded curtly.

"Understood."

A moment given to the Sun Lord in his sorrow, then:

"We must move as swiftly as the bog allows, no slower and no faster," instructed Eldurion. "None now live that know this place better than do I, but as you can hear in the gurgling of the moors, Coldmire is ever changing, ever altering, shifting, morphing. And that which may have been solid ground at dusk may be quickmud at dawn. Remain close, and do not stray from my course, or surely the mires will have you." His face was but a shadow within his cowl. "And mind that you refrain from the employ of any power that may alert the spies of Suru-luk to our presence here, lest this little venture be for naught and in vain."

And with no further word the former Marshal of the Grey Watch of the Fiannar strode away into the mists of the marsh.

Yllufarr's cool achromous eyes moved from the dismal wastes of wetland and memory to the solid heavy hulk of the Darad beside him.

"I believe that dissertation was directed toward you rather than me, my friend," suggested the Sun Lord with a small smile, though one yet shaded with grief. "But fear not, good Rundul, I will not permit the swamp to swallow you."

"*Urth ru glir*," growled the Captain of the Wandering Guard irritably as he hefted his war-axe. "First forest, then fen. What must a Darad do for some deep dark delvings of subterranean stone?"

"In time," assured Yllufarr softly.

Rundul of the Wandering Guard was still muttering and mumbling as he moved away in the wake of Eldurion.

The Athain Prince's smile immediately faltered and vanished and an ancient anguish clouded his comely countenance.

Much death, reflected the bereaved Sun Lord in muted melancholy. *So much death. And so very undeserved.*

A moment later, watchful and wary, Yllufarr melted into the misted mire at the Darad's back, a dark guardian gliding into the grey dreariness of dying dawn.

And eyes were on him as he went.

Formed over long slow centuries of the paludification of dead Eldagreen and the terrestrialization of the eastern reaches of the Ruil, Coldmire was a wetland waste of spongy peat deposits, stagnant waters and oozing muds suffocating under the covering carpet of colourless sphagnum moss. The vegetation there was of the harsh and hardy kind – cotton grasses, tamarack, sturdy sedges, carnivorous pitcher plants. But nothing that grew there was green. And nothing there blossomed bright and beautiful. All was grotesque. Stunted. Warped. And all was cloaked in unbroken gloom, clad in a death shroud of dull and mottled grey.

The company moved through the morass of Coldmire as quickly as caution allowed, meandering in the mists like lost souls seeking to return to cadavers long decomposed and reclaimed by the earth – the grim grey Fian an eidetic extension of the everhaze, the Darad melding mercurially into the mist for the dusking of his *inrinil*, the Ath but an ash floating through the fog. But even such spectres were forbidden any course that might have been efficient in Coldmire, and Eldurion led them along a route selected for its sure and solid ground rather than for its directness to their destination.

They carefully circuited still stream and poisonous pool, keeping to the high ground when possible, prudently shunning the heavily hazed hollows and sunken places of the moors. Often would their grey leader pause briefly, nostrils twitching at a subtle shift in the stench of the fen. He would then turn aside from a perceived peril, avoiding a discerned danger that those who followed him had neither seen nor sensed.

Somewhere above the evergrey mantle of the mire the unseen sun had arced toward middleday when Eldurion drew to an abrupt halt. He squatted on his haunches, grey eyes aglitter, fingers tracing over the sphagnum and muck at his feet. He rose shortly, turned and nodded to his companions.

"We are fortunate, my friends," the Fian revealed. "Doubly so. We have lucked upon the trail of the marsh moose. And the way leads eastward and does not wander as wildly as that upon which I have taken you. I determine that we can move with some speed now."

Rundul glowered at the moss-covered mud.

"Are you sure, Fian?" he rumbled doubtfully. "The earth doesn't speak to me in this wretched place."

"I am certain, Stone Lord," came the reply of greased iron. "The mire can accommodate some haste now. Where the ground might support the mass of the marsh moose, so surely can it support you." Beneath eyes as grey as the haze of Coldmire a slow smile creased the Fian's face. "Or mayhap you are fatigued?"

The hulking Darad growled, but his ebon eyes were bright with humour.

"Lead, old man. And I will follow."

And so the Fian led, and the Darad followed.

But Yllufarr of the Neverborn lingered momentarily, pushing a lustrous black lock that had fallen free back beneath his hood. He bowed his head slightly, listening intently to the slick wet voice of the fen. Harkening, hearing. His uncoloured eyes glowed with a thinly veiled light.

Something. Something was out there. Something was there, somewhere in the mists.

Something somewhere.

The glow in Yllufarr's pale eyes grew to a gleam of long-kindled loathing. But he pushed the urge to strike out in search of the thing aside and away, and took to the trail of the marsh moose.

And eyes were on him as he went.

The trio looked upon the ruin of the immense marsh moose in a detached silence.

Only the great grey bull's forelimbs, prominently humped shoulders and regally racked head remained above the surface of the quickmud that had claimed it. The animal's hide was covered in slime and sphagnum. The creature's maw had fallen open and was thickly frothed in exhaustion. Tattered sheets of moss hung from the bony tips of its massive rack. Its wide round eyes had rolled up in their sockets, exposing whites made pink by burst blood vessels. The exertion of the creature's fight to free itself from the fetters of the fen had served only to hasten its doom.

A single pale plume of breathmist fluttered feebly from one flared nostril into the grey fog of the bog.

"The beast lives," observed Rundul.

Eldurion nodded slowly.

"His heart is shattered within him. His end is near. But he yet suffers..."

There came a sound like that of the plucked string of a harp. An arrow black of shaft and vane appeared, protruding from the pierced eye of the animal, vibrating visibly. The moose died instantly

Yllufarr slung his blackwood bow back across his shoulder.

Eldurion inclined his head.

But Rundul of the Wandering Guard chuckled lowly.

"Stone and steel! If the beast hadn't foundered here that may have been *me* lying in the muck with an Athain arrow in my eye!"

"Perhaps the Prince would not have been inclined to show you the same mercy, Stone Lord."

Rundul's breast rumbled with laughter for the Fian's words and for the small eerie smile playing on the Sun Lord's lips.

"If not for mercy, then surely for the sheer *fun* of it," agreed the Darad.

Then something else rumbled within him, and he eyed the carcass speculatively, one finger tracing the edge of a blade of his axe.

"Shouldn't we butcher the beast?"

"Hardly, Stone Lord," refused the Fian. "All that exists in Coldmire, flora and fauna, are a poison most lethal to those that do not dwell here. Should we not perish for the poison blackening the blood of the animal, then we should certainly die of disease for the filth of its flesh."

"The Daradur are susceptible to neither poison nor disease."

"Then you would surely die of the taste."

Rundul frowned, but said no more, and reluctantly dismissed the hunger panging in the hollows of his belly.

"Let us away from this place," Yllufarr suggested softly.

And Eldurion took them around the moose and its misted muddy grave and led them away into the east.

They paused atop a grey-heathered hummock and studied the growing gloom of the northern skies.

"Night comes," Eldurion announced. "And night in Coldmire comes swiftly and is most utter, unfavoured by either moon or star, and forbids safe navigation. We will halt here and continue come the morrow's dawn."

And indeed, the dusk was unnaturally brief, and in little time the misted mires were bound in a pure and perfect black. The temperature plummeted to a hard arctic chill, freezing the fog, cladding the flora of the fens in a thin film of ice. But beneath the rigidified mosses and stiff cotton grasses, the saturated soils of the moor did not harden, as though the wet of the waterlogged earth was a constant thing, never varying, never altering. And the call of Coldmire, that constant sound of slimy things seeping and oozing, seemed to intensify in the icy air as though great greasy hands had risen from the roil to wring the very night.

Rundul of the Wandering Guard rummaged through the party's provisions that he had borne through forest into fen, retrieving for Eldurion a bear brush cloak which the Fian quickly wrapped about himself, warming fur inward. Yllufarr was of the Neverborn, and as such was not subject to the infirmities imposed upon mortal beings. The Darad was as innately immune to the cold as the rock from which he had been Made.

As Rundul erected a small tent, Eldurion struck a small fire and prepared a hot meal of stew and brew, confident that the frigid fogs would sufficiently conceal the lowly leaping light of the flames from the eyes of hungry things that roamed the wet-land night.

Rundul soon joined the Fian beside the little yellow blaze, and they supped in a shared silence, the quiet of two souls bound in purpose and brotherhood. The stew warmed Eldurion from within, a healing heat that swam through his veins, chasing the chill from his heart. The Darad consumed dried cuts of bacon and bison beef hungrily, and drank deeply of the boiled brew. The meal soon finished, the two leaned back in something close to contentment, staring silently into the deep of night.

Some distance away, Yllufarr stood atop a mossy mound, his cowl pulled close, his eyes shut in concerted concentration as he harkened to the noises of the night. He heard the morass move, heard the thick gurgle of thixotropic silt swallowing a stricken swampdeer, heard the soft padding a prowling lynx, the quickened heartbeat of its wary prey, the whispered wind of a great grey owl's wide wings, the quiet squeak of its quarry. There were many voices of death on the mires, and somewhere within and around them he found the sound he sought.

There it was – below the wet writhing of the bog, above the feeble frightened cries of dying things. A voice. No...*voices*. Vague and vacuous. Remote, removed. Yet close and contiguous to all. At once both near and far. Like the very mist. Everpresent. Ethereal.

Sublime.

So it was that Yllufarr of the Undying first heard the soft sorrowful song of the Shaddathair.

Dawn descended dark and dismal on the wretched wastes of the wetlands. The sky seemed a vast slab of slate bearing down upon the bogs, compressing cloud and cold into a corporeal thing, palpable and substantial. Eldurion felt the hovering haze fall upon his shoulders, driving down, pushing him into the peat. His nostrils twitched at a conspicuous change in the air.

"We will have rain this day," the Fian foretold. His face was as fell as the firmament.

Rundul groaned.

Yllufarr stood silent and still at their sides.

"Come," commanded Eldurion, his voice an alloy of resolve and commitment. "We will make haste while we are able, and pray the rains when they come do not make a sea of this place."

The rain began in the bleak fullness of morning. Cold and hard it fell, torrents of tapered teeth, fine fangs of steel slicing into the sludge, manifoldly magnifying the misery of the mistbound mire. And the rains ripped and rent with neither relent nor surcease for the duration of the day, greasing the grey of the ground, swiftly supersaturating the spongy soil into a roiling soup of oily slime.

All pretense of path or trail disappeared, vanished, drowned in the deluge. Yet the party persisted, tenaciously trudging the seething sludge of the fen.

Eldurion led, head hooded and bowed against the cataract of the cracked heavens, steadfast and silent, his body warded from the wet by an oilskin cape Rundul had pulled from his pack. But a deepening damp chill seeped into his soul.

The hulking Darad slogged along, often sinking up to his knees in muck and mud, but his immense strength and stamina permitted him to persevere. He muttered and mumbled at whiles, rumbling at the rain, but his ranting was more for dislike and displeasure than for any real discomfort.

Only Yllufarr of the Undying was unthwarted by the storm, the long lean Ath softly treading the surface of the sog as though it was as solid as stone. And the torrent did not touch him, deigning to dampen neither cloak nor cowl, but rather parting and pulling aside to allow the darkling Prince of the Neverborn passage unharried.

Nevertheless, despite their defiance and determination, the party's progress was minute, minimal, agonizingly slow, measured not in miles but in mere fractions thereof.

And the rain-wracked wastes of Coldmire seemed to know no end.

Time died. The bog knew neither day nor night, no sunrise and no darkfall. But only rain. Hard cold grey rain. Torrents, cataracts, tears of heaven falling as though in endless and inconsolable grief for ruined Eldagreen. And Coldmire drank of the bitter waters, thirstily sucking on the shriveled breasts of the blasted sky. And what had been a mire became a place of shallow and silted lakes, moving and morphing, blindly seeking one another with twisting tentacles, then combining, becoming more than they had been.

Becoming a sea.

Head bent against the rain, Eldurion led with inhuman resolve and determination, pressing through the bog like a man bereft of reason. In the world beyond Coldmire, where the skies were clear and time yet lived, three days passed. But Eldurion did not rest, did not relent. And he sought no reprieve.

I will do this thing.

The soaring shards of stone rose from the muds of Coldmire like teeth from the diseased gums of a dying dragon. Tall and grey, they were, rearing against the rain, tearing great gashes in the mists of the marsh. There were dozens of them, mighty monoliths erected in an age long-passed by hands long-dead for purposes long-forgotten. The stones marked the foot of a significant mound in the mire, entirely encircling the hummock in a henge of gargantuan granite, unsleeping sentries warding the rise from the wastes and the wet and the wicked things of the night.

"Impressive," muttered Rundul into the rain as he ran one hand over the weathered face of the nearest rock. He traced the swirl of a chiseled symbol with one finger. Something of admiration kindled in the bright black of his eyes. "What does this place signify?"

"Carricevan," replied Eldurion quietly. "*Carrioch Duin Spiarradh* – the Gate of Gods and Ghosts." Dark rain dripped from the rim of his cowl like the woeful weepings of those very spirits of whom he spoke. "This cromlech was erected by the Tuathroth, the primal progenitors of the Rothic people, long before the coming of the Fiannar to this World and the rise of the Daradur from the womb of Mother Earth. Similar formations remain throughout the lost realm of the Tuathroth – of these, that which embraces Arrenhoth would be most familiar to you. We know from the songs and stories of the Rothmen that the Tuathroth held Eldagreen a sacred place, hallowed and holy, where the immortal folk of Faerie once walked among mortal Men."

Yllufarr's eyes glowed with a pale fire. He knew of the folk of Faerie, though the Athair of Gith Glennin called them by another name, and then only in voices hushed with dread and loathing. The Shaddathair. The Shadowfolk of Sammayal. But of these ugsome Unforgiven, Yllufarr of the Undying said nothing.

Eldurion glanced upwards into the rain.

"The day dies. We will take shelter in Carricevan this night."

And like a phantom that may have once haunted that place in the time of Tuathroth, Eldurion of the Fiannar floated into the confines of Carricevan.

The otherwise barren hill of Carricevan was crested by a single and simple structure of stone – three titanic triangular shards of granite leaning inward upon one another and forming a rough pyramid, and this capped at its point by a circular slab of gleaming white rock, like the flat face of the full moon balanced upon the summit of Eternity.

"Doras Serrin," announced Eldurion. "The Portal to the Stars."

One by one, the party slipped from the rain through a crevice where two of the supporting stones fell loosely together. Within the angled walls of the dolmen was a broad open space, sufficiently tall and wide to accommodate a dozen large men, and the air and earth there were neither as cold nor as damp as they were otherwhere in Coldmire. And upon the faces of the three walls were carven oghams of the lost Tuathroth, simplistic swirls in the stone, symbols depicting broad ideas rather than individual words.

"The Tuathroth had no written language of their own," explained Eldurion. "Theirs was an oral tradition, one in which knowledge was passed along and preserved in the form of the spoken word rather than in texts and tomes. But on occasion they employed symbols such as these, where and when their beliefs warranted. Here they have graven 'That Which Was', 'That Which Is' and 'That Which Will Be', respectively. The Tuathroth believed Doras Serrin to be the place where one might find passage from this Earth to the Otherworld of their religion, and from the Otherworld to this one – and so here it was that they would lay the great among their dead to rest."

Rundul frowned.

"Aye, my Daradun friend," smiled the Fian as he ducked back out of the dolmen. "Doras Serrin is a tomb, and here the ghosts of thousands haunt."

The Darad did not fear the dead. But nor did he care much for them. He followed the Fian out into the rains.

Yllufarr remained within Doras Serrin for a moment, his pale eyes pulsing with an ancient and eldritch puissance, secretly probing both shadow and stone. But whatever power that had once been there had long since deserted the place. The Prince prayed that so too had those who had surely come by way of that portal. He slipped from the shelter of the stone and rejoined Eldurion and Rundul beneath the fallings of rain and night.

From the crown of Carricevan, the three surveyed their surroundings. The comparatively solid haven of the hill was closely bounded on sides north and east and south by an impassable lake of liquefied earth. And from this morass there arose another – a sea of spears and tapered spikes, slim pikes of petrified wood, branchless and bare – the blackened bones of drowned Eldagreen stabbing skyward from their watery grave.

"The rains have caused this," said Eldurion, glaring darkly at the spiked seas about Carricevan. "We should have been able to proceed eastward from here, parallel to the southern marches of the marsh. Now we cannot."

"I will seek a way," stated Yllufarr simply. "Rest this night within the walls of Doras Serrin, friend Eldurion. Whatever ghosts that may have once visited there are now gone. Go easy into a good sleep." He smiled strangely, an echo of the eeriness of Carricevan. "The Darad will willingly watch and ward you – from without the walls, or I am very much mistaken."

Rundul harboured little love for either rain or revenants, but of the two he loved the latter least.

"Ah, good Prince – what better way to watch the night than without walls to obscure my sight?"

"This from a Darad who only recently was heard wishing for halls of stone," the Prince smirked.

Rundul scowled, growled.

Grinning, Yllufarr disappeared into the dense dark deluge of the rain-ravaged night.

And eyes were on him as he went.

"Is it heavy?"

Eldurion's steely voice seemed to startle Rundul, as though the fullness of the Darad's attentions had been riveted elsewhere. Risen from a short slumber, the Fian emerged from the rocky shelter of Doras Serrin into the beleaguered deeps of night on Carricevan.

The rains had changed, altered, hardened in the swelling cold of the night. They had degenerated into a deluge of driving sleet, shards and slivers of ice fraying the fog and tearing the bog. An unceasing cascade of shattered glass.

Rundul made a guttural sound that sounded like "What?"

"Heavy," repeated Eldurion, pulling his cloak close around him. "Your burden."

The Darad squinted against the sleet, glancing back through the aperture in the stone to the massive pack he had borne through Ravenwood, across Coldmire. He shook his head, and sleet fell from his hair and beard.

"Not that burden," said Eldurion. "The true burden you bear. The destruction of the Illincarnadine."

The *urthvennim.*

Rundul did not immediately respond.

It is within you.

"Yours is the greater of the two burdens, Fian," stated the Darad flatly.

"Your own may be the more difficult," replied Eldurion.

About them, the sleets of Coldmire fell like arrows of dark iron. The cold deepened. The night was impenetrably black.

The Darad chuckled lowly.

"Insomuch as the nearly impossible differs from the almost impossible."

Eldurion smiled grimly. "You can do this thing?"

Rundul did not respond. His black eyes roved the night atop Carricevan. Through the darksome sleet. The mist. The deeps of centuries. Seeing.

Seeing a thing.

Eldurion saw it also. Or sensed it. A change. The hushed whisper of intuition. A coming.

"We're not alone," murmured the Darad.

The Fian nodded. His eyes were thin silver slits of stellar light in a forgotten corner of the world that had not known stars for centuries, for millennia.

"We are not," agreed Eldurion. "Nor have we been since we first crossed into Coldmire." He paused. "The Ath knows this, but says nothing."

Rundul grunted something incoherent.

Eldurion's eyes sparkled in the dark. Sleet snaked along the length of his bare blade like shards of crushed crystal.

"They come," said the Fian.

Rundul nodded. Readied his war-axe.

"Each to his burden," he growled.

Yllufarr of the Undying moved unaccosted through the moil of the moors, the tumult of the tempest turning aside and away from the pale-eyed Prince of the Neverborn. He glided with impossible grace across the waterlogged wastes, treading peat and pool with like lightness and ease, slipping silently through the sleet in his search for a path through the fen.

Ever did he harken to the voices of the night, seeking the song of the Shaddathair, that melancholy melody overlaying and underscoring the constant call of Coldmire. But the sad song of Sammayal was faint that night, feeble and far, and Yllufarr discerned little of that deathless dirge of dismay and despair.

The night aged. The storm raged.

And Yllufarr soon slid from himself into the halfworld between the Three Earths and the Light, that eternal and ethereal place of peace where all Athair in part abided, the paradise of waking dreams they named Eilla Evvanin.

There Yllufarr rested his mind and spirit, the perfect beauty and serenity of Eilla Evvanin soothing his soul as a salve might mend a physical hurt. And his sorrows passed from him into the Evvanin, and became lovely things – here a flower in beauteous bloom, there a silver stream, there the light of a lustrous star.

Yet Yllufarr also remained aware of all that was about him in Coldmire: The hammering of the sleets; the oozing wounds of the wastes, the ancient agony of eviscerated Eldagreen; the sad and sorrowful song of the Shadowfolk of Sammayal.

And he was aware of the eyes upon him in the night.

Yllufarr was of the Athair. He perceived all.

But he was many miles from Carricevan when he heard the sounds of battle break before the ancient stones of Doras Serrin.

17

NORTHERN LIGHTS

*"Some hold the Lights to be natural luminous aspects of the
ether. Others presume them to be spirits and gods at play in
the heavens. Mariners insist they are but reflections of the
distant ocean upon the black canvas of the night sky. I say,
what matter? Such beauty need be neither investigated nor
evaluated, nor even truly understood – but only appreciated."*

Cornileus Bruca, Grand Master of Astrology, Ithramis
On the Aurora

"Beautiful!" exclaimed Axennus Teagh, clapping his hands together enthusiastically. His eyes shone in delight, damp with
pride. "Absolutely beautiful!"

"Still needs work," grumbled the Iron Captain.

The Commander and the Captain of the North March Mounted
Reserve sat astride their mounts atop Lar Thurrad, the most northerly
of the Seven Hills' three grassy rises, their backs to the rush of the River

Ruil and the dark hard walls of Rothrange. Before and below them, the men of the Reserve rehearsed one of the new and strange exercises that their Commander had brought to them from the Hall of the Ways of War.

"*Beautiful*," insisted Axennus, almost petulantly.

"Still needs work," repeated Bronnus. His own obstinacy lacked the childishness of his brother's. "Much work."

But the Iron Captain's admiration for the display of horseman-ship before him was betrayed by the glint in his dark gaze. He glanced to his brother.

"This maneuver is quite unorthodox, Axo. Even for you."

Axennus grinned.

"Necessarily so, brother," he explained. "The foe we await can easily withstand a charge of light horse. The Unmen are thick of trunk and limb, swift and sturdy, and extremely powerful. And they employ great crude pike-like weapons that would gut our mounts with savage efficiency. Should we charge them in formation or attempt a frontal assault of any sort, we would most certainly be utterly destroyed."

Bronnus frowned, but nodded.

"Better we stay to their flanks."

"Indeed."

It was the eighth morning since a decidedly dour Commander Axennus Teagh had emerged from the ancient Halls of Lore and had requested and received permission from the Lord of the Deathward to drill the Reserve on the Seven Hills.

"You have made them good fighters, Bronnus," the Commander had said to his brother, "but I shall teach them to fight well."

And so to the Seven Hills they had come. There the dedicated men of the North March Mounted Reserve had trained tirelessly and without complaint, from dawn till dusk, day after day. And as each day passed, they approached mastery of several markedly complex maneuvers that their Commander had discovered in the yellowed war-tomes of the Fiannar. Between exercises, the men of the Reserve investigated the terrain, calculated distances, tested the texture and hardness of the ground, measured slopes and grades, marked the placement of rocks and roots – and committed all to memory.

And Axennus' mood had lightened appreciably as the men's knowledge of the Hills and their grasp of the ancient-but-novel tactics grew – for his strange sternness had been born of a profound concern for the lives of those under his command, of those he and his brother had convinced to stand with the noble Fiannar at the Pass of Eryn Ruil. The Commander may not have ensured his men's survival – none but the Teller might accomplish such a thing – but he may have delayed their deaths. And each and every beat of his men's hearts was a thing precious to the younger son of Jophus Teagh.

Bronnus did not fail to mark his brother's return to self.

"I liked you better when you were skulking about like a prophetic Recitor who saw the sky fall in his dreams," growled the Iron Captain.

"So you admit it at last."

"I admit what?"

"That you *do* like me – albeit less some times than others."

Bronnus grimaced.

"I admit no such thing. I have never liked you. And I am not about to start doing so now."

"A small matter, dear brother," laughed Axennus. "I like myself enough for the both of us."

"Never was a truer word spoken."

Axennus' laughter subsided into a small and silent smile as the brothers watched the Reserve complete the complicated exercise with competence, confidence, precision. Right Tenant Hastiliarius peremptorily commended the performance, and the men of the Reserve cheered and congratulated one another boisterously.

The Commander raised an eyebrow to his Captain.

"Better?"

"Much. They were too near upon one another earlier." Bronnus stroked his new growth of dark beard. "Unorthodox, still. But a useful addition to our repertoire. Effective, even. Does it have a name?"

A subtle change on the wind, a warming and a sweetening, the scent of summer – these things came then and stilled Axennus' tongue even as he parted his lips to reply.

"It is called Hiridion's Helix, Captain," a third and familiar voice answered in the Commander's stead, "and when executed properly, few moves on the gameboard of war are more effective."

Caelle.

"Though I cannot recall it ever having been attempted with a mere one hundred riders."

Ah. She returns. Yes.

Axennus felt his heart leap within his breast. He turned, smiled. There was a strange shyness, a rare uncertainty to his smile.

The Shield Maiden straddled her *mirarran*, the gold of her *rillagh* gone white in the light of the morning, the curves of her small feminine form yet apparent despite the shirt of chain mail she wore over her close-fitting hunting garb. Her raven hair was ashine in the sun and westering with the wind, stray tresses falling across her fine fair face in a manner that seemed sultry, seductive, that would set afire even the coldest of men's hearts – a passive allure, for surely it was not *her* hand that held the wilding whips of the wind. Over certain things, even the most beautiful of women could claim no control. But there was an anonymous heat, a longing, perhaps, or a passion, warming the winter-silver stars of Caelle's blue-flecked eyes. And the crook of her comely lips was a knowing one as she saw Axennus Teagh reflexively avert his gaze.

"Shield Maiden," the Commander welcomed softly.

"Commander," nodded Caelle. "Captain."

The Iron Captain inclined his head wordlessly in return.

"I trust I find you both well, my friends," said Caelle.

"You do, Shield Maiden," replied Axennus. He had neither seen nor spoken to the daughter of Eldurion since she had escorted him from the Halls of Lore to the Hearthhold of the House of Defurien. Tentatively, he ventured, "We have missed you these past several days."

Caelle lips curved beautifully.

"You have been...distracted...by other concerns, Commander."

"Yes."

The Shield Maiden tilted her head to one side, disarmingly demure, and a twinkle took her eyes.

"Do you remain distracted, Commander?"

Axennus felt the warmth of the flush that swept across his face.

But it was the Iron Captain that responded to the Shield Maiden's question.

"We endeavour to prepare the men for the tasks and tests that await them, Shield Maiden. In five days these hills will become a battleground, the like of which they have never before imagined, let alone experienced."

"Thus this excellent display of Hiridion's Helix." A strangeness lent itself to Caelle's smile. "The mighty Hiridion was not only a formidable warrior, but also a brilliant military strategist. The Lords Defurien and Vallian relied on him heavily in their wars against Shadow." She looked appraisingly upon Axennus. "It becomes increasingly evident that Master Hiridion's blood does indeed flow in your veins, Commander."

Axennus waved one hand dismissively.

"Should that be so, Shield Maiden, then I have inherited more from the tactician than from the warrior," said he with genuine humility. He glanced at the sturdy and stalwart Bronnus. "And my brother has inherited more of the warrior than...well...than anything."

The Iron Captain scowled in the silence specific to one who suspects he has been insulted, but is not entirely certain.

Laughter leapt in Caelle's wondrous eyes, but only quivered quietly upon her lips. Prudently, she steered the conversation in another direction.

"I am pleased that your time in the Halls of Lore was of some benefit,Commander. When first you emerged from the libraries you seemed...other than yourself."

Axennus' throat tightened. "My apologies, Shield Maiden, if I seemed –"

But Caelle held up her hand. "You did nothing wrong."

The Commander bowed his head.

The Iron Captain looked to his brother, then upon the Shield Maiden, then to the heavens. He sighed forth fatigue, frustration.

War comes upon us swiftly and savagely, and these two are as adolescents only a little past the change...

"But I have come here for reasons other than simple pleasantries, Southmen – however pleasant said pleasantries might be."

Axennus looked up.

Bronnus looked down.

"Marshal Varonin has informed me that the Ithramian flotilla – nay, *armada* – approaches Druintir on the white waves of the River Ruil." The Shield Maiden's voice was oddly detached, devoid of emotion, of inflection. "The Marshal promises, in his ever-understated way, that this armada is a true wonder to behold. The Ithramians will begin to arrive above the Silver Stair come middle-day. I come to bring you thither."

Axennus blinked.

Ahhh...I understand. Marshal *Varonin. Odd as it might seem on the eve of war – and doubtless there is purpose and wisdom in this – the father has gone into the Wilderness, and will not return. And the daughter remains. This is why she has been so long in coming. This is the reason she delayed so. She was not leaving me to my distractions – but attending her own.*

The Fiannar do not mourn.

Like hell.

Several miles upstream from the embassies of the Free Nations, the long ivory-white Arms of Branne stretched westward into the rush of the Ruil. Twin peninsulas of marmoreal stone worn smooth and white by wind and water, the Arms created a pair of deep calm coves, natural harbours with surfaces as smooth and as clear as glass save for where they were broken by the prod of prow and oar.

The southern inlet the Fiannar called the Bosom, and there they harboured their fleet of tall proud warships, marine miracles of wood and iron, some several centuries old, all as noble and as able as the folk that fashioned them. Mariners of the Fiannar moved about and upon the vessels, hard hands readying rope and rigging, oiling oarlocks and mending sails. They were grim of face, these dour Deathward, for they understood their tall ships would see no combat in the coming war, but might only bear survivors from slaughter should the Fiannar come to ruin at the Pass of Eryn Ruil.

But at whiles these same Deathward would glance to the relic resting high and regal upon the rounded rock of Branne's southern Arm, and light would shine from their eyes, and they would banish all darkness within them. For there, at once both darksome and gleaming under the cool northern sun, were the petrified remains of mythical *Dal Starrys*, the flagship of the armada that had taken the Deathward from the devastation of the First Earth to the promise of the Second. *Dal Starrys* slept now, her bright sails long stripped, her polished wood become blackened stone, her mighty masts soaring like a troika of scorched obelisks. But the majesty, the glory of *Dal Starrys* remained, the gold of her wales glittering like sunfire upon dead waters, the fair face of Fircuine flashing at the bow, starry eyes gazing ever westward to a beckoning sea.

And then the Fiannar who worked the ships would return their attentions to tasks they were confident would prove unnecessary.

Upon the northern Arm reared a great beacon tower, an upright shaft of shining stone thrust from the peninsular rock like a tremendous white femur protruding from a primordial giant's barrow mound. The Fiannar named the magnificent structure *Idallinimir*, proud monument to hope and liberty, and cradle of the brilliant beacon-sphere that was the Sea Star of Defurien.

Idallinimir. The Light of Idallion.

Most simply called it the Bone.

Axennus and Bronnus followed Caelle's svelte form as she ascended the spiraling stair within the hollow of the Bone. Black hair flying at her back, the Shield Maiden sprang up the stone steps like a sprite, her feet light and sure. The brothers bounded behind, striving to keep pace with the fleet-footed Fiann. Initially, the Commander intentionally distracted himself from Caelle's compelling curves by counting the steps of the winding stone staircase, though he soon abandoned this endeavour, not only for fatigue of mind and muscle, but also for his keen appreciation of feminine beauty. The Commander passed the greater part of the climb in guiltless pleasure, happily enrapt by the lithe motions of the woman above him.

"Spectacular!" exclaimed Axennus as he emerged from the hollow of the Bone into the cool white glare of the sun and gazed upon the vista about him. His legs yet burned with the rigours of the climb, and his heart still hammered in his chest, but it was the panoramic view rather than the effects of exertion that stole his breath from him. "Such a wondrous sight!"

"I am sure it was, Commander," said the Shield Maiden slyly, the specks of her eyes twinkling in the northern sunshine. She cleared her throat, her comely countenance assuming an exaggerated expression of sobriety. "*Is*, rather. It certainly *is*."

Axennus winced as he felt the fire that burned in his legs rush unimpeded to his face. He moved away from the lovely Fiann, looking in every direction but at her, then rested his elbows on a stone rail of the platform and hung his head sheepishly. As surely as he could feel the flush of his face, so surely could he feel the flutter of Caelle's silent laughter at his back.

Does nothing escape this woman?

The Commander and Caelle stood atop the Light of Idallion, the wind wilding in their hair, the sun bright and white in their eyes.

They were not alone.

Silent sentinels of the Grey Watch stood by the crenellated balustrade, one to each point of the compass, hard hands folded before them on the hilts of long silvery swords, grey gazes fixed north and south and east and west. Their forms differed from statues of stone only in the whipping of their hair and cloaks.

Behind them upon a tall pillar of marble rested the fabled Sea Star of Defurien, a flawless sphere of opaque crystal easily five feet in diameter, its convex surface patiently catching and collecting the light of the sun. Like the Stone of Scullain, the Star had been carried by the Fiannar to Second Earth from the First, where it had been discovered long before by the Lord Defurien in the depths of the darkling ocean. The Sea Star retained much of the power and the properties it had possessed in the First World, for come each fall of dusk and every rise of darkness the Sea Star released its gathered light, illuminating the night as would a small shining moon, safely guiding river-farers to the waiting Arms of Branne.

There came a thud and a muffled curse, and the Iron Captain accomplished the landing with a scowl and a grimace, stumbled toward the encircling balustrade, leaned upon its sun-warmed stone and veritably *willed* air into his lungs. Pained moments passed as the elder Teagh devoured oxygen. Then, his breath not quite his own again, he raised his eyes and fixed the Shield Maiden with the blackest of looks.

"Teller of...the Tale...woman!" panted Bronnus. "You might have... *walked* up the steps and then simply...*thrown* me over the railing...the result would be no different."

Caelle laughed aloud, merriment in her dazzling eyes, sunlight flashing across her perfect teeth.

"Oh, come now, Captain," she said good-humouredly, "surely the 'Iron' of your epithet does not refer to the composition of your legs."

"Nor my...constitution," Bronnus half-gasped, half-growled.

Caelle's wondrous eyes narrowed.

"I see now why you abandoned the Legion Foot for the Legion Horse."

The Iron Captain glared, waiting for his heart to slow. "Shield Maiden, you are...a cruel woman."

"And one wonders that you remain unmarried, Captain."

Bronnus grimaced, sucking air.

"Oh?" chuckled Axennus. "Really? I don't wonder. Who wonders?" He looked toward a stony sentinel of the Grey Watch. "Do you wonder?"

No response.

"See? No one wonders."

Caelle cocked her head to one side, regarded the Iron Captain with an intentionally wicked gleam in her eyes.

"Well, there is a certain animal magnetism about him..."

Axennus looked genuinely shocked. "There is?"

Caelle's laughter was like the dance of a northern aurora, a thing one could not experience and remain unchanged.

"Oh, come now, Commander." She flashed a flawless smile. "Envy does not become you."

Axennus found himself flushing again.

"This is one of those rare times that Bronnus is actually quite right," he muttered in exaggerated misery. "You *are* a cruel woman."

The Shield Maiden laughed once more, then patted the Erelian's arm lightly.

"And you would do well to remember that, Southman."

Axennus' mouth dropped open, then flapped closed and curled into a happy smile.

Count your losses, Axo...there is no winning with this one.

Caelle came to the balustrade where Bronnus yet wheezed for wind. She merely placed one fair fine hand on his shoulder, whispered the word *breathe*, and immediately air flooded the Iron Captain's lungs, and his heart settled to slower, more regular thud. The Erelian looked upon her with brief surprise in his eyes, then inclined his head gratefully.

The Shield Maiden shone a small smile in return. She then turned her starred grey gaze to the northern inlet below them, the harbour known simply as the Bund.

"Prince Arbamas makes good on his promise, Southmen," she said softly, her words afloat on the whisk of the wind. "Ithramis has come."

Axennus and Bronnus followed the Fiann's gaze.

The Bund was bustling with activity as barge after heavily laden barge rode the Ruil into harbour under the watchful eyes of *mirarra*-mounted warders of the Grey Watch. From the extreme height of the brothers' vantage, the Ithramen seemed so very small, like a horde of bipedal mice hurrying to and fro, scurrying back and forth. Even the hoarse barking of the Ithramian officers' commands and the answering cries of the labourers reached the brothers' ears as little more than a half-heard symphony of chirps and squeaks.

"Indeed, Shield Maiden," mused the Commander. "It would appear *all* Ithramis is here."

War horses and work horses, carts and wagons of all shapes and sizes, innumerable crates and sacks, cattle and sheep and goats and chickens, weaponry and armour, foodstuffs for the Ithramen and feed for the livestock – all were unloaded onto the docks of the Bund with remarkable speed and efficiency. The organization of the Ithramen was superb, supported by thousands of workers labouring in the cold with neither curse nor complaint.

"Such efficiency and practiced precision speaks to long preparation," mused the Erelian Commander, one hand on his chin. "It is as though the Black Prince *expected* this call to arms."

"So it would appear, Commander," agreed the Shield Maiden from beneath slightly knotted brows.

And the splendidly helmed warriors of the Ithramen were a spectacle in themselves: One thousand heavy foot, clad in solid plate, bearing great shields at their backs and long swords at their sides, and carrying tall halberds in their strong hands; two thousand light foot in chain and banded mail armed with swords and spears; five hundred bowmen with long slender bows of ash; four hundred heavy horse in chamfrons of shining steel; one hundred brilliantly armoured knights of the Prince's Own, long lances tapering to the heavens, the Three Lions of Ithramis emblazoned on steel breasts and shields; and Prince Arbamas himself, standing tall and black at the prow of the *Prodigal*, great bear brush cape undulating about him like the shade of a sea serpent of olde.

"How well do you know the Black Prince, Shield Maiden?" queried Axennus quietly.

Caelle looked upon the Commander, and there was a quirk to her lips.

"Well enough, Commander. But would your question be asked of curiosity alone? Or mayhap you seek something insidious in the Prince's intent?"

The Erelian's mouth answered the Fiann's quirk for quirk.

"Humour me, my friend, if you would."

The Fiann peered at the Commander, striving to read the riddle in his keen grey-green eyes. But despite the brightness and honesty of their light, the eyes of the Southman betrayed nothing to the Shield Maiden, save an active intellect and the hint of thoughts well hidden.

"I think not, Commander," Caelle responded at little length. "Rather, I would hear tell your own thoughts of our friend Arbamas of Ithramis."

The quirk of Axennus' mouth quickened to a smile. An odd light played in his gaze as he looked from the Shield Maiden to the Ithramian army mustering below, its serried rows of swords and spears glittering in the sun. Even the non-combatants among the Ithramen – metalsmiths, armourers, wrights, teamsters, physicians, cooks, scribes, runners – were impressive, assembling themselves with such martial efficiency and orderliness as to suggest they were a single creature, or many of one mind.

The Commander's smile shone whitely, but did not reach his words when next he spoke.

"I know little of the Black Prince," said Axennus, "and likely less than most. But the little I do know only leads to wonder and gives rise to questions."

"Wonder and questions?"

The Commander nodded. And then a shiver took him. For Prince Arbamas of Ithramis had turned upon the prow of the *Prodigal* and was gazing upwards at the Light of Idallion, his head curiously cocked as though harkening to a half-heard whisper. Despite the considerable distance, Axennus caught a flash of shining silver in the tall Ithraman's eyes.

"Such as, Southman?"

The Shield Maiden seemed oblivious to the Black Prince's scrutiny.

The Commander cleared his throat, chasing the chill from his spine.

"The noble intentions of the recipient aside, Shield Maiden, do you not consider the gifting of the first city of the Fiannar in this world to a moneyed stranger from the South somewhat...irregular?"

"Ithramis was abandoned long ago, Commander," explained Caelle, "and long ago did she become a derelict of sea-washed stone – a dead thing. *People* are a city's flesh, a city's blood, its very heart and soul. Verily, a city is not a city without citizens, but a skeleton of rock and wood only."

"Nevertheless, I find the situation odd, and the more so when I consider the heritage and legacies that define the Deathward folk. One would think the Fiannar might be loath to part with the treasures of their past. Was Ithramis not the very place where Vallian first set foot ashore this Second Earth?"

"The Fiannar possess and are possessive of nothing, Commander, save liberty only." Caelle smiled, but there was little humour in the curve of her lips. "Might you doubt the Lord's wisdom in this matter?"

"Nay, Shield Maiden, not that. Never that. I do but remark upon the singularity of the gift, and wonder of the motivations that underlie the giving."

"Giving is its own reward, Commander, and needs no motivation," Caelle responded. "But should you need to further rationalize Lord Alvarion's generosity, you need only look below you – for there be four thousand swords here this day that were not here yesternight. A fair return, I would say, on the giving of a thing long disused and abandoned, though that return has been thirty years in the coming."

"But those thirty years are a curiosity in themselves, Shield Maiden," the Commander said enigmatically.

Caelle raised one fine brow. "How so, Commander?"

"Thirty years has Arbamas governed in Ithramis," Axennus replied, "yet he appears little older than do I, and certainly no older than Bronnus."

The Fiann shrugged and smiled, but her eyes were thoughtful.

"Some men age well, Commander."

Axennus shook his head.

"Not *that* well, my friend. And I wonder that you did not mark it aforetime. Tell me, has the Black Prince aged at all since first you made his acquaintance? Have you never considered the prolonged youth of the man?"

Caelle's brows fell and furrowed.

"Mayhap the blood of the Fiannar yet runs hot in the Southman's veins – as it does your own, Commander. Some among the Erelians enjoy unusual longevity for this very reason."

But Axennus only shook his head once more, and his eyes were focused and strangely fierce.

"But you did not think on this until *now*, Shield Maiden, and would not have done had I not raised the issue." The Commander's gaze narrowed. "Ever alert, ever watchful daughter of the House of Defurien and protector of its Lady, and this thing you did not mark? If nothing else, then this absence of observation alone should alarm you."

The Fiann's frown darkened and she turned from Axennus to peer down upon Arbamas from Ithramis, and was startled to see the man staring up at her with bright besilvered eyes. Something stirred within her then – a memory, perhaps, or the feel of a familiarity half-forgotten – and it seemed that a mist that had lain long upon her mind was parting.

"Odd indeed, Commander," she agreed, her voice little louder than a whisper, "that it appears I and my Deathward brethren, father and cousin included, have never considered this Southman's evident fraternity with the Fiannar."

"Odder still that you choose the term *fraternity*, Shield Maiden."

"And why is –"

But Caelle's question died unfinished on her lips as her sidesight caught a brisk movement near to her right.

There the warder of the Grey Watch who kept vigil on the west stood like a living replica of the Colossus of Defurien, his weapon raised high, swordpoint to the heavens, its bare blade glittering bright and brilliant in the white light of the sun.

Silvery steel flashed in immediate answer from the shores both north and south, and mounted companies of the Grey Watch sprang westward, riding swift and hard.

Caelle hastened to stand at the sentinel's shoulder, her sapphire-specked eyes as intent as his own upon the west. The sentry remained motionless, not a muscle moving to acknowledge the presence of the Shield Maiden. Then Caelle spoke "Where?" in a voice as cold and as hard as her father's had ever been, and the sentinel lowered his sword arm, and with no word he extended the blade westward.

The far-seeing gaze of the Fiann followed the line suggested by the shining length of steel, peering over and past the last stragglers of the Ithramian flotilla, along the thinning blue thread of the River Ruil to the distant place where the sky knelt upon the earth.

And she saw there the coming of dragons.

Out from the horizon they came. Dozens of them. Great pine-masted longboats of oaken plank stained scarlet beneath square black sails, the carven figureheads of horrible sea monsters and fell gods rearing at their prows. Onward they came, dread dragon ships riding the Ruil in a long single line that seemed to mimic the undulations of an enormous sea serpent, though this was likely a trick of mind and distance only. Arrays of colourful circular shields lined wales where toiled burly oarsmen, muscles wet with sweat and spray, heavy oars hammering water with a fury marching on frenzy. But ever at their fore was the largest of their number, a great *drakkar* dyed entirely crimson, plank and keel, mast and sail, and ribbed with the bones of a leviathan of the sea. The figurehead had been fashioned of the leviathan's draconic skull, and upon this, high above the tall and terrible men massed on the deck of the dragon ship, stood a huge blond warrior with eyes like glacial ice.

A shiver shook the Shield Maiden's spine, and a sound like a serpentine hiss escaped from between her clenched teeth. One to each of her shoulders, the brother's Teagh strained to see the thing that she saw, but their eyes had not the long sight of the Fiannar. Caelle felt Axennus' hand close upon her own, strong and sure.

"What is it, Shield Maiden?" the Southman asked, his smooth voice soft and near at her ear. "What thing do you see?"

Tightening one hand about that of Axennus, the other about the haft of her sword, Caelle suppressed her shudderings, sent them away. Her eyes, when they turned to meet Axennus' own, were cold and clear, and a wary wonder swam in their depths like silver-tailed mermaids beneath the ice of winter.

437

And in time came her reply, and it was one word only, and had long been the watchword for terror and doom descending from the fjords of the great white north –

"Nothirings."

"Nothirings?"

Lord Alvarion stared into the glow of the Hearth's ever-burning stones.

"Of this you are certain?"

Marshal Varonin nodded.

"Thirty-seven longships carrying nearly five thousand men," he confirmed. "Ingvar Dragonsbane son of Eleric Bloodhand leads them."

"Dragonsbane? The Mad Earl of Invarnoth?" A storm of consternation blackened Alvarion's noble brow. "How is this so?"

But Varonin only shrugged.

Alvarion turned from the Hearth, closed his eyes and sighed. In days counted upon the fingers of one hand, the host of the Blood King would fall upon Eryn Ruil from the east. And now an entire army of heathen Nothirings were come from the west. He reached for the pommel of *Grimroth*, but the Blade of Defurien was not at his girdle, and for the first time Alvarion felt a pang of regret for sending that ancient talisman of his House into the murky wastes of Coldmire.

"What is the Dragonsbane's intent, Marshal Varonin?"

"I do not know, Lord Alvarion."

"What of the Nothiric Ambassador?" asked the Lady Cerriste, her eyes not leaving the form and face of her husband. "What knows he of this?"

The Marshal shook his head.

"Ambassador Sunderstrum was as surprised as are we upon learning of Ingvar's approach. More so, or I am much mistaken."

"You are not mistaken, Marshal," spoke Sarrane, Seer of the Fiannar. Violet swirled in her cool clear gaze. "It is in my heart that Ingvar comes to us at the behest of a friend to the Fiannar, though that friend's face remains shadowed in my sight as one hooded and cowled."

Cerriste stepped nearer to her husband, and touched his hand to still its restless search for the sword that was not there.

"The Dragonsbane was *sent* to us, sister and Seer?" asked the Lady. "You know this to be true?"

"That is my thought, Lady, though I cannot discern whence it came."

Cerriste nodded, sighed.

"And it is *my* thought that we shall have no answers to our questions, save from the tongue of the Earl Ingvar himself."

Alvarion gazed into Cerriste's glittering grey eyes, took her calming hand into his own, and a smile warmed the corners of his lips. But his words when he spoke were as cold as the icefields of Nothira.

"Bring the Dragonsbane to the Colossus, good Marshal," commanded Alvarion. "We shall treat with him beneath the long shadow of Defurien."

Nearly four hundred years had passed since the first dragon ships of the Wulfings of Var had been sighted off the western coasts of Second Earth. What followed were two centuries of Wulfic raiding of coastal Rheln, of the Dice, of the southern shoals of the Erelian Republic and of the sandy strands of the Southfleetian Empire. Terror ever spread like wildfire at word of a Wulfic raid, for the huge horn-helmed marauders were a cruel and bloodthirsty race to whom war was but sport, and death in battle a glory to be sought and savoured. And none, it seemed, could withstand them.

None but the Wulfings themselves.

For then, in the farthest northeastern reaches of the known Second Earth, the Wulfings descended into a long and catastrophic civil war between the Kyetniks, those loyal to the hereditary king, and the Ustashnir, the supporters of a pretender to the Ice Throne of Var. The Ustashnir were backed by a deep dark power far to the south, and strange and fell creatures flocked to their black banner. In time, the loyalist Kyetniks were defeated, and the king was killed, and his rightful heirs and family hunted down and annihilated. All but a few of the mighty Clan Kyet went to their ends on the iron blades of Ustashnik axes.

But Noth the Red, the eldest of the king's many bastard sons, escaped the slaughter of his kin, gathered to him the surviving Kyetniks that he could find, a mere two thousands all told, and in fourteen water-weary ships did he come by storm and sea, sailing south then west then north again to the harsh and rocky fjords of northwestern Second Earth. There he was met by Ri Donnal, High King of Rothanar, who had crossed the Steppe with a mighty army of Rothmen, a great force of fierce and fearsome *caelroth* at the fore. The Wulfings had never before encountered upon Second Earth a host whose might and battle-fury matched their own – as they had never pressed any significant distance inland for rumour of the *Fynnir*, a fair and fell folk that would see the Wulfings swift and soon to the Halls of Valdarra – and in his wisdom, Noth the Red laid down his battle-axe and sued for the High King's mercy.

Advised of the horrors of war-ravaged Var, and aware that the Kyetnik refugees would find no welcome elsewhere in the world, Ri Donnal took pity on the barbarians, and left them unaccosted to their fates in the icy fjords of the north – but not without first, however, extracting from Noth the oath that no Kyetnik would ever make war upon the Rothic nation or its allies. And to this Noth the Red did readily swear.

The Kyetniks then settled the hard unforgiving northern coasts, calling the land Nothira in honour of their new king, and that hardy people thrived and prospered and multiplied where a lesser folk would have found only despair and icy death. Noth instituted a functional timocracy, where only those of proven honour, regardless of bloodline, were given land and title, though to the King these *huskarlar* and *jarlar* still owed their loyalty and paid tribute. And the people of Noth honoured the pledge of peace, going to war only in alliance with the Erelian Republic against the Southfleetian Empire, defending trade routes and sea roads so vital to the prosperity of the Free Nations, and providing mercenaries to stand with the Legion on dozens of battlefields across the war-torn Republic.

But the Wulfic raider yet lived in the Nothiric soul, never to perish until the Wolf of World's Ending howled at the shattered moon and the Serpent of Eternity swallowed Second Earth.

The shadow of Defurien was indeed long.

The marmoreal ridge made a perfect half-disc of the setting sun, a semicircular crown of reddish gold fire on the pale pate of the ancient city of Druintir. Beneath the glow of sunfall, the Colossus cast lengthy black shade eastward, cloaking the company that had gathered there on the Ruil's shore in premature night. And the rush of the clear cool waters was hushed and quiet, as though the very river sought the solace of slumber as dusk descended on the world.

Alvarion looked upon the Nothiring on bended knee before him, the man's massive shoulders braced low, his long blond hair splayed upon the moon-white marble of the road like so much straw strewn on ice. The Lord of the Deathward then looked to his Lady, who responded with a vague smile and a nearly imperceptible nod. Alvarion turned once more to the kneeling Nothiring.

"Worship countenances servility only in all things or in nothing, Northman," spoke the Lord of the Fiannar, cool warmth to his tone. "And we are neither here nor there. I therefore bid thee rise, Earl Ingvar, son of Eleric Bloodhand who rules in Nothira, and treat with us as a friend among friends."

And Ingvar Dragonsbane, the Mad Earl of Invarnoth, rose.

The Northman was a giant. Of those who gathered beneath the Colossus of Defurien – the Lord and the Lady of the Fiannar, the Master and the Mistress of the House of Eccuron, Marshal Varonin and several wary warders of the Grey Watch, tall men and women, all – only dour Tulnarron surpassed the Nothiric *jarl*'s great height. And like Tulnarron, Ingvar was broad of chest and shoulder, his arms thick with sinewy strength, his legs as stout and as sturdy as oaks. Balled at his sides, his hands were huge and hard, their knuckles inflamed and knotted by oar and axe and many a brawl. His hair was long and wild, but clean, and retained its flaxen sheen even in the coupled shadows of the Colossus and the gloaming.

"Friendship is the greatest of gifts, Lord Thyrkin," said the Dragonsbane, his thickly accented voice like the distant rumble of Thyr's own thunder. "No greater compliment may there be than friendship offered, and no greater slight than friendship refused."

Stone Defurien reflecting in the blue waters of his eyes, the Earl forwarded a closed fist in the Nothiric gesture of fraternity.

Thyrkin?

Alvarion glanced questioningly toward Cerriste, but she only smiled bemusedly.

Mistaking the Lord's confusion for hesitation and uncertainty, the Earl lowered his fist, nodded in erroneous supposition.

"But it is also ever wise for the husband to gain the wife's approval before allowing a new friend to cross the threshold." His lips twisted into what might have been a wry smile. "Especially when that friend is a northern barbarian, heathen and uncouth."

"Hardly heathen and less uncouth, noble Ingvar," remonstrated the Lady Cerriste. "It is known in Druintir that the Nothirings select their princes, and that they select them well."

The Dragonsbane lowered his head respectfully.

"It is also known, friend Ingvar," continued Cerriste, "that you were reared in Ciaran's court and then educated at Ithramis before selling your sword to the Erelian Republic for gold and glory. It is known that you went to war an anonymous son of the north, and that you returned a prince."

And indeed, Earl Ingvar had the manner and bearing of a prince. He was cloaked in the white fur of the great winter bear, the heavy pelt fastened at the left breast by a brooch of gold in the shape of Thyr's Maul. Beneath the bruin's brush glinted a well-wrought birnie of ring mail over a colourful woolen tabbard, and these pulled tight at the waist by a broad leather belt. His boots and trousers were also of leather, both bearing the look of long wear and much travel. The golden torc at his throat was of Rothic design and make, a relic from the years he had been fostered with King Ciaran of the northern province of Uladh in Rothanar. He was weaponless, for he had surrendered his enormous sword and battle-axe to the care of the Grey Watch prior to his reception by the Lord and the Lady of the Fiannar. But his sheer size and strength were weapons enough in their own right, and spoke to the battle-crazed berserker he had once been, and also to the honoured prince of the Northmen he had become.

"I would say much is known in Druintir, Lady Thyrkin," said the Dragonsbane, the twist to his mouth softening to a true smile, warm and surprisingly wise.

For the Earl's face was that of a young man, unspoiled by weather and wear, his skin smooth and unscarred as though neither war nor woe had ever touched him. His eyes were large and bright, the cool clear blue of a cloudless winter day's sky. And although Nothiric men were given to heavy beards in which they took great pride and tended with great care, Ingvar wore no whiskers. Only in this was the youth of the Earl betrayed, for his manner was that of a much older man; only in this were the Lord and Lady reminded that the Dragonsbane had seen but twenty-five winters of that world.

"That is true, Earl Ingvar," answered the Lady. Her eyes narrowed slightly. "But some things remain unknown, even in Druintir."

"Lady Thyrkin?"

"What brings you hither, Prince of Invarnoth?" asked Cerriste, her tone as direct as her question.

A keen light shone in the giant *jarl*'s clear blue eyes.

"Much is also known in the lands about Invarnoth, Lady Thyrkin," he replied, "and the more so since the god appeared before me of a recent night."

Alvarion and Cerriste exchanged a grey look.

"It is known that the *Fynnir* are descendants of the very gods," expanded the Dragonsbane, "that you lie now in grave peril beneath the shadow of war and ruin, that you cannot hope for victory without the swords and axes of the Sons of Noth – and that you would surely fail and fall should I not come to Druintir."

"Some among these things are more certain than are others, Northman," the Lord of the Fiannar stated coolly. "Nevertheless, I would know how you learned of them."

"The men of my warband would tell you Thyr himself, the great god of thunder and war, came of a night of wild lightning and white rain to our encampment on the Chillor, where we gathered in preparation for our departure to Southfleet – for the Empire is yet beyond the Ban of Ri Donnal, and we thought to winter there in the manner of the old ways." There was dark humour under the rolling breakers of Ingvar's voice. "My men would tell you that Thyr spoke to me of the rise of an abominable evil in the East, and that he did bid me hasten to the land of the *Fynnir* whom he called his kin."

Ahhh...hence 'Thyrkin', deduced Alvarion.

Sarrane's eyes swirled strangely. "Are we to understand that your god Thyr came to you in a dream, Northman?"

The Earl shook his huge yellow head, an insightful expression upon his face as he looked upon the Seer.

"You are to understand no such thing, Witch," he replied respectfully. Witches were held in high honour among the Nothirings of the North. "I do not dream, nor have I ever done, though mayhap it is only that I cannot recollect that which I have seen of the Other Side in the night."

"So you contend that Thyr the Thunderer descended from Valdarra, strode into your camp of a rainy night, and sent you to us on a mission of salvation," said Tulnarron, a touch haughtily. "Small wonder that they name you the Mad Earl."

The Nothiring peered at Tulnarron with the eyes of a wolf sizing up a rival. A small taut silence passed, the still between the footfalls of giants.

Then, "I was named *jarl* for my feats on the fields of the Republic and for the slaying of the serpent whose bones strap my ship. I was named *mad* for the manner in which I accomplished these things, for the bloodlust that takes me when I do battle." A hint of that madness clouded the sky-blue of the Earl's eyes. "But no, Master Tulnarron of the Thyrkin, I do not contend that the Thunderer *strode* into my camp on the Chillor. Rather, I would tell you that the god *rode*."

Tulnarron's rising wry retort did not pass his lips for the august glare of admonishment given him by the Lady of the Fiannar.

"Did the god name himself?" asked Alvarion from beneath narrowed eyes.

"He did not," replied the Northman flatly.

Still holding the Master of the House of Eccuron in the steely vise of her gaze, Cerriste said, "I have not seen the god, friend Ingvar. I wonder, does he resemble those whom he counts as kin? I would know his look, that I might recognize him should he come to me even as he came to you, that I not fail to mark his divinity."

The Nothiring's eyes seemed to shine with something akin to religious ardour – or it may have simply been humour.

"You would not mistake him, Lady Thyrkin," he answered, "for he is tall and mighty and fair to look upon. His locks are of sunfire and his eyes are shining stars. His skin is as smooth and as white as mammoth ivory. The cloak he wears close about him is surely a cutting of the very evening sky, only softer and more blue. His armour is of a divine white metal that glistens of its own accord, like silver but not, and his sword is made of golden flame. Light and power and majesty emanate from him as though these are his flesh and blood and bone. And his voice is the song of a thousand thunders."

Alvarion and Cerriste shared a swift look. And in that moment a thing passed between them. A memory of wistful words spoken in the light of the Stone of Scullain.

I only wish I could do more, and do so more immediately.

Freed from the shackles of the Lady's gaze, "But does your god of thunder and war not wield a maul, noble Earl?" Tulnarron contested. "Or did this escape your scrutiny for all the sunfire and starshine?"

Alvarion started in vexation, but his wife's calm expression stilled the cool remonstration reflexively rising to his tongue. Tulnarron had never weathered waiting well, and now the prolonged tedium that frequently preceded war had withered him, made him irritable. And Alvarion could not truly blame him. The Lord made a mental note to find something for the Master to do.

Lord Alvarion looked upon the Nothiring, expecting to see anger colouring the Northman's countenance.

But the Dragonsbane only smiled.

"Nay, Master Tulnarron," he replied, a wisdom that belied his youth swimming beneath the waves of his words. "But then, I toiled many a long night of my later boyhood in the libraries at Ithramis, seeking there tales and histories that my own folk do not know. Thus I have some knowledge of the Athair who dwell so near to Nothira in secrecy and silence behind holy Vallagard."

"Why do you speak of the Neverborn, Earl Ingvar?" asked Alvarion grimly.

"Because I saw upon the banks of the Chillor what my *huskarlar* and *hird* did not, Lord Thyrkin. My captains and warriors saw a god come to earth upon the eve of our departure for Southfleet, a god bringing word of great glory awaiting us upon grasses much nearer to home than are the beaches of Bhaskar, asserting also that Ustashnir march in the ranks of the enemy." He cast Tulnarron a sardonic smile. "That my captains did not mark the absence of the Thunderer's maul was likely more for mead and thoughts of blood and death than for sunfire and starshine."

"And what is it that *you* saw, friend Ingvar?" plied Cerriste.

The Dragonsbane's smile broadened into a disconcertingly childish gap-toothed grin, and the last light of the sun glittered upon the broad blue of his eyes.

"It is in my heart that I saw a Sun Lord of the Neverborn, come from Gith Glennin to call the Sons of Noth to war – though I cannot profess to know his name."

Another look shared by the Lord and the Lady of the Deathward in the descending dusk. Another thing passed between them. A thing in the tales and histories that Ingvar's own folk did not know.

A name.

Evangael.

"It is quite fortuitous," observed Axennus Teagh with exaggerated gravity, "that the Nothirings take their name from their country rather from their first king..."

Caelle's gay and glorious laughter rose into the night, and the very stars seemed to twinkle with mirth.

"Truly spoken, Commander," the Shield Maiden replied, her laughter lingering at the corners of her lips. "The thralls of the Blood King would hardly quail at the rumour of a march of 'Nothings'."

The young Commander grinned whitely, happy in his heart and soul, then inhaled the cool black air above Druintir. The scent of hope was there, soft and sweet, floating lightly upon the fresh dark wind of night.

Axennus lay upon his back atop a grassy hillock above the Bund, hands folded behind and pillowing his head, his legs crossed at the ankles, his eyes to the distant diamonds of the skies. The Shield Maiden sat near to him upon the blanket of his cloak, slim arms hugging her shins, her fine chin resting on drawn knees. Bronnus had returned to the White Manor, and the Ithramians and the Nothirings had departed for the lands about their embassies, leaving Axennus and Caelle essentially alone in the night above the Bund – though silent spectres of the Grey Watch were never very far from them.

Axennus moved his gaze to rest upon his comely companion, and she smiled upon him, and her smile outshone the Sea Star on Idallinimir above her. The Erelian was for a time content to bathe silently in that perfect light.

Then, at some small length, "Have you thought more on the Ithramian Prince?" asked Axennus.

"On Arbamas?" Caelle's lovely brows formed a small frown. "What is there to think upon concerning the Black Prince? He is our loyal friend and ally."

A shadow darkened the Erelian's features, and the Shield Maiden did not fail to mark the knots of confusion and concern in his brows.

"When we were atop the Bone...before the Nothirings came...we were discussing Arbamas."

But Caelle only shook her head.

"I do not recall doing so," she smiled softly. "Perhaps you have... charmed me."

Charmed, certainly, the Commander thought, *but by no magics of mine.*

Caelle's smile quivered at his silence.

Axennus sighed, raised one hand, ran his fingers through Caelle's silken tresses.

Caelle turned her face from him, but did not pull away. His touch was tender, intimately so, yet innocent. A warmth stirred within her. Her heart fluttered.

And then his hand was gone.

An intake of breath, a small pause, a composition of self. And then, knowing not what else to do, the Shield Maiden sang.

And here words fail. For the Westspeech has neither the elegance nor the eloquence to adequately depict a thing of such pure and profound beauty as the song of Eldurion's daughter in that night above the Bund. It was the sound of silver moonlight on still waters. It was the cry of the golden eagle under the white fire of the sun. It was the glitter and twinkle of stars in the firmament. It was the very beat of the earth's own heart. It was all these things and so much more.

And at first she sang alone, a single voice rising to the heavens, and there was a beautiful sorrow in its tone, like the sadness of a last farewell, or like the loneliness of love gone unrequited. But then, from the breast of one nearby but unseen, another voice joined in the song. And then another, and another. A few became several, and several many, from the island of Hora Erdine to the Seven Hills of Eryn Ruil, in the Arms of Branne and aside the Silver Stair, on the Miramarch and in the Gardens of Galledine, throughout the streets of Druintir and in the Hearthhold of the House of Defurien, until every Fiannian throat in Lindannan shared the soaring song of the Shield Maiden in a chorus of risen thousands.

And upon the height of Idallinimir, the Sea Star of Defurien blazed bright and white, and its brilliance scattered the night. And the sky became a canvas of colour, broad strokes of violet and emerald, soft highlights of sapphire and gold, slowly swaying and mingling, moving to the melody of the Shield Maiden's song. And for a time, beneath the light of the aurora, within the sweetness of the song, there seemed there was no evil, no ill, no wrong in the world.

And then the song was done.

Long and sorrowful was the silence that ensued.

In time, "Other than that which is your own, Shield Maiden, I had not thought such beauty remained on this earth." Axennus' words were breathless, like the voice of a lover in the after-moments.

"It is called the *Laleth Mennillad*," Caelle said softly, "the 'Lament of the Departed', sung by fair Aeline long ago upon her departure from the First Earth."

"A song for your father, then," Axennus surmised sympathetically. Caelle shook her head slowly, sadly.

"Nay, Southman. Eldurion is far beyond shot of ear now." A poignant pause. "Rather, the *laleth* of this night was sung for *me*."

Axennus started, rose to sit at the Shield Maiden's side. A terrible foreboding took him, shook him, and his heart trembled as he reached for the Fiann's hand.

"For you, my friend?" he whispered past the chill of a cold intuition.

Caelle received Axennus' hand in her own, and there was little to distinguish between the desperation of their grasps. She then turned, faced the man she had come to love so soon and so surely, and there were silver tears ashine in the corners of her wide and wondrous eyes.

"I am to leave Druintir in the morning, Southman. I am to leave and I know not when or whether I might return."

And in that moment the only thing of which Axennus Teagh was aware was the bitter breaking of his heart within him.

18

FIRST BLOOD

"To stand against a thing that cannot be conquered
Is not stubbornness, nor even dogged determination,
But only sheer stupidity."

"To insist that there even exists a thing that cannot
Be overcome is the conclusion of fools and cowards –
And is stupider still."

Gavrayel and Eccuron, *The Scullain Dialogues*

S trange things happen in the night.
Day dies, dusk bleeds away, darkness falls. The night rises, rules. A black velvet cloak swoops over the world, flutters down and settles, and then is snapped back. Leaving the dark. And things disappear. Hope, faith, courage. Eyes widen, thirsty for light that is not there, drinking in only the bitter black elixir that is the earth's solar shadow. Fingers claw blankets, teeth grind, bodies curl into balls. Into the void

left by vanished things come imposters, interlopers. Imaginations rubbed raw by sleeplessness seep terror into the darkness, fertilizing seeds of doubt, birthing dead men and demons. Fiends prowl the deep pockets of the dark, talons clicking on floorboards, moaning their miseries into ears that cannot close, that must hear, that must listen. Men and women whimper, whine, pray for light. Phantom fingers play over pebbled skin. Hearts shudder and shatter. Death sweeps down.

Indeed, strange things happen in the night. When that conjuror's cape comes down. But the night is no market-kiosk magician, no practitioner of sleight of hand, and needs neither smoke nor mirrors to effect its power. The night is not illusion, its creatures no clever trick of chicanery. The demons exist. The monsters are real. Children know this. Children and cowards. They are wiser than the rest.

They know.

They just...*know*.

"I know nothing of this."

Varonin of the Grey Watch sat astride his smoke-grey *mirarran* beneath the great curved stone of the Andalorian Arch, his wintry eyes glittering in the blackness of his cowl, diamond chips in the darkness. The white marble of the Arch glowed like a crescent moon, the naked steel of Varonin's sword gleaming coolly under the rock's argentine radiance. The warders to either side of him were motionless upon their mounts, mere extensions of the night, shadows in the black.

"Lord Alvarion has only just sent us, Marshal," explained Tulnarron, his voice a deep rumble of thunder. "Word will not have come to you yet."

"You have your entire House with you."

"Hardly, Marshal. Half, at most."

A nearly imperceptible incline of Varonin's hooded head indicated Sandarre.

"The woman – is she not to depart come the morrow morn for Allaura?"

"She has been given...special dispensation."

"Indeed. And this endeavour – it is the Lord's will?"

Tulnarron nodded.

"You are aware the Blood King's army moves faster than we first calculated, Marshal Varonin. Our allies require time to prepare. And the Rothmen are not yet here. Lord Alvarion would have the enemy's advance tardigraded, would see their march slowed. We seek to fulfill that desire."

"This is Lord Alvarion's will, Master Tulnarron?" repeated Varonin, emphatically.

The Master of the House of Eccuron glared coldly at the Marshal of the Grey Watch, and the line of his lips was thin and severe.

"It is."

Varonin stared at Tulnarron in algid silence, his breath misting before his hooded features, cloud and cowl concealing the entirety of his countenance save the crystalline chips that were his eyes. He neither moved nor spoke, but only breathed.

Tulnarron waited. Equally still, equally silent. The roar of the Ruil seemed remote and removed, the cold of the night pressing in upon all sides, reducing the world and all in it to two hard men facing one another beneath the stark white rock of the Andalorian Arch.

"Very well, Master Tulnarron," breathed the Marshal. His *mirar-ran* stepped to the side. The warders with him followed wordlessly.

The night wind sighed.

Tulnarron inclined his head, nudged his own mount forward. The thud of hooves on stone sounded so very like the beat of a burning heart. Through the ancient span of stone, along the marble-paved road, beneath a riot of stars.

With nearly three hundred riders of the Host of Arrenhoth at his back.

Silver-white mists crept out from the muskegs of Coldmire, crawling across the faltering flow of the Ruil to obnubilate their going. Fiannar and *mirarra* faded into the fog, grey into grey, meagre ghosts in the gasping breath of night. Outriders before them, wary wingmen at their flanks, a rearguard in their wake, they followed a narrow path a mile south of the river, angling north and east, the ground oddly soft and pliant beneath them, cushioning the crush of rushing hooves on earth. They called it the Soft Road, specifically for the strange spongy nature of the soil, soil that remained plush and forgiving even in the deeps of winter. Soundless and unseen, they went, quick, quiet, grey wights in the blackened white, revenants of the night.

Hours passed. Leagues swiftly swallowed in the night. Death racing.

When Tulnarron finally decided to slow the pace, the two nearest riders brought their mounts up to the flanks of his own, one to each side.

"Is it, cousin?" Sandarre asked.

Tulnarron cast a cold glance the Fiann's way. His eyes were as silver stars, shining, shining. Like a beacon. Or a warning.

"Is it what, exactly, Sandarre?"

The Fiann looked across the neck of the Master's *mirarran* to the phantasmal form of Gornannon, but her friend did not meet her eye, only resolutely chewed his unlit cheroot against the compelling urge to smile. She found no ally there.

"Is what we mean to do indeed Lord Alvarion's will?"

Tulnarron's face was as inscrutable as stone.

"I said as much, did I not?"

Sandarre nodded, gripped the reins of her mount a little tighter, the supple leather crunching in her fist.

"Yes, you did say as much, cousin. But Lord Alvarion did not fare us well, nor even send a delegate to do so in his stead. You delivered no apopemptic address. Furthermore, I know you. Thus I cannot help but wonder, did the Lord expressly order this strike?"

The Master of the House of Eccuron stared straight ahead. Tendrils of fog snaked about his broad shoulders.

"Something of the sort."

Sandarre's brows bunched beneath the brim of her helm. Her breath misted before her eyes, white and wispy.

"Something like it, but not exactly?"

The Master was silent for a heartbeat, two, three.

"Even so."

They rode in silence for a while, the haze hiding them, the humectant turf of the Soft Road sucking away all sound of their passage.

"What, exactly, did Lord Alvarion say, cousin?"

A heartbeat.

"He told me to find something to do," replied Tulnarron bluntly.

Gornannon guffawed, losing his precious cheroot in the process. Sandarre grinned generously, her grey eyes gleaming gaily.

"Fair enough, cousin."

Lord Alvarion did not look up from the map upon the table.

"Thank you for your swift and precise report, Marshal Varonin. You performed admirably. That will be all."

The Marshal of the Grey Watch brought a gloved fist to his breast, turned upon his heel, vanished.

Alvarion frowned in the brownish-yellow candlelight, his grey eyes glinting out from amidst cracked craters of fatigue. He moved a single horse figurine towards a black mass of miniatures obscuring a large portion of the map depicting the Northern Plains. His frown blackened.

"So it begins."

"It is precisely as you predicted, husband," said Cerriste from across the table. She lit a few more tallows to ease the strain on her husband's weary eyes. "Tell me, how did you know Master Tulnarron would ride tonight?"

From frown to scowl.

"I know the Master well. Better than he knows himself, perhaps. Tulnarron is a man of action, at his best when he is doing something. Something, anything. Inaction makes him restless, irritable. Idle, he can become burdensome, something of a liability, as was evidenced in his reception of the Earl of Invarnoth this evening. Irascibility is oft the familiar of a driven man, and the Master of the House of Eccuron is the very definition of the driven man. Abandoning the Rock of Arren yet eats at him, gnawing his soul, devouring him from the inside out. The ghosts of the red wind's victims ceaselessly beseech him for vengeance, retribution. He hears them. Even in his sleep, he hears them. I knew he would ride because he is who and what he is – Tulnarron, Master of the House of Eccuron – and because Arrenhoth must answer. I knew he would ride because he *must*."

Cerriste flashed a knowing, needling grin.

"So Sarrane spoke to you."

Alvarion glanced up, straightened, stretched. He managed to keep the smile from his lips, but not from his eyes.

"Well, that, too."

The Lady laughed. The sound soothed and eased, so very much like a cooling lather upon a soul scraped raw.

"You might have simply *ordered* Master Tulnarron to strike the enemy camp, husband," she suggested. "That would have been the straighter road."

Alvarion shook his head.

"Straighter, perhaps, but hardly as effective."

"Oh?"

Alvarion nodded, grey eyes roving the map on the table.

"Tulnarron is the ultimate scion of Eccuron. A good friend and a great leader, but overly prideful and a decidedly poor, however loyal, follower. Any expression of authority or delivery of restrictive decree demeans him, even debases him, in his own estimation. This sensitivity is founded not in insecurity, but in its extreme opposite – an irrefrangible belief in himself, his abilities, his opinions, in the rightness of his convictions. Combine this inflexibility, this intransigence, with a desperate need to act rather than watch and wait, and our sharpest remaining blade can become a razor at our own throats – this despite all love, loyalty, martial discipline and fair intentions."

Lady Cerriste reached toward the solitary horse figurine, moving it slightly northward on the map, just beneath the grey marches of Coldmire.

"The Master's fealty is indeed a complicated thing, husband."

"Complicated, but fierce and firm, beloved. He is as unyielding in that as he is in all things. But he is no recusant. Never that. Tulnarron is the great hound that gnaws and strains against its chain, growling and snapping at the hand that feeds it. But remove the chain and the beast rests quietly at the master's side, docile and dutiful, connected, prepared to do the master's bidding with little or no guidance and direction. Instinct, insight, initiative – these are the hound's sharpest teeth and claws, but are rendered entirely impotent by collar and chain. Retain the chain and the hound can only howl as the wolves ravage the herd."

Cerriste's smile was like a curved blade.

"I understand, husband."

The Lord of the Fiannar grinned grimly.

"Yes, I thought you might."

The Lady pushed the lone horse around behind the black mass on the map. Looked up. Her eyes glittered, gleamed above the scarlet scimitar of her lips.

"Unleash the beast."

Dawn came, dull, drear. A semblance of day followed.

The Host of Arrenhoth rode the Soft Road at a gait approaching a gallop. Never slowing, never faltering. Urgency in their effulgent eyes, in every corded muscle, in each and every stride. Above them, the sky was a dingy and dirty umber, a damp clay sheet suspended low over the earth; about them sullied fog swirled, an eidolon of mist as fell as the folk it enfolded in its miserable embrace; below them the ground oozed grey filth, first sucking at the hooves of the *mirarra* as they passed, then filling the prints with greasy muck in their immediate wake, rapidly resiling the spongy ground once more, leaving it level, unmarred and unmarked, as though the party had never come, had never passed. Had never even been.

Onward they rode, the dour Host of Arrenhoth.

Hours slid, slipped, seeped by.

Dusk descended. The mists thickened to a tangible film, like pale colourless blood congealing over a sopping sore in the world. A forerider appeared from the fog, in apparent conversation with the haze to his right. Tulnarron slowed his steed, squinted, and the fog to the outrider's side solidified, became another mounted Fian, the bare and blackened blade in his hand marking him as a scout of Grey Watch. A ghost in the night. Forerider and Watcher came up, stayed their steeds, brought fists to their breasts. Tulnarron halted his muscled *mirarran*, received the outrider and the warder with a curt nod and a thump to his heart. His eyes glittered, cold and bright.

"Report, Castadon."

"Master, I have with me –"

"Gostullian of the Grey Watch," Tulnarron inserted. "Yes, I see that."

The Master's icy gaze swept over the phantasmal form of the Watcher. The Fiannian scout was utterly unlike any other among his fair folk. He was lean and gaunt, his cheeks sunken, his sockets sallow. The skin of his thin face was cracked, creviced and cross-hatched with pale scars, as weathered and worn as the ancient oilskin cloak draped about his narrow shoulders. His prominent nose was crooked and crumpled, his bony chin bristling with irregular patches of uncoloured stubble. He wore his hair long, but it was long past thinning, mere strings hanging from a mottled scalp. One ear was a bulbous cauliflower of ruined cartilage, the other was entirely gone.

"Looking a little haggard, Ghost."

The Fian called Ghost grinned – a gruesome, near toothless grimace.

"Oh, been a rough few weeks."

"I can imagine." The Master moved his gaze back to Castadon. "Continue."

"The enemy has divided, Master. Three camps. The northmost one is the largest, about one hundred thousand souls strong, and lies a six hour hard ride east and south of here. Unmen of Mroch Durva and the Hebbingore. Urkroks. Norians and Wulfings. Others. Near upon this main encampment lies a smaller one to the south. Twenty thousands or so. Maybe fewer, not more. Unmen of Waldard, Urkroks. A small company of grey-skinned, black-clad, mean-looking giants with whom we are unfamiliar, somewhat less than seven hundred. The third camp lies another day's march to the east and is composed entirely of Graniants. Some two thousands, I'm told. They serve as a rearguard, marching only every second or third day, most likely due to the substantial length of their stride."

Tulnarron nodded slowly.

"And the train?"

"The wagon train lies beyond and between the two main camps," replied the outrider. "Thousands of supply wagons pulled by all manner of beasts of burden. War machines, as well. Catapults and the like. A seven hour ride."

"Munitions trucks?"

"Twenty-six, at least. At the heart of the wagon train. Precisely as you expected. Covered carts and drays full of incendiary missiles, shatter bombs, stonebreakers, shells of dragon's breath. Fodder for the machines."

"I see. And the Graniants remain an entire day behind?"

"They do."

"What can you add, Ghost?"

That ghastly grin. "Oh, a little. This and that."

"Watcher Gostullian is overly modest, Master," protested Castadon. "He has been tracking and surveilling the enemy for weeks. His espial is exceptional, without equal. He has intimate knowledge of their crasis, their formations, routines, habits. When they sleep, when they wake, what they eat for breakfast. Their watches and their pickets. Strengths and weaknesses. He may be of some service to you."

Tulnarron's smile was thin, sere, arctic in its warmth.

"I suspect he might. Very good. That is all, Castadon." He then called over his shoulder. "Sandarre. Gornannon. We will rest here for the moment."

"As you will, cousin."

The Master of the House of Eccuron looked upon the withered Watcher once more.

"You should have it from me, Ghost – the Rock is lost."

A liquid blink, the shrug of gaunt, knobby shoulders. "Oh, well. Never felt much like home anyway."

"Indeed." Then, "I will hear you, Ghost. Ride with me, if you would."

That most grisly of smiles.

"Oh, I would. But don't expect me to call you 'Master'."

Tulnarron turned away, north into the night.

"Even so."

Among a modest people, he had always been described as proud. And he was. He knew this. Not only did pride describe him, it defined him.

Pride was his armour and his shield. Pride was the cutting edge of his sword. It was a true and tangible thing, gripped in the Crimson Fist of his standard, blazing in the *rillagh* across his breast, towering tall upon the titanic Rock of Arren. Pride in himself, in his family, in the history of his House. Pride in his name, his deeds, his strength, his sword. Pride in his past, his future, his here and now.

But Tulnarron's pride was not an arrogance. There was no vanity, no suggestion of conceit in him. His pride was not an exaggerated egotism, neither inflated self-importance nor smug superiority. Rather the Master's pride was a sureness, a certainty. Confidence and conviction. An unshaking trust in himself, in his beliefs and in his abilities. In what he could accomplish. In what he *must* accomplish.

Having heard Ghost, having listened and brooded, deliberated and planned, Tulnarron now stood alone some distance from where the warriors of the Host of Arrenhoth recovered from their wild ride and prepared for one even wilder. He stood upon a small hummock, mighty arms folded across his chest, his countenance hewn and hard, cold eyes looking north into the night. As he gazed out upon the vast grey morass of Coldmire, Tulnarron did not consider that his terrible pride might be an appalling fault, a dreadful flaw in his character, his own personal hamartia. He did not contemplate the horrible hubris of his planned attack upon the enemy encampment. That his small company of fewer than three hundred Deathward warriors should strike, and strike successfully, at the heart of a force more than four-hundredfold their number did not seem illogical in his estimation. Not even for a moment.

Tulnarron's eyes glistered like glace. Somewhere out there in the wet wastes of Coldmire another Fian strove to do that which so many others would have deemed impossible, another Deathward soul endeavoured to achieve a thing considered unachievable. A valiant attempt, others would say, valiant and vain. But Eldurion yet lived, Tulnarron knew, for the gold of the Colossus still shone, declaring that *Grimroth* remained in or near the hand of a living scion of the House of Defurien. And where there was life, there was hope. And with hope, possibility. Possibility, potential, promise.

Promise.

Despite his heavy cloak and hood, a chill slithered over Tulnarron's skin, beginning at the nuque of his neck, then quivering and shivering down his spine. He stiffened. His face tingled as though pierced by a thousand tiny pins.

He was no longer alone.

He sensed a manifestation somewhere to his left. A presence. A power.

"I thought you might come," murmured the Master of the House of Eccuron without turning.

There was no reply.

"My wife sent you, I assume. An intolerable combination, that, wife and Seer. She cannot help herself. The woman is always meddling."

There came a deep coughing sound, and a large dark figure formed in the fog and moved silently to Tulnarron's side. Bright silvery eyes swept over the vapid vista of Coldmire.

"Have you come alone, old friend," the Master asked, "or have you brought with you some of your kin?"

As though in answer, the mists eddied before a bitter earthbound breeze, swirled back and away, revealing rank upon rigid rank of shadowy grey forms standing silent and still in the night. Hundreds, thousands of fierce fulgurant eyes gleamed, glowed. Argent and angry.

"Ah. I see. You have brought *all* your kin."

The regal head inclined slightly.

"I suppose you would have me relinquish command of this little enterprise. You being a Lord, after all, and myself a mere Master."

A throaty growl and the shake of a great black mane.

"Very well, Lord of Galledine. Your modesty far surpasses my own."

Tulnarron looked upon the massive beast at his shoulder, reached over, ran a surprisingly tender hand over the dark, thick coat.

"We have a long hard run ahead of us, old friend. Think you can keep up?"

The wolf-king of the *warokka* peeled back broad black lips, baring wicked white teeth in a feral, eager grin.

Promise.

Tulnarron smiled thinly, ruffled the mighty Alpha's midnight mane. Then he and Teraras turned away from the misted misery of Coldmire and headed back toward the waiting Host of Arrenhoth.

And in the churning fog of their wake, silent and sleek and stealthy, the spectral shapes of a thousand war wolves.

Kor ben Dor did not scream.

Every aspect of his being – the taut skin encasing his hard flesh, the molten marrow of his bones, the persistent impulses firing in his brain, the wildly raging inferno of his soul – urged, insisted, *demanded* that he scream until his throat shredded.

Yet the Halflord did not scream.

But he had never known such pain. Such utter agony. Excruciating, blinding, universal. Ripping through his flesh, every nerve rended, his brain torn, his soul shredded. A maleficent misery so very far beyond physical hurt. His eyes bulged, white and wide, his back arched, his body thrashed, legs kicking violently, his fists bunched into hammers of flesh and bone and pounded the ground. Blood seeped angrily from his ears, his nostrils, weeping red anguish from his eyes. His heart slamming, ramming, battering his ribcage, fast, furious, on the verge of breaking, bursting.

And still he did not scream.

"You must *stop*, Umbar'hal!" demanded Ev lin Dar, tears streaming from her wide white eyes, her fists balled at her thighs. "You will *kill* him!"

But Umbar'hal only shook his head earnestly, emphatically, as he clung desperately to the Halflord's head cradled in his lap. The witch-doctor sat cross-legged on the earthen floor of Kor ben Dor's tent, the Prince's tortured form twisting before him, black hair splayed across the shaman's thin thighs. The dragon's heart hanging from Umbar'hal's neck, withered as it was, glowed a brilliant red and pulsed rhythmically, vigorously beating, beating, beating. The Graniant's gigantic gnarled hands struggled to hold the Halflord's head motionless as the body writhed, the shaman's fingers replicating the tattooed talons, cracked nails tearing into the Prince's temple and cheeks, drawing blood.

"Stop! Cease this madness!" commanded Ev lin Dar as her sword whispered from its sheath. She took a step forward, her eyes wild for fear and weeping. *"Stop or die!"*

But a strong hand fell upon her shoulder, staying her advance.

"I like it no more than do you, Ev," hissed Gren del Mor at her ear. "But I gave my word. As did you. We promised our Prince we would see this through, come what may. We must endure. We must honour that word."

Ev lin Dar haughtily shrugged her friend's hand from her shoulder, seethed, sheathed her sword, but did no more. Only watched. And listened.

A soft chant, almost a cooing, issued from Umbar'hal's scratched and raspy throat, seeking not only to soothe, but to push Kor ben Dor past the pain. Past and back. Back into a yore where there existed no pain, no hurt of any kind, in any sense, in any measure. Back to the time before the pain.

Kor ben Dor thrashed in agony.

Ev lin Dar bit down on her lip, weeping freely.

The lullaby was constant, unceasing. Consistent, persistent, insistent. Never faltering, never failing. Sung every night for a fortnight in the halflight of the Prince's tent, that hoarse and ancient voice murmuring over the stricken prostrate form of Kor ben Dor, comforting and encouraging. At once a calming nightsong and a coaxing reassurance, urging the Halflord against the towering black wall of phantasmal pain in his mind.

Phantasmal, yes.

For the pain was not real.

The agony that the Halflord remembered was not genuine, had never been, but had been only a terrible illusion, and remained so. The pain had been purposely placed in his mind, an artifice insidiously inserted, potent and pervasive. Put there as a barrier to other memories, a barricade to the forbidden knowledge of self.

To the truth that was Kor ben Dor.

The Halflord's fists came crashing down one last time with such furious force that Ev lin Dar felt the earth tremble beneath her boots. Somewhere, deep within the palmed prison of Kor ben Dor's skull, in a place profoundly submerged and subliminal, walls came crashing down. And then Kor ben Dor's thrashing suddenly subsided to a spasmodic shaking punctuated by short pronounced sporadic convulsions that soon dwindled into a sustained shuddering. And finally, a silent shivering.

"This...this is different," whispered Ev lin Dar.

"Very," agreed Gren del Mor at her shoulder. Then, to Umbar'hal, "What is happening, shaman?"

The ancient Graniant looked up, obviously perplexed. His wasted countenance was pallid and drained from the strain he had endured. He shook his head, the yellowed skull fetishes clattering hollowly in his greasy green hair. His shoulders slumped, his hands sliding wearily away from the Halflord's head. Upon Umbar'hal's sunken chest, the desiccated dragon's heart fell still once more.

"The Prince shivers," Ev lin Dar observed, "yet he perspires. Is he fev –"

But the Black Shield never completed her question.

Because the world exploded.

Night is.

Night conceals, night hides.

Night is a slumbering god, and the world is its dread dream of horrors. Night is a monstrous maw stretched in a silent scream. Night is the cloak of the lurker, the spotted coat of the hunter. Night is the padded feet of the predator, the reed-woven blind behind which kill-ers crouch, the cover beneath which stalkers creep up quietly on their prey. Night secretes and secrets sin in its alleys and alcoves, screens the sinner from scrying eyes. Night obscures, obfuscates, disguising deeds dastardly and perverse. Night is the black hand of murder.

Night guides the pieces on the gameboard, masking their move-ments, conveying them behind the lines, arraying them in ambush. Night is the wolf on the ridge silhouetted upon the pale white face of the sinking moon. Night is the hand of vengeance, the raised dagger in the dark. Night is the band of raiders crawling on their bellies over frosted grass, blackened knives clenched between their teeth, death in their cold grey eyes. Night whispers with arrows aflight, softly thudding as steel barbs pierce a hundred hearts. Night is the black blood seeping from so many slitted throats. Night is a thousand grey ghosts slinking among the sleeping. Night is a spark in the dark.

Night hides, night conceals.

Night is.

A blinding flash. The world went white. Nothing but light.

Light.

Silent light.

Only an instant. Barely enough time to blink. But to those for whom death is imminent an instant is as a thousand years.

Ev lin Dar squeezed her eyes shut, threw up a shielding arm.

Then the sound. That sound. So impossibly loud. The sound of detonation, massive, monstrous, like the abrupt eruption of an enor-mous volcano, the roar of angry gods waging their war of ages, break-ing the earth.

Gren del Mor covered his ears, his own scream lost in the thunder of the sonic blast.

And lastly, concussion. Exploding, radiating outwards, an incred-ible release of energy. Absolute. The shock wave toppling, flattening all in its path. For miles. Razing the Plains.

Fire. Billowing smoke. Ash.

Death.

Ev lin Dar did not believe she had gone blind, though all she could see was a formless darkness. She did not consider that she might have been deafened, despite hearing naught but a constant hollow humming, as though struck tines of metal had been held to both ears, vibrating vigourously, endlessly. Her tongue was pasted with dust, her nostrils stuffed with dirt, depriving her of all taste, of all smell. She felt no pain, no discomfort, only the soft weight of a descending darkness persistently pressing her body into the earth. On some level, deeply subconscious, she realized that she was not breathing.

Ev lin Dar was certain she was dead.

Powerful hands hauled the heavy canvas of the toppled tent from her fallen form. Hands hooked under her armpits, urging her to a sitting position. Darkness took her for a time, and her soul slid away down a steep black slope greased with oblivion. Then she was snatched back. Something – someone – pounded her back between the blades of her shoulders, then the cleft between her breasts. Voices, the words muffled and indecipherable yet unequivocally urgent, thrummed upon her traumatized eardrums. She blinked against the chaos of colourless shadows swirling before her eyes. A hand struck her face. Hard.

And Ev lin Dar returned.

"What...?"

"Up, woman," came Gren del Mor's insistent growl. "We have been attacked."

Something wet and warm oozed from her brow, trickling down her cheek. The terrible tickle of blood on skin.

"You took a blow to the head, Ev. A bad one. But you're tougher than you look. Up, now."

Her feet beneath her, the Black Shield teetered upwards, vying against the last vestiges of vertigo. Her nostrils twitched. The air smelled of sulphur, tasted of chemicals, caustic and sour. Acrid ash floated on the black breath of night. The stench was strangely vivifying. Ev lin Dar's vision floundered into focus as her mind won the battle for balance.

Before her, Gren del Mor had raised his hand once more.

Ev lin Dar's own hand automatically found the haft of her sword.

"Hit me again, lizard-face, and I will relieve you of the offending hand."

Gren del Mor grinned like a gargoyle, his thin saurian face begrimed with dust and dirt, blood and ash.

"Ah, there she is. The ever demure and grateful Ev lin Dar. Welcome back."

Ev lin Dar glared at Gren del Mor, then past him.

The eastern section of the camp was leveled. Tents had been toppled, carts were overturned. Everywhere, chaos and destruction. Nothing moved there save a large tattered Black Jack banner which had been torn from its pole and was undulating rhythmically over the devastated camp like a winged serpent of death.

Ev lin Dar's eyes shone white.

"Casualties?"

"Half a hundred tents, some steamy dreams, a few egos," replied Gren del Mor. "Nothing that cannot be repaired or revisited. We Bloodspawn are a resilient folk."

Beyond the ruin of the camp, the edge of the world was on fire. The night to the northeast was glowing orange and red and yellow, shot through with fluorescent blues and greens, as though the northern aurora had descended to earth and set the prairie ablaze.

"The train?"

"Obliterated. Or so I assume. I hope you are partial to the distinctive flavours of grubs and grass, Ev lin Dar."

Sporadic sounds of battle floated down from the north. The intermittent and distant din of steel on steel, shouts and screams, the enraged roars of men and monsters fighting, dying. And oddly, the horrible howling of wolves in the night.

Fire and blackness flitted over the white of Ev lin Dar's eyes.

"We are attacked."

"Yes, I did say that."

"What of Prince Kor?"

Gren del Mor flashed a little lacertilian grin, grunted.

"Besotted as you are, I thought that would have been your first question."

Ev lin Dar glared at him, the fire in her eyes swelling heatedly.

Gren del Mor shrugged, gestured behind her with his pointed chin.

"Ask him yourself."

Ev lin Dar turned.

Immediately before her, Kor ben Dor sat astride his teratoid steed. Beside the Prince loomed the hunched and weary form of Umbar'hal; at the Halflord's back, beneath the billowing Black Jack, were assembled the entirety of the Bloodspawn, fully armoured in shining black steel and mounted on *mar rendera*, ready for war.

Beneath Kor ben Dor, his render growled anxiously, its eyes raging with red fire, a pinkish froth dripping from its maw as it champed at its bit. Its wickedly clawed forefeet gripped and gouged the ground, eager, earnest. Broad black nostrils flared fervently for the scent of blood in the night.

The Prince himself was completely calm, utterly composed. His back was straight, his shoulders square, his tattooed face the very picture of peace. He was clad in full battledress, his black armour reflecting fire and refracting darkness in equal measure. His hair had unfurled into wings so terrible and black as to inspire envy in an angel of death. The muscles of his naked biceps and thighs gleamed with sweat and firelight.

"I am gladdened that you are unhurt, Ev lin Dar."

The Black Shield inclined her head. She opened her mouth to speak, but the Halflord preempted her.

"We have been anxious for your recovery."

"How long was I –"

"Overlong, Shield."

Ev lin Dar blinked. There was no tone of admonishment to the Prince's voice, only a soft and simple relation of fact. And underlying it, perhaps, maybe, just maybe, another thing. Her heart fluttered, something flitted in her belly.

He waited for me?

Aside from streaks of dried blood on his chiseled cheeks and chin, Kor ben Dor seemed entirely unaffected by his own ordeal and the subsequent devastating explosion.

"Remain here, Umbar'hal," commanded the Halflord. "I need not remind you to say nothing."

The fatigue upon the Graniant's face was utter, absolute.

"Of course, Halflord," wheezed the shaman.

Kor ben Dor then met Ev lin Dar's damp gaze. A brief but certain silence shared.

"We ride now."

The Black Shield nodded mutely. Her throat felt suddenly sore.

He waited for me.

Two renders rumbled out of the night, manes and fetlocks flowing like flames. With reptilian alacrity, Gren del Mor swung upon his steed. Entirely recovered, save the tightness in her throat, Ev lin Dar leapt lithely astride her monstrous mount, taking the reins in an iron grip, nudging the monster northward toward the diminishing din of battle.

But the beast did not move.

"No, Ev lin Dar," said the Halflord softly. "Not north. West."

West?

The question must have been etched upon the Black Shield's blood-streaked, tigress-tattooed mien, for Kor ben Dor answered.

"Yes. West. Fast and hard. Then north. I am sure you can reason why."

Ev lin Dar nodded dumbly once more. West, north, east, south. What matter? She did not care where, did not care why.

He waited for me.

With no further word, the Halflord spun his render about, the monster rearing as its mighty master hefted his massive mace high.

And the black tide of the Bloodspawn roared once and thundered away.

The Host of Arrenhoth rode like a great grey wind.

West. Fast and hard.

Bent low over their majestic mounts, cloaks and pennons flying, Tulnarron and company raced headlong and heedless along the Soft Road. Caution sacrificed for speed. The hooves of the *mirarra* devoured league after league, even as the hours consumed the last morsels of night. The sun slid slowly above the rim of the world, red spears of light hurling at the backs of the riders as they chased their shadows westward. Far behind them, a surly scarlet dawn shone its shadowlight upon the ruin that had been wrought, the death that had been dealt.

The explosion had been utterly devastating, its destructive force several-fold more powerful than Gostullian had calculated. But the Watcher called Ghost had not survived centuries in the unforgiving wild by being incautious. Neither rashness nor recklessness were in his nature. He had considered and reconsidered that the explosive potential of the munitions train may be far beyond his expectations, well past his predictions, and had advised and ensured that appropriate measures and precautions be taken.

Nevertheless, *someone* had to light that first fuse.

The riders of the House of Eccuron sped after their shortening shadows. Westward, ever westward. After the explosion there had been pursuit, there had been a pitched and running battle, one that ended unceremoniously and of a sudden when the Norian cavalry were led through a waiting gauntlet of silvery spears and were thoroughly scuppered, sliced to bloody ribbons in a threshing whirlwind of Fiannian steel. Teraras and the *warokka* had decided the rest. Teeth bared and gnashing, the war wolves of Galledine created such havoc in the night that all other pursuit from the northern camp had been abruptly abandoned. The Unmen of the Hebbingore had suffered the worst of it – a thousand warriors' throats torn open as they slept, a thousand more ripped wide as they woke. Even now, the *warokka* lingered somewhere in the wake of the Host, loping fluidly over the grasses, a ferocious rearguard of fang and fury.

West. Fast and hard.

When the morning wind at their backs had warmed, and their swift shadows on the Soft Road were become significantly shorter, Tulnarron at long last slowed his well-lathered *mirarran*'s gait. His troop of Deathward shared a silent sigh of relief.

"That was close thing," said Gornannon at Tulnarron's left side, the everpresent cheroot clenched between his teeth.

"Very close," agreed Sandarre upon the Master's right.

"Too close," corrected Tulnarron, a touch sharply. "Far too close. For Haldarian and Lorradien, at least."

The pair of Fiannar, Haldarian and Lorradien, had been in the rearguard, fighting fiercely to protect the retreat. There was an earnest engagement, a contest made desperate by the unexpected intervention of wandering band of Urkroks. A dozen Deathward led by their mighty Master detached to do battle. The blow from an enormous Urkrok's club crushed Haldarian's skull, spattering his brain. A stray Norian arrow took Lorradien in the eye. Tulnarron saw them go down. Took his revenge, cold and deadly. Painted the Plains with enemy blood. The bundled bodies of both valiant fallen Fiannar now lay across the backs their *mirarra*, borne in honour beneath the banners of the Golden Strype and the Crimson Fist.

"And for Gostullian," Gornannon added gravely.

"A brave and selfless deed, his," said Sandarre, both a sadness and a particular pride to her tone.

Tulnarron grunted doubtfully.

"I would not mourn the good Ghost oversoon, cousin. Death has come for that man a hundred and a half times. And a hundred and a half times Death has departed in disappointed dejection. I will say my eulogy for Gostullian of the Grey Watch when I have seen his cold dead corpse with my own eyes."

Sandarre and Gornannon exchanged a strange look. The former cleared her throat a touch nervously.

"Cousin, the explosion will have –"

But the certainty in Tulnarron's small smile silenced Sandarre's assertion. The Master did not articulate aloud the two little words which that specific smile signified, but Sandarre heard them murmur in her mind:

Even so.

Before the band of riders, the road dipped and rose in a series of valleys, some shallow, some deep, the interceding hills between limiting the line of sight. Clouds clung to the earth, obscured the morning sky, scuttling the sun. The air was cloying and chill. Fog crept out of Coldmire, gathering in the low places, thick and grey.

At the head of the Host, Tulnarron scowled as they descended a slope, following the Soft Road into an elongated hollow, a sunken stretch of misted miles walled on both sides by high rounded hills. With every step the fog cooled and congealed, thickening into a swirling soup, so dense about the legs of the *mirarra* that the riders could not see the ground. A feeling of floating gripped them, strangely soothing and sedative, stultifying the senses.

The furrows of Tulnarron's frown deepened, darkened. There was no reason to assume anything that wished ill or intended harm awaited them between there and Eryn Ruil. No thrall of the Blood King could outpace the *mirarra*. Nothing on the Northern Plains was fleeter. Naught but fog ever came out of Coldmire. And the *warokka* warded their backs.

Nevertheless, the Master was uneasy in his mind. The night flight had been too wild, too reckless by far.

And then the ears of his mount twitched.

Tulnarron called sharply for Castadon and his contingent of outriders.

But another voice answered him.

"No further, Fian."

Too wild, too reckless. And too late.

The Master held up his hand. The Host halted, instantly effecting a defensive formation, shields raised, spears seething outwards in all directions, like a great plated prehistoric beast bristling with long lethal spikes. Weapons ready, Sandarre and Gornannon edged closer to Tulnarron, their steel-grey eyes constantly sweeping the fog before them. Nothing but mist beneath them, cloud above them, fog before them, each seemingly seeking a state of translucent equilibrium with the other.

The Master of the House of Eccuron gritted his teeth, grinded his jaws, but otherwise did not move. His eyes glittered, cold and angry. The error had been his. And grievous. But self-flagellation, however much deserved, would of harsh necessity have to wait.

"Come."

The voice was soft, but swollen with power, with command. Should the fog before them have been alive, an entity both animate and aware, that voice would have suited its spectral throat more than adequately. And it sounded close. So very close.

Tulnarron deftly slid his greatsword from its harness.

"I need to *see*, cousin," he hissed beneath his breath.

Sandarre nodded silently, raised her bow above her head, left arm outstretched and upright, strong right arm bent and drawing the string back to her bosom, the nocked arrow pointed to the heavy overcast heavens. The bow *thwacked*. The missile launched skyward, vanishing almost instantly into the grey. And Sandarre sang. Her voice light and lilting, soft and smooth like a warm summer rain. A few words only, in the Old Tongue, words of power that remained unforgotten to some among the Fiannar.

To some, like Sandarre of the House of Eccuron.

High above, a lone flash of lightning lashed the heavens, and a single roar of raw-throated thunder shook the earth. Sparks showered down from the sky, a crackling cascade of fiery rain. The cloud cover parted, scattered, pulled back and away, as though a great grey shroud had been ripped from the cadaver of the world. The mists withdrew, crawling back to Coldmire. The fog faded, fell away.

Tulnarron bit back his breath.

Hundreds of great grey giants astride huge horses from Hell lined the rises upon both Fiannian flanks and to the fore. To the east, behind the Deathward, more mounted giants swiftly and efficiently pinched off the lane of retreat, effectively surrounding the Host of Arrenhoth. Though their horrific horses huffed and heaved and clawed at the earth, the giants only stared down upon their snared prey in cool, contemplative aphony. Black-armoured, white-eyed, winter-cold of countenance. Angular visages tattooed with totem animals. The universally black hair of the males worked into a variety of odd shapes and figures; that of the females worn long and loose, veritably shining with darkness. Armed with an expansive assortment of armaments, some recognizable, some not, all forged of the same strange blue steel, all held loosely, almost casually, somewhere between at the ready and at ease. To a man, to a woman, the gargantuan grey warriors radiated a chill calm confidence. Above them fluttered unfamiliar colours – a copper and a silver stripe crossing one another upon a field of pure midnight.

And upon the Soft Road, only thirty strides away, their leader.

"Come."

Tulnarron peered up at the apparition, his grey gaze glittering with silvery fire. None of the alien giants surrounding the Host bore any type of bow, and few wielded weapons that were even remotely designed for throwing. All seemed armed and armoured for extreme, intimate, close fighting. But not one weapon was held in a threatening manner. Even the leader's huge-headed mace remained strapped at his back. The ambush had not been orchestrated to effect immediate mass slaughter of the Fiannar. But if not that, then what?

"*Stay. Come.* You are indecisive, giant. And I am not your dog."

The leader of the giants regarded Tulnarron with impassive ice-white eyes, then languidly rolled his broad shoulders. The morning wind rippled the impressive black wings of hair stretching from the sides of his head. He closed his eyes briefly, seemed to sigh in the sunlight. And then his nightmarish steed coughed, stepped slowly forward, terrible talons sinking into the spongy earth, bloody froth drooling from its savagely toothed jaws.

Fifteen paces farther, the rider stopped his steed.

Said nothing. Waited.

Tulnarron cursed under his breath, biting back a bitter *"Bastard"* between bunched teeth, then moved his *mirarran* forward five, ten, fifteen paces. Unsummoned, Sandarre and Gornannon followed, remaining a length behind and to each side. In response, two mounted giants, a male and a female, detached from the ranks behind their leader and descended to take up similar and opposite positions.

For a time, nothing was said. Simply silent observation, wordless regard. Curiosity struck dumb by an overwhelming perception of peril.

Tulnarron marked the well-defined lines of the leader's faceted face, the chiseled cheekbones, the squareness of the jaw. He frowned inwardly at the seeming familiarity of that grim, purposeful, yet handsome countenance. The authoritative austerity exuded there thrummed the strings of recognition, but made no melody, stirred no memory.

"Do I know you, giant?"

"Unlikely, Fian. We have never met."

Tulnarron nodded. "I would remember you."

"Likely, Fian. Name."

"This is my country, giant," scowled Tulnarron. "You first."

The giant shrugged indifferently.

"I am Kor ben Dor. Prince of the Bloodspawn. I am called the Halflord."

The Master failed to suppress a smile. "Only 'Half'?"

Kor ben Dor sighed, but otherwise ignored the jibe.

"Name."

"I am Tulnarron, Master of the House of Eccuron, commanding the noble Host of Arrenhoth."

"You should know, Tulnarron of Arrenhoth, that your home remains as you left it, unbroken and unplundered. Such deplorable action I could never allow."

"Why, giant?"

"Why not, Fian?"

"The Blood King is not known for such restraint."

"I am not the Blood King."

"Yet you follow him."

The Halflord said nothing.

"And you command his army," the Master deduced. "How else could you forbid the sack of Arrenhoth?"

"No. I command only the Bloodspawn."

"Then why should the Blood King's army listen to you?"

"I am...respected."

"Feared, you mean."

"The line between the two is often blurred, Tulnarron of Arrenhoth."

"Indeed. And who commands you?"

The Halflord paused for a moment, white eyes aglow.

"Leeches command the army of the Blood King, Tulnarron of Arrenhoth."

Leeches.

The revelation struck the Master of the House of Eccuron like a physical blow. A sharp intake of breath, hissing inward between clenched teeth.

Leeches!

"Leech, really," amended the Prince, watching the Master's face intently. "The little girl dominant. The little boy, submissive. Or so it seems."

Little girl? Little boy?

"The Leeches have stolen the bodies of human children, Fian. A girl and a boy. Young, and of an age. Ten summers, perhaps. Twins, by the look of them, but I cannot be sure."

Tulnarron's eyes flared. Shades of grey rage. White fire, black ice.

No! The little twins from Maple Creek! And I do them the dishonour of forgetting their names. Teller, do not tell this tale!

The Halflord regarded the Master ruefully.

"I do not condone what the Leeches have done, Tulnarron of Arrenhoth. Indeed, I am appalled, and would undo it, if it was within my power to do so."

Tulnarron gritted his teeth, his eyes iridescent with ire.

"There are powers greater than you in this world, Bloodspawn."

"So the Leeches keep reminding me."

Tulnarron glowered. But the sincerity of the chagrin etched upon the Halflord's features and evinced in his words cooled the wrath rising within. And with coolness came clarity.

The revelation that the Blood King's army was commanded by Leeches had astonished Tulnarron. That those demons had taken the little twins had shocked him. But even in his shock and astonishment, Tulnarron had not failed to mark that the leader of the Bloodspawn had answered a question he had not asked, whilst adeptly avoiding the one he had. The Master consciously shoved all surprise and anger aside, recovering swiftly.

"But the Leeches do not command *you*, do they, Prince of the Bloodspawn?"

The Halflord stared. Rolled his massive shoulders once more. Cocked his head slightly to one side, broad black wings buffeting the wind.

"I am commanded by my conscience." Kor ben Dor glanced to his left, to his right. "And by the consciences of my friends."

The Master had not expected that answer. And by the looks on the faces of the two flanking Bloodspawn, neither had they. Indeed, the entirety of the parley was not proceeding along predictable paths.

Tulnarron's grey gaze met the Halflord's ivory eyes evenly.

"What are we doing here, Kor ben Dor?"

"Conversing."

"Conversing?"

"Yes."

"Is that all?"

"What else would you have us do, Master of the House of Eccuron?"

Tulnarron frowned.

"You have skillfully surprised and surrounded a war party of Fiannar. More, the Host of Arrenhoth. A feat not easily achieved. Yet you keep your weapons lowered, make neither menace nor threat, and speak of abstractions like conscience, a concept completely alien to thralls of the Wraithren. Indeed, until recently I had heard neither whisper nor rumour of you and your Bloodspawn. You are something different. Something...other."

Kor ben Dor raised his eyes to the fluttering Golden Strype, then swiveled about, looked upon the Black Jack billowing on the hill behind him. Turned back, looked left upon Gren del Mor, right upon Ev lin Dar. Then at Gornannon and Sandarre. And lastly returning to the Master of the House of Eccuron.

Something like a smile touched the Halflord's lips.

"We are not so different, Tulnarron of Arrenhoth."

The Master's frown blackened. Had there been something profound in the Bloodspawn's assertion? Something enlightening, insightful? Tulnarron brushed a stray tress of hair from his eyes. Philosophy was not his strength.

Neither was patience.

"Are we to do battle here, Prince of the Bloodspawn? Should that be so, we had best desist with idle chatter and be done with it."

"You would not fare well, Fian."

"You would fare far worse, giant."

"You are fewer than three hundred. We are six hundred three-score and six. And you discount the fury of our mounts, the *mar rendera*."

"As you do the might of the *mirarra*. An oversight that has frequently proved fatal to foes of the Fiannar. And moreover, we Deathward are not the ones outnumbered, Kor ben Dor. We have you two to one."

"You count strangely, Tulnarron of Arrenhoth."

"Be honoured that I count you at all, Bloodspawn."

In a moment of purest poignancy, Sandarre met Ev lin Dar's ever-watchful eye, and the two female warriors shared a certain knowing, weary smile common to women wherever and whenever men insist upon participating in prolonged pissing contests.

And then the long and lingering howl of a lone lupine throat shivered the cold northern morning air.

Tulnarron grinned triumphantly.

Kor ben Dor tilted his head back, closed his eyes, sighed.

"Ah, the *warokka*. The war wolves of the Fiannar. I had forgotten them. A terrible error." He looked down upon the Master once more, his eyes wide and white with warning. "Nevertheless, do not lose your head, Fian."

Ev lin Dar's smile died instantly.

Instinctively, Sandarre nocked an arrow to the string swifter than the eye could follow.

Gazes locked, Master's and Prince's, grey on white. Assessments and costs. Choices and consequences. Cause and effect. And unbeknownst to either warrior, the very fate of the world hanging haphazardly in the balance.

Until wisdom prevailed.

"I will keep my head if you will keep yours, Kor ben Dor."

The Halflord nodded. "I intend you no harm, Tulnarron of Arrenhoth."

"Not, at least, until we meet again at Eryn Ruil."

But the Prince of the Bloodspawn shook his head.

"I do not go to the Seven Hills."

"No?"

"No."

"Why not?"

"The Leeches do not want me there. I suspect they have their reasons."

"Where, then?"

"I am to go to the southern pass, there to meet and destroy its lord in battle."

Tulnarron blinked incredulously. "You are going to Doomfall to fight Drogul of Dul-darad?"

"Should he be there, and willing, yes."

"Drogul the *kirun-tar*. The Mighty One."

"Yes."

"On purpose?"

The Halflord angled his face toward the sun. Inhaled deeply.

Tulnarron shook his head slowly, almost sadly. "Well...good luck with that."

Kor ben Dor dismissed – or simply missed – the mordacity in the Master's words.

"I am grateful for your good wishes, Tulnarron of Arrenhoth." He inclined his handsome head. "I have enjoyed our conversation. We will leave you now."

The Master nodded, paused, considered, then fisted his breast in rare raw respect for an esteemed enemy.

The Halflord raised his hand, hesitated, the giant fist hovering before his breastplate for four, five palpable pulses of blood in the veins at his thick wrists, then tentatively tapped the blackened steel over his heart. Once, twice. He then turned silently away.

"Kor ben Dor."

The Prince of the Bloodspawn stopped, looked over his shoulder, waited.

"Why did you come? Certainly not to...converse."

Kor ben Dor closed his eyes. "You would not understand, Tulnarron of Arrenhoth. Only a Bloodspawn could comprehend."

"Try me, Halflord."

The Prince lowered his head, his chin nearly touching his chest.

"I came because the pain is gone," he said softly, so very softly. "And because I *remember*. I remember everything."

19

THE UNFORGIVEN

*"Often it is easier for one to forgive others their sins
than it is for one to forgive oneself one's own."*

Rafayel, *Book of Laments*, Chapter XX11, Verse 24

The beasts burst from the black heart of the night, leaping past the ring of rock that warded the rise of Carricevan. Dozens came – great feral creatures crashing through the sleet, hungering for flesh, thirsting for blood. Rundul of the Daradur and Eldurion of the Fiannar met them before the stones of Doras Serrin with mettle and metal. And the swamp-things of Coldmire began to die.

Rundul's war-axe whirled like a wild thing, slicing through sleet and mist and foul flesh in a fury of blood and iron. And the ever-bare blade of Eldurion danced in the darkness, sweeping aside fog and foe as effortlessly as a stormwind would do withered leaves. Death was come again to Doras Serrin that night, a tempest of doom riding the wings of wrath, wielding sickles of Daradun and Fiannian steel.

The bog-beasts were large and loathsome, partly lupine, partly crocodilian, entirely abominable. They swarmed the sleet-slicked mosses of Carricevan, surging against Rundul and Eldurion in a roiling sea of fur, fang, scale and claw. But Darad and Fian stood as did the very stones of Doras Serrin, hard and grey. Stalwart, steadfast. Immovable. And the swamp-things died in droves upon their steel.

There were dozens of them.

And then there were none.

"What on Mother Earth were these things?" growled Rundul in the hushed aftermath of battle as he brushed sleet from his beard and brackish blood from the blades of his war-axe.

Eldurion slipped his sword from the belly of a bog-beast. The Fian's visage was past grim, past grey, and his eyes were slits of silver in the sleets of night.

"I know not, Stone Lord," Eldurion replied lowly as he crouched to study the carcass of the creature. His nose wrinkled for the rancid reek of the thing. "Long have I traveled and tread the bogs of Coldmire, but I have neither seen nor sensed these things before, nor even heard rumour of them."

The beast was broad and bulky, easily seven feet from elongated snout to humped hind, with a perilously plated tail of like length. The creature's jaws were ferociously fanged, its body alternately armoured in scale and matted with fur. The legs were stout but long, swift and strong, terminating in wickedly curved claws. The thing seemed an inexplicable anomaly of evolution, the product of mutation run amok, at once a horrible progenitor of the wolf and a hideous antecedent of the alligator.

"I cannot determine with any certainty whether they are reptile or mammal," Eldurion mused in the mist. "They appear to be...both."

"They are neither," came a third voice into Carricevan.

Eldurion rose. Rundul turned.

Yllufarr of the Neverborn stood amidst the slime and slaughter of the swamp-things, his form a shadow in the night of the storm-bound bog, a long-bladed Athain dagger glimmering in each deft and deadly hand. A subtle shift of his presence, and the pair of pale blades vanished into invisible sheaths within his vestment. The Prince's eerily luminous eyes glowed like pearls under moonlight, moving from carcass to carcass, then meeting the respective grey and black gazes of his companions.

Rundul spat into the storm.

"Is it the curse of the Athair that they must ever come late to the battle, or come not at all?"

Yllufarr disregarded the gruff banter of his Daradun friend.

"They are neither mammalian nor reptilian," he repeated. Something deep and dark swam in the pale pools of his eyes. "Nor are they of this Second World, but of the First. And I have seen their like before. They are the *ulviathoi*, the spawn of Ulviathon, and have not been seen on this Earth since the *Angar ban Gan Gebbernindh*. Their presence here now is...unsettling."

Rundul leaned on the haft of his war-axe, his midnight gaze contemplating the Athain Sun Lord intently.

"Ulviathon was destroyed at Gan Gebbernin," Eldurion stated succinctly, "as were his spawn. These cannot be *ulviathoi*."

"They are *ulviathoi*," reiterated Yllufarr softly yet emphatically, "though lesser in size and power than those of olde, as these are more mortal animal than deathless demon-spawn." Darkness swirled beneath the pale sheen of his eyes like the coils of a sea serpent undulating under ice. "I have reason to remember them."

Eldurion inclined his head. Slivers of sleet slid from his hood. He well knew what had occurred at the Battle of Gan Gebbernin. He knew what had been won there – and what had been lost.

"What aren't you telling us, Sun Lord?" Rundul rumbled. "You're hiding something – what is it?"

Yllufarr met the Darad's midnight gaze evenly. He decided to withhold that which he knew from his comrades no longer. Their suspicions aroused, such suppression served no good purpose, but could only seed division, derision. The Fian was wise beyond his mere three hundred years. And the Darad could not be deceived.

The night swelled. The storm raged. The sleet became hail and hurtled down like hammers from an angry heaven.

And the Prince of the Neverborn said simply –

"We are not alone."

The three companions gathered within the stone walls of the Doras Serrin, sheltering from the night and the wet and the frozen rains of Coldmire. Eldurion stood tall and straight, as grey as a ghost, the Blade of Defurien bound at his back, his own blood-sullied sword yet gripped in one hand. Rundul of Axar, Captain of the Wandering Guard, positioned himself by the aperture of the dolmen's leaning stones that served as sole entry and egress. Vapours rose into the chill from the blades of the Darad's great war-axe like white wisps of the souls it had slain. Yllufarr of the Neverborn stood at the centre of the structure, a wraith of the Otherworld wrapped in midnight. And the hails rapped unrelentingly upon the capstone of Doras Serrin, the skeletal knuckles of unnumbered wayward wights, knocking, knocking, wanting in.

"I have sensed something vast and vile in the bog," whispered the Prince of the Folk of Gavrayel. "A great and powerful evil."

Eldurion's eyes narrowed to silvery slits.

"When did you sense this thing?"

"I felt it as we entered," replied Yllufarr softly. The serpent swam the pearly pools of his eyes. "And I have felt it since."

Rundul's face darkened.

"And you're only telling us now?"

The Sun Lord looked to the Captain of the Wandering Guard.

"I did not wish to distract you, Stone Lord. The Athair sense much that others do not. There are many powers, both good and ill, of which the Athair may be fully or partially aware, but which take little or no interest in the affairs of this world. Were I to speak to you of all that I sense, friend Rundul, you would surely tire of my voice."

Rundul bit down on the obvious retort that teased the tip of his tongue.

"What is this great evil of which you speak?" asked Eldurion. "And need we take cautions against it?"

"I can be certain of neither, friend Eldurion. I know only that it is out there, somewhere, and that it slumbers now, and has done so for a long time."

"It sleeps?"

"Soundly."

Rundul peered into the pale eyes of the Prince, and saw no untruth there, no falsehood, neither misdirection nor deception – only a serpentine thing moving beneath their pale sheen. And a rolling rock of warning rumbled in the Darad's breast.

"There's more, isn't there, Sun Lord?

"I have at times felt eyes upon me in the mist," revealed Yllufarr, "though in those eyes I perceived neither ill nor malice, but only some little curiosity – and something else."

Eldurion raised a greyed and grizzled brow.

"Sorrow, friend Eldurion. Sorrow was in those eyes in the gloom. The black sorrow of shame."

The Fian frowned. And he recalled the words that Tulnarron, the brash young Master of the House of Eccuron, had spoken to him in the eaves of Ravenwood.

Beware the Moor Walkers, Eldurion.

A small dark silence, but for the ghouls of Coldmire knocking, knocking, knocking upon the capstone of Doras Serrin.

"One thing more, friends Eldurion and Rundul."

The Darad glowered.

The Eldest of the Fiannar remained motionless for a moment, his countenance cast in clays pondering and pensive, and then he nodded for the Prince to proceed.

Yllufarr's pale gaze glowed in the dark of Doras Serrin. The serpent swam like the swirling script of the oghams on the walls.

"I have heard the Song of the Shaddathair," said the Sun Lord. He paused as one listening to a whisper on the wind. "I hear it sung even now."

Knocking, knocking, wanting in.

"I hear nothing," muttered Rundul, peering warily into the night, his eyes and ears searching the darkness about Carricevan.

Eldurion cocked his head to one side, his leathery face a mask of concentration. He then looked up and shook his head slowly.

"I too hear nothing, Prince Yllufarr. And unlike the Darad I am well-attuned to Coldmire. Perhaps the song you hear is for the ears of the Undying alone."

"Or perhaps the Ath has at long last gone entirely mad."

The Prince smiled blandly, beautifully, but dignified the Darad's riposte with no retort.

"I have not heard of these Shaddathair," said Eldurion. Doubt darkened his tone. "And none know Coldmire better than do I."

"You know of the Shaddathair more than you suppose, and less than you should, friend Eldurion. For in your travels here you have often seen and sensed them, though your people name them the Moor Walkers."

"Ah. As I suspected. Harmless shades, then. The Moor Walkers are mere shadows. More or less."

"Less. And more. They were not always the Shaddathair, friend Eldurion."

"Is that significant?"

"Is the past not always so?"

The Eldest of the Fiannar frowned. "You say they are aware of our presence here."

The serpent swam the colourless seas of Yllufarr's eyes.

"Most certainly. They were once Eldagreen. They are now Coldmire."

"And they have been...watching us."

The Sun Lord nodded. The serpent swirled.

Rundul's hand tightened involuntarily about the haft of his axe.

"Do the Moor Walkers mean us harm, Yllufarr?" Eldurion asked evenly. "Will they seek to thwart us?"

The dark Prince of the Neverborn shrugged slightly.

"I do not know. The Shaddathair have ever showed little concern for the travails of this World. Nor for those of any other."

The Darad grumbled gutturally and kept his vigil on the night, taking comfort in the feel of the steel upon his palm.

"Tell me more of the Moor Walkers," said the grim Fian. "I would know their nature, and decide the peril they may or may not pose."

The Prince of the Folk of Gavrayel hesitated for an ancient hurt in his heart, then inclined his hooded head.

"It is fitting that the tale of Sammayal and his Unforgiven should be told here in this place, this Portal to the Stars – for it was here, in this very place, that the Unforgiven first set foot on Second Earth."

Rundul turned, glancing about the darkness of Doras Serrin warily.

Eldurion waited in silence.

And the serpent sank into the deepest depths of the Sun Lord's glimmering eyes.

"My friends, I would sing you the Song of the Shaddathair."

And Yllufarr, Prince of the Folk of Gavrayel of the Golden Voice, spread wide his arms, and the movement seemed to stir the music and the Light within him. For he shone as a star, ever bright, eternal, soft and white and beautiful. And about him there arose the tender tinkling of bells under silver moonlight, the haunting fugue of a harp plucked at the peak of a misty mountain, the rhythmic resonance of a lyre strummed upon a calm sea. And he summoned and set free the song within him, a song of tragic and terrible beauty, of magnificent melancholy and majesty, of the sublime and ceaseless sorrow of Sammayal and the Shaddathair.

Yllufarr sang of the treachery of Asrayal the Accursed, that dark and dreadful Ath who wrought war and ruin upon the paradise of First Earth, and of the misfounded loyalty of his lordly lieutenants, Ingallin and Sammayal. He sang of battle and bloodshed, of the might of Sammayal, tall and terrible, of the strength of his arm and the swiftness of his sword, of the wrath and wreckage he bore with him in battle against his brethren. Sang of the final fall of Asrayal to the fury of Defurien and the flaming brand of *Grimroth*, of the trial of the Folk of Asrayal at the Stone of Scullain, of the pardon granted them by the Kings Micyll and Gavrayel and by the gallant Lord Defurien. Of the rift in the ranks of the Folk of Asrayal, of those that followed Ingallin and accepted the absolution offered them, and of the shame and sorrow of Sammayal and his faction, and their refusal of all forgiveness.

Yllufarr sang of the coming of folk of Sammayal to Second Earth, of their emergence from the Portal to the Stars, of their making a home in elegant Eldagreen, of their abiding there in peace with the primal Tuathroth. But he sang also of their incredible sorrow, of their naming themselves the Unforgiven, for though it was true that they had been shrived of their sins by those that ruled the First Earth, they could not remit themselves their own wrongs, and ever did the galleries of ancient Eldagreen weep to the song of their shame and sorrow.

Yllufarr sang of the coming of Gavrayel and his golden folk to the shores of Second Earth, of the welcome given them by Sammayal, of the sureties sought by the King and his Queen Aeline. He sang of Sammayal and the Unforgiven vowing against all violence, of the setting down of their swords and the shedding of their armour. Sang of Gavrayel and his fair folk taking their leave of Sammayal and going far into the north, of the founding of the hidden realm of Gith Glennin. Of their removal of themselves from the woes and worries of Men as that mortal people emerged from the bindings of their primitive past.

And then he sang of the Unforgiven's withdrawal from the world of the living into the deepest depths of Eldagreen, of their walking over-often in the halfworld of Eilla Evvanin, of their becoming the shadowy *shee* of Rothic legend.

The stone walls of Doras Serrin shimmered with the light of the Sun Lord, and the music of his voice was as a wistful wind weaving through the leaves of living Eldagreen in her ancient glory. Eldurion harkened, aswoon with the love for song that all Deathward possessed, and the lids of his eyes fluttered and fell closed, and his sword slipped from his grasp. But Rundul listened, unmoving and unmoved, a rock within rock, his axe fast and firm in his fist, and ever did he retain his vigil on the night.

Yllufarr sang of the rise of the Wraithren, and of war ravaging the Second Earth, of the resolute resistance of the Roths, and of Sammayal's steadfast refusal to intervene. He sang of the arrival of the Fiannar, that fierce and fell folk, and of their gathering unto them the beleaguered tribes of Man, and of their riding into the wars of the new world under banners bold and brave. Sang of Vallian and of Eccuron and of Hiridion, of glorious triumph and victory in the vale of Caen-al-Morra, and of the ensuing years of peace and prosperity. Of Sammayal knowing little of these things and caring even less.

Yllufarr sang of the return of the Wraithren and war, of the *Angar ban Maelmorradh*, the apocalyptic Battle of the Barrens. He sang of the grievous defeat the Fiannar and the Men that stood with them suffered there, of the Lord Vallian's long retreat to the seeming sanctuary of Eldagreen. Sang of the cool reception by Sammayal of those wretched refugees of war, of dour Vallian's outright dismissal of him. Of the subsequent invasion of glorious Eldagreen by the swarming armies of Shadow.

Yllufarr sang of the great and terrible battle fought at Gan Innivir, the vale the Athair named the Valley of Dreams, but which would ever afterward be known as Gan Gebbernin, the Valley of the Dead. He sang of the gallant last stand of the Deathward and their allies. Sang of the courage and fortitude they displayed in defiance of death, doom and destruction. Of Sammayal's refusal to receive the emissary of the Fiannar who came to him begging aid of the Unforgiven.

And then he sang of the sudden coming of the shining *Sul Athaifain* of Gavrayel to the devastated Valley of Dreams, of the valour of the Sun Lords Evangael and Thrannien and Yllufarr at the *Angar ban Gan Gebbernindh*. He sang of the failing of hope and fortune as Zan-zurak, Death King of the Wraithren, unleashed his hidden hordes of heinous things upon the Sun Lords and their shining Knights. Sang of Evangael bidding Yllufarr seek Sammayal to sue for assistance, for Yllufarr and mighty Sammayal had of a time been fast in friendship. Of Yllufarr finding Sammayal weeping in the wood.

And he sang of Yllufarr, Prince and Sun Lord, returning to battle alone and without answer from Sammayal, come to find his Knights slaughtered and utterly destroyed beneath the unholy might of Ulviathon and its horrid demon-spawn.

And then did the Prince's voice thicken with rage and wrath, and his light dimmed, darkened, and the stone walls of Doras Serrin took a crimson sheen as though the shining of the moon had fallen upon a world awash with blood.

Yllufarr sang of the fallen Hiath become the demon-god that the Athair called Ulviathon, the great beast that had haunted and hunted the eastern seas of First Earth, voraciously preying on ocean creatures and mariners and even its own twisted spawn. He sang of the dark and potent sorcery of Zan-zurak summoning Ulviathon to the *Angar ban Gan Gebbernindh*, of the beast crashing into battle against the Sun Knights of Yllufarr with countless thousands of *ulviathoi*. Sang of the doom and ruin the demon and its spawn wreaked there. Of the seven hundred Sun Knights that fell there, ripped and rended and trampled into the mire of their own blood.

And he sang the name of each Sun Knight lost, one by one by one by one by one...

Cold tears streamed down Eldurion's cracked cheeks.
Rundul watched the night.

Yllufarr sang of the earth erupting and of the coming of the mighty Daradur to Gan Gebbernin. He sang of the scattering of the shrieking *ulviathoi*. Sang of their slaughter under the axes and hammers and mighty mauls of the Stone Lords. Of the great Demon-god Ulviathon itself turning to flee before the power and might of that new enemy.

And he sang of Yllufarr, the bereft and knightless Sun Lord, seeking and finding Ulviathon amidst the carnage and chaos of Gan Gebbernin, of the ringing challenge that burst from Athain Prince's breast. He sang of Yllufarr, grim and glorious in his grief, standing alone before the monstrous Ulviathon, of the clash and clamour of the *Angar ban Gan Gebbernindh* receding as the two Immortals faced one another, the one as huge and black as a mountain of obsidian, the other a solitary sapling shining in its shadow. Sang of Yllufarr crying aloud in sorrow and rage as he sprang into battle, ablaze with Light, a long sword in one hand, a tall spear in the other. Of the ground quaking as the two fought, of the skies shaking to the roars of the demon, of the tears that spilled from the Sun Lord's eyes as he dodged the talons and tail and teeth of the beast. He sang of the fires burning about the two combatants in their struggle, of the ebb and flow of the fight beneath sun and moon and sun again. Sang of the demon-god frothing in frustration for the fleetness of its foe, of the blows and thrusts of the Ath falling back from the steely hide of the beast in futility. Of a duel of might and muscle and magic that the Second Earth had seen neither before nor since.

And then he sang of Yllufarr at long last launching his spear like a lance of lightning into the crimson orb of Ulviathon's left eye, of his lithely leaping atop the gigantic beast and sinking his sword past scale into skull. Sang of Ulviathon shrieking, thrashing, threshing the air, throwing Yllufarr into the eldritch fires that burned where they fought. Of the beast fleeing the field, returning, it was said, to the distant seas, there to lie down and die.

And lastly he sang of the stricken Prince coming in the aftermath of battle to stand before Sammayal, cursing the cowardice of the Unforgiven, calling them well-named and swearing that the deaths of his seven hundred were sins upon Sammayal's craven soul that would never be absolved.

And then a silence fell within Doras Serrin. The wights of night ceased their knocking as the hails softened to rain and the rain faded to fog. Even the gurgle of the bog quieted, as though the muds and sludges of the swamp slumbered at long last.

"Thus is the Song of the Shaddathair sung among the Folk of Gavrayel," sighed Yllufarr, Prince of the Neverborn. "The Unforgiven of Sammayal sing it otherwise."

Eldurion nodded slowly. Wiped his cheeks with his sleeve. Gathering himself, he stooped to retrieve his sword from the ground at his feet. When he straightened once more, his eyes were dry. He cocked his head to one side, harkening to sounds he did not, could not hear.

"Do they sing still, Sun Lord?"

Yllufarr shook his head.

"Nay, friend Eldurion. The Unforgiven are silent. They have heard my song. They know I am here."

"Surely they were already aware. You have said as much."

Something like a smile curled Yllufarr's fair lips.

"They knew one of the Undying was come to Coldmire, but they would not have known me for myself, as I have remained cloaked and cowled, and my Light is dimmed. But now...Sammayal has heard my voice."

Rundul frowned deeply, and sparks crackled in his black gaze.

"What have you done, Ath?" he growled.

The Sun Lord shrugged.

"Perhaps nothing. Perhaps overmuch."

The Darad muttered something as unintelligible as it was obscene, then resumed his stalwart vigil at the door of Doras Serrin.

"Why, Sun Lord?" Eldurion's voice was as oiled steel. "Why alert the Shaddathair to your presence here?"

"Because we are in need of them," the Ath answered simply.

"In need?"

"Verily, friend Eldurion. Coldmire is become an ocean of black-water and hungry muds, and we may progress no further. The lands north and east and south are drowned, and the way west is nearly so. Carricevan alone remains above the sludge. The rains have con-quered all else."

"And you suppose the Shaddathair might guide us from this place?"

The Prince of the Neverborn nodded.

"How might they achieve this, Sun Lord? As you have said, Coldmire is a drowned thing."

A certain strangeness slid across the Prince's fair features. "The Shaddathair *are* Coldmire, old friend".

"And why would these Unforgiven wish to aid us?"

"They will want me removed from Coldmire. I remind them of their failings." A pensive pause. "I am their shame."

Eldurion's eyes became silvery slits in the dark of Doras Serrin.

"And should they wish to rid themselves of you in ways other than guiding us from this place?"

But before the Ath could answer, Rundul spoke gruffly from the aperture in the stone.

"These Moor Walkers, Shaddathair, Unforgiven – whatever – they're a lot like wraiths, right? More fog than form, things of shadow not substance."

"That is so, Darad," replied the Prince of the Neverborn. "They have walked overlong in the Evvanin."

"And they wear no armour, bear no weapons, wear ragged raiment. Their beauty is lost, their strength is as withered as their limbs, and their only power over others now is fear – should one be inclined to fright."

"All true."

"And their lord," continued Rundul, his voice a bestial growl, "this betrayer called Sammayal, he's tall and dark and terrible to look upon."

The Sun Lord eyes glittered. "Indeed."

Eldurion frowned. "How do you know these things, Stone Lord?"

"I know them, Fian, because I'm not blind."

And with no further explanation the Captain of the Wandering Guard hefted his war-axe and moved from Doras Serrin into the fog-fettered night on Carricevan.

Eldurion directed an enquiring look toward Yllufarr and saw comprehension both brighten and shadow the glint in the Sun Lord's colourless eyes.

Spoke the Prince of the Neverborn:

"Sammayal has come."

They were the Shaddathair. The Shadowfolk of Sammayal. They were the Unforgiven, those followers of fallen Asrayal whom so long ago had refused Gavrayel's absolution. And they had wandered the

493

wastes of Coldmire for centuries. They had borne woeful witness to the ruination of Eldagreen. They had shared its sorrow, had endured its pain. They whom had once been Eldagreen were become Coldmire, sentient extensions of the moor's own death-in-life existence. Such was their fate. Such was their doom.

And this doom was now come to Doras Serrin on Carricevan.

Neither Rundul nor Eldurion could ascertain the number of Shaddathair that were before them, so indistinguishable were the Unforgiven from the fogs and the mists of the marsh. But there must have been thousands, perhaps tens of thousands. They were as wraiths, formless but having form, half-shadows. And their collective essence twinkled with the gleams of little lights, like distant stars and suns, as though the Shaddathair were the very skies of night fallen to earth.

Sammayal, Lord of the Unforgiven, towered tall and terrible before his phantasmal folk. His being was dark and ominous, like a thunderhead crackling with electrical antipathy. His countenance was cold, his lips thin and severe, his eyes white and baleful. Death itself was surely a warmer thing.

"Why have you come, Prince Yllufarr?" Sammayal's voice was almost lost among the resurgent seething sounds of Coldmire, so like was it to the wet vociferations of the bog.

"I have come because I must," replied the Sun Lord simply.

So intent was Sammayal's gaze upon Yllufarr that he seemed completely oblivious to the presence of the Darad and the Fian at the Athain Prince's shoulders. The Sun Lord's companions were not of the Undying. They were irrelevant, inconsequential. They mattered nothing.

"And you have summoned me with my own people's song, however ill-sung, also because you must?"

Yllufarr nodded.

Sammayal stared in spectral silence. The Shaddathair about him wavered like stilled whispers, mute phantoms aflutter in the fog.

Then, "What must is so dire that you deign to summon one for whom you harbour a hatred as undying as the Athair themselves? Surely not these inferior imitations of the *ulviathoi* of olde. These are weak and ineffectual and pose one such as you little true peril. What then, good Prince? Two thousand years have passed since you cursed me and my folk with eternal guilt and shame for deeds we did not do. Two thousand years since last we saw or spoke to one another. *Two thousand years.*" A cold hard pause. "What desperate need compels you now, Prince Yllufarr?"

Without hesitation, "We seek passage through Coldmire," Yllufarr replied.

The Lord of the Shaddathair glared whitely.

"I did not rouse Coldmire against you, Prince Yllufarr. I am not your enemy."

Yllufarr responded with neither word nor motion. Beside him, Eldurion stood stone-still, his naked blade hidden within his cloak. Of habit, and because he knew not what else to do, Rundul tightened his grip on his war-axe.

"Hatred, like love," continued Sammayal, "is a thing that might go unrequited, old friend. And yours is a hatred that is wrongly placed. I did nothing to cause the fall of your *Sul Athaifain* at Gan Gebbernin."

"My Sun Knights fell precisely *because you did nothing,*" Yllufarr retorted. His eyes flashed with ire. "There is little to distinguish those that commit evil from those that stand idle whilst evil is committed."

Sammayal's spectral arms spread in supplication.

"Would you have had me compound the sin of kin-slaughter with that of oath-breaking? I was and am oath-bound to neither bear nor raise arms in this World. That I stood idle at Gan Gebbernin was not my desire, but that of another. Had I not been fettered by my sworn word, I would have stood with you and your Sun Knights against Ulviathon and its horrid spawn. The blame for your Sun Knights' ruin lies not with me, Prince Yllufarr, but with him whom extracted from me the oath of pacifism."

The ire in the Sun Lord's eyes became pale fire.

"You will *not* place this fault at the feet of Gavrayel." Faster than the eye could follow, blades of Athain steel flashed into Yllufarr's hands. "Withdraw your foul words, Unforgiven, else I slay you where you stand and regret only that I had not done it two thousand years sooner."

Eldurion's longsword leapt from his cloak. Rundul braced his stout legs and hefted his war-axe.

Sammayal disregarded them entirely.

"Hold, Prince Yllufarr." The Shaddath raised one phantasmal palm. "Good King Gavrayel is not the one of whom I speak. No, Gavrayel offered me and my folk clemency when we had no claim to it, and pardon where none was deserved. And though he required of us a pledge of peace, that we never again bring arms to bear against the Athair or their allies, he did not demand of us a pledge of absolute pacifism. Perhaps he saw that one day the sword of Sammayal might serve him well. No, Prince Yllufarr, 'twas the voice of another, one most dark and perilous, that extorted from me my most lamented promise."

Yllufarr's eyes remained wild with pale wrath. But he lowered his weapons. And he said only, "Speak."

Sammayal's sigh was slow and soft with sorrow.

"I followed Asrayal to war of loyalty and love for him rather than of loathing for those he deemed his foes. In this, I was certainly swayed by Shadow, for it is ever the nature of evil to render foul event from fair intent. Thus was my love for my King become corrupt and the agent of my own damnation.

"But another, one whom ever had Asrayal's ear, was willingly and willfully seduced by Shadow, and his became the voice of Ilurin at the court of Asrayal. 'Twas this provocateur, this minister of Shadow, that preyed upon Asrayal's pride and urged him to rain war and ruin upon Yriel and those who stood with him. 'Twas he, this servant of Ilurin, that first compelled Asrayal to sully the Teller's Tale of First Earth with blood and murder." A cold damp pause. "And 'twas that same servant that pried from me my promise of pacifism when he and Gavrayel encountered me in Eldagreen so many millennia ago."

Yllufarr's eye-fire chilled and he sheathed his shining steel. Beside him, his companions relaxed their martial stances, the Darad slightly less so than the Fian.

"As I have said, Prince Yllufarr," the Lord of the Unforgiven reiterated, "your enmity is misplaced."

"Name him," commanded the Prince of the Neverborn. "Name this agent of Shadow."

The shade that was Sammayal bowed, then straightened. His ghostly countenance was bleak with gloom and foreboding. His white eyes narrowed to slivers of ice in the Coldmire night.

"We Unforgiven call him the Marralin, the King-Whisperer." A profound pause. "You know him as Ingallin."

Rundul and Eldurion shared dark and startled glances, the Daradun warrior growling lowly at the memory of the Athain Chancellor's deceit and derision.

Yllufarr blinked once, then nodded slowly.

"Ingallin." The Prince's voice was as an echo of Sammayal's own, both word and tone. "The vileness of his nature was glimpsed at Druintir, though its depth and breadth we did not guess." Something grim tugged at the corners of his mouth, and a darkness crossed his countenance as though he was considering his own failings. "He has been...removed."

The dark Lord of the Shaddathair stared coldly.

"There is no greater peril than the one that goes unperceived, Prince Yllufarr, and few greater than those that are perceived but mistakenly believed to have been...removed." His voice was no more than a hiss, yet the warning there could not have been more forceful had it been shouted. "Do not underestimate the guile of the Marralin. His machinations are most devious and deceptive. The possibility remains that he desired to be removed."

"To what end, Shaddath?"

Sammayal shook his head slowly.

"I know not the movements and motivations of the Marralin's black soul. I know only that he has ever served the Shadow...and ever will."

The Sun Lord's colourless eyes shone cold and clear.

"When I have done that which I have come to do, I will deal with Chancellor Ingallin," he vowed. "Personally."

Something of a smile softened Sammayal's visage, and he turned his white gaze to the black unstarred skies. He stood thus for a moment, still and silent, then moved his eyes to meet Yllufarr's own once more.

"I would have you know a thing, Prince Yllufarr. I would have you understand."

The Sun Lord inclined his head.

"Eldagreen did not fall to war, Prince of Gith Glennin," uttered the Shaddath. His form shimmered blackly. "The ruin of Eldagreen came of the fathomless anguish of my people, and of the ancient malignance that slumbers at the heart of these marshes. Know that Coldmire is the sickly spawn of a deed I did not do, and of the deed you left undone." His gaze shifted evocatively to the carcasses of *ulviathoi* sprawled at his feet in a grisly morass of mud and blood. "Understand, good Prince, that *we* are the cause of Coldmire. *We*. You and I."

An invisible blade scored Yllufarr's spine and he shivered for a chill born not of the cold. But he spoke naught, and the serpent stirred and swam again beneath the pale sheen of his eyes.

Ancient malignance...the deed you left undone.

Yllufarr knew of what Sammayal spoke.

He knew. He understood.

The Prince of the Neverborn nodded his comprehension.

Sammayal slowly lowered his chin to his chest. The movement held the sound of a sigh. He then straightened as though a great burden had been shed from his shoulders. Something of a long-forgotten and fast-fettered pride shone past the shadows of his timeless misery.

"I would be released from the bond of the Marralin, Prince Yllufarr," declared the Lord of the Shaddathair.

Yllufarr saw the terrible sorrow and shame in Sammayal's moon-white stare. He felt the Shaddath's despair in the marrow of his own bones. But he also sensed in the roiling thunderhead of Sammayal's essence a thing that could only have been hope.

Nevertheless –

"I cannot release you from your bond, Sammayal," said the Sun Lord quietly but emphatically. "Nor can I forgive you."

The Shaddath remained still for a moment, and the tempest of his being was calmed. Then a tear like molten pearl slowly slid down one sallow cheek. And he gave the slightest nod.

"I cannot fault you, old friend," he whispered past his shattered and broken hope. "Your loss was most grievous."

But the Sun Lord was not done.

"A covenant made with the King may only be unmade by the King," he explained gently. "And I can offer no forgiveness where there is nothing to forgive."

Sammayal blinked.

Nothing to forgive.

The Sun Lord's lips twitched to a small smile.

And the Lord of the Shaddathair wept. And his phantasmal folk wept with him. The sound was not unlike that made by Coldmire's rains, only softer and sweeter. A catharsis of pale tears cleansing sullied souls. A release and a rebirth. The soft sweet song of hope renewed.

Yllufarr's own eyes welled wetly. Eldurion felt his throat tighten with emotion. Only Rundul appeared unmoved, though his thick fingers fidgeted awkwardly on the haft of his war-axe.

Then Sammayal lowered his chin to his chest in deference and reverence.

"The night is old, Prince of Gith Glennin," spoke the Shaddath, raising his brightened eyes once more. "Take some rest and think on happier times. Come the morn I will guide you through this horrid place."

And with no further word the Lord of the Unforgiven turned and faded with his phantom folk into the fetid fogs of the fen.

"Is he to be trusted, friend Yllufarr?"

But the Athain Prince seemed oblivious to the oiled iron of Eldurion's voice, and he answered not, but only stared stiffly and silently out over the dank darkness of Coldmire.

"There's no Shadow in the shade," responded Rundul of the Daradur in the Sun Lord's stead. "His sorrow and shame are sincere."

Eldurion raised one greyed brow. "You are certain of this, Stone Lord?"

The Darad nodded. "I don't have any great familiarity with sorrow, Fian, but I'm sure his is genuine. And I know something of shame."

A sound like a sigh passed Eldurion's lips. He was acutely aware of the Blade of Defurien in the bundle at his back. The memory of the day that he had first borne *Grimroth* scored his mind with demonic claws. One hundred years past. The sands of the Dunelands. A sword recovered. A brother lost.

"As do I," whispered Eldurion empathetically, emphatically.

"As do we all, my friends," rejoined Yllufarr of the Neverborn, his voice resonant with regret.

Fian and Darad looked upon him.

The Sun Lord's pale eyes glowed strangely, as though a thing they had seen yet remained within them, casting a light both bright and dim.

"Shame is the thing that most separates us from Shadow," stated the noble Ath pensively. "Our individual dignity defines each of us. That we can know disgrace distinguishes us from those who are ruled by Darkness. For it is shame that differentiates the fair from the foul." The eerie halflight in his eyes flared and faded. "Darkness has no conscience. Evil knows no guilt."

Grey Eldurion nodded. Rundul grumbled.

"Sammayal can be trusted," Yllufarr concluded. "It is not he but another that has earned our mistrust."

"The Chancellor Ingallin," stated Eldurion. His voice was hard, and the Sun Lord was no longer ignorant of the iron there. "He readies Allaura for the women and children of the Fiannar." *And my own and only daughter goes with them...my Caelle.* "It is in my heart that my people walk into the peril of a scheme yet unrevealed."

But the Athain Prince shook his head.

"Ingallin is under the careful scrutiny of a score of Sun Knights, each of whom has been advised of his wickedness, though they cannot know its true measure. I am content that he can do no harm whilst in the company of First Knight Lalindel and the *Sul Athaifain*."

"And Warder Mundar of the *mara Waratur* is with your folk, Fian," Rundul reassured. "Mundar will not be tricked by this Ingallin creature. He was not deceived at Hollin Tharric, he will not be deceived elsewhere."

Eldurion frowned but did not dissent.

"That aspect of Daradun nature is the very cause of the Chancellor's disdain and derision for your kin and kind, Captain Rundul," considered Yllufarr. "He hates you because you cannot be corrupted. He fears you because you cannot be deceived." A pause profuse with pain. "Would that my own folk were so blessed."

They descended the eastern shoulder of Carricevan under the pall that passed for dawn in Coldmire. They emerged from between the tall silent stones of Carricevan's encircling cromlech into a ghastly grey half-flight of mist and morn. And there they stood in the muds at the edge of a stagnant rain-born lake, eyes straining to pierce its shroud of fog, ears harkening to hear past the lubricious gurgle and gush of the bog.

"Will he come?"

Prince Yllufarr peered into the gloom over the stillwater lake, his eyes as pale as the pall of the dawn. Where the fogs were thin there could be seen great black spikes of petrified timber rearing from the thick water, multitudinous funerary monuments marking the unnumbered graves of murdered Eldagreen.

"He will come."

Rundul grumbled, unconvinced.

"By what means does the Shaddath propose we travel these bog-waters?" asked Eldurion of the Sun Lord. The silver of the Fian's hair was tarnished in the dun light of dawn, but his eyes were cool and clear. "You may walk on water, and I might swim it, but the Darad would surely sink like a stone."

Rundul glared blackly at the dark water, then frowned at the grey mud oozing about his broad feet.

"Fish swim," he growled. "The Daradur build bridges."

The Prince of the Neverborn smiled through a sigh. Even the stalwart former Marshal of the Grey Watch allowed himself a wry grin.

"My axe alone weighs more than either of you," Rundul rumbled irascibly. He shifted reflexively beneath the great weight of his pack. "Not to mention the indignity of being made into a mule." A black scowl shadowed his mien for the mist-mantled morass before him. "I can't traverse this place."

"I am confident our guide will provide some manner of transport," Yllufarr replied. "A craft of some sort, or a vessel."

"A craft? A vessel?" The Stone Lord actually sputtered. His beard bristled. "Is he mad? Are *you*?"

But before the Athain Prince could respond –

"He comes," Eldurion stated with the succinctness of well-oiled steel.

The Lord of the Unforgiven approached, seeming to glide upon the fog-fettered waters, as straight and as tall and as black as the petrified trunks through which he navigated. Soon it became apparent that he rode a craft comprised of those very timbers, a raft less than two yards across and little more than six long, loosely lashed together with scraggly grey weeds and thorny vines. Contrary to the shabbiness of his craft, Sammayal seemed more substantial than he had been, more significant, no longer a wraith of rags and shadow, no longer a withered mendicant of melancholy, but once again a lord of a lordly folk, a true prince of the Neverborn who despite his impenetrably black raiment was resplendent with the twin shinings of Light and Hope.

"*Urth ru Glir*," Rundul swore softly, somewhere beneath the surge and gurgle of the tundral swamp.

"Your friend is changed, good Prince," observed Eldurion, his breath streaming into the gelid air.

Yllufarr nodded. If he breathed, he did so invisibly.

"*Urth ru Glir*," repeated Rundul, somewhat more emphatically. His fists tightened reflexively about the haft of his war-axe.

The Darad's companions peered at him quizzically.

Rundul's black gaze followed Sammayal's approach with an apprehension nigh upon dread. His apprehension, however, was not for the restoration of the Shaddath's essence – indeed he likely did not so much as mark it – but for the dilapidated craft that bore the Lord of the Unforgiven across the chill stillwaters of Coldmire. The Darad muttered miserably as he watched the raft fade and form and fade again within the fogs.

And then –

"*Urth ru* fuckin' *Glir!*" erupted the Captain of the Wandering Guard, spittle flying. "That mad wraith intends we ride on *that* thing? I won't do it! I won't!"

Eldurion raised one silvered brow.

"What have we here? A Stone Lord in the fullness of his might intimidated by a little water when a decidedly old, tired, decrepit Fian is not?"

Rundul's glower was as black as midnight in Hell.

"The Daradur are Made of Earth, Fire, Love and War," he retorted roughly. His beard and brows bristled. "Not a drop of water in the mix. Not one drop. But do not mistake practicality for trepidation, Fian – one need not be a son of Earth the Mother to know that wood which has become rock most certainly does *not* float."

"Indeed," considered Yllufarr, his hand to his chin. "Sammayal employs power eldritch and arcane." Concern cooled the pale pools of his eyes. "I fear..."

The fogs thickened.

"Fear nothing, Prince Yllufarr," spoke the Shaddath as he slid through the gloom. His voice was no longer the hapless echo of the bog's own, but was become strident and sonorous, the crack of thunder in the van of a storm. "The power I employ is Coldmire's own, and is neither natural nor unnatural, and cannot be detected however vigilant the watchers. I am Coldmire. Coldmire is me." The prow of his impractical craft struck the muds at Yllufarr's feet. "Your secret is secure, old friend."

The Sun Lord stepped back.

"My secret?"

Sammayal's moon-white eyes glowed eerily.

"Secure. From your foe." A strange curling at the corners of the Unforgiven's fine lips served as a smile. "And I intend that it remain so."

"Speak plainly, Sammayal," commanded the Sun Lord.

The Lord of the Shaddathair made no move to disembark from his rickety craft, but only stood there, tall and dark, cloaked in power and wreathed in fog. The odd smile remained upon his mouth. He did not deign to cast even the briefest of glances to the Athain Prince's companions. They were not of the Neverborn. They remained of no consequence. They mattered nothing still.

"Your purpose is plain and easily perceived, Prince Yllufarr."

"How so?"

"War marches upon the west beneath the banners of Blood and Shadow. The Guardian Peoples prepare for battle. Druintir of the Deathward and Doomfall of the Daradur await much blood and death."

"You perceive much, Sammayal."

"Yet you enter Coldmire beneath Ravenwood in stealth, and hasten eastward as swiftly as the terrain and the limitations of your companions allow. You remain within a few miles of the moor's southern marches, but never strike for the more traversable lands beyond that boundary. You employ no magic, yet powerful magics you surely command. And you move with an air of urgency, of necessity. You have purpose, specific and certain."

The Shaddath paused, his moon-white eyes aglow and reading the Sun Lord's tautness and tension as easily as he would words on a scroll. He wondered whether his own death was also written there. His smile faltered, fell. For he well knew that some secrets should, of necessity, remain secret.

Nevertheless.

"You seek Ungloth Reborn," the Lord of the Shaddathair said boldly. "You would slay the Blood King on his Throne of Bone. You would expunge the Earthbane. You would win this war far from the fields of battle."

Sammayal saw the dark Prince of the Neverborn balance on the balls of his feet, pantherine, muscles bunched and set to spring. He sensed the Darad's grip on his axe-haft tighten, heard his teeth grind beneath his beard. He perceived the readied blade concealed within the Fian's sealskin cloak.

And he descried his own death in their eyes.

Nevertheless.

"You will fail."

The Sun Lord took one stride forward, retracing the step he had taken backward. He peered upon Sammayal, pale luminous eyes glimmering softly. Nothing swam within them. They were eerily still. Still and unblinking. Deathly.

Neither Eldurion nor Rundul moved, though their breath steamed into the dawn in slow and steady drafts. They did not glance at each other. Nor at the Prince of the Neverborn. Nor he at them. No words passed between the three. Yet in some subliminal manner, they came to a decision.

And Yllufarr spoke a single word.

"Explain."

The Shaddath bowed gracefully. Gratefully.

"Your quest is doomed, Prince Yllufarr." Sammayal's voice was mellifluous, but solemn. "The Blood King has been alerted to his vulnerability. At best, he fears the Guardian Peoples will attempt to strike him in his lair. At worst, he *expects* them to do so. Thus all ways to Ungloth Reborn are well watched and warded. The Northern Plains about Ungloth Reborn teem with the thralls of Shadow. Every path that leads there is patrolled. Those ways that are not patrolled are mined with glyphs and wards. Foul raptors – creatures taken, altered and corrupted by Shadow – watch from the skies. Fouler things slink within the earth. Even should you strike for Ungloth Reborn from where Coldmire is nearest, you will need to hike more than a dozen leagues, over open ground or under, with little or no cover but your own cloak and cleverness. Neither will suffice. You will be discovered, Prince Yllufarr. Discovered – and destroyed."

The Sun Lord folded his arms across his chest, his glare as pale as the undulant veils of dawn. Yet he said nothing.

"There is one way," revealed the Lord of the Shaddathair, "a way so well warded that the enemy would not cast his gaze there even should he have the power to do so – which, I assure you, he does not."

Yllufarr waited. Said nothing.

"Beneath the stilled heart of Coldmire," Sammayal continued, "a tunnel bores through the earth, snaking southward to the dark catacombs beneath Ungloth Reborn. The passage has but a single guardian." The moons of his eyes waned to crescents. "One with whom you are...familiar...good Prince."

The deed you left undone.

"Verily," confirmed the Shaddath, as though Yllufarr's thoughts were as clear to him as his own. "Do this thing and the way to Ungloth Reborn lies open to you. And the canker that poisoned glorious Eldagreen will be removed."

The deed you left undone.

"Do this thing, and though the very empyrean does shatter, your quest shall remain secret," Sammayal ensured. "I am Coldmire. Coldmire is me. That which occurs in Coldmire shall remain in Coldmire, Prince Yllufarr. I will see to it. This I swear. And *this* oath I freely take."

The Sun Lord's pale eyes darkened with the swirling shadows of serpents. He mourned the ancient loss of his sword and his spear. They would soon be most sorely needed – and never more sorely missed.

"Knowing these things, Prince Yllufarr," said Sammayal, "shall we aborn or abort your most noble quest?" His white eyes glistered with expectant, enervated light. "Do we proceed?"

A momentary pause, then Yllufarr turned slowly and cast a raised eyebrow toward Rundul of the Wandering Guard.

The Stone Lord's fierce gaze shot black bolts of loathing to the Shaddath's unworthy craft. But Rundul inclined his great maned head, a nod so slight as to have been imperceptible to all eyes save those of the Undying.

Yllufarr turned back to Sammayal, then and leapt lissomely upon the raft.

The deed you left undone.

"We proceed," stated the Prince of the Neverborn.

They floated through the fog of the flooded fen as though they themselves were made of mist. The Lord of the Unforgiven and the Prince of the Neverborn stood side by side at the prow of the craft, each cloaked and cowled in midnight, so alike as to be indistinguishable from one another. Eldurion, Eldest of the Fiannar, kept a steely vigil at the stern, foregoing sleep in favour of silent meditation, taking sustenance only when absolutely necessary. And Rundul, Captain of the Wandering Guard, huddled amidships, perched atop his cumbersome pack, putting as much distance between his chronically chthonic feet and the water as possible – though he was actually unsure which he loathed more, the cold dead waters over which they moved or the arcane *athamancy* that propelled them. Nevertheless, he endured both with a garish grin, an exceedingly grotesque expression reminiscent of the rictus of a hirsute skull.

No one moved. No word was spoken. Utter stillness and silence for a time measured neither in minutes nor in hours, but in days. Only the strange and unsettling sensation of floating over still water, propelled by a power stranger and more unsettling still. Floating, floating. Forever floating.

Then in the lugubrious light of the fifth day from Carricevan, the fogs thickened, forming veritable walls of mist, impenetrable and impervious. The tundral chill plummeted to a polar cold. The sensation of floating faded and fell away, leaving in its absence a void of static immobility, a surreal tranquility so complete, so pure, as to surpass that of Death itself.

Then Yllufarr turned.

"For the sakes of stealth and secrecy, we have entered the Everworld at the edge of Eilla Evvanin," explained the Prince of the Neverborn calmly. "The Everworld knows not Time. We may soon look upon this Earth and see it as it was long ago, as it was many thousands of years past, perhaps thousands of thousands of years. We may see creatures that lived on this Earth uncounted millennia before Man or Fian or Ath or Darad ever walked this land. But fear nothing. We are in the Everworld. Whatever beings we might see cannot in turn see us. And they can affect us no more than we can them."

Eldurion nodded curtly. Rundul grumbled.

"Even so, that which you might see may be...disturbing," allowed the Sun Lord as he turned away from his companions once more. "Close your eyes if you so choose."

Rundul twisted to cast a prolonged and rather profane complaint back to Eldurion, but no sound beyond a gasp passed the Darad's moustached mouth. His eyes widened to round black moons, his jaw fixed itself agape, and he shuddered – as much as one of his kind might shudder.

For the walls of fog had condensed to form a watery membrane about the raft, a diaphanous dome through which the outer world could be seen – should one be inclined to look.

And Rundul had looked.

Coldmire was gone. The mistbound moor was no more. Gone was the turbid tundral swamp. Gone was the muskeg made into a torpid tarn by festering floodwaters. Gone and no more. But the appalling gloom and the water remained.

A slate-grey sky sagged threateningly above a world that had become nothing but water. Water, water, so much water. Water with neither beginning nor end, nor apparent bottom, an angry ocean heaving great dark waves to the heavens, a shoreless sea surging to drown the falling sky and make naught but water of the universe.

Mighty Rundul of Axar closed his eyes.

And so he did not see the world change once more and become a primeval jungle, verdant and virile, where small dark dragon-things darted in the lush undergrowth, and large dark dragon-things pursued them.

And Rundul did not see the world become a snow-racked winter wasteland, ice without end, where enormous furred behemoths trekked a cold hard white world under a colder and harder and whiter sun.

And he did not see the world become a magnificent gallery of holy oak, of ash and elm, and of regal redwood, a sylvan wonderland bedecked with dappled sunlight, effulgent, shimmering, beautiful.

And he did not see the Ath and Shaddath before him spread their arms in warmest love and welcome.

But he heard Eldurion's awe-hushed whisper –

"Eldagreen."

Rundul eyes creaked open.

But the Darad had scarcely glimpsed the glory and grandeur of ancient Eldagreen before oak and elm retreated before a broad deep hollow that held thunder and blood and ruin and death like a great dark chalice frothing with doom.

"Gan Gebbernin."

The awe in the Eldurion's whisper had degenerated, devolved to unadorned horror. Then it was he that looked away, and Yllufarr and Sammayal averted their gazes, whilst the Darad bore willing witness to the *Angar ban Gan Gebbernindh*, that great and terrible battle of olde waged by men and gods. And Rundul watched as his own ferocious folk rose from the bosom of Mother Earth, an eruption of fire and stone, of power and rage, irresistible, overwhelming, and a pure untaintable pride glistened in the black of his wide wet eyes.

And then Gan Gebbernin was gone. Two thousand years passed in a fraction of an instant. And there was only Coldmire again.

Coldmire.

And one thing more.

It rose from the water like the rounded hump of a sleeping sea serpent, a monstrous mound, high and horrible to look upon. Its surface was rough and uneven, as though scaled and plated like the rough hide of a reptile. But the mound was composed of densely interwoven matter, fashioned of indeterminable things twisted and tied together, perhaps of branches broken from their boughs and of roots ripped from the earth – the debris and detritus of ruined Eldagreen.

And then, as the company floated nearer through the fog, Ath and Fian and Darad saw that which they had not seen before for mist and dark and distance.

Bones.

Bones, bones, countless bones.

The skeletal relics and remnants of unnumbered thousands, woven into an enormous osteophyte of ghastly grey wicker, with warps of rib and wefts of femur.

A monstrous mound of the dead.

"*Maol an Maalach*," announced the Lord of the Shadowfolk. His voice was itself a shadow. "The Dam of the Damned."

A silence like the hush of descending death.

Then –

"Good name for it," grumbled Rundul as he clambered from his perch atop his pack. The Darad's deep black gaze became deeper, blacker. "What do you know of this place, Fian?"

Eldurion stared. Dread darkened the wonder in his widened eyes.

"I have walked Coldmire long and often," he rasped as though something had scored the iron of his voice, "but never have I encountered this place. I know it not, and have no wish to know it."

Yllufarr's eyes shone with a pale light, like moonlight on bone. In their depths the serpent swam, sleek and silent, seeking the surface.

"I know it."

In the Sun Lord's voice was a throttled rage overlying immeasurable grief, both ancient, both impossibly bitter.

"Or rather I know these bones. They are the dead of the *Angar ban Gan Gebbernindh*. And there" – one arm swept up from beneath the impenetrable blackness of the Sun Lord's cloak – "lie my seven hundred, slain and slaughtered by slaves of Shadow. And even unto this late day, their deaths have gone unavenged, and the evil that took them remains unanswered." Pause. "Unto this late day, but not beyond."

Rundul and Eldurion exchanged an uneasy glance. They felt a certain disquiet snake its way within them. Certain but indistinct.

Yllufarr strode to where the Darad stood and gestured for Eldurion to join them. The Athain Prince placed one fair hand on Rundul's shoulder, the other on Eldurion's. Yllufarr's hood fell away from his head and his face shone with a pale but pure light. And

Rundul and Eldurion saw in the Sun Lord's eyes the thing that slinked within them as surely as one might see an eel swim the clear shallows of a mountain stream. And they knew it for what it was.

The thing he had left undone.

"I leave you now, dear friends," Yllufarr declared with a gravity surpassing all but that which comes beneath the shadow of looming death. "There is a thing I must do, a thing from which I cannot turn away. I may not return to you. And should I not, then do not attempt to follow me. Sammayal will take you to the borders of Coldmire, and from there you must strike southward across the Plains and continue our quest. The way is closely watched, and death and failure will await you, but no death is certain, no failure assured."

"Remember your own words, good Prince," said Eldurion with uncharacteristic softness. "We will await you here."

And Rundul rumbled, "You will return."

Sammayal of the Unforgiven said nothing, but bowed in sincere reverence of the Sun Lord, then rose, turned and looked away.

Yllufarr smiled grimly but beautifully, lowered his hands from his companions' shoulders, and with no further word dove gracefully from the raft, and instantly vanished into the cold grey dead waters.

He did not hear the Darad mutter *Madness!* at his back.

Frigid water filled the Prince's ears, assaulted his eyes and skin with cold. But Yllufarr was of the Athair, and the Athair were Light, and Light knows no cold. *Ulviathoi* swam about him like strange and terrible sharks, vile and voracious, but long knives flashed in the Prince's hands and he slew two of the beasts with swift strokes, and the remainder converged to tear at the bleeding carcasses. Black things like great leeches swarmed about him, then scattered, for they were spawn of Shadow whose only power was fear, and both Shadow and fear flee the Light. And then the grey water became like oil, thick and black and viscous, and the Prince passed through an aperture near the sunken base of *Maol an Maalach*, arced his body upwards, and in moments broke the surface within the deep darkness of the Dam.

The Sun Lord emerged from the water to stand upon a rough and uneven shore. Something crunched underfoot. He did not need to see his feet to know he stood upon a bank of bones. He was unmoved. For he had come there as Death, and Death does not esteem the dead.

He waited.

The air was arctic and acrid, its blackness near complete. But Yllufarr's heart was colder, his pale gaze more caustic, his own blackness absolute.

He waited.

The water lapped the bones at Yllufarr's feet. Something had moved. Something was stirring, waking. Something incredibly massive.

The Sun Lord waited.

And then a single great slit of bloody light cracked the black within *Maol an Maalach*. An eye. The sole remaining eye of the thing that had slumbered there for two thousand years, of the thing whose power was so terrible that its very presence had poisoned Eldagreen and had cast that place of wonder into the warped and wretched ruin that was Coldmire.

And for that thing Yllufarr waited.

The deed you left undone.

Ulviathon rising.

20

THE MUSTER OF THE NORTH

"Nothing there is that binds disparate and desperate
peoples more surely than the threat of a common foe –
thus does the enemy of our enemy become our friend."

Ri Connall, thirty-third High King of Rothanar

"The Shield Maiden is leaving, I presume."

Axennus Teagh seemed to not hear his brother's words, but only peered past the misted pane of the chamber's window, watching the night waver before the first glowings of dawn – watching, but seeing only shades of darkness. The aurora of Caelle's *laleth* yet lingered there in requiem. There, and in his aching heart.

"I suppose she is leaving," repeated the Iron Captain.

The word *yes* remained in Axennus' throat unspoken, as though voicing confirmation of his brother's assumption would make the painful truth more painful and truer still.

Blue cloak billowing, Bronnus Teagh crossed the chamber to stand at his brother's shoulder. The Iron Captain was clad in full battledress, his bronze breastplate and greaves polished to a sheen, his sword at his hip, his crested helm held securely in the crook of one arm. He waited for Axennus' response in silence and with uncustomary patience, as though the rapid approach of war and the prospect of a glorious death had calmed his turbulent warrior spirit.

And then Axennus nodded slowly, sadly. "How did you know?" His voice was hoarse with sleeplessness and sorrow.

"The gardener's daughter," was Bronnus' immediate reply.

The Commander cast a damp look his brother's way.

Bronnus smiled through his new beard, and the smile was strangely gentle and comforting. His gaze, too, was uncharacteristically warm.

"When you were but three you developed a fondness for the four-year-old daughter of father's gardener," explained the Captain. "She was a little wisp of a thing, a happy child, and very pretty. You would follow her around like a puppy, from dawn till dusk, professing your undying love for the little waif and proposing marriage thrice daily."

Axennus smiled softly. "Crissia."

The memory was vague, but had not altogether vanished.

"Then, when you were four," Bronnus continued, "the gardener inherited his family's modest estate in Anthum, and –"

"And Crissia went away," Axennus finished wistfully. "I remember."

"Well, little brother, you have the same dismal slouch to your shoulders and the same pathetic look on your face now as you had then. The deduction that the Shield Maiden is leaving is not a difficult one."

"You surpass yourself, Bron."

The Captain disregarded the comment, both word and tone.

"And I will tell you now, Axo, that which I told you then: There are other flowers in the garden."

Axennus smiled, saving the pain that dwelt in his heart for another place, another time.

"And do you recall my response to those words, dear brother?"

Bronnus frowned, pondered, shook his head.

"I told you then that you were as full of manure as any garden in Hiridith."

Bronnus chuckled. "Ah...I remember now."

Axennus turned away from the window and from the optical echoes of the Shield Maiden's *laleth*. The night was done and day was dawning. Mourning ended with morning. The Commander wrapped a lean arm about his brother's broad shoulder and grinned widely.

"Now I would tell you, big brother, that you are as full of manure as *all* the gardens in Hiridith."

Bronnus scowled.

Axennus laughed.

"Come, dear Bronnus," bade the Commander, his cerulean cloak snapping brusquely as he turned toward the door. "We must answer the call of kings."

The morning sun fell upon the Gardens of Galledine like the forlorn smile of a failing father upon the face of a favoured child.

Mounted upon his noble *mirarran*, Lord Alvarion swept his metallic grey gaze over those assembled before him. Fully half of the folk of the Fiannar were gathered there at Galledine's most northerly eaves, three thousand noble souls whose fates lay not at the Pass of Eryn Ruil, but elsewhere. War would not claim these sons and daughters of Defurien. Nay, they would not be taken. Not soon, at least. Alvarion had seen to this, had ensured this with his decision to send the women and children of the Fiannar away to Evangael's refuge at Allaura. Thus removed, they would survive. Thus, even should calamity strike his forces at Eryn Ruil, Alvarion's people would survive. The Deathward would endure.

The Lord of the Fiannar nodded to himself.

We will endure.

Alvarion had awoken to those words, silken softnesses in his ear, a hushed whisper at the edge of consciousness, ere the dawn scattered the night. Cerriste had smiled down upon him, stray tresses of her hair playing tenderly, teasingly at his temple, a single fingertip lovingly tracing the raised lines of his scarred cheek. Her eyes shone like heavenly stars, defying all darkness, shining past all sorrows. A single tear, shed not of sadness but of love, slicked one fine cheek with molten silver, and a slight tremble shook but did not chase the smile from her supple lips.

Such courage. Such beauty. Such perfect love.

"All have come, Lord," Varonin's voice intruded upon Alvarion's unintended reverie. "All are here."

The Lord of the Fiannar nodded gravely.

"Very well, Marshal."

Two thousand women and one thousand children of the Fiannar faced their Lord with uplifted faces and shining eyes. In serried ranks of green and grey they silently awaited Alvarion's address, the gold of their *rillagha* glittering like sunfire beneath banners bold and beautiful. And at the fore, under the Golden Strype, the Flaming Sword and the Crimson Fist, were those nearest and dearest to the heart of their Lord.

Taresse, wife of Eldurion, was there, her eyes implacably grey, like shards of stone chipped from rigid rock walls of defiance.

And there also was Sarrane, worthy wife to tempestuous Tulnarron, her strange Seer's eyes aswirl with shades of things both seen and unseen. Her husband's absence there did not irk her – they had nodded farewell the previous evening. And then the Master had excused himself to 'address a situation that demands my immediate attention'. He was, she knew, riding hard and fast to deliver his immediate attention even now.

And Arumarron, heir to the House of Eccuron, whose glower and glumness of countenance belied the glory that beckoned him, a glory that would in time not only eclipse that of his father, but rival that of Eccuron himself.

And Caelle, daughter of Eldurion and Taresse, Shield Maiden to the Lady of the Fiannar, as fair of face and form as an Athain princess, as deft and as swift of sword as any scion of Defurien.

And the Lady Cerriste with infant Aranion.

The Lady of the Fiannar sat astride her steed, her shoulders straight and square with the dual irons of pride and determination, her eyes like argent fire veneered with ice. From the caring cradle of one arm, the babe Aranion cooed quietly in dream-sweetened slumber.

Alvarion inclined his head toward them, those to whom he would ever be bound in thought and heart and shining soul.

"May your tale not go untold, dear woman, nor ever be forgotten. And may that of our beloved son be far more glorious than my own."

A small smile creased Cerriste's lips and eased her otherwise flinty expression. And when she fisted her bosom in salutation and farewell, the gesture was gentle, made tender by the depthless love her heart harboured for her husband. Briefly, baby Aranion raised his curly-haired head from the pillow of Cerriste's shoulder, yawned, peered through eyes heavy with sleep, and blessed his father with a little laugh.

Alvarion felt a certain tightness in his throat, and tiny tears tugged at the corners of his eyes. His heart, his very soul, ached.

"Go," the Lord rasped through a resignation that surpassed sorrow. "Allaura and asylum await you. Do not want for haste. Mundar of the Wandering Guard will meet you on the far side of Galledine and guide you through the Hard Hills. Go now, my Lady – and should the Teller deem it proper, his Tale will reunite us in time, whether it be in this world or in the Light."

Cerriste gifted her beloved husband with a soothing smile, bowed her head slightly, but said nothing.

And then the Lord of the Fiannar raised his voice, and it burst from his breast like the call of a war horn across a field of battle:

"Go! Go, good sons and daughters of Defurien! Go and know no fear! Believe that those whom you leave behind will prevail, though the price of their victory shall be most terrible and dear. Many homes will be empty of fathers and sons and husbands upon your return. Such are the wages of war. Such has ever been the fate of the Fiannar. But the Light awaits us all, and only the Teller of the Tale might know when it is to shine upon each Deathward soul. Go now, and take peace with you, for there shall surely be none here!"

Then Alvarion nodded to Cerriste, a damp gleam whispering in his eyes –

Go.

And the Lady of the Fiannar turned.

And most that had assembled there turned with her.

But there were many among the Deathward there that did not. Fully one third of those gathered at the eaves of Galledine, one thousand stalwart souls, remained facing their Lord and leader, static and staunch in silent stillness.

And then Taresse, wife to Eldurion, ushered her magnificent mount forward. The woman bowed her head toward her Lord and nephew, then met his hard gaze with one that was yet harder. Her lips were set, her face firm, the knuckles of one hand whitening for the tightness of her grip on the pommel of her sword.

"I remain, Lord Alvarion," she pronounced, her voice calm with certitude. "I and these one thousand with me."

The Lord Alvarion peered through a frown.

"I will countenance no disobedience in this matter, uncle-wife," the Lord said sternly. "You will go to Allaura."

Cerriste and Sarrane turned upon their steeds to gaze questioningly at Taresse. They then glanced at one another, then upon Caelle, whose lips quivered betwixt strange humour and sorrow, and belated understanding played across both their visages.

"I obey only your own desire, my Lord," spoke Taresse above an outthrust chin, "that the Fiannar survive. That we endure."

Lord Alvarion bit the ire from his tongue.

"Hear her, husband." Cerriste's calm cool voice struck the rising admonition from his lips unuttered. "Permit no pride to deafen you."

Alvarion glowered, but nodded for Taresse to speak.

"You seek the survival of our folk, Lord," said Taresse, "and your wisdom in sending the greater of the number gathered here to sanctuary is sound. For our women whose wombs are yet viable and the children among our people must be spared the horrors of this war. They must survive."

Alvarion's frown darkened.

Taresse continued unperturbed.

"But those women among us who are barren of womb need not be sent to waste and worry away at Allaura. Verily, our arms are yet strong and our swords still sharp. Our absence from the field of battle would avail the fate of our folk nothing – indeed, it would but serve to imperil the fortunes of the Fiannar unnecessarily."

"I will not have your deaths upon my –"

But the Lady Cerriste clapped her husband's mouth closed with a swift gesture and a reproving glare.

"There is no argument, my Lord," Taresse stated implacably. "The Lady shall have Caelle at her side should your wife need aid in Aranion's care – my daughter is as able as I in this, and such duty would well prepare her for children of her own. Motherhood is a thing she contemplates even now."

Caelle felt her cheeks redden in rare discomfiture. Evidently, her blossoming love for the charismatic Erelian was no great secret.

"The logic in these things cannot be challenged, Lord," avowed Taresse.

A smile stretched across Cerriste's features to threaten the stony set of Alvarion's own.

"And this also cannot be challenged, Lord Alvarion," Taresse concluded, "that upon his departure my gallant Eldurion did bid me look to my own death. I have heard him. And I intend my death be a glorious one."

The Lord of the Fiannar looked from Taresse to Cerriste – found neither ally nor any inkling of support in the gleaming grin he saw there – then back again.

At some length, "Very well," Alvarion conceded quietly. "Taresse and her one thousand shall remain – though there is a dark misgiving in my heart and a cold certainty in my soul that no death at Eryn Ruil will be a glorious one."

Taresse lowered her head, easing her *mirarran* back and away.

Cerriste laughed lightly, and the sound teased a grim curl of the lips from Alvarion.

"It would seem, beloved husband, you now have good uncle Eldurion's twenty thousands."

And flanked upon one side by the Shield Maiden Caelle and upon the other by the Seer Sarrane, the Lady of the Fiannar turned from her love and her Lord once again and led a mere two thousand Deathward into the waiting green of Galledine.

Long and longingly did Alvarion gaze after her.

He would not see her again in that world.

"Why has Lord Alvarion chosen the White Manor?" asked Bronnus of his brother as they strode the long sunlit corridor toward the sunken theatre that held the Council Circle. "Why have we been selected to host this council of war?"

Axennus shrugged. "Why do you ask, brother?"

"Perhaps because we are of the House of Hiridion," ventured the Iron Captain in answer to his own question, whilst ignoring the Commander's. "These Fiannar are a discriminating folk."

"Perhaps," pondered Axennus, "though likely not."

"Why does he not host the thing himself?"

"He does not want to impose himself upon his allies. He seeks to avoid making them feel that they are something...less...than he is."

Bronnus nodded. "Then why us?"

"I would suggest that Lord Alvarion seeks to unite the Nations of Men that have come to stand with him at Eryn Ruil. Rothanar, Ithramis and Nothira have each provided sizeable armies, but Lord Alvarion knows that a fist is far more powerful than four fingers and a thumb."

"I do not understand," grumbled Bronnus.

"The whole is greater than the sum of its parts, dear brother," explained the Commander with an exaggerated sigh.

The Captain frowned.

"That seems clear enough – but why choose the Erelian Republic to host this council? The Rothmen, the Ithramen and the Nothirings count their gathered swords by the thousands, and they are captained by kings and princes – we have only our one hundred, led by...well...*you*."

Axennus laughed aloud. "I see the source of your confusion, brother."

Bronnus lifted an eyebrow.

"Yes, dear Bron, you are *thinking* – and thought is not your greatest strength. Should you cease to think, then you will no longer be confused."

Bronnus scowled, opened his mouth to retort, then clapped it closed once more. Silence seemed a safer thing.

"The thumb," Axennus proffered past puckered lips, "knows that the index, middle and third fingers respect the little finger, and have no cause to fear it, for though it is useful, it is comparatively weak beside the other three."

The Iron Captain stared at Axennus in utter bewilderment.

"Thumb...finger...what the hell?"

The Commander grinned, chuckled softly, then enlightened, "Should the Lord Alvarion have chosen the Black Prince, say, to host this council, surely the High King and the Mad Earl would have seen it as a slight. And there is little love lost between the Rothmen and the Nothirings, and each is a haughty folk and swift to anger, so neither Ri Niall nor Ingvar Dragonsbane would have made a suitable host. Thus the logical choice left to Lord Alvarion – indeed, the only remaining choice – is *us*, the Commander and the Captain of the Republican Legion's fabled, if somewhat reduced, North March Mounted Reserve."

"Ah...I understand...*we* are the little finger."

"Surpassing yourself is becoming a habit, dear Bronnus," Axennus smirked as they approached the arched entrance to the Circumforum.

Voices, some heated, others harsh, each revealing its own explicit irritability, came from within. Evidently, foes to a common enemy needed not be fast friends.

The Iron Captain's brows furrowed once more, sending his face into shadow.

"The fools bicker."

"Come, brother," replied the Commander, resolve to his tone, determination in his manner. "Let us make a fist of these fingers."

"All have come, Lord. All are here."

The Lord of the Fiannar winced inwardly. When last Marshal Varonin had spoken those words, Alvarion had bidden his beloved wife and son farewell. The memory was yet fresh and vivid, as was the pain. But the Lord's face revealed no pain, neither loss nor sorrow. Only the iron resolve that comes of grim hope marked his countenance. And in the gleaming grey of his eyes shone the strength of well-tempered steel.

Secreted in the same shadows of the upper tiers of the Circumforum that had concealed Caelle several days earlier, the Lord of the Deathward, the Marshal of the Grey Watch and two other figures gazed down upon the Council Circle, upon the seven lords and captains of Men who had become their allies, had sworn to stand and die with the Deathward at Eryn Ruil.

Save Prince Arbamas of Ithramis, who sat in deep black silence at the far side of the round table, and his equally dour First General, they were a quarrelsome lot. Despite Nothira's adherence to Ban of Ri Donnal, the sons of Noth and the great Roths of the North had ever been wary of one another, and though they had never been foes on the field, tension between the two was an everpresent thing when Roth and Nothiring did meet.

Alvarion watched, listening to the rather rotund Rothic Battle Druid passively yet aggressively goad his Nothiric counterpart, an aged priest of the martial Cult of Thyr, for words were as weapons to the Rothmen, as sharp as swords, as heavy as hammers. The Thyric priest blustered and blasphemed, and the Mad Earl of Invarnoth met the silent glower of Warthane Connar with an icy glare, whilst the High King of Rothanar chuckled to himself for some private joke that the others had neither heard nor likely could have comprehended.

The Lord of the Fiannar shook his head slowly, sadly.

Lords of Men, indeed.

Then the Erelians entered the Circumforum.

Though the elder Teagh was stern and stalwart and strong, a man of distinction and decisive action, the younger brother's stature was the greater. Axennus Teagh's very presence almost immediately pacified those gathered about the Council Circle, and all tension fled the chamber as would woodland creatures from a forest aflame. The Southman strode with a jaunt to his step and an irresistible smile upon his face as he greeted each there by name and made some small remark that drew from each a grin, if not laughter. All eyes, all attentions were fixed upon the Erelian Commander, and all former hostilities were abandoned and forgotten.

The Lord of the Fiannar nodded his head slowly, gladly.

A lord of Men, indeed.

"Alvarion, son of Amarien, Master of the House of Defurien. Lord of the Fiannar."

Varonin of the Grey Watch moved aside as his Lord and leader entered the Circumforum.

All there stood and fisted their breasts, then sat as Alvarion fisted his own. A hush like the hollow between heartbeats fell upon the theatre. The Lord's steely gaze met the eyes of each man there in turn, lingering a moment longer upon those of the Erelian Commander – a subtle gesture of appreciation and gratitude.

"Welcome, friends of the Fiannar," intoned Alvarion. "Welcome and well-met. We will forego all formalities, as each man here is a king of men, in stoutness of heart if not in title. And we need not make gifts of our names, as I am quite aware that all here have become... familiar with one another."

Nods, murmurs of assent, a flushed face or two.

Axennus' flashed a knowing grin.

"Very well," said Alvarion. "I will not make a brief thing long. The Fiannar are grateful for your friendship in this time of woe and war. You have brought hope to the Deathward where there was little, and you have dashed doubt where there was overmuch. These things will be forgotten only when the Teller's Tale itself goes unremembered."

Nods, murmurs.

Alvarion inclined his head toward Axennus Teagh.

"The table is yours, Commander."

Axennus stood. The Erelian's smile was bright beneath shining eyes.

"Kings of men, indeed, Lord Alvarion," spoke the Southman, "for though the Republic counts more men than all the other Free Nations combined, it cannot boast the quality of those that have gathered here. I am truly humbled."

Bronnus frowned, but did not speak the thing stinging the tip of his tongue.

Others muttered appreciation.

The Black Prince only peered at Axennus, his silvery eyes sufficiently sharp that they might pierce the Southman's very soul.

Axennus held up his right hand, fingers splayed widely.

"This is what we are."

He then curled his fingers, clenching them into an upright fist.

"This is what we must become. We must think as one. We must act as one. We must fight as one."

He lowered his arm and paused meaningfully.

"My lords, we must *unite*."

The ensuing silence was profound.

"We must unite," repeated the Commander, "and we must do so under the leadership of *one*."

Frowns and murmurs.

The Erelian Commander unsheathed his sword. Light from the fires in the surrounding sconces gilded the edges of the blade with golden flame. He placed the weapon on the table before him.

"I submit my sword to the command of Alvarion, Lord of the Fiannar."

Silence once more.

And then –

Arbamas, the Black Prince of Ithramis, stood. His presence was powerful, his demeanor dark and dour, his countenance a thunderhead of peril. But his eyes were bright with argent light, and that light shone also in his voice.

"My own sword is thine also, my Lord Alvarion."

And Niall, High King of Rothanar, rose from his seat, smiled through his scarred visage, and said in the odd Rothic manner of making statements in the form of questions, "Sure, do I not know that there are worse fellows to follow? And as she ever has, will Rothanar not go where Lindannan leads?"

The High King placed his bejeweled blade upon the table.

And then Ingvar, the Mad Earl of Invarnoth, towered to his feet, his youthful features honed but yet unhardened by weather and war, and his blue eyes sparkled with a keen killing light.

"You command my axe, Lord Thyrkin."

And Alvarion, Master of the House of Defurien, Lord of the Fiannar, palmed the golden *rillagh* which lay like a slash of sunfire across his heart. He stood tall, straight, rigid. His eyes shone. Regal, royal, a king of kings, a lord of lords.

"Your trust is not misplaced, my lords, and your faith not mis-founded," said he in a tone accustomed to command. He inclined his head to each in turn. Then, "Because of you, we thirteen are become Everfriends. May these bonds born of war also bind us when peace arises anew."

The men about the table cast uneasy glances at one another, all thinking the same thought, but none deigning to speak it aloud – save one only.

"Lord Alvarion," said Axennus quietly, delicately, "there are thirteen seats about this table, but we are only eleven here."

The smile that softened the Lord's hard lips was singular and strange.

"Nay, Commander," he countered. "Long ago, in another age, another world, would the high ones among the Undying and the Deathward gather about the shining Stone of Scullain in times of trouble and tribulation, and those lords that gathered there would ever be thirteen in number. That the round table of this Circumforum has thirteen seats is not a thing of chance, but of design. For months ago did my Seer inform me that when war next fell upon the Fiannar, a son of the House of Hiridion would unite the kings of Men as Everfriends, and that he would do so *here*, in this Circumforum. And she foresaw that, even as the lords about the Stone of Scullain before them, those Everfriends would number thirteen. *We* are those Everfriends. And we are thirteen."

Axennus' clear hazel eyes swept about him.

Lord Alvarion and the Marshal of the Grey Watch. High King Ri Niall, his Warthane and his Battle Druid. The Black Prince and his First General. The Mad Earl and his Thyric priest. And himself and Bronnus.

Eleven.

The Erelian Commander shook his head in palpable perplexity.

"Lord, we are eleven."

Alvarion's smile flickered once more, then fell into a thin severe line.

"Nay, Commander," he repeated, his voice as faint as a whisper but as forceful as a roar. "*We...are...thirteen.*"

And before the next breath or beat of heart, one fantastic form flowed from the stone floor at Alvarion's right, black and mercurial, and another shimmered into the air to his left, white and luminous, as though materializing from nothing. Both solidified and became beings that surely had emerged from the lyrical lays of legend, or from the very mists of mythos.

The first figure was massive, a moving mountain of might and muscle, broad and black and bearded, and upon one thick shoulder he bore a huge hammer that seemed to have been forged and formed of midnight. His eyes were as burning coal, entirely black, and wetted with invisible flame. And about him the air verily pulsated with power.

The other was a being of bright and boundless beauty, his face and form so fair as to have been fashioned of the lights of both sun and star, and his very eyes seemed wrought of gleaming gold. His figure was lean and long, but exuded a supernatural strength, and about him was the incandescent mist of music, soft and sweet and achingly sad. He leaned lightly upon an ivory bow as long as he was tall, and peered upon the assembly as a god might gaze upon beasts – without pride, but certain of his supremacy.

All those gathered in the Circumforum shared a collective and audible gasp, and all instinctively stepped back. All save dark Arbamas of Ithramis, who remained as still as silent as a standing stone.

"Everfriends of the Fiannar, I give you Brulwar of Dangmarth, First Made of the Firstmade, Earthmaster to the Wandering Guard of Raku Ulrun."

Alvarion's words were met only with a stunned silence.

"And I present to you Thrannien, Prince of the Folk of Gavrayel in Gith Glennin, and a Lord of the Sun Knights of the Athair."

Nothing but silence.

And then the Darad and the Ath lowered their weapons upon the table.

The Lord of the Fiannar unsheathed *Findroth*, raised the glorious sword high, and flames flickered along the length of the blade.

"My lords! Everfriends all! Be comforted in spirit and joyous of heart, for though the trials that lie before us will be truly terrible and heavy with horrors that no mortal should ever meet, know that we do not face the Shadow alone. The mighty Daradur of Ora Undar and the Athair of Gith Glennin have come to Druintir. The Stone Lords and the Neverborn stand with us!

"My lords, *we cannot fail.*"

Silence.

And then Axennus Teagh stepped forward. The smile upon his handsome lips was irrepressible, the light in his eyes like sunlight on steel.

"Ah, yes. Thirteen."

Alvarion nodded austerely.

Axennus' smile broadened.

"Be seated, my lords and Everfriends," gestured the Southman with a flair and flourish unique to him alone. "I do believe we have a war to plan."

They worked through the day, into the night. Planning, calculating, strategizing. Options were considered, reconsidered, accepted. Alternatives deliberated, deconstructed, discarded. Maps were unrolled. Methods of communication were developed. Logistics were discussed, specific responsibilities determined. Positions of strength and weakness debated. Possibilities, probabilities, potentialities were postulated. Histories were shared, vast knowledge and experience was pooled, tales of triumph and tragedy told. Tactics, methods, manoeuvres. Some tried, tested and true; others new and exciting. Strategic defenses against monsters, magic, munitions. Glowing victories, terrible failures, costly draws. War in all its glory and horror.

Then, in the small darkest hours before the dawn, as the constant concentration demanded by their deliberations was causing some among their number to tire, the stone floor beneath their boots trembled. An unmistakable shaking of the earth. A quivering, a quaking. Figurines on the war map wobbled, a few toppled. Eyes shadowed by scowls and bright with alarm met above the table.

"Earthquake?" guessed the Rothic High King.

"I think not," Brulwar answered, his eyes black and shining. "This was no casual shrug of Mother Earth's shoulders. She has been struck, and struck hard."

Wordlessly, Alvarion turned away and strode from the Circumforum. The others followed him, one by one. Out into the night. Halting in the centre of the courtyard, peering east. East, past the Silver Stair, past the city, the Colossus, beyond the Fend, the Seven Hills, across the Northern Plains to where the night sky pressed down upon the distant horizon. A horizon glowing red and orange, a level laceration of lurid light ripping across the night, as though the rim of the world was afire.

The Lord of the Fiannar smiled.

"It would seem, good Everfriends, that the enemy's munitions are no longer a major concern."

Beside him, Brulwar chortled beneath his black beard.

"Nor even a minor one." The Earthmaster glanced at the Prince of the Neverborn, clapped heavily him on the back. "You are outdone, Sun Lord."

Thrannien's golden eyes shone.

"Decidedly more effective than a single arrow, I must admit."

"We have a little more time than we first thought," suggested the Mad Earl of Invarnoth. "This will certainly slow the enemy."

But Alvarion shook his head. "Nay, friend Ingvar, the enemy will hasten westward now with all possible speed."

"How can you know this, Lord Thyrkin?"

But the Lord of the Fiannar only smiled, somewhat blithely, and sent a searching gaze in Axennus' direction.

"Their supply train is obliterated, Dragonsbane," the Southman responded. "They will have naught but very limited supplies – less than a week's worth, I would wager – and the prairie offers little in the way of foraging, insufficient certainly to sustain any sizeable army. They will move fast now, day and night, hoping to strike hard and achieve a swift and decisive victory. They cannot do otherwise. A starving army will not – *cannot* – fight."

"Ah...of course. Should we not oppose them in this accelerated approach?"

Axennus discerned a curious curl colouring Alvarion's smile.

"Perhaps we already do so," mused the Erelian Commander.

The giant Northman stared, then shrugged, seemingly satisfied with Axennus' obscure answer.

Yet transfixed upon the gory red gash of the burning horizon, Prince Arbamas of Ithramis murmured, "How was this thing accomplished, Lord Alvarion?" His silver eyes were ashine with wonder – wonder and something that could only have been pride.

Alvarion's smile broadened, brightened, and for a moment all woe and worry and weariness were forgotten.

"I made a suggestion."

Toward evening of the following day, word came of the Rothic army's long-awaited arrival at Druintir. Seven thousand warriors. Six hundred miles. Fourteen days. A long and arduous journey over hard unforgiving terrain. A truly superhuman feat.

Have we Roths not accomplished greater deeds in times of lesser need?

The High King and his Warthane had then excused themselves from the protracted council of war that they might welcome the warriors who had made – and instruct the provincial Kings and Princes who had led – the difficult, grueling, punishing march.

Subsequently, the council of war was adjourned.

But long after the others had departed the Circumforum, Axennus Teagh remained at the Council Circle, intent upon the many maps and charts cluttering the table, moving carved wooden markers here and there and back again, frowning, tapping his fingers, stroking his chin, moving the markers again, his mind churning with battle concepts and calculations. The solitude seemed to stimulate him, and he saw war rage across the table, the markers become companies of foot and cavalry, the time-yellowed parchments become autumn-greyed grasses of the battlefield. He frowned again, gazing intently, then lowered his chin, closed his eyes and sighed.

It would be a close thing. A very close thing.

"We will prevail, Southman," came a voice from the tiered seating behind the Commander. The voice was deep but soft, like water washing over stone. "Of that, I am certain. You can be as well."

Axennus turned and bowed his head.

"Prince Arbamas."

The Black Prince of Ithramis peered from the half-dark where he reclined, his eerily silver eyes glistering coolly, like chips of ice catching stray bits of moonlight in the night.

"Lord Alvarion has said you are a son of the House of Hiridion. I see that this is surely so. Your understanding of battle is masterful. The signaling system you developed is remarkable; your notion of turning the sunrise against the foe is nothing short of brilliant. I do not doubt that Master Hiridion himself would have been impressed."

Axennus bowed his head once more, then met the Black Prince's argent gaze.

"You speak of Hiridion as one who knew him, Prince of Ithramis."

Arbamas did not reply, but only stared silverly at the Erelian, his face inscrutable for the blackness of his beard and the dimness of the lighting. The Ithraman then stood, a great dark presence, and slowly descended to the Council Circle. There he came and stood before the Erelian, and their eyes locked in mutual scrutiny, silent and sublime.

"You have guessed," stated the Black Prince.

The Commander nodded.

"Yet you have said nothing," said Arbamas.

Axennus shrugged indifferently.

"I see no need for secrecy, Prince, but I am only a mortal man, and such things are likely beyond me. I do not doubt the wisdom of the Athain King and your father in the matter."

The Black Prince nodded. "Secrecy was...is...necessary."

"Surely the Athair know."

"A select few only, and those who do are beyond reproach. Most among the Neverborn would look upon me and see only another of their own kind with little or nothing to distinguish him."

"A glamour?"

The Prince nodded. "A courtesy of Gavrayel. Among the Four Kings of the Athair of First Earth, Gavrayel was ever the foremost practitioner of arts eldritch and arcane, illusion being his personal specialty."

"I have heard the Daradur cannot be deceived."

"Indeed. But they for their own reasons say nothing, and neither Shadow nor any power in this world or any other has devices that might extract information from them should they not desire to share it. But Men and Fiannar are fallible beings, and no secret may be considered completely safe with them. And so my...existence...has been kept from them."

"Another glamour."

The Black Prince nodded.

Axennus regarded the Ithraman with keen, shining eyes.

"You have considered killing me, haven't you?"

"I have."

"Should I be worried?"

Arbamas' beard moved slightly, betraying the small smile that lay beneath.

"Not overly so."

"Somehow that doesn't make me feel much better."

"I believe my secret is safe with you, Southman."

"And why is that? Why am I to be trusted where the noble Fiannar and the greater number of Athair are not?"

"Because the enchantment does not deceive you."

"But why?" asked Axennus. "Why am I not likewise charmed?"

"Perhaps you were not meant to be so."

"Not meant to be so?"

"While sequestered in the Halls of Lore, did you perchance happen across a certain disturbingly apocalyptic book concerning the Folk of Defurien?"

Axennus' eyes narrowed. "I did. A work of both history and prophecy. The *Lament for the Fiannar.*"

"*And the Great King will be father to the Last Son,*" recited the Black Prince, "*and he alone will know the First Son, and these three will conspire to defend the Earth, and the Sons combine to bring Shadow to its final Doom.*"

Axennus' features furrowed into a frown, and he shook his head slowly.

"I have no son. I am no king."

But Prince Arbamas of Ithramis only turned and strode toward the door, the scent of sea salt lingering in his wake. He then turned once more, captured the Erelian in a strange and silver stare.

"My time has not yet come, Southman. Nor has your own."

And then he was gone.

The next day saw much activity and preparation.

The ever-ready Deathward assembled in and about Druintir, stern and silent, almost cold in their courage, sure of their strength and that of their Lord.

The Nothirings ate and drank and brawled upon the grounds about their Embassy, and though their behaviour seemed reckless and wild to the foreign eye, Earl Ingvar seemed satisfied with their display of restraint.

The army of Ithramis massed upon the stony fields north of their Embassy, formed themselves into perfect squares and wedges, bright and shining, their precision and efficiency meeting the discriminating approval of first their captains, then of their generals, and lastly that of the Black Prince himself.

Only the weary Roths rested.

Dusk sighed over the dense woods north of the White Manor. A grey pall fluttered atop the canopy, filtering down through the intertwined leaves and branches, settling slowly and silently on the forest floor. Into a realm of shadows, an eventide deeper and darker than mere dusk. Where magic ruled.

"Nice one, Ruby!"

The big black man stood in a wide clearing, some distance from a significant mound of ash and crackling cinder. His eyes blazed with scarlet fire, the flames substantially more than metaphorical, and his balled fists smouldered and hissed at his thighs. The air smelled of sulphur and smoke.

"Thanks, Riff." Rooboong's white teeth gleamed in the glowing gloom. "It came naturally this time. It just *flowed*. So easy."

"Never thought you had it in you, Ruby," said Decan Regorius from off to one side, his pink eyes shining in approbation as he peered at the place where a towering thick-trunked tree had once been. "You're getting rather good at this."

"His folks must've been bloody witchdoctors back in the jungles of Unga Boon," Maddus theorized from the other side. "Maybe Ruby picked something up from all those years of dancing around communal fires and iron cauldrons full of boiling captives. That's why it's so bloomin' easy for him."

Rooboong's burning gaze scorched the air between him and Maddus.

"Actually, I just pretended the tree was you, Maddy."

"Oh, very bloody clever."

"Maybe next time I don't pretend."

Maddus made a face. "I don't burn as easy as bleedin' sticks and twigs, Ruby."

"Everything burns."

"Starting with your eyeballs, mate. Shut those bloody things off, will you? It's really creepin' me right freakin' out."

Rooboong grinned macabrely. The fire in his eyes flared from red to white, then swiftly faded to tiny twin embers glowing softly behind his pupils. At his sides, the last wisps of smoke fizzled from his fists.

"Better?"

"Much. What did that bloody tree ever do to you, anyway?"

"Like I said, it reminded me of you, Maddy."

There came the disembodied sound of slow, deliberate applause – rather of one man applauding slowly and deliberately – and Teji Nashi stepped from nowhere into the soldiers' midst.

"Well done, my friends," commended the Diceman, his smile white and wide. "Very well done, indeed. Good, good. Novices nevertheless, but as new adepts you are quite, well, adept, yes?"

Teji Nashi was dressed in Erelian blue and bronze, his ornate helm held beneath his arm, the matching curved *katana* and *wakizashi* at his hips, a hand loosely wrapped about the grip the former. His brown eyes glittered, as though flecked with gold or bright with pride, or both.

"You exceed all expectations, my friends. Your dedication and commitment have been more than admirable, and now you reap the rewards, yes? The rivers of your power have been dammed overlong by ignorance or, more accurately, by obliviousness, but now they flow freely, you see. I am simply a humble guide, for the most part, and when paths are walked often enough, the guide eventually becomes obsolete. Still, you yet have much to learn, so very much." His glanced disconcertedly at the mound of ash and ember. "The tree was dead, yes?"

Regorius nodded. "Dead and leaning. Ruby rested against it and it creaked."

"I see. Should my age ever catch up to me, Master Rooboong, remind me never to creak around you, yes?"

The big man grinned.

"I got a question, Doc," interjected Maddus.

"Please."

"Well, I'm not a religious man, not by no means, and the only school I ever seen was a bloody carpenter's workshop, but I remember a Recitor once tellin' me when I was a lad that sorcery was wickedness. So I was wondering, if I do have a soul, is it in any danger of being damned by all this bleedin' witchery...errr...warlockery?"

Teji Nashi smiled pleasantly.

"An interesting concern, my good Maddus. Interesting but invalid. I will make but two comments. First, you *are* a soul – you *have* a body. And secondly, any Recitor worth half his weight in wisdom would do better to look to his own soul, for surely the peril presented it is by far the greater, yes?"

Maddus frowned.

"That means, 'Don't worry about it', Maddy," sighed Riffalo as he brushed a shock of blond hair from his eyes.

Maddus smiled awkwardly. Muttered, "I knew that."

"I have a concern, too, Doc," revealed Regorius, his arms crossed over his chest. "I don't like all this sneaking and hiding from the Commander and the Captain. Doc, you say the Lord of the Fiannar knows we're here and what we are and what we're doing, and he happily leaves us to it, and I understand why he has to know and why he leaves us alone. But it just feels so wrong not telling the Commander and the Captain. Our loyalties lie with them first, right?"

The Diceman regarded the Decan with cool, flat eyes. His closed-lipped smile was small, but warm and genuine.

"Your fidelity is admirable, good Decan. But do not equate discretion with disloyalty. All things have their proper place and time, yes? The Commander and the Captain see that which they either wish to see or are capable of comprehending. To allow them to see more before they are properly prepared to do so would be of grave disservice to them and to us all, you see. The first shadows of suspicion stir in the Commander already. We should let those shadows solidify naturally and at their own pace, for I am aware that the Commander harbours some secrets of his own. Secrets are weighty things, and even a man of the Commander's strength might buckle under too heavy a burden, yes?"

The Decan nodded. "I get it. Discretion is not disloyalty." He eyed the smouldering mound. "Besides, I suppose they'll find out soon enough."

"Quite so." Teji Nashi placed his helm on his head, then clasped his hands together. "Enough practice, yes? A quick nip at the Folly, and then to bed with us. An early night and a good long sleep, for tomorrow we muster and march."

The four soldiers exchanged guarded glances.

"So soon?" murmured Riffalo.

The Diceman smiled broadly, his round bronze face glowing, soft and serene. Atop his left shoulder the air shimmered, and for the briefest of moments two slits of golden light blinked in the halfdark.

"War waits for no one, yes? And I, for one, grow weary of waiting for war."

In the courtyard of the White Manor, the men of the North March Mounted Reserve sat straight and silent upon their steeds beneath a brisk Blue Banner and the White Eagle of the Republic. The blue of their cloaks and the bronze of their armour shone pure and pristine in the lustrous light of the morning sun. Their Commander and the Iron Captain watched as the men submitted themselves and their horses to the careful inspection of Right Tenant Hastiliarius. Each man there knew that his death might well be written into his tale upon the morrow, but none had it writ upon his face.

The Right Tenant turned his mount toward Axennus and Bronnus, fist over his heart.

"We are ready, little brother," declared the Iron Captain. His eyes flashed darkly. "Tomorrow comes war, comes death, comes doom. But we are ready."

The Commander nodded silently, then raised his fist to beat the bronze of his breastplate, once, twice.

"Tomorrow is a thing ever uncertain, Bron," he replied calmly. "War even more so. We can never truly be ready."

But before Bronnus could speak the question that tightened his tongue, the clear clarion call of a battle horn rose from somewhere within the nearby delvings of Druintir, bold and bright, like a shining shaft of light striking out to spear the very sun.

The War Horn of Defurien.

"Come, brother," bade the Commander coolly as he nudged his mount around. "War calls. We ride to meet it."

And they rode.

They marched.

Led by silent shades of the Grey Watch, they marched. From the grounds of their Embassies, across bridges spanning the rush of the River Ruil, down narrow crevasses cloven into the cliff alongside the Silver Stair, they marched. Erelians and Ithramen, Nothirings and Roths. They marched. The Erelians, few but fabled warriors of the North March Mounted Reserve, singing the accolades of their famous Commander and the Iron Captain. The Ithramen marching and riding in perfect precision behind their Prince upon his great black charger. The Nothirings at the back of the Mad Earl of Invarnoth, bawling out brazen challenges and vowing brutal death to foes yet unmet. Weary but willing Rothmen braying ballads of battle behind their Princes and Kings, the indomitable *caelroth* and their High King. Along the stone streets of deserted Druintir, last city of the Fiannar, they marched. Through the Andalorian Arch, upon the marble road above the green Gardens of Galledine, they marched.

Onward they marched.

Together they marched.

Then, beneath the towering Colossus of Defurien, they were met and hailed by the noble Lord Alvarion at the head of his dour host of Deathward. The Lord of the Fiannar sat like a gold-sashed god of war astride his splendid *mirarran*, his flaming sword raised high, his hair flowing from beneath the lofty winged Helm of Defurien, his stature seemingly as enormous and as majestic as the Colossus itself.

Briefly, the Lord of the Fiannar allowed his eyes to stray to the bright gold of the Colossus' *rillagh* and blade, taking comfort and staking hope in the fact that *Grimroth* was yet in the hands of a son of the House of Defurien, in the hands of his uncle – grim, grey Eldurion.

They did not tarry there, for though the miles were few, the going was slow and tedious. Twenty thousand men and nearly half as many horses move not swiftly over narrow ways and close ground. The day aged, and the sun was well into its long descent when Lord Alvarion led the Fiannar and their friends into the deep green halfdark of the Fend.

When they emerged from the verdure and nettle-strewn nearness of ancient Faendomin, dusk had fallen, and night threatened like silent thunder from the east. They were met upon the flowered Field of Cedorrin by an uncharacteristically fatigued Tulnarron and his stalwart Host of Arrenhoth, and there was blood on their blades and death in their eyes. The Master of the House of Eccuron spoke in low tones with his Lord, and soon cheers arose from the ranks of the Deathward as details traveled of the destruction wrought upon the enemy munitions trucks and supply train. All but two of the Host's *mirarra* had returned with their riders seated upon rather than slumped across their backs; those warriors of the House of Eccuron who had not accompanied the Host roared with pride and the promise of revenge.

First blood.

First victory.

"Of this you are certain, Master Tulnarron?"

The huge Fian nodded wearily, his cold grey eyes regarding the Lord of the Fiannar somewhat blearily. His breath streamed like smoke into the algid air of descendent dusk. Beneath him, the froth-drenched flanks of his *mirarran* heaved heavily. Unbroken days and nights, hours upon hours of constant, relentless running battles with the enemy vanguard in effort to retard and delay the Blood King's army's final forced march had drawn and drained Tulnarron's vast reserves, had enervated the warriors of his House and pushed them toward exhaustion, had sorely tested the limits of even the mighty *mirarra*.

"Leeches, yes," the Master verified, his voice low, slow, almost laboured. "There was no lie in this Kor ben Dor's words, nor any reason for one."

"Even less cause to speak the truth, I should think," muttered Alvarion. Beneath him, his *mirarran* shifted slightly, as though the beast somehow sensed his unease. "And these Leeches are in the guise of children?"

Tulnarron grimaced as one might for a hidden hurt, ducking even, almost like he had been struck. Recovering himself, "So spoke the Prince of the Bloodspawn. The little girl shall lead the assault upon the Seven Hills; the boy and the Bloodspawn strike for Doomfall. I have already sent word to Drogul."

Alvarion studied the Master of the House of Eccuron momentarily.

"Prince, is it? It is unlike you to give such credence to an enemy."

Tulnarron blinked blurrily. "He seemed...familiar."

"Oh? How so?"

The tired Master managed a wry smile. "Well, I have thought on it, Lord. And if you must know...he reminded me of you."

Alvarion stared at Tulnarron for one heartbeat, two. Then, despite himself, he laughed abruptly.

"That being so, I am surprised you considered him credible at all."

Tulnarron scowled, then shrugged. "I deserve that, I suppose."

Alvarion reached out, settled one strong hand upon Tulnarron's broad shoulder.

"I am glad, Master Tulnarron, that you...found something to do." The Lord withdrew his hand, reined his mount about. "Take some rest now – you will find much more to do come morning."

Tulnarron grinned, and blood shone on his teeth.

"Even so."

The forces of the Free Nations set camp upon the flowered Field of Cedorrin, while the indefatigable Fiannar rode the sloping grasses to the foot of the Field, into the broad mouth between Sentinel Ridge and the Warwatch. Those rocky rises loomed bleak and black into the falling night, like sentries of soaring stone, all-seeing, unsleeping. A few phantasmal figures of the Grey Watch descended Sentinel Ridge in haste and hurried to their Marshal at the shoulder of Lord Alvarion. More low words were spoken, and soon the Deathward were riding hard and hurriedly to the three grassy hills of Eryn Ruil.

Then, as the black hand of night took the Seven Hills in its deep dark grasp, a second cry of terrible joy burst from the breasts of the Fiannar, and the Lord of that fell and fearsome folk held high his blade and called her aflame.

For there, strung along the troika of grassy hummocks and the vales that lay between, stood a single line of massive figures, darker than the fallen night and equally ubiquitous and unyielding. They faced eastward, their broad backs to the Fiannar and their friends, to the Field and to the Fend. They confronted the night, the black, and the deeper dark that lurked therein – the Shadow that had come from the east. They made no motion. Unmoving. Immovable. Statues hewn of stone and steel. And though they numbered no more than fifty, and the spaces between each and the next were measured in strong stone-throws rather than in strides, the figures seemed to form a wall so impervious, so impenetrable, so impassable that no foe might ever breach it.

Despite the immediacy of the enemy, the Deathward and their allies could rest in comfort that night, knowing that they were well-warded, that the only danger they might encounter before dawn was that which dwelt in the deep dark of their dreams.

For the mighty Daradur had come to the Seven Hills.

He had been given many titles:

Lord of Doomfall. Chieftain of the Wandering Guard. Captain of Captains. *Kor uri Korr*. Master of Raku Ulrun. Lord of the Axe. *Kiruntar*. The Mighty One.

Yet he had but one name –

Drogul.

The greatest Darad ever Made stood within the soot-black socket of the Dragon's Head's southmost eye, his own ebon eyes blacker still, the dual darknesses of death and doom glittering in their immeasurable depths. A chill white wind huffed, whistling shrilly through the huge high hollows, driving cloud before it to billow like angry smoke from the dead eyes of the Dragon. Drogul's black gaze followed the fog as it crawled down from the Dragon's Head, down the scarred stone face of the beast, seeing it settle upon the hard lands before the Pass of the Guard, watching it mix and meld there with the hot vapourous breath of Mother Earth, then slink eastward across the Northern Plains.

There, a thousand paces from the gash in the night and stone that was Doomfall, the fog-fettered fields were dappled with thousands of opaque orange specks flickering feebly in the haze. Quickly calculating the number of fires and the distances between, Drogul evaluated the strength of the enemy that had come to destroy him at Doomfall. And that strength was truly terrible.

Twenty thousand.

Iron-armoured Unmen of Waldard. Powerful Urkroks. Gargantuan Graniants. And great grey giants that Drogul had not yet met in battle, had neither seen nor heard of before Tulnarron had sent word with the *throkka*. Bloodspawn, they named themselves. And their leader, Kor ben Dor. Impressive, Tulnarron had called him. *Impressive.* High praise from the Master of the House of Eccuron. Drogul could only guess the might of this Kor ben Dor, of the fiends that were the Bloodspawn, but he was certain that it was tremendous indeed. Not that it mattered.

Twenty thousand.

More.

The Mighty One moved his gaze to gap of Doomfall, where his own force was gathered in the gloom, keeping a calm and confident vigil on the vapour-bound night. Fewer than one hundred Wandering Guard.

One hundred.

Less.

Drogul felt a hot and powerful presence behind him, and rage and madness seemed to burn the blackness at his back. He summoned Dulgar to his side with the slight shrug of one massive shoulder.

The Wild One grinned through a fiery mane of hair and beard at the spectacle of the foe so far below them, and an insane hunger crimsoned the black of his solitary eye.

"Mundar would suggest we surround the mudfuckers," Dulgar grated, his great bare chest rumbling with conjoined humour and wrath.

Drogul nodded stiffly, but said nothing. Warder Mundar of Duldarad was not there – he guided the Lady of the Fiannar somewhere south of Galledine. His axes would be badly missed.

As would Rundul's.

And Brulwar's hammer also.

Eastward, far beyond the furthest marches of the Northern Plains, a deep dark redness leaked languidly into the black of night, like blood seeping from a festering wound in the world. Night was dying. Dawn approached. Death was coming.

Death and doom.

"We should go down, *kor uri Korr*," declared Dulgar, an odd urgency, a certain *need* to his tone. War and battle and killing defined the one-eyed Captain. Sometimes he seemed but an animated extension of his bloodthirsty axe. "Our brothers wait for us. Fuck."

Drogul nodded once more, still said nothing.

A crack in the earth's crust called Doomfall.

Twenty thousand foes.

One hundred *mara Waratur*.

The Mighty One hefted his great black war-axe to his wolfskin-mantled shoulder, and turned to begin the long dark descent down the Dragon's Head. In a voice that rumbled like boulders rolling in the heart of the earth, the laconic Chieftain repeated the very same oath he so recently had given his Fiannian friends in Hollin Tharric.

Three words.

Simply spoken. Indisputable. Irrefutable.

Three words that enticed a laval tear-stream of blood from beneath the worn black iron of Dulgar's eyepatch.

"Doomfall will hold."

Axennus laboured up the steep pinnacle of the Warwatch. The going was arduous and difficult, made worse by the deep dark of a night that knew but little light of either moon or star. The path – an obscenely charitable description in the Commander's estimation – was narrow and winding, oft slippery underfoot where the rock was greased with moss and black frost, and in places he found it necessary to pull himself up to the next stone shelf of the incline by strength of arms rather than of legs. In other places, where the face of the Warwatch was essentially vertical, Axennus was forced to splay like a spider clinging to the stone, inching himself upwards by utilizing the smallest of handholds and footholds.

The way was called Dead Man's Climb – a most apt and likely literal name.

Axennus clambered, scrambled, scraped and clawed his way up the Climb, grittily determined, minutes seeming like hours, until at long last he achieved the summit of the soaring stone of the Warwatch. Outwardly relieved, he slowed his quickened breath, brushed his cloak smooth and frowned at the marks scoring the bronze of his greaves. With some reluctance, he unclasped the rope and harness that his taciturn guide had insisted he wear.

Two warders of the Grey Watch looked upon him with pale, placid eyes.

One appeared significantly older than the other, his hewn, once handsome features become hard, almost haggard. He was seated in an odd metal chair with large wheels for back legs and small ones on the front, his grey woolen cloak bundled loosely over his lower body. By the formation of the cloak's folds, Axennus guessed the man had lost both lower limbs at the knees.

The other Watcher was tall and lean and as straight as a spear. He seemed very young, younger than Axennus. His hair was fair, his eyes sparkling and bright, the small sardonic smile upon his full lips appeared permanently fixed as he coiled the rope that had been attached to the Southman's harness. His features were flat and flawless, the kind of face that causes men to bridle with envy and makes women swoon.

A scuffling sound behind Axennus, and Harlastian of the Grey Watch vaulted lithely over a natural parapet in the rock. The Watcher was unwinded by the climb, the bare blade in his belt and the *rillagh* across his breast flashing faintly in the cloud-filtered moonlight. He shrugged out from the straps of a fairly ponderous pack, knelt, neatly arranging the pack's contents on the peak's wind-smoothened floor. Some meagre provisions, a collection of various coloured pennons, several plates of polished steel.

"A long climb," Axennus complained, his chest heaving.

"The way down is faster, Southman," replied Harlastian evenly. "Much faster."

The Commander grinned grimly. "I'm not sure what that means, exactly, and even less sure that I'm looking forward to it."

"I will not allow you to fall, Southman. Lord Alvarion would be... displeased."

Axennus grimaced. "My confidence in you knows no bounds, Watcher."

"Nor should it. You will be safely back with your company before the battle begins – for whatever that is worth." Harlastian jerked his chin. "These are Silmarien and Spedamon of the Grey Watch."

The young Watcher flashed a smile that would outshine even the most brilliant of Axennus' efforts.

The Watcher in the wheeled chair nodded. His neck creaked.

"Call me 'Speedy'," he insisted, his ancient voice pocked with irony.

"I am Axennus Teagh, Commander of the North March Mounted Reserve."

"The March Fox of the Ghost Brigade," said Silmarien, still smiling. "I am honoured."

"Don't let that go to your head, Southman," muttered Speedy. "The boy honours very easily."

"Forgive the old man," smiled Silmarien. "He's been sitting in that chair too long. It has made him combative and overly competitive. He refuses to concede that he will never get a leg up on me."

"Careful, boy. It's a long way down," grunted Speedy as he wheeled over to inspect Harlastian's collection of signal flags and mirrors.

A wink and a nod, and Silmarien followed.

Axennus managed an awkward half-grin, cast a quick look Harlastian's way. The Fian only shrugged dismissively.

"Have a look around, Southman."

The apex of the Warwatch was roughly circular and somewhat concave in shape, a little less than thirty yards in diameter, the rock floor curving toward a high stone lip that ringed the summit like a round rampart carved by wind and time. At the center of the circle was a tall pyramid of piled timber from which came the slight pungent scents of tar and oil – a beacon of warning, long disused and unignited. And now superfluous, as the Fiannar had been only too aware of the advance of the enemy.

To the north, the Warwatch fell vertically to the white-crested wash of the Ruil, the river's rush and roar dulled to a quiet rumble for the sheer height of the pinnacle's titanic rock.

To west, past and below the blackened mass of the Fend, Axennus caught the pale golden sheen of the Colossus' upraised blade, though Defurien's gargantuan stone likeness was itself invisible in the aging night.

Southward, small and barely visible in the darkness, men and horses were moving in close formation through the nightbound gap between the Warwatch and Sentinel Ridge, assembling about their lords and the banners of their nations on the flats at the western feet of Eryn Ruil's three grassy rises.

Behind the southmost hill, beneath the cloud-weakened gleam of moon and star, the Sunburst of Rothanar, the Emerald Trefoil of her

High King, and the Black Hand of the *caelroth* fluttered proudly in rebellious defiance of the dark.

At the back of the central hill, the Three Lions of Ithramis waved almost winsomely in the whisking wind of night.

And behind the northern hill flew the Scarlet Serpent of Nothira, ever hungry for battle and blood.

Axennus nodded to himself in satisfaction. The three hills effectively concealed the presence of the Fiannar's allies from enemy eyes. The foe need not have knowledge beforehand of the strength gathered to oppose them. Surprise and the intentional stimulation of over-confidence in the enemy, the Commander knew, were oft sharper weapons in war than any blade forged of steel.

Atop the crests, along the slopes and in the vales of the three hills were mustered most of the might of the Deathward.

The defiant Crimson Fist of the mighty House of Eccuron and the Raging Bull of the House of Cilcannan marked the southern rise.

The bold banners of the Houses of Dalorion and Mirmaddon, and of Serra-Collean and Shon Roidain flapped from the crown of the northmost mound.

And from the central hill flew the noble Golden Strype of the Fiannar, flanked by the unadorned and colourless standard of the Grey Watch and the fiery Flaming Sword of the great House of Defurien.

And somewhere before the Hills were hidden fifty hammers and axes of the Wandering Guard under the command of broad black Brulwar of Dangmarth.

Axennus could not see the hundred riders of the Republican Legion's fabled North March Mounted Reserve led by the unconquerable Iron Captain. But he knew where they were, where they waited. He would join them soon enough.

The Erelian Commander swept his gaze over the landscape once more.

The only thing lacking was the enemy.

Harlastian made a vague gesture with one hand toward a shadowed corner of the eastern parapet, and Axennus moved his attention there. He sensed more than saw the figure standing there, a phantasm in the night, long-limbed and tall, cloakless in the chill, eerily ethereal. And then he heard the soft sad song of bells, and marked the pale curved sheen of polished ivory at the figure's back – and he knew Thrannien, Lord of the Sun Knights of the Athair, stood with him atop the Warwatch.

Axennus and Harlastian moved toward the Sun Lord, each to a side. They followed the Ath's golden gaze out into the eastern night. Harlastian's lips parted for that which he saw there – parted but made no sound. Axennus observed that the Fian's hand had curled quietly about the pommel of his naked sword. The Southman squinted eastward, but he saw nothing save the night, bleak and black.

"They have come?" he wondered in little more than a whisper.

Thrannien nodded.

Harlastian withdrew his blade from his belt.

Neither spoke.

The Commander shared his companions' silence, the trio standing stern and still in the dying night, like statues wrought of the stuff of shadow. They watched. They waited. And night passed like the fleeing soul of dead god.

Axennus saw the first gloaming of dawn rise deep and red in the farthest east, the earth bleeding into the heavens from some hideous hurt in her heart, her life leaking westward across a stricken sky.

A red dawn.

Such a sunrise bodes danger to the traveler.

A chill shivered Axennus' spine as he recalled the Rhelman's words.

The wind sleeps, but does not die.

And a dark wind woke and rose in the east, hastening westward on howling, bloodied wings.

We must beware the wind's return.

Dawn broke in a burst of bloodlight over the Seven Hills.

Peril awaits us, Master Teagh.

And then Axennus saw the thing that had been lacking. Saw the army of the Blood King amassed there under the ruddy light of ruby dawn, upon the frosted grasses of the Northern Plains. Saw the immensity of that army, its sheer and utter monstrousness. He saw, and wished that he had not, for doubt and darkness then gnawed his heart as surely as a leech sucks the blood from the vein.

Less than a league before the scarlet-stained slopes of the Seven Hills, beneath banners crimson and cruel, the Blood King's army was assembled, its vastness encompassing the entirety of the eastern vista for as far as Axennus' mortal eyes could discern. An ocean of enemies. Thousands upon uncounted thousands. Foes arisen from the darkest realms of nightmare. Fiends. Beasts. Demons. Barbarians. Evil incarnated into the most massive army the Southman had ever seen.

Before that enormous force, the mustered might of the Fiannar and their allies seemed so small, inconsequential, ineffectual.

But the Erelian Commander knew better than to delve into the depths of despair, and soon and swiftly did doubt and darkness desert him.

For he saw another thing.

Alvarion, son of Amarien, Master of the House of Defurien and Twelfth Lord of the Fiannar, urged his great grey *mirarran* from beneath the proud pennons of his House and his folk, forward through silently parting ranks of the Grey Watch and dour Deathward warriors.

Alone rode Alvarion, the pristine metal of his bewinged helm and the glittering gold of his *rillagh* catching and cleansing the crimson rays of the befouled sun, sending them forth once more, glorious and golden.

Alone rode the Lord of the Fiannar, cantering out upon the Plains, his cloak and hair flying about him like the very wings of war.

Alone he rode across the frost-greyed grasses, drawing ever nearer to the foremost enemy line, calling his mount to a halt just beyond bowshot.

Alone he sat there astride his steed, strangely serene in his stillness and his silence, a rendering in stone but for the windmade movement of cape and mane. There he remained in rigid and resolute defiance of the Darkness that had come to devastate his land and destroy his people.

And alone did he then hoist his golden sword high, becking her ablaze in a voice of strident thunder. And the golden fire of the Lord's blade flamed like the fury of avenging gods, and in his cry was the wrath of each and every Lord that had gone before him. Verily, the battle-call of Cothra himself was a thing less terrible.

Somewhere far away the soulless spirit of the Blood King trembled in its dark demesne.

And then came silence.

Deceptively peaceful. Deceivingly pure.

The poignant still that heralds the storm.

And then the rolling peal of drums rocked the world. Pounding, pounding, as though seeking to shatter the very earth. Booming, booming, like the last quaking of tectonic plates at the breaking of the world. And then came another sound, a screech so heinous that it might shred the ear, a shriek so dreadful as to rend the heart and rip the sturdiest of souls.

And the host of the Blood King moved.

And so, at last, the thing that breaks the bravest of hearts, that destroys men in the thousands of thousands, that lays waste to civilizations and wreaks ruin on worlds, came to Eryn Ruil. The thing that the greatest of gods do dread, the thing cherished by demons for the pain it promises, for the evil it permits, for the annihilation it allows, descended upon the Seven Hills of Lindannan. The thing that even the Teller is ever loath to speak of in his Tale for the sorrow it sows and the harvest of shining souls it reaps – this foul and fatal thing at long last came beneath a bleeding sun to fall upon the fair fell folk of the Fiannar.

The thing that should never happen.

The thing that should never be.

The thing called –

WAR.

EPILOGUE

"The angel Hope and the demon Fear
both reside here,
in this place so dreadful and strange,
combative cohabitants of the
e'er-whirling sphere
the Teller of the Tale calls Change."

Omereo, *Tranformations and Transpositions*

P ale sunsheen fell on the fog over the Ford of Findarron, casting the nascent morn in a monolight of ghostly grey. Autumnal frost silvered and stiffened the grasses, and slicked the stones of the shore-line with a thin skin of ice. And the ghosts of departed night fled along the fogbound banks of the North March, the muted murmur of the river mimicking the sound of phantasmal fetters rattling or. rock, the wind awhisper with the sad song of shamed and sorry sculs flying from the light.

In agile imaginations, such a drear and dismal dawn gave easy rise to plentitudes of spectres and restless spirits.

The young goatherd marshaled his meagre trip of goats through the mist toward the water's edge, leading his bleating charges to drink just below the shallows the local folk called Findy's Ford. Long ago a terrible battle had been fought there, he had been told. The superstitious held the place to be haunted. The boy knew better. He feared more tangible things, such as the land to the north. North of the river lay lands unknown, lands that did not fall under the rule of Republican law and order. North was the Wild.

The young goatherd frowned, wondering what twisted things haunted and hunted in the haze of the northern shore. He glanced to the brightening sky. He had heard rumour of winged demons over the prairie. He had dismissed the tale, for he knew that his friends were oft overly fanciful. He was the rational one, the logical one.

He lowered his gaze, glowered at the fog.

The mist was moving. Altering. Becoming something more than it had been.

Things were changing.

His father had at long last entrusted him with the herd, thirty-or-so long-haired goats, mostly white, a few tans, two greys, one black. The harvest was done, but the animals would graze until the grass was browned beneath its veneer of frost. His older brothers were away with the Legion. Only he remained to tend the trip. The herd had become his responsibility. Understandably so, as he was the sensible one. It was his first time, alone with the goats. Some among his friends would surely find some humour in that.

The goats grazed, the river ran, the wind rose white and chill.

And things changed.

The ghosts came.

They approached the Fords of Findarron without hesitation. Proudly, arrogantly. Horses. Hundreds of horses. Twenty hundred horses. Twenty hundred riders. Blue and bronze, bold and strong.

They should not have been there, the young goatherd knew. Not there. Not then. They had been disbanded. They were no more.

How was it that they were there?

There. Then.

A double blue standard rippled above the riders like a strip of the morning sky. Flapping in the risen wind. Dark blue over light. The banner of a brigade long defunct. Long gone. No more. Disbanded. Defamed. Worse – forgotten.

Dead – yet not.

The Ghost Brigade.

They would not believe him, he knew. Not his friends, those who spun fantastic stories of winged and wicked fiends from hell. Not his father, now. Not his brothers, later. His sister, perhaps, though she was but three and would believe anything. His mother, yes, were she yet living.

The Ghost Brigade. A power of the past. There. Then. Blue and bronze and bold and gold. Spears bristling, armour glistering, horses huffing great clouds into the cold morning mist. Crossing the Fords, riding northward. Two thousand strong.

And at their head a dark-skinned heathen upon a brilliant white steed from the very fields of heaven.

The mist swirled, faded, fell. The day brightened. The ghosts passed. North into the Wild. And were gone.

The boy lowered his eyes. No one would believe him.

And so he would tell no one.

The War For The North
concludes in...

Book Two:
Roars Of War

Available soon!

Visit *Whispers of War* on Facebook
www.facebook.com/whispersofwar

Made in the USA
Charleston, SC
09 May 2014